Lisa,

I truly appreciate your encouragement. You are wonderful, and your smile is delightful.

Thanks for everything!

Best Wishes,

Tesa Jones

Cobwebs
of
Time

Cobwebs
of
Time

Tesa Jones

Rutledge Books, Inc. Danbury, CT

This is a work of fiction. The characters in this book are the product of the author's imagination. Any resemblance to actual persons is coincidental. Those references to real locations or actual people (living or dead), sporting, entertainment, historical or political events are included only to give the fictional story a sense of authenticity.

First Edition

Rutledge Books, Inc.
107 Mill Plain Road, Danbury, CT 06811
1-800-278-8533
www.rutledgebooks.com

Manufactured in the United States of America

Cataloging in Publication Data
Jones, Teresa

Cobwebs of Time

ISBN: 1-58244-193-6

1. Fiction.

Library of Congress Control Number: 2001096109

To my parents
Richard and Barbara Ranney
Thank you for believing in me.
I still feel your loving presence—even from the grave.

Acknowledgments

I wish to thank the following people for their assistance and suggestions:
Preston Abbott, Joe Burdette, Jan Curtis, Mary Annie Harper,
Mike Guiles, Christie Masters Janssen, Ticee Jensen, Arnie Jones Jr.,
Becky Littlepage, Ellen Phillips, Betty Politte, Dr. Brooks Ranney,
Pitter Bautz Ranney, Mary Coolidge Ruth, Peggy Taylor,
Maureen and Cary Sinn, Dave Vennell, Kathy Wicks,
all of the people at Rutledge Books especially Marilyn Smith, John Laub,
Katherine Breen, Kim Phipps, and Timothy Daly.

With a tremendous amount of love and a feeling of great loss,
I thank the following individuals posthumously:
Gertrude O'Keefe, Richard and Barbara Ranney.

I especially want to thank Kimberly Ranney, Brian Ranney, Dustin Ranney,
Shelby Jones, Rick, Debi & Brooke Sorber,
Carol Guiles, and Kathye Geary;
you gave me the encouragement I needed to reach for my goal.

Carol, *little friend,* I love you. And I truly appreciate all of your help.
I will forever remember the hours we spent in the kitchen.
You have taught me so much; one thing is for sure, I could have
never done this without you.

Kim, thank you for seeing talent in me, when I had trouble finding it in myself. I want you to know that I see the same talent mirrored in you. You are an amazing woman. Keep those dreams you had as a child, and never give up!

Brooke, thank you for making me realize *Cobwebs of Time* is a story that transcends the generation gap. Your enthusiasm gave me strength to continue. Rick, thank you for opening my eyes to the fact that this is a story men can enjoy too. That day I spent in the hot tub with you and your family will forever be imprinted on my mind.

Brian and Dustin—I know it's been years since you read the manuscript, but I want you both to know that your comments were the very foundation that kept my dream alive. Whenever I became discouraged, I focused on your words and your expressions when you spoke of *Cobwebs of Time.* Brian—especially you—you are the reason I never gave up! I have truly loved watching you and Dustin grow into such fine young men. I am so proud of both of you!

Shelby—thank you—you have been with me every step of the way--even when you did not realize it! I cannot thank you enough—for your love—for your friendship—for your encouragement—for your wonderful ideas, especially the one regarding the cover. And thank you for being there the day I mailed the manuscript away. You touched my heart more than you will ever know.

With enormous gratitude, I wish to thank Debi and Kathye, because—bottom line—it was *your* words that made me believe I could follow my dream to completion. I want you both to know that I truly treasure your friendship.

I wish to thank my dear friend, Kelly Myatt St. Clair, who is an immensely
talented artist.
Your beautiful illustrations exceeded all of my expectations.

I also wish to thank Robert James, my English teacher at
Fort Hunt High School.
When I ran into Mr. James several years after graduation, he asked me,
"Have you written a novel yet?"
When I replied, "No,"
he responded, "You should; in fact, I suspect that someday you will."

And finally, I want to thank my family:
Roger, Shelby, and Rick Jones.
You are the joy in my life.

Contents

Part I
The College Years

Part II
The Changing Years

Part III
The Awakening Years

Epilogue

Part I

The College Years

1

Laura

I DISTINCTLY REMEMBER HOW HOT AND STICKY IT WAS THE DAY I TOOK the train to North Carolina. Nixon was in his first year as president. Many in our country were protesting the Vietnam war. Neil Armstrong had walked on the Moon the previous month, and earlier in August, at Woodstock, Janis Joplin had called the hippies "a new minority." However, my mind was focused on being a college freshman: excited, nervous, yet a little apprehensive about the future, and what it might hold for me. It was the first time I was more than a few miles away from home. My heart was racing with the experience. I would soon be nineteen, and although an objective observer might describe me as naive and innocent, I considered myself a mature woman.

My parents saved every penny they could in order to send my brother Kurt and me to college. It seemed that my mother and father, being products of the Great Depression, were determined that their children would have the education they had missed. Although my parents were far from wealthy, neither Kurt nor I ever felt financially deprived. Granted, we didn't have many tangible luxuries, but we were comfortable. In addition, we had something money could not buy; we had a home filled with love.

Most girls go off to college with a truckload of possessions, but I had only a purse containing $25, a box of school supplies, linens, an Underwood portable typewriter (which was a high school graduation gift from my parents), a tennis racket, and one suitcase. Packed inside were five different mix-and-match Lady Bug outfits, a light blue A-lined Villager dress, a pair of heels, a pair of flats, a pair of worn-out Keds, a nightgown, some make-up, several pairs of panty hose, and an 8-x-10 picture of Tom.

Tommy Ladley was beyond a doubt the most kind, considerate, and gentle guy any girl could hope to know. I had met him two years earlier. He was so shy that it took months to get him to smile in my direction and an additional three weeks before he spoke to me. I had almost given up on him when he finally asked me to a sock hop after a Friday night football game during my junior year. I'd never had a real boyfriend before him. Of course, I had my share of crushes and an occasional Saturday night date to the movies or a school dance, but Tommy was different. He gave me confidence. He made me feel important, secure, and safe—even now, when he was fifty miles away at High Point College. It was not long into our relationship that he became my whole world, and I became his. We were so happy, so attuned to each other, and so desperately in need of the other's strength. There was no doubt in my mind that I would absolutely and positively love Tom Ladley for the rest of my life.

At eighteen, college bound, young at heart, emotionally and mentally unblemished, I thought I knew it all; I had the world on a string, and life was one big bowl of cherries.

2

My first day at Elon College was a whirlwind experience: never-ending lines, welcome speeches, rules, faces, and names. I was one of five hundred freshmen seated in the gymnasium as we listened to President Danieley's greeting. After his opening speech, Dean Strum rattled off the list of rules I had already read in the pamphlet. She very firmly stated that freshmen girls were not allowed to stay out overnight unless they had written parental permission; girls were not permitted to wear pants to class; and freshman girls were confined to their rooms Monday through Thursday from two to four and eight to ten for a close study. This rule was established in hopes that the girls would develop good study habits. The young men, of course, were free to roam. Dean Strum added, "Since the girls are not available, perhaps the young men will also choose to hit the books." Soft laugher drifted through the audience. The girls had to sign in and out of their dorms if they were going anywhere off campus. Last, but certainly not least, we were told that although the drinking age in Alamance County was eighteen, there was a no drinking policy on campus, which was strictly enforced. If caught, the penalties were severe. Students rustled around in their seats; a few chuckled inwardly. There were several who actually laughed. I heard comments about what a foolish and archaic rule it was, but I refrained from expressing my opinion because the regulation meant nothing to me; I did not even drink wine at dinner. Perhaps the school was old fashioned, but I didn't care. After all, I was a rather old-fashioned person; the rules seemed fair to me.

After orientation, I met my roommate Sue. She was a quiet, reserved girl whom I liked immediately. Without a great deal of chatter, the two of us fixed up our room and divided the closet space and drawers. She had bell-bottom jeans, T-shirts and beads; I had skirts hemmed four inches above my knee, vests, and blouses with Peter Pan collars. We hung posters. Hers were Woodstock, Steppenwolf, and Led Zeppelin; mine were Neil Diamond and Johnny Rivers ("Sweet Caroline" and "Summer Rain" were Tom's and my favorite songs.) We put up some inexpensive curtains, sprinkled a few knickknacks around, set up my picture of Tommy, and put our toothbrushes in their holders; suddenly, it felt like home.

Sue and I could not have been more different. She was quite tall; I was only two inches over five feet. She played acid rock loudly while I played mellow music quietly. She wore a headband with a feather in it; I wore tiny tortoiseshell barrettes. She had patches on her jeans; I did not even own a pair. She was reserved; I was gregarious. She admitted to smoking pot; I confessed I'd never seen it. She was from an affluent family; I was not. She was into physics; I was going to be a teacher. The honor roll came easily to her while I needed to study my head off in order to excel. She played the guitar; I played tennis. We had nothing in common, but I liked Sue. I honestly felt that she liked me too. Even though I instinctively knew we would never be close friends, I did think we would make good roommates.

After dinner, Sue and I took a walk around the spacious grounds. The campus was lovely. I had never seen anything quite so refreshing in my life. Harper Center was the newest building and was set aside from the rest. It stood three stories high. Even though it was called a coed dorm, in actuality, it was two: Staley Dorm for girls and Moffitt Dorm for boys. Both dorms were connected by a cafeteria and lobby, which were jointly shared by all the inhabitants. The quality I liked best about Harper Center over the other dorms on the main campus was the magnificent view. Forests on two sides and a small lake on its right bordered three quarters of the building; the front of the dorm overlooked the track, tennis courts, and gymnasium. Everything was so clean; even the path leading up to the lobby door was immaculately groomed.

The main campus—as everyone referred to it—was one city block in size; it consisted of Whitney Auditorium, McEwen cafeteria (for those in that area), Long Student Union/Recreation Center, three female dorms, five male dorms, a library, and four classroom buildings. The buildings on main campus were surrounded by a four-foot red-brick wall, which gave it a compact look. Everything seemed to match as if it were a coordinating outfit. Even the freshly painted white trim that circled each window and door drew the buildings together in a structural unity.

Elon College was a town in itself with a population of approximately two thousand. Jokingly, I wondered if the census counted the enrolled students because it did not seem as if there were many townspeople to be seen. There was a gas station on the corner and a convenience store called the Tiny Tote next to it. On the main street, there was a laundromat, the police station, a diner, a barbershop, and a church. Railroad tracks ran parallel to the back wall. The town had one streetlight that flashed yellow. Everything was so peaceful. After leaving the hectic Virginia suburbs of Washington, D.C., it seemed amazing to me that a place like this actually existed.

While exploring our new environment, Sue and I tried to locate the buildings in which our classes would be held the following day. With nervous laughter, we mapped out our route. In the courtyard between the Alamance Building and Long Student Union, Sue and I crossed paths with a small group of guys. One of them was taking pictures of us. He kept focusing and snapping shots one right after the other without saying a word. I looked at Sue. She was smiling into the lens, but all I seemed to be able to do was blush and look awkwardly in another direction. When he took the camera away from his face, the first thing I noticed was that the young photographer's eyes were so incredibly dark brown, they appeared black. I saw nothing else: just those eyes.

I snapped out of my trance when I suddenly realized that one of the guys directed a statement at me. "I'm sorry, I didn't hear you." I stumbled over the words.

He repeated himself. "My name's Richard Malone. My friends call me Rick. I'm a sophomore." He pointed to his companions. "This is my brother Brad and his roommate Bill. They're just freshmen."

"I'm Laura . . . Laura Davis, but everyone calls me Lori. This is my roommate Sue." As an afterthought, I added, "We're just freshmen too."

"The voice of an angel."

I turned my attention to the one who had just spoken. Mr. Brown Eyes nodded, then raised his camera, focused, and took several more pictures in rapid succession. Was his name Brad? I could not remember. After lowering the camera, his lips turned upward forming a smile. He winked in a confident way. I felt defenseless against his penetrating gaze. He seemed so cool, so self-assured, and cocky; it was unnerving. I began to blush. I could actually feel the heat radiating from my face. I tried to moisten my lips several times, but they remained parched.

Brad winked again and added to his initial comment, "Definitely the voice of an angel, but the body of a Greek goddess." His words had a soft purring quality to them.

For some strange reason, I wanted to strangle him. Where did he get off—talking like that and staring at me as if I had no clothes on? It was infuriating. Despite my best attempt at remaining calm, I continued to turn even brighter shades of red. If only he would look away; if only I could take my eyes from his!

An arm was gently placed around my shoulder as Rick's voice broke the silence.

"Ignore my baby brother. Brad thinks God put him on this earth for all women to worship." Rick steered me away from the others. He kept talking to me and telling me pointers about campus life and certain professors. It was not long before I realized that Rick did not appear to be as confident as his brother Brad; instead, he seemed more self-conscious.

Several minutes passed before Rick casually invited me to go "to a movie or dancing or whatever" on Saturday night.

I accepted. After all, the invitation seemed harmless. Tommy and I discussed dating other people since we would not be seeing each other during the next few months. Rick would be a good companion.

On my first day at Elon, I was in bed by midnight. Surprisingly, I was not homesick; instead, I felt very comfortable. I had met a few nice people. I liked my roommate. I had a Saturday night date (something I hadn't had with anyone except Tommy in almost two years), and I was totally and completely in love with being a college freshman.

3

On Friday, things began to get a little more confusing. It was the second day of classes, and I was on my way to becoming a dedicated elementary school teacher. Education was my major; teaching was my dream. In addition, it was also what my guidance counselor, Mrs. Jo Williams, emphasized when she said, "The country really needs good teachers." More than anything in the world, I wanted a classroom of my own.

After I came out of Professor Byrd's western civilization class, I noticed confident, cocky Brown Eyes leaning against the wall with two books under one arm and a handful of wildflowers in the other. Not in my wildest imagination did I think that he was waiting for me. I turned and started walking to my dorm.

He suddenly materialized at my side. "Been waiting for ya." Brad Malone's rapid Northern accent had a way of making four words sound like one.

His voice sent a trail of chills down the back of my spine. For some unknown reason, I felt leery of him. I picked up my pace and ignored him; nevertheless, he kept right up with me. I refused to look in his direction. I was not going to give him the satisfaction.

"Thought you might be the type of girl who likes flowers. Sorry they're not roses." He was walking sideways, watching me, and flashing the bouquet in my face.

It was amusing. He really did look a bit silly waving a combination of wilting violets, dandelions, and colorful weeds. I stopped in my tracks; I could not help but smile.

Brad laughed. It had a pleasant ring to it. "So, the lady knows how to smile."

I looked up at him. He was nearly six feet tall. I asked, "Do you do this often?"

He laughed again, and his eyes lit up; in fact, his whole face radiated affability. Brad's smile only magnified his incredibly handsome face. "To be perfectly honest with you, Laura, I've never done anything like this before." He continued exposing his white teeth as his eyes pierced their way through mine.

"Is that what you say to all poor, unsuspecting females?" I stifled a smile and tried to mask my face with the coolest stare. Why did he have such a strong effect on me?

"You really are a very frustrating individual to get to know." His expression took on a puzzled look as the corner of his lip cast sideways giving him an even more devilish appearance. At first, I thought he was angry, but then I realized Brad was teasing me. I felt agitated at him . . . at myself, too, for allowing him to make me feel so nervous and uncomfortable. During the silence, he handed the flowers to me.

His lips curved upward once more as he began to speak again. "I don't have a car so I can't take you any place special, but I wonder if you'd have a soda with me tonight at the student union. We could talk . . . get to know each other." He paused a moment. When I did not give him an immediate answer, he laughingly added, "Don't worry, Laura, I won't drag you off into the local bushes and compromise your virtue . . . although it is a tempting idea."

I blushed, which only caused him to laugh a note or two higher. It was maddening. I kept thinking. No . . . don't accept. Danger . . . keep away! But I actually heard my voice reply, "Okay." Why?

"I'll pick you up at 7:30."

Before I could answer his final statement, he was gone. Just like that . . . vanished. Brad turned around and walked away as if he knew—even before he asked—that I would agree to go.

4

I felt like a high school kid preparing to go out on my first date. I did not know why, but I took extra time on my makeup. I fussed with my hair for an hour combing and curling it. (I never fussed with my hair.) I polished my nails; then I took the polish off and started all over again because I was not satisfied with the color. I even put on a splash of my suitemate's perfume, Wind Song. I kept glancing at Tommy's picture, wishing it would speak to me and give me a reason to reject Brad's invitation. I wanted Tommy to be here with me—to hold me—to protect me, but I was not sure exactly why I needed protection.

At 7:30, I started pacing the room like a caged tiger. Confusing thoughts resonated through my mind. There was a part of me that hoped Brad would not come, yet another portion of my mind wanted the chance to see him again. I could not remember my stomach ever being so tied up in knots.

By the time the intercom announced I had a visitor, I was in such a state of turmoil that I nearly tripped on my own feet getting to the door. I raced down the stairs. Before entering the lobby, I slowed my pace. I wanted to appear sophisticated, or at the very least, calm.

Brad was the first person I saw. He was leaning against the receptionist's desk and watching me as I approached. Silently, he appeared to be taking a mental picture of me as I walked toward him. All I could think of was how magnificent he looked in brown. The shade of his shirt was just a touch lighter than that of his eyes and hair. Each of the brown tones accented the other.

"Hello," he whispered as a half smile covered his face.

"Hi." Without another word exchanged between us, he turned. I followed. With the exception of a brief comment regarding the pleasant evening weather, we took our strides in silence. He did not reach for my hand or lay an arm around my shoulder. I tried to think of something to say in order to break the silence, but I could find no words. The only sound we heard was the steady, even beat of our footsteps as I kept pace with his movements.

Upon entering the student union, he purchased two Cokes and a couple of orders of fries. We sat in a corner booth. Just as if it were the most natural thing in the world, we both started talking. From that moment on, there was not one ounce of strain between us. Words poured out.

Brad spoke of his desire to be a freelance photographer, about his roommate Bill, who was his best friend since elementary school, his home, his kid sister Rosaline, and his parents, who were divorced. In fact, he talked about anything and everything except his brother Rick.

I, in turn, told him about my dreams of becoming a teacher, my home, my parents, and my brother Kurt. I said things to Brad that I could not remember ever telling anyone. I found myself talking about anything and everything, too, except for Tom.

At first, I did not mention Tommy because for a brief moment in time, I forgot he existed. Then, it became more than that . . . I didn't want Brad to know. I felt like a traitor. I hated myself for what I was doing, but I could not control the thoughts and emotions that were swirling around inside of me.

We talked the entire evening. Brad's expression became particularly animated when he discussed photography. I enjoyed watching his facial features dance with enthusiasm and listening to the ring of his laughter.

"I've never wanted to do anything but take pictures. As long as I can remember, I've had a camera. I get such a high off capturing reality and freezing it forever in a photograph."

"The way you talk about it sounds so exciting."

"Have you ever heard of Eddie Adams?"

"No." I pondered his question. "I don't think so."

"You might not know his name, but you've seen his work. It was on the cover of *Newsweek*. He took a picture of a police chief executing a Vietcong prisoner on a street corner in Saigon. He won a Pulitzer Prize for Feature News Photography."

"Yes. I know that picture. I'll remember it for the rest of my life. It was so dramatic."

"*That* is what I'm talking about!" Brad was extremely intense. "It's my dream that someday I'll take a picture the world will see and remember." Making a conscious effort to relax, he leaned back in his chair. "A picture isn't any good unless it tells a story. A person should be able to look at a photo and hear words . . . see images . . . be able to create an entire dialogue from what is seen. If not, the photographer failed to capture the subject."

A portion of Brad's hair slipped down over his brow. I wanted to reach across the table and slide it back into place, but I didn't dare. Even though I was finally feeling comfortable speaking to him, I was still afraid of any kind of physical contact. Why was I afraid to touch him? I was a touching person. I came from a touching family. My parents embraced us warmly; I felt comfortable hugging my brother. It was easy for me to throw my arms around acquaintances and relatives whether I knew them well or not. Why couldn't I simply reach across the table and touch Brad?

As the hour grew late, Brad escorted me back to the dorm. We spoke freely as we took our strides. He did not offer his hand or put an arm around me. I half expected him to guide me away from the sidewalk as he had mischievously threatened to do earlier. But nothing happened.

I became apprehensive at the door. I was not sure what to expect. Was he going to kiss me? Was he going to shake my hand? Did I want him to kiss me? I mustered the courage to look at Brad. He gently touched my cheek with his hand. His middle finger traced my lower lip. He stared into my eyes—deeper and deeper. It seemed as if I were suddenly floating. I closed my eyes and gave in to the very touch of him. Softly, he brushed his lips across mine. As unbelievable as it might sound, I actually felt as if electricity passed between us. I wanted to encircle him with my arms, but my muscles were frozen. I could not move.

Suddenly, I realized he had taken his palm from the side of my face, and his lips were gone. My eyes snapped open. I was positive he would laugh at me, but he did not. Brad was watching me. My God! Those eyes! They were so mesmerizing. I could lose myself in them. I wanted to say something . . . anything, but I was speechless. I couldn't remember another moment in my life when I was at a total loss for words.

Brad broke the spell. "Laura . . . thank you . . . I had a wonderful time." There was no devilish smile on his face, no mischievous glint in his eyes, no joking quality in his voice . . . just a sincere, warm expression.

My muscles started functioning again. My fingers moved. My sense of touch was restored. Even my voice worked, because I heard myself answer, "Yes . . . yes it was fun, wasn't it? I'm glad I went with you."

"Still think I'm a terrible wolf in sheep's clothing?" He was laughing again, but I didn't mind; I was laughing too.

"It'll take more than one evening to convince me to change my mind."

Brad leaned his shoulder on the wall next to me as a low, deep laughter came from his throat. "Are you proposing that I take you out again . . . and here I thought that you were such a demure, inexperienced little girl."

Little girl! He called me a little girl. How dare he refer to me as a child!

I was infuriated. I simply stood there, transfixed in one position, and wondered how this guy was capable of catapulting me into such a wide range of emotions. I felt like a Ping-Pong ball. One moment, I was relaxed and comfortable; the next, I was nervous and apprehensive. Now, I was on fire with fury! I wanted to choke him for creating such havoc in my mind and making my body turn traitor to my better judgment.

The expression on my face must not have changed with my conflicting emotions because his eyes did not reflect any alterations. Gently, Brad touched the tip of my nose with his index finger and smiled pleasantly. "Whether you were planning on seeing me again or not, Miss Davis . . . " Contemplating his words, Brad paused a few seconds. He locked my eyes to his as he softly stroked the skin of my cheek. His words were spoken so quietly that they were barely audible. "You will go out with me again, Laura. I insist upon it. See you tomorrow." He smiled, pivoted, and walked away.

I slowly mounted the stairs to my room. After taking a hot shower, I donned my nightclothes and crawled into bed. Sleep! I needed sleep. In the morning, I would be able to sort out all these new and confusing feelings; hopefully, I could put them into perspective. Giving in to weariness, I closed my eyes. As I drifted off into a peaceful slumber, I wondered why Brad called me Laura when everyone else called me Lori.

5

The following night I went out with Brad's brother Rick. He took me to see *Romeo & Juliet* in Burlington. I had seen it a couple of months earlier with Tommy. I loved the movie. It was so romantic and beautiful, yet such a tearjerker. For some reason, it did not seem appropriate to see this particular movie with Rick.

Rick Malone was a very nice, gentlemanly type of guy, extremely attractive, maybe even more so than his brother Brad. Rick's features were perfect in the classic sense of the word; whereas, Brad had the type of face and body a person expected to see in a magazine ad for Marlboro Country: eye catching, dark hair, tanned skin, a little rugged looking, lips slightly parted exposing perfectly formed white teeth, eyes challenging a person to step into the imaginary picture with the snow capped mountains in the background.

My God! What was the matter with me? I was daydreaming in the middle of the balcony scene when Romeo was proclaiming his love to Juliet. I had to snap out of this. I felt so strange . . . not at all like myself. I concentrated my thoughts on the film and did not allow my mind to wander in any other direction.

After the movie, we went to Pizza Hut. As we ate, Rick told me a lot of the same things about his family that Brad had mentioned on Friday night. I listened to every word and noted only one difference. Rick described his father in a completely opposite manner than Brad had. To Rick, their father was intelligent, kind, sensitive, and loving; but to Brad, he was aggressive, domineering, and overbearing. I wondered how two sons could see their father in such different ways.

After finishing our food, Rick took me back to Staley. He kissed me goodnight at the door. The earth did not tremble under my feet; lights did not flash. I didn't even feel remotely shaken by the experience. It reminded me of the way Tommy kissed. It was at that moment I had my first real foreboding of an impending problem.

6

The days melted into weeks as I concentrated on my part-time job in the cafeteria, studying, making new acquaintances, "broadening my horizons"—as my mother would say—and spending time with Rick and Brad periodically, but never together. I enjoyed being with both of them. It was very hard for me to believe that the two of them came from the same family. I didn't see them as brothers because they neither looked or acted the part. Both were attractive but in their own unique ways. Brad seemed easygoing while Rick appeared a little too serious. Brad was witty, charming, and gregarious. He had a vibrant quality surrounding him that made me feel alive. Rick was more reserved, pragmatic, and affable . . . qualities which had a calming effect on me. I developed new and distinct feelings for both of them. I felt like a friend toward Rick. I enjoyed his company. On the other hand, my emotions toward Brad were a little more difficult to define.

I liked Brad and didn't like him all at the same time. When I was with him, I felt like another person. Brad made me laugh. He made me nervous. He had the power to make my hands tremble, my stomach do flips, and my cheeks blush. He made me smile to myself even when I was alone, and somehow, mysteriously, he made me crave his company.

I pondered my thoughts and discovered that I harbored friendly feelings toward Rick, but the emotions I had for Brad went past platonic. It did not take long to realize I couldn't date them both, and I shouldn't be seeing either of them. Both brothers distorted my feelings for Tommy.

Tom and I spoke of marriage, children, and a lifetime together. We wanted to buy a small Cape Cod house with a white picket fence around it. We were going to have a dog and a couple of children. Both of us were going to teach in neighboring schools. That was our dream; those were our goals. Why was I trying to ruin it all by allowing two brothers to invade my world and destroy my security? I made a pact with my emotions and promised to tell both Rick and Brad that there could be no relationship with either of them.

While I was in the McKwen Library studying for my general psych test, Rick approached me and asked if I wanted to go with him to a party at The Lodge the following weekend. I watched him silently for a few moments and tried to find adequate words to explain my feelings. Before I gave myself enough time to plan my statement, the words started coming without any real structure to them. "Rick," I paused. "I like you. You're a very nice person . . . one of the nicest people I've met since I came here . . . "

"I like you, too, Lori," he interrupted. "I like you a lot." He reached for my hand and started caressing it in more than just a friendly way. Rick looked so sweet and so very honest.

I felt awful. I felt as if I purposely deceived him, and I had no one to blame but myself. I withdrew my hand before speaking again. "Rick, please . . . don't say anything else. Let me talk for a minute and try to explain. I can't let this go on any longer. I wish . . . "

"Never mind, Lori." A hostile expression covered his face. "I think I already know what you're going to say." It was the first time I had ever seen him angry.

"No . . . no, you don't know what I'm going to say." I lowered my voice a notch as I tried to put my thoughts into words. "I can't go with you this weekend; in fact, I really shouldn't be seeing you at all. . . . "

"It's Brad. Isn't it? You've made up your mind that I'm not good enough for you, but my brother is. Brad won. Didn't he? Brad always wins. I don't know why I thought this would be different." Rick sounded bitter—a characteristic foreign to his nature. "You're making a mistake, Lori. I'm the one who cares about you. Not Brad! He doesn't know how to feel or care about anyone but himself. He will hurt you like the string of other girls in his life. He'll cleverly snare you into his little trap and destroy you. I've seen it a dozen times. Don't be such a fool."

"Stop it!" I said it a bit louder than I intended. Several heads turned, investigating the commotion at our table. I lowered my voice and continued. "I can't stand this feeling of competition. It's as if the two of you think I'm some kind of prize. You don't understand. This has nothing to do with you or Brad."

"Oh really! Cut the B.S., Lori. I've seen how you look at him. And I know exactly the symptoms he creates in girls."

"You're not listening to me. Rick, I'm trying to explain. . . . "

Rick stood up. "I'm not interested in your excuses. He leaned on the table and made a fleeting attempt at touching my face, but he withdrew before contact was made. "Perhaps when you get tired of my brother's games, or he gets tired of toying around with a nice girl and goes on to someone more suitable to his needs . . ." Rick paused as he swallowed. He glanced around the room before allowing his eyes to wander back to mine. He seemed calmer when he spoke again. "Maybe, when that happens, Lori, maybe I'll still be around to pick up the pieces."

"Rick . . . "

"Spare me, Lori. Don't bother." The bitterness was gone from his voice.

Tesa Jones ❧ 17

"I'll wait. It won't take long. If I'm still interested, I'll let you know." He leaned over my shoulder and gently placed a kiss on the side of my face. "Take care of yourself and watch your step . . . that's good advice. I hope you're listening to it."

Before I could say another word, Rick vanished. I felt so bewildered. Rick misinterpreted everything I said. I covered my face with my hands and let out a deep sigh. Tommy was wrong. I should not have gone out with anyone. I should have made it perfectly clear from the beginning that I was practically engaged and happy to be in that state. Seeing other guys put such a strain on my nerves. God! I wished Tommy were here. I wished he could hold me and make all these confusing emotions go away.

Later in the evening, Brad waited for me to finish my dinner shift duties in the cafeteria. I felt his eyes upon me as I wiped down the last of the tables and cleared the few remaining trays left by lazy students. I knew it was the right time to explain my relationship with Tommy and to inform Brad there could no longer be any kind of relationship between us. I hoped the conversation would go more smoothly than the one with Rick. Unfortunately, I instinctively knew telling Brad was going to be a great deal more difficult than the encounter with Rick.

There had been no further physical contact between Brad and me since that initial chaste kiss. A strange part of me wanted his touch, and another part wanted to push him away for fear that he was becoming mentally too close. But I knew tonight—after our discussion—all those mixed emotions would disappear. I would put a stop to this transition and go back to the person I was when Tommy kissed me good-bye at the station. Tonight . . . everything would be fine . . . no more stress. My life would be in order again.

Brad walked up to me and gently placed an arm around my shoulder. "Hello, sunshine." He smiled warmly.

"Hello, Brad." I could not help but return a smile. He had a way of making me glow inside. "Can we go somewhere private and talk?"

"Those were my exact thoughts."

Brad guided me out of the building. We took steps in the direction of the man-made lake adjacent to the dorm. Nestling my frame inside the curve of his arm, he gave me a gentle squeeze.

We sat several feet from the edge of the water. Brad was talking, and I was trying to figure out the right words to say and the proper time in which to interject them when he stopped speaking. He looked directly into my eyes. His fingers were lightly brushing strands of my hair away from my face. His touch made all my prior thoughts take flight. That wild, new sensation started spreading through my veins, and I felt a sense of weakness wash over me. Tiny goose bumps appeared wherever he trailed his fingers and then spread like a rash covering the rest of my body. I wanted to look away. I wanted to push his hand from me. I wanted to stop the turmoil he was creating in me and talk, but I didn't move. He cupped the back of my neck with one hand as he gently drew me toward him. Run . . . get up and run . . . but instead, I closed my eyes as his mouth touched mine. I felt ablaze as his lips drew sensations from my toes, through my abdomen, to my mouth, and back again. He was using not only his lips but also his teeth and his tongue. His fingers were kneading the back of my neck as if they were dancing through my hair. I was pulsating with an inner fire.

I had never been kissed like that before. Tommy certainly never kissed me that way; his were always chaste and dry. Neither one of us had the experience to know any differently. Sweet Jesus! This was a whole new world. This man holding me now was casting a spell over me, and I seemed to have no choice in my reactions. Never in my life was I so thrilled. I wanted time to stop. I wanted past and future to disappear. I wanted only now—this moment—this second to go on forever. As our lips parted, his hands guided my head to his shoulder. His fingers drew imaginary pictures on neck and burned invisible patterns wherever they touched. I heard his voice. It was like music but miles away . . . soft, steady, and relaxing.

Firmly, he stated, "I understand you bid my brother a fond farewell."

Those words snapped me into reality. Tommy! Now was the time to explain the reasoning behind my motives. I could not allow these crazy, wild sensations to make me stray from my future. Tommy! Think of Tom, marriage, children, and goals . . . reality!

Before I was given a chance to utter a word, Brad spoke again. "I'm glad you're not going to see Rick anymore. I don't want to share you with anyone, Laura. I want you all for myself."

Like black magic, the whole image of Tom vanished. All I could think about was the gentle, soothing feeling of Brad's fingers tracing my jaw, my lips, and my cheekbone. I closed my eyes and continued swimming in the ecstasy of his touch.

Brad talked about his home in New Jersey. I didn't move. I simply rested my head on his shoulder and closed my eyes. I could picture everything Brad said: dozens of oak trees scattered over acres of land, the rippling brook in their backyard, the two-story Georgian house with black shutters, the boxwood hedges, the marigolds and petunias in the gardens. The picture he painted with his words sounded beautiful, but what I really relished was the soft melody of his voice.

I was so mesmerized by his tone, I didn't realize he directed a question toward me. "What?" I inquired without lifting my head from its comfortable position on his shoulder.

"I said, maybe next summer you'd like to come and see my home."

Because I needed time to think, I reacted slowly. I was completely stunned. Was his statement a casual one or a definite invitation?

He smiled that confident grin of his. "I just invited you to come home with me. Don't you have anything to say? A simple 'yes, I'd be delighted' would do."

"But Brad. That's months and months away."

"Well, perhaps then, if you're so eager . . . you might consider Thanksgiving or maybe the Christmas holidays." Smiling, he tapped my nose softly. Brad had two totally different ways of smiling. One minute he could appear very mischievous, almost wicked; the next moment, he could look as innocent as a child. At this particular instant, he appeared to be a babe in arms . . . content, satisfied, and happy. "Laura, I want you to meet my family. We live with my father in the house I was describing to you. It's a grand place. My mom lives on the other side of town. She's remarried to a nice enough guy. She'd like you, Laura . . . I just know it. I want you to meet my sister too. Rosaline's a typical teenager . . . a good kid." Brad was brushing my hair with his fingers again . . . slowly, methodically, sending me into another trance. "We live about ten miles from the Passaic River. My dad keeps his boat there. Have you ever been sailing?"

I laughed slightly. "No. I've never been on any kind of boat."

"You'd love it, Laura. It's like being totally free. The breeze blows through your hair; water splashes gently against the hull. It's quiet and peaceful. It's my favorite place in the world. I want to share it with you."

"Your home sounds marvelous. It must be a very happy place."

Brad looked away and became suddenly distant. I knew I said something wrong, but I was not quite sure what it was or how to correct my error. I touched his face with my hands and turned it toward my own. His skin felt warm; his eyes were melancholy. I searched for words that might take away whatever was causing his pain. "I'm sorry, Brad. I didn't mean . . . "

He smirked as he interrupted me. "No sweat. It's really no big deal. I guess I just made it sound a lot happier than it actually is. We're not very close. We don't do things together like most families. My sister's a sweet kid. Sometimes, I can hug her to death, but she's into her own thing now. And my brother . . . I don't want to talk about him. God! He aggravates me. Unfortunately, I don't even see my mom that much. She's busy with a new husband, a new kid to raise, and a job, which consumes most of her time. And my father . . . hell, he's so wrapped up in making money, he doesn't care about anything else. He's loaded, but money only buys surface beauty and artificial happiness . . . doesn't it?"

I didn't know what to say, so I remained silent. Brad reached for my hand. The gesture felt comforting.

He continued speaking. At first, it was in a steady, calm fashion, but gradually his voice became raised and filled with a pent-up anger. "My father . . . he is nothing more than a bastard at heart. He was so ambitious and so busy making his own fortune in restaurants and other investments that he didn't even notice or care when my mother fell in love with another guy. He's a selfish son of a bitch." Brad stopped a moment as if he were contemplating thoughts deep inside his mind. "When my father found out about the whole affair, he went through the roof. He couldn't stand that someone dared to take *his* property. He spent thousands of dollars and two years in court making sure that he got custody of Rick, Rosaline, and me just to spite my mom. On top of all that, he never gave her one damn dime of his precious money for settlement.

"I suppose my mother wasn't right in what she did but, damn it, neither was he! Do you know, Laura, my mother lives in this dinky little apartment they're renting? They don't even have enough money to buy a home. Her husband works for the post office. They have a kid of their own now. He's three. She gave up everything . . . money, prestige, nice clothes, expensive cars, the house, Rick, Rosaline, and me. She gave it all up . . . just to be free of my old man. I hope to hell she's happy."

He was squeezing my hand so tightly at this point that I was afraid he might break one of my fingers. Brad seemed oblivious to what he was doing. I used my free hand to stroke his; some of the tension seemed to ebb. Deep in thought, he kept staring out across the water. Finally, he began to speak again. "My father . . . what a jewel he is. God! I can never do anything right as far as he's concerned. Always Rick . . . Rick is perfect. Richard Malone Jr. As far back as I can remember, Rick always got the good grades; he's always well mannered and polite, never talking back, never getting into trouble; he listens endlessly to my father's stupid stories. And Dad is always saying, 'Rick this' and 'Rick that' and, of course, to top it all off, Rick wants to go into the family business. I don't give a shit about the family business! I never have and I never will. I don't want his money. I don't need him. I want to be a freelance photographer. I certainly don't want to sit behind a desk and count piles of receipts, watching paper money grow. I want to take pictures. I want to watch them develop, and most of all, I don't want to be compared to my big brother anymore. Jesus! Do you know how hard it is to follow perfection? No matter how hard I try, I can't succeed. It's a losing battle. Just once! Just one time, I wish I did something better than Rick." He stopped.

It was as if we were in a hurricane, and the eye of the storm was upon us. Silence! He let go of my hand. Slowly, Brad ran his fingers through his hair and pulled it all straight back. After taking a deep breath, he let it out in one long sigh. Lying on the ground, he closed his eyes. "I'm sorry, Laura. I didn't mean to say all those things." He ran his hands through his hair again and took another deep breath. "I don't know what to say. I've never spilled my guts like that before. Never! Not even to Billy. God! I don't know what came over me. I haven't had hostile thoughts like that for a long time. In fact, I thought I'd mastered them. I really thought I'd come to grips with it all."

I still could not find the right words to say. I quietly lay down beside him on the grass, rested my head on his shoulder, and wrapped an arm protectively around his chest. Silently, we stared up into the massive oak branches over our heads. It was dark. I couldn't see his face; I could only listen to the erratic beating of his heart. He encircled me with his arms. As the minutes ticked by, I noticed his heartbeat gradually stabilized and his breathing regulated. He started stroking my hair again. With every touch, I felt a tightening develop in the pit of my abdomen. A strange sense of desire came over me, which made me want to press my body even closer to his; I wanted to feel his warmth. It was a unique urge I had never felt before, like a warm, or rather hot, fluid was racing through my veins. I wanted to protect him. I wanted to cradle him. I wanted to kiss him. And God help me! I wanted to make love to him.

"Laura . . . "

"Yes?"

"I really would like you to come home with me." His voice invaded the quiet. "I mean it. I'm not just kidding around."

"Sure," I heard myself reply. "I'd love to, Brad, I'd really love to." But how could I?

Shortly after my last comment, he stood up and helped me to my feet.

It was nearly 11:00—way past close study—almost time to lock the doors to Staley. Where had the time gone? I hoped the housemother had not done a random room check. I didn't need the demerits.

Together we walked back to the lobby. Both of us were silent until he bent over and kissed the side of my face. A pleasant, warm smile exposed his teeth as he muttered softly, "Sweet dreams, Laura. Can I see you tomorrow?"

I nodded. I wanted him to kiss me again as he had done earlier. I had the strongest desire to put my arms around him and press myself firmly against his body. I wanted to feel those wonderfully warm sensations he created inside of me, but mostly I just didn't want to let him go. I watched him smiling at me. I had so many things I wanted to say, but the words didn't form.

He touched my face lightly one more time as if I were a precious metal. "You're good for me, sunshine." There was an intangible bond between our eyes.

As I mounted the stairs, a wave of depression swept over me. I intended to confront Brad with the truth about Tommy; instead of succeeding in that task, I was drawn closer to him.

7

Playing cards was a favorite pastime for many of the girls in the dorm. I enjoyed the craze as much as anyone else. When Mary and Janet asked Sue and me to join them, we accepted. They smuggled two six-packs of beer into our room and were drinking and laughing at their latest caper. I didn't mind. It didn't seem to bother any of them that I was not sharing their beverage of choice. It was common knowledge that alcohol was taboo in the dorm, but the three of them were so spirited and fun-loving that it was infectious.

As the cards were dealt and each game of Spades was played, the girls exchanged ideas and experiences on sex. I played my hand and listened. Using sensual, descriptive vocabulary—right down to the act itself—Mary described her first time. Her language was so colorful as she laughed and spoke of segments during her first sexual encounter that we, too, joined in laughter. Mary giggled wildly as she acted out how the guy's zipper got stuck. She rolled on the floor when she explained how the police car interrupted them; finally, she became somber when she finished her synopsis by saying, "And then the next day, he didn't even look at me. The creep had been chasing after me for months, sending me flowers, calling me every night on the phone, proclaiming eternal love and devotion. Then, after he'd gotten his notch in the belt, all that crap went out the window. The bastard didn't even have two words to say to me. He'd gotten what he wanted and no longer had any use for me. The next day, I saw him rubbing up against another girl; that was the end of him." Mary took another gulp of beer and a long drag of her cigarette, exhaled, and then laughed in a plaintive way. "But it's okay. The whole thing's behind me now, and I don't have to worry about which guy to save it for any longer. In fact, it's been my experience over the last couple of years that guys aren't necessarily the only ones to have all the fun. There are plenty of good times to be had by women; men don't have a monopoly on it. There ain't nothing like a good lay."

Janet jumped into the conversation. She waved her hands frantically. "Me! My turn." She had consumed quite a few beers making her uninhibited. "Since it's confession time, I want to tell my story. My virginal bliss ended of my own accord. I simply didn't want to be in that puritanical state any longer. I was tired of trying to decide which boyfriend to give it to so I willingly and unforgettably gave it to a stranger. It was the best I've ever had. No lie! The guy was a lot older, and he really knew what he was doing, not like these young punks who think they're king jock!" Janet closed her eyes, clasped her hands together, and rested her chin on the pyramid it made. "He was smooth and considerate. This guy knew all the right places to touch and fondle. He had the most terrific moves. Good God! I'm getting wet just thinking about it." Her eyes flashed opened and a mischievous glint appeared in her eyes. "I felt freed. I still do."

Sue began to describe her long-standing boyfriend and their intimacies.

My mind began to wander. I drifted back five months to when life seemed less complex . . . to when my whole world was centered around Tom Ladley. At that point, we had been dating nearly a year and a half. It was spring, and graduation was just around the corner. Tommy and I discussed sex at length, experienced all kinds of foreplay, and fogged up more car windows than I could count; but still, we had not become lovers. I was too frightened to give my consent. Tom was so inexperienced that he didn't really know what he was missing any more than I did. Of course, he was terribly frustrated and even irritable at times, but being the gentle, loving guy that he was, he waited patiently.

One weekend in late May, after we watched *Good-bye Columbus,* Tommy became inspired by Richard Benjamin's performance and wanted to take advantage of the fact that his parents were out of town. We were driving home from the movie theater when I gave him my simple but affirmative answer. "Yes." He was speechless. At an intersection on Richmond Highway, he took a right turn and drove into the 7-11 parking lot. Even though he was a bundle of nerves, Tommy was in control of the situation.

He very bluntly said, "I need to buy something . . . Trojans, I guess. I mean, we can't take the risk that you might get pregnant." He leaned over and kissed me. I could still remember how his hands trembled. I watched him as he looked in his wallet and noticed there was only one dollar left. "Do you think this will be enough?"

"How should I know?" I answered tersely, already regretting my spur of the moment stab at courage.

Tommy jumped out of the car, walked into the store, and returned a few moments later empty-handed. He leaned in the window and whispered, "I didn't get them. There's a woman behind the counter. I mean . . . what do I say? I can't go up there and ask some strange lady for a rubber. My God! I'll die."

"I don't know, Tommy. Maybe we ought to just forget it." I was on edge. I feared that I might burst into hysterical laugher in order to cover my trepidation. The whole thing was a terrible combination of comedy and tragedy.

"No!" Tommy answered. "I'll think of something." He disappeared a second time and reappeared carrying a small bag in his hand. He smiled as he waved it in my direction. "Success!" Tommy whispered as he sat in the car. "Three for sixty-seven cents . . . a real bargain in my book, despite the embarrassment."

We drove back to his house. Tommy talked incessantly. I, on the other hand, did not say a word. I could still remember how nervous I was. Upon entering the house, he ran directly to his bedroom, turned down the sheets, lit a candle, got undressed, and chatted away the entire time.

Wearing only my slip, I sat quietly on the mattress. Nervously, I twisted the birthstone ring Tommy had given me for my eighteenth birthday. It felt so wrong. Nothing was how I imagined. There was no romance, no spontaneity. It seemed so calculated. I gave in to my emotions. As my face fell into my hands, I began to cry—sob would be a more precise description. At that point, Tom took a seat next to me and cradled my body in his arms. I cried for a long time. In between choking sobs, I said, "I guess I'm just not ready."

Tommy rocked me in his arms and whispered quietly into my ear. "It's okay, baby, it's all right . . . really it is." Over and over again he said the same sentences. Tommy was so kind . . . so patient. When I was finally calm, he put the unwrapped Trojan in his hand and placed a second, wrapped one in mine. He was laughing. "I have an idea. Follow me." We both walked into the bathroom. Tom placed the lifeless piece of rubber under the faucet and turned to me. I recalled how quickly Tommy brought a smile to my face. He was going to make it all better. Tommy was always capable of making everything okay again. "Will you do the honors?" He laughed as he pointed to the water faucet.

I turned the valve counterclockwise; the water poured out. It was amazing how much liquid the Trojan held. It expanded and grew until it looked like a white replica of the Goodyear blimp. We both laughed uncontrollably. It was so ridiculous; it was actually funny.

"You know, Lori, this would make a great advertisement for the durability of these things." He tied the end into a knot, and we proceeded to do the same to the second one. It was just as funny the second time as the first. Tommy put the third Trojan in his wallet, as he casually commented, "This one's for whenever you're ready."

I knew he was disappointed, but it was hard for me to explain how I felt about sex. For as long as I could remember, my mother subtly connected virginity to honeymoon and intercourse with marriage. I wanted the traditional white gown, and I wanted to be carried over the threshold in breathless anticipation of my wedding night. In my own naive way, I had the perfect honeymoon picture painted in my mind. I was so innocent . . . such a romantic at heart.

A couple of months went by after that incident with Tommy. We graduated and were making plans for our futures. Tommy and I were packing a lifetime of experiences into one last summer before college would divide us for months at a time. Despite Tom's gentleness, he became more and more frustrated and impatient with me. I tried countless times to explain to him how I felt, but it did not seem to release the physical pressure that was building inside of him. He was no longer satisfied with innocent fooling around. His frustration caused a breach between us. Consequently, one very hot July night, in the back of his parents' brand new 1969 Mustang, we made use of that third Trojan Tommy was concealing in his wallet.

It was not at all like the books and movies said it would be. I was disappointed. I had always read that upon initial entry, there would be one stabbing pain, which ultimately converted to ecstasy with each new thrust. The books lied. Authors compared making love to skyrockets and fireworks. They claimed that the act itself was a physical unveiling that immediately changed a girl into a woman. All that was just plain bullshit! There was no other word for it. Not only were there no skyrockets, fireworks, or ecstasy, but there was no pain either. It was just kind of tight and uncomfortable for a few seconds, and then it was over.

I wanted to feel something—*anything*—but there was no physical or emotional feeling at all. In fact, at first, there wasn't even any guilt. I cried no tears, felt no joy or jubilation. The worst part about it was that I did not even discover an overwhelming closeness toward Tommy. No! It was nothing like Hollywood or authors professed, and I resented them for teasing me with false words and images.

Tommy, on the other hand, rode on cloud nine both during and after the occasion. He was so overcome with happiness that he totally missed my quiet depression. I was glad. I didn't want to explain my thoughts. That night, he said a lot of things to me, but the only sentence I remembered in its entirety was, "There will never be anyone but you, Lori . . . our lives are so perfect." He held on to me as if I was his salvation.

"Lori."

I kept hearing my name far off in the distance. I jerked my head up. It was Sue. I snapped out of my personal thoughts and returned to the present.

"Lori, my God, where have you been? Were you sleeping through my tales of love?" Sue laughed gaily. "Jesus, no respect!" Everyone joined in laughter; so did I. "Well, tell us what was so engrossing that you missed out on my life story. We're all dying to hear."

"It was nothing," I answered. "I was just thinking of something that happened a long time ago." I couldn't tell them. I never spoke about it . . . not to anyone. I wouldn't even know how to put it into words.

"So, tell us, Lori, about you," Janet encouraged with a teasing voice. "We've all confessed. Let's hear your story."

I flushed with embarrassment. I didn't know how to politely withdraw from the conversation.

"Janet, come on . . . cool it!" Mary spoke. "Can't you see a virgin when she's right in front of you?" She was smiling at me in a warm, friendly way. "It's okay, kid. Sometimes, I wish mine were still intact. Save it . . . it's a good thing to have around. But a word to the wise, Lori . . . don't hang around that Bradley Malone character too long. And whatever you do, don't listen to any of his fancy talk. He has a reputation that followed him all the way down here from New Jersey. The Brads of the world are the type of guys sweet kids like you should stay away from." She took a long drink of her beer and lit another cigarette.

"Yeah, and if I were you, Lori . . . " Janet added. "I wouldn't break off with that nice-looking honey you have in that picture frame over there for Brad Malone . . . no matter how sweet talking he is. You play with fire, kiddo, you might get your ass burned."

That night, after close study, I didn't go down to the lobby. When Brad called, I told the girl who answered the phone to tell him I was out of the dorm.

8

I ran into Brad between classes. He walked up to me, put his arm around my shoulder, and kissed me softly on the forehead. "How's my girl? I missed you last night. Where were you?"

Just the touch of his arm sent my nervous system into turmoil. When his lips brushed against my forehead, I felt ablaze. What power was this that he held over me? "I went out and had pizza with some of the girls." *Why was I lying?* I had never deliberately lied to anyone in my life. Why was I afraid of having him so close to me . . . yet equally afraid of letting him go? Why was it, whenever I was close to Brad, I couldn't even conjure up an image of Tommy in my mind?

"Laura, what do you say if I get a bottle of wine tonight and we take a sunset walk?" Brad was staring at me and smiling that charming, irresistible smile of his. "Hey, sunshine . . . what's up? Cat got your tongue? Come on, say yes . . . it'll be fun."

I looked into those brown eyes as he worked his magic on me. "Okay, that sounds nice." My voice betrayed me again.

Brad called for me after dinner. By the time we walked a short distance and laid the blanket down in a secluded spot, the sun was already nestled peacefully behind the trees. The evening hue produced a yellow glow on the changing leaves and made them an even deeper shade. Birds created their own melodies, and squirrels scampered playfully from branch to branch. It was like a private, secluded world where only nature invaded our lives.

"This is nice . . . like a world all its own. So quiet and tranquil." I sat down on the blanket. "I like it here."

"I'm glad, Laura. I stumbled on it quite by accident while I was doing a nature layout for my photography class." He pointed to a fallen tree several yards away. "See that branch over there? The other day there was a chipmunk perched on it. I almost didn't notice him. He was so cute; he watched every move I made. That little critter actually stood posing while I got my camera, changed lenses, focused, and took five pictures." Brad paused, looked around, and took in the view. "I like it out here . . . there are no problems—no rules—no right or wrong—just peace and quiet. Solitude! It's so beautiful . . . like you." Brad was still standing; his attention suddenly directed toward me. He stood there silently for several seconds with an unreadable expression on his face. "My God! Laura, do you have any idea how truly pretty you are? You're so fresh and new and utterly delightful. You fit in with all this beauty." He sat down beside me and gently pulled the hair away from my face. It appeared as if he were going to kiss me, but instead he whispered, "Are you aware that in certain lighting your hair seems to have flecks of cinnamon streaked through it? Other times, it's highlighted with honey tones." He quietly twisted a few strands around his fingers. "Your eyes are like pools of spring water—so crystal blue and pure—I could lose myself in them." He was running his fingertips ever so delicately over my lashes. As I closed my eyes, he traced a complete circle around each one. "And your smile . . . it's bright and warm . . . like sunshine."

He dropped his hands from my face and laughed in his confident way. "Good God Almighty! Would you listen to me. Jeez! I sound ridiculous."

He reached over my lap and picked up the bottle of Boone's Farm, twisted off the top, and poured some in two paper cups. As he handed one to me, he jokingly commented, "You deserve Dom Perignon and long-stemmed crystal, but this is the best I can do."

I sipped the wine. At first, it made my nose crinkle, but after a few tastes I decided I liked it. There was a fruit flavor to the liquid and a mild calming effect on my nerves. I drained my cup and reached for more. He poured us both another.

As I drank from the second glass, Brad pulled out a shoebox from the bag he had been carrying. "Close your eyes, Laura." He spoke softly.

I could hear the rustling of paper and a match being struck. The sulfur burned my nose. I was so curious I nearly opened my eyes prematurely when Brad finally spoke again.

"Okay, Laura . . . you can look now."

I was totally surprised by what I saw. There, on the blanket in front of me, was a cupcake with a lit candle on top of it. In the palm of Brad's hand was a beautifully wrapped package with a bright yellow bow. My heart leaped into my throat, and tears stung my eyes.

"Happy birthday, Laura."

"Oh, Brad . . . this is so sweet."

"I heard through the grapevine that you were turning nineteen today. I can't believe I had to find out from someone else. You should have told me."

"It's my first birthday away from home. My parents called. I talked with my brother for almost an hour, but it's not the same as being with them. I miss my family. To be honest, I think I've been a little homesick, and I've been feeling quite melancholy." After I blew out the candle, I leaned over to kiss his cheek. "Thank you, Brad. You've made today special."

"When you blew out the candle, did you make a wish?"

"Of course."

"What was it?"

"That all my days can turn out to be as wonderful as today."

He handed me the gift. Savoring the moment, I unwrapped it slowly. After the paper was stripped, I opened the box. Inside, I discovered a tiny gold ankle bracelet. "Oh, Brad! It's gorgeous." I was stunned.

"Not nearly as gorgeous as you are." He carefully took it out of the box. "Let me put it on you." Gently, he adjusted the clasp and placed it around my ankle. "There . . . fits perfectly . . . now you'll never be able to forget me." His voice was light and jovial. "I'd like to make a toast." He picked up his paper cup and lifted it into the air. "To Laura Davis . . . who looks as beautiful in warm sunshine as she does in this moonlight. May her days always be wonderful and filled with happiness." He lifted it slowly to his lips and took a sip.

Soft shadows, which made his eyes shine like stars, danced across Brad's face. A gentle breeze blew his hair out of place. I reached over to put the few strands back in order. He immediately stopped talking in mid-sentence. Reaching up, he touched my hand. Without holding on, he led my hand back down to my side. I saw him leaning toward me. I felt myself falling backward . . . gently . . . slowly . . . until I could feel the earth on my back.

The moon, the stars, and the trees were gone; all I could see was Brad's face descending upon mine. That wonderful, wild feeling was playing havoc with my body again. Every part of me was already on fire by the time his lips touched mine. My arms automatically encircled him; I pulled him firmly to me. I could feel the entire length of his pulsating body. Oh, Sweet Jesus! This had to be heaven.

Over and over again, he kissed me: my neck, my face, my shoulders, my lips. The wine only accentuated my mounting desire. I felt as if I were transported to another dimension, which made it hard to comprehend the words Brad spoke.

He whispered while his lips worked their magic. "You've cast a spell over me, Laura." Brad was burning my neck with light touches of his tongue sending trails of electricity throughout my body. "You must be some sort of witch. My God! I haven't looked at another girl since I set eyes on you." His hands were everywhere . . . on my face, my neck, my shoulders, running down my sides. "I think about you all the time . . . I even dream about you." His breathing was erratic as he kept moaning and muttering words I no longer understood.

I felt pressure on my breasts and realized he was touching me and sending wild currents of excitement through my veins. I felt as if waves were crashing around my ears. I reveled in the wonderful sensations he created inside of me. He pulled at my clothes. I heard fabric rip, but I didn't care. All I knew was that this moment was ecstasy at its peak.

Suddenly, I felt a great weight lift off of me. The sound of waves started melding back into birds and crickets; my burning skin felt a cool breeze upon it. I opened my eyes. Brad's back was all I could see.

"Sit up, Laura."

"What?"

"I said, sit up . . . damn it." He was angry. As I reached over to touch his back, he snapped a retort. "Don't . . . don't touch me, Laura. Don't say a word . . . just sit up."

As I did what he commanded, I felt a rush of cool night air hit my chest. I looked down to see the entire front of my blouse was opened. I used both hands to cover myself as best as I could. Some of the buttons were missing. I felt so helpless. I didn't know whether to be sad or grateful. I had been plunging headfirst into an ocean of excitement with no self-control; a part of me was disappointed it had stopped so abruptly.

"I'm sorry about your clothes." He still was not looking in my direction. Why was he so upset with me? Had I done something wrong?

"Put on my jacket." His voice was stern as he stood up, collecting his radio and blanket. Without another word, he started walking away. He took several steps before turning around, "Don't just stand there. Come on! I'm taking you back to the dorm."

We walked toward campus in silence. I was too afraid of his wrath to say a word. What was he thinking? Why was he walking so rapidly? I could barely keep up with his pace. Why wouldn't he talk to me? "What did I do wrong?" Did I actually say those words or were they only my thoughts?

"Nothing." His voice was more gentle now, more relaxed. "Nothing . . . Laura . . . you didn't do anything wrong." He made a short grunting sound in his throat that resembled the beginning of a laugh. He drew me closer as he put an arm around my waist. "I hope I didn't hurt you." He squeezed me with his hand, and I nestled my head against his shoulder as we continued walking. Brad threw his head back in laughter; the whole forest echoed the sound. "Lord, girl . . . you do weird things to my head." He was teasing me. He reverted to that confident style of his, laughing and joking, toying with my lack of experience. "Oh, if the guys could only see me now!" He started whistling as we picked up our pace. By the time we got back to the dorm, we were practically running—arm in arm—laughing and singing the entire way.

When I reached my room, there was a message taped to my door: "Tommy called". I should have been sorry I missed him; strangely enough, I felt no loss. I picked up some change and went to the pay phone down the hall. After a few moments, I heard his voice.

"Hi, babe . . . Happy birthday! Did you get my card and the flowers?"

"Yes. They are very pretty. Thank you."

"I miss you, Lori."

"I miss you too." I choked on the words, but at least I managed to get them out and even made them sound convincing. I should have had *some* feeling—eagerness, excitement, joy—but none of those old emotions surfaced.

"Hey, listen, Lori . . . I've got some great news. There's a guy driving past Elon this weekend. He told me I could have a lift. I'll be there by 3:00 tomorrow. Try and find a bed for me to sleep in."

My heart sank. I had a date to the football game with Brad on Saturday. I'd have to break it. I'd have to tell him about Tommy, and I wasn't sure how I was going to do that. All these weeks, Brad thought his brother was his rival; he didn't know a thing about Tommy or my future or my dreams. To top off my deceit, Tommy didn't have the first clue about Brad. I wrote Tom faithfully each day, and I never mentioned dates of any kind. I even managed to make the letters light and happy to cover my growing emotional stress. It was all going to come to a head, and I had no one to blame but myself.

"That's great, honey." Trying to sound enthusiastic, I added, "I'm looking forward to seeing you. It's been a long time."

"I love you, Lori. I can't think about anything else but you. Being separated is driving me crazy." He paused and waited for a reply.

I knew he expected a similar response, but my tongue seemed to be tied up in knots. I finally spoke. "Me, too."

"I'm miserable here. I can't wait to be with you and hold you again. Just to have you in my arms." The operator came on announcing that our time was up.

"See you tomorrow, Lori. God! I can't wait."

"Yeah . . . " We were disconnected. I hung up the phone. I stood there for what seemed like an eternity with one hand on the cradled receiver while the other massaged my temple. Oh, Tommy, please . . . I prayed. When you come tomorrow . . . bring me back down to earth.

The next morning, I confronted Brad. I explained that I had to cancel our date. I also admitted that Tommy and I had been dating for two years. I was honest and frank about Tom's and my relationship, and I only left out the fact that we had been intimate. I didn't think that was necessary. As difficult as it was, I managed to keep a pleasant expression on my face. I received another lecture from a couple of the girls on the hall about Brad's reputation, and I didn't want to let him know how apprehensive I was about his response to my honesty.

During my entire confession, Brad's expression never wavered. It appeared as if he was not even the slightest bit upset by my news. His apathy caused a sinking sensation in the pit of my stomach. I did not want Brad to know how much he hurt me by not caring that there was another person in my life. I wasn't sure what I expected. Anger? Resentment? Perhaps a part of me wanted him to be jealous, but he showed none of the signs.

"Do you love this fellow?" Brad's voice was very casual.

I looked away and watched as a jogger ran around the track. I heard car doors slamming in the distance and voices far away. I pressed my lips together tightly and rubbed my thumb against my index finger until I thought my skin would go raw. "I don't . . ." I muttered quietly. "I don't know anymore." I couldn't believe that I actually said those horrible inner thoughts. It was almost a relief to express them. I took a deep breath and looked back at Brad.

"How long will this hometown honey of yours be here?" His voice remained steady.

It was unnerving. How could he be in such control when my entire stomach was flipping over? "He'll leave on Sunday."

"All right then, Laura . . . I'll see you Sunday night . . . after dinner." Without waiting for a response, Brad pivoted and walked away.

What was I going to do?

9

The moment I saw Tommy, I knew that the feelings I once had felt were gone. I tried to act lovingly. I even managed to control my facial features and appear happy. I knew it would be far too cruel to blurt out everything without warning. I needed to do it slowly, gently. I knew how much I meant to Tommy—his letters and phone calls reeked of his emotions. "You're all I have and all I ever want." How many times had Tommy said that to me? Over and over again.

He was hugging me, kissing me. There were no skyrockets, no sense of weakness, and no music in my ears. Had it always been like that? Yes! But before it hadn't mattered; I had known no differently.

We had dinner in the cafeteria. I heard subtle innuendoes all around us; luckily, Tommy didn't grasp their meanings. I saw Brad out of the corner of my eye. He was taking his tray to the garbage conveyor belt. He was with some friends. They appeared to be laughing at him as he banged his stuff around rather rudely. Brad was wearing a rancorous expression. Was he angry? Billy must have said something to provoke him. They walked past my table on their way out. When Brad discovered that I was looking at him, his hateful sneer turned into a smile.

"Hi, Laura." He appeared just as cool and confident as he always was. He nodded his head pleasantly first at me and then at Tommy before continuing his steps.

"Hello, Brad," I replied. My face started to flush. Before I finished my greeting, Brad put an arm lazily around a pretty blonde and proceeded to walk out of the room. I had never seen him with another girl. I felt my first pang of jealousy. Jealousy was another new emotion for me. It seemed to eat

Tesa Jones 37

at my heart. Even though my expression was stoic, I wanted to race up to that girl and tear her eyes out. I was livid. I clenched my hands under the table as I witnessed Brad nuzzling his nose in the girl's hair. He let out a deep, throaty chuckle. Obviously, Brad Malone did not give a damn about me. He had already found a replacement.

Somehow, I made it through the weekend. I felt like a robot going through the motions. Tommy and I played tennis. Saturday evening, we watched a Bob Hope special on television, played bridge with another couple, and joined in a few gab sessions in the lobby. I did everything I could think of to keep from being alone with him. Why? Why didn't I want to be alone with Tommy? Was it because I was afraid he might want to make love? Yes. That was part of it. I didn't want to resume our sexual relationship. But there was more. The feelings inside of me were so frightening, so indescribable.

When it came time for Tommy's departure on Sunday, I clung to him and begged him not to leave. I cried. I couldn't explain why, not even to myself. I was so confused. For some reason, I felt sure that Tommy represented my sanity; I wanted desperately to hold onto him. I was so sure that if we stayed together, everything would be okay; my confusion would be erased.

After Tommy left, I went back to my room and tried to concentrate on my term paper for Dr. Blake's class. Many times, I jotted down sentences relating to the thesis, but each time I ripped the paper up and tossed it in the basket next to me. My mind wasn't functioning to capacity. No matter how hard I tried, my eyes kept drifting over to the ankle bracelet, which rested on the corner of my desk. I had taken it off on Saturday before Tom arrived because I knew it would be difficult to explain. I couldn't decide whether to wear it or not. My mind constantly flipped between memories of Tommy, which seemed to meld uncontrollably into thoughts of Brad. I didn't want Brad on my mind. I felt completely out of control of not only the situation but my feelings as well. These new overwhelming emotions terrified me.

As the hours slipped by, I discovered that I was watching the clock tick.

I waited for the moment when Brad would come to see me as he had promised. Seven o'clock . . . eight o'clock . . . nine o'clock . . . ten o'clock. Brad did not come. Mixed emotions battled it out inside my mind. At first, I was hurt, angry, and jealous. As much as I fought the emotions, I simply could not keep them away. I envisioned him with that gorgeous blonde. I slammed books and kicked furniture. I paced back and forth feeling my body grow taut from tension. Damn him!

By ten fifteen, I knew Brad was not going to show. After a long shower, my common sense took command. This was for the best. Brad was making the choice for me.

I did not see Brad at all during the next four days. He didn't eat his meals in the cafeteria, I didn't see him in the library or in the student union, and I never saw him with his brother or Billy. It was as if Brad vanished without a trace. Rumor had it that he was eating off campus and spending a great deal of time with a sophomore from West Dorm.

It wasn't until I was returning from my French class on Thursday that I got a quick glimpse of him. He was leaning against a wall and smiling into the face of the sexy blonde I'd seen with him last weekend. Twice I watched him plant a more than friendly kiss on her cheek. He ran his fingers up and down her arm as if he knew what her skin felt like underneath the material. I was furious and jealous, but then I calmed down long enough to remind myself that I had been warned. I was finally seeing Brad for what he really was. I had been just foolish enough to think that I had been right about him and everyone else had been wrong.

Brad was so intent on capturing his next victim that he totally ignored me as I passed. Well, so be it . . . at least now I knew the score.

That evening, I studied diligently for several hours and accomplished a great deal more than I had in the four days prior to it. After close study, I sat back in my chair and relaxed. My muscles were stiff from sitting so long in one position. I decided a walk would be nice before the dorm closed for the night. After circling the lake one full time, I chose a large oak to sit under. Leaning against it, I watched Mother Nature undress her trees for winter.

Multicolored leaves floated gently to the ground. The air was fresh, which made it a joy just to breathe. I closed my eyes to get full benefit from the cool autumn breeze. It was the most relaxed I had been all week.

There was no sound of footsteps—no rustling of cloth—when I heard my name being spoken very softly. I knew that voice. The sound of it created a fever-hot rushing sensation in my loins. I did not move, nor did I open my eyes.

"Laura," he repeated.

I refused to look at him; instead, I stared out across the water. "Hello, Brad."

"Can I sit down?"

"It's a free country, isn't it?" I couldn't believe how harsh my voice sounded. He sat down a foot or two away. Thank God, he wasn't any closer. I watched the silhouettes of a couple in the distance and concentrated all my thoughts on them.

"Billy told me he saw you playing tennis the other day. He said you were pretty good." When his comment was returned with silence, he continued. "Maybe we could play sometime."

"Why? Don't you have anyone else to play with?" My God! That sounded catty. What had gotten into me?

Brad ignored my question. "How'd it go last weekend?"

"Fine . . . everything went fine . . . marvelous in fact," I lied.

Several minutes passed before he made another comment. "It's a nice night, isn't it?"

The weather! How could he be so collected and in control? How could he talk about the weather when my whole mind was in complete chaos? Another minute and I'd have to get up and run for safety, or I would explode from the tension his closeness created inside of me.

"I see you're not wearing the bracelet."

"It's on my desk." Get a grip, Laura . . . before you make a fool of yourself.

"I thought you liked it."

"I do . . . it's nice." My fingers were trembling. "I've . . . I've just been so busy I haven't had a chance to put it on since . . . since last weekend."

"Laura . . . look at me." His voice was a whisper. "Please . . . just look at me."

As I turned my head to face him, I saw his hand reaching for mine. I instantly jerked it away. "Don't!" I snapped as I rested both hands in my lap. "Don't touch me." I knew I could not bare the blinding and powerful effects of his touch. It was hard enough to look at him . . . touching would be more than I could stand.

"We have to talk, Laura." His eyes were drilling through me. "I have to know."

I stood up, brushed grass from my pants, and started to walk away. I could only think of the sanctuary of my room. I must not think of anything else . . . my room. "I have to go inside now, Brad. I have some more studying to do." I took a few steps in the direction of the dorm when suddenly I felt a firm grasp around my forearm. I was spun harshly to face him.

There was nothing gentle about the way both his hands tightly held my shoulders. He jerked me, which caused my head to swirl in circles. I wanted to scream. I wanted to free myself. Escape!

"You won't walk out on me!" Brad demanded. "I'm trying to talk to you, damn it. You will not walk away from me. Do you hear?" The vibrations stopped. There was silence, but his fingers still dug into the soft skin of my arms. "Damn it, Laura! Say something."

Those eyes. God! Give me peace from those mesmerizing eyes. His arms were suddenly enclosed around my back, and my body was crushed against him. He was kissing me, forcing my lips open, and bending my neck so far back that I could not fight. I became consumed by him . . . captured by the fire he set throughout my body. I tried to resist, but it was a losing battle. I returned his passions. Every part of me was pressed into the form of his frame. Every ounce of my energy was devoted to his touch.

I didn't know when or how it happened, but I was free of his embrace.

Miraculously, my legs still supported me. I felt out of breath; my chest heaved with the simple task of breathing.

"Now, tell me, Laura . . . look at me and tell me that your precious Tommy kisses you like that!" He spat the words out like venom.

I found my tongue. "How dare you!" My brain was pounding with so much excess energy that I was sure it would burst. Repeatedly, my fists beat at his chest, hitting him as hard as I could. "How dare you! You son of a bitch!" I could not remember ever raising my voice or losing my temper at anyone; and here I was screaming, using scurrilous words I had never uttered before in my life. "How dare you talk to me like that . . . you damned rotten . . . bastard! You . . . with your harem of women! Why don't you leave me the hell alone? I hate you! I hate everything about you." He grabbed my wrists, which made it impossible for me to strike out at him any further. "Let go of me! I don't need you! I don't want you! Let me go!"

His laughter was like a splash of cold water on my face. It echoed over and over again in my ears. I stopped screaming in time to hear his chuckling turn into words.

"If I'm not mistaken, sunshine, I think we're having our first argument."

"You're incorrigible."

"And you, my sweet Laura, are a very spirited young lady." I snapped my hands from his grasp. He ignored my actions as he added, "And I was thinking all this time what a demure and reserved creature you are."

I rubbed my bruised shoulders. "You bring out the worst in me."

"No! That's where you're wrong! I bring out the best in you. You come alive with me. You radiate when we're together. Don't think for a moment I can't see the effects I have on you."

"You conceited . . . smug . . . "

"Shhh . . . relax. Don't fight what's between us, Laura." He whispered softly into my ear.

"There's nothing between us. Nothing at all!"

"Oh, yes there is, and we both know it."

I was calmer now; my breathing was less erratic. The tension started to subside. Gently this time, Brad drew me protectively into his arms and stroked the side of my face with tender fingers. "I'm crazy about you, Laura Davis. I don't know why or how it happened . . . I just know that the feeling's there."

My common sense told me he was just saying the words in order to get my defenses down, but the sound of his voice was like music. What was this power he held over me? I felt myself falling into his trap.

"I wish I'd met you a few years from now." The tone of his voice was low, barely audible. "You're exactly the type of girl I'd consider settling down with." He tilted my head, and his lips curved into a smile. "Hey, how would my best girl like to spend Homecoming Weekend with me?"

"What?" He changed the subject so fast, I lost my train of thought.

"Homecoming . . . spend it with me."

"I . . . I don't know . . . that's a few weeks away."

"What's this? The stall? Are you trying to hold out for a better offer?"

"No, of course not."

"Then say yes, I'd love to go with you."

"All right . . . yes, I'd love to go with you." The words slipped out before I had the time to think about them.

He lifted me effortlessly into his arms, spinning me around, laughing and kissing me simultaneously. "Do you know that you're as light as a feather? How can such an enticing body as yours weigh so little?" He carried me all the way back to the dorm, through the lobby, and deposited me at the door to Staley.

10

The next several weeks were heaven. Brad and I spent every free minute together. We played tennis, ran laps around the track, attended the football games, studied, saw a few movies in Burlington, and watched every game of the World Series. I had never seen Brad so excited as he was when the Mets won the fifth game and the championship. He was yelling and hooting and throwing his arms around everyone in the room. There were even tears in his eyes. Never at any time in my life could I remember being so happy. I was parading around on clouds and loving every minute.

I should have known it would not last.

The second Friday in November was exceptionally pleasant and warm, so Brad suggested that we lay the blanket under the gigantic oak tree next to the lake. We listened to the radio and drank wine coolers concealed in Coca-Cola cans just in case a campus cop should stumble upon us. Over the past several weeks, I had acquired a taste for the refreshing combination, and I no longer became tipsy after just a few swallows.

Brad was discussing his latest photo layout when out of the blue, he interjected a sentence that was completely off the subject. "I rented a room at the Holiday Inn for next weekend."

"What?"

"A room . . . I rented a room . . . it's Homecoming . . . everyone does it. You know, stay up half the night partying and raising hell. It's not only Homecoming; it's the last game of the season. Just about everybody on campus will be celebrating."

I sat up and crossed my legs. "What do you do with the other half of the night?"

"Huh?" He stared at me with that innocent little boy look on his face that he must have practiced on hundreds of girls before me.

"You said, everyone parties half the night. What happens during the other half?"

"Oh come on, Laura, be a sport. If you don't sign out for the night, you'll have to be in the dorm by 1:00, and that's when the parties really start rolling." He began to nibble at my ear.

"You know I can't. All freshman girls have to get parental permission in order to stay off campus. My parents wouldn't let me do that."

"It's easily remedied, Laura. Call 'em. Tell them you want to go with a bunch of girls to Raleigh for the weekend. They'll send you a letter." He spoke in a cajoling manner as his tongue traced circles on my neck. Between words, he gently sucked small portions of my skin into his mouth. He was rewarded by my reactions as I melted toward him.

"Brad, stop that. I can't concentrate."

"Who said anything about concentrating."

"I can't lie to my folks. Besides, they know me too well. They'd see right through it."

"Well, how about this idea? Pretend you're your mother, write a letter to Dean Looney or the housemother or whoever you need to, stamp it, address it, have it ready to go. Mail it to a friend back home and have her mail it to Elon so it will be postmarked from Virginia. How about that? Ingenious, right?" He gathered a section of my hair, pulled it away from my neck, and continued to kiss that area. "Oh, you taste so sweet."

"Brad, that's forgery." I was trying to stay rational, but his actions made it extremely difficult to stay focused on the conversation.

"You could always go in at 1:00 and then sneak out after bed check."

He turned my face toward him and kissed me deeply on the mouth. His actions sent charges of electricity through my veins. My breath was caught in my throat. I closed my eyes giving into the ecstasy he created. His fingers massaged the back of my neck, danced through my hair, and left trails of excitement wherever they touched.

"I can't do that either, Brad." It was hard to speak. The words seemed trapped below my throat. "I could get kicked out of school for sneaking out after hours."

"You could get kicked out for drinking wine coolers and skipping close study too . . . but you've been doing that for weeks." He chuckled inwardly as he continued to tease me with his tongue. "If they kicked out every kid in school who broke a rule, there wouldn't be anyone left. Say yes, Laura . . . "

"I don't know."

"Say yes . . . it'll be fun . . . " Again, he kissed me, long and lingering. "Laura, this isn't the puritanical 50s."

"I don't know, Brad . . . maybe . . . I'll think about it."

Slowly, he pushed me to the ground and rolled on top of me. His body felt solid and warm. I was losing myself in the very feel of him. At first, I thought Brad was going to continue kissing me; but instead, he began to tickle my sides. I was laughing uncontrollably, shocked by his actions. He was also laughing as his lips turned from passion to teasing movements. He pecked playfully at my forehead and nose as I squirmed underneath him.

"Are you afraid to go to the motel with me, Laura?" Brad began a new assault to my side; as a result, fresh peals of laughter came from both of us. "What do you think is going to happen if you go? Do you think I'm going to pump you full of booze, chase you around the bed, capture you, and attack you on the spot?" He bit me softly on the neck. "Laura . . . I could seduce you anywhere . . . in the car last week, in the forest, behind one of those big boxwood hedges on main campus . . . or maybe right here . . . under our oak tree. I've had plenty of opportunities." He stopped laughing; I did too. "I don't need a bed in order to make love to you." He was watching me intently and waiting for some kind of response. "And if you're not ready . . . that's fine . . . I won't push you. I swear to God, Laura . . . I won't touch you. I won't come near you if you don't want me to." He spoke with a serious tone in his voice. "I just want to hold you in my arms while I sleep. I want to wake up beside you in the morning. It's a fantastic feeling."

His face descended upon mine . . . lips like fire. The weight of his body felt like a warm cozy quilt. He transported me into a realm where everything was magical. The rustling branches sounded like musical instruments. I could smell his aftershave; the scent made me delightfully dizzy. Circling him with my arms, I pulled Brad as close to me as I could and savored the very feel of him.

Amidst the passion of the moment, I heard voices. Something alerted me to one particular voice. All feeling drained out of my body; Brad immediately sensed the transition.

"What's wrong?"

"My God!" I pushed Brad off me and rolled onto my stomach. Twenty, maybe twenty-five yards away I saw that my fears were a reality. "It's Tommy!"

"What the hell's he doing here?" Brad's voice was agitated.

"I don't know. He must have gotten a ride up or something. He didn't call or anything. He must have wanted to surprise me."

"Why don't you tell him that you don't like surprises."

I couldn't think clearly. Everything seemed to be happening too rapidly for thought.

"Are you sure it's him?"

"Of course, I'm sure." I saw Tom disappear into the dorm. "What am I going to do?" I had to think fast because I was sure the girl working the receptionist's desk would tell Tommy I was out here. She was that blonde I had seen with Brad a few times; I imagined she would think it was a real joke to point Tommy in our direction.

"Laura." Brad grabbed my arm. "Listen to me. Don't break our date for tomorrow night. I've borrowed a car. I'm taking you dancing. Billy has a date . . . the four of us . . . we're going to Greensboro. You *are* going with me. I'm not going to share you with anyone . . . not anymore . . . do you understand? You tell him to go back where he came from . . . tell him that you're finished . . . it's over. Do you hear me, Laura?"

"Okay . . . okay, Brad. Just get the blanket and leave . . . I don't want to make a scene." I was frantic. I could barely hear Brad's words. I only knew I had to move quickly. "Please, Brad. I can't let Tommy see us like this. Please just go."

"Damn it, Laura! You've already broken one date with me because he showed up. You're not breaking another one!" His fingers were wrapped tightly around my arms.

"I'm begging you . . . " I picked up the blanket, thrusting it in his direction.

"Okay . . . this one last time . . . but this is it." After kissing me quickly, he turned and headed in the opposite direction.

I walked toward Harper Center; immediately, I knew I was too late. Tommy stood beneath a lamppost, far enough away so he could not possibly have heard our conversation, but close enough for him to see. I didn't know what I was going to say. When I reached him, I looked into his face and tried to think of the right words.

Tom broke the silence. "You conniving, snotty bitch . . . I hope you rot in hell!"

I thought he was going to hit me. His fist was balled up, ready for the punch. His face was masked with rage. I flinched awaiting the blow, frozen and unable to speak. He stood there for what seemed to be an eternity before he lowered his hand, turned, and walked away.

There was no time for words, hardly even a moment to think, before Tommy raced back to me. Throwing his arms around my body, he clung to me . . . sobbing. The rage was gone from his expression; only pain remained. "I can't lose you, Lori. I'll do anything, but Jesus . . . don't leave me."

11

"Lori." Someone was shaking me. "Lori, wake up. You have a phone call."

I opened and closed my eyes several times as I tried to get my bearings. Where was I? In bed. I fumbled around for the alarm clock. Squinting, I read the time. My God! It was 4:00 in the morning. Who would call at this hour?

I had one arm in the sleeve of my robe before I realized that it was on backward. I attempted dressing again, this time with success. Making my way to the door by the light in the hallway, I stumbled over the makeshift table in the center of the room. "Damn!" I held my toe until the pain subsided. By the time I reached the phone, my eyes were fully opened, but my mind was still half asleep. "Hello."

"Laura."

I immediately recognized the voice. What was I going to say? I had lain awake for hours trying to think of exactly the right way to phrase my thoughts. I didn't want to lose him. Brad had become so very important to me. He had stormed into my life, changed my whole outlook; somehow without my realizing it, he had transformed me into an entirely different person from that creature I had been last summer. Was it really such a short time ago? It seemed like years.

"Laura . . . I only want to know one thing." Brad paused as if he were taking in a deep breath. "Are you going out with me tomorrow?"

Tomorrow? Tomorrow was today. It was 4:00 in the morning. Didn't he know that? What was he doing still awake? His words sounded slurred as if he might have been drinking. I wished he had given me more time to think. But what did I need time for anyway? Hadn't I already committed myself? Hadn't I already promised Tommy I would not desert him?

"I don't know, Brad. I just . . . " The phone went dead in my hand. That steady humming sound was all I could hear. He hung up before I was able to finish my sentence.

It was all for the best anyway. I replaced the receiver and slowly walked back to my room. I had never felt more alone in my life.

I crawled back into bed. Staring up at the ceiling, I tried desperately to make my mind void of thought. I lay awake the rest of the night, motionless. Flashes of fond memories raced through my mind, but I knew—no matter how much I wanted to—I could not go out with Brad tomorrow. There would be no Homecoming Weekend for us. No more long walks. No more hovering over books as we studied. No more cuddling in front of the television. No more lengthy conversations mixed with laughter. No more dancing, or movies, or football games together. No more passionate kisses, or warm arms, or gentle touches. I had promised Tommy that I would cut the ties between Brad and me; I had to keep that vow if I intended to share the rest of my life with Tom. And wasn't that what I really wanted?

At dawn, I rolled onto my side, hit my pillow a few times, and concentrated on sleep. I had made my choice. Tommy and I had our dream . . . our future. Tommy needed me; I couldn't let him down. I was not going to deceive him or lie to him either. Not anymore. Nor was I going to act the martyr. My road was paved. Tommy and I belonged together. We knew each other . . . inside and out. He knew my strengths and my weaknesses; he understood my motives and my dreams. Tommy was my future; Brad was only an illusion.

Somehow, even though I was drunk from lack of sleep, I managed to make it through the day. I was amazed at how I masked my anxiety with a pleasant facade. No one, not even Tommy, could guess the anguish I concealed.

Tommy chattered aimlessly trying to get me to relax. I watched him as I would a stranger. Was he really so different than he had been last summer? What had changed? He was still the same attractive, sensitive person he had always been . . . still warm, attentive, and loving. No. He had not changed. Tommy was still the same. Because of his patience, I knew he would help me over this hurdle. With only a little effort on my part, I was certain we could recapture our past; I would feel safe and secure again, comforted by his love.

"You won't see that guy anymore?" Tommy interrupted my thoughts. There was a pleading quality in his voice that tugged at my heart.

"No . . . I won't."

"You swear?"

"Yes . . . I promise."

He seemed to relax as he reached over with his arms and embraced me fondly. Holding me tighter than I thought possible, he whispered quietly into my ear. "Thank God," he paused. "I really need you, Lori."

I urged myself to feel something, but only compassion emerged. That would have to be enough for now; the rest could be rekindled with time.

"I'll buy a car, Lori. I have some savings. I think it's enough to get a used one. I'll come every weekend and see you, or I'll send you money for a bus ticket, and you can come to High Point. We'll see each other as often as possible. You were just lonely. I can understand that. But it's all over now. I won't let you be lonely anymore. Everything will be okay. I swear to you. Everything will be fine."

I buried my face in his shoulder and let him cradle me in silence.

12

Monday morning as I returned from a lecture, I saw Brad emerge from behind a grove of trees several yards away. It was the first time I'd seen him in three days. He was coming toward me with a blank expression on his face. I wanted to walk by without saying a word, but he stopped directly in my path. His usual friendly demeanor was unreadable as he stood staring down at me.

Hands by his side, one eyebrow lifted, a half smirk covering his lips, Brad broke the silence. "I'm sorry I called you in the middle of the night only to hang up on you. I knew when you answered the phone that you'd been sleeping."

"It's okay," I answered in the most polite tone I could manage. "I went right back to sleep." I lied. I looked past him, around him, and down at our feet, but I would not look directly into his eyes. I wasn't going to allow myself to be pulled back into his web. I knew I was just a toy to him . . . a challenge . . . a new game. Wasn't that what everyone kept telling me? "I have to go, Brad. I have to work the lunch shift at Harper Center." I proceeded to take a step around him when I felt his hand grasp my arm.

"Please stay just a minute . . . " His fingers, as well as his words, were tender and gentle. He watched me intently, but I refused to make contact with his eyes. "Are you afraid of me, Laura?" He allowed several seconds to let his words sink in. "Do you think I'll make you do something you don't want to do?"

I remained stationary, silent, repeating constantly to myself not to look into his eyes.

"Have I *ever* asked anything of you, Laura? Damn it! Look at me." He jerked me to the side, forcing me to face him. "I've never pushed you . . . never asked a thing from you physically, have I?" He was starting to raise his voice.

I chanced a brief glance at his expression and saw a trace of anguish marked in the lines around his eyes. Was it my imagination?

"And I never would push you . . . never." He whispered the words. "I know I've been coming on strong recently. I realize that you're not use to it. . . . " He paused, shifting his weight. "We don't have to make love. . . . I can wait as long as you feel it's necessary. I swear to God, Laura, I would never force myself on you."

"I can't . . ." I could think of no other words to say. I watched his eyes . . . those dark brown eyes that could drive me into madness. I saw nothing reflected in them.

He turned his head, spat on the grass next to his feet, and silently stared out into the cluster of trees in the distance. There was no other reaction. "So . . . you're going to go back to that guy. I suppose you consider him safe and secure . . . no risk. You'll probably marry him someday, have a pack of kids and an unsatisfied life." His mordant words reeked of sarcasm.

A tiny voice in the back of my mind kept nagging at me. I found myself praying that Brad would not let me go . . . that he'd fight for me. I want you! The thought vibrated continuously inside my head. I pushed the notion aside. No! Don't think of such silly things! Think of Tommy. Think of the future. Think reality, not fantasy.

"Maybe, we can be friends." What a stupid comment!

"Friends? No, Laura . . . we will never be *just* friends." He was watching me again. Our eyes locked. His face was void of any internal emotion.

I wanted so desperately to feel his arms around me, to have his skin touch mine, to feel his soft breath on my neck, and to let the flood of sensations overwhelm me. Open your arms, Brad . . . open your arms and let me come in. Don't allow me to simply walk away from you.

The intangible spell our connected eyes made was broken when his lips curled up into a contemptuous grin. Smirking quietly, he rubbed the back of his neck. "Well, ya can't win 'em all, I guess." He laughed. It had a devil's ring to it. "It's no big deal. I got a chick on main campus just dying for a little action. I'll take her Saturday night, and we'll really let hell break loose."

I felt a sinking sensation in the pit of my stomach. Everyone was right! I really wasn't important to Brad . . . just a game. I was nothing more than a new and different toy for the rich kid. He would have tossed me aside when boredom set in, like a used train set or a broken bicycle. The very thought was torture.

I reached into my pocket and fondled the chain I was concealing. After swallowing several times to force away the pending tears, I pulled the ankle bracelet out of its hiding place. Without a word, I handed it to Brad.

"I don't want that!" Brad snapped as he stepped back a foot or two. "I gave that to you for your birthday. It was a gift." He sounded angry.

"I can't wear it anymore." Each syllable hung in the air, which caused an electrified tension between us.

After what seemed an eternity, he snatched it from my palm. Brad fingered the links for several seconds before making an attempt to toss the chain in the bushes. He made the motion, but at the last moment he stopped, glanced at it again, and jammed it into his pocket. "Why throw away a good piece of jewelry? It might come in handy." He sounded confident again. His shoulders squared, he added, "If you ever get bored of that mister nice guy of yours, Laura . . . give me a call. If I'm not booked up, I'll ring your bell for ya."

I couldn't look at him. I didn't have the courage to face his caustic sarcasm. I hated him. God, how I hated him! How could I have been so incredibly blind? Why couldn't I have seen what everyone else had been warning me about all along? I held my head up. I would not allow him to see how badly he crushed me. I took steady, even steps back to the dorm . . . one foot in front of the other as calmly as I could. When I reached the sanctuary of my room, I grabbed Tommy's picture, held it to my chest, and cried.

Two days later I saw a girl wearing the ankle bracelet Brad had once given me. She sported it like a trophy and made sure everyone, including me, knew who had given it to her; the blonde receptionist wore a spiteful and victorious smile on her face.

2

Brad

I WAS DRIVING BACK TO ELON WITH MY BROTHER RICK. NIGHT DRIVING is so tedious. Interstate 85 passing through Virginia is so straight and monotonous that the oncoming flow of headlights can lull a person to sleep. I frequently shook my head and blinked my eyes to stay awake. Several cups of coffee and a pack of chewing gum were helping to some degree, but the drowsiness was still there.

Thank God, Christmas vacation was over. Damn! I hated Christmas Day. I dreaded the occasion. Every year, it was always the same. The morning was spent with my father. We opened dozens of expensive presents. I knew my dad never bothered buying his own gifts for us; instead, his secretary picked them out and charged them to his account. Each Christmas, I received a couple of silk ties (which I never wore), half a dozen of the finest shirts, a cashmere sweater or vest, and an assortment of costly colognes. The gifts were inevitably the same, no thought or originality to them. Even before the boxes were unwrapped, I knew the contents. Why the hell did he bother? It was so superficial. My father did not give a damn about Rosaline or me. Just Rick . . . always Rick.

Then in the afternoon, the three of us—my sister, Rick, and I—ate dinner with our mother and her husband. She was a terrific cook. I knew Mom spent a small fortune and a whole day's time on the meal. I felt guilty because I saw dollar signs with every mouthful. It was obvious that the spread she put on the table took up a good portion of a week's salary, but I imagined the joy on her face was the expression of her rewards.

After our bellies were filled with homemade pecan pie and chocolate cake, she handed each of us a beautifully wrapped package. We, in return, gave her several brightly decorated boxes that Rosaline wrapped for us. Each year, we knew to expect only one gift apiece, but I realized that the present she selected for each of us was carefully chosen. Mom watched us individually—as she did every year—while we stripped off the paper. Her eyes moistened with the anticipation of our reactions. Each year, as I did this year, I stood up and kissed her lightly on the cheek, telling her, "Thank you, Mom; I really wanted this." In truth, I always did. It never ceased to amaze me that she was able to find something I secretly wanted. Unfortunately, Christmas did not leave me smiling. It only magnified the feeling that my mother was deprived of what was rightfully hers; every year, I resented my father more for denying her the money she needed and deserved.

Seven years ago, after a Christmas very similar to this one, I came home from my mother's apartment only to find my father in his study. He was slouched in a chair and drinking brandy. Even at my young age, I realized that he had consumed quite a bit of alcohol because he not only reeked of the scent, but his normally immaculate attire was in total disarray. I recalled that my first thought was sympathy; he must be sad and lonely because his children left him on Christmas Day. I went into the room and took a seat in a big leather-bound chair opposite him. Looking both unhappy and angry at the same time, he silently stared at me. I scanned the walls lined with hardback books and tried to think of something to say in order to break the silence, but my father succeeded in vocalizing his thoughts first.

"Get out of here, kid. Don't bother me." My father's voice was not raised; instead, the words were spoken in a calm, quiet manner. "I don't need you . .

. I don't need you sitting around here and moping with that pathetic look on your face." He swirled the brandy around in his glass and concentrated on the movement the liquid made. "Didn't you get what you wanted for Christmas? Sometimes you never get want you want in life, kid . . . so you'd better get used to it." We watched each other in silence for a few moments before he added in a rather sharp tone, "Stop looking at me like that!" He waved his hand several times toward the door. "Scram . . . get lost . . . go play with your new toys."

Even though I was not quite twelve years old, I bit my lower lip, pushed back the tears, and pretended to be a man. A knot formed in the base of my throat. It was hard to swallow. Even though I did not feel strong, I held my head proudly. I was not going to let him know how upset I was. Quietly, I left the room. After putting on my coat, I went outside to walk in the snow.

A few hours later when I returned, I saw Rick in that very same room with my father, but Dad wasn't telling my brother to get lost. No! He was holding him in his arms. Or was Rick holding my father? One of the two was crying. I did not stick around long enough to find out who; but even now, I still remember the sound of the sobs. It was *that* day when I realized my father loved Rick so much more than either Rosaline or me. He wanted Rick around him all the time. My old man never held me like that; he never gave a shit about me one way or the other. It was *that* night— over a half dozen Christmases ago—I started my campaign against loving my father. I promised myself I would never give him the power to hurt me again.

"Jesus, Brad. Watch where you're going!"

I snapped out of my memories just in time to look to my left and see that I had merged halfway into the other lane. I turned the wheel slightly and steered the car back on track.

"This is my car, Brad. I sure as hell don't want you to wreck it."

I immediately pulled off onto the shoulder and slammed on the brakes. "You don't like the way I drive? Damn it! You can have the honors." Without saying another word, I pushed the door opened violently and walked around to the passenger side. Rick slid behind the wheel. He put the transmission in drive and pulled out.

That was another thing that ticked me off. Why the hell did my father buy Rick a car and refuse to give me one? Shit! Rick had everything.

I leaned back in my seat and relaxed. It was Rick's turn to bear the monotony of the road. Glancing out the window, I recalled the only exciting moment during the whole two-week vacation. I coaxed Bill into calling Laura on the night of the twenty-fifth to wish her a Merry Christmas. Billy frowned at the idea and complained that he didn't want to do it because she might think he was interested in her as more than just a friend. At first, I only toyed with the notion; but the more I thought about it, the more I pushed Billy into doing it. I bugged him for an hour and a half until he finally dialed the operator. I was nervous as a grade school kid as I sat on the edge of my chair, but Laura never even asked Billy one single word about me. Damn her! She was probably moaning over that son-of-a-bitch boyfriend of hers. Well . . . he could have her. Laura wasn't worth the trouble. What the hell did I care anyway? Shit! Face it, old buddy! The witch put some kind of spell on me, and I just plain wasn't functioning normally. God knows, under any other circumstances, I would never have let a juicy morsel like her get away. Well, damn it, that was the last time I let some chick catch me off balance.

At least I got laid a few times while I was home to make up for all those monkish months last fall. God! It was good to be in circulation again. That Jill! She always was sweet meat . . . good for a fun time with no strings. My God! She knew some moves that would embarrass a hooker. Then there was Toni. Take her a box of candy and give her a few compliments, she would spread her legs for anyone. A couple of hours with her was always worth the buck ninety-five for a pound of Russell Stover's. The sad and unusual thing about the experiences with both girls was that I went home each time feeling sated but not really satisfied. Something kept nagging me, and I could not quite put my finger on it.

Man, Jill wore me out one night until I could hardly walk; surprisingly, I still was mentally unfulfilled. It about drove me crazy. Then on another occasion—the day after Christmas if I remember correctly—I just barely got it up. It was the first time since I was thirteen when the maid lifted her skirt that I had any trouble performing. I almost panicked. I mean, Jesus Christ! It wasn't like I didn't want that snatch!

New Year's Eve was a good time. Billy and I went to this crazy party. Everyone was acting wild. Our dates were tripping and passed out cold before midnight. Billy and I found these three dynamite-looking chicks who were more than willing to share themselves with both of us on a king-size waterbed. What a way to kiss the 60s good-bye: My mouth on one broad's gigantic tit and my pecker between another's. That was heaven!

"Hey, Brad, aren't you coming?"

I looked over at the driver's side only to find that it was vacant. Rick was standing outside the car looking sleepy and worn out. We were back at Elon.

"Come on, Brad . . . jeez . . . you've been somewhere else the whole trip down here."

We carried our suitcases up the stairs of Moffit. I crashed fully dressed on my bed. It was 2:00 in the morning. I had an 8:00 class. I was wiped out.

2

I saw Laura working behind the cafeteria line the next day. Damn! She looked good. I watched her for a few minutes as I waited for my turn to be served. There was an innocence about her; yet she was so incredibly sexy. She had taunting, sensual, blue eyes that sparkled when she smiled. Her lips curved upward at the corners, which made her appear happy all the time. Her face was so naturally pretty that she didn't need any makeup. Plus she had a body that screamed to be set free. I contemplated taking another crack at her. Maybe I should give her another chance. Perhaps I could even convince her to leave that jerk boyfriend of hers. Hell! I had to admit Laura was worth a little effort on my part. We really did have fun last semester.

I stood in front of Laura and smiled as pleasantly as I could. She returned a feeble grin. I was just about to speak when I glanced down as she spooned a healthy amount of spaghetti onto my plate. I saw the shiny stone on her left hand. The diamond was not that large, but for one instant it looked as if it were a gigantic rock, which glittered blindingly off the overhead lights. I was so mesmerized by the tiny prisms it created that I was unable to look back into her face.

Stupid Bitch! She could go to hell with that asshole jerk of hers if that was what she wanted! I could give a flying fuck anyway. Laura was nothing but a royal pain in my butt! I was better off rid of her. I never returned my eyes to hers; instead, I moved through the line and collected vegetables, a salad, and dessert. After pouring myself some iced tea, I picked up my tray and went to the table. I chose a seat between Rick and Billy, who were already in a conversation about a couple of transfer students at the next table.

Rick took a spoonful of Jell-O from his plate as he changed the topic of discussion. "Hey, Bill, hear the news? Lori is wearing a diamond." He was talking around me—obviously rubbing it in. "Heard there was no date set yet . . . just tentative plans."

"Yeah . . . looks like wedding bells are going to chime," Billy answered laughing slightly and waiting for a reaction from me.

"Suppose so," Rick replied, glancing in my direction to see if I would take the bait.

"She looks really happy," Billy added.

I was getting pissed. I knew they were only drawing out their comments to egg me on and see how long it took before I jumped into their conversation.

"It's a shame," Rick said. "I kind of wanted a crack at her. I guess it's no great loss."

"No great loss!" I finally interjected, fed up with his bullshit. "You always had the hots for her, Rick. You'd have moved heaven and earth to get to her before I did last semester. Don't pretend you didn't. You moped around for weeks like some sick dog when she put you down."

"Look who's talking!" Rick swallowed the rest of his milk before adding, "She really had you dancing like a puppet on a string." His voice was a bit more antagonistic than the teasing tone he had used earlier.

I flipped him the bird. "Sit on it and rotate!"

"Gotta admit, Brad," Billy interrupted. "You really were acting strange last fall. In all the years I've known you, I've never seen you date just one girl. Even when Laura's boyfriend got into the picture, you didn't date anyone else. You sat in your room and got plastered for four straight days. Then you played second string while you waited for Laura to make up her mind."

"Shit! Laura Davis wasn't anything to me but a prospective piece of ass." Smiling, I waved my fork in Bill's face. "You wait . . . she ain't married yet. In fact, I'll bet you ten bucks I get into those puritanical pants of hers before she slips any wedding band on her finger."

"Lori!?" Billy truly looked surprised by my statement. "You've got to be kidding. She's not the type for balling. Girls like her are virgins on their honeymoon."

"Hey, buddy, no sweat!" I retorted finally feeling my old confidence again. "She may act as if she's holding an aspirin between her knees, but Laura would be like putty in my hands. You forget . . . I'm a pro in these matters. I can turn her into melted butter if I want to." I did not know why I was talking like this. Hell! What did I want with her anyway? Laura was probably the kind of broad who turned into a sniveling idiot the moment I entered her.

"Bring me the red sheet!" Bill mocked. "I'll believe it when I see it. My money's on Lori."

That night I tore up every picture I had taken of Laura except the one of her sitting by the lake with her legs crossed, her elbows on her knees, and her chin resting on her fists. The sunset in the background was incredible. My Nikon really captured her that time. Surprisingly, I could not bring myself to destroy that one particular pose; instead, I stuffed it in the bottom of my desk drawer and piled paper and envelopes on top of it. All the others, I ripped into shreds as I repeatedly tore them over and over again. The hell with her! She was not even worth a ten-dollar bet!

3

By the end of the week, I met a really foxy momma who lived about a mile and a half down Haggard Avenue, this side of Gibsonville. Annie was a native of the area and a working girl with no hang-ups about what she did in her spare time. She was not all that great looking, but she did have a dynamite body; in fact, when I watched Annie walk, her ass twitched in a way that made my mouth water.

After sharing a six-pack of beer and a half a bag of pretzels one night, she led me into her father's barn. I had always heard the slang term rolling in the hay, but until I actually experienced it, I could not appreciate the words. We burrowed ourselves into the straw. Our body heat was enough to combat the cold winter air.

Annie was a moaner, and God knows I love a moaner! I told her that she was the sweetest honey I'd ever had; in actuality, it really was not that far from the truth. I was starting to feel like my old self again. Some tender loving care from a good woman was the best medicine any doctor could prescribe. Lord knows, I needed a little R & R (rutting and relaxation), and Annie had the right combination of both.

After we exhausted ourselves, I rolled off onto my side and closed my eyes. Taking a long deep breath, I uttered, "God, Annie, that was sheer heaven."

She turned herself into a position that enabled her bare breasts to lie on my chest. There was nothing like a protruding nipple making teasing sensations on the skin. She knew I liked her actions. I could tell by the upward curving of her lips and the twinkling in her eyes. As I plucked fragments of straw from her hair, she gently rubbed her body against mine and purred like a kitten.

"You sure must have plenty of experience under your belt," she whispered as she ran her fingers down my abdomen. "A girl could go mad with your moves."

I chuckled to myself. "I really love women like you, Annie." I kissed her on both cheeks and massaged one firm boob with my hand. "And, God, I love these babies too." I kissed each breast and fluttered my tongue over the taut nipples.

"Oh, don't stop . . . that's marvelous." A soft humming sound came from her throat as she closed her eyes and relished her own private pleasures.

"Don't you ever wear out?"

"Not with a guy like you . . . I've got energy stored up for a lifetime."

"Got to tell ya, babe, I simply can't get it up again. You'll have to save it for later."

"Ya mean, you'll come back?"

I pulled the hair away from her face and smiled. "Are you kidding? I'm no fool. I'd never let a treasure like you get away. You're better than a chocolate sundae with mountains of whipped cream, nuts, and a cherry on top . . . even better than a cold beer on a hot summer day, and almost as good as a royal flush in a table stakes poker game. No way am I letting you get away!"

We both laughed. She knew I was exaggerating. Annie also knew that I would return, but that there were no strings attached and no commitments.

For ten consecutive nights, I saw Annie. No fancy talk, no cares, no worries—she was on the Pill—God, I loved women on the Pill—and no burdens whatsoever.

Then, out of the blue, I started getting a burning sensation and a lack of desire for sex. Never in my life had I turned down open arms, but I just plain wasn't interested. Tiny white open sores were forming on the tip of my penis. By the time Jill called on the pay phone outside my room, I already had a faint idea what the problem was.

"Brad, this is Jill. We've got trouble." Before I could comment, she continued. "I got a blood test yesterday."

"You're pregnant?" My God! That was a horrible thought!

"No." She paused, then blurted out her next words. "I have V.D. . . . so do you."

"Did you give it to me, or did I give it to you?" It was the only thing I could think of to say. I was completely caught off guard by her blunt statement.

"What difference does it make? The point is, Brad, you need treatments."

"It makes a hell of a lot of difference to me." I was beginning to lose my cool. "Damn it, Jill, how long have you had this?"

"I've probably had it since sometime last fall, but I didn't know it until yesterday."

"Why don't you check yourself out more regularly?" I was angry. "Who the hell gave it to you anyway?"

"Damn it, Brad! I can't help it if some jerk paid for a little action one night and started passing it around the neighborhood."

"Shit!" I grumbled as I tried to control my anger. "Of all the rotten luck."

"It's going to be okay . . . I mean, it can be cured. The only problem is that the health officials insist that you contact all the people you've slept with since you contracted it."

"Oh, great!" I thought of Toni. Then a flash of the three nameless girls from the New Year's Eve party popped into my mind, and finally I thought of Annie. Christ! Annie and her Irish temper. She would go through the roof. I tried to calm down. I figured the disease would not last forever, and I better not lose my connection with Jill. After all, she was good to keep around. I changed the subject. "Well, aside from all this crap . . . what's new?"

"Oh, you know me, babe . . . footloose and fancy free. As soon as I get this cleared up, I'll be looking forward to your next weekend home." She paused waiting to see if I was so mad at her that I wouldn't want to see her again.

"You are something else, Jill." I laughed. It really was comical if I thought about it. In fact, it was amazing the way I played around that it took this long to get the dreaded disease.

"You know, Brad, if you ever said the word . . . " Her voice became more serious than her usual carefree tone. " . . . I'd drop those other guys and stick with you." There was no response on my part so she laughed slightly and continued, "I always have had a special feeling for you. I'm just waiting for you to settle down and mend your wild ways . . . I'm hoping one day you'll boomerang back to me."

"My wild ways! What about yours?"

She laughed that jolly way of hers and added, "Shit, Brad, you ought to know by now that I'm mostly all talk and little action. Basically, you're the only guy . . . if you know what I mean. I only went out with that other guy last fall because I heard you were kind of involved with some girl down at your school." She paused briefly. "I really am crazy about you."

"Don't get mushy on me, Jill. This is not the time or the place . . . besides you know how I feel. I don't want any ties . . . no strings. Right? We agreed on that a long time ago."

"Hold on a second." I heard her put down the phone. I thought she was blowing her nose or something. Women! The minute I thought I had 'em all figured out, they threw a curve ball and destroyed the score. Jesus, I hoped she wasn't going to start that routine again about having some kind of serious relationship. I liked it just the way it was.

"I'm back. Everything's cool." Her voice reverted to its normal happy sound. "By the way, I saw your dad last night. I was having dinner at a restaurant. He was having a drink at the bar. He was all by himself. He looked real lonely, so I asked him to join my girlfriend and me."

"Don't go hitting on my old man, Jill. That'll really piss me off."

"Brad! You really do have the wrong impression of me, don't you? My God! What do you think I am?" She was agitated. "Well, anyway, we talked a little while. Your father looked good, Brad, at least he looked good until your mother came in. He went over to her table and talked to her for a few minutes. Then he came back, paid his bill so fast it would have made your head spin, and flew out of there like the place was on fire. He really looked ticked."

"No surprise to me. My old man doesn't much care for my mom."

"That wasn't the impression I got."

"What the hell do you know!" Dime store psychiatrists! Shit! Jill didn't know my old man like I knew him. "Hey, Jill. Can we change the subject?"

"I gotta hang up soon anyway. You just be sure and get yourself to a doctor." There was a moment of silence over the wire. "And, Brad, I really am sorry about all this. I'm as ticked off about it as you are. God knows, I would never do anything like that intentionally."

"I know that, babe. It's okay. Like you said, in a couple weeks I'll be good as new."

We both said our farewells and hung up simultaneously. I did feel better after talking with her a while. Jill was the type of person I couldn't stay angry with for long, especially when she was putting extra effort into being pleasant. Jill! She was an all-right chick. Not the type I'd take home to Mother, but still fun all the same. We had some great times together. From the sound of it, we were going to have some more.

I rumbled through the phone book until I located a nearby clinic. After putting a dime in the phone, I dialed the number and made an appointment for Annie and me.

That was the easy part . . . now I had to tell Annie.

She didn't take the news too well; actually, that was putting it mildly. I took her a few little gifts: a fancy comb for her hair and an inexpensive bottle of cologne. I figured they'd make a good peace offering, but I made the mistake of giving them to her *before* I told her, instead of using them as a consolation afterward.

The woman went crazy. She grabbed a pitchfork and started forcing me toward the wall. "You son of a bitch! I swear to God I'm going to stick it to you but good." Annie was jabbing the tool and missing me by only inches with each thrust. Her eyes, glaring viciously while she spoke, were big as saucers. As she continued her forward movement, her nostrils flared, and the muscles in her jaw flexed repeatedly.

"Annie, for Christ's sake, calm down. It's not terminal."

"Don't tell me to calm down!"

She had me backed into a corner. I was trapped. I felt perspiration forming over my lip. I couldn't make myself believe she'd actually hurt me, but damned if there wasn't fire in her eyes. The points of the fork were creating indentations in my skin. Even though the pressure wasn't enough to draw blood, it was enough to put the fear of God into me.

"What the hell's going on in here?"

I looked to my right in time to see Annie's father appear in the doorway carrying a shotgun. Oh, terrific! Now, I was going to get my head blown off as well as my gut transformed into a sieve. I knew all too well that her old man was a Bible beater from way back. With my luck, the least I'd get was an altar, a preacher, and a wedding ring for my indiscretions.

Annie lowered the pitchfork as she laughed. "Nothing, Pa. I'm just joshing around here, having a little fun." Her father didn't move. The gun was still pointed directly between my eyes. "No kidding, Pa. Don't be so serious . . . we was just funnin'."

I took a deep breath as I saw him lowering the barrel and placing the butt under his arm.

"You sure, child? This guy ain't done nothing wrong, has he?"

"No, Pa. We was just playing around. I was only teasing him. You go on now. I'm sorry we disturbed ya." At the end of Annie's sentence, her father turned and walked outside. As soon as he vanished, Annie broke into hysterical laughter. She tossed the pitchfork to her side. "I really had you scared shitless this time. Another few minutes and I'd of had ya cleaning out your britches." Still laughing, she added, "You should have seen your face . . . white as a sheet, eyes bulging outta their sockets. I wished I'd owned a camera. It woulda made a funny picture."

I didn't know whether to be angry or pleased, but I heard myself laughing too. Christ! That was close. She was wrapping her arms around me still laughing uncontrollably.

"It's no big deal, puddin'. I've had V.D. before. After a couple of trips to the doctor, we'll be good as new. Don't much care for shots, but I reckon we ain't got a choice here, do we?"

I felt my heart begin to beat normally again. Annie sure had a weird sense of humor. "Hey, I've got another little present for you to make up for all the trouble I caused."

"Oh, good, I love presents."

I reached into my pocket and pulled out two tickets. "I have front row seats for the Sly and the Family Stone concert in Greensboro Saturday night. You want to go?"

"Who are they? I ain't never heard of 'em."

"You've never heard of Sly? They're a rock group . . . real big back home."

"Don't like all that loud stuff much . . . Country music's more my style. Hank Williams and Johnny Cash know how to strum a good guitar. Or get me tickets to see Loretta Lynn. I ain't never been one for all that hippie screaming and yelling stuff . . . that ain't music."

I couldn't help but chuckle. "It's not hippie music. Come on, Annie, you'd like it."

"I cain't. Already have plans for Saturday night."

As usual, it didn't matter. I didn't care one way or the other. Girls! They were all the same; one was as good as the next. "No big deal. I'll catch you another time."

As I turned to go, she grabbed my arm. "You ain't leaving, are you? Don't you have some time for a little fun in the loft?"

"Annie, I'm not much good for that right now. As soon as we both get fixed up again, we'll hit the hay, okay?" But even as I said the words, I already knew that the novelty of Annie had worn off. She'd be good for a bang every once in a while, but basically the newness was gone. And when that was gone, I usually lost interest.

During the walk back to campus, I toyed with the tickets in my pocket. Who should I ask? Hell! Maybe I'd give them to Rick. We hadn't been getting along very well recently, which was probably more my fault than his; perhaps the tickets would be a good peace offering to break the ice between us.

4

The next evening, I saw Rick talking with Laura as they ate dinner together. I'd seen them in each other's company a lot recently. It kind of pissed me off in a way. Rick was looking at her like she was a goddess. He was practically foaming at the mouth and making childish goo-goo eyes while Laura smiled back at him. They both were acting as if there was no one else around. Didn't Rick realize that he was behaving like a first class idiot? Shit! Why should I care if my brother acted pussy-whipped when he wasn't even getting laid?

I returned my thoughts to eating my meal. A dynamite-looking blonde came to my table and asked if the seat across from me was taken.

"Are you kidding?" I flashed her a friendly smile. "That seat's always available for any girl who has a pair of wheels like yours." She really did have nice-looking legs. (Thank God and the fashion world for the miniskirt!) The rest of her wasn't bad either. Perhaps she was a bit skinny for my taste and her tits were a little small, but what the hell . . . you couldn't always get perfection. "Name's Brad. What's yours?"

"Cindy . . . Cindy Wilder."

"Pretty name. Haven't seen you around before."

"I just transferred here this semester."

I listened as she told me about her hometown in West Virginia and a few experiences prior to Elon. Most of the conversation was a bunch of B.S., ending with me drawing the conclusion that Cindy was too nice of a girl for me to invest time or money. After finishing my dinner, I excused myself and went back to my room. I had every intention of opening my English lit book, but the idea bored me. We were reading Chaucer's *Canterbury Tales* in Professor Bland's class; I hated it.

It wasn't five minutes before Rick sauntered into the room and casually plopped his carcass on my bed. "Hey, little brother, whatcha know?"

"You've been down here too long, Rick. You're starting to sound south-ern," I answered as I closed the book and looked in his direction.

"Must be Lori's accent rubbing off on me. By the way, thanks for the tickets. I asked Lori. Tommy's not coming up this weekend, so she's going with me."

"You asked *her*?" I could feel the muscle in my jaw twitch spasmodical-ly. "Jesus, Rick, you got gall asking Laura!"

"She doesn't belong to you. You already had your shot at her, and you lost out. It's too late for you to lay claims on her." He shifted his weight so he could lean against the pillow.

"Rick, I'm asking you real nice. Don't take her. Don't mess around with Laura Davis."

"Ah, come off it, Brad. Just because she didn't fall victim to your macho tactics doesn't mean she has to be off limits to everyone else. Besides, I kind of like the girl, and I plan to change her wedding plans."

Every muscle in my body was taut with tension. My teeth were so tight-ly clenched I thought I might crack a filling. An image of Laura lying in Rick's arms swept repeatedly through my mind. I could actually visualize Rick's hands touching her skin. I imagined his lips kissing hers and his fin-gers dancing through her brown hair. Blood started pumping rapidly through my brain; I was certain that at any second a vessel might pop.

"Lori's my kind of girl. I could settle down with her. She's nice, pretty, and smart. I bet she'd be great in bed too." Rick was grinning from ear to ear as each word rolled off his tongue.

Before I knew what happened, my right fist connected with his jaw. My punch caught him so off guard that he immediately fell backward, off the bed, and onto the floor. I dove onto his body. Together, we rolled across the floor hurling jabs and shouting insults, oblivious to the fellow classmates who entered the room. It wasn't until I felt strong arms around me—every-where—like an octopus—that I stopped.

When my head finally cleared, I realized Billy and two other guys were holding me down. I looked at Rick. He was sitting up and dabbing at his face.

I hadn't punished him as badly as I imagined. He had a slightly bloody nose and the makings of a whopping shiner circling one eye, but other than that, my older brother appeared all right. I felt soreness on the left side of my mouth and a pending bruise on my ribs. I, too, appeared relatively unscathed.

Both of our chests heaved as we simultaneously struggled for fresh oxygen. I couldn't imagine what came over me. The whole thing was absolutely ridiculous. Why should I give a damn anyway? "Sorry, Rick . . . really, buddy, I don't know what my problem is." I walked over to the built-in sink and splashed cold water on my face. After drying the drops from my forehead and cheeks, I returned my gaze to Rick and added, "Do what you want with those tickets. It's no big deal who you take."

As my brother rubbed the side of his face, he cocked one eyebrow and grinned. "I did a good job teaching you how to fight when we were kids. I gotta admit, Brad, you have one hell of a left." He tenderly massaged the lower part of his jaw and winced slightly from the pain.

I reached my hand out toward him. When he clasped onto it, I helped him to his feet. We stood silently for a few moments as we waited for the other's reaction. Before I could think of words to say, Rick grabbed me with one arm in a friendly hug.

Rick's laughter broke the tension. "No sweat, baby brother. I guess I sorta had it coming. After all, I did come in here specifically to egg you on, and I think I succeeded at that." He softly touched the skin around his eye. It was already beginning to puff up and darken. "I better get some ice on this before it swells and gives you more credit for that punch than you deserve." He winked with his good eye and laughed.

I couldn't remember the last time I heard my brother laugh in that way. He sounded so friendly. To me, Rick was serious and aloof—more like a stranger than a brother. "I really am sorry, Rick," I said. Ironically, I meant the words. So many times I wanted to strike out at him, thinking I would feel relieved or even victorious, but strangely enough I didn't feel either emotion. I was two inches taller and weighed nearly a dozen pounds more than Rick, which gave me one sense of superiority toward him. In every other category, my older brother was better. Everything he did was a notch above me. Good grades came effortlessly to him, so did the honor roll. Both my parents thought he was the "perfect" son. How many times had I heard that? He was better looking than I was even if he was more shy and reserved. In the athletic arena, a person might think I was more successful; but no, he was. Because of his size and speed, my older brother was faster on his feet and could run with a football through a maze of tackles without getting touched. I always wanted to play that pigskin sport, but Rick was constantly picked, and I was ultimately cut from every roster. Thank God for baseball. I played four years in high school, two of them on varsity. It was my one athletic triumph over Rick, but barely a victory because he had no passion for the sport. An additional slap in the face was when I couldn't make Elon's baseball team. I was cut after the second week of tryouts.

Billy gave Rick a damp washcloth. He pressed it against his eye. My brother stood there looking about as guilty as I must have appeared. It infuriated me that I was no longer angry with him; instead, I was beginning to warm up toward him.

"It's okay, Brad. No hard feelings. I didn't know you were so sensitive about Lori, or I never would have mentioned it in the first place."

"I'm not sensitive about Laura. It's no big deal." I sure as hell didn't want to talk about it. If Rick wanted to get mixed up with her, that was his business, but I didn't want to know anything about it. "Let's drop it."

A few hours later Rick came back into my room. I had all the lights turned out and was laying on the bed listening to a Rolling Stones album and drinking a Budweiser.

He turned on the overhead light. "It's dark in here, Brad. My God, you'll go blind if you keep this up." He reached in the cooler and pulled out a beer. "Mind if I join you?"

I couldn't remember a time when we had shared a friendly drink together. "Yeah, sure. Help yourself." There was a first time for everything. I couldn't make my mind up whether I wanted to sit back, relax, and enjoy his company or get up and walk out of the room.

"Just finished talking with Lori."

I made a move to leave. I didn't have to listen to his bragging. Shit! The last thing I wanted to hear was *her* name.

"She broke the date," Rick added as he popped the top off the can.

My curiosity got the best of me. I sat back down on the bed and watched him as I waited for him to continue. When he didn't speak, I broke the silence. "I suppose that fiancé of hers is coming here this weekend. I warned you not to get involved with her, Rick."

"No . . . that's not it. She said Tommy's not coming this weekend."

"Oh, really? What excuse did she give you?" Waiting for his answer, I sipped my beer.

"Well, to be honest, Brad . . . I think it's you."

Every nerve in my body came alive. I jerked my head and glared into Rick's eyes while he silently teased me by withholding further information. I wanted to strangle him until he told me what he meant by that little tidbit of news, but I was amazed at how outwardly calm my reactions actually were.

Finally, he continued. "It's incredible how fast gossip flies around a small campus. Seems like Lori got a hold of the scoop about our little fight even before she saw my shiner."

"Yeah, so what? I mean, what difference would that make to her?"

"I thought it wouldn't matter at all." Rick twisted the can around in his hands as he watched the circular movement it made. "But instead . . . she broke the date and said that maybe it was better if we didn't go out together socially."

"She didn't give you any explanation?" I felt my heart pounding away at the walls of my chest. "I told you to stay away from her, Rick. She's so damn fickle and not worth the trouble."

"To be perfectly honest with you, Brad, I think I painted a picture about Lori's and my relationship that really isn't true. I like her. I'm crazy about her, but she only thinks of me as a friend. There's nothing romantic between us." He fiddled with the top of the can, tapping his fingers monotonously on it. "Hell! I haven't even kissed her . . . maybe once or twice last fall . . . but not recently. If I had my way, that would all change. Unfortunately, she's made it clear she isn't interested in me on that level. I know she's engaged, but I don't think that's the barrier."

I couldn't help myself as I heard my own voice asking, "What makes you think I'm the reason she broke the date?" I was actually holding my breath as I awaited his response.

"It's nothing she said. Lori didn't have to say anything. It's the way she looks at you when you happen to walk by or how she perks up when she picks your voice out of a crowd. She pretends to be inconspicuous about it. Perhaps she doesn't even realize she's reacting that way . . . but I see the signs." Rick took his eyes from the beer he was drinking and stared directly at me. "I'd do anything to erase you from her mind, because I don't think it's her fiancé who stands between us . . . it's you."

We had been sipping beer and talking casually about a subject that was obviously gnawing away at both of us. Intently, he observed me and waited for my reply. Rick probably wondered why he was making this confession to *me* of all people.

"God! I wish I could be as callous and cold as you are about girls." He sounded angry.

"She left me, Rick!" I sat up, finally allowing a bit of my own hostility to surface. I stood and paced the room. "Laura went running back to that guy and got herself engaged. I didn't dump her, or are you forgetting that?" When I realized how loud my voice was, I took several moments to calm myself before speaking again. "As far as I'm concerned, you can have her with my blessings. She's nothing but a royal pain in the ass."

"You mean you really don't care? It doesn't matter one way or the other if I keep seeing Lori?" Rick seemed relieved.

"Hell, no! I couldn't care less what Laura Davis does."

"Why did you give me this black eye?"

I shrugged. "I was pissed off about something else when you walked in.

I guess I took it out on you. I've already apologized twice for that mistake. You don't need to keep rubbing it in."

"I wasn't. But somehow . . . it just seemed to me that it was connected with Lori." He reached for another beer, opened it, and swallowed several gulps. "What kind of relationship did you two have anyway? Lori never talks about it. I even asked her once, but she instantly changed the subject."

"Not the kind you seem to think it was." I glanced out the window into the darkness. "I didn't sleep with her." I could see Laura smiling at me. If I concentrated a little harder, I knew I could imagine her body pressed against mine, feel her warm skin on my fingers, smell her scented hair. Never had I wanted a girl more than I wanted her, and never had I exhibited such self-control. Why didn't I take her when I had the chance? Then, maybe, she wouldn't haunt my thoughts like this. Laura seemed so willing on more than one occasion, but I had stopped because I didn't want to take advantage of her innocence. What a fool I was! So what if she'd been a virgin. When had that stopped me before? God! I wished I were able to pound my head and strip all thoughts of her away. I looked straight at Rick and willed all the memories of Laura to die. "She meant nothing to me, Rick . . . absolutely nothing. But I warn you . . . if you get involved with Laura, you're going to get hurt. You don't know how to handle yourself with chicks."

"Yeah . . . you're probably right on that account. I've always been envious of you. You're so cool about it all, and you always have more girls than you want."

"Damn! But you have everything else." I couldn't believe I was actually admitting my jealousies to him. "Everything comes naturally to you . . . you're president of your class . . . next to Richard McGeorge, you are the best wide receiver in the conference . . . you'll probably be valedictorian. I have to bust my ass for everything. Christ, you even have Dad on your side. Our father dotes on you so much he doesn't even know I exist."

"You've got to be kidding me!" Rick smirked. "Me and Dad? Hell no! You're the one Dad really loves. You're the one he pushes to excel, and you're the one he wants to come into the business with him. All my life, I've tried to do things in order to please him . . . but it's you, Brad, not me, he really wants. You're the one he watches at the dinner table. You're the one he disciplines and tries to motivate. Hell, I work my butt off for a little encouragement from him, and all he ever says is a polite 'nice work . . . keep it up'. He doesn't give a flying fig what I do so long as you're around." Rick drained the liquid in his can, smashed it with his fingers, and tossed it into the wastepaper basket across the room. "I told him I wanted to work with him in the business, and what did he answer? 'How about Brad? Does he sound interested yet? Try to get him to come in with us.' Dad is always asking about you. Shit! You're more like our father than I could ever hope to be."

"Me and Dad . . . no way."

"Yeah, you are, Brad. You may look just like Mom but you act exactly like Dad, and I'm sick of hearing him say, 'Brad reminds me of myself when I was his age.' He's always saying that shit to me. It's like salt in an open wound. God knows how I've tried to please him but you're the son he wants to follow in his footsteps . . . not me."

"You're wrong, Rick. You couldn't be more wrong." I didn't know where my brother was getting these ridiculous ideas, but I knew the real score. My old man couldn't stand the sight of me; I hated him just as much. "I don't want anything to do with our father or his restaurants. I never have . . . I never will. I don't need him or his precious money. He knows I want to work with cameras; he knows my love for photography. That son of a bitch would not give me a dime. He wouldn't even lend it to me . . . not if it had anything to do with cameras. Hell no! I bought all that stuff myself . . . in spite of him. I'll show him someday. He won't stop me."

"You're just as stubborn as he is. You and Dad. A mountain couldn't move either one of you when your minds are made up."

"For Christ's sake, don't compare me to him, Rick. I can't stand it. The man turns my stomach. I can hardly wait for the day when I can be rid of him for good."

"I don't see how you can be so blind."

"Hey, let's cut the crap! Change the subject! I don't want to talk about him." Dad and me . . . what a crock that was! The only thing the two of us had in common was an address in New Jersey, and that was only temporary.

"You know, Brad, this is the most we've talked at one time in years."

I could feel my lips forming a half smile. Rick was right. We hadn't said more than two consecutive sentences to each other since I was in elementary school. In a strange way, in spite of the suppressed hostility, it felt good to talk with him. There were even moments when he seemed more like a friend than a competitor. It was almost as if Rick and I were reaching out to each other. That was a crazy thought!

I raised my beer and chuckled. "Maybe it took a few punches and a shiner to bring us together. I'm game to try our hand at friendship if you are." I swallowed the rest of my beer. "There are just two subjects that are off limits . . . Dad and Laura Davis. If you want to date her or just be friends . . . that's cool . . . I don't care . . . I just don't want to hear about it. Okay?"

"It's a deal."

5

Easter vacation was finally upon us. It was amazing how North Carolina had a way of welcoming spring and simultaneously putting winter to rest for another year, as if in one day it could draw an imaginary line between the two seasons. Bitter, cold, windy days and nights were replaced with soft breezes, scented air, brilliant colors, and warm sunshine.

I enjoyed photography most in the springtime. It was as if I could capture nature with my lenses and a few rolls of film. I shot countless pictures of daffodils, budding trees, and birds migrating north, but my greatest passion was photographing a pretty face while using nature as a backdrop. I loved using shadows and breezes to enhance certain features while at the same time infiltrating the natural background behind the subject.

It was a noted disadvantage that color film was my choice over black and white. As hard as I tried and experimented, I could not get that special quality from a colorless shot. I knew, if anything, *that* would be my downfall in the profession. Over and over I took hundreds of black and white glossy prints. The shots were good—even if I did say so myself—but they weren't exceptional. Landscapes, single objectives, groups of subjects, or even just one stationary item . . . I tried every kind of pose, lighting, and filters, but eventually I always reverted back to color film. Black and white was the real art—everyone knew that—but mixing colors was what I enjoyed most, and what I succeeded at best.

Instead of going to Florida along with thousands of other college students, Rick and I went home for spring break. I had cajoled him in a hundred different ways to use his car in order for the two of us to enjoy the week in sunny Fort Lauderdale, but Rick had remained firm. He was such a stuffed shirt when it came to partying. How the two of us had ever been born into the same family, I'd never know! My older brother was so formal, so correct, such a proper guy. And me . . . well, I loved a good time, wild women, and a nice cold beer.

Rick had refused to take my vacation idea to heart, stating he had responsibilities at home with Dad and the business. That had been the only reference Rick had made toward our father since the night we had reconciled. The past several weeks had been rather nice. My brother and I had started developing a friendship for the first time in our lives.

I saw him with Laura quite often, but Rick was true to his word; he never mentioned her name. There were occasions when my curiosity was eating away at me, but I bit my tongue and refrained from asking. Her fiancé still came up on alternate weekends; occasionally, I noticed Laura was not on campus during a Saturday or Sunday every now and then, but nevertheless, Rick still hung in there.

Laura looked as happy as ever. My ego resented the fact that she seemed to have recuperated just fine from our fall experience. Obviously, I had never been very important to her. Shit! What was I doing thinking about her anyway?

Although being home for a week was no great thrill, it did give me the opportunity to sever all ties with Annie. She had started up a new affair with a wealthy farmer and had been trying to juggle her calendar between this fellow and me. I had stated that I didn't want to be part of her harem and joked about the shoe being on the other foot for a change. She had claimed that this other guy could be her ticket to society and money. Annie had begged me to stick around, but I had no real desire to stay in her life. Even though she had been a great lay, I was glad it was over. The novelty had worn off. It was time to move on.

Thank God my social disease was cured by the time Easter came, which enabled me to find peaceful solace with Jill. What a woman! That creature never ceased to amaze me. It was a real shame every girl couldn't be like her. Jill was always as hungry for sex as I was, which made it simple. She was out on her own, had a reasonably good job, and a nice apartment. I spent hours lounging around in bed with her and toying with all her secret treasures. It was delightful. She had stopped that love-caring routine which made it even better. Jill always made me nervous when she spoke seriously and planned a future . . . our future together. There was no future for the two of us—not together anyway—but damned if Jill didn't fit nicely into my present. She was one dynamite chick . . . insatiable and loving every minute of it. There was always a certain look in her eyes that teased and taunted me even after we'd just had sex. It was unreal and absolutely fabulous.

One night, after spending hours drinking George Dickel on the rocks and sampling Jill's treasures, I returned home. Upon opening the door, I found my father in an uproar. He'd been drinking too. Despite the fact that I had consumed quite a bit of alcohol, I could still smell brandy on his breath and see the disquieting effects it had on him. I couldn't imagine what had ticked off his fury, but I instantly knew—no matter what the initial cause—I was going to get the butt of it all. I tried to sneak passed him and up the stairs to my room. Before I reached the first step, he saw me.

"It's almost four in the morning." His eyes were blazing. His voice was harsh and throaty, which was the tone he used when I was about to get a lecture.

"Jesus, Dad. I didn't know I had a curfew." Laugh it off. That was the only way to get around him.

"When are you going to grow up and start acting like an adult?" His words were slurred, but he continued speaking as he took the steps between us. "Look at you! You turned nineteen a few months ago. You think you know it all, don't you? You think the entire world is your personal playground, and life's just one huge fun game with you being the center of it all."

I turned to go up the stairs. I didn't need this hassle. It had been a terrific evening; I didn't want to top it off with one of his fights.

"I'm not through with you yet, Brad. You get your tail down here and listen to me. I'm still the one paying the bills around here, not to mention the fact that I'm flipping the tab for the education you seem to take for granted. You spend most of your time partying instead of hitting the books, and your grades show it."

"I bust my ass in those classes. I didn't want to take most of that shit anyway. I would have been perfectly happy going to a vocational school and taking nothing but commercial arts courses. But no! You wanted me to get a degree in business. You insisted that I go to Elon where Rick can keep an eye on me and make sure that you're informed about everything I do." My father had me going now. I was too pissed to keep my mouth shut. I walked toward him and faced his wrath. I was his height, which enabled me to look at him eye to eye. I squared my shoulders, tightened my jaw, and raised an eyebrow. "What the hell's got your shorts in a knot, Dad? Bad day at the office?" My rebellious tone oozed with cynicism.

"You impudent, young punk. I'm sick and tired of your back talk. I'm fed up with you carousing all night long, sleeping with every bitch who'll spread her legs for you, and doing nothing . . . nothing about planning any kind of a future. You've been sowing your wild oats—to coin an antiquated phrase—since you were fourteen years old. It's about time you cut all that shit out and start acting like a man."

"And what exactly do you consider a man to be?" I kept my eyes on his, refusing to yield under his scrutinizing stare. "Is a man someone who slaves his life away for some stupid business nobody gives a shit about? Someone who's so damn busy his wife gets fed up with it all and leaves? Is a man someone who is so fucking selfish that he separates a mother from her kids and so damned tight that his ex-wife can't squeeze a dime out of him? Is that what you consider a man to be . . . someone like *you*?" I screamed the words.

It wasn't until a couple of seconds later that I actually felt the impact. My father had hit me—not with an open palm but with his fist. My head reeled, but I concentrated all my efforts on keeping my feet firmly planted on the floor. I wouldn't give him the satisfaction of looking away. Instead, I stared him down without moving a muscle.

My father lowered his hand. "I'm sorry, Brad. I shouldn't have done that." He paused. "You don't know what happened between your mother and me." He appeared pained by his thoughts. "And don't you ever . . . *ever* accuse me of neglecting your mother again." He turned to go up the stairs. After taking a few steps at a slow pace, he faced me. "Why can't you be more like your brother?"

I detected a hint of anguish in his voice as he stood there watching me. I wanted to make a stab at his momentary weakness. I wanted to verbally lash out at him for comparing me once again to my perfect sibling, but before I had the chance to speak, he broke the silence between us.

"You *will* stop screwing around. You *will* take your business courses more seriously. And you *will* go into the business with me, Brad. I created all of it for my sons. I will not stand by and watch you waste your life free-loading off my money. Money you make a point of not wanting—but you don't mind spending it—do you? You *will* finish your education. I'll give you one year after graduation to try and make it in photography, if that's what you think you really want . . . but after that, you come back here. In the meantime, you work off your debts during the summer in one of my restaurants." He steadied his voice. "I'm a fair man, Brad. You can decide to work in whichever one you want . . . but you will work in one of them during all holidays and summer vacations. You're through getting a free ride. I'm being reasonable with you. I'm giving you a choice. Don't be a bigger fool than I picture you right now. Think about my offer because I'll throw you out on your ass if you don't comply." He paused a long moment. It seemed as if he was going to walk away without another word but instead he finally added, "I only want what's best for you, son."

I watched him climb the stairs. He had never looked older in my eyes. His shoulders were slumped. I noticed that each step he made seemed to be an effort. Some of the fear drained out of me as I got back my self-control. The son of a bitch! He only wanted what was best for me . . . my ass! My father never gave a shit about me in his whole life. I was nothing but a pawn to him . . . someone he could rule and manipulate. It was a little late for him to pretend to care for me. I could go upstairs, pack my bags, and leave this friggin' place! But then what would I have? Nothing! Not a damned thing. No! The smart move was to play his game. Milk the bastard for all he was worth. He deserved it! I was nobody's fool! Perhaps I should stick it out three more years, get my degree, cut loose, and make it on my own. He won't be able to do a thing about it either. By then, I will have bought all my equipment; with the professors' connections and a little luck, I'll be on my way. Yeah, that was the game plan for now. Just lay low and do what the old man wanted. Hell, that wasn't so much to ask. I could live through it.

When I reached my room, I found Rick awake in his bed. Silently, he watched as I stripped down to my boxers and crawled between the sheets. Jesus, my head hurt. I hoped Rick wasn't up for some kind of gab session. All I wanted was to hit the pillow and fall into a dreamless sleep. No such luck. Before I reached over to turn out the light, I heard Rick's voice.

"That was quite an argument."

"You heard it, huh?"

"How could I miss? My God! They probably heard it two miles down the road. What did he have to say when your voices got low?"

"Nothing important." I flicked the switch, putting the room in darkness. "Hey, Rick, mind if we call it a night? I'm really beat." I hit the pillow with my fists a couple of times and then settled into the alcove it made.

After a minute or two, his voice broke the silence. "Mom came by tonight to give Rosaline her birthday gift."

Damn! I'd forgotten to give my sister her present. I'd bought her a charm for her bracelet. I'd wrapped it myself and tucked it under my T-shirts in the top drawer of my dresser. Tomorrow I'd take her out for a burger and give it to her then.

"Mom and Dad had words in the library." Rick interrupted my thoughts. "I don't know what they said, but when she left, Dad sure was mad. He was cussing and carrying on like a wild man. That's when he started drinking and looking for a fight."

"So what the hell do I care?" Why wouldn't Rick just leave me alone? I wasn't interested in my parents' postmarital arguments. Hadn't I heard enough of them while they'd been married? I could visualize Rick in the darkness, shrugging defensively during my last statement. He didn't add anything further so I gathered I was finally going to be granted sleep. I closed my eyes, but the drowsiness I had felt only moments ago had vanished. I concentrated on making my breathing regulated and my mind void of thought, but my mother's image kept dancing in front of my veiled eyes. "How'd she look?"

"Mother?" Rick sounded wide-awake too. "Physically, she looked pretty well. But emotionally? She looked sad." He paused. "When she first arrived, she seemed happy enough, but after she came out of the library, she looked worn out. I asked her what was the matter and if I could help, but she only shook her head in a depressed way and left."

"That's our father for you. Divorced all these years and he still has to show his power by bringing her down every time he comes in contact with her. I never could understand why she married him in the first place."

"Brad, Mom wasn't the only one who looked sad. Dad looked depressed too."

"My ass! He was probably loving every minute of it."

"I wish you could have been there to see him for yourself."

"Let's cut the crap, Rick. I know Dad's made out of iron. If you had any eyes, you'd see it too." My words resonated in the darkness leaving my brother quiet for a few moments.

"All right! Have it your way." Rick rolled onto his side. "There's no talking to you about Dad. I don't know why I bother."

I had no idea how much time passed before I heard his steady breathing. I knew Rick had fallen asleep. I was envious. Sleep! How I wanted to be in that state . . . to have my mind drift into nothingness. I tossed and turned until I saw the faint light of daybreak peeping out from behind the curtains. The sun was completely up by the time my thoughts were laid to rest, and my body floated into a restless slumber.

6

I worked alongside Rick and my father in the restaurant for the remainder of the week. No further comment was made about the words we'd exchanged. My father took it for granted I'd simply show up the next afternoon, and that galled me. But what other options did I have?

To my amazement, Dad put me in charge of the entire bar area instead of the usual table clearing and temporary host positions I had done in the past. He told me to watch everything carefully because this summer I was going to be responsible for the whole section. He informed me that my duty would be to have all liquor and mixers in stock, keep a running tab of expenses and profits, pay the employees in my area, and make sure that my section brought in a cash flow that ran in the black. His only sarcastic statement was, "You seem to feel at home with booze and beer, so I'll start you in the bar where I'm sure you'll feel most comfortable."

As hard as I tried to resent my mandatory position, I ultimately started to enjoy it. The atmosphere was exhilarating. Everyone worked in an energetic and organized manner. The air seemed electrified by music, laughter, and activity. Although the bar was nicely decorated and well organized, I couldn't help but think of ideas that would increase productivity. If Dad knocked out one wall into the banquet area, set up a sound system or a bandstand, and moved some tables around to form an empty space in the center of the floor, it would enable people to dance, thus draw in a larger crowd who would spend more profitable dollars. I already knew liquor sales were where the big money was and dancers always developed quite a thirst. If I weren't so stubborn, I probably would have suggested the idea, but I didn't want to give him the satisfaction of knowing I was forming an interest . . . no matter how small.

Because of the fact that I worked well into the night, I no longer had time to wrestle and roll with Jill. By the end of each evening, I was too exhausted even to make an attempt at sex. I appreciated the fact that Jill was being very good about the situation. She came in every night, sat on the bar stool in the corner near the cash register, sipped on a Tom Collins, and kept me company during the slower moments of the evening. As often as I could, I took a few minutes to exchange words with her, but mostly she just watched me running my tail off doing the best I could with what little knowledge I had.

On the last night of vacation, I leaned on the bar next to her and gave her a promising wink. As I flashed her a suggestive smile, I said, "I'll take off early tonight. The two of us can have a night to remember. What do you say, babe?"

She grinned causing her green eyes to sparkle mischievously. "That sounds like a good idea." Jill drew her fingers through the back of her hair. She grinned seductively as she ran her tongue across her teeth in a very provocative, teasing way.

Good God! She was sexy.

Leaning back slightly in her chair, Jill propped one leg over the other at the knee. "Brad, if I didn't know you better . . . I'd swear you were really enjoying this little job of yours."

"Don't be absurd."

"No kidding. Your face is all lit up. You run around here like a ball on fire. Everything seems to be smooth as silk under your supervision. You're a natural . . . even for a rookie."

"Jill, you know me better than that. I have no intention of sticking it out here any longer than I have to." I softly stroked her cheek as I tried to divert her from the conversation she had started. "You run along home now. Get ready for me. I'll be there in an hour or two. And put on that nightgown you wore the other night. I love the way it clings to you."

7

The trip back to Elon seemed endless as usual. The only difference was, this time Rick and I communicated better than we ever had. Words flowed, as we exchanged boyhood memories. On several occasions, I laughed until I thought my side would split wide open.

Rick reminisced about his first date, and how he just about passed out as he tried to muster up the courage to kiss the girl. He was sixteen years old at the time and scared witless. He remembered that every time he leaned over in the car to kiss her, the girl's father flicked on and off the front porch light. Rick confessed that he finally extended his hand, shook hers with his clammy palm, and expressed something that sounded a little like—if his memory served him correctly—'You had a wonderful time, and I hope I did too.' Rick claimed he tried numerous times to correct his misuse of words, but every time he attempted he just made a bigger fool of himself. The thing that I found so amusing about his tale was that my brother actually blushed from the five-year-old memory.

I laughed. "You think that's funny? You ought to hear about *my* first time. I had never even experienced a chaste kiss before I got thrown into the whole shebang. Remember our maid Gretal? She was the one we had when you were probably fifteen because I was thirteen at the time, or was I fourteen? No, it was the week before my fourteenth birthday. She was foreign. German, I think."

"I remember her. A little on the plump side. Bright red hair. I bet she dyed it. Slightly bucked teeth. Man, could she make fantastic pastries."

"Yeah. She's the one." I was no longer laughing. Instead, I drifted back into the past, reliving memories. "I came home from school one day. She had just finished baking a pile of sweet-smelling stuff. There wasn't anyone home. I walked into the kitchen and filled my hands with donuts and cookies. She gave me the strangest look and then took all the snacks from my hands. Gretal said something like . . . let me see if I can remember the exact words. Yeah, this was it . . . she said, 'I've got something you're going to like a whole lot better than those treats.' I, of course, being completely innocent at the time, had no idea what she was talking about."

"I can't imagine you ever being innocent," Rick laughed.

I chuckled too. The thought was amusing. "Well, anyway, she took my hand and led me into her bedroom. At first, I thought she wanted to show me something, but I had no idea what that something could be. When she pulled her dress up to her waist, I thought for sure I was going to piss in my pants right there on the spot. Good God Almighty! The woman wasn't wearing anything underneath but a flimsy slip, and that was over her waist too. I felt my dick stand up so hard I was sure it was going to pop right through my clothes. I'd never seen the real thing before. Oh, sure, I'd seen it in pictures—like the ones in Dad's magazines he always had hidden under the bed—but never had I seen a real genuine pussy. Jesus! I remember I could not decide whether it was pretty or ugly. Her snatch was the color of a carrot. By the way, I don't think she did dye her hair . . . I saw living proof of that. Her skin was so white and fleshy by contrast; I thought for sure it had to be some kind of sick animal.

"Anyway, back to the story. Gretal said something like 'don't you want to feel what it's like? Come on, come over here and touch it. It won't bite.' I swear my feet were made out of lead. I couldn't move, so she came to me. I remember my first thought was how curly and coarse it looked, but really it was kinda soft to the touch. It wasn't at all like I imagined. I felt like such an idiot. I had no idea how I had gotten there, what I was supposed to say, or how she wanted me to act. I just kept looking around the room. Then I remember I said a really stupid comment like . . . 'nice weather we're having.'"

"You didn't?"

"Not those exact words, but I'm sure it sounded just as asinine. No kidding! I acted like a total moron. She told me to drop my pants. Of course, she said it more delicately than that. I fumbled and stammered. When I yanked down my zipper, I think I ripped out a few dozen hairs. God that hurt. I cringe just thinking about it.

"There I was with my pants around my ankles, her skirt pulled up to her waist, and humping a woman almost three times my age. She couldn't have gotten much of a thrill from it, because I went off like a skyrocket two seconds after I popped her. She was ticked off. I could tell that much. She let go of me, and I just kind of landed on the floor. Legs and arms sprawled every which way, and my head was somewhere else. It took me a few minutes to realize that she'd left the room. I was alone.

"At first, I was sure my dinger was going to fall off—that's what I called it back then—but nothing happened. Two days later, Dad was working late, you were out doing something, and Rosaline was at a Girl Scout meeting— Gretal approached me again. It was fantastic.

"After that, we developed a routine. Two, three, four times a week . . . sometimes I'd skip school when I was certain no one but Gretal was home. Other times, it was at night when everyone else was sleeping. I think the secrecy was half the thrill for Gretal . . . but for me . . . I just loved being with her." I paused as I let past memories race rapidly through my mind. "In the beginning, I was shy and scared, but the more we did it, the more confidence I felt. She taught me so much. Sex was an art form to Gretal, and I lapped up every lesson. Believe me when I tell you, Rick, Gretal was phenomenal. It wasn't just the sex. She made me feel so special—so important—so grown up. Now, looking back, I realize it was only a childish sexual attraction that I felt for her, but at the time I truly fancied myself in love with her. I even told her once that I loved her. She laughed at me. She said I was 'adorable . . . cute and cuddly.' I felt like one of her stuffed animals she'd collected from around the world." I hesitated as the painful part of the memory began to meld with the pleasant ones. "It damn near crushed me when I came home from school one day several months later to find her gone. She never even said good-bye. I swore from that moment on . . . nobody would ever make a fool out of me again."

"Did you ever find out why she left?" Rick spoke quietly.

"It took me a week to gather the courage to ask Dad what happened to her."

"What did he say?"

"He told me that she'd gotten another job in upstate New York." I gazed out the window watching the scenery pass and sipped several times on my Pepsi.

"Do you think he knew, Brad?"

"I don't know. I was always too scared to ask," I commented wistfully. To try to lighten the mood I added, "What a way to get broken in, huh?"

"It's actually kind of sad."

"I've never told anyone before, Rick. You better never say anything to anyone. Swear!"

"I'm not telling. Trust me." Rick paused before asking, "Is that why you steamroll over girls the way you do?"

"What do you mean?"

"You take girls for granted. They never seem to mean anything to you. It's almost as if they are toys to keep you from being bored."

"Hey, Rick, I think you've got me all wrong. I adore the ladies. The more the merrier."

"How about Jill?" Rick seemed cautious.

"Now there's sweet meat. That girl is really good in bed . . . one of the best."

"I didn't mean that, Brad. I meant—aside from sex—how do you feel about her? After all, you two have been dating off and on for a couple of years. You must love her."

"Shit! Love? You've got to be kidding. What the hell's love anyway? That's for poor dumb schmucks who are too afraid of being alone in life so they settle down to one steady for security only to find out that one of the two is cheating on the other or bored or lonely or demanding or possessive. No way! That's not my bag. I have no intention of ever falling in love. Besides I think it's a crock of shit anyway. People don't *love* each other. They *use* each other. That's all. They do it in the name of love to make themselves feel better about it. I'm not a hypocrite. I've never told a chick that I love her . . . and I never will. Every girl I've ever dated knows how I feel, and that I have no intentions whatsoever of getting serious."

"How about Jill?"

"What about her?"

"I mean, Brad, she seems serious about you."

"She's got dozens of guys. She's always telling me stories about them."

"That's exactly what they are, Brad, stories. You're blind if you don't know she's head over heals about you. She only pretends to date other guys hoping that you'll get jealous. I know . . . she told me."

"I know better, big brother." I thought of my unfortunate case of V.D. As far as I was concerned, that was proof positive Jill had been with at least one guy in the last year. "Besides, Jill's a great date, lots of fun, and terrific in bed, but there's no love . . . just a good time."

"What about Lori?" Rick's voice seemed more guarded with his latest question.

A flood of warm sensations ran through me: cinnamon hair blowing in the breeze, the moonlight reflecting off her magnificent blue eyes, a sunshine smile that radiated warmth. Laura . . . laughing at my jokes and talking of pleasant thoughts and memories. Laura . . . in my arms. Laura . . . staring up at me, telling me she was going back to that creep, and saying 'maybe we can be friends.' Friends! My ass!

I answered Rick in a controlled voice, "The Lauras of the world are for unsuspecting romantics like you." After the words were spoken, I felt the tension start to ease from my body. "Laura! Now that's a real laugh. If I were ever to get mixed up with a woman, it sure as hell would not be with any-one like her. No . . . not Laura. She's not my type. Besides, I thought we weren't going to discuss her anymore."

"Yeah. You're right. I was just curious."

There was that nagging feeling again. That urge to know what went on between the two of them. Were they still just friends? I finished my soda in silence. There was no point in trying to teach my big brother the facts of life.

He had to learn them on his own. If he wanted to screw his mind up with a girl like Laura . . . well, that was just his problem, not mine. I leaned my head back, closed my eyes, and dozed as we crossed the Virginia-Carolina border.

8

The bulk of the remainder of my freshman term was spent cramming for exams and writing what seemed like infinite papers. Each day just piled on more of what I considered to be useless crap. I couldn't wait until next year when I could concentrate on courses I enjoyed, like commercial art and photography. Elon had a lot of new equipment: an enlarger I was dying to try, a filter for shots directly into the sun, a telephoto lens that could focus on a fly a hundred yards away, and several programs for apprentices. Those were the courses and the experiences I wanted. To hell with the rest of this shit! My father demanded I major in business which consisted of classes in accounting, statistics, and economics. I had to take them next year. Fortunately, it wouldn't hurt my grade point average if I did take those classes because all types of math came easily to me. But the rest of this garbage was for the birds. I was sick to death of wasting my time on history and English courses. Those subjects had been pumped into me since grade school; I considered them a waste of time. As for Overton's religion class, I really resented having to take a mandatory Old Testament course. But there was no way around that one; I couldn't graduate without it. Unfortunately, Professor Overton was a lot more difficult than I had thought at the beginning of the semester; I would be lucky and thankful if I passed his class. I contemplated cheating, but bagged the idea. It went against my grain to cheat. For as long as I could remember, Mom preached honesty in the classroom. My mother smacked me across the butt with her hairbrush when I was in the third grade because my teacher caught me copying off a kid's paper. I could still hear her words. "No son of mine is going to be called a cheat. You learn what's in those books, Brad. When you grow up, it's knowledge that will help you succeed. Knowledge is the key to everything. You'll be nothing without it." After she calmed down, the two of us sat on the bed.

Mom spoke quietly. "If you don't know the answers, Brad, what makes you think the kid next to you does?" It was *that* sentence which registered the most. My mother wasn't quite the tyrant I made her out to be. It was just when it came to what she referred to as "book learning" that she had an iron hand. She married my father directly out of high school. I imagine she must have felt cheated when it came to her own education. Mother had planned to earn a college degree. She gave it up in the name of love—another bonus against the emotion. How many times in my childhood did I hear my mother scream? "I gave up everything for you." Dozens of times! And my father always answered, "Don't you think I have the right to throw that same statement back in your face?" It made me want to cry when I overheard her say, "You son of a bitch! I could have busted free of that town. I could have done anything I wanted . . . been anything I wanted to be. I was smart. Some people even told me I was gifted. My family could have been the only one in that stinking town to send a girl to college. They had the money, and I had the brains. It was our dream for me to go to Radcliffe. I'd even been accepted for the following fall term. But no! No! You wouldn't have it any other way. No! I *had* to marry you. You thought you were some kind of knight in shining armor, and I should fall at your feet in gratitude. Some knight you turned out to be."

Although the words changed slightly and the pitch in their voices often altered, the subject was always the same. Even as a kid, I figured that my father was the culprit. Well, so be it. That was their private war. I had picked sides a long time ago.

I shook my head and massaged my temples. Enough daydreaming! I had to get back to this paper. It was due in the morning. As hard as I tried, I couldn't get my mind back on *The Tale of Two Cities*. I started fanning the pages of the book. It was no use. My concentration was shot!

I got up and walked to the window. I leaned my shoulder on the sill and gazed outside. What a fantastic day! It would be perfect for sailing on the river. Sunshine glistening off the water and just enough breeze to catch a sail. This time next week, I'd be out of this dump and doing just that. A whole summer to lounge around. Not the whole summer, of course, I had to work nights for my father, but the days were mine; I planned to make full use of them.

In the distance, I saw a girl walking up the path. She was carrying an armload of books and fighting the wind from her skirt. She had great-looking legs. I kept wishing that a big breeze would come along and raise her skirt up above her waist. Now that would be entertainment on a dull day like this! As the figure passed the windy tunnel the absence of trees made, I focused on her face. It was Laura. I stepped back a foot or two so I was not visible in case she happened to look up in my direction. She appeared despondent, not at all her usual vivacious self. I wondered what had happened to make her so unhappy. Maybe Laura and that fiancé of hers weren't working out too well. I stepped back another foot when I noticed her looking up toward my window. Or was that only my imagination? I closed my eyes. Oh, Laura . . .

"Don't be a fool," I muttered to myself.

As I returned to my desk, I wiped all daydreams from my mind and delved into my essay. Much to my amazement, I finished it in less than three hours. It was pretty good.

9

The night before my last final in western civ, I pushed myself away from my studies and decided that both my eyes and my brain needed a break. After splashing cool water on my face, I decided that wasn't enough. A walk would help. Some fresh air and muscle activity were in order. I went down the flight of stairs, out the side door, and headed toward the lake. All the stars were out; the moon was so full and bright it created huge black shadows out of the trees.

By this time tomorrow, I'd be home. I'd give Jill a call and nestle up inside her lush body.

I stopped dead in my tracks. Several yards to my left, sitting quietly under an oak tree staring out across the pond, was Laura. She hadn't heard my footsteps. If I turned now, she probably wouldn't even know I'd seen her. I wouldn't have to speak to her; I wouldn't have to look into her eyes. I did not turn away.

Silently, I walked up to her. She still didn't notice me. I wondered what she was thinking that enabled her to be oblivious to the sounds of my approach. The reflection of the moon off the water cast a beautiful shadow over her face. I wanted to reach down, touch her cheek, and feel my fingertips on her warm skin.

"Laura." It was the first word I had said to her since that November day so many months ago. We had not spoken . . . not even one casual greeting in all that time. I must have startled her because the sound of my voice caused her to jerk slightly and gasp in surprise.

"Hello, Brad." Her voice was soft and low. She kept staring up at me.

I wasn't sure what to say next. I was beginning to regret interrupting her thoughts. I should not have come. Shit! We didn't have anything to say to each other. Despite my thoughts, I heard myself speak, "Mind if I sit down?"

"No, of course not," she replied amiably but kept her eyes straight ahead avoiding mine. "It's a nice evening, isn't it?" Jesus! Why did I have to talk about the weather? That wasn't what I wanted to say. But what did I want to say?

"Yes, it is. I love springtime. Everything is so fresh and new." Laura looked down at the grass running it through her fingers and caressing each blade. She smiled, and her eyes lit up. "Sometimes, I wish it could be spring all year around."

I pulled up a few blades of grass and started building a pile with each handful. I felt awkward, but she didn't seem the slightest bit disoriented by my company. "How's it going with the exams?"

"Oh, not bad. My last one's tomorrow morning. I'm really looking forward to going home." Pulling up grass must be contagious. She was doing the same as she spoke. "With a little luck, I think my grades are going to be good enough to get a scholarship next year."

"That would be great! I know how hard it is for you and your family. And I know how much you want to be a teacher."

She laughed gently. "I suppose you do at that. I sure talked enough about it, didn't I?"

Laura was looking at me. If I could have moved, I would have reached out to her. Touched her. Instead, I spoke. "You'll make a good teacher, Laura. You have all the natural talent for it."

"Thank you. I take it that's a compliment?"

"Of course it is." I felt so stilted, so unnatural, but I wanted to keep talking because her voice was like soft music to my ears. Every word she said was a sweet melody. I knew if I quit speaking, she might get up and leave. I didn't want that. The crazy thing about it was . . . I didn't know why. "What are you going to do this summer?" I asked.

"Oh, I don't know. I might work at the Variety Store like I did last year. It's close by and transportation wouldn't be a problem. Or I could wait on tables. Unfortunately, the jobs are limited as a waitress because you have to be twenty-one in Virginia to serve liquor."

I threw a handful of grass at her and grinned. "That's right! You're just a spring chicken."

"So are you!" She threw her head back in laughter. It was such a pleasant sound. The ice was broken. In its place was a steady flow of conversation. It was so easy—so natural—to talk with Laura. We touched on a half dozen subjects, including the terrible tragedy at Kent State; she was close to tears when she talked about those four dead students. We also discussed a movie, *Airport*, which I had seen the previous weekend; I mentioned the acting was average, but the movie was worth seeing. Lastly, we talked about the winning season our baseball team had. All the subjects were noncommittal, but it didn't matter. The only thing that did matter was that she was speaking directly to me. I was lulled into a sense of warmth by the sound of her voice.

I threw blades of grass into her hair and on her body. She retaliated with her own attack; I was showered with more of the same. We both laughed hysterically when suddenly the laughter stopped. I was only inches from her face. I wanted to kiss her so desperately; I craved the feel of those warm lips I knew so well. She watched me as if in a trance. As hard as I tried, I couldn't move my body toward her. I willed my muscles to react, but only my fingers reached for hers.

As she caught my gesture from the corner of her eye, she withdrew her hand and sat up straight. "No," she said firmly. "Please don't." She turned her face away from mine.

I could no longer see her expression. What the hell did she think I was going to do? Attack her? All I wanted was to kiss her, but she pulled away and clammed up, tight as a drum. "Laura, I wasn't going to hurt you." I couldn't believe how soft my voice sounded.

"I know."

What the hell kind of answer was that? She still wasn't facing me. I wanted to see her eyes, read the thoughts that were in them. I wanted to stroke the back of her hair and feel the strands run through my fingers. I longed to pull her into my arms and cradle her. What made her turn away?

"How's Tom?" I tried to make my voice gentle, but it came out rough and antagonistic.

"He's fine."

I wanted to ask her a question. Why can't you look at me? But I could not gather the words together to form the sentence. It felt like hours were passing in silence, but I was sure it was only a minute at most before I spoke again. "Are you happy, Laura?"

A long time passed. An ambulance zoomed by with a blaring siren followed by a fire truck and a police car. Then the silence was upon us again. She still wasn't looking in my direction.

"Yes . . . Yes, I'm happy."

A solid answer! Why couldn't she have said "Maybe," "Sometimes," "Once in a while," *or* "Occasionally?" Anything but "Yes." It was so positive, so sure. The truth of the matter was, I didn't want Laura to be happy; I wanted her to be miserable. I wanted Laura to miss me.

"Have you and Tommy set a wedding date yet?" I was holding my breath.

"Yes."

"When?" I spoke like a robot.

"Christmas Eve."

"*This* coming Christmas Eve?"

"Yes," she paused. "Tommy is going to transfer to Elon next spring. We are going to get an apartment off campus."

For the first time since I reached out to touch her hand, Laura returned her eyes to mine. "Are you happy, Brad?"

I certainly was not going to give her the satisfaction of speaking my thoughts of the moment so I quickly answered, "Yes, of course. I'm always happy."

For one moment, she looked sad; then it passed as a smile spread over her lips. "Good, I'm glad."

God, how I wanted to wipe that confident expression off her face, crush her beneath me on the grass, and force her into submitting. My fists were clenched, even my toes were wadded up in a ball inside my tennis shoes. Outwardly, I must have remained passive because I saw no sign of change reflected in her expression.

After a brief period of silence I stood up, brushed grass from my shorts, and gazed down at her. "Well, I better get back to the books." She didn't comment, so I added, "Have a nice summer."

"You too."

I walked back to my room and glanced out the window. Laura was still there . . . staring out over the water.

Damn her!

3

Jennifer

I TOOK ONE LOOK AT ELON COLLEGE AND KNEW I WAS NOT GOING TO cut it. It wasn't the school's fault. The campus was small and really quite beautiful in a quaint sort of way with its huge sprawling oaks and gigantic magnolias. Everything was so colonial: white pillars on every building, ivy growing over red brick, and boxwood lining the main paths. There was no doubt about it; the place was really pretty.

No! It was not the school's fault. I just plain did not want to be there. My parents knew it, I knew it, and David knew it. But here I was anyway. I would have been perfectly happy going to the secretarial school in Washington, D.C. and living at home. It was cheaper, and it was also what I wanted to do.

But no! Mom and Dad could not have that. No way! Their kid had to go to college and get some stupid, useless degree. After all, what on earth would the neighbors say if the general's daughter didn't do the correct and proper thing? And God help the gossip if Jennifer Carson did not follow the path of the elite.

"Blend in, don't make waves, and don't you dare flunk out!" Those were my father's final words of encouragement. It did not seem to bother him one iota that I just plain did not have the brains to be college material. No! I had to do it anyway—for the family image, for the neighborhood, for the country club, for everyone but me.

All I ever wanted to do was get a two-year secretarial degree, get a nice office job, and marry David. But no! Being a secretary and marrying David were too low class for the daughter of a general. My father thought I should come to this wealthy school and find a nice upper class jerk to marry. "Someone who will make your mother and me proud to call a son-in-law." My parents did not want much. Their description of an ideal husband for me was some smart guy who came from good breeding and had plenty of money. They even said, "If the guy's good looking, it's a nice extra." My father sounded as if I were in the market for buying a sports car instead of meeting a husband. My God! Wasn't there anything more to life than money and prestige? After all, David was not poor. He made a nice salary as assistant manager of the drug store. He even owned a townhouse. The two of us could live quite comfortably off both our incomes. But Daddy would not hear of it! And who was I to go against dear Daddy's word?

"You haven't got any guts." That was what David always told me. And the truth was—I didn't—not where my father was concerned. I would give anything to have the courage to stand up to him, but I couldn't. So here I was—bag and baggage—at the base of the stairs of a three-story dorm. Just my luck, I was on the third floor.

My folks dropped me off in this predicament and stated, "It'll give you a reason to make new acquaintances. They'll help you carry your stuff. By the way, this place is loaded with kids from well-to-do families so you'll fit right in."

Oh, great! That was just what I needed: a bunch of rich, pretentious snobs. I started carrying my things. I did not need any friends. I was in too bad a mood to meet new people anyway. I found my room number and discovered that the door was already opened. When I entered, I immediately saw a girl perched on the bed by the window.

She was pretty. My new roommate had long, brown hair and a pair of the bluest eyes I had ever seen. Smiling, the girl got off the bed. She seemed so much taller sitting down. I was five feet seven inches, and I knew I had quite a bit of height over her.

"Welcome to room 315." She walked over to shake my hand. "That was my bed last year, but you're free to choose. I really have no preference. Oh, I'm sorry. I forgot to introduce myself. I'm Laura Davis, but everyone calls me Lori. You must be Jennifer Carson. Your name's already on the door."

Terrific! I was going to get a perky kid with a sunny disposition. She probably was the type who liked to sit up half the night and chat. That was just great! She was all I needed in the frame of mind I was in right now!

"I'd be glad to help you carry the rest of your stuff. I know what a long haul it is."

"Sure, why not?" How could I refuse? Lori might be small, but she was strong. She picked up my suitcase as if it were stuffed with cotton. "This bed will be fine." I pointed to the one that was unmade. We both deposited the luggage on it.

Together, we walked down the hall. I could tell that Lori was one of those people who walked fast, fully of energy, get up and go. Jeez, of all the luck.

"Are you a freshman or a transfer student?"

Questions! She was already on me with questions. Why couldn't I have gotten here first and had a little peace and quiet before bombshell rolled in? "I'm a freshman," I answered trying to sound as polite as I could. "And you?"

"This is my second year. Elon's a wonderful school. You're going to love it."

Oh, marvelous! She already had my life decided for me. Just like my father. "Yeah . . . I'm sure it'll be just peachy." As hard as I tried, I still could not keep the sarcasm out of my voice. Lori looked a little set back by my curt attitude. I figured I probably hurt her feelings. "Hey, Lori, I'm sorry. It's been a hell of a day." I apologized. After all, she could not help it if she was bubbling over with friendliness, and I had a rotten trip down here.

Besides we were going to have to live together; I didn't want to get off on the wrong foot.

"Yeah, I remember. My first day here last year was pretty hectic and confusing too. Leaving home, you kind of miss your family and old friends. It's sort of scary. I understand. It'll be okay, though. You'll meet new friends."

We reached the rest of my luggage about the time she finished her pep talk. "Listen, Lori, don't psychoanalyze me and we'll get along just fine." I stuck a bag under my arm and picked up two more suitcases. Without glancing at her, I turned toward the door.

Lori and I climbed the stairs, dumped the load off, and walked back down the steps again in silence. The only thing left was my trunk. It was pretty hard to carry a trunk up three flights of stairs without talking to the person on the other end. By the time we reached the landing on the third floor, I started softening toward her. Hell! I was not such a bad person; normally, I was friendly enough. I shied away from close female relationships, but there was no reason to take out my hostilities toward my parents on this unsuspecting kid who really did not deserve my verbal abuse. There was no law stating we had to be bosom buddies, but I didn't have to be so hard on her either. I tried to break the ice. "Hey, Lori, want to rest here for a minute?" She put down her end of the trunk at the same time I did. I stopped to catch my breath. I never, as long as I could remember, had as much stamina as everyone else. This was no exception. Lori barely seemed winded as I gasped for fresh air. My heart beat erratically against my chest. It must be the cigarettes. The doctor told me I was an idiot to smoke with a heart murmur, but I refused to quit. It was my one successful rebellion against my father.

I looked at Lori. She still hadn't said a word. "Where ya from?"

"Virginia," she replied softly still unsure of me.

It was the first pleasant thing I had heard all day. "Really? Where abouts?"

"Outside D.C."

"Me too." I saw a smile forming on her face. I asked her to be more specific.

"Near Mt. Vernon."

"We live in Georgetown . . . that's not far from there at all." I was feeling a little better. Somehow the fact that she was from my old stomping ground helped my disposition. We talked about places we both knew as we carried the trunk the remainder of the way to the room and dropped it onto the center of the floor. "Now, I'm all moved in."

"Hey," Lori laughed. "That's the easy part. The hard part is putting it all away."

"You're right about that. They sure don't give us much space here. A few drawers and a tiny closet will never do."

"I don't have much stuff, Jennifer. You're more than welcome to use a couple of my drawers and some of my closet space."

I looked inside. She was right. Lori didn't have much at all. A couple of dresses, a few skirts and a blouse or two. Her drawers were just as spacious. It was so refreshing not to see a closet stuffed with name brand labels. I laughed. This was irony! Daddy sent me down here to his so-called rich kids' school, and I got a roommate who could not afford more than a few outfits that were probably bought at what my father always referred to as peasants' stores.

"Why are you laughing?" Lori looked bewildered.

"Nothing. Everything. This is marvelous," I laughed again. "Just perfect. I think we're going to get along fine." As I said the words, I realized that she probably thought I was some rich snob who gloated over the fact that I was going to be able to take advantage of her disadvantage. "Hey, Lori, you wouldn't believe what I've been thinking. I don't even know if I should try to explain." I paused for a moment. "Please don't take offense."

"I won't," she answered guardedly.

"You see," I was really laughing, practically in hysterics. I stopped and tried to get my breath before I continued my explanation. "My father sent me here to this barless jail away from home. He actually thought there was no one here but country club kids. Wouldn't he just die if he discovered that my roommate didn't have a closet full of Bloomingdale's, Saks, and custom-made everything?" I watched her for a moment. "See, you are offended. I didn't say it to hurt you. I wished to hell they were my clothes." I paused a moment. Pointing to my five suitcases and trunk, I continued, "I don't want all these things. I never wear half of them. I hate those clothes, I hate North Carolina, and I especially hate this place." I was crying. No—crying wasn't quite the word for it—I was sobbing. My God! Where did all the tears come from? I never cried! Lord, I couldn't remember the last time I shed a tear. Dad always said, "Keep a stiff upper lip!" And here I was clinging to this stranger and bawling my eyes out. My father would kill me—not only was I crying—I was doing it on a poor kid's shoulder.

After I had exhausted myself, Lori placed a glass of cold water in my hands. She brushed my hair away with a cool, damp cloth. I began to relax. Surprisingly, the water and the damp cloth did make me feel better. Lori had not said a word. I suppose it was because she was waiting for me to speak. I muttered, "I may be a weak person in general, but I'm certainly not used to reverting into a blubbering idiot in front of a person I've only known a few minutes."

Lori finally spoke. "I'm sure you're not weak at all." Her tone was filled with patience. She guided me over to my unmade bed and gently sat me down on it. Lori sat on the trunk across from me before adding, "I'm sure that it's just what you said earlier, and if I may quote you, 'it's been a hell of a day.'" Lori grinned slightly. She seemed to understand. Her eyes reflected wisdom and concern.

The world was filled with people who couldn't give a damn about anyone except themselves, but this girl seemed sincere. I managed to return a half smile and mumbled, "No, it's not just the fact that it's been a bad day." I blew my nose. I could not for the life of me understand why I was talking to this girl. I never confided in anyone . . . not even David. I was a private person, but this girl was catching me off guard; the fact that she seemed so genuinely attentive made it easier to express myself. "No. I'm basically weak in nature. You see," I blew my nose a second time. "I'm a Pisces . . . the fish . . . wishy-washy. I've got no backbone. No spunk. No guts." I ran the cloth over my face a couple of times before continuing. "I shouldn't be here. It's not what I want. But my father was bound and determined to make something out of me that I'm not. Unfortunately, I've never had the courage to stand up to him."

I watched Lori. When I realized she was not going to interrupt me, and she was actually listening to every word I spoke, I continued, "My father always wanted a son. Someone he could be proud of to carry on the family name and follow in his footsteps. He wanted a son who would go to West Point . . . a real Army man. He never gave a damn about me because I did not have testicles and a dick." I looked up to see if my words had shaken her, but Lori's expression had not changed. "He always pushed me to be athletic. It was futile. Not only am I weak in mind and spirit, I'm also physically unable to do any of that crap. I'm so uncoordinated, and if that's not enough . . . I'm short-winded, too."

I reached for my cigarettes, drew one out of the pack, and offered her one. Lori paused a moment before taking the cigarette out and holding it between her fingers. I lit mine, took a long puff, and kept the match going for hers. I could tell by the way she drew smoke in, held it in her mouth a second before releasing it in one big white cloud, that Lori had never smoked before. She coughed slightly and put the filter to her lips again. I may be a coward and a combination of a lot of other things, but I wasn't stupid. It took me just a moment to realize Lori only accepted the cigarette to give me a sense of unity. I gave her another point for trying. I wasn't going to embarrass her by saying how silly she looked, so I continued to drag off my cigarette silently until she put hers out halfway through. As I watched her in silence, I noticed that Lori was unusually pretty in a quaint way. With the right clothes and a little touch of makeup, she could be a real knockout.

I finished my cigarette and then confessed. "I usually don't spill my guts to anyone . . . stranger or otherwise. I'm sorry if I've imposed on you."

She finally spoke. "Not in any way has this been an imposition. I'm glad I was here.

I couldn't decide if she was passing judgment on me, or if she was remembering my statement about not psychoanalyzing me. She had not conveyed one opinion about my confession. It felt odd talking about my innermost feelings to someone instead of holding them inside. For some strange reason, I was waiting for a response from her. Lori remained silent, so I added, "About that statement earlier . . . you know . . . the one about practicing elementary psychology. Well, I was just spouting off. I didn't really mean it."

Lori grinned. She had pretty teeth. I had worn braces for three years, and mine weren't as perfectly formed and spaced as hers were.

"Say something, Lori. Please."

She sat up straight and paused for a few moments as if she were gathering her thoughts.

"Personally, I don't think you're weak at all. And if you don't mind my saying so, I think that father of yours sounds like a real tyrant."

I chuckled, "I've never heard my father described quite like that before, but I suppose you're right. I have always thought of him as an unmerciful god, but I think tyrant is much more suitable. I have never been able to decide whether I love him or hate him, but one thing's for sure . . . I don't like him very much.

"When I was a little girl, I wished with all my heart that he'd let me sit on his lap. I wanted my father to cuddle me in his arms and tell me stories." I glanced around the room and paused for several seconds before continuing. "He seemed so big in my eyes. Ribbons and stars decorated his uniform. He looked so handsome, like a movie star. He carried this huge briefcase, and he drove around in his black Lincoln Continental. He was larger than life. All I ever wanted from him was a kiss, a hug, or to be tucked in at night, but he never had the time . . . or maybe he just didn't make the effort. He seemed so gigantic . . . so powerful . . . so damned busy." I sighed despondently. "I guess I was six or seven before I realized he didn't love me. It was really a rude awakening when I overheard my father yelling at my mom because she couldn't have any more children and bear him a son. That's when my mom cut my hair short in a pixie and dressed me in jeans and boyish shirts. On Christmas and birthdays when all the other girls were getting dolls and tea sets, I was getting baseball mitts, trucks, and footballs. I guess my father figured if he couldn't have a son, he'd have to make do with his only alternative . . . me."

"That's so sad. What about your mother? Didn't she have anything to say?"

"Mom? I imagine she tried in the beginning. But she's a lot like I am. No guts. I think she's scared to death of him. She has a right to be. Every time she defies him . . . he beats her."

"You're kidding!"

"Why would I kid about something like that?"

"I didn't mean it like it sounded, Jennifer. It's just that I can't imagine something like that actually happening. I don't understand why a man would do something like that, or why your mother would put up with it. I mean, why doesn't she leave?"

"Who knows? My mother's always seemed like a little mouse to me." I lit another cigarette, but this time I did not make the mistake of offering one to Lori. She noticed and smiled shyly. "If my mother doesn't have the guts to stand up to him, she probably doesn't have the courage to leave him either. Who knows what goes on in her shallow little mind? She rarely talks. I think she drinks a lot. I've never seen her, but I smell it.

"Only once did she come close to making a stand against my old man. I was in my early teens. My dad was just about to hit me for some reason. I can't remember what it was about." I shook my head sadly. "My mother jumped between us and screamed hysterically. The doors and windows were all opened. My father must have been afraid of what the neighbors would say because he stopped in his tracks and left. Mom, without saying a word, ran to her room—by the way, they had separate rooms. She locked the door. I remember hearing her cry. I knocked. I wanted to talk to her. I wanted to protect her. But she wouldn't even open the door.

"That night, I was in bed but I could still hear it. God, it was awful! He beat her. She kept screaming and crying. All I did was lay there and listen to

it. I thought he was going to kill her, and I couldn't even lift a finger to help."
I blinked back the tears. I was not going to allow myself the luxury of crying anymore. "The next day my mother was still there. She made breakfast as if nothing happened. She was wearing a lot of makeup, but I could still see the bruises. She didn't say a word. Nothing! That's when I realized she wasn't going to do anything to change the situation. I'm sure she has her reasons. Maybe, in some sick way, she loves the man. Maybe she's too scared of him . . . maybe it's because she has a blind sense of loyalty to the church. We're Catholic. Anyway, my father has never laid a hand on me since that day. Of course, he still beats up on my mother, but he doesn't touch me. I'm always too scared of unpleasant confrontations so I don't do anything that might tick off his fury."

"You think you're weak because of that?"

"Don't you?"

"No, Jennifer, I don't. I think you're frightened. You have every right to be. But I don't think you're weak. From what you've said, your father sounds like a very sick man. I pity him. I think it's terrible what he's done. But you mustn't bear a cross you don't deserve." Lori leaned over, touched my shoulder, and smiling reassuringly. "Perhaps coming here is a blessing in disguise. Being around your father has obviously confused you. You consider yourself weak when you've never had the opportunity to be just you. Jennifer, give yourself breathing space and some time. Don't let your father corrupt or brainwash you into thinking you're something you're not."

I smoked the cigarette all the way to the filter. I flattened it in the ashtray and concentrated all my efforts into shaping the butt into one small accordion ball. As hard as I tried not to like Lori, I discovered a bond growing between us. Never before had I talked with anyone like this. No one had ever taken an interest in me for who I was. Not even David knew most of the things I just said to this girl. Maybe this place did have a silver lining; it was worth a try. I looked at Lori and grinned, "Perhaps Elon won't be so bad after all." She returned my smile. I slapped my hands together a couple of times and stood up. "Feel like helping a poor, depressed freshman unpack?"

"I'd love to . . . where do we start?"

I watched her for a few seconds before stumbling over words I'd never said before. "Do you think, Lori . . . that maybe we could be friends?"

Lori's eyes shone. Her grin was wide but exposed no teeth. Pausing only a moment, she answered, "I'd really like that."

2

September blended into October, and October started whizzing by. With each day, I realized what a true friendship Lori and I had blooming. We studied together, we ate our meals together, we went to movies, we listened to rock 'n roll, and we mourned Janis Joplin's death. Just as I had predicted, we spent hours talking every night. But I was wrong about one thing; instead of resenting the friendly conversations, I found myself looking forward to them. Talking with Lori was relaxing. I could be myself with her. I didn't need a stiff upper lip or hard-core facade. We exchanged words about everyday occurrences, boys, hang-ups, other girls, and inner feelings. Lori learned a great deal about me, but in the six weeks I'd been at Elon, I only learned two basic characteristics about her personality. The first was that she never spoke unpleasantly about anyone; the second was that she rarely discussed her own emotions.

I knew Lori had a fiancé. Despite the fact she never said anything concrete about him, I sensed she was not in love. She simply didn't glow the way I imagined someone like her would radiate if she were truly in love. I was tempted to ask about Tommy but decided against it. My roommate was a private person. When she was ready to discuss it, she would voluntarily.

The thing I liked the most about Lori was that I knew anything I said to her was held in confidence. She was my own personal sounding board, and she wouldn't rat on me. The only thing that bothered me—and this was my own hang-up—was Lori seemed so popular with everyone—girls and guys. Having to share her with so many people made me jealous. I'd never had a real friend before; it seemed slightly unfair that others monopolized so much of her time.

During my first six weeks at Elon, I went out on several dates. I knew David wouldn't be happy with my actions, but I figured . . . what he didn't know wouldn't hurt him. Most of the guys I went out with were people Lori introduced me to, but one particular date was with a guy I met all on my own. His name was Brad Malone.

We met in the library one night when I was doing research on a paper. From time to time, especially when Lori and I were in the cafeteria, I noticed Brad watching me. I always returned his smiles. He'd wink at me, and I'd grin. Knowing full well about his reputation, I still encouraged his attention. After all, he was incredibly good looking.

One afternoon, Brad approached me while Lori and I were walking back from class. He nodded silently at Lori and then directed his attention to me. "How you doing, Jennifer?"

"Fine . . . and you?" I responded. Immediately, I detected my roommate's agitation. Lori shifted repeatedly from one foot to another, but she remained silent.

"I'm doing well, too, thank you." Brad looked at Lori and then at me again. "I was wondering, Jennifer, if you might be interested in seeing a movie with me Friday night?"

"Sure . . . why not?" I answered, still perplexed at Lori's obvious apprehension. I glanced dubiously at her, but she turned away without a word. She was probably concerned about my lack of judgment accepting a date with Brad. Didn't Lori know that I could take care of myself? Brad Malone wasn't going to get the best of me. I knew how to handle guys like him.

"I'll pick you up at 8:00." He smiled congenially at me and then glanced at Lori. His eyes were unreadable, but his lips were curved upward in a devilish grin. "See you around."

Lori refused to comment on the subject as we walked to Staley Dorm. I was extremely curious about her attitude, but I didn't pursue the matter. Getting her to say anything was like pulling teeth if she wasn't in the mood to discuss it.

The date with Brad was a complete disaster. His idea of a movie was sitting in a parked car at the Circle G drive-in theater. It was a night to remember. The guy was all hands—like an octopus. He nearly drove me insane. I never dated anyone who didn't take "no" for an answer like Brad Malone. He was persistent, arrogant, vain, stubborn, and egotistical. I could think of a million adjectives to describe him; none of them were good. The weirdest thing about the whole evening was his constant referral to my roommate. He slipped questions into conversations that started out having nothing whatsoever to do with Lori. He was subtle when he inquired, "How do you get along with your roommate?" or "What's your roommate like?" I wondered if he knew my roommate was Lori. I never mentioned her name; neither did he.

After I physically pushed him away for the hundredth time, I demanded that he take me back to campus immediately. He was irritated, commenting, "You're a friggin' prick teaser." I was so revolted by his whole nature that I didn't even dignify his words with a reply.

When I returned to the dorm, I felt nothing but relief. Obviously, it was no great shakes to him either, because I saw Brad the next day with a cute blonde named Cindy Wilder. I knew Cindy casually; she was constantly in our room chatting with Lori. The poor kid! I hoped she wasn't going to get herself mixed up with Brad. Cindy was too nice a girl for the likes of him.

David called and wrote occasionally. I missed him, but not nearly as much as I thought I would. Of course, I missed making love and lying in bed stoned afterward; I missed the easygoing nature of our relationship and the massive snacks he made for me when I was too wrecked to handle a kitchen knife. But David—the person—I didn't miss him all that much. Somehow, I associated him with my life at home, with my parents, and my hostility. He belonged to another place, another time, and another me.

In the weeks since I came to Elon, Lori had somehow transformed me. It was as if she had waved a magic wand, which turned me into someone new and special. Maybe I hadn't really changed all that much, but it felt as if my eyes had been opened and weights had been lifted off my shoulders.

It was amazing how my outlook on life had changed and how my self-esteem had grown. Not once since I'd been at Elon had I taken a toke off a jay. It seemed as if I no longer needed the numbing effect the marijuana created or the blissful forgetfulness that had always surrounded me with its dulling nature. I felt like a born-again Christian, but instead of finding Christ, I had found myself.

Needless to say, I was barely holding my own in my classes. That was no great surprise. I hadn't chosen a major as of yet, so I was taking non-committing but mandatory courses and struggling with all of them. If it weren't for Lori and her endless hours of help and patience, I probably would have already been shipped home by now, declared a failure, and sentenced to my father's wrath. Thankfully, with Lori's encouragement, I was slowly plugging along.

3

It was a Sunday night toward the end of October when I entered our room and immediately noticed that the pictures of Lori's fiancé were gone. They had been stripped from the wall and stashed somewhere out of sight. The shower was running. I assumed it was Lori since I knew our suitemates still hadn't returned from their weekend at home. I sat on the bed, lit a cigarette, and waited for Lori.

By the time my cigarette reached the filter, Lori entered the room. She was wrapped in a terry cloth towel and had a turban around her head. I decided not to wait for her to broach the subject, so I very frankly pointed to the wall where the pictures had been and asked, "What's up?"

"Something that should have happened a long time ago," she answered despondently.

"I see you are not wearing your diamond. Does that mean you're a free woman now?

She whispered in a soft, sad way, "I guess that's what it boils down to."

"I know Tommy was here today, Lori. I saw you two together in the lobby." I made my voice sound as firm but gentle as possible. "I'm not going to let this pass. It's your turn to spill your guts. You've listened to me for almost two months. It's time you have enough confidence in me to share your problems too."

"I've never talked about it, Jennifer. I don't know where to begin." She pulled the towel from her head and started brushing her hair. "I guess if Tommy had been accepted to Elon as a transfer student, we might have had a chance, but when his application was rejected . . . I knew it was never going to work for us." She stared out the window with a blank expression on her face. "I guess I kinda outgrew the relationship. That sounds so cold, doesn't it? I don't mean it to be. It's just that I tried as hard as I could . . . but it just wasn't enough. I wanted to love Tommy. God, I tried so hard." She put the brush down and sat on the chair crossing her legs Indian style. "He was so good to me . . . so patient and considerate."

"How'd he take it when you told him?"

"I'm not sure. Outwardly, he took it better than I anticipated. He said he'd seen it coming for months. But inwardly . . . I don't know. It's hard to explain. You'd have to know Tommy to understand. I was his whole world . . . and he had become only a fraction of mine. I was living a lie. I knew I couldn't do it any longer. It wasn't healthy . . . not for him . . . or me." Lori paused. "He cried a little. I half expected that. I cried too. Three years is a lot of time to share with one person. There's this huge void." Lori was quiet for a moment before continuing, "It's odd. I don't feel any pain. I only feel relief."

"Do you think it's really over, Lori?"

"Yes. It's over. I'm not the person Tommy fell in love with . . . that person died last year. No matter how hard I try, I can't resurrect her."

"What happened last year?"

"That's another story . . . for another night." As a despondent expression covered her face, Lori looked squarely in my eyes. "I can't talk about it, Jennifer . . . maybe later, okay?"

My curiosity was killing me, but I let the subject pass. Lori was finally opening up to me. I didn't want to push too hard; therefore, I stayed on the subject she was willing to discuss. "How did you tell him?"

"I just said it."

"You mean, you just said 'it's over' . . . just like that?"

"Yeah . . . kind of. He asked me if I still loved him. Tommy must have asked me that question a hundred times in the last year. This time instead of saying, 'yes, of course,' like I usually did, I said, 'no, I don't . . . not anymore.' I don't know how I could have been so cruel, but the words just slipped out. It was as if someone else spoke them. In a way, I wanted to take them back, but it was too late." Lori picked up a pencil and silently began to doodle on a blank piece of paper. "He very calmly asked me if the problem had to do with sex." She suddenly looked up as if she had just then realized she was speaking thoughts instead of thinking them.

Lori watched for my reaction, but even though I was surprised by her revelation, I tried not to show it on my face. "If you think I'm going to be shocked by the idea that you've lost your virginity . . . don't. You've known for weeks that I lost mine three years ago to some dip at a wild party." I sat back and waited for her to continue.

She looked away and stared at the walls. "It's just that I've never talked about it before."

To be honest, I *was* a bit surprised. The rumor mill claimed that Lori was the only virgin left on campus. In a way, I admired her for it. Her secret was safe with me; I'd never tell.

"Well, to put it bluntly," she paused momentarily and flipped the pencil back and forth. It made a drumming sound on the desk. "I wasn't very good at lovemaking."

Lori was so proper; even her vocabulary was refined on the subject. Just once I wanted to hear a foul word come from her mouth, but she was a lady all the way. It was almost unnerving.

"We dated almost two years before Tommy and I actually did it. I was disappointed and scared . . . and guilty. I wanted to be like other girls . . . loving it and being free about everything . . . but I couldn't." She shrugged her shoulders. "I guess I'm just one of those cold women."

"That's bullshit, Lori. Tommy just wasn't the right guy." I couldn't see the expression on her face because Lori immediately turned away from me and expelled a sorrowful moan. "What did you have to say?"

"About what?"

"When Tommy asked you if the problem was sex."

"Oh, that." Lori looked at me again. Her expression was the same . . . stoic. She looked away a second time. "I told him no, that wasn't the root of the problem, and then I told him it was basically just that I didn't love him enough anymore."

"He accepted that?"

"Yeah. I don't think it was a big surprise to him. He said he'd been preparing himself for the 'Dear John,' as he put it, for quite some time. He also told me he'd always be there for me if I ever wanted to come back."

"The guy is nuts about you, Lori."

"I know. I think that's what bothers me more than anything else. I feel awful. I didn't want to hurt him. I didn't want to wreck his dreams—what had once been our dreams. But I was so stagnant and unhappy. I didn't know what else to do."

"What did Tommy do after you told him?"

"He left."

"Just like that?"

"Just like that. He said, 'Good-bye' and 'I still love you,' got in his car, and drove away."

"Are you going to be all right, Lori?"

"I don't know. I feel so guilty, and I don't know if I'm ever going to feel okay again."

"It will be okay, Lori. I know it doesn't seem like it right now, but some-day, it will be okay."

Lori smiled weakly. "That's enough about me for one night. Thanks, Jennifer; thanks for being here. It felt good to talk about it. I don't express myself too well. I'm kind of new at it." She let out a long sigh that puffed her cheeks out and seemed to release some of her mental pressure. "You've been a big help. It felt good to kind of unload some of the tension."

Tesa Jones ⚘ 115

You've been a big help! In my entire life, no one had said anything so special to me. It was as if the full circle of our relationship was finally formed. There were never two more different people than Lori and me; but in a strange way, I was closer to her than anyone I had ever known. I felt that now, not only did I need her, but she needed me. I drew a unique sense of strength from that thought.

"Not to change the subject, Jen, but my brother's coming here next weekend. Would you be interested in a blind date?"

"Sounds good to me," I replied.

"He's a pretty terrific guy. Kurt is so cute, and he's smart too. I think he might be borderline genius or something. When I was struggling through elementary school, he was skipping grades. He's studying pre-law at Chapel Hill. I think he'll make a great lawyer."

"Lori, you don't have to sell me on your brother. If he's anything like you—I'll like him."

"Who knows . . . maybe I can scrounge up a date and we can double," Lori laughed as she crawled into bed and snapped out the light on the table next to her.

4

I was right. I did like Lori's brother. Kurt was handsome, funny, and polite. Lori and Kurt looked so much alike. All of their features were similar. Kurt had the same extraordinarily large shining blue eyes; both of them had wide friendly smiles; the shape of their faces were a little rounded with high cheekbones and ever so slightly pointed chins. The only surprise was Kurt's hair. It was the same brown color with honey and red highlights as Lori's, but the length was not what I expected. Although The Beatles had long since made the crew cut and the flat top out-of-date, the average guy south of the Mason-Dixon Line still wore his hair neatly trimmed. Kurt didn't look at all like the standard jock who was running around Elon. I liked his shoulder-length style, and the independent aura it gave him.

We doubled with Lori and Rick Malone. The four of us danced up a storm at the Castaways in Greensboro. Kurt was interesting, witty, and fun. Of all the guys I had dated since I came to Elon, he was the only one I wanted to see again.

Conversing with Kurt was almost as easy as talking to Lori. He had the same attentive expression on his face, as if every word I said was registering in his mind. Of course, I didn't speak with Kurt as openly as I did with Lori, but it gave me a warm sense of security to think that perhaps—if I wanted to—I could.

That night in the dorm, Lori and I talked. I repeated numerous times how I thought Rick Malone was a perfect match for her. "It's obvious, Lori. The guy's crazy about you."

She answered, "We're just friends, Jennifer, nothing more. He knows that, and so do I."

"But now that you're not engaged anymore . . . don't you think all that could change?"

"No." She shook her head persistently. "I have no romantic feelings for Rick."

"You're nuts, Lori. Jesus, if I had a guy like Rick on my doorstep, I certainly wouldn't put him off. He's so nice and gorgeous too! I hear his family's loaded. I can't believe he and Brad are actually brothers. They are like night and day. They don't act alike; they don't look alike. And have you ever noticed the way Brad treats Cindy Wilder? It's disgusting."

"Jennifer!" she snapped angrily. "What Brad Malone does is none of our business. As for Rick, you're assuming I'm shopping for a husband. That's your father's idea of college—not mine."

"You're right. I'm sorry. I guess it's kind of hard to forget an idea that's been pounded into my brain ever since I can remember. But I can't help it if I still think you're crazy. I mean Rick is 100 percent perfect in every category."

"Except one," Lori replied shyly. "It just isn't there."

"You're right," I answered. "You usually are."

Lori changed the subject with a pleasant smile. "Did you have a good time tonight? How'd you like my brother?"

"I had a wonderful time. It was the best time I've had since I came here."

"Really? That's wonderful. Kurt told me he had a good time too. In fact, he asked me to find out if you'd be interested in going out again sometime."

"I would. I really would." I slipped my nightgown over my head and kicked the dress I had been wearing into the corner of the closet. Lori and I were different in a million ways, but I imagined tidiness was probably the biggest gap. She was extremely neat, immaculate almost to a fault. I was the exact opposite. Her clothes were always folded properly and placed on top of each other in the two drawers she used. Her few dresses hung crisply from the hangers. Her bed was always made unless she was in it, and her desk was always cleared unless she was studying. Her shoes were always in a row just inside the closet door. I knew I probably drove her to near insanity with my clutter and disorganization, but she never said a word. Lori never commented on how my drawers would not close properly because I jammed too many unfolded garments into them, or how I piled dirty clothes in heaps scattered around the room, or the way I draped unused blouses and slacks over the backs of chairs, or even about the fact that my bed was only made on room-check days. At first, I made a mess of my clothes just to see how far I could push her. When she didn't comment, I figured she was going to let me do things my way, and she'd do it her way. That was just one more extra in her favor. I finally realized Lori wasn't going to try to change me; she simply liked me for *me!*

I flicked off the light and crawled into bed. It had been a good evening. I knew the small buzz I had acquired from the beer was going to grant me a peaceful night's sleep.

5

I saw Kurt the following weekend. The two of us hitched a ride to Whitman Stadium in Burlington to see Elon's football game. Our team lost 6-7, but I never understood football jargon well enough to figure out why Catawba was victorious. It seemed ridiculous to me to see all those massive guys running around, chasing each other, working their asses off, when the real fun was up in the stands with the laughter, cheers, and booze.

It was obvious that Kurt enjoyed the sport, so I made a mental note to study the rules of the game. He told me that he was an avid Redskins fan. Apparently, last year some coach named Lombardi led them to their first winning season in fourteen years. Kurt was bursting with all the statistics.

It was a wonderful weekend. I discovered almost immediately upon Kurt's departure Sunday afternoon that I missed him and couldn't wait to see him again. I liked him . . . even more than I was willing to admit.

The Wednesday after the football weekend, I received a card from Kurt. He thanked me for a marvelous time and stated his plans to return on Saturday. He asked if I would like to go out again. I replied by phone, "Yes . . . I'd love to see you again."

Kurt arrived Saturday afternoon. We walked around campus. At first, he was shy. Gradually, as the hours slipped by, he managed to drape one arm comfortably around my shoulder. It felt good.

He asked about David. My first thought was to lie, but then I realized Lori had probably informed him about the relationship, so I decided the truth was better.

"David? Well, to put it in a nutshell . . . David and I have a relationship that goes beyond the goodnight kissing stage." I watched to see if Kurt comprehended my meaning. By the look on his face, I thought he had. "It's serious . . . but not necessarily permanent."

Kurt grinned and squeezed my shoulder firmly as he kissed the end of my nose. "Nice, tactful, honest answer. I like that."

I let out a deep breath. A point scored for me. It seemed as if I made the right decision by being honest with him. "Did Lori tell you about David?"

"No. She just told me you had some guy you were dating back home. She didn't fill me in on any of the details."

Terrific! I might have known Lori wouldn't break a confidence. I was beginning to regret my confession.

"Jennifer? It's all right if I keep seeing you . . . isn't it?" He appeared apprehensive.

"Yes."

We doubled again with Lori and Rick. Because Rick could provide transportation, we saw *Patton* in Burlington. Kurt was totally engrossed in the historical aspect of the film. He talked for over an hour after the movie about World War II and the strategies behind the battles. His words held little meaning for me, but I did enjoy listening to him talk. Being around him made me feel smart.

Later, the four of us parked in a deserted elementary school lot and drank a six-pack of beer. The radio was playing a tribute to The Beatles. I enjoyed every song. They were definitely my favorite group. I was delighted to discover that Kurt felt the same way.

It wasn't until the song "Something" came on the radio that Kurt kissed me for the first time. Oh, he'd brushed his lips across mine once or twice and kissed my cheek several times, but he'd never really held me with any kind of passion. I'd like to think that the slow rhythm and the beautiful words of the song had something to do with his actions, but I imagine it was simply the right moment. Kurt had been working his way up to the embrace for thirty minutes. I, feeling like an inexperienced kid for the first time in years, hadn't been able to rush the awkwardness along. But once his lips touched mine, all that initial tension vanished. As the evening progressed, I found myself hoping his hands would roam and explore my body, but he never took them from around my shoulders. He kept kissing me endlessly, each one melding into another, until he finally traced a pattern up to my ear and muttered very softly, "I've been wanting to kiss you since the moment I met you."

I held him tightly, forgetting that there was anyone else in the car. It had been a long time since something as simple and innocent as a kiss had stirred such thrilling reactions within me. I kept my eyes closed, savoring the moment.

"Let's take a walk." Kurt broke the silence.

We left Rick and Lori. Neither of us spoke as we took our steps. After finding an isolated area under a group of trees, we sat down. I wanted him to make love to me—right there under a heaven full of stars—but I knew he wouldn't. I instinctively knew Kurt was the type of guy to do things by the book, and the book never mentioned making love in a public place to a woman who belonged to someone else. I wanted to denounce David—cast aside the good year we had shared together—but I thought wiser of it. A bird in the hand, as the saying goes.

I couldn't believe how much I had changed since that fateful day I came to Elon. Had two months changed me that much? I no longer felt like the clinging vine who held on to David in a state of near panic the night before my departure. I had mixed feelings. Part of me wanted Kurt and a new beginning; yet, another part of me whispered that I loved David. Two months ago, I wanted the courage to defy my father and marry David. I wanted a simple career and a life with the man who made me happy. I knew no decision on my part could be made until I returned home. I needed to find some answers. But, for the time being, I was going to enjoy Kurt.

Kurt didn't see me as some rich bitch who lived on top of the hill with all the other wealthy people in town. He treated me like I always wanted to be treated—special. He seemed enchanted by me, not because of my father's pocketbook or his rank, but because of *me* and who I was. He always asked my opinion on things, as if he valued what I thought. Nobody had ever asked me—aside from Lori—one single question that required an opinion. Certainly not my father or mother and definitely not David, who always jokingly referred to me as his "dumb blonde in a sexy package." Kurt asked me not only everyday questions, but what I thought about political parties, the economy, and President Nixon's promise to pull 40,000 U.S. troops out of Vietnam by Christmas. Since our first meeting, I spent each night in front of a news broadcast and tried to take in all the information I could so I would be able to answer intelligently. I was not one to know the difference between a Republican and a Democrat or what was going on in Southeast Asia. Kurt was shocked to discover that I didn't even know the Jets had won the Super Bowl in '69. I wanted to sound knowledgeable and interesting, so I learned all I could about each subject he mentioned. Whenever groups of people formed to discuss current events, I stayed and listened. Eventually, I hoped to have the courage to speak my opinion.

Kurt seemed pleased when I actually knew that Brooks Robinson was the Orioles' third baseman who won the Most Valuable Player award during the World Series. He loved discussing sports. And, although I didn't understand why our country was in a recession, Kurt seemed thrilled to explain to me how the 60s had been a flourishing decade for business expansion, and the last year had left us in a recession, where our cost of living soared and the purchasing power of our dollar declined, which made money tight and credit expensive, especially if a person wanted to buy a house. It all seemed like Greek to me. I was still too timid to voice my opinion around other people, but I did find that expressing myself with Kurt was becoming increasingly easier. The best part about our rapport with each other was the fact that if I stumbled on any specific fact, he enlightened me without criticism. It gave me new encouragement to learn.

Kurt's gentle voice broke the comfortable silence. "I love your hair. It's so blonde it's almost white. You are so gorgeous, Jennifer." He stroked my hair. "Why so quiet? Don't you realize how beautiful you are?"

"No one has ever made me feel beautiful before. You're so good, Kurt . . . so warm and gentle and good. I don't deserve anyone like you."

"That's the silliest thing I've ever heard. Why would you think such a thing?" He cuddled me in his arms and kissed my forehead.

I felt very safe.

"My God! Look at the time," Kurt's voice blurted out in the pleasant night air. "Hurry or you'll be late."

"It's ridiculous the way they lock all the girls up at one thirty! It's a coed dorm, but the male section stays open all night. I don't think they've ever heard of women's rights down here. Someone ought to call Gloria Steinem. I bet she could get the rules changed." We both laughed as we jogged hand in hand back to the car where Rick and Lori were anxiously awaiting our return.

6

I awoke completely disoriented and in a pool of sweat. Trying to get my bearings, I sat up and looked around. I was in bed . . . that much I knew. As my eyes adjusted to the darkness, forms in the room began to take shape: the desk, the closet, and the bed. Lori was in that bed. Yes, I knew where I was. Why did I awake with such force? It must have been a dream. What was I dreaming about? As hard as I concentrated, I could only grasp part of the memory.

It was about David and my father. They were laughing at me and calling me a stupid fool. The two of them wore all black with masks over their faces, but I knew who they were. Their high-pitched voices were hideous as they danced around me singing some horrid song about how I was no good for anything or anyone. Then they joined hands to form a circle around me. The melody changed to the nursery rhyme, "Ring Around the Rosie." Over and over, they laughed and sang the words. I tried to break away from their hold, but their wrists were like iron.

In the distance, far away, I saw Lori dressed in yards and yards of pastels. The material circled around her like a warm mist. Beside her stood Kurt—tall and magnificent. He was dressed all in white with a gigantic Panama hat crowning his head. I jerked, kicked, and scratched at the hold my father and David had on me, but to no avail. Kurt and Lori came closer, but with every step they took, they interchanged. One moment, Lori had Kurt's face; the next, she had her own . . . and vice versa. The closer they came, the more I realized they were laughing, too. Everyone was laughing at me. Lori wasn't wearing pastels anymore, and Kurt wasn't in white. All of them were draped in black and laughing so loudly I had to cover my ears. I could still hear it even now. Then I fell. My father, David, Kurt, and Lori— everyone was gone, but the laughter remained, magnified and vibrating. It was as if I were descending in slow motion through huge white billowing clouds. I tried to grab on to something, but there was nothing tangible within my grasp. I kept falling and falling. That was all I could remember.

It was just a bad dream . . . a stupid silly dream, but it left me so cold. I was still shaking from the memory of it.

I longed to awaken Lori, but when I looked over at her sleeping figure I realized that despite my restlessness, she was still in a deep slumber. I lay back on my pillow. I was not going to analyze the nightmare. It was obvious the meaning pertained to the fact that I knew my father and David would never approve of my new relationships. So what? It was my life! I could choose to live it as I saw fit. That was my first burst of courage. I knew it was fleeting, but it felt good all the same.

A few weeks passed. I saw Kurt every weekend he was able to hitchhike to Elon—even when it rained. We became closer, but there still was nothing physical between us. Kurt made me feel like a princess. I loved every minute with him. I felt like I was riding on the top of a big fat bubble and praying like hell it wouldn't burst. I stopped dating other guys. I had no interest in forming any new relationships. I wrote home religiously to David describing the school, the girls, and how dull it was on campus (I lied a bit.)

Surprisingly, my grades were much better than I expected; they were nothing to wave banners about, but for me a C in English lit and math, an A in typing, a B in religion, and a D in history were pretty good grades. I made a habit of getting up early on Saturday mornings, eating breakfast, reading the paper, and getting to the campus library at 9:00 when it opened.

It was on one such Saturday morning when I knew Kurt wasn't coming to visit, that I got up to start my routine. Lori was already gone. Her bed was made. She was downstairs in the cafeteria working the breakfast shift. Poor kid! It must be hard trying to hold down a job while going to school. She never complained. Lori just divided her time wisely among her studies, her work, and her friends. She even had a few hours left over for a bit of a social life.

When I got to the cafeteria, it was empty with the exception of Lori, cloth in hand, wiping down tables in one corner, and Brad Malone, who was quietly eating his breakfast, at the other end of the room. Lori waved. As I picked up a tray, I returned the gesture.

By the time I got my eggs, coffee, and juice, I noticed that Lori was talking to Brad. I couldn't imagine why she wasted two seconds on that creep, but knowing Lori, she never slighted anyone. I watched them for a moment and wondered whether or not to join them, but decided against it. It was strange; Lori seemed unusually happy. Her cheeks were flushed, her eyes had a mischievous look to them that I'd never seen before, and she was smiling in a unique way, as if her entire face were involved in the expression. The two of them were laughing about something. I shrugged my shoulders and walked to the far table in the corner, opened my paper, and proceeded to eat my breakfast and drink my coffee.

After thirty minutes, I folded my paper, took my tray to the garbage, and left. I decided to take a relaxing walk to the library before delving into the books. I went out the side door and took a left only to be shocked to find Lori wrapped in Brad Malone's arms. They were kissing, oblivious to my presence.

I stood motionless, trying to find a discreet way to get out of the situation. I couldn't imagine what Lori was doing with *him* of all people. Didn't she realize what type of person he was? Had she forgotten that her friend, Cindy Wilder, was dating Brad? Cindy was crazy about him. What on earth had gotten into Lori?

I took a step backward. My foot snapped a twig. The two of them came apart like repelling ends of a magnet. Lori's eyes were big as saucers when she saw me, and her face glowed with guilt. She ought to feel guilty. My God! I never figured her for a fool. I didn't see Brad's face. I was too busy watching Lori's. She didn't say a word; neither did I.

I went to the library and tried to concentrate, but it was futile. After a couple hours of looking mindlessly at pages in my textbook, I slammed it shut, gathered my work, and walked back to the dorm. Lori was sitting on the bed reading *Love Story*.

Silently, I paced the floor banging drawers and throwing articles of clothing around the room. When I realized Lori wasn't going to comment on my sudden entry or my burst of pent-up energy, I lashed out at her. "Just what the hell do you think you're doing?" I spoke the words a little more loudly than I intended. I couldn't believe how angry I was at her stupidity.

Without looking up from the pages of her novel, she very softly answered, "It's none of your business, Jennifer." Not a muscle on her face altered, not even a batted eyelash. She continued to read.

I was infuriated. "Don't shut me out, Lori." I tried to control my temper. Yelling wasn't the way to reach her. I lowered my voice and continued, "I'm your friend. I don't want you to get hurt. Please, don't get involved with Brad. He's no good. He's a despicable character who's only out to get what he wants from people. He's on such an ego trip. Can't you see that?

Lori looked up from her book and stared at me as she very calmly stated, "You don't understand, Jennifer. And I can't explain it to you. Don't worry about my virtue. I have no intentions of becoming involved with Brad Malone."

"That's not the way it looked a couple hours ago."

"You walked in on a situation you know nothing about. Don't sit in judgment of me." Lori was very firm—almost callous—with the tone of voice she used.

"You're not going to tell me anything?"

"No." She didn't look up. "Some things are best left unsaid." As an afterthought she added, "And unremembered too." Her face looked pained. Tiny lines were etched around her eyes. I could tell her teeth were clenched by the firmness of her jaw.

I softened. I wanted to share her thoughts—whatever they were. I sat down on the bed beside her. "Please talk to me, Lori. I'm your friend . . . you've listened to me so many times. I thought we trusted each other with our problems. Please tell me what's going on."

"I can't . . . I can't talk about it . . . not to anyone . . . not even to you." Her voice was unsteady. "The subject's closed." She looked directly at me. A small tear formed in the corner of her eye. "Maybe another time we'll talk about it, Jennifer. Not today. Okay?"

The following few days, I noticed Lori stayed clear of Brad; she avoided verbal and even eye contact of any kind. On the other hand, Brad was not so obviously snubbing her. I saw him watching Lori constantly whenever they were in the same room. It amazed me that Brad could carry on a complete conversation with Cindy while his eyes bored holes into Lori's back. I wondered if Cindy noticed—I wondered if *anyone* noticed but me.

I couldn't decide by the expression on Brad's face whether he looked like a wolf sizing up his next victim or a child cherishing his favorite toy. Knowing Brad through rumor as well as experience, I gathered it to be my first impression. I discreetly asked a few people who had been at Elon last year whether there had ever been anything between Brad and Lori. I was informed they had dated a year ago, but no one seemed to know to what extent or the outcome of the relationship. I was tempted to ask Rick Malone but brushed the thought away. It would be better not to question him. Rick and Lori saw each other quite regularly. He might tell Lori I pumped him for what she called scoop; Lori hated gossip.

Neither Lori nor I brought up the subject of Brad again before Thanksgiving vacation. I found that when I didn't talk about him, our relationship reverted back to the easygoing friendship we had before the quarrel. She appeared to be her old self again: happy, carefree, and friendly. There were only a few occasions, when she didn't know I was watching, that I saw signs of any anguish on her face. I longed to have her confide in me, but I knew the words would come only when she was ready to speak them.

7

The Thanksgiving holiday was a mixture of arguments, confusion, and bliss. The arguing was with my father, of course. He was furious about my midterms and my continued escapades with David. The confusion was within my own mind, because I didn't know whether to stay with David. Finally, the bliss came with each bursting orgasm. Our physical relationship was never better. I was hungry for the touch of a man and starved for inner release and fulfillment. Kurt frustrated me with his lack of sexual activity; therefore, David was the only way to open the floodgates. Two and three times a night, I encouraged his desires. I didn't want to talk to David; I just wanted to make love and to drown in the feeling of each climax. David was a master in bed. He was the best; I couldn't get enough of him.

Even though we lived in the same vicinity, I didn't hear or see either Kurt or Lori during the entire vacation. I was glad. I didn't want them to become part of my world with my parents and David. My roommate and her brother belonged to another place and another me. I didn't want to spoil the beauty of our relationship by mixing it with my old fears and hostilities. I thought the two and a half months spent with them cured my hang-ups and inferiority complex, but it hadn't. Five minutes after walking into my parents' house, I felt the towering influence my father still had over me. If only he could have hugged me, said he missed me, even patted me on the back or given me a kiss on the cheek. Sadly, there was nothing. He simply said, "You're late for dinner. You'll have to make your own." My mother welcomed me warmly with open arms, but my father told her that she was acting like a blubbering idiot. Mom dropped her arms from around me and quietly said, "It's good to have you home. You've gained a couple pounds. It looks good. You were always too thin as a child."

That was my homecoming.

An hour later, I saw David. Immediately, I asked him to take me to bed. A few times, I tried to talk to him about all the new knowledge and ideas I had regarding current issues and foreign affairs. He only laughed. I got so nervous around him that all my facts became confused and jumbled making me sound ridiculous instead of intelligent. He chuckled, "All this college nonsense is going to your head, but you are still my crazy, wild, gorgeous, blonde with a peanut for a brain and a body that won't quit." It had always been a joke between us; I had actually laughed along with him in the past. But now I was hurt and slightly humiliated. I rationalized the situation as best I could and discovered that I could handle it. I didn't need to share my mind with David. I had Kurt for that. What I did need from David was his body and his touch.

By the middle of Sunday afternoon, I had exhausted all my sexual needs and clipped my horns. Mentally, I was close to being a basket case, but physically, I was sated and relaxed. There was no doubt about it—I needed David, but in a different way than I needed Kurt.

When I returned to Elon, I reclaimed my newfound self-esteem that had vanished while I was home. I did not have the courage to break up with David, but I was not going to let go of Kurt either. They were both very important to me in their own separate ways. I could not afford to lose either of them. I needed time. Time would help me sort it all out. Time would help me make the right decision.

4

Kurt

"SURPRISE!"

"Happy Birthday!" A chorus of voices shouted in unison.

Needless to say, I *was* surprised. Several of my closest friends were in my room. Jennifer and Lori were sitting on the bed. There was a chocolate cake in the center of the table. It was surrounded by a variety of different size packages. My spirits were immediately lifted.

All day I was pissed off because I thought no one remembered my birthday. I walked around campus in a bad mood and ignored just about everyone because I was feeling extremely sorry for myself. Birthdays were special occasions at home; I resented this one going unnoticed. For as long as I could remember, my parents made a big deal about what they referred to as my special day. Traditionally, each year Mom made waffles with warm syrup and a side order of extra spicy sausage. That was my favorite breakfast. For dinner, she served a medium rare roast beef, mountains of mashed potatoes, corn on the cob, and a huge salad with homemade croutons. They inevitably embarrassed me by singing "Happy Birthday" off key. Even though I felt too old for the tradition, I still missed it all the same.

The best part about this birthday was seeing Jennifer again. Last weekend, much of North Carolina was hit by a horrible February snowstorm, which made hitchhiking to Elon virtually impossible. We were apart for two weeks. I missed her terribly. It seemed like a miracle to see her sitting on my bed. I stood patiently as everyone finished singing.

I was finally eighteen years old. I no longer felt like the only kid in town. Being seventeen on a campus full of students years older had made me feel out of place. Everyone told me I looked older than my age, but it was not always that way. There was a time not so long ago when the girls were taller than I was. Through most of my high school years, I was short, had two left feet, and acne. I was the worst-looking kid on the planet. Thankfully, around Thanksgiving of my senior year in high school, I noticed I had grown six inches in one year's time, my face cleared up, and my voice finally hit a consistent pitch that did not sound like a soprano. At first, I was gangly and awkward, but then my weight and my coordination caught up with my increased size. I worked out in the school's weight room, which actually produced biceps worth displaying. Halfway through my senior year, I looked in the mirror and realized I was no Burt Reynolds or Robert Redford, but I was not so bad looking after all.

My first semester at the university went very slowly until I met Jennifer Carson. I dated quite a few girls my last year at home but none like her. She was special. Every minute I spent with Jennifer was like a trip I wanted to take over and over again.

"Say something, birthday boy."

"I don't know what to say." I was still at a loss for words.

Jennifer placed a warm kiss on the side of my face. "Were you surprised?" She smiled and wrapped her arms affectionately around my neck.

"Definitely."

"Happy Birthday, Kurt." It was Lori's pleasant voice. She was grinning mischievously, knowing full well they had succeeded in tricking me.

"Now you're old enough to buy beer."

"Hey, Kurt." My roommate Charlie was addressing me. "I didn't get you any real present. My gift is transporting these two gorgeous females back and forth."

"That's the best present I can get. Thanks, buddy." I kissed my two favorite women. "I'm really glad you're here. I've missed you both."

Lori and Jennifer smiled warmly as they simultaneously returned my physical affections. It felt like a wonderful dream to be so close to Jennifer again. She smelled wonderfully sweet. It seemed as if a lifetime had passed since the two of us had been alone. I craved privacy.

Charlie cracked open a bottle of champagne. We drank it out of Dixie cups. I cut the cake and kept a piece to smash playfully into Jennifer's mouth. She had traces of icing on her lips and nose. I kissed them off. God! I wanted to be alone with her. After great encouragement from the crowd, I opened my presents. I received a bottle of Jim Beam from Mike, a fluorescent jock strap from John, a UNC T-shirt from George, a pipe and a gram of hash from Tim (I was a little embarrassed—neither my sister nor Jennifer knew I smoked,) a bottle of Canoe cologne from Lori, and the Beatles' *White* album—which completed my collection—from Jennifer. All in all, it was quite a nice haul for a birthday.

After we finished the champagne, Charlie's voice interrupted the silence. "These other guys are going to split, and I'm going to take your sister out to see *Five Easy Pieces.* That ought to give you two lovebirds some time alone." He laughed. "I've seen you two eyeing each other wishing the rest of us would get lost."

"Charlie, don't make any moves on my sister, or I'll kick your ass." I said it in a joking tone, but Charlie knew I meant it. "She's not really your type—if you get my drift."

"Hey, man, I'll be good. I'm just giving you an added bonus for your birthday—privacy," Charlie joked as he steered Lori toward the door.

We were alone. I took the Grand Funk album off the record player and put on the album Jennifer gave me. After switching off the overhead and turning on the black light, I went over and sat on the bed next to her. She looked so good.

"I didn't know you smoked." She pointed to the hash.

"On occasion. Nothing really heavy, though."

"Want to share some of your birthday present with me? I never smoke around Lori. I really don't think she'd understand what it's all about. Your sister is rather prudish in that category." She extended her hand and allowed me to take the hash from her palm.

It only took a few seconds to feel the effect. "This is good stuff," I commented as I took another hit. I leaned back and encircled Jennifer with my arms. "It's great to see you, Jen. And having Lori here is groovy too. I can't imagine a birthday without her." I grinned as childhood memories flashed through my mind. "Lori and I shared everything when we were kids. In fact, when we were really young, we slept in the same room. Actually, we had separate rooms, but we were both afraid of the dark, so there were many nights when she snuck into my room and slept in the other twin bed. Some nights, we talked for hours. One particular Christmas Eve, we tried very hard to stay awake so we could catch Santa Claus. We told each other stories until we both crashed. I laugh now when I think how frustrating it must have been for Mom and Dad to wait for us to fall asleep so they could put the presents under the tree. We never caught them—not once—not even when we were teenagers." I smiled as I reflected upon the memories. "And that wasn't all we shared. She was always wearing my pants, my coveralls, my sweaters—until there came a time when my clothes no longer fit her. We took tennis lessons together. We were even in a few mixed doubles tournaments. I have the trophies to prove it." I pointed to one on my dresser. "We both learned how to drive on the same old beat-up Ford Falcon. That was an experience! I will never teach my kid how to drive a stick shift before he or she learns how to drive an automatic. On my first day, I had to stop at the light on a hill. When I tried to go after the light turned green, I wasn't sure exactly how hard I should press on the accelerator. Needless to say, when I let out the clutch, I messed it up and stalled the car. It rolled backward into a ditch—another dent in the bumper. Dad was ticked; I was frustrated. But Lori laughed. She told me that she did the exact same thing and even showed me the dent she caused. Somehow, it made me feel better." I took another hit. Smoke circled us like a cloud. "Lori was always there for me. In fact, when I was in the first grade, there was a kid who picked on me unmercifully for weeks without letting up. The kid was verbal and physical—on the playground—on the bus—in the hall. He was a nasty ass bully. Then, one day, Lori intervened. The guy was taller and weighed more than Lori. She didn't care. Lori went toe to toe with him and belted him right in the nose. The kid cried. His nose bled all over his shirt, but he was too embarrassed to admit that a girl hit him, so he didn't fink on her."

"I can't imagine Lori hitting anyone," Jennifer chuckled.

"Yeah. I know what you mean. It is rather funny, isn't it?" I laughed too. I was in a wonderful mood. It was great reliving these memories and sharing them with Jennifer. "Lori was always there for me. She listened a lot. She set me up on my first date. I was scared to death because I didn't know how to slow dance. Lori taught me how. I was no Fred Astaire, but I made it through the evening. And during my junior year, I ran for class president. Lori was my campaign manager. She helped write my speech. She made my posters. She handed out flyers. I won! She was so proud of me." The hash was almost gone; the sweet smelling smoke permeated the air. I paused before taking in the last hit. "Those were good days. She's a great sister."

After the bowl was finished, I leaned back and closed my eyes. "I remember the first time I smoked grass. It was the day after Bobby Kennedy was shot. I was in my sophomore English class when the principal announced over the PA system that we would have a moment of silence in memory of him. Jesus! It was like an instant replay. It had only been a couple of months since Martin Luther King was killed, and the school was still reeling from that shock.

"I really believed in Bobby Kennedy. He could have changed the world. It sounds silly to say it out loud, but he was my hero. He kept idealism alive inside of me. He could have started off where John Kennedy had stopped. Back in JFK's time, people were proud to be Americans: flag waving, trusting, and patriotic. I was just a kid, but I remember it. Bobby could have brought all that back."

"My father has never liked the Kennedys. He calls them liberal prigs."

"Yeah! He probably likes Nixon."

"He does," Jennifer responded softly.

"It figures." I let out a sarcastic laugh. "Your old man has the best of both worlds as far as he's concerned: Nixon in the Oval Office and Vietnam as his play toy. Fucking generals!"

"You sound so angry, Kurt."

"I am. Damn it! I am. When Bobby Kennedy died, a part of me died too. I skipped the rest of my classes that day. I went out with the kid who shared my locker. We got so wrecked. When it was time for dinner, I didn't go home. I had him drop me off at Fort Hunt Park. I sat on a bench and stared at nothing in particular. Just staring. Actually, I cried. God, I cried! It wasn't fair! He could have been President—maybe not in the '68 election—but eventually, he would have been President. He could have righted a lot of the damned things that are going wrong in America. I feel like this giant snowball is rolling down the mountain, and it's going to crush all of us." I paused. "I just want a chance—a chance to go through life—for it to be whole and happy. I want to be able to say, when it's all over for me, that my life was good—worth living. Does that make any sense to you? Or does it sound like I'm talking out my ass."

"I don't know, Kurt. I don't have any of the answers."

Several minutes went by before I spoke again. "I remember when I was in elementary school, JFK was president. Do you remember the Cuban Missile Crisis?"

"Only slightly."

"I remember it like it was yesterday. The first time that civil defense siren went off, I was so scared I almost wet my pants." I sighed letting out all the air in my chest. "The teachers told us to line up. They marched us out into the hall where they instructed us to sit against the wall, put our heads in our laps, and cover them with our arms. Ha! As if we stood a chance living so close to Washington. If the bomb hit, there'd be nothing but a gigantic crater left where I was sitting." I did not move. I focused my eyes on my roommate's Iron Butterfly poster on the wall. "Lori and I had planned a Halloween party that year—our first joint party—our first party of any kind other than birthdays. We each invited seven friends. We decorated everything in orange and black. We even had a haunted house set up in my bedroom, games, the whole nine yards. My mom made the costumes. Lori was a black cat, and I was Davy Crockett." I frowned slightly as the memory flashed through my mind. "Only three kids showed up—three out of fourteen. Their parents were so scared. That's when I realized how bad the situation was. If my friends weren't allowed to go across the street to a party, then things were a lot worse than I imagined. It seemed like all the adults were holding their breath; parents tried not to talk about it in front of a kid. But I heard bits and pieces—enough to know what was happening. Plus, the evening news was always on at our house. That was enough to scare anybody." Trying to relax, I paused and took several breaths. "Kennedy got us through it. He was one tough guy. He ordered a naval blockade around Cuba and went head to head against Castro and Khrushchev." I puffed out my cheeks with a long sigh. "Damn it! Damn it to hell! If you kill off all the good guys, then all you have left is shit."

I suddenly realized I was in a raunchy mood. It was my birthday for crying out loud; Jennifer was with me; I did not want to be in a bad mood. I needed to snap out of it. I wanted to enjoy the time I had with her. I pulled her close to me and started kissing her, tasting her. This was where I wanted to be. She began to respond.

There was nothing like kissing Jennifer when I was stoned. It felt as if she were everywhere. She felt heavy and light at the same time. I ran my fingers through her hair; each strand seemed endless and smelled like lemons. Her tongue tasted vaguely of champagne and mint. I slowly lowered her on the bed. Her breasts pressed against mine—mountains on my chest. Every time she inhaled, it felt like a volcano erupting against me. I closed my eyes and savored every touch. My hand slid down her side and cupped one firm mound. Even through the material of her blouse, I could feel her nipple expressing her passion. I gently rubbed my thumb back and forth across the protruding tip as she moaned silently in response to my actions. Jennifer's hands firmly held my back, and her nails dug into my skin. It seemed as if she and I were suspended in midair with no bed beneath us as if we were floating together with only the other's embrace for support.

Far away in the distance, I heard the monotonous tone of the record player announcing the music was over. Around and around it went, stuck on the same beat. The sound grew louder and more pronounced. I tried to block it from my mind, but it became even more magnified. I sat up realizing that the intrusion was probably for the best. In another moment, I would have been stripping the clothes from her body. Patience! Patience! I repeated to myself. I would not take Jennifer until I knew she was all mine. Without saying a word, I walked over to the stereo and turned the album to the reverse side.

When I faced Jennifer, I noticed that she was undoing the buttons on her blouse. She never looked more appealing. As she slipped each button from its place, she stared into my eyes. My God! I wanted her. I felt as if my entire insides were screaming for release. I was not even sure I could walk back to the bed because holding back was causing great pain.

"Don't do that, Jenny," I muttered, as I tried to regain control of my body.

"Make love to me, Kurt. I want you so much." Her voice was husky and low.

A groan came from the base of my throat. My knees were weak. Leaning against the wall for support, I tried to combat the urge to throw myself upon her. I instinctively knew if she were within reach I would lose control, so I did not dare take the steps between us.

"No! No, Jennifer. We are not going to make love." I could not believe I actually formed the words and made them audible enough for Jennifer to understand.

"How can you put me off like this? Don't you want me, Kurt? Don't you know how long I've waited for you to make some kind of attempt?" Jennifer was pleading as if she were having difficulty controlling her own passion.

She looked beautiful. Jennifer was real, not a dream, not a picture in my imagination! I was rock hard, and my pulse was resonating in my ears. I wanted her, but I was not going to settle for only possessing her sexually; I wanted *all* of her. I knew my best trump card was to hold back. Jennifer would never leave David if she could have the best of both worlds. Even with the few things she had told me about her home life, I realized David was important to her. He was her escape from reality. She had to break that bond before I could claim her for my own. I did not want her for one night, one month, or one year. I wanted Jennifer for a lifetime! I had no intentions of sharing her with anyone else. I had thought about this a lot. If I took Jennifer now, she would remain two split individuals: one insecure person hanging in limbo in a place that represented her home and David, and another person who was stable and confident in a niche consisting of North Carolina and me. The way I saw it, David was the type of guy who thought of Jenny as a dimwitted blond; he wanted to keep her barefoot and pregnant and waiting on him hand and foot. He did not want to give her a chance to express her own philosophies and opinions. Jennifer deserved so much more than his caveman attitude.

Of course, the fact that Jennifer was sleeping with David drove me to near insanity, but I learned to cope with that element in our strange love triangle. The one thing that gave me confidence was the fact I knew all about David, but he knew nothing about me. Patience! I had to have patience. Jennifer was worth the wait.

"You're not going to make love to me are you, Kurt?" Her eyes glistened with tears.

"Jenny, my beautiful, Jenny." I cupped her face in my hands. "I'm in love with you." The words slipped out. I had no intention of letting her know how strongly I felt about her, but I could not help myself. "I love you too much to share you. Can't you understand?"

"I don't know what you want from me," she mumbled the words as the tears streamed down her face. "I can't let go of David. I can't explain it. I'm too afraid." She glanced up, looking forlorn and confused. "I don't love David. I don't. I really don't, but I can't let go."

As she placed her head in my lap, I held her and willed her to draw strength from my touch. "It's all right, baby. Everything will be all right."

She gripped me tighter. "I need you, Kurt. You and Lori are everything to me. Without you, I'd be lost."

Even though I could not see the tears, I knew she was crying. My shirt was damp from the moisture, and her shoulders heaved with the silent shutters. My physical and mental high was gone; it was replaced by a depression we both shared.

2

I took advantage of the fact that a friend of mine was traveling through Washington over the weekend and hitched a ride home to visit my folks. Jennifer also went home. She promised to cut all ties with David.

On several occasions, I picked up the phone to dial Jennifer's home number. Before I finished the seven digits, I always hung up. No! I was not going to push her. Let her make her own decisions. She needed space and room to breathe. But God! I wanted to hear her voice.

While I was home, my parents had another one of their long-winded fights. The argument was a combination of threats and verbal abuse. My father, as usual, had a low harsh tone to his voice; my mother's words were boisterous and wailing. During this particular argument, my mother griped that my dad was never home. My father, in return, complained about the incompetence of my mother's talents as housekeeper, cook, and bed partner. My mom fought back with how tired she was of being an unpaid whore and how sick she was of being the chief cook and bottle washer. My dad retaliated by pointing to the door. "You know the way out!"

It turned my stomach to hear them quarrel so violently.

In a way, I envied Lori. She was blind to our parents' situation. She never even saw the tension between them. On a couple of occasions, I was tempted to inform her of the actual facts but trashed that idea. It was better for Lori to be ignorant of our parents' true relationship. Sometimes I thought that my sister lived in fantasyland where there was no evil, no injustice, and no reality. She saw beauty in everything; she was so idealistic, so romantic, and so completely naive. I dreaded the day she discovered that life was not like that. This was a nasty world we lived in where people scratched and clawed to get to the top. It was often ugly.

No! I could not tell her about our parents. Lori needed the security her naiveté gave her. Perhaps with a little bit of luck, she would never have to know.

3

I had been back in Chapel Hill for several weeks and had not seen or heard from Jennifer during the entire time. I studied my ass off every night and forced Jennifer's image from my mind. When I was not studying, I was stoned, trying to forget. The only highlight during that time was when everyone on campus celebrated Congress's decision to propose the Twenty-sixth Amendment, which would change the voting age from twenty-one to eighteen. Hopefully, it would be ratified; if so, with eleven million young voters we might have a chance to bump Nixon in '72. The news gave me a temporary reprieve from my depression, but it was fleeting. I realized I was playing games by not attempting to contact Jennifer. I thought if I could just make her come to me or call me, it would be a step in the right direction. Sadly, each day passed without word from her; there was not even a post-card in my mailbox. My sister wrote three times without once mentioning her roommate. I answered each of Lori's letters, omitting every time the sub-ject of Jennifer.

During the hiatus with Jennifer, I went out several times with Pamela Woods, a girl in my sociology class. She was above average height, slightly overweight, and cute in an ordinary way. Pam was what everyone referred to as a nice person. I enjoyed her company. We were good friends. I discov-ered a growing dependency toward Pamela when I started confiding in her about Jennifer. As close as I felt toward my sister, I could not talk to Lori about her roommate. Every time I mentioned Jennifer to my sister, she just listened attentively but never commented. I felt no comfort from her. As for Charlie and my other male friends, they would never comprehend the situation. They would think I was a fool not to screw Jennifer, as they would put it, and be done with it. Pam, on the other hand, was extremely patient and a much better confidant on the subject of Jennifer Carson. She understood my attitude. I was grateful for her company.

After talking with Pamela through an entire evening, I walked with her to the dorm. She stalled at the door. I got the distinct impression she was waiting for me to kiss her. I knew I could not do that. If I kissed Pam, it would ruin everything. I did not want to destroy or complicate our friendship. There was no room for intimacy. She looked at me with those thickly lashed brown eyes of hers, paused, and then said, "Goodnight." She waited for me to exchange some kind of physical embrace. I did not do anything; instead, I left.

That night the phone rang. When I answered it, I heard Jennifer's voice on the other end. After discussing the weather, our classes, my sister's good health, and last night's *Marcus Welby, M.D.* show, I detected an uncomfortable break in the conversation. I toyed with the phone wire and twirled it around like a jump rope.

"I miss you, Kurt."

"Why didn't you call me, Jen? Why did you leave me hanging?"

"Why didn't you call me?" Her voice sounded just as anxious as mine. "I waited, but you never wrote or phoned. You didn't even mention my name in the letters you wrote to Lori. I was afraid you didn't want to see me anymore. I was so scared."

"Oh, Jennifer! I thought—oh, never mind. It's not important anymore." I paused. "Can I come see you this weekend?"

"Yes! Yes, of course." Her voice became a whisper as she continued, "I tried to tell David about us, but he wasn't listening to me. He never listens to me. Nothing's changed."

"I love you, Jennifer. Isn't that enough?" I lowered my voice a tone, but each word still dripped with passion.

She was quiet a long time. "I don't know how to explain it, Kurt. I need you. I need your love. I need your strength. Isn't that enough? The worst part is, I don't even know why I can't leave David."

I could tell she was crying as she disclosed her emotions. I melted toward her. Immediately, I realized it did not matter what she said. It was not important whether she loved me or not. It did not matter if she stayed with David or not. Nothing mattered! The only thing that mattered was I loved her and I could not do a damn thing to change that. No matter what the cost, I could not risk losing her. As much as I resented David and wanted him out of both our lives, I knew that I would do nothing to change it myself. That was Jennifer's decision. A fraction of Jennifer was better than no Jennifer at all.

"It's okay. We'll work that out later."

5

Laura

I<small>T HAD BEEN NEARLY A YEAR SINCE</small> I'<small>D BROKEN MY ENGAGEMENT TO</small> Tommy. During that time, Rick and I had developed a strong friendship. I felt very comfortable around him. We even dated on occasion. Sometimes I saw him with other girls; frequently, I dated a variety of guys, but no one of significance for either of us. It was hard to explain, even to myself, why I had no desire to form anything concrete with Rick—or anyone else for that matter—but I just was not interested. I was starting my junior year in the fall, and the last thing I had on my mind was a permanent or serious relationship.

My happiest memories during the summer of '71 were those spent with Jennifer. Because of my waitress job at the Jolly Ox and her family circumstances, there were not a lot of occasions, but I treasured those we did share. Never in my life had I been closer to anyone, including my parents and my brother. Together, and without any warning, Jennifer and I had bonded. The idea of being without her was unthinkable now that I knew what a trusted friendship was. In a way, I had become just as dependent on her as she had become on me.

Rick called long distance on a hot July night. He said he was traveling through the Washington area on his way home from summer school and asked if I might like to spend some time with him. If so, he would drive me to New Jersey for a long weekend. I was delighted. It was a wonderful diversion from the mundane schedule I had developed of working, watching TV, and sleeping. I answered "Yes" without thinking. Immediately, I regretted my reply. Visiting Rick at his home meant seeing his brother Brad.

Brad! I had not thought about him in ages. For the longest time, his face had appeared on the pages of books, his laughter had echoed in my ears, and his voice had blended in with the melodies on the radio. But now, all of those memories of him had been locked away; cobwebs had formed around my emotions. Thank God, the pain had finally died. It had been nearly two years. I was definitely over him; we were ancient history.

After pondering Rick's invitation, I realized that a short trip to his home would be a nice break after all.

My parents instantly adored Rick. Mom said, "He is so charming and attractive." Of course, she was right; Rick looked wonderful, all tanned and healthy. I tried to explain to my mother that Rick and I were just friends, but she brushed my comment aside and stated, "You two are such a darling couple!" I blushed, hoping Rick didn't hear her.

The car ride to New Jersey was a pleasant journey. I had never been further north than the nation's capital, and each road was a new experience. It was fun to be with Rick. The conversation never lagged, and his witty sense of humor made me laugh most of the time.

When we parked in the driveway of his home, it felt as if verbal pictures finally took tangible shapes. The big oak trees, the beautiful flowerbeds, the bushes, the winding brook, and the brick house were just as I imagined them; Brad's descriptive words were very accurate.

Rick ushered me through the front door. After placing my suitcase at the bottom of the stairs, he guided me into the family room. I saw Brad lounging on a black leather couch. He was watching a baseball game. He looked good. I was very proud of how nothing in my body betrayed me. I felt no nervousness, no apprehension, not even my knees were weakened.

"Hi, Brad, I'm back," Rick stated in a friendly tone.

"Hi." Brad waved his hand without looking at either one of us. His eyes were glued to the TV, and his concentration was devoted to the double play on the field.

"I brought someone with me. We're going down to the river. Want to join us?" Rick asked in a warm, gentle way as he placed an arm around my shoulder.

For the first time, Brad glanced in our direction. Surprise registered on his face. Seconds later, it was replaced with irritation—or maybe it was anger—before a confident smile masked his emotions. "Laura." He immediately stood. "Well, this is quite a surprise." Even though there was a half smile spreading across his lips, his voice had a cynical tone. "You're the last person I ever expected to see here of all places." Brad put his hands in the pockets of his jeans. As he continued to stare at me, his eyes became an even darker shade of brown.

I shifted my weight slightly and leaned gently against Rick for support. "Hello, Brad." I nodded pleasantly. "It's nice to see you again."

"Oh, really? You could have fooled me."

Why was he being so sarcastic? His stare never wavered. The eye contact between us began to make me feel quite uncomfortable. I was finding it increasing more difficult to look away from him.

"Well, Brad," Rick interrupted the momentary silence as he gave my arm a tender squeeze. "What do you say? Want to come down to the river and sail with us?"

"No, thanks." He never even glanced at his brother; instead, Brad gave me one more intense glare before returning to his baseball game and devoting his attention to the pitcher's curveball. "I think I'll pass."

Rick showed me around his house. Never in my life had I seen a place more elegant. Spacious rooms were beautifully decorated. The kitchen looked as if it were just remodeled; all of the appliances were avocado green, and the wallpaper accented the tones. It amazed me that the kitchen was at least twice the size of my parents' living room. In the dining room, there was a table big enough to seat a dozen people. Thick gold carpet covered all the floors. There was a chandelier a yard wide hanging in the foyer. In the back of the house, overlooking the brook, there was a library lined with more books than any one person could read in a lifetime. Every room was an adventure in itself, but despite all the luxuries, it did not radiate any warmth. I had never seen a house that appeared less lived in; everywhere I looked I saw the signs. The Waterford crystal ashtrays were wiped clean. The candy dish on the coffee table in the formal living room was filled to the brim as if it hadn't been opened in years. The magnificent crushed velvet drapes were closed excluding the sun's rays. And there was not a plant in sight—not one green leaf in any room. It was obvious they had a maid to keep the place clean, but what the house really needed was a woman's love.

The second floor showed more signs of being inhabited. There was a guest room for my temporary use decorated in warm spring colors. I fell in love with it on sight. Rosaline's room looked like a typical teenage girl's dream. It had dainty pink curtains with matching bedspread and pillows. The furniture was French provincial. Dozens of new, as well as old, stuffed toys were displayed. A blouse draped on a chair and a few articles of clothing lay in a heap on the mattress. Rick and Brad's room was the average male's quarters. Predominately red and blue colors with splashes of white and yellow gave the room a masculine flare. A water-skiing poster hung beside one of a football player being tackled. Next to it was a picture of a sailboat at full mast; hanging over the dresser was a Playboy calendar with the 1971 July centerfold in all her glory. Several college banners and a half dozen of what I knew to be Brad's pictures were displayed on the wall closest by the door. The photographs were good; even with my lack of experience in photography, I knew that Brad had talent.

After we left the room, Rick pointed to a closed door at the end of the hallway. "That's my father's room."

"And what's that?" I asked as I pointed at the only other closed door in the hallway.

"That," Rick answered, "is the master bedroom. My father hasn't used it since Mom left."

"Why?"

"I don't know," Rick replied as he guided me past the two bathrooms on the second floor, pointing them out to me and showing me where I could find clean towels. "I suppose there are just too many memories for Dad in that room. The door's always closed. Every once in a while, I'll hear him rustling around in there, but I never ask him about it. I figure it's something he has to handle in his own way."

Rick encircled me with one arm and led me back to the guest room. After placing a gentle kiss on my cheek he said, "I'll give you fifteen minutes to get ready. Then, we'll go to the river and do a little boating."

I unpacked a few things, hanging them up in the closest. After tying my hair back and donning my bathing suit and a T-shirt, I bounced down the steps in search of Rick. He was in the TV room watching the baseball game that had been on earlier. Brad was nowhere in sight.

Rick and I took a short ride to the Passaic River. The Malone's boat was far from small. It had a cabin that slept four with a private bath and a small galley. It was called *Caroline Sue.*

As I stepped aboard, I inquired, "Who's Caroline Sue?"

"That's my mother's name," Rick replied casually as if I should have known the answer.

"Oh."

"You're wondering why it's called that, aren't you?" Rick asked as he stepped onto the deck and started showing me around the twenty-five-foot vessel. "My father doesn't sail anymore. He used to. I remember as a kid, my mom and dad spent every free moment on this boat. Those are the best memories. It was great. Then, for some reason, my mother stopped going. But my father still enjoyed it. He used to take Brad and me out a couple times a week. Rosaline rarely came because she was too little, and Mom wouldn't let her go. That ticked my dad off. My parents fought a lot about the three of us. Hell! My parents fought a lot about everything."

He steered me through the galley and pointed out the refrigerator and the stove. "Dad loved to sail, so did Mom." We went back on deck; both of us blinked from the sun's brightness. "My father hasn't stepped foot on this boat since the divorce was finalized. But he won't sell it either. He refuses, and he said it was too much trouble to change the name so he just left it *Caroline Sue.*"

"It's a gorgeous boat. How old is she?" I said as I ran my fingers over the newly varnished rails and glanced at the workmanship of the deck.

"This baby's been around a long time. Dad bought her seventeen years ago. He used to maintain it himself; my mom helped, but now he pays some guys to keep it in top-notch condition. They paint the bottom once a year, sand and varnish the brightwork every spring, and scrub the teak decks several times a summer. Nobody can guess her age. It's a shame Dad won't even drive here and look at her."

Rick hoisted a sail, untied the lines, and pushed the *Caroline Sue* from the dock. A gentle breeze immediately caught the raised sail and carried us away from the shore. It felt heavenly. I pulled my T-shirt over my head and leaned back on my hands basking in the sunshine. Before I knew it, the other sails were in place, and Rick was at my side.

"Like it?" He asked as he smiled warmly in my direction.

"It's beautiful! Everything is beautiful."

Rick kissed me quickly on the lips. "This is just the way I imagined you would look, Lori. Sprawled out on that exact spot, hair blowing in the breeze, smiling just the way you are right this moment, and looking incredibly gorgeous." There was a serious expression on his face as he kissed me again—longer this time.

I looked away for a moment. The tone of his voice concerned me. He sounded so serious. I wanted to reverse the mood before it became something I could not handle.

"I'm glad you came, Lori. I hope you like my home and my family." He paused for a few seconds. "It's really important to me that you're here."

After that comment and another slightly more passionate kiss, his mood changed to carefree and friendly again. The rest of the afternoon was spent with noncommittal chatter. I began to relax and enjoy every minute.

That night Rick, his father, Rosaline, and I ate dinner at the large table in the formal dining room. The remaining eight chairs were empty. Brad did not join us for the meal. I had the impression his father was a bit agitated by his absence.

"I apologize, Lori, that my other son has no manners," Mr. Malone spoke as he carved into the roast and served each of us several slices of meat. "He disappeared early this afternoon, and no one's seen him since."

"It's his day off, Dad. He's probably out having a good time," Rosaline interjected in her absent brother's defense.

"I guess he does deserve some fun. He's been working very hard. I've been rather proud of Brad's attitude lately. What do you think, Rick? Do you think Brad's finally shaping up?"

"I suppose so, Dad," his eldest son answered as he swallowed another mouthful.

I studied their father. Rick looked like a younger version of him. Mr. Malone had what most people would call classic good looks. I guessed from previous information that he was around forty, but he looked even younger. There was no gray in his hair and barely a wrinkle on his entire face. He was not at all like I imagined. Brad always made him seem so hostile and overbearing. I pictured an ogre, but their father was quite friendly and very pleasant.

Rick's father inquired warmly about me. He asked where I was from, what my family did, how I liked Elon, what I was studying, and what I wanted to do with my life. Never once did I get the impression that Mr.

Malone was sizing me up; instead, he seemed genuinely interested. I felt as if he were truly listening to me. And he didn't snub me because I came from a poor background and had what I feared he would consider simple-minded goals. He seemed to like me. I discovered that I was having a great deal of difficulty seeing him as the raging tyrant Brad had once described.

Rosaline was a rather cute sixteen-year-old who was not quite as striking as the others in her family, but had all the potential of blossoming into a real beauty in a few more years. She was a little on the shy side. Rick's sister had a pleasant smile and features that resembled those of her father and oldest brother. I wondered where Brad had gotten his looks. It was certainly evident that no one at the table even remotely looked like him.

After dinner, Rick took me to meet his mother. I wasn't sure what I expected, but what I saw when the door opened was certainly *not* what I anticipated. When Rick's mother greeted us, I faced the mirror image of her middle child. Brad was a male duplicate of his mom. She had the same blackish-brown hair, the same dark enchanting eyes, and the same warm, friendly, confident smile. I envisioned seeing a woman older than her years and worn out from too much work and not enough money, but Caroline Sue was far from haggard looking. Quite the contrary, she was beautiful.

After seeing their mother, I expected her husband, John Harrod, to be equally attractive, but I discovered that he was a rather ordinary-looking man. He was at least a dozen years her senior. He had crew cut, light-brown hair, dark-rimmed glasses, and stood approximately three inches taller than his wife. Mr. Harrod was a friendly fellow whom I liked immediately. He was soft-spoken and kind. His wife, on the other hand, was another personality entirely.

They offered us seats and a cup of coffee. We accepted. During our conversation, the same questions were asked as those around the dinner table earlier, only his mother was not as affable as his father had been. I felt as if I were on trial, and each answer I gave was another step to the gallows. I got the impression she thought I was trying to railroad her little boy to the altar. Didn't she realize that nothing could be further from the truth? Rick and I had no intention of ever becoming serious, but obviously Caroline Sue didn't know that. I was beginning to feel quite uncomfortable.

During the conversation, I subconsciously scanned the room. Their apartment was very neat. Early American seemed to be their taste in furniture. On top of the television, I noticed pictures of all her children: those from her first marriage, as well as one from her present. The room did not express wealth, but by no means did it show signs of poverty either. I wondered why Brad always visualized his mother in rags and slaving to make ends meet. It definitely was not the impression I received.

I was relieved when Rick finally suggested that we leave. It was very unsettling to be in his mother's home. Unanswered questions kept jumbling around in my thoughts. I had no intention of pursuing the answers; but nonetheless, they still nagged at the back of my mind.

After we descended the stairs and crossed the parking lot to his car, Rick asked, "Well, how'd you like my mother?"

"She seems very nice."

"Good, I'm glad." It was Rick's only reference to the meeting.

We went to his father's restaurant for a drink. I was impressed with the decor. Everything was so elegant. Red and black were the primary colors. Multicolored tiffany lamps hung over every table, wicks flickered tiny lights from scattered candles, and soft music drifted through the air. The ambiance was romantic. People were lined out the door, but the two of us walked right in and took a seat at the mahogany bar.

Rick ordered two fruity drinks. "Don't drink too many of those. All that sweet stuff will give you a terrible headache in the morning."

I looked around. "This is lovely, Rick."

"It's only one of my dad's restaurants. He has three, but this is his favorite. My father spends most of his time here, probably because it was his first, and he considers it his baby."

"I imagine it requires quite a lot of work."

"It does. Since Brad and I help out during the summer and on holidays,

Dad's been able to relax a bit—thank goodness. He even took a small vacation this summer."

"Brad works here too?" I remembered how he hated his father's business.

"Yeah, he fights it constantly, but I really think Brad enjoys working here in spite of all his bitching," Rick answered as he bit into a pretzel.

I did not pursue the subject. Rick and I rarely talked about his brother. I figured it was best left that way. I had no idea what Brad had said to Rick in the past, and I definitely didn't want to know; neither did I wish to inquire what Rick might have said to Brad. As far as I was concerned, the two of them were from two different worlds. I had no intention of allowing them into the same realm—at least not within my own mind.

The remainder of the evening we spent curled up on the couch watching an old Cary Grant movie on television. Around midnight, I climbed the stairs to my room. After slipping into my nightgown, I crawled into bed. I read a couple of pages from a magazine, which was on the bedside table. In less than five minutes, I was asleep.

I woke up suddenly. Lying quietly in bed, I tried to figure out what had invaded my dreams and disturbed my sleep. I heard a soft click. Was that the door closing? Or was it only my imagination? There was a very faint odor lingering in the room; it was a combination of beer and cologne. I craned my neck. Were those footsteps I heard? No. It couldn't be. It was almost four o'clock in the morning. Who would be up at that hour? I rolled over and went back to sleep.

The following day was eventful. Rick and I had a picnic at the local park, played a few sets of tennis, and talked constantly. I enjoyed Rick's company. It was relaxing and peaceful.

In the evening, he took me to another one of his father's restaurants for dinner. Afterward, we saw *Summer of '42* at the local movie theater. When the movie was over, Rick drove to a secluded spot and parked the car. He leaned toward me and drew me to him. His embrace was more than casual; in fact, he was rather passionate. He kissed me several times. Each one grew increasingly more demanding. I was not sure how to react. In all of the time we had spent together, we had never parked. His kisses had always been rather chaste, often on the cheek.

Rick began to tug slightly at my clothes. His hands were exploring parts of my body he had never touched before, and I was shocked by his actions. This sudden aggressive change in his behavior was overwhelming to say the least. I tried to draw some kind of feeling from his actions, but my body was all but warming up toward him. I wanted to feel something. Rick was such a gentle and kind man. Why was it that I could not summon any desire for him?

He loosened his hold on me and withdrew his lips from mine. Without any preliminary warning, he muttered, "I love you, Lori. I've always loved you."

I was too shocked by his confession to comment.

He smoothed my hair away from my face and lightly kissed each of my features. "I'll be graduating next spring, Lori. I want to start a life on my own. I want you to be a part of it."

I still had no idea what to say. I tried to think when I could have encouraged these statements from him. Had I not made my true feelings clear? Did he misconstrue my emotions? Did he not realize I only felt friendship toward him? Was I to blame for this situation?

Rick looked directly into my eyes. "Marry me, Lori. Be my wife. All I want in this world is to spend the rest of my life with you."

I found my voice. "I don't know what to say." It should have been easy to accept his offer. Rick could give me so much. He had so many qualities I wanted in a man: attentive, kind, loving, handsome, and smart. I felt certain he would be loyal, and I was confident he would be financially secure. It could be such an easy life. All I had to do was fall in love with him—that was all! Was that so much to ask?

"Is it too soon? I'm willing to wait, Lori."

"No. No, Rick. Time isn't the problem." I stumbled on my own words. How was I going to say this? What had I done to deceive him? "I can't marry you because . . . because I don't love you." The words just slipped out. They sounded so callous. Why couldn't I have said it in a kinder way?

His face was immediately covered with a hostile expression. "It's my brother, isn't it? He's the one who keeps you from me. Two years and you still can't settle for me."

"No! Where did you get an idea like that? Brad has nothing to do with this! Nothing at all!" I replied.

"Why the hell did you come here then, Lori?"

"I came here because I thought we were friends, and you wanted to spend a weekend with me." The words sounded ridiculous even to my own ears. I *had* been blind! I had been drifting through the relationship shrugging off any type of commitment he offered and passing it by as friendly conversation. "I didn't come here to see Brad. I swear to you. He means nothing to me. I had almost forgotten he was your brother."

"Don't play innocent with me, Lori." He gripped both my shoulders. His face was twisted with rage. The hateful mask he wore was so out of character. Rick's fingers dug into my skin as he forced me down onto the seat. He laid his entire body weight on top of me.

I felt crushed by him. I struggled to free myself, but with every move I made, his strength just seemed to increase. "Rick . . ." I begged. "Rick, you're hurting me. Please let me go." I was more frightened than I was willing to admit.

He stopped moving. His hands loosened from around my arms. Suddenly, he sat up. Rick was quiet for a long time. Staring out into the darkness, he finally spoke. "I'm sorry, Lori." He sounded defeated.

"No, Rick. I'm the one who should apologize. Obviously, I've led you to believe that I felt something that isn't there. I wish I could change how I feel. I wish there could be something between us, but there isn't. Rick, I'm sorry."

"Don't apologize. You didn't lead me on. It was just that I wanted you to care for me. I wanted you for myself. I guess I misinterpreted the signs. I thought that Brad . . . I thought maybe . . ." He continued to stare out into the blackness refusing to look at me. "When you broke your engagement last fall, I thought I had a chance. I just kept hoping that you'd grow to love me. I wanted it so much that I even pretended you did."

"I'm so sorry."

"So am I," he sighed. "But for God's sake, don't treat me as if I'm some poor sick animal. It was my own stupidity. You're not to blame."

I reached over to hold his hand. He returned my comfort by latching onto it. We sat in silence listening to the chatter of wildlife.

"I always seem to fall in love with girls who don't love me in return." He sounded more exasperated than unhappy.

"Rick, someone will come along someday who will be worthy of your love. She will love you in the way you want." I squeezed his hand firmly in mine. "I only wish I could have been that girl. You're a wonderful person. I admire and like you very much, but you must not settle for just that. You deserve so much more."

Several minutes passed. He turned to face me as he spoke in a soft calm voice. "I think, subconsciously, I've always known we could never have a future together. I just kept hoping." He paused. "Can we be friends, Lori? I won't force anything on you. I don't expect that eventually you'll change your mind. I think I know you well enough to realize you would never intentionally hurt anyone, and you didn't mean to hurt me. You know I love you, Lori, but I like you too. You're a fabulous friend."

"I've always wanted to be your friend, Rick."

He wrapped me in one arm and let out a long sigh. "Oh, Lori. I sure have a way of screwing up my life. Don't I?"

He didn't wait for a reply; instead, he started the car. We rode back to his home in silence. During the short ride, I contemplated his words. Had I really been so blind or did I subconsciously depend on the fact that Rick loved me? Did I draw some kind of strength from his emotions? Was I not craving a type of tenderness from him, even though I was unable to return it? Was I not searching for the love I feared did not exist?

I awoke on the day of my departure knowing that Rick had to work the lunch shift before driving me to Newark Airport. I had told him the night before that I was more than willing to take a taxi, but he brushed my comment aside and said, "Don't be ridiculous. That would cost a fortune. I'm mature enough to handle this. I'll take you to the airport."

I spent the morning in conversation with Rosaline, who was a very vivacious individual, on a one-on-one basis. She told me about her high school life, her teachers, and her current boyfriend. She seemed so young and so very wrapped up in her own world. More than once, she stated firmly that she never intended to grow up and that she considered twenty years old to be ancient. As far as Rosaline was concerned, life would end when she left her teens behind.

I listened to Rosaline and her stories without comment. Instinctively, I knew she would not comprehend my philosophies regarding the fact that life most certainly did not end when a person left high school. I knew she would have to learn that particular lesson for herself. Had I sounded like that? Had I been so wrapped up in Tommy's and my relationship that I had actually thought my high school years would be the best? Had I been that oblivious to the world around me? I imagine to an objective observer, I probably had been; maybe I still was. In a way, I feared my college years ending and dreaded the world outside my protective cocoon. Was that not the same thing Rosaline was saying: except instead of eighteen, my cutoff age was twenty-two?

I could hear voices in the other room. I knew instantly that they belonged to Brad and his father. I had not seen Brad since the first day Rick and I had walked into the room invading his privacy and his baseball game. Brad had always left early and returned late, never joining us for meals or any other activity.

"Dad, I need the car. Can I borrow it?"

"Sure, Brad, but you'll have to drive Lori to the restaurant. I promised Rick that I'd take her, and if you use my car, I won't be able to get her there."

"Shit!"

"It's no big deal, Brad. Just drop her off, and you can have the car until the dinner shift. Then come back and pick me up. We can go together."

"Damn it!" I heard the sound of keys jingling as they hit a wall. Then their voices became raised and more antagonistic.

"Where are your manners, son? It's a simple task. It will only take you a few minutes." His father was angry.

"You don't understand!" Brad snapped a retort. "Oh, just leave me the hell alone."

There was silence again in the corridor outside Rosaline's room. I felt uncomfortable at the thought that Rosaline knew I had overheard every word.

Thirty minutes later I stood in the foyer with my baggage and wondered how I was getting to the restaurant and Rick. Brad jogged down the stairs in an ill temper, snatched up my suitcase, and headed out the door without a comment. After turning the knob, he looked over his shoulder and said in a gruff voice, "What the hell are you waiting for—a limousine to come through the living room?" Then, he turned and walked outside.

I followed him. He literally threw the bag in the backseat of his father's car, sat behind the wheel, and slammed the door. We drove several minutes in an uneasy silence. It was quite apparent that Brad was extremely put out by having to chauffeur me around.

I noticed an unopened envelope on the dashboard with Cindy Wilder's return address. I broke the silence. "I see you got a letter from Cindy. How is she?"

"Nosy, aren't you?" His voice was very hostile.

"I'm sorry. I didn't mean to be." I was only trying to make conversation. "Cindy and I were pretty good friends last year. I was just wondering how things are going for her."

Without looking in my direction Brad stated, "I suppose you heard that the rabbit died on her last spring?"

"What?" I had no idea what he was talking about. I tried to read the expression on his face, but it was blank.

"Don't act so goddamned innocent, Laura!" He retorted as he turned his head in my direction and shot imaginary needles from his eyes. "You know exactly what I'm talking about."

"No, I don't, Brad. Cindy and I used to be pretty good friends, but she hasn't spoken to me in months." It was true. Cindy Wilder and I had been good friends last fall, but she had snubbed me and cut me off without a single word. I could not figure out why.

We stopped at a red light. "Cindy was pregnant. I figured you knew; in fact, I thought the whole campus knew about it," he said in a very apathetic tone. The light turned green. He accelerated before adding, "But it's all taken care of now."

"Cindy had an abortion?"

"Hell, yeah! Cindy had an abortion."

"I'm sorry." So that was the reason for his foul temper.

"Well, I'm not! I'm the one who talked her into it. It was a pain in the ass to get one too. It's not like you can walk into any doctor's office. It took a lot of research, if you get my drift."

"Oh, how sad." I had a sick feeling in the pit of my stomach.

"Don't be such a fool! What would either one of us do with a kid at this point in our lives. I certainly don't want any baby tying me down." His words were cruel.

My God! How could he talk like that? Brad sounded like some kind of monster! I dropped the subject.

We drove another mile in silence before Brad spoke again. "What the hell are you doing here anyway, Laura? Why don't you stay away from my brother?" Every word was spat out of his mouth like a poison that was choking him.

"I suppose he told you about last night?" I replied sheepishly as I suddenly realized his attitude was probably based on the fact that he knew I had hurt Rick. No wonder Brad seemed so agitated with me.

He took his eyes off the road and glanced in my direction. It was obvious that Brad's curiosity increased. "Rick hasn't told me anything. I haven't seen him all weekend."

For one split second, I saw something other than anger in his eyes. What was it? "Well, don't worry, Brad." I answered softly. "I won't be seeing your brother very much anymore." I wished I didn't have to discuss the subject with Brad.

"Good." That was the last word he spoke.

Brad looked slightly relieved. I imagined he thought I was a bad influence on Rick. He probably realized that his brother loved me, and I did not share in the emotion. Rick had told me the two of them had gotten closer over the last year or so. Brad seemed to be having a protective reaction toward his older brother.

We exchanged no further conversation before he pulled into the restaurant parking lot, turned off the ignition, got out of the car, and entered the building. I remained in the car for a second or two before removing my suitcase and walking in the door. I flagged Rick down and sat at a vacant table.

"You're a little early," Rick said as he walked up to me and kissed my cheek. "That's good, we can have lunch before you leave."

I saw Brad at the bar practically inhaling a beer before he ordered a second and drank it in the same manner. He was watching us with an expression that distorted his features. After finishing his second drink, he walked out of the restaurant without so much as a good-bye. Thank God, Brad was gone! I no longer had to be subjected to his hostile silence or his cold unreadable stares.

After our meal, Rick drove me to the airport. Before I boarded the plane, he said, "I'm glad you came, Lori, despite the outcome."

"I'm really sorry, Rick." I had that same guilty feeling I experienced when I told Tommy good-bye for the last time.

"Don't be, Lori. I knew from the beginning there could never really be anything more than friendship between us. But I kept hoping. It's not your fault. You can't help how you feel." Rick ran two fingers across my cheek and smiled. "I really do have a wicked crush on you, Lori, but it's not incurable. I'll be all right. I certainly won't go through my whole life waiting for something that won't happen. I know now you will never love me, and I know why."

The intercom paged the final boarding call for my flight. Rick smiled and kissed me lightly on the forehead. I smiled back at him before turning and walking to the plane.

6

Kurt

DESPITE THE FACT THAT JENNIFER HAD GOTTEN A CAR DURING THE SUM-mer, which enabled us to see each other more often, I was growing increas-ingly more impatient about the fact that our relationship was still hanging in limbo. Although the brand-new, all-white TR6 made it possible for Jennifer to come to Chapel Hill at least once a week, it also allowed her to go home more frequently. Jennifer still was not committed enough to our rela-tionship to leave David which, of course, made me feel completely inade-quate and extremely jealous.

Last year, we had spent countless, comfortable, relaxing hours talking. Now, it seemed there was tension in every conversion we had; many of those conversations ended in arguments. I had given up the idea of celibacy regarding Jennifer. I wanted her so much—my willpower lost the battle to my physical passion. After all, I was only human. Jennifer, on the other hand, had become distant when it came to sex. She pushed my advances away and would not even broach the subject.

Lori and Jennifer rushed the Zeta Tau Alpha sorority at Elon in the beginning of the semester. Jennifer spent more time with her Zeta sisters than she did with me. I secretly wanted to kidnap her and take her away from all the people who were keeping us apart. In my frustration, I turned to Pamela Woods for friendship. If it were not for Pam, I probably would have gone totally insane by the middle of October. She became not only my sounding board but also my date to all the activities that Jennifer could not attend with me.

Over the weeks, Pam finally opened up to me. We shared secrets. Pam's life was a sad one. No wonder she was so shy and quiet. Her father was extremely wealthy. In fact, from the sound of it, Pam's father made Jennifer's old man seem like a pauper. It was odd. I had never pictured Pamela as a rich bitch; when she told me, I was more than surprised. Apparently, her mother died when she was very young. A governess raised her because her father was away, traveling on business all over the world. Pam told me she attended boarding schools since she was eleven years old. Every two weeks a check came in the mail. Her face looked dejected when she added, "The checks were not even personally signed by my father." Visits from him were few and far between all through her youth. In fact, one year she had only seen him for two days; neither was Christmas nor her birthday. On holidays, he never forgot to send expensive gifts from foreign countries, but actually all Pamela ever wanted was his love and his time—two things that seemed too valuable for him to give.

Although our problems were not common, the suffering was. Pamela and I drew closer by sharing our emotions. It felt good to confide in someone instead of stifling my anger. Pamela had the softest shoulder and the most attuned ear of anyone I knew. We were terrific friends.

2

Jennifer came to UNC on a Friday afternoon after finishing her classes for the week. It was so good to see her. We spent the evening at a pub talking and mingling with acquaintances. Jennifer was loving and attentive, which made me happier than I had been in a handful of months.

Unfortunately, the next day was not as pleasant. After breakfast and three cups of coffee, Jennifer and I took a drive. We parked in a harvested field, got out, and walked around. It was a beautiful Indian summer day not uncommon for October in North Carolina. The sun was delightfully warm. We took our sweaters off and draped them around our shoulders. Rays of light caught Jennifer's hair and made it glisten. She was irresistible. I stopped to kiss her. I could not help myself. I pulled her blouse up slightly as my hands searched to unhook her strap. This was the ideal secluded place and the perfect day to consummate our relationship.

"Don't, Kurt." She pushed at my chest. "Please don't."

I became agitated with her persistent negative responses. Jennifer knew how much I loved her. She knew I craved her. Why the hell did she hold back? Why did she keep pushing me away? Something snapped inside. I unleashed my bottled frustration. I verbally attacked her with stinging words. "It's not like you're a virgin or anything. For Christ's sake, you're even on the Pill!" The tone in my voice was anything but patient. "How long do you expect me to wait?" I had never threatened her before, but the rage was flooding through my veins. "If you push me away one more time, I won't be around whenever you decide you're ready and willing to spread those fancy legs of yours." I had not meant to sound so crude. I loved Jennifer. I did not want to force her, but it was getting more and more difficult to control myself.

"Kurt . . . "

"Don't say no, Jennifer. Don't refuse me this time. I can't take anymore of your unconvincing answers. You want David . . . you don't want him. You want me . . . you don't want me. You need him in a different way than you need me. Shit! You're fucking him, and it's driving me crazy. You decide, and you decide right here and now . . . this very minute. I will not tolerate you screwing that bastard back home and leaving me high and dry down here to jerk off in the bathroom." My God! What had come over me? How could I be so crude?

Her face was ashen. Tears formed in her eyes. Her expression was marked with pain. Despite her obvious horror at my words, I continued, "I haven't laid a girl since the first night I met you. I'm not going to put up with this crap any longer."

She pivoted and took two steps toward the car.

"Don't you dare leave!" I grabbed her arm and spun her around. "We are going to start a new beginning right now . . . or we are going to end it for good. Do you get my message, Jennifer?" I was angry. I could no longer control the fury that welled up inside of me. The flesh of her arm was pressed tightly between my thumb and fingers. I let go of her and stared into her eyes. They were blank. I wanted to encircle her in my arms and confess that I did not mean to say such terrible things. I was just crazy with jealousy, and I would keep her any way I could. Why was she looking at me like that? Why wasn't she saying anything? I reached a hand slowly out to her, but she turned again. Without a word, Jennifer walked to her car. Before I even had a chance to move, she drove away.

What had I done? Jennifer . . . my Jennifer! Oh, God! Jennifer. I screamed her name repeatedly only to have it echo back into my own ears.

Slowly, I walked the five miles back to campus. Each step was tormenting as I remembered the words I had spoken. I dug into my pocket and pulled out a joint. After lighting it, I took a half dozen tokes before tossing it onto the ground and squashing it with my foot. I hoped the numbing effect would dull my pain, but it only served to magnify it. By the time I finally reached the campus, I was so wrecked I could barely walk. I bought a beer at the corner bar to drown my sorrows. One was not enough, so I bought another, and then a third, and even another after that until I lost count.

I also lost track of time. I had no idea how long I sat there before I noticed Pam standing by my table. Oh, Pam! Talking will not help me now! Without saying a word, I wrapped my arms around Pamela and let her guide me back to the dorm.

When I woke, it was to blackness. My head hurt so badly. I felt as if the muscles in my body no longer functioned. As hard as I tried, I could not move. Finally, after commanding my fingers to operate properly, I reached for my alarm clock on the nightstand. It was not there; in fact, neither was the table. I fumbled around in the darkness and realized that nothing was in place. Everything was disorganized. Instead of the bed being up against the wall, it was jutting out into the room. The table was where the desk should be, and the desk was on the opposite side of the room. Where was the damn light? Who rearranged my room? Where was Charlie?

"Kurt."

That definitely was not Charlie's voice. That was a woman's voice. Why didn't someone turn on a light? I tripped over something that immediately fell to the floor and made musical notes like a guitar. What was a guitar doing in my room? The overhead light turned on. I covered my eyes, because the sudden brightness caused a jarring pain to my eyes. Jesus, I would give my soul for an Alka-Selzer and a hot shower. When I finally lowered my hands, I looked around the strange room. Where was I? My eyes finally managed to focus properly. I immediately saw Pamela. Dressed in a floor-length robe, she sat quietly in a chair in the corner. Pamela! What is Pamela doing here? Is this her room? How did I get here?

My memory started returning. Jennifer! Oh, my God! Jennifer left me. I got wasted. Too much pot . . . too many beers. But how did Pamela fit into this picture? Yes! It was coming back to me. I vaguely remembered Pam at the bar.

The room began to spin. My stomach was doing nonstop flips. Slowly, I sat on the edge of the bed. "Did we make love?" I asked very meekly. "I'm sorry . . . I don't remember."

"No, it's all right, Kurt. Nothing happened. I was going to take you back to your room, but Charlie was having a wild party. There wasn't any room left on your bed, so I brought you here instead."

She rinsed a cloth in the sink and pressed it against my forehead. Pamela appeared to be walking in slow motion and weaving with every step. I held my head firmly between my hands as I tried to steady the rising bile in my throat. If I did not find a bathroom soon, I was going to make a hell of a mess all over the floor. I covered my mouth with my hand. Pam comprehended my predicament and quickly pointed to the bathroom door. I raced passed her. There was no time to close the door behind me. I leaned over the toilet and violently threw up the entire contents of my stomach.

I felt a cold compress on my forehead and realized that Pam was on her knees beside me. She was wiping my face. "It's all right, Kurt. Everything will be all right. I'll take care of you."

I heaved again and again even after nothing came up with each gag. The muscles in my stomach ached from the constant action, and the taste in my mouth was so awful I could barely stand it. I looked at my clothes. There was a mixture of undigested food and liquid on each sleeve. I reeked of the foul scent, and I hurt all over. The coolness from the cloth was my only savior; each stroke was comforting.

"It's all right, Kurt. Everything will be all right." The same soothing words were spoken over and over again.

I looked up at Pam. Before I knew what happened, I was in her arms. She held me tightly; I drew comfort from her embrace. As Pam rocked me back and forth, she repeated her gentle words. A long time passed before I asked if I could borrow a towel and her shower. She handed one to me and left the room. I scrubbed my entire body raw with fresh-smelling soap. Finally, I felt as if I might live through the experience.

When I reentered the room, I noticed that the bed was freshly made, and the sheets were turned down for me. It was a very inviting sight.

"Lie down, Kurt. I'll give you a massage. "I let Pamela work her magic on my aching muscles. Her fingers dug into my back. I closed my eyes and relished the relaxing effect her hands had on me. I started drifting off to sleep. Sleep! I needed sleep. Sleep granted forgetfulness. In sleep, I'd find peace. My mind entered darkness as I fell into an undisturbed slumber.

Someone was moving beside me. I felt snug and comfortable. There was soft skin touching mine, and the faint scent of lilacs drifted past my nose. I cuddled up close to the warmth. I must have died and gone to heaven.

When I opened my eyes, I saw tiny rays of light peering out from behind closed curtains; it was nearly dawn. I turned to my partner. Instead of seeing flaxen hair, I saw a mass of black strands resting on the pillow. It was Pam. Jennifer was gone . . . this time for good. Pamela was here. I touched her shoulder. My fingers felt bare skin. It was smooth and soft. She rolled over and opened her eyes. They were misted with sleep. The double row of lashes accented their almond shape. She smiled. I gently touched her cheek and ran my fingers slowly over her face. She took my hand in hers and silently invited me to explore her naked body. I cupped a breast as she pressed the other tauntingly against my chest. There was trust in Pamela's expression. I watched her in silence, and then gathered her in my arms. She willingly encouraged my embrace. While holding the full length of her, I realized that she was not wearing anything. I could feel her furry mass rubbing against my hip, and I grew hard with desire. As we kissed, I rolled Pamela onto her back and placed my body over hers. She felt hot. I repeatedly kissed her. After tracing a pattern of kisses down to her breast, I placed my mouth over one pointed nipple. I teased it playfully with my tongue. She moaned softly which only enhanced my own excitement. Running my hands down her legs, I gently separated her thighs and maneuvered myself. Her outer rim was bursting with fire. I wrapped my arms around her. She, in turn, clung to me.

I gave one thrust before I realized I had penetrated the thin skin that protected her virginity. For one brief moment, I stopped, "My God, what have I done?"

She continued to press her body rhythmically against mine. It was too late; I could not stop. I tried to be as gentle as possible as I penetrated deeper into her. She was hot and tight and wet. I felt her juices trickle around the inside of her thighs. My God! It was wonderful! She was wonderful! I clung to her. With each repeated movement, I felt the ultimate explosion mounting. Everything rushed to my loins. I tried to pace myself. I tried to slow down the process, but I was out of control. Rapidly, I thrust myself into her warmth until I finally pumped myself dry and filled her with the tangible evidence of my lust. In a pool of sweat, I shuddered and collapsed on top of her. The room went blank. I was aware of only two things: her arms clung tightly around me and my heart pounding wildly inside my chest.

Eventually, I felt her hands stroking the back of my head, and I began to focus on the present. I slowly rolled to my side and cradled her with my right arm. As I drew her head to my shoulder, I spoke, "Pamela." I was not sure if she heard me.

Without looking up, she muttered peacefully, "Yes."

"I hope I didn't hurt you. You should have told me . . . I would never have made love to you if I'd known."

"That's why I didn't tell you, Kurt." She lifted herself up on one elbow and thoughtfully stared into my eyes. There was no regret on her face—only pleasure and contentment. "I wanted you to make love to me. I've wanted it for a long time." She lowered her head onto my chest.

I squeezed her tightly with both arms and buried my face in her hair. She smelled sweet.

"Kurt . . . there's no need to patronize me. I understand how you feel. I know you love Jennifer. I know you only made love to me because I'm here and available." She paused for a moment. Pam lifted her face, which enabled me to see her expression. She appeared serene and angelic as she smiled. "I want you to know . . . it was all worth it, Kurt. Everything! You were wonderful. I will treasure today for the rest of my life." She spoke in a calm and happy manner.

"I care about you, Pamela. You are right about Jennifer though . . . I am in love with her. I won't deny that." I clutched her in my arms and smothered my nose in her hair. "But . . . I need you, Pamela. I need you." And I meant it.

"I understand." She buried her face in the hair of my chest. Her body quivered slightly.

Pamela! You deserved so much more. Virginity should be given to someone you love; it should be shared with someone who loves you in return.

I felt guilty about abusing her friendship.

"Don't, Kurt," Pam muttered quietly as her lips pressed tenderly against my skin.

"What?"

"Don't think those thoughts." She perched her chin on my shoulder and looked into my eyes. "Don't feel guilty. Don't think that you've taken something away from me."

"Oh, Pamela . . . you are so sweet."

"Don't!" She placed a finger over my lips. "Please don't! I don't want your pity. I feel wonderful. I feel beautiful . . . and I'm so happy. Don't take that away from me." Each word was spoken as if she caressed the syllables before they came out of her mouth.

I enveloped her with both my arms and pulled her securely against me. Every ounce of her nakedness felt beautiful. We held each other in silence until we fell into a peaceful slumber.

7

Jennifer

THE SMARTEST THING I DID AT ELON WAS RUSH THE ZETA SORORITY WITH Lori. She was extremely interested in the organization and the girls involved with it. I was jealous of the time she spent with them. Lori was branching out with new relationships, both male and female, whereas I still clung only to her for friendship. The fact that I had Zeta sisters helped balance my life.

She told me at the beginning of the semester about the episode with Rick Malone. I thought she was a fool for letting him go, but I realized that Lori would never settle for anything less than what she so idealistically called true love. Didn't she realize that there was no such thing? Rick could have given her everything: loyalty, tenderness, devotion, security, and plenty of money. Wasn't that enough?

But then again . . . I was one hell of a person to be preaching love. After all, was I not far more confused than Lori? I certainly had screwed my life up royally! I still had David, but I had lost Kurt. And Kurt was more important than a hundred Davids. Aside from Lori, I depended on Kurt more than anyone in my life. He gave me strength.

I had no idea why I could not make love to Kurt. It wasn't as if I had no attraction for him! I wanted Kurt as much physically as mentally, but there was a barrier in our relationship I could not overcome; ironically, I was incapable of putting a label on the problem. Perhaps I was developing a sense of post-virginal hang-ups. Who the hell knew? I thought about it constantly, and although Lori and I could not have been closer, it was the one topic I did not feel comfortable discussing with her.

Why had Kurt backed me into a corner? Forced me to choose? Didn't he know I couldn't handle it? Hadn't I repeatedly told him how insecure I was about everything in my life from leaving David to introducing Kurt to my parents? My father was still not used to the idea of David; I could only imagine what he would say if I brought Kurt home with me. Kurt, with his long hair and his liberal attitudes, would surely send my father over the edge. I felt as if I were between the proverbial rock and a hard place.

Although I depended on David for sexual fulfillment, I realized I did not love him; I wasn't even sure I liked him anymore. Thankfully, David no longer had the ability to break my heart; he could not hurt me. His attacks on my intelligence and my insecurities did not bother me anymore, because I viewed David as a habit. I was addicted to the sexual release he gave me. I feared more than anything that Kurt would be unable to grant me that feeling; as a result, I clung to David even more.

2

"Jennifer! You have got to cut this out!" We were sitting on the bed cross-legged hovering over a history book and dozens of sheets of notes. Lori propped her elbows on the inside of her thighs and cleared her throat. "Why do you keep putting yourself down like this? You're beginning to sound like a broken record, and there is absolutely no reason for it. Contrary to what you seem to believe . . . you are not stupid!"

"This crap is all bullshit for people with higher IQ's."

"Oh, stuff it!" Lori interrupted. "Listen to me and don't give me that garbage talk anymore! You are not stupid! I want to know what's bothering you. And don't tell me that there isn't anything wrong, because I told you who Thomas Paine is five times. The only possible reason you can't remember him is because you aren't concentrating. You're not dumb, Jennifer . . . you're just not listening." Lori hit the book with her fist to accent her statement. "Cough it up, Jen. What's bugging you?"

As I watched Lori, I realized that she was covering up her anger with what little patience she had left. I could not really blame her. After all, she had spent the last two hours devoted to teaching me the facts for tomorrow's American history test. Lori always said she enjoyed helping me, but she insisted that I had to help myself too. I could not depend totally on her. "Can we talk, Lori?" I finally muttered when I knew that a discussion would be my only therapy.

"I'm listening, Jennifer . . . you know I always do." Her voice was calm and caring.

I paused for a long time and tried to figure out where to start. "You know Carl . . . that guy I went out with Saturday night?"

"Yeah," Lori nodded her head and waited quietly for me to continue.

"Well, he's your typical asshole, like every other jerk around here. I don't know why I bothered to go out with him. I guess I was just bored." I folded my arms across my chest and rubbed my shoulders firmly. "He came on to me like a German tank. He was all hands and groped around as if he was a kid in a candy store where everything was free. I wanted to slug him. I was so turned off. He was utterly revolting. Every time he kissed me, the son of a bitch drooled all over me. The jerk really thought he was tough shit with his tongue. I mean he believed that the answer to everything was sticking the entire thing into my ear. It was all sloppy and wet. I felt like the Atlantic Ocean was having a tidal wave against my eardrum."

"Jennifer!" Lori spoke gently but firmly. "Why do I get the impression that you're skirting the issue?"

I pushed my hair behind my ears and glanced around the room. Lori said nothing else. I knew her tactics all too well. She was waiting, giving me time to ponder my thoughts. After taking a couple of deep breaths, I continued. "I miss Kurt." It was the first time I had mentioned his name in a month. Lori knew nothing about what had happened; I had only told her that it was over between Kurt and me.

"Why don't you call him? I'm sure he'd like to hear from you."

"Did Kurt say anything to you while you were home last weekend?" I held my breath and awaited her reply.

"No."

"At least that's an honest answer."

"Jennifer, he didn't talk about you at all. Not one single word. That's why I know he misses you. If my brother didn't care, then talking about you wouldn't have mattered."

"I can't call him, Lori . . . don't you understand? If I call him, it means committing myself. He won't settle for anything less."

"Why are you so afraid of that?"

I closed my eyes and pressed the palms of my hands firmly against their sockets. My voice was muffled but still audible. "I don't know. If I did, maybe I'd be able to sleep better at night."

"Is there anything I can do to help?" Lori was genuinely concerned.

"No . . . " I rubbed my temples. Oh, for a good night's sleep! I was smoking too much lately, and my chest hurt. Sometimes, it was hard to get a full breath; as a result, I often woke up and struggled for more oxygen. I hurt all over. I was always tired. Straightening my back, I smiled slightly. "On second thought, Lori, there is something you can do. You can dump all this studying crap and go to a movie with me . . . anything. I need to get out of here. I need to think about anything but books, Kurt, and me. I can't stand another moment of it."

She watched me intently. "Are you sure you don't want to talk anymore?"

"Positive! Let's go see something exciting."

"Last time I looked, there wasn't much of a selection in Burlington," Lori said as she picked up the paper.

"What's playing in Greensboro?"

"I don't know yet . . . hold on, I'll see." She rummaged through the section on entertainment looking for the ad. "*Play Misty for Me*. It has Clint Eastwood in it. It's probably a cowboy movie. Do you think it'll be worth the drive?"

Play Misty for Me was not a cowboy movie as Lori had thought; in fact, the plot's suspense and romance were the perfect ticket for a temporary cure. When Jessica Walters came out of the closet with that seven-inch kitchen knife, I nearly flew out of my seat. Neither Lori nor I expected to see a thriller on the screen, and we clutched each other's arms throughout the entire climax of the film. By the time the credits were shown at the end, I was feeling better.

The drive back to campus was filled with friendly conversation. We talked about the movie and the sorority before the topic turned to Lori. I asked her, "Does it bother you that Rick is dating one of our sorority sisters?"

"Not at all." Lori seemed honest in her response.

"I get the impression that he likes her a lot."

"I know. I think it's marvelous. Valerie and Rick are good for each other."

"I can't believe that you are so blasé about this, Lori. I mean, after all, you dated Rick off and on for two years. Aren't you even the slightest bit jealous?"

"We were just friends."

"There must have been more to it than that, Lori."

"I already told you about last summer. You know that I didn't care for Rick the way he wanted me to. Why should I be jealous if he finally found someone who does?"

"I guess I understand. It's just that I have always thought you were nuts to let that guy get away. He was perfect for you."

Lori laughed. "You know my philosophy on that subject."

When it started to rain, I rolled up my window and extinguished my cigarette. Before we had gone a few hundred yards, the raindrops began to fall in torrents; the wipers could barely keep the window clear enough to see. I felt blinded by the sheets of water that pounded the windshield. Lori was silent in the passenger seat next to me, and I concentrated all my efforts on the road. With each car that passed heading from the other direction, an additional splash bombarded the glass and temporarily blocked my vision.

Before I even saw the fence, I felt the impact. My head flew toward the dash; then all action stopped. Everything was still except the steady beating of the rain. I sized up the situation and realized I had crossed over a draining ditch and slammed into a cedar-railed fencepost. I shook my head and tried to focus. Immediately, I touched my brow. There was an egg-shaped knot beginning to grow above my left eye. I must have hit the steering wheel. It sure was going to hurt in the morning. I glanced over at Lori. She looked in the same condition that I was: nothing serious, just stunned.

"Are you all right?" Lori spoke before I could get the words out.

"Yeah, I think so. How about you?"

"Fine, I guess," she replied. "What happened?"

"I couldn't see . . . I must have run off the road," I answered. I tried to start the car but nothing happened. "I guess I really made a mess of things this time."

"What are we going to do? There isn't anything between here and campus, not even a phone."

"It's okay, Lori. The dorm is about a half mile away. We can run for it."

"You mean leave your car?"

"Who the hell's going to get it out on a night like this?"

"But, Jennifer . . . a half mile is a long way in this storm."

"You chicken or something?" I teased knowing Lori's main concern was for me.

"I'm game if you are. Here, you take my hat. I have a scarf in my purse." Simultaneously, we opened the car doors and darted in the direction of the dorm. Before we reached the railroad tracks, we were completely drenched. My legs hurt so badly I did not think I could take another step. Lori noticed my struggle and fell back to grab my hand. She slowed her pace so we could stay together. I took short quick breaths. No matter how hard I tried, I could not get enough oxygen. In spite of the fact that I was perspiring, I felt extremely cold.

"Lori . . . Lori . . . I can't run anymore!" I stopped. The rain continued to hit us full force. The hat she had loaned me was saturated. I felt as if every raindrop pelted me directly on the skin instead of hitting my clothes. I heaved for air. I wanted to lie down. My legs felt heavy; I feared they might buckle under me.

"Jennifer . . . it's okay. Harper Center is right over there. Come on! You can make it. We're so wet now it doesn't matter if we run or not. We'll just walk. You can do that, can't you?" Her voice was patient . . . always patient, competent Lori. I was forever relying on her. This was no exception. She wrapped a protective arm around me. As we walked, I leaned against her.

By the time we reached our room, I was chilled to the bone and shivering so much that my teeth actually chattered noisily. Lori helped me take off the soaking clothes, wrapped me in a blanket, and towel dried my hair before she even started disrobing herself.

"Jennifer, you're going to have to take a hot shower. You're blue around the mouth. My God! You're freezing." Lori looked frightened.

"I can't . . . I can't move, Lori. Just let me lie down." All my limbs felt like putty. I rested against the pillow and closed my eye.

"Jennifer, stand up. Come on! Do as I say. A hot shower will help." She guided me into the bathroom and sat me gently on the toilet seat before starting a steamy hot shower. The water beating down on me felt more like ice than heat. Finally, Lori steered me back to bed and helped me into it. Even after she covered me with layers of blankets, I still quivered from the cold. She stripped her own bed and placed the blankets on top of me. My entire body quaked from the chill inside of me.

Lori disappeared. When she returned, she had a cup of hot soup. Where did she get soup at this hour? She held the brew to my lips and allowed only a few drops at a time to trickle down my throat. It helped. I huddled down deep into the bed, pulled the pile of blankets up under my chin, and drifted off to sleep. When I woke up hours later my entire body was blazing. I imme-

Tesa Jones ✿ 179

diately pushed everything, including the sheet, off of me. God, I was hot! Perspiration drenched me. Lori was sitting next to the bed reading a paperback book by candlelight. Why was she still awake and reading in the dark?

"Here put this into your mouth." She placed a thermometer under my tongue and pulled half of the blankets up over me again. "Don't, Jennifer . . . don't push the blankets away. You're only hot because you have a fever. You don't want to catch another chill on top of the one you already have, do you?"

When she removed the thermometer, I saw the surprise register on her face.

"I'm going to go call the infirmary."

"What is it?" I asked.

"It's almost 103. I think you need some professional help."

It seemed like Lori was gone forever. I dozed off and on but not peacefully. I had not been feeling well recently, but this was worse than even my worst day. When Lori returned, the campus nurse was with her; she gave me a shot. Everything became blurry and blended together. Lori and the nurse faded away as I closed my eyes.

Sometimes when I awoke, it was daylight, and on other occasions, it was dark. Each time I was blazing with fire, and each time I ran to the bathroom to vomit blood and bile. The room was always spinning. What was happening to me? I was frightened, but too weak to ask questions.

One time I awoke and noticed that the sun was streaming in through the semi-closed blinds. I searched the room for Lori, but I was alone. Looking around with half opened eyes, I saw a tall glass of water and a bottle of aspirin next to my bed. Everything hurt. With all my strength, I reached for the bottle and the glass. My fingers were numb, but I succeeded in grasping the uncapped container and emptied two white pills into my hand. After placing them in my mouth, I returned the bottle to the nightstand only to realize that I laid it on its side. All the remaining aspirin fell on the floor. I groped for the glass and managed to take a small sip before it, too, slipped from my hand and crashed to the floor. Fragments of glass sprayed everywhere. I did not have enough energy to get myself completely back onto the bed. My head and one arm were draped over the side. It was easier to give in to the drowsiness than to fight it. I closed my eyes and let the blackness swallow me.

Someone was holding me and continuously crying my name. I tried to open my eyes. Nothing happened. "Don't let me go . . . just keep holding me!" Was I saying the words or was I thinking them? I simply wanted to die quietly in the warm arms that surrounded me. No! Wait! I did not want to die. God! Help me! Did I say that? Maybe I was already dead. No . . . death would cease the pain, and I definitely felt too awful to be dead.

"Jennifer . . . Jennifer . . . wake up!"

Who was talking to me? "Lori?" My voice was a husky, raw whisper. Did she hear me? "Lori." I tried forming the word again.

"I'm here, Jennifer. Open your eyes. Come on now . . . just open them."

She rocked me rhythmically. I tried to do as she commanded. Again, nothing happened. Again, I tried. Finally, after blinking several times, I began to focus on an image. It was Lori. She was crying. Why was she crying?

"Oh, thank God. Oh, Jennifer . . . I had the worst feeling when I walked into the room. You were so white . . . and you were lying there half out of the bed. You didn't move at all."

"I feel like I'm dead." Every word was such an effort to speak.

"No, don't say that! You're going to be okay. An ambulance is coming. They're taking you to the hospital. Don't worry, Jenny . . . everything will be all right."

"No . . . don't let them take me away. I want to . . . stay . . . here with . . . you." Even though I knew Lori's arms were around me, I could barely feel them.

"Jennifer." She was clinging to me, sobbing. "Shhhh . . . it's okay. They'll take good care of you. You're going to be all right . . . I promise . . . everything will be all right."

Was she saying that for my benefit or her own? There seemed to be dozens of people floating all around me. I felt myself being picked up and transported to a hard board. I wanted Lori. Lori! In the distance, I kept hearing this persistent monotonous humming sound. It must have been a siren. Noises . . . people were making all kinds of noises. Shut up! Everybody shut up! I can't stand all these noises. Someone was putting a device over my nose and mouth. I used what energy I had left to brush it away.

"Miss Carson . . . don't fight it. It's only oxygen. Let us help you."

Who the hell was that? I breathed deeply and found a little relief. It was so hard to take each breath. The pain was excruciating. There was a sharp, quick stab in my arm. A needle? I felt warmer. Lori . . . I wanted Lori. Where was Kurt? Hold me, Kurt! Make love to me. Make me climb mountains and explode. Make me reach heights I have never felt before. I need you, Kurt! I ran and ran through a mixture of cold flames and hot snow. Everything was confused. Lori! I'm coming. Slow motion . . . everything was in slow motion. Lori was smiling and her arms were outstretched, welcoming me. When I reached her, I threw myself into her grasp and looked up into her face. It wasn't Lori; it was Kurt. Oh, Kurt! I need you. Help me!

I crawled back into oblivion.

3

I lay quietly in the bed. Without opening my eyes, I placed my hand slowly over my other arm and felt needles penetrating my skin. There was a strange material surrounding it. Must be tape . . . the needles were secured by some kind of tape. I tried to peel it off, but it pulled at the tender hairs of my forearm so I stopped the painful procedure. Where was I? Breathing was such an effort. There was an odd scent in the air. What was it? Why did I hurt so much? When I finally managed to open my eyes, everything was blurry. I squinted. There must be something wrong with my vision because I could not see anything. Finally, I realized that I was surrounded by a plastic structure. It was some kind of tent. What was I doing in a plastic tent? I tried to speak but my throat was parched. I swallowed. God! That hurt. My mouth felt dry as a desert. I even swore I could taste sand. My lips were cracked and swollen. I wanted something to drink. I made another attempt to speak but only a groan emerged.

"Hello, baby."

Who was that? The voice was vaguely familiar, but I could not see through the plastic mist.

"It's Momma. I'm right here, baby. Mother's right here. You're getting better . . . all the doctors say so. You're going to be just fine."

"Momma?" I sounded raspy and hoarse. My mother? What was she doing here? I could not remember anything. Where the hell was I?

"Don't try to talk, honey . . . just rest."

"Lori . . . "

"Who?" My mother responded questioningly.

I tried to form the word again. "Lori."

"Oh, Lori . . . your roommate. She's been here every day. She always stays during the entire visiting hours. She'll be here soon . . . another fifteen minutes or so."

"I want Lori." I was so afraid I would be unable to stay awake for fifteen minutes, and I wanted to see her. I tried to sit up as I dug the palms of my hands into the mattress for leverage. I barely moved, but I kept on struggling.

"Don't get yourself worked up, dear. Just lay back and relax . . . It'll be okay."

"Where am I?"

"You're in a hospital. We wanted to take you home to George Washington Hospital, but you got so hysterical at the idea, the doctors thought it best that you stayed here." She patted my hand as if I were a family pet. "I've been so frightened, Jennifer. I've been sitting here every day, and I've been so scared. You're all I have. I was afraid I'd lose you." My mother choked on her words as if she were crying.

"Is Dad here too?"

"He calls. He's very worried. He wants to be here with you, but he has those meetings."

My father! Sure! That was a big laugh. My old man did not give two cents and a tinker's damn about what happened to me. If he did, the Pentagon sure as hell would not keep him away. "Sure, Mom . . . whatever you say." If my mother wanted to pretend that my old man was the good and loyal father, then so be it. I did not have the strength to argue with her. Why in God's name did she protect him? He had molded her into the meek little creature that he wanted; she would never disobey, never talk back, and never reveal their secret brutal life. My mother fit right into his wishes, and the habit was hard to break. But why did she feel that she had to lie to me? I knew the score. I knew what he was really like.

A nurse came into the room, noticed I was awake, and rushed back out to find a doctor. A few moments later, the doctor walked in. He and the nurse pulled the plastic aside and started examining me. A thermometer was placed under my tongue, and the nurse felt my wrist for a pulse. The physician listened to my heart in silence. He smiled warmly and winked in a pleasant way. "You have pneumonia along with a few other complications, but I think the worst is over."

I did not feel like the worst was over. I felt horrible. It was difficult to believe that my body could actually hurt so badly and still function. I wanted to appear brave to the young doctor so I managed a weak grin and listened to his analysis.

"You've given us all a real scare, young lady. You've been in here for over a week, and it seemed like you were fighting everything we tried on you. But things are looking better now. I think with a lot of rest, the right foods, and some tender loving care . . . you'll be as good as new in a month or so."

A month! I wished I had the energy to voice my questions. The doctor stood back, looked at my mother, and gave her a sign that only she understood. The two of them left the room. I did not have enough time to worry about the meaning of their silent message because at that moment, Lori quietly entered.

Before either one of us spoke, the nurse addressed my roommate. "You're friend's coming along nicely, Miss Davis. You're welcome to stay and talk with her but only for a few moments. Our patient needs her rest."

"I understand . . . I promise not to tire her." Lori's voice sounded worried. "I'm just so glad she's finally awake." She watched me a moment in silence. "Hi." Leaning against the bed, she clasped onto my hand and grinned. Lori looked as if she had not slept or eaten in days. "Don't try to speak, it's all right." She smiled. "I'll do the talking, okay? You just lie there and relax. God . . . it's so good to see you awake for a change. You just can't imagine how guilty I feel, Jennifer. I've been so worried. I feel awful that I didn't call the hospital earlier. I didn't realize how truly sick you were. I thought I could take care of you in the dorm, but that day I walked in and found you looking like death warmed over, I knew you were getting worse, not better. I hope you can forgive me."

I squeezed her hand trying to give her comfort. Poor Lori! It was not her fault; but knowing her, she would shoulder all the responsibility. No matter how hard I tried to speak, I could not even manage a syllable.

"I've met your mom. She seems real nice. She's been so worried, Jennifer. I don't think I've come here one single day that I didn't catch her crying over your bed. She loves you so much." Lori paused as she wiped a few strands of my hair away from my eyes. "I met your dad too. He was here the day after you were admitted. He's quite a character. You wouldn't believe the ruckus he made when the doctors suggested that you stay here instead of sending you home to DC. Jeez, he nearly tore the place apart. I gather from everything you've told me that your dad is used to getting his way. No kidding! He pitched a royal fit when the doctors didn't give in to him. He ranted and raved . . . cussing . . . I'd never heard some of the words he said." Lori smiled sheepishly and blotches of red appeared on her cheeks. We exchanged knowing grins before her expression changed, and she continued. "But, I think in spite of it all, your father really was concerned, Jen. He seemed quite worried."

"Don't . . . don't defend him."

"Okay, Jen . . . I'll change the subject."

I was glad she understood. Lori always understood.

"You're looking pretty good considering." Lori smiled and sat back in her chair.

"You . . . look . . . awful." It was such an effort to speak.

Lori grinned again. "That's a hell of a thing to say." She was laughing. "Now I know you're getting better."

I made a grunting sound that was intended to be laughter. My shoulder jerked from the response, and I felt a jutting pain race down my side. I grimaced. Immediately, I noticed concern register on Lori's face. I wanted to tell her not to worry, but I felt too tired to comment. I kept trying to keep my eyes opened. I did not want to go to sleep. I was afraid that if I closed my eyes, Lori would be gone the next time I awoke.

"You're sleepy. Get some rest. Don't worry, Jennifer, everything's going to be fine." Her words were soothing.

I latched on to her hand and drifted off into a peaceful slumber.

As the days passed, I began to feel stronger. Finally, the doctor removed the oxygen tent. My mother was constantly with me except when Lori came to visit. Even though there was rarely a conversation between Mom and me, I did feel better knowing she was there. Every day, she mentioned that my father called, but I never instigated further comment, and the subject was always dropped.

When Lori arrived Saturday for her daily visit, she was bursting with excitement. The feeling was contagious. She popped her head in the door, handed me a bouquet of flowers, and said, "Jennifer, I have a surprise for you." She was grinning widely. "You like surprises, don't you?"

I nodded my head and managed a smile. "You know I do."

Before I finished my sentence, another figured stepped into the room. It was Kurt. For a second, I thought my heart stopped. I knew I must look ridiculous with my mouth hanging open and a dumbfounded expression on my face, but Kurt was a surprise I never expected.

He ran the steps to my bedside and grabbed my hand in his. Kurt kissed each finger several times before making any statement. "Oh, Jennifer! I've been so worried about you. So afraid to come and see you. I didn't know whether you wanted me here or not." He had tears sparkling in his eyes.

I lifted his hand, still entwined in mine, and kissed it gently with my lips. He buried his face in my lap.

"I've missed you, Kurt."

I was crying. He was crying. Despite the tears that rolled down our cheeks, we both were laughing. I felt wonderful . . . better than I had since before this whole rotten mess had started. Kurt was here.

Thank you, God! My prayers were answered.

8

Laura

It was lonely in the dorm while Jennifer recuperated in the hospital. I saw her every day, but it was not the same as sharing our room. Thankfully, Jennifer regained a few of the twenty pounds she lost, her coloring was natural, and her spirits seemed lifted. I was thrilled she was doing so well. The doctors predicted she'd be home long before I left for Christmas vacation.

Kurt, who was happier than he had been in nearly a year, was drifting along on cloud nine. He still could not believe Jennifer actually broke all ties with David Henderson. My brother was the only person I knew who was more excited than I was about the fact that Jennifer would return to Elon for the spring semester.

Unlike Kurt's life, mine had become rather confusing. Brad Malone had, for some reason, started approaching me in a friendly manner on Wednesday nights during Professor Byrd's American history class. For two years, Brad had barely spoken to me; but during most of the fall semester, it seemed as if everywhere I turned, Brad was there. He always entered class after I was seated and chose a desk near mine. He was constantly initiating a conversation or passing silly notes to me while Professor Byrd wasn't looking. Oddly, Brad appeared nervous around me. He strained to find topics of interest that would draw a response. After class, he always found a reason to accompany me to Harper Center.

I heard through the grapevine that Brad terminated his rather long-standing relationship with Cindy Wilder. Because I knew Cindy had been pregnant last spring with Brad's child, I felt sorry for her. It was obvious that she loved Brad, but perhaps she was better off without him. It was common knowledge that he was not very good to her.

As far as I was concerned, Mr. Bradley Malone was off limits. He was poison in my book. Brad had hurt me more than I was willing to admit. I certainly was not in for a replay of the same treatment. Nothing he could do or say would ever change my opinion of him.

I had learned my lesson, and I never made the same mistake twice.

2

One unseasonably, warm afternoon in the beginning of December, after I played two sets of tennis with a girl on my hall, I turned to walk off the court. I instantly noticed Brad leaning against the chain-link fence. He waved and called me over to him. Casually, I walked in his direction. Why was he intruding upon my time?

"Hi, Laura. You look pretty good out there."

"Thanks." I drew the back of my wrist across my forehead and brushed the hairs into place. After picking up the cover of my tennis racket, I walked through the gate.

He followed. "Can I buy you a Coke?"

I stopped in my tracks and faced him. Why was he doing this? Why did not he just leave me alone? After staring at him for several seconds, I rather harshly answered his question with one of my own, "What for?"

Brad looked stunned by my response. I could not remember seeing him with that particular expression before. It was quite amusing.

He timidly answered, "I'd like to talk to you."

"Talk? I can't imagine what we have to talk about."

"Come on, Laura. You have anything better to do?" Brad looked like a little kid who was afraid someone was going to punish him for putting his hand in the cookie jar.

"Okay, I guess there's no harm in a free Coke."

We walked together to Long Student Union. His jovial attitude was contagious. I felt myself melting toward him. It was approximately twenty minutes into our conversation before I broached the subject of Cindy. Why did I mention her? It was none of my business.

Brad drifted into thought for a moment before he answered. He chose his words carefully. "Cindy is a really nice girl. I liked her . . . a lot. It was good for a while, but then she became so possessive and demanding. I felt like I couldn't breathe." Brad paused. "I don't love Cindy. She wanted me to love her . . . but I couldn't." He shrugged his shoulders and continued, "Contrary to what everyone seems to think about me . . . I did not set out to hurt the girl."

"Well, you have a strange way of showing it, Brad." I felt like I was sitting in judgment of him. I had no right to do that. It was his life—his decisions, his choices.

"Laura." Brad said my name in a manner which made me instantly look at him. His expression was serious. "You've ruined everything for me." He paused waiting for a reaction. When I made no comment, he continued. "My life was so simple until you came along. I tried to forget . . . forget about you . . . forget about what it was like when we were together. Cindy helped. In her own sweet way, Cindy reminded me a little of you . . . but she wasn't you." He paused. "I made a mistake our freshman year, Laura. I never should have let you go."

I felt something crack inside of me. It was that protective wall around my innermost thoughts and feelings. Patch it up! Patch it up quickly! Don't let him get the upper hand! Don't fall for Brad's act! He was conning me . . . I knew it. What was his game? What did he want?

"Laura . . . I don't know how you did it. I wish I did because then I could cure myself . . . but the fact of the matter is . . . you're in my system, and I can't get you out." He paused for a moment draining his cup dry. "I would give my soul to be rid of thoughts of you." Brad looked directly at me as he continued his confession. "I've watched you, Laura. I watch you all the time. I even watch you from my window when you come back from class. As hard as I try, I can't look away. Lord, help me . . . I even dream about you."

Did he really expect me to fall for this? Did he actually think I was gullible enough to believe him? Who did Brad think I was anyway? A simpleminded idiot? I had seen him chase every skirt on this campus . . . and he never gave a thought to those girls' feelings. Did he really think I'd believe all his bull! I stood up to leave. I didn't have to sit here and listen to him!

Gently, Brad grabbed my arm. "Don't go . . . please stay and listen to me."

I could not help myself. Obeying his request, I sat down again. I was shaking all the way to the bone. Why didn't he just leave me alone?

"I know what people think of me, Laura. I realize that everyone considers me to be an outrageous bastard. I don't give a damn what they think. All that matters to me is what *you* think!"

I started to speak.

He interrupted. "Most everything people say about me is all blown out of proportion. The majority of it is gossip that isn't even close to the truth." He paused. "When Cindy got pregnant, I really tried. For a little while, I thought it might work between us. Unfortunately, it was hopeless. She thought marriage would cure everything. I didn't love her. People can't make other people love them." He squeezed my hand. "You have to understand."

"Why? Why is it so important that I understand?" Why did I sit here and subject myself to this? It hurt being close to him.

"Because . . . Laura . . . I want you back." He watched me in silence.

Those brown eyes of his were driving me crazy. I did not move. I could not trust myself to speak. Of all the nerve! Did Brad actually think he could waltz into my life without any regard as to what I wanted? Did he expect me to jump at his command? Where did he get off thinking he could simply snap his fingers, and I would come running?

"I want a second chance. Laura . . . give me . . . give *us* another chance." He spoke in little more than a whisper.

I felt myself slipping into his web. How could he lie with such a straight face? What were his motives? What was his angle?

"I'll think about it, Brad. I can't say anything else right now. I'll let you know."

3

The following week was filled with bombarding efforts on Brad's part. I received numerous phone calls, a single red rose was delivered to my dorm room, and sweet notes were left in my mailbox. I felt myself weakening. Brad Malone at his best was definitely hard to resist. My mind was filled with indecision. I kept telling myself to ignore him; perhaps he would go away. But he didn't. He only became more persistent. My willpower began to slip. I admitted, even if only to myself, that I still had feelings for him—feelings that had never really died. They merely lay dormant, buried deep inside, and covered by the painful memory of his last stinging verbal abuse.

After a week of rejections, Brad finally convinced me to have dinner with him at Le Chateau. He acted so strangely, like a teenager on his first date. Brad gave me a corsage, opened doors for me, pulled out my chair, made polite compliments, and catered to me in every way. For the entire evening, I knew how Cinderella felt at the ball.

After dinner, as we finished the bottle of wine, Brad's conversation became more personal. "Laura . . ." He blushed slightly.

I had never seen Brad blush.

"It's amazing but I feel like a second grader who has a crush on his teacher. I can't remember the last time I felt more apprehensive about being with a woman." He took a sip of wine. "I feel so nervous about every sentence. I'm worried I'll say or do the wrong thing."

His words were making me uncomfortable. There were dozens of girls on campus who were dying for the chance to go out with Brad. Why was he here with me? "Brad . . . can I ask you a question?"

"Certainly . . . anything."

Externally, I was very calm. I wanted to be straightforward. I wanted to ask the questions that were nagging at my mind; but instead, I avoided those issues. "Why do you call me Laura when everyone else calls me Lori?"

Brad paused for a minute before he answered, "Because Lori sounds cute and sweet . . . which you are. But Laura sounds like poetry . . . soft and warm . . . beautiful . . . which is the way I see you."

His expression was so sincere. Was it a facade? I wanted to believe Brad. I wanted to let my defenses down and feel the way I had in the beginning of our freshman year. I was so happy then. It was such a magical time. Perhaps if I just reached across the table and touched his cheek—held his hand—maybe it would all become real.

No! I could not allow myself to be vulnerable to Brad. I instinctively knew if that were ever to happen, he would have the power to crush me with hardly any effort at all.

After a long silence, I spoke. "I see." I could not think of any other response. I started asking questions about Cindy. I had seen Brad with her on several occasions over the past week, and even though I tried to conceal my emotions, I realized that I felt pangs of jealousy. Brad swore that there was nothing between them. I hated to admit it, and I'd be a fool to say it to him, but if I were truly honest with myself, I realized that seeing Brad with Cindy, or any woman, had a negative effect on me. I was not willing to let Brad see how vulnerable I was; therefore, I remained composed. "I hear Cindy isn't taking the separation well. She's very unhappy, Brad."

"Cindy said that she'd take me on any terms. I'm not going to lie to you, Laura. I have seen her, but I don't initiate the meetings. She corners me. I don't have the heart to walk away. I won't go back to Cindy. She deserves someone who really cares about her . . . and I never will. I hurt her. I know that . . . and I'm sorry, but I can't change the fact that I don't love her."

"Cindy still loves you."

"I know. At first, I really liked the idea that someone loved me as much as Cindy did. I don't think anyone's ever loved me like that . . . not really loved me for who I am . . . except maybe my mother. But then I realized that it wasn't enough. I was only hurting her more by sticking it out. I had to let her go. I would never be the person she wanted me to be, and it wasn't doing either of us any good trying to pretend that I would change."

"I feel sorry for Cindy."

"Cindy wouldn't want your pity, Laura. She hates you."

"I've never done anything to Cindy . . . never. We were pretty good friends last year, but she moved to Sloan Dorm. We hardly see each other anymore. Why should Cindy hate me? What have I ever done?"

"You didn't do anything, Laura. It was nothing you ever did. She hates you because she's always known that I'm attracted to you . . . and as hard as she tried, Cindy couldn't compete with you."

Brad was watching me with those mysterious brown eyes of his. I wanted to believe him. I wanted every word to be true. Even though I knew it was selfish, I wanted Brad for myself even at Cindy's expense. Desperately, I wanted to fall into his arms and let him capture me with his passions.

Don't! Don't let him catch me off guard. What was I thinking? Don't let his flattery weave a trap around my emotions.

After paying the bill, Brad and I walked to the car. We drove to Elon in silence; each of us contemplated our own thoughts. He parked his brother's car, walked around to my side, and opened the door for me. As I stepped out, he gently reached for my arm and pulled me close to him. It was the first physical contact of any kind that we had shared since that day countless months ago. Brad paused only a moment—searching my eyes—before he lowered his mouth to mine. I closed my eyes and awaited his lips. He was gentle and chaste in his actions but that made no difference. I still felt a pulsating fire race through my entire body. Why did I get so weak at his slightest touch?

Slowly, he withdrew his warm lips and pressed them against my forehead. Brad's eyes were closed. "I've been wanting to do that for so long," he whispered softly.

I rested my head against his chest. It was too late. No amount of common sense could save me now. Brad had unlatched the floodgates, and all the old feelings came pouring out. My God! What had he done to me?

We stood together for several quiet moments before Brad gently wrapped an arm around my shoulder. "I'll see you tomorrow . . . okay, sunshine?" Brad had not stated his words, he had asked them as if bidding a favor from me.

I nodded. How could I refuse him?

4

After exams came Christmas vacation. I had no idea eleven days could seem so infinite. I missed Brad. He called every day, but it wasn't the same as being with him. Our relationship had blossomed during those final weeks of the fall semester. We had spent a great deal of time together, which made being apart seem that much worse.

Three days before we were due back at Elon for the mini winter term, Brad arrived by train at the King Street station in Alexandria. I took him to see some of the sights in Washington. I had never enjoyed being a D.C. tourist until I was able to share it with him. We saw the Capitol, the American History Museum, the Washington Monument, and the Jefferson Memorial. It was bitter cold, but neither of us felt the winter chill because our arms were wrapped protectively around each other sharing our warmth.

On the second day, I dragged him to see Mt. Vernon. Brad said that he really wasn't interested in George's home, but I think he enjoyed it more than he anticipated. Afterward, we took a lazy, long walk by the Potomac River, and I pointed out Fort Washington on the Maryland side. We held hands. For part of the afternoon, we sat on an old piece of driftwood and watched the airplanes headed for National Airport. We created fictitious stories about passengers on board. I found myself laughing uncontrollably because his anecdotes were far more original and amusing than mine.

When it came time to return to Elon, we both took the train. I had never enjoyed the trip more.

5

The month-long winter term, where students concentrated on only one course, flew by so quickly I could hardly believe four weeks passed. Brad and I signed up for the same elective, Ms. Yesulaitis's public speaking class, so we spent almost every waking hour together. The month seemed more like one long party than a college course. Aside from studying and writing speeches, Brad accompanied me on two Zeta functions; we went to a couple of movies; and we saw a Three Dog Night concert in Raleigh, but my favorite moments were spent in the lobby of Harper Center after dinner. He rested his head on my lap as I read from Rod McKwen's *Listen to the Warm*. Brad commented on more than one occasion that the way I read the poems made them come to life for him.

The only good thing about the mini-term coming to an end was the fact that Jennifer was returning for spring semester. I couldn't believe how glad I was to see her again. Even though she was not completely her old self, she looked basically well. I immediately suggested she crawl into bed and rest after the long trip. Jennifer agreed but insisted that I sit with her and talk. She propped herself up on pillows and pulled the blankets around her.

"Are the doctors satisfied with your recovery?"

"I don't know, Lori. I'm never sure whether or not they're being honest with me. Christ, it's hard enough to understand all their long technical words without trying to read between the lines."

"Do you feel back to normal again?"

"Pretty much . . . except that I tire so easily. I never was one to have a lot of energy like you do, Lori, but now I don't seem to have any at all . . . not even enough to make it through a quiet day."

"Do you think it's wise to be at Elon?"

"You think I'm going to stay home in that morgue? Get real! At first, everything was peaceful enough. Even my father was acting human to some degree, but the minute the doctors told him I was out of danger, my old man reverted to his usual patterns. Shit! Just last week, he knocked my mother around again. It's disgusting. I don't understand why she puts up with it. I mean . . . just because he's some goddamned general working out of the Pentagon doesn't give him the right to play army in his own home and use my mother as his own personal punching bag. One of these days, I swear I'm going to kill him. He's the meanest son of a bitch I've ever known." She paused. "There's no way I was going to stay there. You can bag that idea! Besides, the doctors said that if I followed all their rules, it would be okay for me to come back to Elon. I have to let them check me over every once in a while. It's no big deal—just routine."

"How are you emotionally?"

"Are you kidding? I feel like a new person," Jennifer answered as her face lit up with enthusiasm. "Saying good-bye to David wasn't as hard as I feared. The only problem was when he laughed at me. He actually laughed at me and said that I'd come running back to him before the year was out. I'll prove him wrong! I have no intentions of ever going back to David. He isn't good for me, and even though it took me a long time to figure it out—I finally succeeded." Jennifer yawned and tried to stifle her actions. Her eyes were slowly drooping closed. "Lori . . . I'm so glad to be back here with you . . . and Kurt just around the corner. I've missed you so much. You can't imagine how lonely I've been."

"I've missed you too. We have plenty of time to talk. You look exhausted, and I think you need to get some sleep." Jennifer slid her body deeper into the comfort of her bed and closed her eyes to the light. She muttered, "Lori, you're so strong. I wish I had your strength. I don't know what I'd do if you weren't here for me." She fell asleep almost before the sentence was finished.

I tucked the blanket around Jennifer's neck. After grabbing my jacket, I left the room and ran down the steps to meet Brad. I knew he was waiting for me outside the dorm. Every moment I spent with him was precious. I reached for each second as if it were a gift.

When I passed through the lobby doors, I immediately saw him leaning against "our" oak tree a few dozen yards away. He ran the short distance toward me with his arms outstretched and his voice ringing with laughter. The moment he encircled me, I felt the wonderful magic of his touch. "Laura, you're late. I was afraid you weren't coming." Brad picked me up and whirled me around as peals of laughter penetrated the afternoon air.

Each complete circle he turned made me feel dizzier, not just from the movement but also from the very feel of him. Nothing mattered. Nothing else in the whole world mattered to me, except him—his bright smile, his pleasant laughter, his warm body, his sparkling eyes—the very magic of him. The trees, the sky, the clouds, the building—everything spun around me, but I saw nothing except Brad Malone.

"I know I must sound silly, Laura . . . but I missed you. Even overnight, I missed you." He pulled me tightly against his chest and nearly crushed me with his strength.

"Didn't you know I'd be here? Didn't you know I couldn't stay away?" I spoke in a teasing tone, but I knew in my heart that each word was true.

Brad stopped holding me so tightly. Gently, he lowered me. My feet connected with the ground. Brad was no longer smiling. His expression was still warm and caring, but the smile was gone. His soft brown eyes mesmerized me.

"Laura," his lips barely moved. "I will never let you go again." Burying his nose in my hair, he wrapped his arms securely around my shoulders.

I had never in my life felt more alive, more euphoric, more bursting with pleasure.

*

6

The weeks all ran together; each was more wonderful than the last. One weekend was spent in Durham at the Daniel Boone Inn where Brad's fraternity was having an all night TKE party. It was so much fun. We laughed, talked, danced, and took a midnight walk in the moonlight. Around 4:00 in the morning, when all the other couples drifted into their rooms, Brad silently pulled the blanket off the bed, wrapped it around both of us, and guided me onto the balcony where we watched the sun rise. I dozed for a while. When I awoke, I found Brad watching me. There was a warm smile on his face. I felt so close to him.

In late February, Brad and I went to the mountains with Rick and Valerie Hunt, a Zeta sister of mine. The four of us had a fabulous time walking in the forest, laughing and talking. Brad brought his camera, and he busily took several rolls of film. I had a wonderful time with Brad, but the day was even more enhanced because we spent it with Rick and his date. It was especially nice to see Rick so happy. He and Valerie had been dating for several months, and it was obvious that they were falling in love. I also enjoyed watching Brad interact with his brother. There seemed to be a strong bond growing between them—a bond I had never noticed before. In addition, they seemed to have a mutual respect for each other. It was rather strange; in the past, I had not seen any similarities between the siblings, but now I constantly noticed little likenesses. Both Brad and Rick had the same hand gestures when they talked. More often than not, when they were excited about an event or an idea, their voices picked up speed in the same manner, and their accents were magnified. When I first met them, they never touched—never. But recently, I noticed that they'd fondly slap each other on the back or shake hands or exchange bear hugs once in a while. They still argued about their differences, but it seemed as if they genuinely liked each other. It was nice to watch them. The day was a huge success. On the way back to Elon, we stopped on the crest of one of the foothills and ate dinner at a lovely restaurant. The view of the sunset was magnificent. I will never forget the reflection of it in Brad's eyes.

On more than one occasion in March, we spent the entire night at Your Place, a tiny diner in Burlington that had twenty-four-hour service. It amazed me that Brad and I could talk until dawn while drinking coffee and eating danish. I had no concept of time when I was with Brad.

And then, there were the bluegrass bands we saw on Tuesday nights at the Brown Derby in Burlington, and on several Saturday nights, we danced, at The Castaways in Greensboro with Bill, Rick, and their dates. Other days, Brad would sneak me into the photography lab to show me how he developed his pictures. When weather permitted on Sundays, we played in those fabulous fraternity-sorority softball games. Brad was so patient with me. He showed me the proper stance when I approached the batter's box. Then, with both arms circling me, he demonstrated the swing and follow-through. After I succeeded, he nibbled playfully at my neck, which caused me to giggle until he stopped. It only took a few short lessons to get the hang of it before I connected with a pitch that caused Brad to cheer loudly. He was so proud of me.

Every moment we could, we spent together. Brad was so attentive, so loving. I was convinced he had made a transformation, and that egotistical individual everyone made him out to be was gone. All those old emotional and physical feelings that laid dormant for over two years were finally reborn. It was very overwhelming. Mentally, he symbolized a type of foundation for me that I couldn't even begin to describe, but that wasn't the only power he held over me. I was drawn to him sexually. I had never wanted anyone the way I desired him. It was never like this with Tommy. When I was with Brad, I felt constantly breathless and out of control. It was electrifying and terrifying at the same time; consequently, I knew I was completely vulnerable.

In spite of my insecurities when it came to Brad, I remained steadfast and closed my ears to Jennifer's warnings; I shut my eyes each time I saw Cindy—or any woman—in Brad's company; and I tried desperately not to dwell on the fact that Brad may be trapping me for his own personal reasons. I repeatedly told myself that everything was perfect.

During this blissful period, only two occasions dampened my mood. The first was when my brother's birthday drew number eleven in the army's lottery for the draft, and the second was when Jennifer confronted me about my relationship with Brad.

The US government stated that any male turning nineteen during 1972 would be eligible for the country's last mandatory draft. And, of all the luck,

Kurt fell into that category. President Nixon promised that no more of our boys would ever have to serve unless they voluntarily enlisted, but it was necessary at this particular point in the war to have one more call. No one could quite understand the need for it when they were pulling troops out of Vietnam, and it just made me crazy to think that Kurt was riding on the tail end of it all. Everything seemed to be going so well in most of Asia. Nixon had a very successful trip to China where he and Mao Tse-tung bridged twenty-two years of hostility. That meeting made Russia's Brezhnev more willing to discuss peace agreements. But Vietnam was a different story. The year began with an increase in American bombing of North Vietnam. And on March 30, the North Vietnamese made a full-scale invasion across the demilitarized zone. Not since 1968 had there been such a large Communist offensive launched. No one could believe it. We had been so close to peace. It was like a nightmare we kept having over and over again. I couldn't believe that my brother was going to be part of it. A rumor was out that only the first ninety-nine birthdays drawn would be called, but that was of little comfort when Kurt's number was much lower.

My brother went crazy when he heard the news. There would be no college deferments. All healthy males who were at the right age—or the wrong age, depending on how you looked at it—would be called, with no exceptions. The only thing that kept Kurt stable during this period was that he had Jennifer's support. Despite Jennifer's lack of energy, she gave Kurt strength to cope with the situation.

Jennifer had confessed to me that the two of them were finally sleeping together. I was not shocked or surprised. I was overjoyed for both of them. It had been a long, hard road paved with many disappointments on both sides; thankfully, they were now together . . . at least for as long as the US Army permitted.

The second unpleasant incident that tarnished my ebullience was when Jennifer confronted me with her newfound knowledge about the fact that I was seeing Brad.

"Lori, do you love him?" Her voice was gentle.

I thought about the question for a long time before replying, "I don't know," I stumbled. "All I know is that it would kill me to lose him again."

"Have you told him that?"

"No!" I quickly responded. "I haven't told him anything about the way I feel."

"Well, at least you're not completely nuts." Jennifer's words were harsh. "I think you're a fool, Lori. He's trying to get to you . . . manipulate you. Can't you see that? Brad Malone doesn't love you . . . and he never will. People like him don't even know the meaning of the word. Open your eyes, Lori. Don't be so damned naive. I've seen him with Cindy more times than I can count. Just yesterday, I saw him talking to her on the steps of Whitley. If you want my opinion, I certainly don't think it's over between the two of them . . . not by a long shot. If Brad was as crazy about you as you so blind-ly believe, then why the hell does he hang around Cindy so much?"

"Stop it!" I was angry and hurt. Why was Jennifer trying to burst my bubble? But I had to admit it was true. I, too, had seen Brad with Cindy several times. I was jealous. Jealousy was an emotion that went hand in hand with all the other emotions I felt for Brad. My God! Why couldn't I control my feelings? Somehow I had developed a possessive attitude toward Brad. I wanted him all for myself. The thought that he might care for someone else burned holes in my heart. As my only defense, I vowed never to state my real feelings . . . not to Jennifer and most certainly never to Brad.

I was in love with Brad. I hadn't quite come to terms with my emotions yet, but I knew it was true. Brad had crept back into my life and stolen all my thoughts and dreams leaving nothing for me to fall back on. There was a fear growing inside of me that if he left me, I would surely die. I knew it sounded melodramatic but God help me, it was true.

Jennifer and I bickered for an hour until finally I said, "You don't under-stand, Jen."

"No! You're the one who doesn't understand. You're so trusting. You're so damned naive you believe every word anyone says to you. Wake up, Lori!

This is real life . . . not one of your daydreams. When are you going to realize everyone is not as nice or honest as you are?"

"Stop it . . . I won't listen to you!"

"This guy's a creep, Lori. Can't you see that?"

I couldn't stand another word. I picked up my coat and raced from the room. There was no talking to Jennifer. Why couldn't she see my side of this? Why was she intentionally trying to hurt me? I let Jennifer's words manifest inside my mind until I couldn't hold them in any longer. Finally, I confronted Brad. "Is it really over between you and Cindy?" My voice was very matter of fact without a hint of any inner stress.

"Yes! It was over between Cindy and me even before you and I started up again."

"Why do you keep seeing her?"

"Huh?"

"I've seen you two together."

"What's this . . . the third degree?" He wasn't angry, just mildly amused, and his voice had a teasing tone to it. "Don't tell me you're jealous. Are you?" When he got no response, he continued. "I see Cindy because she corners me, not because I plan the meetings. I've told you that before. It's over between us. I swear! I admit that it took a long time to finally cut the ties, and maybe it lasted longer than it should have, but I have no intentions of going back to Cindy."

"How do you feel about her? Emotionally, I mean?" I was sitting on the edge of my seat.

"Of course, I have feelings for her, Laura. I feel compassion, a little pity, and a lot of guilt." He looked directly into my eyes. Brad tapped his fingers together lightly as he spoke. "You ought to know those feelings, Laura. You had them two and a half years ago with Tommy Ladley."

I didn't move. My eyes traveled around the room fearing to look into Brad's face. How well I remembered those emotions.

"I didn't understand then why you chose to stay with Tommy . . . but I do now, Laura." He reached for my chin and forced me to look at him. "I don't have the blind loyalty that you had. I would have given anything to spare Cindy all the grief I caused her. It was never my intention to hurt her. But I can't devote my life to sparing her feelings; that would make me a worse cad in the long run than what everyone is accusing me of now. They all say I deliberately set out to mess up Cindy's mind but I didn't. Laura, you have to believe me."

Brad or Jennifer! Whom should I trust? Brad looked and sounded so convincing. I wanted to believe him. More than anything in the world, I wanted to believe him.

7

One Saturday afternoon in early April, Kurt came to Elon. He and Jennifer were walking around campus. I was lonely and restless because Brad had traveled with the baseball team to see them play against Catawba. I paced the room and finally decided that what I needed was a change. I needed something to make me appear more mature, older, and sophisticated. I bummed a ride to Holly Hill Mall where I selected a hair frosting to give my ordinary shade of brown a more vibrant look. After purchasing it, I asked a friend down the hall to help me. She placed the cap on my head and used the tool to pull out sections of my hair in order to color it. The procedure took hours. By the time she was finished, I was very apprehensive. I had never touched my hair with anything but shampoo and creme rinse. What possessed me to do this?

When the cap was removed, all my fears came to life. I shouldn't have done it! My God! I looked awful. Awful was not really the proper word for it; I looked horrible! My friend apologized many times over, but the damage was already done. Where my brown hair had been stood a crop of straw white mass that jutted out in every direction. I felt sick. Nothing I did helped. I tried conditioners, ribbons, clips, and even rubber bands but the outcome was always the same. I looked as if I stuck my finger in an electrical socket, and my hair took the butt of the reaction. I had only intended a slight change—a few highlights of blonde—but instead, my entire head was whiter than Jennifer's and totally unmanageable.

My only alternative was to try to regain my original hair color. Before I got out of the door, Jennifer walked in. Her first reaction was that of utter disbelief, and then she was angry.

"What the hell did you do to yourself? Look at you, Lori. My God!"

"I was just trying something new." I felt timid in front of her verbal attack.

"Why didn't you wait for me? I would have helped you. Jesus Christ! You look awful."

I didn't need Jennifer's comments. I'd seen myself in the mirror. I knew exactly how I looked.

"You did this for him, didn't you? I suppose you think Brad Malone prefers blondes. Is that why you did it?" Jennifer's voice was hostile. "Lori . . . you look like a two-bit whore. Well, all I can say now is that the two of you are perfect for each other—the ideal couple—the campus stud and a local streetwalker."

I wanted to yell back into her face. I wanted to tell her that I couldn't care less what she thought, but I was too hurt and humiliated to utter a word. I draped a large scarf around my head and jogged all the way to the Tiny Tote in hopes that it carried hair dye. I was lucky. They had a small selection. I picked out what I thought was the closest color to my original shade and raced back to Staley Dorm.

When I returned, Jennifer was gone and so was her suitcase. She left with Kurt to spend the remainder of the weekend in Chapel Hill. I was relieved that she wasn't in our room and grateful for the solitude.

After using the dye, I realized that the color I had might be better than the straw white disaster of only an hour ago, but it wasn't by any means my original brown. Instead, my head was covered with something similar to pea green with silver highlights. I lay on the bed and cried. Jennifer was right. I shouldn't have done anything to my hair. There was nothing wrong with it in the first place. Now I was stuck with the weirdest shade I'd ever seen. I felt awful, and all the tears in the world weren't going to bring back my natural brown tones.

About the time I had brushed my hair for the millionth time, Brad called announcing his return. I tried to beg off of our date, but he refused to listen to any excuse. All afternoon, I'd heard nothing but laughing comments about my "new look," and I feared more of the same from Brad. I stalled for as much time as I dared before walking down to the lobby. Surprisingly, he didn't say a word about my appearance. We talked for over an hour until I simply couldn't stand the tension any longer.

"I did something terrible to my hair. I know it looks dreadful, and I can't get it back to normal again."

"Laura . . . it looks fine."

"I just wanted to look better . . . older maybe . . . I don't know. I felt that maybe you . . . oh, it's not important."

"Of course, I liked your hair better before. I loved the cinnamon in it, but I don't care, Laura. Don't you realize by now that I don't give a damn what color your hair is. I don't think I'd even mind if you were bald." He was grinning.

"Jennifer said I look like a whore, and she said you . . . "

"I don't give a shit what Jennifer Carson says. She's nothing but a bitch in heat. Don't listen to her, Laura."

"She's my friend, Brad. Don't talk about her like that, please. Jennifer's the only real friend I've ever had. I love her . . . even if I am angry with her right now."

"And what the hell am I? Aren't I your friend too? You talk as if Jennifer's the only person in the world you care about. It's always the same . . . Jennifer this and Jennifer that. Jesus! I'm sick and tired of hearing about her. She monopolizes you, Laura. She leeches off you. Can't you see that? She uses her illness as a crutch to bind you to her. You feel guilty as if it were your fault, and she plays on that. My God, Laura! Why can't you see her for what she is? She's got you so wrapped up in her life that you let everything else pass you by."

"Don't be angry with me, Brad. You don't understand. Jennifer needs me, and I need her too. She's the only person . . . ever . . . in my life whom I could confide in. I trust her . . . she knows me and understands me and cares about me. It's a relationship that I've never been able to form with anyone else. I treasure it."

"You're really pissing me off, Laura. If you can trust and understand and care about Jennifer Carson so damned much, then why can't you spare a few of those emotions for me? I want those things from you, Laura." Brad seemed truly annoyed. His agitation surfaced when he stood up and glared down at me. "I'm not asking a whole hell of a lot, you know. Just a token would do. We could build on that."

"Brad . . . " I reached for his hand, but he jerked it away.

"I can't talk about this right now! I hate that Carson bitch. Nothing you say is going to change my opinion of her. And I'd appreciate it if you just wouldn't bring her name into any more of our conversations. I don't want to hear anything about her."

"All right . . . all right. What ever you say." I was so frightened he'd leave me that I was willing to make any agreement with him. If he didn't want to discuss Jennifer, then it was a sacrifice I would make. Jennifer and I could still be friends. Brad and I could still have our relationship. After all, I couldn't discuss Brad in a civil manner with Jennifer, so what would be so difficult about not discussing Jennifer with Brad?

Brad sat down again as a bit of the tension vanished from his face. He drew me into his arms and held me in silence. I was so grateful that he was still with me. I would do anything to keep him . . . anything at all.

8

Jennifer made an attempt to apologize on Sunday night when she returned from Chapel Hill. At first, I was going to ignore her feeble statement, but then I realized that she was just as crushed as I was over our argument. Jennifer walked into the room and only glanced in my direction before starting to unpack her suitcase. Quietly, she put dirty clothes in the hamper and clean ones back in the drawers. I continued to read *The Godfather*, still too angry and hurt to make any stab at conversation. As Jennifer draped a blouse over a hanger, I noticed from the corner of my eye that she was watching me.

"Lori . . . "

Still boiling with inner hostility, I looked up from the pages I was pretending to read. I refrained from comment, knowing that any words I might say would sound negative and angry.

"I'm sorry, Lori." Jennifer's voice was so soft and muffled it was barely audible. "I had the most terrible weekend. Nothing Kurt said or did helped. I just feel so badly about everything I said to you." She sat on the bed waiting for me to respond. When nothing was said, she continued. "I can't stand it when you're mad at me. I don't know why I said those awful things, Lori. I'm really sorry; please forgive me. You just have to forgive me."

I couldn't stay angry with Jennifer for long, especially when she looked so forlorn. "Oh, Jen . . . "

Before I had finished my sentence, she had fallen into my arms weeping with a combination of relief and joy. "Lori . . . I was so miserable. I couldn't stand myself for saying those terrible things. I knew I hurt you, and I didn't mean it. I swear to God . . . I didn't mean it."

"It's okay . . . I'm all right now."

Jennifer stroked a few strands of my hair. "You fixed it. Your hair looks a lot better now. Really it does. I wished you had let me help. I was just so upset that you asked someone else to do it instead of me. I wouldn't have messed it up like that . . . I would have done it right."

"Don't worry about it, Jenny. Everything's fine now. It'll grow out. And I've learned my lesson. I'll never touch my hair again with anything artificial." We both laughed. I softly patted her on the back and tried to calm her down. I changed the subject. "How's Kurt?" My brother seemed to be the only neutral topic that the two of us could discuss anymore.

"I'm worried sick about him. Kurt isn't studying at all. And you know how he's always prided himself on making dean's list. Well, now he couldn't care less. He doesn't even open his books. He's just waiting to get that damn draft notice, and more times than not, he's stoned. I don't think he goes to his classes anymore. Charlie says that he just sits in his room and gets smoked up. It's scary. I don't know what to do. I don't know how to help him."

"You help him, Jennifer. You're the only reason he hasn't split the country. He told me that if it weren't for you, he'd be in Canada. Just keep hanging in there for him, Jen."

"I'm so scared. I get this feeling in the pit of my stomach that something awful is going to happen. I feel so helpless."

"Just be with him, Jennifer. Keep loving him. Stand by him; he needs you more now than ever before. Besides, maybe he'll be lucky. They haven't drafted him yet. Maybe they won't. Maybe something will happen, and he won't have to go."

My name was paged over the intercom. I knew Brad was waiting for me in the lobby. There was a long, silent pause as we stared at one another and waited for the other to comment.

"I suppose that's Brad," Jennifer muttered.

"If you don't have something nice to say about him, I would appreciate it if you didn't say anything at all." My voice was firm as I held my ground.

"I don't like him, Lori."

"That's fine! You have a right to your opinion, but I don't want to hear another word."

"But Lori . . . "

"Not another word. I'm not kidding, Jennifer. I don't need your foreboding comments."

"All right . . . if that's the way you want it. I can't stand fighting with you. I'll do anything to keep you from being mad at me. Even if it means keeping my mouth shut."

Jennifer threw her arms around me again. I was glad that we had formed a truce.

I raced to the lobby and ran into Brad's arms. It felt glorious to be held by him. He picked me up and carried me out into the moonlit beauty of the night. I couldn't see or hear anything but him. After placing me gently on the ground, Brad encircled me in his arms and kissed me with so much passion I felt surely I would faint from the ecstasy of his touch.

"Laura . . . my beautiful Laura. I will never let you go." He smothered me with his lips as each of his fingers ran an electrifying dance through my hair. Laughing merrily, he lifted me into his arms again and whirled me around. Brad teasingly threatened to throw me into the lake feet first. After I called his bluff, he placed me back on the ground, flew on top of me, and rolled both of us over three times before positioning me on my back while he laid on his side. The smile vanished from his face. His eyes were somber and quiet, and his voice was serious. "I'm crazy about you, Laura Davis. There has never been anyone in my life whom I've cared about more than you. I don't know how many ways I can say it or how many times I must repeat it, but . . . Laura . . . as hard as I've tried to block you from my mind . . . you simply won't go away. I've spilled my guts to you, but you've never returned any kind of emotional response." Brad seemed to be waiting for a reply from me.

"Do you love me, Brad?" I couldn't believe I was so blunt. Did I have no pride? How could I have asked that question? Yet wasn't that what I really wanted to know? I held my breath and awaited his answer.

"Are you kidding?" He seemed not only perplexed but annoyed as well. "Love? Why is it that women always want to hear that word?" He smirked. "No, Laura . . . No. I won't ruin what we share by allowing that overly possessive emotion into our relationship. Love destroys everything. It's a harness! It's a prison! A person can't bend or stretch without causing the other person frustration or jealousy or anger. I have no respect for love! I won't condemn myself to that kind of false commitment." As he brushed warm lips against my cheek, the twinkle reappeared in his eyes. His voice became more serene. "Isn't it enough that I'm absolutely crazy about you? I adore being with you. I'm wild about the very touch and scent of you. I want you like I've never wanted any other woman. And I think I've been pretty patient too." Tenderly he kissed me. "I happen to think you'll be worth the wait." He lowered his voice to a whisper. "Isn't that enough, Laura?"

Jennifer was right! Brad didn't love me. He didn't even know how to love anyone! What had I gotten myself into? "Brad," I paused and watched him as he waited for my response. How could he belittle such a beautiful emotion as love? How could he honestly believe that love could not be linked with a caring relationship? I couldn't tell him how important he had become to me. How was I going to keep him from breaking my heart? "I'm not really sure how I feel." My words sounded like a token comment.

"There's going to come a time, Laura, when you have to face the fact that we *are* attracted to each other. We can't keep seeing each other without it developing into a more physical relationship." He gently placed one finger under my chin and raised it just high enough to force my eyes to look into his. "I want to make love to you."

I was spellbound. It took me several seconds before I spoke. "I'm not ready, Brad." My heart was pounding rapidly against my chest. "I need more time."

"More time? Why? Either you want me, or you don't. It's as simple as that."

Words were caught in my throat. I found it hard to breathe. I wanted him. I craved him! I had an aching for Brad that I'd never known before, but I wasn't going to be his victim. I tried to remain calm. I laughed in a nonchalant way and feigned an indifferent attitude. I was not going to let him know how deeply I felt. "Of course, I care about you, Brad." My voice sounded more relaxed than I actually was. "You are incredibly adorable in a teddy bear sort of way. As the saying goes . . . what's not to like?"

"A teddy bear! I remind you of a teddy bear?" Brad seemed hurt by the comment. After several seconds passed, he masked his initial reaction with a confident grin and merrily added, "Lady, you will drive me to insanity yet! I will be totally gray and completely feebleminded by the time I graduate from this place."

We both laughed. He rolled me over. Our bodies were covered with a mixture of grass and evening dew. Brad kissed me several times. Nestling his face in my neck, he whispered, "Someday, Laura, we'll make love . . . and I promise . . . you'll love it."

10

I awoke the next morning to the sound of birds singing outside my window. It was a lovely tune. I hummed along with them. During the night, I came to the conclusion that I would settle for whatever part of Brad he was willing to give. He meant so much to me. I held on to the fact that Brad had told me he would never let me go. I had to believe those words! And wasn't that a type of commitment in itself?I dressed quickly and raced down to the cafeteria to do the breakfast shift. Sleepy students paraded into the room filling and refilling coffee cups and eating a choice of scrambled eggs, French toast, grapefruit, bacon and sausage. I smiled at everyone. What a glorious day! How could anyone look so drowsy on a beautiful day like today?

As the hour drew to an end, I wondered why Brad hadn't come through the line. He never missed breakfast on the days he had his 8:00 accounting class. As I started wiping down the tables, I hummed "The First Time Ever I Saw Your Face," and the face I saw in my mind was Brad's. I was so happy. "Ain't life grand!" I whispered.

After finishing my duties, I picked up my books. Out of the corner of my eye, I saw Rick approaching me.

Rick Malone was such a nice guy. He was always smiling and had a positive attitude. I was so glad we'd been able to salvage our friendship, and that it had weathered the transition when Brad and I had started dating again. As Rick came closer, I noticed a wary expression on his face. Immediately, I detected bad news. I hoped that there wasn't anything wrong with Valerie. I was certain that the two of them were getting quite serious, and I had the feeling that there might be an announcement in the near future. I liked Valerie Hunt. She was one of my favorite Zeta sisters, and I thought she made a perfect match for Rick.

The moment Rick stopped in front of me, I tensed up. There was definitely something wrong. My heart beat wildly, and my hands started to tremble.

"Good morning, Lori."

"Hello, Rick," I answered as I tried to stifle the growing panic in my voice. "Is Valerie okay?"

"Val's fine."

Why was he looking at me like that? The hair on the back of my neck instantly stood on end. "What's the matter, Rick?" My knees began to buckle. My stomach churned violently. Something awful had happened, and my intuition was tuning in to it. "Is Brad all right?"

"He's okay, I guess," Rick paused. "Cindy went home last night. I don't know how to tell you this, Lori. I'm sorry." Rick paused for what seemed an eternity. "Brad went with her."

I don't know why I was so shocked. I believed I knew exactly what Rick was going to say even before he said it. They were together again. "Did Brad ask you to tell me?"

"No . . . no, Lori. He didn't say anything. In fact, I didn't find out from him. I read a note on his door that said he'd gone to West Virginia, and he'd be back in a few days. A guy down the hall told me he left with Cindy. I just felt you had a right to know. And I didn't want you to hear it through the campus grapevine."

"I see."

"I'm so sorry, Lori. My brother's a fool. He doesn't know a good thing when he sees it. I wish there was something I could do. It's rather odd . . . I finally thought I had my brother all figured out, and then . . . well . . . I guess I don't understand Brad at all."

"It's all right, Rick." I pivoted and left.

Games! That was all Brad knew how to play. He left without a single word. He never cared about me. Lies! It had all been tricks and lies. How could Brad be so unfeeling? How could he pit Cindy and me against each other? Brad was a cold, unfeeling bastard, and I hated him. I despised him for what he had done to Cindy and what he had done to me. How in God's name had I let him get so close? I opened the lobby door and drank in the air.

It had all been a dream . . . a fairy tale. And now the fairy tale was over.

9

Brad

It was a long drive north through the Shenandoah Valley and into West Virginia. Cindy remained in a shocked silence the majority of the time. Periodically, she released a pitiful sounding moan; but mostly, she gazed into the darkness. Even though I knew it was only hours, it seemed like an eternity since she called me on the phone and hysterically begged me to come with her. No one in her dorm was capable of calming her including the housemother. Cindy pleaded with me. Sobbing, she begged me to accompany her. She accepted no one else's kind words. I tried to explain to Cindy that there was nothing I could do to help, but she cried like a mad-woman until I gave in to her request. Her mother's death could not have come at a worse time for Cindy. She was still strung out about her father's death from cancer the previous summer. I didn't know how much more grief any one person could handle.

A part of me wanted to turn my back on Cindy because I finally felt I had succeeded in cutting the ties between us, but then compassion and my conscience took over. In the end, I agreed to go with her; subsequently, I knew I would have to suffer the consequences later. During the time that Cindy and I dated, I hurt her more than I cared to remember. When I broke up with her last September, it was the final blow. For the first time in my life, I actually felt guilty about my actions. In no way did I intend to hurt her. It just happened.

Since our separation, Cindy tried numerous ways to "win me back," as she put it. I couldn't count the occasions she begged, cried, and tried to persuade me to change my mind, but each time I firmly stood my ground and refused to yield to her ploys. I explained to her over and over again that there could be no future for us, but she was so tenacious.

And now this! The roads in life have many forks—thousands of decisions that lead to ultimate destinies. By this unforeseen quirk of fate, I knew that I had chosen a new path, and the one I had just been on was closed.

Laura! Every mile I drove took me further away from her.

"Take the next exit," Cindy muttered. She was pale and fragile—balled up with emotional pain. She was wearing the same grief-stricken expression she wore on the day of the abortion. Even though a year had passed, it seemed like yesterday. On that fateful weekend, Cindy did not cry—not one tear. She was stoic when she walked out of that hellhole of a room where that so-called doctor took care of our problem. I heard horror stories about women dying from the procedure; but luckily, Cindy recuperated very well.

Cindy made no secret about the fact that she wanted our baby. I knew from the beginning that the conception was no accident. Cindy even admitted she purposely forgot to use her diaphragm a few times in hopes that I would marry her if she got pregnant. She felt a child would bind me to her.

Marriage! I never had any intention of marrying Cindy or anyone else for that matter, and certainly not because of a forced pregnancy. For over a month, Cindy was stubborn and stated firmly, "If I can't have you, I'll settle for our child." I knew that was bullshit from the word go. She considered a baby to be a product of our love, and she wanted me in the equation. It was a scheme. There was no way Cindy would stand by and allow the father of her child to simply drift away into the woodwork. She would have been after me constantly to tie the knot. No way! I wasn't falling for that old trick. She set a trap for me, but I didn't take the bait.

What Cindy was not aware of were the many nights I laid awake and wondered whether or not I was doing the right thing. Part of me wanted our unborn child.

In the end, I knew we made the right decision.

After the abortion, Cindy became even more demanding. She accused me countless times of being in love with Laura Davis. I was infuriated by Cindy's comments. I hated Laura. But, in retrospect, perhaps Cindy was partially right all along. Of course, Cindy was wrong about the fact that I loved Laura. I didn't love her! But I wanted her! I wanted Laura Davis more than I wanted any woman in my life. She haunted my dreams and even plagued me while I was awake. There were moments when I contemplated crushing her and stripping her of the willpower that kept her from succumbing to me. And then, there were other occasions when I was completely satisfied holding her in my arms, smelling her hair, watching her eyes, listening to her voice . . . just being with her. It was odd. I actually felt comfortable with Laura.

I had to give Laura credit. She had enchanting powers. It was a total mystery to me how she did it, but she constantly invaded my thoughts. She made me desire her; in fact, I had this incredible urge to conquer her. Any other woman, I would just have lured her in . . . but Laura was different. Virgins! It was so much harder to get to them. But it was more than virginity with Laura. There was something else, and I couldn't put my finger on it. There were times when I knew she wanted me. I could see it in her eyes, but she always stepped back right at the point when I thought I was gaining ground. She frustrated me to no end.

Never once in all the times Laura and I dated did she say how she felt about me. That bruised my ego. It was exasperating. I must be losing my touch. Well, I wasn't going to be led around by her anymore. And I wasn't going to chase after her like she was some kind of sweepstakes grand prize either. I'd wasted enough time on her. I didn't need Laura Davis. I didn't need anyone!

No! Cindy was wrong! I didn't love Laura Davis. Love was an intangible, destructive crutch used to manipulate and control people. I was one hundred percent certain I was incapable of that useless emotion. I would never love anyone. Never! And certainly, I would never love Laura Davis. But I did have to admit that she bewitched me. Bewitched and in love were different. There was a fine line between the two, and I was never going to cross over that line.

"Take the next two right turns. It's the fourth house on the left." Cindy's muffled voice cut through the morning air. The sun was rising, which gave everything a rich, red hue. A patchwork of spring flowers lined the sidewalk, birds chirped merrily, the paperboy delivered the news, and a neighborhood lady walked her dog. Morning had begun, and life continued. "How is it that everything seems so normal?" Cindy mumbled the words more to herself than to me.

There were not many people who came to pay their respects. Cindy did not lie when she told me that there was no one else. She was virtually alone. As she wandered around her tiny home, Cindy touched objects and ran her fingers over furniture that brought back memories. She looked so pitiful and small standing there with an ashen color covering her face. It was as if Cindy was in a numb stupor, which protected her from facing reality. She didn't speak very much, only a few words when the next-door neighbor dropped off a casserole and when the minister came to pay his respects and plan for the service.

I approached her silently and put my arms around her sagging frame. She buried her face in my shoulder. I felt the moisture of her first tears.

"Oh, Brad." She choked on the words. "This can't be real! The day before Daddy died last August, Mom told me that she didn't think she could live without him.

"When the doctors first diagnosed my father with cancer, we were so hopeful and so sure that the operation and the drugs would succeed." Cindy seemed to regain some composure as she spoke. "Daddy had a positive attitude which was contagious. My mother and I truly believed he would get well. It never dawned on Mom or me that Daddy was already dying." Cindy paused, "He knew it . . . everyone knew it . . . except Mom and me.

"Within two months, he was bedridden. The doctors recommended a nursing home, but my mother wouldn't hear of it. She insisted on taking care of him. She fed him. She bathed him. She shaved him. She dressed him . . . every single day. It was their ritual. And toward the end, she even changed his diaper." Cindy sucked in a long, laborious breath of air. "You can't imagine what it was like to watch my mother do that. It broke my heart." Tears silently streamed down Cindy's cheeks. "And through it all . . . they both had such dignity . . . such love . . . so much devotion.

"Then, my father had to face another ugly adversary. The pain. What little energy he had left, he devoted to concealing his agony so my mother wouldn't worry. But she knew. It was horrible. Finally, to give him some relief, they elected to increase the medication. When the amount of morphine was finally great enough to take away his pain, it also took his memory. When he was not in a drug-induced sleep, he would gaze at my mother with dark, blank, empty eyes—no recognition mirrored in them. He spoke strangers' names and described imaginary events only he was capable of seeing. He didn't have a clue who she was or who I was. The drugs robbed us of those last weeks. Even then, Mom continued to sing to him and read to him and talk to him. She prayed that somewhere in the dark recesses of his mind he would remember her voice." Cindy lowered her voice and continued, "My father aged a decade in that final month. He was so frail. His eyes were hollow—void. His skin was an ominous shade of gray." Cindy brushed the tears from her cheeks. "Toward the end, there was a smell in the house. It was faint and lingering—a distinct odor. I can't describe it, but it is forever imprinted on my mind. It was the smell of death." Cindy closed her eyes as she momentarily drifted off into her own private thoughts. When she spoke again, her voice was stronger. "You cannot understand cancer until you have lived with it—until it has invaded your home, robbed your heart, stolen your future—sucked the life out of someone you love. Yes! You can sympathize. You might even think you understand, but you don't . . . not until you have actually lived with it.

"After the funeral, Mom told me that she didn't know what was worse—watching him suffer from the pain or living without him." Cindy glanced to her left. "Mom was sitting in that chair—the one in the corner— wearing a worn-out sundress with daisies on it. I can still hear her voice. It quivered when she said, 'I feel so guilty. I would rather have him here with me—suffering—and in all of that agony. But I should be thankful he's at peace now. His struggle is over. I should be grateful, but I'm not. I don't think I can live without him.'" Cindy paused as she glanced around the room. "Mom didn't die of a stroke. I know that. She died of a broken heart." Fresh tears streamed down her cheeks. "And she left me alone. I'm all alone. How could she do that to me?"

Cindy looked at me. It was as if she just remembered I was there. "Brad . . . take me upstairs . . . make love to me." She picked her head off my shoulder and stared longingly into my eyes. "Help me to forget . . . if only for a little while."

I lifted her effortlessly in my arms and carried her up the flight of stairs that led to the room of her childhood. Subconsciously, I took in the signs of her youth: the high school graduation picture on her dresser, the raggedy teddy bear on the pillow, Nancy Drew paperback novels scattered on the shelf, the remnants of a prom corsage pinned to her headboard. The room was filled with bright, friendly, welcoming colors and its warm reminders of the past.

Cindy's face was buried in my neck. Her arms clung to me. After slowly lowering her onto the bed, I freed myself long enough to undress. I watched her as I unbuttoned my shirt and draped it over the chair next to her desk. She looked so fragile, so lost and confused. I instinctively knew that if I lay beside her now and sheltered her with my body, it would represent a commitment.

After I finished stripping my pants, I methodically disrobed Cindy thinking with each article of clothing I dropped to the floor that I was stepping into a new world with her which would alter my own plans for the future. A thought kept nagging in the back of my mind: Cindy loved me . . . she needed me. I hung on to that. Cindy was trusting me with her sanity and of all the things I'd taken away from her in the past, I was not going to let her down now. I could think about the future tomorrow . . . but I was going to think about Cindy today.

Never in my life had I been gentler and more aware of my partner than I was of Cindy at that moment. I took my time and allowed her to dwell on the sensations that the act of love could create. I used all my skills to bring her to physical heights that would block out mental thoughts and pains. I teased her body with my tongue, my lips, and my teeth until Cindy was squirming with my every gesture and begging for the ultimate release. Slowly at first, I entered her and toyed with all the private areas that bring mounting desires to their peak. I could feel her nails digging into my shoulder blades, hear her moans of ecstasy and squeals of delight, feel her thrusting up toward me with her pelvis as she silently begged me to bury myself deeper into her warmth. Instinctively knowing she was not quite ready, I paced myself and gave her just a little more time to reach the summit.

With each new thrust I concentrated all my efforts on pushing the image of Laura's face from my mind. I tried to think only of Cindy. Cindy loved me. Cindy needed me. Cindy wanted me. Cindy could give me all the emotions that Laura was incapable of showing. Laura! How I hated her for teasing me with her innocence and taunting me with her aloof manner. How I wanted to strangle her. I envisioned myself tackling Laura on the ground and forcing her into succumbing to her own desire—making her scream for the release I could give her. Laura!

Her imaginary face vanished as I felt a combination of exploding sensations rush to my loins. It was as if all the blood was stripped from my veins and concentrated in only one fraction of my body, which jabbed continuously into the tightness that represented Cindy's warm, snug haven. Cindy . . . Laura . . . this bed . . . this body . . . this house . . . everything went blank, as the zenith was reached, and the crest of the wave was ridden out. I collapsed, thoroughly exhausted, onto Cindy's body. My mind was void of any thought—relishing only the beauty of the moment. Every pore of my body ejected perspiration. My heart was pumping rapidly and with such force that I was sure it would beat itself out of my chest, and my lungs expanded and contracted with quick, shallow breaths straining for needed oxygen.

"Brad."

A voice . . . there was a voice calling out to me. I struggled to push all thoughts of reality away. I wanted nothing to disturb my bliss—nothing to enter into my own private world of darkness and contentment.

"Brad."

There was that sound again. Go away! Leave me alone! Slowly, I began to focus on the situation. My memory brought me back to reality and snatched me from the top of my mountain.

"I love you, Brad." Cindy repeated her words over and over again like the steady beating of a jungle drum. She held me tighter than I thought humanly possible as she cried out to me. "Don't leave me. I can't lose you."

I lifted my head off her shoulder and watched Cindy's expression alternate from the contentment of physical release to the pain of verbal and emotional begging. I smoothed her damp hair and brushed the tears from her cheeks.

"I need you, Brad. I have no one but you . . . please . . . please don't leave me."

"It's all right, baby," I whispered as I drew her into the protection of my arms. "I'm here. I won't leave." Cindy had won. Through no fault of her own, she had gotten me back into the position she wanted. Now, I would have to resign myself to the fact that at least for the present I was committed to her.

"Say you'll marry me, Brad; say we'll always be together. Promise you will never leave me." Cindy was near the breaking point.

As hard as I tried to skirt the issue and divert her attentions to another subject, Cindy clung to me with every ounce of strength she had and begged me to answer her pleas.

"Yes, Cindy . . . "

"You'll marry me? You'll really marry me!"

"Yes."

A combination of laughter and tears expressed her jubilation. I knew she was hysterical and blinded to the fact that I did not share in her enthusiasm. I also knew I would take care of Cindy. She needed me. No one had ever needed me before. I would give her the reassurance and comfort she craved. I owed her that much. God help me . . . I owed her that much and more.

2

I went to the fraternity-sorority mixer at The Lodge. Because Cindy had the flu, she didn't join me. Billy and I had been drinking all day and by the time the beer blast started I was well on my way to feeling that wonderful buzzing sensation only alcohol created. It was fun to dance and party in a world foreign to Cindy and her unrealistic outlook on life. I felt free. I was enjoying my independence. These were the first relaxing moments I'd been able to savor since that night nearly two weeks ago when I'd gone to West Virginia. That day seemed so long ago. How different my life would have been if I had not been sleeping in my bed at that moment, if I hadn't accepted her request, if I simply hadn't answered the phone. Ifs! Always ifs! It was too late to dwell on them now.

I was dancing with a cute little redhead when I saw Laura enter the room. I froze for one split second. It was treason! I hated how my body betrayed my mind. Laura! It was the first time I'd seen her since before my departure. I had purposely stayed away from all the places I knew she'd be. I avoided the student union and the library. I ate my meals at McEwen instead of Harper Center where she worked. If I wasn't with Cindy, I stayed in my room.

Laura was standing in the corner with Jennifer Carson. Both were smiling tauntingly into the eyes of several men. Laura! The ice princess . . . beautiful enticing Laura with the sweet purring voice, the smiling eyes, and the heart of stone.

She glanced in my direction. I immediately detected that she noticed my presence. Her eyes were cold and unfeeling. Her expression was completely empty of any trace of emotion. I watched her circle the room, avoiding my path, and refusing to have visual contact with me. She started a conversation with some guy I recognized from main campus. I saw him put his arm around Laura in an overly friendly fashion. I was outraged. It took all my self-control to keep from walking up to them and jerking his arm away. How dare that asshole hold Laura in such a suggestive way, and he was looking at her as if she were going to be his next meal. What made it worse was the fact that Laura was encouraging him. She was smiling invitingly up at the jerk and using her eyes as a sexual tool. Why the hell didn't she ever look at me that way? Where did she get off acting like a tease? I'd strangle her if she left with that guy, and I'd knock his teeth down his throat if he laid a hand on her. My body was shaking with controlled rage. I could not tolerate it another moment. Without saying a word to the redhead, I turned and left the building.

Trying to calm the turmoil that was racing through my body, I closed my eyes and drank in the crisp night air. When I realized I was holding a cold mug of beer in my hand, I put the glass to my lips and drained the liquid in a matter of seconds. It helped. I took in steady even breaths of oxygen until I felt the tension start to subside. I was drunk—very drunk—probably more so than I'd been in a long time. That had to explain it. That must be the reason for my reactions toward Laura. I had consumed so much alcohol today—two or three six-packs—I'd lost count. That had to be the reason. It was the fucking beer that was making me act this way.

Billy came out of the backdoor. He was laughing and saying something about the way I'd jilted the redhead when I left her standing in the center of the floor. I wasn't listening. I didn't need his jolly comments. I wanted to be alone. Why the hell couldn't he see that?

"Hey, buddy." He slapped me on the back playfully. "Do I owe you that ten dollars yet?"

"What?" I questioned. "What the hell ten dollars are you talking about?"

"You know, Brad." Billy was drunk too. He was weaving almost as much as I was. "You know, Brad . . . the one about popping Laura Davis's cherry . . . remember? You bet me ten bucks when we were freshmen that you were going to make her melted butter in your hands and screw the hell out of that sweet ripe body of hers. Come on, old buddy! You know what I'm talking about. You've been hanging around her for months. I figured you'd made your move, popped it, and that's why you're back with Cindy." When I didn't comment, he slapped me playfully on the back again, "What's the matter, champ . . . losing your touch?"

I pushed him with both of my hands. He fell as if in slow motion. "Shut up, Billy. I don't want to talk about that fucking cunt."

"Now that's funny!" Billy roared with laughter. "Don't you think, Brad, that it's a bit of an oxymoron to use the words fucking cunt to describe Lori Davis? Give me a break, Lori doesn't qualify!"

"Damn it, Billy. I don't want to talk about her. I don't care about her. She means nothing to me!"

"Me thinks thou dost protest too much," Billy chuckled.

"I wouldn't waste my time on her." I walked back into the building and slammed the door behind me but not soon enough to shut out the ringing of Billy's laughter. I stomped feverishly down the hallway. The walls were lined with couples pawing and groping at each other's bodies. Everywhere I looked there were people intermingled in arms and legs . . . mouth to mouth . . . fingers on breasts . . . hands fondling round soft asses . . . moans and sighs that were driving me to madness. I wanted to push them all apart and slug the first person I could get my hands on; but instead, I entered the room where the music played loudly and the majority of couples were danc-ing, talking, and laughing . . . having a grand old time. I reached for anoth-er beer and drank it dry before filling it up again from the tap.

I scanned the room. Even in the partial darkness, I immediately saw Laura dancing to a slow melody in the arms of that guy. She was smiling—taunting him with that wonderful look I knew so well. Those incredible blue eyes were shining, her cheeks were flushed, her smile radiated warmth, and

Tesa Jones ❦ 227

her body pressed intimately against her partner. Her firm round tits rubbed against his chest. Was she doing it intentionally? I'd kill her if she didn't stop swaying against him like that. He was touching her hair and whispering into her ear. What was he saying? Don't touch her like that!

Before I knew what happened, I was standing next to Laura and jerking them apart. "Dance with me!" I demanded. The room was spinning. I concentrated on Laura's face and stabilized the sudden urge to pass out.

"It's all right, Johnny." Laura spoke to her partner. "Let's keep calm. I don't want any problems—no scenes, okay? Let me just dance with him for a minute, and I'll come right back."

"Lori . . . you sure you want to talk to this creep?" He jabbed my shoulder as he spoke.

"Get me a beer please, Johnny." Laura's voice was firm and unruffled.

I thought I'd go mad if she didn't show some token sign of emotion. I felt oppressed by not only Laura's cold stare but also the noise and the smoked-filled air. My anger made me so rigid with tension that I barely noticed when Laura's partner disappeared. Her cold gaze was all I could see. I desperately wanted to take her in my arms—hold her and caress her body—touch her breasts and make them swell with desire for me. I wanted to make her moan softly as I stroked her skin—entice her into yielding to me of her own free will. I wanted more than anything to see her smile at me with the expression I had seen her wearing only moments ago.

Laura didn't say a word.

There was so much I wanted to say. I wanted to tell her how much I've missed her, how little Cindy actually meant to me in comparison, and most importantly, I wanted to tell Laura that I only went with Cindy because she needed me. I felt obligated to help her.

Still, Laura did not speak.

None of my thoughts took verbal shape. Nothing I wanted to say formed words on my lips. All those traitorous thoughts I'd had while I was staring down into her face vanished as I saw only contempt in her expression. How could she be so cold? So distant? Bitch!

Suddenly, I wanted to hurt Laura. I wanted to lash out at her and make her feel pain—if not physical, then emotional. I finally spoke and broke the silence that had been thick between us. "Cindy and I are engaged."

Laura's expression didn't change—not one muscle in her face altered. Her eyes still had the same blank look to them, her lips held the same fixed tightness, her nostrils flared ever so slightly, then reverted back to the same stilted shape. Nothing! She said nothing. How the hell could she be so in control? Hadn't I meant anything to her at all? Was she so fucking callous that my desertion left her totally apathetic and unmoved? Why didn't she say something?

I couldn't let her go without adding to my first comment. I needed to wipe that smug determined look off Laura's face. Again words formed on my lips before I had complete command over my thoughts. "Laura . . . we are the right two people for each other." Why was I saying this? That wasn't what I meant to say! Why was I letting down my veiled emotions for Laura when she was obviously insensitive to my desire? "We *are* the right two people . . . we just always seem to find the wrong times . . . the wrong places."

Laura stood quietly. I couldn't bear her silence. I was not going to let her see that her lack of reaction was humiliating me. Why couldn't Laura have cared for me? I had admitted that I was wild about her. What had she said in response? Her words still vibrated in my ears. "You are incredibly adorable like a teddy bear." Sweet Jesus! I didn't want to be a friggin' teddy bear. Teddy bears were toys girls collected and put on shelves when they were worn-out or forgotten. She wanted love from me when she wasn't willing to give me anything in return. Teddy bear . . . my ass!

"Laura . . . " I stared deeply into her eyes and searched for some sign—any sign. Nothing! "I'm going to marry Cindy." No change. Nothing registered on Laura's face. What were the words I could say to inflict some pain? "There's no right time or right place for you and me, Laura . . . there never was . . . there never will be. I don't need you. Hell, I don't even like you. But I sure did want to get into your pants. How about we get a room . . . shack up for the night? I've got something swollen here I'd love to share with you." I reached for her hand and placed it on my crotch. I forced her to hold me and refused to let go of her hand. She struggled, but my fingers were like a vice. "Come on, Laura . . . we both know what you want." Smugly, I grinned as I noticed a small twitch circling her right eye. I pressed myself harder against her and tightened my grip. "You want it, Laura. Admit it! Come on . . . let's do it . . . you and me . . . satisfaction guaranteed!" That ought to do it! The cunt! The cold-blooded cunt! The guy who ended up with her deserved her nonchalant bitchy ways.

Before I had the opportunity to say another word, Laura yanked her hand free, turned, and walked over to Jennifer Carson. Not once had she spoken . . . not one single word. I spat on the spot where she had been and left the room.

3

Rick and I went home for Easter break. I was extremely thankful to be away from Cindy with her constant clinging and Laura with her cold, uncaring glances. I needed freedom from Elon, because the walls seemed to be closing in on me. Everything was going wrong. My life seemed so screwed up that even drinking wasn't helping anymore. Rick sensed my foul mood and neither one of us made conversation during the long trip home. I appreciated the solitude.

I hadn't dated Jill for almost a year but immediately upon my arrival home, I dialed her number. Perhaps there was a chance I could find some solace in her inviting arms. At first, Jill seemed stunned when she heard my voice. She spoke hesitantly and refused to commit herself to an evening with me.

"Come on, Jill. It's been a long time." I coaxed her, as I tried my best to tempt her into agreeing to see me. "Can't two old friends get together for a drink?"

"Is that what we are, Brad . . . old friends?"

I knew what she was thinking. I knew Jill was remembering our last encounter when she had clung to me. She'd cried and pleaded with me not to leave her. Jill had admitted to being in love with me, and I had been agitated by her confession and blew it off without considering her feelings. Jill had known better than to pull that routine on me. I had warned her repeatedly that I never had any intentions of getting seriously involved with her, but Jill had still backed me into an emotional corner until I had no alternative but to leave her crying.

In retrospect, I was sorry for my actions. I had been cruel. It was inexcusable.

"Come on, Jill . . . be a sport. Have a drink for old times sake."

"Do you want a drink or..." She paused making her voice as controlled as possible, "Or do you just want to hop into bed?"

"Hey . . . come on, Jill . . . I just want to talk. I don't need the drink, and the bed isn't necessary . . . really. I just need someone to talk to." It wasn't until that moment when I realized how very much I wanted Jill's acceptance . . . her company. I had so many mixed feelings scrambling around in my brain. I needed desperately to talk them out with someone. Anyone! I could not tell Billy. He wouldn't understand. Neither would Rick. Jill was my only candidate. Jill didn't know Cindy. She didn't know Laura. Jill could be objective. She would listen.

"Please, Jill . . . I just want to talk . . . please let me come over."

There was a long moment of silence before her voice came over the wire. "All right." She sounded exasperated. "I guess there's no harm in talking. Give me thirty minutes and then come on by."

"Thanks, Jill. I really appreciate it." I felt relieved. "See you shortly."

4

When Jill opened the door to her apartment, I immediately saw that she was no longer the vibrant, healthy person she had been a year ago. Jill was far too thin for her height, her cheeks were much more concave than the fashion, and the natural color that had once covered her face had disappeared. She was wearing a great deal of makeup—much more than usual. She appeared ghostlike.

"You look good, Brad. It's nice to see you." Jill was distant.

"You're looking pretty good yourself."

"There's no need to lie, Brad. I know what I look like. I don't need any false compliments."

"Are you all right?"

"Yeah . . . I suppose so. Things haven't been so terrific lately. I lost my job last fall, but I have a new one now. At least I'm paying the bills and getting the creditors off my back."

"How'd you lose your job?" I was still standing in the hallway waiting for her to step aside and let me in.

"My boss said I wasn't concentrating hard enough on my work . . . and I was screwing up so badly they had to let me go. I can't blame them. I really was messing up a lot. But I'm doing better now. This new job is coming along. I finally have my head on straight, and my attention is where it ought to be."

I knew without her saying another word that I was the reason for her present situation. I was thankful that she wasn't verbally blaming me. "I'm sorry, Jill. I'm really sorry."

"It's okay, Brad. It was my own fault anyway. After all, didn't you warn me enough times? I should have known better. Right?" She stepped aside and gestured for me to enter the room. I walked into what looked like a rapid job of cleaning around her apartment. "Besides, I like this new job. There's more work and more challenge. I have to bust my ass every minute, and there's no time for my mind to wander . . . if you know what I mean." She paused briefly then spoke before I had a chance to interrupt. "I'm getting over you, Brad . . . I thought it would never happen, but I'm really beginning to feel normal again." Her voice became harsh. "I hope you're not intending to shatter what little structure I've started to rebuild in my life. I don't need any more grief."

"I really hurt you . . . didn't I, Jill?"

"I loved you, Brad. I loved you more than you will ever know. But my head's out of the clouds now. Things are starting to fall back into place for me. I'm getting a new perspective on life in general."

I reached for her and wrapped my arm comfortingly around her shoulder. She willingly allowed her body to slip into my embrace. "I'm so sorry, Jill. It seems as if I hurt those people who care the most about me. I really am sorry, Jill."

She gently slipped from my hold and walked confidently to the bar in the corner. Her voice was stronger when she said, "As much as I'd like to blame you, Brad, I know it's not really your fault. I knew in the beginning that you didn't love me. I guess my heart wasn't listening to my common sense." She poured herself a glass of bourbon on the rocks and added a splash of water. "Can I make you a drink?"

"Yeah . . . but make it straight, okay?" After fixing it, Jill sat in a chair on the opposite side of the room. In the silence, I scanned the apartment. Soft music played on the stereo, and there was a faint scent of Lysol in the air. I sipped my drink as I contemplated my thoughts.

"So, tell me . . . how's Cindy?"

I set my glass down on the end table and leaned back. "You're not going to believe this, Jill, but I'm engaged." I saw the surprise and hurt register on Jill's face. I could tell by her expression that it was as if I poured salt on an open wound. I downed my drink and went to refill the glass. Refraining from comment, Jill watched me. I drank another few ounces and discovered the blissful numbness it created in my body. I poured myself a third drink and went back to my original position on the chair facing Jill. "I don't love Cindy. I tried. I wanted to . . . but I don't love her, and I can't marry her."

"Then what the hell are you doing engaged to the poor kid? Don't you have any conscience at all?"

"I don't know how it happened, Jill. It was all so fast. I thought I was doing the best thing for her at the time, but Cindy's living in this dream world. I don't know how to bring her down to earth without hurting her. I don't know what to do."

"Are you asking for my advice? You've got brass balls, Brad." There was anger in her voice. "You have a hell of a lot of nerve coming here to me . . . "

Tesa Jones ❧ 233

"I need someone to talk to, Jill. I need someone who will listen." I was frantic.

"You actually think that I will quietly sit back and play your Dear Abby . . . listen to you talk about your endless string of women and your never ending victories over them." Jill stood up and screamed. "You get the fuck out of here, Brad Malone! Get out! Get out!" She was yelling and hurling obscenities with each breath she took.

Covering my face with my hands, I slouched in the chair. I pressed the fingers tightly into each socket. I had never felt more defeated in my life. Everything had gone wrong. Cindy had me backed against a wall; I was plagued with thoughts of Laura; and now Jill was turning her back on me. I was hurt, confused, and miserable. My body ached. All I could hear was the shrill screeching of Jill's voice.

I had no idea when the tears formed, but I suddenly felt them burning my eyes, struggling to break free, and pour down my cheeks. I swallowed repeatedly and tried to gain some composure. Men don't cry! Tears were for babies and weak women. Before I realized what was happening, the salty liquid was streaming down my face, and my shoulders were jerking in spasmodic sobs.

Out of nowhere, Jill was cradling me in her arms. Somehow, without my realizing it, she had taken my chair and I was kneeling in front of her with my head in her lap. When had the transition taken place? Had Jill come to me or had I gone to her? The answers didn't matter. All I knew was that the floodgates were open, and I was soaking her slacks with my tears. I tried to put an end to my humiliating outburst but my efforts were futile. Nothing helped, so I gave in to my weakness and let the choking sobs fill the room. In the distance, I could hear comforting words, but I could not grasp their meaning. All I knew was that Jill did not betray me. She was holding me and gently allowing me to use her lap as my safe haven.

As my emotional heaving began to subside I started to speak. Each word was a struggle, but I managed to tell Jill that Cindy's mother had died and how I didn't want to go with her, but she had needed me so much. I explained how I had finally succeeded in breaking off the relationship only to be pitched headfirst back into it again. I kept saying over and over again how helpless Cindy was and how dependent she had become. And I repeated more times than I could count that I was so confused.

Before I knew what I was saying, fragments of sentences came from my lips about Laura. I couldn't recall when or how the subject changed, but suddenly I was telling Jill about sweet beautiful Laura . . . Laura and her innocence . . . Laura and her radiant smile . . . Laura and her soft purring voice. Laura and how happy I was when we were together. I even told Jill that I was comfortable with Laura . . . she made me feel like a whole person. Laura . . . sensual . . . sultry . . . warm . . . kind . . . gentle . . . tender Laura. Laura and my insatiable desire for her . . .

"I remember the first time I took her out. There was something unique about Laura . . . something special. The entire evening I kept staring at her while she spoke, and all I wanted to do was feel her in my arms. When I took her back to the dorm, I was actually nervous about kissing her goodnight at the door. She stood there, eyes closed, head tilted up slightly. I barely brushed her lips, but the impact was incredible. I have never felt anything like it. Magical—it was magical." I devoured my drink. My mood switched from pleasant to hostile. My voice grew angry when I spoke again, "Then do you know what that bitch did? The next day . . . the next damned day, she went out with my brother. Do you know how that made me feel? My own fucking brother!" I was having difficulty controlling my rage as I went on to discuss Laura and her nonchalant manner . . . Laura and her apathy . . . Laura and how she'd walked away from me twice without a second glance or care . . . and finally, "Since the day I met her, I've wanted her. God! How I've wanted her. And do you know what she did? She had the audacity to come home with Rick. She was in my home with him! I asked her to come home with me. She's the only girl in my entire life I've ever invited home. What does she do? The bitch comes home with Rick!

"While she was sleeping in our guest room. I walked in. I stood over the bed and watched her. Down deep in my gut I ached for Laura. I wanted to lie next to her—make love to her—force her if I had to. But I knew she did not want me. I was so angry I could have strangled her while she slept. How dare she come home with him and flaunt it in front of me!"

"Then this last time . . . everything was so good between us. I even met her folks over Christmas vacation. It was great. I thought I was in heaven. She seemed happy too. I thought she might even start to care for me. It was the best time of my life. We were always together. I knew with a little more effort we'd wind up in bed. But that didn't seem so important anymore. When I was with Laura . . . I didn't really think about sex. I can't explain it. All I know is that I wanted her . . . I craved her . . . but I was happy just being with her." I hesitated before continuing. "And do you know what? She did not give a shit. She didn't give a damn the first time . . . and she didn't give a damn this time either. When she found out I was engaged to Cindy, Laura didn't even bat an eyelash. She couldn't have cared less. I don't mean a thing to her . . . nothing! She made a fool out of me! Twice!"

"I hate her! I hate her! I'd kill her if I had the chance. She's a callous, self-righteous bitch, and I hate her more than I thought possible to hate anyone." The moment the words were expelled, I felt the tension begin to drain from my body. I heard the peaceful humming sound Jill made as she ran her hands repeatedly over my head. It was soothing.

"I wish I could be this Laura that you've been talking about." Jill's voice had a melancholy quality to it. "I wish I could trade places with her."

I lifted my head from her lap and stared into Jill's sparkling green eyes. There were tiny tears forming in them. "Why would you want to be Laura? Why in God's name would anyone want to be her?"

"Because Laura has what I've always wanted. She has your heart. Brad, you're in love with her, and you don't even know it."

I stood up. "You're crazy, Jill." I began to pace. "I don't love Laura Davis! I hate her! You're confused. I must not have made myself clear . . . you've misconstrued my words."

Jill's voice was very patient and soft as she continued to speak. "You're wrong, Brad. You better think about your emotions a little more. There's a very fine line between love and hate. You only think you hate Laura because it shelters you from your fear that she won't love you in return." Jill glanced away as she quietly dabbed at her eyes and sniffled several times. "I don't know why I should talk to you like this. I would rather think that you actually did hate her. It would be more comforting to me and probably to Cindy in the long run, but you have to face the fact, Brad. There's someone in this world who can hurt you as badly as you've hurt Cindy and me and countless other unfortunate women. It's about time you got a dose of your own medicine. In a way, I'm kind of glad I'm around to see it."

Quietly, I watched Jill and absorbed her comments before I spoke again. "Since you think you're so clever in your evaluation, just what the hell do you think I should do about it?"

"Now, there's the $64,000 question. You've certainly come to the right person if you want to ask about how to get over someone you're in love with."

"I told you, Jill, I'm not in love with her."

"Call it what you will. It makes no difference to me." She laughed slightly and tried to make a joke out of her sarcasm. "The way I see it . . . you have two choices. You can go about your business in hopes that the feeling will go away—but take my word for it—that doesn't work." Jill stared straight into my eyes and took another sip of her bourbon, then placed the glass on the table. "Your other option is to keep after her . . . keep pursuing her and try to make her love you in return. I'm a real pro in that category. And take it from me . . . the odds of that working aren't so hot either. Unfortunately, that particular tactic can be even more painful than the first." Jill drained her drink and left the room.

I walked to the window and stared out into the darkness below. Was there any truth in Jill's words? Did I really hate Laura as much as I proclaimed, or was I simply hiding behind a facade that protected me from hurt? When had I become drawn to Laura? Was it the first time I saw her through my camera lens? Was it the first time she smiled when I handed her those wildflowers? Or perhaps it was the first time I heard her laugh? Or was it that first kiss in the dorm lobby? Or maybe it was when I saw her cheek blush crimson as I touched it?

Or was it the first time she rejected me? Was I drawn to her simply because I couldn't have her, or did I want her even before she walked away?

No! Jill was insane! I didn't love Laura Davis! I didn't love anyone. I was just driven to Laura because I had never been denied a woman I wanted. That had to be it! Of course, that was the answer. Or was it?

The reason was not important. The fact of the matter was, I wanted Laura and I would never be free of her until I finally conquered her emotionally or physically, thus pushing her completely out of my mind. It had been over two and half years. I knew that blocking her image from my thoughts was virtually impossible. Therefore, I would have to win her sexually if I wanted to be rid of her haunting memories. That was the only option available to me.

Jill re-entered the room and chose a seat opposite the one we had been sharing. I returned to my chair and relaxed for the first time since I'd come into her apartment. I felt slightly the fool for falling apart, but the effects were comforting after the fact. "Thank you, Jill. I really appreciate . . . "

"No problem. Glad I could help," Jill interrupted. "I hope that you will come to me in the future if you should need to talk again. I think perhaps we can be good drinking buddies if nothing else." She lifted her glass for a toast, and the corners of her mouth turned upward in a smile. "Here's to a new kind of friendship. Whatcha say?"

"Sounds good to me, Jill. I rather like the idea."

5

A few evenings later, I came home from work only to find our house in an uproar. The moment I opened the door I heard screaming from both sexes. I knew Rick wasn't home because his car was not in the driveway; but my mother's was. I hung up my jacket in the hall closet. Before I closed the door, I picked my father's bellowing tones out of the conversation in the library. My mother's voice followed. My parents were at it again. Jesus!

Didn't they even take a break for Easter? The library door was ajar, which allowed each syllable to ring clearly in the hallway. I hadn't intended to eavesdrop, but the first sentence I heard in its entirety peaked my curiosity. I stood completely still; my feet were planted firmly on the floor outside the door.

"I don't care if she is pregnant . . . I will not stand by and let her ruin her life." My mother's shrill voice echoed in the hall.

"Caroline," my father interrupted. "What if she wants to marry him?"

"It doesn't matter. She's not eighteen years old. She may be legal age in a court of law to have sex, but she isn't legal age in this state to get married without parental permission."

Who the hell were they talking about? It couldn't be Rosaline! Not my kid sister! Jesus Christ! Rosaline wouldn't go and get herself knocked up. Not Ro! My God! She was just a kid!

"I won't stand for it, Richard! I mean it! I won't let my little girl destroy her life the way I did." She lowered her voice slightly, but the words still traveled into the foyer. "Rosaline will not make my mistake. I wanted an abortion . . . but you wouldn't let me! No! Not you! You wouldn't think of such a thing. I simply *had* to marry you and do the "right thing"! But what you really wanted was a free ticket to my father's money."

"Come off it, Caroline. You know that's not true. And besides, would you rather that Rick were never born? For that matter, would you rather none of our children was ever born?"

"Richard! How can you say such a thing? You are always twisting my words. I hate it when you do that. You know I love my kids. I love them more than you ever could. You don't love them. You never have!"

"That's not true! And you damn well know it!"

I wanted to walk away. I didn't want to hear this conversation. As hard as I tried to take a step, my feet wouldn't move. God! Get me out of here! I heard glass shattering against the wall opposite where I was standing and words immediately followed.

"You seduced me with your pretty words. You conned me into sleeping with you, and what did I get for my weakness? A baby and a marriage I never wanted."

"That's not how it happened, Caroline!"

"Shut up! I'm sick of listening to you. You and your declarations! You and your stubbornness! You wouldn't let me go! You wouldn't let me have my own life. No! You had me cornered, and you knew it. You saw the easy way to get rich—old family money. And you—so smug—thought you could walk right in and take it. How I hated you, Richard! I hated you for stealing the best years of my life. I wanted so much more than you could ever offer me. I had a boyfriend who was twice what you are. My father approved of him. Everything would have worked out perfectly. But he wouldn't touch me with a ten-foot pole after you'd ruined me."

"Caroline," my father was screaming. "I never wanted your father's money. After all these years, you must have figured that out by now!"

"Don't you try and talk around me anymore. I'm through with your flowery speeches! Rosaline will *not* make my mistake. I know what it's like to have a child when I was little more than a child myself! And I still remember what it was like to live with a man when there is no love. I wouldn't wish that hell on anyone . . . least of all my own child."

"An abortion isn't that easy to get. You can't just waltz her into your doctor's office."

"I know a place where it can be taken care of—a safe place—but it's going to cost a lot. I want the money, Richard, and I want it now . . . or it will be on your head if she goes to some butcher for a cheaper price."

"I will not be party to this, Caroline!" My father's voice was stern. "I can't believe that you are encouraging our daughter to do this. This is unbelievable!"

"I will not listen to you! You are through running my life!"

"Damnation, Caroline! This isn't about you and me! This isn't about what we've been through. This is about our daughter! For God sake . . . this is about our grandchild!"

Suddenly, my mother was silent. In fact, the entire house was deathly quiet. I was afraid to move. I feared that if I made an attempt to escape, it would sound like a magnified roar rebounding off the walls. The last thing I wanted was for my parents to know that I had witnessed their horrifying conversation. I stood completely still for more than a minute before I heard faint whimpering noises coming from the library. At first, I was not sure what it was. Then I recognized the sound. It was my mother's muffled sobs.

"This is what we are going to do, Caroline." My father's voice was calm and surprisingly gentle. "I've heard of a place in Illinois. It's a home for girls who are in trouble like Rosaline. When she starts showing—hopefully, it will be after she finishes this school year—Rosaline can go there and stay until the baby's born. They even handle the adoption. It's all very safe and very private." My father paused. "You and I will go check this place out. If we don't like it, we will find another place."

"Oh, my God, Richard! How did this happen?" My mother was crying as she spoke.

It sounded as if my father was holding her—comforting her—but I knew that couldn't be true. My father never comforted anyone. I thought I was going to explode from tension. I had to get out of here. As my parents became engrossed in a soft-spoken conversation, I saw my chance to flee. I took careful, quiet steps to the stairs and then flew up them three at a time. My mind was in chaos. Partial sentences, whispered threats, masked hostilities. Everything was beginning to fall into place. My father! The son of a bitch! How I hated him. No wonder my mother left. I had always known that he was the culprit, and my mother was the victim. My father had taken her innocence and exploited her youth to his own advantage. Now I knew where he had gotten the money to start his business. Poor Mom! How she must have suffered.

Rick! I wondered if my brother knew the truth? Probably not! If he did, I would have known too. No! Rick didn't know. I doubted if Rosaline knew either. I was the only one who truly understood. All these years, Mom and Dad had kept their secret only to have it disclosed when the sins of the parents visited the child. What a nightmare this must be for my mother.

Rosaline! Poor little Ro! I wondered where she was. I'd like to get my hands on the bastard who knocked her up. I'd beat the living shit out of him. That son of a bitch ought to be castrated. I stopped in my tracks. Suddenly, I realized I was guilty of the same transgression. How many times had I coaxed a girl into sex with white lies and encouraged her to spread her legs for only a moment of pleasure? Most of the girls had been more than will-ing—some even begged for the act—but a few had been hard to break—pleading virginity or guilt or fear. Had I ceased my maneuvers because of a simple negative response? No! I had continued to chase them thinking the harder they fell the sweeter the meat. My God! I was no better than my old man. He probably chased after my mother, refused to take "no" for an answer, and pursued her until she finally gave in. Oh, my God! I was the epitome of my father.

Cindy! If Cindy had been fortunate enough to have a brother, that brother would probably think the same thoughts I was having now about Rosaline. And with just cause! Cindy was guilty of purposely forgetting to use her diaphragm, but I was even guiltier for putting her in the position to use that tactic. I was a miserable excuse for a man. I lived my life as if it were my own private joke, only to find after all this time that the laugh was on me.

There was a timid knock at my door.

"Yeah!"

The door slowly opened. Rosaline walked in without saying a word. My sister looked so pitiful. I raced to her and swallowed her tiny body in my arms. With my right foot, I pushed the door closed and began to speak. "Ro . . . are you okay?"

"Oh, Brad!" She was sobbing. "He said he wanted to marry me. He said he loved me. We were going to run away. We were going to make a life for ourselves, but now he's changed his mind. When I told him I was pregnant, he said he couldn't be bothered with a baby. Then he said that I had never been important to him at all." Rosaline let out an agonizing wail. "He said I was nothing but a nice piece of ass. He laughed at me. He actually laughed at me, Brad. And then he told me that he never really loved me. He said I was a fool to believe backseat love talk. He told me that those are just words people use when they fuck. That's what he called it. My God! Brad, it wasn't even making love as far as he was concerned. Fucking! That's what horses and dogs do. It sounds disgusting and filthy, and now I feel dirty. Oh, Brad . . . help me."

"Who is he, Ro?" I tried to remain calm.

"What does it matter now? He won't even talk to me."

"Come on, Rosaline. What's the creep's name?"

"Paul . . . Paul Winston."

"The guy who lives on Crestfield Drive?"

"Yeah . . . but he won't talk to me, Brad. I went over there tonight, and he wouldn't even come to the door. I want to die, Brad. I just want to die."

"No, baby . . . you're not going to die. You're going to be just fine. Everything will be all right. You'll see. Pretty soon this will all be nothing more than a bad dream, and you'll be able to put it aside. Don't you worry, Ro, I'll take care of it. I'll teach that son of a bitch not to mess around with kids like you. You don't need him, Ro. You don't need anyone like him."

I guided my sister to her room and laid her gently on the bed. After smoothing her hair away from her forehead and placing a kiss on her cheek, I left the house in search of Paul Winston.

I was filled with rage. I knew my only outlet was to confront the guy. The S.O.B. had it coming, and damn it, I was going to give it to him. I banged loudly on the door of the Winston home. His mother answered my knock. She was dressed in a stained terry cloth robe. Curlers surrounded her head and layers of cream covered her face. She looked like a circus clown.

"Is Paul home?" I asked in a polite way.

"Paul!" She yelled over her shoulder. "Paul . . . there's a friend here to see you." Several seconds passed as Mrs. Winston and I exchanged courteous nods. I rubbed my thumb against my index finger creating a rather loud strumming sound as I glanced passed the woman into her home. The TV was tuned to *All in the Family* and a radio blasted with the sounds of Led

Zeppelin's "Whole Lot of Love" coming from the second floor. The racket was deafening. I continued rubbing my thumb across my fingers as I smiled pleasantly at Mrs. Winston.

Feet hit the stairs on the upper level. Paul Winston came parading down the steps. He recognized me the instant he entered the room. At first, I saw a glint of fear in his eyes. As he took a pace backward, he tried to ease his way up the stairs, but then he squared his shoulders and stepped right up to me. "Well, if it ain't Mr. Bigshot himself." He grinned and saluted with two fingers in an irritating manner. He had an arrogant attitude, which made me want to punch him right there in his mother's house.

I couldn't see what my kid sister saw in the guy. He wasn't even good looking. He had long greasy black hair that was pulled back in a ponytail. A patch of zits covered the left side of his face. His upper lip was too thin, and his smile exposed crooked teeth. He had at least three days' growth covering his jaw. He was disgusting.

I stared into his eyes and dared him to speak. I wanted a reason to hit him. Glancing in his mother's direction, I finally spoke, "Mrs. Winston, ma'am, . . . I suggest . . . " My voice was deep and threatening, "I suggest that you don't bother calling the cops if you know what's good for your son. He's going to get what's coming to him, and he damn well knows it."

"Think you're a tough guy, don't ya?"

"What's this boy talking about, Paul?"

"Shut up, Ma. Shut up . . . I can handle this."

I grabbed him by his collar and pitched him out the front door. He went flying down the porch steps and landed butt first on the ground.

"Get up, punk! Get up and take it like a man."

"Hey, listen, buddy . . . your sister was asking for it. She's no lily-white snow queen, you know. She loved every minute. Ro . . . "

"I never want to hear her name from your filthy lips again." I was standing over him. My feet were planted on each side of his body. I waited for him to make his move.

Slowly, Paul Winston lifted himself off the ground. Before I knew what happened he charged at me. Using his head as his weapon, he drilled it firmly into my gut. The shock staggered me momentarily, but I balanced myself in time to hurl my own punches. He hit me squarely in the ribs three times before connecting one under my jaw. But after his initial combination, it was my fists that became the aggressor and jammed into his face, his stomach, and his chest. Venting my own inner rage, I vigorously threw each jab. Every time I hit him, I saw a collage of Winston, my father, and me. I straddled him as each punch connected and met its target. I could no longer feel my hands as they beat into his flesh.

Finally, I heard his screams echoing in my ears and begging for mercy. My fist was raised—ready for the next hit—when my eyes started focusing in on my subject. The kid was covered with blood, and tears were streaming down his face. Winston's mother was hovering over both of us yelling at me and begging me to stop. I watched him a moment before gingerly lifting myself off his torso. I brushed my hands on the side of my pants as I stared at him.

"You little shit! You're nothing but a pansy."

His mother cradled him in her arms using her robe to wipe away the blood. Winston pushed her hands aside. "Get away from me. I'm not your baby. I can take care of myself."

"I see just how well you can take care of yourself. Let me help you, son. Let's go into the house, and I'll wash you up."

I turned and walked away.

6

Finally, I was back on campus. It had been a hell of a vacation: first Jill, then the enlightening news about my folks, and then Rosaline. At least Ro seemed better when I left. She'd made her decision, and she seemed comfortable with it. Thankfully, it was early enough in her pregnancy to finish the school year before she had to leave. Needless to say, she was still devastated that Paul Winston was not interested in a life with her, but Rosaline claimed that she would recover with time. She also believed that putting the child up for adoption was a choice she could live with. I knew she was try-ing to put on a brave front. My sister was amazing! I was immensely impressed by her fortitude.

Regarding the subject of my parents, I did not confront either one of them about my new-found knowledge. I decided it was their secret—bet-ter left undisclosed and buried in their minds. They had kept it for all these years. Who was I to destroy Rick and Rosaline's security by blurting out the truth? At least now I knew the whole story. It only gave me more rea-son to hate my father, but at least I could understand my mother more. She probably married her second husband in order to have a warm secure rela-tionship that she had been denied in her first marriage. My mother had just wanted love, only to find that she had to settle for contentment with John Harrod.

Jill was the only pleasant aspect of the entire week's break. I liked the relationship we were developing. Instead of sex, we shared communication. It was nice to have her for a friend. The only thing that was annoying was Jill's suggestion that I face my feelings for Laura Davis and follow through on them.

On my second day back from break, I saw Laura walking with Jennifer Carson. Jennifer! Now there was a bitch I could live without! That girl was a tease in skintight pants; in addition, she had a personality that rivaled the devil. What a snob! She flaunted her fancy airs as she turned her nose up to everyone she considered lower than herself! I couldn't imagine why Laura befriended her.

I had an extremely low opinion of Jennifer Carson, but I was not blinded to the fact that Jennifer couldn't stand the sight of me either. No big shakes in my book, but it did make matters more difficult when it came to reaching Laura. Jennifer had too much influence over Laura. That Carson bitch was more like a prison guard than a roommate; therefore, I knew in order to get to Laura, I had to get past Jennifer. Jennifer hadn't helped me when Laura and I were dating. I knew, sure as shit, she would not help me now.

Our paths crossed. "Good morning, Laura . . . Jennifer. Nice day we're having." I tried to sound as polite as possible. My eyes roamed over Laura's body. Her light blue blouse was tucked neatly into the coordinating pair of pants. Her hair hung loosely around her shoulders; it blew slightly in the breeze. She had an impassive smile plastered on her lips and a death grip on her books.

Both Jennifer and Laura nodded simultaneously. "Hello." They proceeded to pass me without another comment.

I couldn't help myself. Before I realized what I had done, my body spun around to face their backs. "Laura, wait." I saw her stop in her tracks. Simultaneously, Jennifer grabbed Laura's arm and coaxed her forward. "Laura." I spoke again. I could see Jennifer whispering into Laura's ear, but I didn't hear the words. I held my breath and waited to see if they would ignore my request or answer me.

Slowly, Laura turned. Our eyes met. Her expression was unreadable. "Yes, Brad."

I was not sure what to say. I only knew that I needed to talk to Laura, and she was making my attempt so difficult. I took three steps in her direction. There was only a foot or two between us. I searched her face for a sign—any sign—to show that I was having some kind of effect on her, but I read nothing in her expression. Cold! She was so damn cold. I had subconsciously started referring to her as the ice princess. As I looked upon her now, I knew why. I saw only ice in her eyes and beauty on her face. I was certain that the nickname ran parallel to her heart. Before I contemplated my thoughts, unplanned words came pouring out, "I need to speak with you privately."

"I can't imagine what we could possibly have to say to each other, Brad."

"Laura . . . all I'm asking for is a little time . . . just a few words."

"Don't you think Cindy might object? After all, I don't . . ."

"Why don't you leave Laura the hell alone?" Jennifer interrupted.

"Stay out of this, damn it! It's none of your business." I didn't look at

Jennifer long enough to see the expression on her face. A nervous sweat was developing all over my body.

"We have nothing to say to each other, Brad. I'm sorry, I really must be going, or I'll be late." Laura turned without another word and began to walk away. Jennifer paused for one second longer in order to flash a victorious grin. Eyes sparkling, squinting slightly, and beaming with confidence, she pivoted and followed Laura.

7

I watched Laura constantly. She was never alone. She was either with Jennifer, a date, a sorority sister, or a group of students. A week passed. I became increasingly more frustrated until one bright May afternoon, I saw her with Valerie Hunt. A fresh idea formed in my mind.

I followed quietly several paces behind them. Of all the people who knew Laura, I realized that Val was my only hope. Valerie had a heart as big and warm as the sun.

Before I had the chance to cut in on their discussion, I saw Jennifer appear out of the Mooney Building. She joined Laura and Val. The three of them spoke for a few moments. The Carson bitch and Laura took off in another direction, which left Valerie standing alone.

I took the remaining paces between us. "Val . . . got a minute?"

"Hi, Brad. Whatcha know?" She smiled warmly. Her pleasant southern drawl accentuated her greeting. She was a cute kid with strawberry blonde hair, saucer-shaped eyes, and splashes of freckles across her nose. She looked exactly like the woman I pictured with my brother. Their personalities were identical. She was shy, like Rick. Val was warm, trusting, and friendly—like Rick. Valerie Hunt was good for my brother. I definitely approved. We discussed the weather, Rick's good health, and Elon's baseball victory against High Point before I broached the subject uppermost in my mind. I had to be careful how I worded my idea for fear that she'd see right through me.

"I have a friend coming up this weekend. I need to find him a date. Do you think one of your friends would accept a blind date? He's a nice guy."

"Well, Brad, most of the girls I know have steadies here at Elon. But Jennifer's boyfriend is at Chapel Hill; maybe he won't be coming by this weekend. No, on second thought, he is coming this weekend. Lori Davis is the only girl I know who doesn't have a regular guy, but I doubt, under the circumstances, that you'd want me to ask her."

"Well, to be honest with you, Val . . . I'm kind of desperate. Being such short notice I can't find anyone. Could you ask Laura for me? But do us all a favor and don't say you're asking for me, okay? She'd never go if she thought she was doing me a favor." I chuckled as if it didn't make one bit of difference to me.

"I'll ask her. I'm already sure she's not doing anything Saturday night because she just told me five minutes ago."

We said our good-byes. I left stifling a grin. My little scheme worked. Now all I had to do was call around and find an old buddy who would be willing to come for the weekend.

8

Doug came to Elon. He had needed several encouraging words and a few dollars for a round-trip ticket, but he had shown up. I was patting myself on the back for my ingenious idea. I filled him in on the plan. The scheme was for Doug to take Laura out—give her a couple of drinks and tell her there was a party at the Holiday Inn. I knew Laura would be furious when she discovered the trap, but I had to be alone with her. I was counting on Doug to give her just enough booze to relax her without making Laura pass out on me. I warned him that Laura wasn't a drinker; therefore, two should be all that was necessary. Loose! I wanted her loose—not falling-down drunk. I gave Doug twenty bucks to cover his expenses and stated very firmly that he was to bring her by the room at 10:30. I told him not to let me down.

I paced the motel room like a caged tiger as I repeatedly looked at my watch. The hands were rapidly approaching midnight. A tiny fear was growing in the back of my mind that Doug might have liked Laura on first impression, and he was standing me up. Damn it! I told Doug 10:30! I insisted on the time because I knew Laura had to be back in the dorm by 1:30. I figured three hours would be enough. Now, I only had an hour and a half! If he showed up at all!

I went over to the table and poured myself another Jack Daniels. My nerves were frazzled, and the liquor wasn't helping. I looked at the bottle and noticed that I'd already consumed a fourth of it. Jesus! I couldn't drink anymore. I had to keep my mind straight. If I were drunk, I'd blow the plan. I walked to the bed and turned down the sheets. No! That was too obvious. I put the blue-green bedspread back in place and smoothed the material. Where the hell was Doug? I looked at my watch again. Damn it! If he stood me up, I'd make him pay.

I heard a faint knock at the door. My heart leaped to my throat, and I nearly choked on my breath. Strategically, I positioned my body behind the door so that Laura wouldn't see me when she entered. Silently, I opened it.

"Are you sure there's a party here, Doug? I don't see anyone." Laura sounded giddy. I detected a faint slur in her voice. Doug had done his job properly. I smiled.

"Lori, I had a good time with you tonight. I really did. I hope you're not going to hate me too much, but I'm going to leave you here. I have to go."

"What are you talking about, Doug? What's going on?"

I stepped out from behind the door. Doug had already vanished. Laura saw me instantly. Her eyes opened so wide, I couldn't imagine what was keeping them in their sockets.

"Brad!" Her angry voice hung in the air like thick morning mist. She was furious.

I tried to think of something to say but no words came. Reaching for her arm, I pulled her away from the door and shut it. Laura kept staring at me with a mixture of confusion and anger on her face; she was speechless.

"Can I get you a drink?" I asked as I walked over to the bottle on the table and poured an ounce in a plastic glass. I was nervous.

"I think I've had enough, thank you." Laura spoke through clenched teeth.

"Enough to drink?"

"Enough to drink and enough of this evening." Her voice was deep and hostile. Laura began to take the steps to the door. I raced passed her and threw myself against it before she could grab on to the knob. My heart was pounding—jabbing at my ribs.

"Let me out of here, Brad! I don't know what this is all about, but I won't stay here."

There was fire in her eyes. I knew if I didn't think fast, Laura would disappear into the night. "Laura! Laura, we have to talk."

"How many times do I have to tell you, Brad? We have nothing to say to each other."

"Then just listen."

She refused to hear what I had to say; instead, she beat the door with her fists and demanded that I move aside. "Let me out!" she screamed so loudly I was certain the entire motel would come to her rescue.

I grabbed her with both hands and spun her around to face me. Her head was reeling as she spoke abusive comments that went deaf against my ears. I pulled her to my body and trapped her with my embrace. At first, she fought me with more strength than I imagined any woman could possess. Her feet kicked my ankles, and her hands tore at my chest. She rotated her head as she tried to avoid my lips, but I firmly gripped the back of her neck and guided her mouth to mine.

Gradually, she stopped fighting me. I pressed her body against the door and molded myself to her. Her breasts were heaving against me; I could feel her heart pounding erratically against my chest. I could smell her hair and her perfume; the heavenly scents were intoxicating. As she began to express her desire, I felt wonderfully dizzy. At first, she returned my embrace with tepid responses, then with a fever that only served to increase my own passion. She kissed me with ardent lips and encircled me with her arms. Laura! Laura! Laura! Was I only thinking her name, or was I saying it? I couldn't believe it. This was surely a miracle. Laura in my arms. This was what I'd planned . . . what I'd wanted . . . what I'd dreamed.

Gently this time, I lifted her chin and placed my lips over hers. She no longer fought me. Instead, she returned warm, slightly parted lips. Her tongue danced with mine. I wallowed in the texture of her mouth and savored every delicious moment. I rested my forehead against hers, and the tips of our noses touched.

"Laura . . . I love the way you kiss." Had I really vocalized those words?

She was silent for a moment before answering, "You ought to . . . you taught me how." Her voice was not pleasant, and her words were spoken with twinges of sarcasm.

I cupped her chin in both my hands and placed a soft kiss upon her lips. Laura! Why was she looking so pathetically sad and wearing such a defeated expression? Why couldn't she be as happy as I was? She looked more like a trapped lioness in a city zoo than a potential lover. Laura! I want you! Don't you know that? Don't you realize the yearning I have for you? Why are you tormenting me with your unfeeling eyes? I tried to speak, but no words formed.

I placed my mouth over hers again knowing that closing my eyes and feeling her lips were better than staring into her blank cold expression. As our bodies meshed once again, I picked her up in my arms and slowly carried her over to the bed. She seemed weightless. I was only conscious of the slight pressure of her head leaning upon my shoulder as if she were surrendering herself to me. It was a miracle. She was no longer fighting. She had ceased struggling with words and actions. I didn't care what her motives for yielding to me were. I only knew that she was allowing me to lower her onto the bed, and my head was swirling with the image of how beautiful she looked with her hair spread out across the pillow. Laura seemed in a trance as I undid the buttons of her blouse and slipped her arms from the sleeves. Without any assistance from her, I drew her skirt from her shaking body. My God! How many times in my dreams had I envisioned this moment? I stood up silently waiting for her to speak, but she remained quiet. Her eyes closed and tension marked the lines of her face. I wanted her to reach out to me. Say something. Do something. Respond in some physical or verbal way, but she just laid there in her dainty slip. Her hands were clenched, and her body was rigid.

"Laura." I knelt beside the bed and gathered her in my arms. I had a combination of lust and animosity growing inside of me. A section of my passion wanted to mount her and drive us both to exploding peaks. Yet another part of me wanted to wrap my fingers around that pretty little neck of hers and strangle the breath from her body. I wanted to destroy her for making me feel so dejected and worthless.

Still kneeling, I ran my hands over the smooth silk of her remaining garment. With great tenderness, I touched her firm round breasts and felt the automatic response of the nipples growing taut even through the fabric that sheltered them. Her eyes opened. For one moment, I read fear in her expression. I didn't want her to be frightened. I didn't want her to simply lay there as if resigning herself to what she believed to be her fate. I craved her. When I was thirsty, I drank; when I was hungry, I ate; when I was tired, I slept. Laura represented a nourishment equal to any of those mandatory basic elements of survival. But I wanted more than a sexual release. I didn't want her limp body. I didn't want her to be afraid of me. I wanted a response from her that was equal to my own obsession.

"Laura, I'm not going to hurt you. I would never hurt you."

She remained silent. Why didn't she speak to me? Why was she torturing me with her silence? I continued toying with her smooth soft skin as my fingers roamed down to her waist and up the inside of her thighs. I felt myself growing harder with each ounce of flesh I stroked. I heard a quiet moan come from deep inside her throat. Or was it my own body projecting its mounting desire? No! It was hers! There was the sound again—a guttural, deep moan. Hearing it augmented my passion. Silently, I laid beside her. In one quick movement, I rested myself on top of her and slipped my arms around her shivering body. Together we rolled in a complete circle until I was on top of her again. I pressed my mouth harshly against her lips demanding a reaction . . . searching for a sensation that was proportionate to how I felt. Finally, after what seemed like endless attempts, I felt the steady movement of her hips pressing against mine. No matter how mechanical it was—whether it was the liquor or the natural instinct—Laura was responding. I traced gentle soft kisses all over her face: her cheeks, her nose, her ears, the hard line of her jaw, the delicate lashes of her eyes. I delighted in every part of her. My hands traveled over her skin. They were everywhere . . . touching every part of her that wasn't hidden by silk or stockings. My God! I wanted her! I wanted to strip the remainder of her clothing and thrust myself into Laura as deeply as I could—ejecting all my bottled lust—punishing her for taking my sanity, for haunting my dreams, and for destroying my self-esteem. I wanted her to pay for all those restless nights when I couldn't sleep, all her aloof rejections of my pursuit, and all the maddening moments that I'd had since the day I'd met her.

Suddenly, without warning, Laura began to tear at my clothing. She jerked the shirt from my back and ripped it as she pulled it over my head. She was muttering something. I couldn't understand the words. I was not concentrating on her voice, only her body. Somehow the clothes that protected her nudity were gone. She was under me with nothing but white gleaming skin for my hands to touch. Had I disrobed her or had she? Every inch of her was on fire, and I gladly placed my fingers on her flames. It was a torture that had no pain—only ecstasy. I feared that I was crushing her with my weight, but she didn't seem to mind as she repeatedly cried out my name. Music! It sounded like music . . . and the tempo went right along with the rhythm of our bodies as we clung to each other with the mutual feverish passion that I craved.

I had no idea when or how it happened, but I suddenly realized I was only a fraction of an inch from entering her warm juicy nest. One slight push and I'd be inside her—stealing the magic of the moment. Laura was ready for me. I could feel the hot fluid flowing from between her thighs—teasing me with its heat. One final push! That was all I needed. One final thrust and I'd be free of Laura Davis. There would no longer be a need to chase after her in order to win her favors. There would be no more constant, provoking thoughts plaguing me and disrupting my life. I would be free! I would be free of her at last!

I saw babies . . . I saw Cindy . . . I saw Rosaline . . . I saw my mother. Images kept flashing distortedly across my mind. They all blended together and formed the shape of Laura smiling trustingly into my eyes. Don't think of them! Don't think of anything! Think of now! I had to escape from the prison that Laura had built around me. I had to think of freedom. Immediately, a picture of Paul Winston lying bloody and battered on the ground transformed itself into a reflection of my father. He was laughing and pointing a finger at me. Don't think about them! Just push! Just one little thrust. Push!

I went limp.

My entire body turned traitor on me. I collapsed into a pool of my own sweat. I was so angry . . . with Laura . . . with myself. I felt Laura's tiny frame pulsating beneath me as she struggled to regain her breath. I was exhausted—humiliated—furious. Nothing like this had ever happened before. Never in my life had I been impotent—utterly and completely unable to perform.

Minutes passed before Laura shoved me from her body. Taking the bedspread, she wrapped herself in it—draping the fabric around her—creating a cotton wall concealing everything but her head. She looked so small, so frightened, and so unbelievably angry. She walked over to the phone and dialed the motel operator. After giving the campus number and the extension, she paused a few seconds before beginning to speak. "Is Jennifer Carson in?" Her back was to me. I couldn't see her face. What was she thinking?

Silence. The room was filled with a pregnant silence that seemed to rebound off the walls. "Jennifer . . . Laura." Another pause. "I'm fine. No! Nothing's wrong. Can you do me a favor? Can you come and pick me up at the Holiday Inn?" She paused. "No. Really. I'm fine." Silence again. Laura shifted her weight as she listened to the voice on the other end of the wire. "I'll be in the lobby. Thanks."

Slowly, Laura hung up the phone. Without turning around, she addressed me in a frosty, deep voice. "Well, Brad, you finally won. You finally managed to prove yourself. Didn't you?"

I had no idea what Laura was talking about. I hadn't done anything. I had wanted to. I had wanted to screw her eyeballs out . . . but I hadn't. What did she mean? I had won? I hadn't won. She was the victor! Laura was always the victor! My damned body had betrayed me, and she had escaped. I thought I would surely go insane if she didn't turn and face me. I couldn't stand looking at her back for another moment. I stood up, put on my boxers, and walked silently to her. "What are you talking about, Laura?" Much to my surprise, there was a genuine concern in my voice. I tenderly touched her shoulders only to see the bundle of material representing Laura spin around and stare directly into my face. I saw loathing in her eyes. A stabbing pain raced through my chest. I didn't want her hate. As gently as I could, I spoke again. "Laura, it's okay. We didn't do anything wrong. It's not like we made love."

With both of her hands, she shoved me. "Don't touch me!"

I was stunned by her actions. "Oh, for Christ's sake, Laura! What are you so upset about?" I hadn't meant for my statement to sound so callous, but the words had just slipped out.

Her jaw grew tight, and her eyes twitched involuntarily. She yanked up the bedspread and ran passed me; yards of material flowed behind her. She tripped several times over her too lengthy hemline.

"Damn it, Laura," I screamed after her. "Don't get so worked up. Your precious virginity is still intact!" I lashed out at her with abusive words. I wanted to cause her a pain equal to mine. I yearned to break those puritanical pillars down and humiliate her as she had done to me. Words came screaming out of my throat as I played my only trump card. "You wanted me, Laura Davis. You can't lie about that fact. I had you begging for it." I was yelling at the top of my lungs—pounding her with words as I watched her pick up her clothes and race into the bathroom. She slammed the door behind her. I was furious. "You wanted to get laid . . . you wanted it!" I beat on the door with both fists. "No amount of haughty innocence is going to cover that up, Laura. Don't play the weeping virgin with me. Admit it!" Why was I saying all these malicious things? Why the hell was I being so vindictive? What I actually wanted to do was beat the door down to her privacy and surround her with my arms. Laura! Laura! "Laura! Come out here!" I tried to regain some semblance of control. "You can't hide in there forever."

The door to the bathroom opened, and she stood basking in the light from the room. I was only a few feet away from her, which enabled me to see the slight trembling of her hands. She was completely dressed: skirt, blouse, shoes, stockings, freshly brushed hair, touched up makeup. Everything was in perfect order.

Her eyes glared. "I hate you, Brad Malone." She took a dozen steps to the exterior door. When she reached for the knob, she pivoted and spoke. "Don't *ever* come near me again." She lowered her voice a notch. "I feel sorry for Cindy." The door opened. Laura walked out and slammed it behind her.

I was alone. I grabbed onto the first available object—an ashtray—and hurled it against the door. It hit with such force that the glass immediately shattered into a hundred tiny pieces.

"Bitch! You goddamned bitch!"

10

Jennifer

I ATE ALL THE RIGHT FOODS, SLEPT WHENEVER I WAS TIRED, QUIT SMOK-
ing cigarettes, and never exerted myself more than I thought I should, but I
still was not feeling like I had before my illness. The doctors said it would
take time; but my God, it had been six months! How much more time was it
going to take? I was always dragging behind, walking slower than anyone
else, sitting while others stood, and sleeping when friends were out partying. I was furious with my body for acting weak when I wanted to run races,
go dancing, and stay up all night making love to Kurt.

The specialists shook their heads in confusion when I questioned them.
They told me that even though there had been irrevocable damage to my
heart, there was no reason why I shouldn't be able to live a relatively normal
life once I had recuperated. It took time. Jesus! I was so sick of that answer.
Time! That was everyone's reply. Even I was guilty of using that word. I had
put Kurt off last year by telling him it wasn't the right time to make love, the
doctors kept telling me I needed more time to heal, and Lori was forever saying it wasn't the right time to discuss this or talk about that. Time! Every
time someone didn't want to answer directly to a situation or a question,
they always said, "Give it time." It was maddening.

As far as Kurt and I were concerned, time was running short. The semester was reaching an end. Any day, he expected to get the letter telling him to report for his physical. The suspense was getting to all of us. He was climbing the walls. Kurt was so bitter about his fate that it altered his personality. He was no longer easygoing; instead, Kurt wasted countless hours wallowing in the protective crutches that booze and pot could give him. He wasn't even studying for his finals. He put up a brave front for my benefit, but I knew he was terrified. I realized that Kurt toyed with the idea of skipping out of the country if they called him. I also knew I'd go with him if he asked. I didn't want to lose Kurt. I'd go anywhere with him—even Canada. Anywhere! I had nothing to lose and everything to gain.

I continued to pack those clothes that had not already been shipped home. Home! In two days I'd be in Georgetown. There were times when I choked on the idea of returning to that house on Fox Hall Road. I envisioned the rich Havana cigar smoke hanging in the air, the crystal goblets accompanying the Irish linen, the Bavarian china, the $400 a place setting silver, and the stuffy rigid guests my parents always invited to surround their table. I could see the Lincoln Continental in the driveway, the gigantic grandfather clock in the foyer that bonged every hour, the Picasso originals that hung in my father's library, and the baby grand piano that nobody played. Masked over all those images, I could see the faces of my parents: my father—stern and overbearing—just waiting for me to make a wrong move and my mother—meek and compliant—wearing a heavy coat of makeup to disguise the latest bruise. No! That was not my home! That was a house where two strangers lived—where a general and his wife had their own private battles, and I was only a fraction of the rope with which they played tug of war. How I hated them. I despised my father for pretending to be the pillar of his community and the genius of the Pentagon while he also played the egotistical, opinionated dictator in his own home. He was cruel, domineering, unmerciful, and violent—nothing better than a common wife beater—hiding from his own sickness. And I loathed my mother, too. She was weak and forgiving. I hated her for standing by her husband's side and playing his barbaric game. I didn't want to go home to that—to them.

Life was so beautiful in North Carolina with Lori and Kurt. The two of them filled a void in my life, and I never wanted to go back home.

Kurt! What bliss the two of us created. Kurt was perfect for me—the ideal lover—so attuned to my desires that he spent hours teasing my most stimulated areas, bringing me continuously through orgasm after orgasm, never tiring of granting me pleasure. Sex was not the only beautiful part of our relationship; we had trust, friendship, and love. The doctors and all their wonder drugs could not have made me feel better than Kurt did each time we were together. I felt as if I lived for him.

Kurt's impending draft was not the only thought on my mind. There was something very disturbing about Lori. She seemed so quiet, and she refused to admit or discuss what was bothering her. A rift had developed between us. Ever since that day I had verbally attacked Lori regarding her hair, she had been aloof. But it wasn't our fight that put the wedge between us. There was more to it. I was certain it had something to do with Brad Malone. They had stopped dating; a few days later, Brad had casually announced his engagement to Cindy Wilder. Needless to say, Lori was completely crushed. Even though I tried to be sympathetic, I couldn't resist saying, "I'm glad he's out of your life;" from that moment on, Lori clammed up and refused to comment on the subject any further. I felt awful about my caustic statement and tried numerous times to make it up to her, but Lori remained distant.

I was certain that given enough time (there was that word again), Lori and I would be able to reestablish our friendship. As for Brad Malone . . . let him marry Cindy Wilder. If Cindy was stupid enough to love Brad and believe in him, then perhaps she deserved his lies.

I attempted to close one of the two remaining suitcases. Damn! It wouldn't shut. I put it on the floor, sat on top of it, and strained to fasten the handles. Finally, after three bounces, I managed to latch it. One down! One to go!

Leaving was not a pleasant thought. I glanced around the room Lori and I shared. The two of us had stripped the walls of our posters and pictures rolling them up and laughing about how nice it would be to hang them up again next year. (It had been the first time in weeks I could remember hearing Lori laugh.) We had taken down the curtains, folded the bedspreads, and rolled up the rug. The room looked barren—so empty. I thought about all the many conversations Lori and I shared . . . all the secrets . . . the times we laughed . . . the times we cried. I loved this room. I dreaded the thought of spending the entire summer away from it—away from Lori. Of course, Mt. Vernon and Georgetown were not worlds apart, but somehow I knew that the time element wasn't what kept us from seeing each other during vacations and holidays. It was more than that, and now it was compounded by the fact that Lori and I had drifted apart.

I started to close the last remaining suitcase and then changed my mind. It was better to leave it open for my few toilet articles and those clothes I would use in the next couple of days. I sat on the bed and pondered what I'd do with the rest of the afternoon. I wasn't tired. I'd just taken a nap. And I knew Lori was in an exam, which would take at least another hour. I felt restless.

As the idea popped into my mind, I stood up and slapped my hands together. I'd go to Chapel Hill and surprise Kurt with an unexpected visit. Kurt loved surprises. My spirits soared. His campus was less than an hour's drive. If I hurried, I'd be there in no time at all.

I took the top down on my convertible TR6 and thanked the Almighty for such pleasant weather. As I drove on Interstate 85, I thought about how wonderful it was going to be to lounge around in Kurt's arms and make love for the rest of the afternoon. I watched the scenery fly by as I pressed the accelerator past seventy-five. Five miles over the speed limit wasn't too bad. The fresh spring breeze felt cool on my face. I sniffed the faint fragrance of honeysuckle mingled in the air. I was on top of the world.

I slowed down for the exit, drove peacefully through the town, and eventually came to my destination. After pulling my car into Kurt's dorm parking lot, I collected my purse and raced up the stairs to his room. I was so thankful that UNC was not as old-fashioned as Elon. His campus accepted new ways, allowed coed dorms, and open hour visitation. Elon's idea of a coed dorm was when the two sections met by an adjoining lobby but neither of the sexes was permitted to enter into the other's domain. That was no fun. The people who wrote the rules for Elon must be over a hundred years old. I bet none of them ever heard of the changing times. It was ridiculous to lock women up like caged animals at a certain hour if they didn't have parental permission to sign out for overnights. It was a good thing I had my mother's signature down pat or I'd have never been able to spend so many weekends with Kurt. I knocked on Kurt's door. There was no answer. I turned the knob and peeked inside. Nobody home. I thought of leaving a message on his door but decided against it. If I couldn't find him at his favorite hangouts, I'd return and wait for him.

Humming happily, I bounced down the steps. Before I reached the bottom, I stopped and leaned against the railing for a moment. I shouldn't be moving so rapidly. It was taking the wind right out of me. I inhaled a couple deep breaths to steady my heartbeat and then started to walk in the direction of the recreation center. Kurt wasn't there. He wasn't in the cafeteria, the lounge, or the library either. He must be taking an exam.

Feeling disappointed, I started back toward his dorm. As I turned the corner of the building adjacent to his, I stopped abruptly. Sitting on a bench under a gigantic oak tree, I saw Kurt talking with a rather attractive dark-haired girl. The two of them had their backs to me; they did not see my approach. At first, I was going to call out to Kurt but something stifled my words. I could hear fragments of their conversation, and I could not help but listen.

"Kurt," the dark-haired girl lowered her head and continued to speak. "I know it was wrong not to tell you about the baby, but I want to have it."

Baby? What the hell was that girl saying? I squinted my eyes slightly in order to focus on the situation. From the angle where I was standing, I could tell that the girl was definitely pregnant. What the hell was going on?

"Pamela," Kurt responded. "I wish you would have told me sooner."

I couldn't see Kurt's expression. I wasn't even sure if I had heard his words correctly. What was this all about?

"I didn't want an abortion," the dark-haired girl continued to speak in a soft apologetic tone. "I was afraid you'd try to talk me out of having the baby. Ever since the first day I realized I was carrying your child, I knew I wanted to keep it. I don't want anything from you, Kurt, and I especially don't want your pity. This was a decision I made on my own. You are not bound to it in any way."

"Is this why you left school?" Kurt asked as he bent closer toward her.

The girl glanced in another direction. "That was one reason, Kurt . . . but there were other reasons for leaving Chapel Hill."

Taking one step slowly backward at a time, I tried to walk away. I did not want either of them to see me; I didn't want to intrude on their private conversation. Before I was out of earshot, I overheard the girl named Pamela say to Kurt, "As you well know, my family has plenty of money, so I don't need any financial support from you. I'm only telling you about the baby because I thought you had a right to know. I realize, Kurt, that . . . "

I could no longer hear what the pregnant girl was saying. Searching for the quickest route to my car, I frantically looked around. I had to get out of here. I had to leave before my mind snapped. I did not want to become a hysterical maniac, screaming at the top of my lungs and crying like a two-year-old child. I darted to my right and raced the hundred yards to my car. I fumbled through my purse for the keys and struggled to push all thoughts of Kurt and that fat creature from my mind. My God! Kurt had gotten a girl pregnant! He betrayed me! I meant nothing to him! Nothing! Making love meant nothing to him. I wasn't special . . . I wasn't important.

I put the stick shift in reverse and spun the wheels across the parking lot. By the time I reached the road, I was already in third gear and burning rubber with every foot I drove.

A baby! There was tangible evidence of his infidelity!

I pushed the speedometer past fifty on the city streets. By the time I was on the interstate, the red dial rested on ninety. I had forgotten to tie my hair back before I'd started the car, and each strand was whipping my face. The pain felt good. I could feel it lashing at my skin; thankfully, it created a diversion from the aching that choked my heart. Did Kurt love this mysterious woman? Did he want to marry her? My God! Kurt was going to have a child! I had toyed with the idea of being Kurt's wife—of someday having his children—I had pondered the idea of sharing a lifetime with him. This was a nightmare!

I pressed down on the pedal even further, hardly aware of the fact that I passed the one hundred mark. My hair was blowing wildly. It produced a screen, which made it difficult to see. I didn't care. I didn't care about anything! Perhaps, if I were lucky, my car would go out of control, swerve off the road, and crash into a ditch or a tree.

Before I realized that time passed, I approached the Elon College exit. I let up on the gas, eased my way onto the ramp, and came to a complete halt at the light. What was I going to do? Certainly my life couldn't go on as usual! I simply couldn't allow my head to stay in the sand like an ostrich and pretend that I didn't know about Pamela and a baby.

The light turned green. A driver continuously pressed his horn; it blew irately behind me. Think! I had to think. I wanted to talk to someone. Who would listen? I instantly knew that Lori was the wrong person, but there was no one else. The only people I cared about in the entire world were Lori and Kurt.

I felt completely alone.

The light turned red. The horns continued to blare out at me and surrounded me with an audible fog that seemed to magnify with each new burst of their increased annoyance. Without looking for oncoming vehicles, I ignored the traffic signal and turned in the direction of my campus. I had to get out of here. I couldn't stay another minute. I would collect my remaining possessions, pile them in the car, and leave before anyone could ask me questions. Yes! That was my answer! That was my plan. Escape! I had to escape!

After pulling into the dorm parking lot, I leaped from the car and took short deep breaths in order to get the energy to flee from my hell. I mounted the stairs two at a time and was amazed my body worked with me for a change. Adrenaline pumped wildly through my veins and created a fortitude I'd never known before. Lori wasn't in the room. Good! It was too late for communication. It was too late for words or explanations.

I latched the opened suitcase and grabbed all the things I could with two hands. After pausing only a moment for fresh oxygen, I raced back down the steps. To hell with this place! To hell with an education! I never wanted one anyway. To hell with Kurt! And to hell with Lori! I don't need you. I hate you! I hate you both! And I hate this place too!

11

Kurt

I WAS IN TOTAL SHOCK! PAMELA WAS DEFINITELY PREGNANT, AND I WAS 98 percent certain that I was the father. It was a nightmare! No wonder she'd dropped out of school after Thanksgiving break. Oh, my God! What had I done? I watched Pam as she bent her head in shame and tried to explain her motives.

"As you well know, my family has plenty of money, so I don't need any financial support from you. I'm only telling you about the baby because I thought you had a right to know. I realize, Kurt, that you don't love me; you never did. I know you're in love with Jennifer Carson." She lowered her voice and diverted her eyes. "I'm truly glad that you and Jennifer are back together. I know it's what you've always wanted, and I'm happy for you."

I wrapped her in my arms. "Oh, Pamela! I'm so sorry. I don't know what to say. I feel awful . . . useless. You say that you don't want any help, but there must be something I can do. I'm responsible for getting you into this situation." I couldn't think of anything else to say.

"I don't want you to be sorry; like I said before, Kurt, I don't want your pity. I'm truly happy about this baby." Pam glanced down at her jutting abdomen and touched it gently with her hands. A pleasant smile spread over her lips, and her eyes sparkled warmly. "I've never been happier about anything in my life. I love this baby, Kurt. I really love it. All my life I've felt as if there was no one who loved me . . . no one I could love in return. My dad and all his millions never gave me what this baby will. My baby will get what I never had . . . a home with love and warmth and caring. My father never had time for me, but my child will have all the time I can give. All I ask of you is please, please don't be angry with me."

"Angry with you? I'm bewildered and guilty and frustrated perhaps . . . but I'm not angry. I can't believe that you're not demanding that I marry you. Aren't you afraid? Isn't your father upset about all this?"

"First of all, Kurt, I don't want a husband who doesn't love me. I've had enough of not being loved. I'd rather not have a husband at all. And no . . . I'm not afraid of being an unwed mother. I don't like that term. I wish I could find another word. It makes everything seem sordid and dirty. I don't feel that way. I feel beautiful for the first time in my life, and this baby has done that for me. I've loved it since the moment the lab confirmed my suspicions." Her voice was very soft and gentle. "As for my father . . . he didn't even find out until last month. It was the first time I've seen him in almost a year. He was ticked off. I guess I can't blame him . . . but he knows it's too late to play Monday morning quarterback with my decision. I thought he would throw me out, but he said he had enough money to ward off a scandal . . . that's what he called his grandchild . . . a scandal. Oh well! I can't expect him to love my child when he never really had the time to love me." Pamela appeared sad for the first time during the entire conversation. Her brow crinkled slightly, and her eyes misted with a thick layer of threatening tears. She laughed in a forced way as she bit her lower lip and gazed upward toward the sun. "You know what my father did when he found out? He made some telephone calls; and the next day, there were three more servants: two additional maids and a nurse. Can you imagine seven servants and me puttering around in that huge penthouse apartment? I haven't the faintest idea what they do with all their time because I certainly don't ask them to perform any chores. It's ridiculous. The place is like a walking morgue . . . silent and stiff. I never hear any voices or laughter . . . nobody talks. The place is so cold . . . so starched and dignified. Butlers in tuxedos . . . maids in little black and white uniforms . . . all of them with plastic smiles on their faces as they say 'Miss Pamela this' and 'Miss Pamela that' or 'what would you like for dinner, Miss Pamela' or 'Miss Pamela, your tea is ready.' I tried to get them to relax and be my friend . . . or just talk to me in more than an employer-employee manner . . . but they won't. I can't seem to break the ice with any of them. As for the nurse . . . she's the exact replica of the nanny I had as a child: plump, gray haired, with rosy cheeks and lonely eyes. I can tell that she is waiting for the birth of my baby so she can take over and pretend to be the mother. I won't stand for it! No nurse or nanny or governess is going to raise my child. That's what my father wants! I can feel it! He thinks that I'll get bored with being a mother, and then the nurse can take over. Then someone will take the baby away like dirty laundry goes to the cleaners. That won't happen! That will never happen! I love my baby . . . I will never, never let someone else take care of my child. My baby is going to know love."

I was amazed at the determination in Pamela's eyes. I felt as if I were seeing her for the first time. I remembered all of those many days and nights we had spent together in conversation and in bed, all those occasions Pamela had listened to me as I had rattled on about my problems, and all the countless times she had befriended me. Much to my surprise, it seemed as if today was the first time I saw her as a person. I suddenly realized that I never really knew Pamela Woods. I thought of her as only studious and dependent. She always seemed rather mousy—what an unkind word—I didn't mean to be unkind. Pam wasn't like that at all. She was strong, determined, willful, and much more independent than I ever gave her credit for. Yet with all those dynamic attributes, she still had that caring warmth surrounding her. I admired her courage.

"As far as financially . . . I have more than enough money, so you don't have to worry about that. If things were different, maybe I'd be forced to ask for your help, but they're not. I have everything I need." She looked down at her hands as if lost in thought and drifted off into an unknown realm that didn't include me. After several moments of silence, she began to speak again. "Money! It's rather ironic in a way. I never gave a damn about my father's money. I didn't want it . . . I didn't need it . . . there were times when I even hated and resented his fortune because it took him away from me, but now I realize that I can use that money to support my child." Silently, with despondent eyes, she searched my face. "Unfortunately, Kurt," Pamela lowered her eyes and erased the sad expression that was mirrored in them. "Money can't buy everything. There are some things that dollar signs just can't purchase." Pamela was quiet for a long time—lost in her private thoughts. Finally, she spoke. "I really must be going. My taxi will be here soon, and my plane leaves in thirty minutes; if I don't hurry, I'll miss it." Sniffing, she ran her fingers gently under her nose and removed the moisture that had formed beneath it. Pam stood up. "I apologize for burdening you with my condition. I just thought you deserved to know." When I started to speak, Pamela interrupted me, "Don't say anything, Kurt. It's okay. I shouldn't have told you. I realize it puts you in a very awkward situation. I didn't mean to put pressure on you . . . truly, I didn't. I just came down here on an impulse. I don't know what made me do it. I had every intention of just writing you someday and telling you the entire story but . . . " She paused a moment as if fighting back impending tears. "Excuse me . . . I've been so emotional these days. They say it's common with pregnant women. I've certainly had my share." She dabbed at her eyes with a handkerchief. Smiling, she continued. "I don't want you to feel trapped . . . I just thought . . . well . . . I just thought . . . you might want to know." She paused again, smiled, and kissed me softly on the cheek. "If you're ever in New York, please feel free to call. I'd love to see you, Kurt."

"Pamela . . . "

"I'm sorry about your draft number . . . I heard the army is practically at your doorstep. I hope it all works out for you."

"I don't know what's keeping them. I can't believe I haven't gotten the letter yet."

"Maybe you'll be lucky. Maybe, they won't draft you . . . or maybe if they do, you won't have to go to Vietnam."

I couldn't believe that Pamela was actually worried about my predicament when she had one of her own. Dear sweet Pamela. She was so unselfish. I felt so guilty.

"I really have to be going, Kurt. Good-bye." A tiny tear formed in the corner of her eye. "I wish you and Jennifer all the happiness in the world. I truly mean that." She turned to make her exit, and then faced me again. "Would it be all right if I write you when the baby's born and tell you whether it's a boy or girl?"

I placed my hands gently on her shoulders. Pamela Woods was the bravest person I'd ever known, and I was such a coward. I hated myself for not taking the responsibility I knew was mine, but I kept seeing Jennifer's face. And Jennifer was all that mattered.

"Of course, Pam . . . please write . . . if ever you need anything . . . just let me know." She closed her eyes as I brushed my lips across her forehead. Before I could add to my last sentence, Pam was gone.

I slowly walked back to my room. I was grateful Charlie wasn't there. Solitude! Thank God for peace and quiet. I lay on the bed and fingered the sheets with my hands. This was where I'd fathered a child. On one of those lost, lonely nights last fall, I had taken comfort from Pamela, penetrated her, and planted my seed. How could I have exploited Pam in such a way? I was ashamed. How could I let Pam carry the entire burden? I had given her nothing but token gestures and polite responses. Pam had told me that she did not want anything from me. But wasn't it an added slap in the face when I hadn't even offered? If I were really a man, I would never have taken her innocence and her trust; I had abused both and given nothing in return. I squeezed my eyelids and forced away the rapidly approaching tears. Pressing my lips together, I stifled the deep throaty moans that strained to be expelled. My entire body heaved with the sobs I could no longer control. To muffle the vulgar sounds of my grief, I rolled over and buried my face in the pillow. I was a poor excuse for a man!

I was finally home. Exams were over and summer had begun. In the remaining days I had spent at Chapel Hill, I had not tried to contact Jennifer or my sister. I couldn't face either one of them, and I had not returned Lori's persistent messages. She had called me over a dozen times between Pamela's visit and my return to Virginia. I had ignored each one and was only slightly apprehensive about the fact that Jennifer had not tried to contact me.

It wasn't that I didn't want to see Jennifer; quite the contrary, I wanted to be with her, hold her, and make love to her, but I stayed away from her because, somehow, Jennifer magnified my weakness. If I saw her, it would only compound my guilt.

Carrying an armload of suitcases, I walked up the path to the front door. As I looked at my parents' yard, I noticed that the tulips were no longer in bloom, and Dad had planted the annuals. They looked pretty. I paused at the door, squared my shoulders, and replaced my frown with a warm smile. I'd give anything to take the oppressive, intangible load off my shoulders. My mom and dad knew me so well. I hoped they couldn't read through my false facade. The last thing I wanted right now was to explain my own private thoughts.

I opened the door. "Hi, I'm home." My parents jumped up from their seats and raced toward me. They both hugged me and repeated several times how good it was to have me home again. After greeting my folks, my first conscious thought was the perplexing expression on my sister's face. Instead of her usual friendly embrace, Lori remained seated staring at me with a mixture of agitation and concern in her expression. I wondered what was the matter. She didn't move. Her arms and legs were as stationary as a statue. All of us were talking at once—except for Lori. My mother joked about the weight I'd lost and told me that she'd put it back onto my ribs in a matter of weeks. She asked about my exams, my return trip, my dirty laundry, and my need for a haircut. She broached a number of subjects except the topic that was on each of our minds: the draft board.

I took a seat on the sofa, and we talked pleasantly for a while. As the minutes ticked by, I became increasingly more curious as to Lori's strange behavior. I wondered what was the reason for her attitude. Why was she shifting her weight around in her chair as if her body had a nervous twitch? Something was definitely wrong. The longer I studied the expression on her face, the more anxious I became. My father excused himself for a moment, and my mother offered to make me a snack; Lori and I were temporarily alone. There was a deafening silence in the room before my sister spoke.

"Kurt! Why didn't you return my phone calls? I must have called you a dozen times in the past couple of days."

"I figured I'd see you this weekend. What's the matter, Lori? You look awful."

"It's Jennifer . . . she's disappeared."

"What?"

"I went back to our room a couple of days ago after taking an exam, and Jennifer was gone. Everything was gone—her bags, her purse, her car—everything. No note! Nothing! She never took her last exam. She just skipped out without a word. I called her parents, but they don't have any idea where she is. I've been so worried. Has she been with you?"

"No." I felt a sinking sensation in the pit of my stomach. Subconsciously, I laid my hands over my abdomen, pressed against it, and tried to push away the spasmodic fluttering that was occurring inside. My body felt numb. My God! I had no idea that Jennifer was the reason for my sister's persistent messages. Jennifer! Where could she be? Why would she possibly vanish like that without a word?

"Kurt . . . has everything been all right between the two of you?" Lori glanced away for a moment. "Things haven't been so hot between us lately, and Jennifer hasn't confided in me very much. I didn't realize there was anything wrong."

"There wasn't anything wrong. We haven't had any problems. I've never seen Jennifer happier. She was worried about my draft number, but other than that everything was perfect between us." I pressed my index fingers tightly against my temples and tried to stop the pounding in my brain.

Tesa Jones ❧ 273

I was trembling all over.

"Think! Think, Kurt! Where could she have gone? Why would she have left like that?"

"I have no idea. Do me a favor, Lori . . . call her house."

"I've already done that. I called three times yesterday. General Carson got really irritated the third time around. He was so ticked off he actually hung up on me."

"Please call again."

"You could call her, Kurt."

"Me? He doesn't even know I exist! "

I followed Lori into the bedroom and watched as she dialed Jennifer's number. My heart was racing, pounding the lining of my chest, and threatening to burst from its cage.

"General Carson . . . this is Laura Davis. Is Jennifer there?" She paused.

I noticed Lori's expression alter from confusion and worry to anxiety, and then to disbelief. Tiny wrinkles formed on her forehead. Her eyes crinkled up before she closed them completely and covered her face with her hand. There was that sick feeling again. Something had happened to Jennifer . . . something awful. I wanted to snatch the phone from my sister and hear the words for myself, but I couldn't move. Lori wasn't talking. She was just listening to what was being said on the other end of the line. Oh, God! What was it? What was the general saying that made Lori's face turn so ashen? She even had tears in her eyes. Jennifer was dead. I knew it as sure as if I'd heard the words myself. Jennifer was dead. It was the only explanation.

Lori's spoke again. "I see, General Carson. Yes, I understand. I won't bother you again. I appreciate you telling me . . . thank you." She hung up the phone and turned her back to me.

I could tell she was wiping her eyes with the sides of her fingers and running the palms of her hands over both her cheeks. I knew I'd go completely insane if she didn't turn around and tell me what had happened. I couldn't stand the silence."Lori?" I cleared my throat as I realized that my

voice had barely been audible. "Lori . . . what happened? Is Jennifer dead?"
I stood up trying to prepare myself for the news. "Say something."

"She's not dead, Kurt. She's all right."

"Then what the hell's wrong? Don't just stand there leaving me in suspense; tell me! I can't stand it another minute."

"Sit down, Kurt."

I lowered my body onto the bed. Lori watched me for a moment in silence. I could tell she was contemplating her next words. If I had had the power to move, I would have strangled them out of her; but I remained still.

"The Carsons received a telegram a few hours ago. It was from Jennifer." Lori took a deep breath that seemed infinite before she spoke again. "Kurt, she's married. Jennifer married David Henderson this morning."

I bent over, jabbing my elbows into my thighs and rested my head on my knees. Far away in the distance I could hear Lori's voice, but the words had no meaning. Nothing she said mattered anymore! I wanted to scream. I wanted to tear the place apart. My head pounded so feverishly I was afraid it was going to explode. Jennifer wasn't dying. She wasn't dead. She wasn't even hurt, but as far as I was concerned I could actually visualize her coffin being lowered into a grave. Jennifer was gone—out of my reach—out of my life. My Jennifer was gone.

I felt Lori's hand touching my shoulder and heard faint, sympathetic sounds that echoed against my ears. I sat up and shoved her with one quick movement. As she fell backward, I saw the surprise on her face. "Get out! Get out! Get away from me." I screamed. "I don't want your fucking pity. I don't need you. Get the hell out of here."

3

The next afternoon, my mother walked into my room; she was holding an envelope. There were tears in her eyes as she silently waited for me to take it from her hand. I glanced at the return address in the upper left hand corner and saw the bold black print: Selective Service. I instantly knew.

Greetings, my friend, from Uncle Sam!

I laughed out loud thinking what an appropriate time for the US Army to drop its own personal bomb on me. The walls of my world were crashing, and this was the final blow. The sons of bitches! I threw my head back and began to laugh. The hysterical choking noise filled the air. My mother must have thought I was crazy, but I didn't care. Without a word, I left my room, walked out of the house, and slammed the door behind me.

4

This past March, while I enjoyed Jennifer and North Carolina in the springtime, the North Vietnamese invaded South Vietnam on four fronts. Once again, the war intensified. It seemed as if the Communists wanted to smash the South Vietnamese government before it could get strong enough to stand on its own without US help. At first, the North Vietnamese gained ground, but after a few weeks the South Vietnamese put a stop to the movement.

On May 8, five weeks after Easter and the invasion (what seemed a lifetime ago), President Nixon gave the command to begin a large-scale air attack and naval blockage of the North to prevent Hanoi from receiving any more weapons and supplies. The US Seventh Fleet mined many North Vietnamese ports, including Haiphong. Our aircraft bombed roads and strategic bridges; this created a disruption and stopped the flow of supplies from China.

Shortly after the bombing, Nixon had a successful visit to Russia, where he and Brezhnev signed the strategic arms limitation agreements, which was nicknamed the SALT Treaty. I wondered if that, compounded with the havoc the bombing and blockade created, was only adding to why the North Vietnamese were no longer getting the help they counted on from either Russia or China.

Two days after Nixon's declaration, the war saw its largest single fighting encounter in the air to date. The first target was the POL storage area north of Haiphong. Later in the day, eleven fighters' mission was to take out the rail switching point halfway between Hanoi and Haiphong. Because the location was heavily defended both on the ground and in the air, it was a classic dogfight and a fierce battle. Both missions were successful, which brought about the beginning of the decline in the opposition.

But still, it seemed that peace was not within reach.

5

Immediately following my physical in early June, I was given a box lunch and pushed onto a bus headed for Fort Benning, Georgia, where I began eight weeks of basic training in Sandbridge. The day we arrived, my hair and sideburns were shaved. I no longer recognized one GI from another. We all looked alike: bald boys in military clothing with bewildered expressions on our faces. For the first time in my life, I was a loner. It didn't matter—I no longer wanted any friends.

On the day I arrived, the sergeant announced that there was an epidemic of spinal meningitis spreading through the camp so everyone had to wear a face mask at all times, except while eating. It wasn't enough that the army snatched us away from our homes and our futures. No! They had to augment the experience. They gave us masks to cover our mouths; needless to say, the masks foamed and dripped from our own saliva especially when we did our exercises and ran for miles in full combat attire.

For the first three weeks, I had a real attitude problem. Because of it, I cleaned more toilets and did more push-ups than I could count. By the fourth week, the sergeant beat into me most of the military procedure, and my spirit was beginning to break. Never in my whole life was I so tired and thirsty. I think I would have done anything for a full night's sleep and an infinite supply of water. The food was the pits; but I was so hungry I blocked the taste from my tongue. Surprisingly, no matter how much I ate, I still lost weight.

By the fifth week, we were into heavy training. They taught us how to shoot an M-14. It kicked like a mule, which made my shoulder ache after a full day's practice. Surprisingly, I discovered that I liked firing at the pop-up cardboard targets, and I was good at it. Finally, I found something I could use to channel my anger. I painted imaginary faces on the targets. Some were Vietcong; some were the sergeant's; some were Pam's; some were Jennifer's; some were even my own. I blew them all away.

I hated my drill sergeant. He was the meanest son of a bitch I'd ever met. He enjoyed pressing my face in the dirt and calling me "hippie boy" if I didn't do a perfect push-up. "Want to go home, hippie boy?" I could still feel his boot in my neck. After a few weeks with him, I stopped being scared. I was too pissed off to be frightened. I wanted to kill him. He was in charge of our PT, and he damned sight made sure we didn't waste one waking moment. He made us beg, "More PT, drill sergeant! The more we get, the more we like it!" And if we didn't say it loud enough and strong enough, he'd double it up until we said it the way he wanted us to. I didn't know it was possible to be so exhausted.

After the eight weeks of basic training, we were given our first promotion from buck private to private, which entitled us to a $7.00-a-month raise. My take home salary increased from $68 to $75. Most of the guys were sent to cushy jobs on a base in the States, or to the boredom of the Aleutian Islands, but I was sent to Fort Polk, Louisiana, nicknamed Tigerland, for Advanced Infantry Training (AIT). It didn't make any sense. Although the navy and their pilots had never been so active, the army's troops were leaving Vietnam. If the war was nearly over, why were more men being trained for combat duty? And why was I one of the "lucky" bastards to get chosen?

God! It was hot in Louisiana. Every morning at 3:30, I woke up in a pool of my own sweat. We had until 4:00 to dress, eat our morning chow, and get to our practice site. We worked all day shooting M-16s, which were much lighter than the M-14s and could fire twenty rounds in three and a half seconds; plus we used machine guns, threw live hand grenades, and learned survival skills that would hopefully keep us alive during a combat situation. We were pushed around the clock until two the following morning when we crawled back into our bunks for the grand total of an hour and a half of sleep before we had to get up again and repeat the procedure. I was so dog tired that I learned how to sleep standing up. I didn't think about home, Lori, my parents, or my education. I didn't dwell on memories of Jennifer, and I had no room for guilt about Pam. That was my past. I was determined to bury it.

By the end of the nine-week AIT, I was a finely-tuned, physically strong, mentally prepared soldier ready to do battle. I don't know how or when it happened, but the army molded me into what they wanted. I actually felt like an animal . . . a stalker . . . a predator. I was ready to kill. It was no wonder I was shocked when I received my orders: not Vietnam—but Germany. Where the hell did the army get off fucking around with my mind? They got me all psyched for battle and then shifted gears in midstream. Damn them! Why were they doing this to me?

6

I sat in Kennedy Airport and waited for my plane. My essential baggage was at my side, and my orders were in my pocket. I watched as lovers reunited, families hugged, wives kissed their husbands hello or good-bye, strangers bumped into one another and casually kept on walking without an apology. The place was a combination of chaos and excitement. People lived in their own private worlds. They disregarded anyone who didn't fit in to their specials molds. Some were laughing; others cried. Some held hands; others embraced. Still others walked separately only touching shoulders when nudged in that direction. They all seemed oblivious to their surroundings as they raced to their own destinations. Were they happy? Content? Satisfied? Did life treat them well? Or were they angry and frustrated—pissed off at the world and only pretending to fit in to our society?

I thought of calling Pam. She lived in this dreadful city. But I rejected the idea. If she wanted to have a bastard baby . . . then let her! After all, it was no concern of mine what she did with her life. Pam had made her choice; she had to live with it. I didn't give a shit what happened to her or anyone else for that matter. The hell with them all!

I heard my flight announced over the intercom. After picking up my duffel bag, I marched to the gate. Good-bye, America. Fuck you! And good riddance!

12

Jennifer

FIVE MONTHS AGO, I DROVE HOME IN A BLIND RAGE. TRYING TO VENT my anger, I did the one thing that would hurt *me* more than anyone else. I was furious, lost, and confused. The two people I loved most in the world deserted me. Lori and I drifted apart because of the wedge Brad Malone created between us, and Kurt was more than likely married to the dark-haired girl with the swollen belly. At the time, David Henderson seemed like the only solution. It was hard to believe I was a married woman. What a fool I was! I didn't love David. I doubted he loved me.

The memory of that day last spring when my world shattered was still vivid in my mind. Moments after knocking on David's door, he opened it. Smiling, he spoke the first words, "I knew you'd come running back. I just didn't think it would take this long." His sarcasm went deaf against my ears. I didn't care about his response. I only knew that I couldn't go home, and I no longer had a haven in North Carolina.

Within an hour after my arrival, David made love to me. During the process, he asked me to marry him. His proposal was spoken in a monotone fashion. I responded affirmatively, more as a desire to lash out at Kurt for his infidelity, than as a wish to be David's wife. At the time, I didn't stop long enough to think of tomorrow or the next day. I only thought about the moment.

Three days later, with license and blood tests in hand, David and I were married at the justice of the peace. Our witnesses were strangers. There were no flowers, nor any music; instead of a chapel, it took place in a cluttered office. The occasion was far from memorable.

After we exchanged vows, David took me to The Tombs in Washington where we celebrated our marriage by drinking several pitchers of beer with a few of his old high school buddies. We remained there through the lunch hour, the happy hour, and even past the dinner hour, as I watched David pour one mug of beer after another down his throat. He laughed and joked with his friends as they exchanged obnoxious stories from the past. I was so disgusted with his attitude that I demanded to leave shortly after nine o'clock. David gave me a cold stare, which spoke volumes. I instinctively knew what he meant. I remained silent. Around midnight, we returned to his townhouse—correction—our townhouse. He casually strolled into the bedroom, turned on the television set, and plopped on the bed. I went into the master bathroom, changed into a sexy nightgown, and prepared to consummate the marriage. I brushed my hair, freshened my makeup, and dabbed perfume behind my ears and between my breasts. When I reentered the room, I saw David perched on the bed completely dressed and captivated by the TV. He was so engrossed in Johnny Carson and his guest star Raquel Welch that he didn't even notice my return. I quietly walked over to the television set and attempted to turn it off.

As I touched it, David snapped, "Don't you dare!" I asked him if he was at all interested in making love, and he responded, "Are you kidding? We can screw any time. But Raquel is a dream a man can really take to bed." Without even once taking his eyes off the screen, he laughed. That night, I slept under the covers while my husband slept, fully dressed, on top of the bedspread. I was totally dejected and completely confused. I should have read the signals; I should have anticipated the future. It was so obvious.

As the weeks drifted by, David started forming a routine. We didn't make love on our wedding night, but we eventually did consummate our relationship. We had sex—that was one thing for certain. David and I had habitual, predictable sex. We screwed twice a week on every Sunday and Thursday—just like clockwork. I could not bring myself to call the act we shared even remotely similar to that of making love. It was hard-core lust— David's own personal lust—no other words could describe it. Without any foreplay at all, he would stick his stiff cock—that was what he called it upon penetration—into me and jerk a few times until he got his fulfillment. He no longer toyed with my body as he had done so long ago. David didn't care whether or not I reached the peaks of satisfaction along with him. He only rolled on top of me, spat his semen, and rolled off me again without ever saying a word. We never talked. We never shared comments about the events of our day. And we never exchanged ideas about what we wanted to do with the rest of our lives. It seemed as if we were in limbo—a limbo from which neither of us attempted to escape.

I had no idea what caused the sudden change in David's reactions toward me. To be honest, I didn't really care. Nothing mattered anymore. I stopped fighting the situation and simply resigned myself to the fact that this was my fate. And I had no control over it.

2

I knew David drank more than he should. I also knew that he smoked more pot than was normally his habit, but during the first months of our marriage, I didn't know about all his other women. It wasn't until Election Day, when Nixon steamrolled over George McGovern in one of the greatest landslide victories in American history, that I discovered the truth.

A week after David and I were married, he insisted I get a job. He told me that he didn't want an idle wife who was nothing more than another mouth to feed. Of course, I had no qualms about working. Feeling jubilation at the fact that I could put to use my newly acquired typing skills, I immediately went in search of a good secretarial position. I looked for work through the entire month of July but nothing was available except a position that required shorthand. By the beginning of August, I finally settled for waitress work at a rather nice dinner theater not far from our townhouse.

The fact that I still tired easily kept me from working more than four days a week. By the end of the six-hour shifts, I was always so exhausted that it took an entire day to recuperate. David had no sympathy for me. He said I was only playing at being an invalid. So, out of some sense of false pride, I dug deep into my physical reservoir and kept on plugging. I was determined not to let him know that I couldn't take the pressure of his unrelenting sarcasm. I worked Tuesday, Wednesday, Friday, and Saturday; in fact, I was glad to avoid my husband on those evenings. David worked day shifts, and I worked nights so we only had to share each other's company a dozen or so hours out of the week.

Sundays were a different story all together. On God's day, we both stayed home. David buried himself in the newspaper through the entire morning and stayed glued to the football games during the afternoon and evening. The schedule was always the same—nothing changed. He never slipped more than a sentence or two into our routine: "Get me a cup of coffee," or "Got any beer?" or "Phone's ringing . . . get it," or "Turn on the light," or "Turn up the sound." There was never a "please" or a "thank you." He always spoke in the same monotone voice. It didn't matter. Nothing mattered anymore.

I was so lonely.

I thought about going home. There were days when I actually became obsessed with the idea. But I knew I could never go home again. After I sent my parents the telegram, they refused to see me. My father irately said, "You are unworthy of my time." He barred me from the house and would not allow me to see or talk to my mother. I didn't really miss my old man. I did not care if I ever saw him again; but in a strange way, I desperately wanted to be with my mom. Somehow, I felt closer to her now than at any time in my life. David wasn't physically abusive to me, as my father was to my mother, but David did strip me emotionally as my mother must have felt a thousand times during her marriage. I wanted to talk to her. I wanted to confide in her. I wanted to explain that I understood—I really understood. But

I couldn't bring myself to dial her number. And it hurt even more to know that she didn't dial mine.

I tried not to think about Kurt. I suppressed all of our memories. I heard he was drafted. I wondered if his wife and child were with him. Probably not—the army didn't allow families in Vietnam.

And I missed Lori. Somehow, without explanation or reason, Lori changed my entire life. She molded me into a person I actually liked. She gave me courage and strength. I felt as if I functioned because of her. Now that our friendship was gone, there was a void in me that reached to my soul. I felt so empty.

I wanted desperately to reach out to Lori again. But I knew I was the one who had created the rift between us. I was the one who had been nasty and vindictive. I was the one who had said horrible, negative comments. And I was the one who had ultimately betrayed our friendship. Why had I been so cruel, when she had always been so patient with me? It was obvious that she was in love with Brad Malone. Why couldn't I have been compassionate and help her cope with her misguided feelings instead of acting like an insensitive beast? Lori would never forgive me. And I couldn't blame her. After all, I didn't deserve forgiveness.

I put the tab on the table in front of my last customer. It had been one hell of a night—a packed house. The Republicans were having a field day celebrating Nixon's reelection. They couldn't stop bragging about the fact that he swept through the country taking forty-nine of the fifty states. I grinned silently to myself; Kurt must be furious. There would be four more years with a Republican in the White House. Kurt hated Nixon.

Personally, I didn't care who won. All I wanted to do was go home. After my duties were completed, I donned my coat and walked to my townhouse. I was tired. Nearly a year had passed since I'd been under the oxygen tent. I was infuriated with my lack of endurance. I was just as exhausted as I had been ten months ago. I hadn't seen a doctor since last spring, but I knew they wouldn't or couldn't help. After all, their diagnosis was always, "Give it time". Well, I was giving it time; in fact, time was something I had plenty of now. There was little to do in my life except eat, sleep, and work twenty-four hours a week. Nothing filled the gaps.

If only David and I could be friends, companions, lovers—anything but the cold, silent relationship we actually shared. At first, I tried to break the ice, but now I resigned myself to the fact that our marriage was one of convenience. There was one thing I didn't understand. What kind of convenience was David getting? It didn't make any sense. We lived in the same house; we shared a checking account; we slept in the same bed, but we rarely spoke. Sex was a twice-a-week routine, and we were anything but friends. I figured David coveted my father's money. But, unfortunately for David, he didn't realize that my father would never give him anything—or me either for that matter. Did David think that time would mellow my father, and eventually he would accept us? I was realistic enough to realize that would never happen.

On Election Day 1972, I was glad I left the restaurant a little earlier than usual, which meant I'd be home and in bed before midnight for a change. All I wanted to do was strip down and crawl between the sheets. I craved sleep. I entered the house, took off my coat, and threw it haphazardly across the Lazy-Boy chair in the living room. I debated about getting something to eat, but decided against it. I wasn't really hungry. I started to climb the stairs. I made a mental note to myself that I really should eat more regularly. The doctors were very strict about that advice. I suppose I should follow their instructions better. Maybe then I might have more energy.

I opened the door to our bedroom, turned on the light, and instantly saw my husband. He was not alone. Next to David was a gorgeous, well-developed, redhead with a Cheshire grin on her face. David immediately sat up; he covered himself and his bedmate with a blanket. We stared at each other in silence for a few moments before I walked into the bathroom and gathered a few personal articles and my nightgown, which always hung on the back of the door. I couldn't believe how casually I was moving around the room as I collected those possessions I needed. David didn't say a word; neither did I. The only person speaking was the buxom bitch who was spread out across my bed, but her words went deaf against my ears. I was too tired to fight and too exhausted to listen. I didn't care; for some odd reason, I wasn't even surprised. If someone had told me that they had seen my husband with another woman, I would not have believed it. But now that I'd seen it with my own eyes, it made perfect sense.

Without speaking a word, I walked out of the room and turned off the light. Carrying an armload of things, I entered the spare bedroom. I shut the door. Just in case David wanted to attempt an explanation, I made sure the door was locked. No matter what his excuses might be, I didn't want to see or hear him. All I knew was David had been fooling around with another woman in our bed when he didn't have more than two lousy minutes a week to spend with me.

The hell with it! What did it matter anyway? I lay on the bed fully dressed and wrapped the end of the bedspread over my body. My eyes weren't closed more than a few seconds before I heard a light tapping at the door. When I did not respond to David's knock, I noticed the knob begin to rattle and heard my name spoken, softly at first, then gradually it became louder.

"Jennifer, please open the door."

I couldn't remember the last time David said my name. It sounded so foreign. I felt like crying, but no tears came. "Go away."

"Jennifer . . . come on . . . open the door. Let's talk."

"Talk?" I laughed. "What for?"

"Jennifer . . . " The pounding continued, but this time it was louder and more persistent. "Let me in . . . let me explain."

I could hear both his fists beating at the barrier between us. Mustering up all the energy I had left, I screamed back at him. "Go away, you son of a bitch! Go away and leave me alone."

"Come on, Jenny."

"I'm too tired to talk tonight, David. Go away!" I smothered my face in the pillow and blocked out his voice. My last conscious thought before drifting off to sleep was of Lori. I wished Lori were here. Lori would help me. Lori would put her arms around me and make me feel better. Lori would take all the pain away.

I woke up the next morning only to discover that I'd slept until noon. Lying quietly in my bed, I listened for sounds of David in the house. When I was convinced he was gone, I got up and donned my robe. After combing my hair and brushing my teeth, I slowly staggered down the steps into the kitchen to make myself a cup of coffee. Coffee! I hadn't had a cup since before I'd gotten sick. The doctors restricted caffeine: bad for the heart, harmful to my condition. Who the hell cared? After blowing on it until the brew was cool enough to drink, I took a sip. It tasted marvelous. Now, all I needed was a cigarette to go along with it. I searched for a pack of David's Salems, but I could not find any. The only cigarettes in the house were a few half-smoked butts in the ashtray, which was sitting on the counter. Two of them had lipstick around the filters. Being very careful not to tear the paper, I straightened them out with my fingers. The redhead had slept in my bed, made love to my husband. I could certainly smoke her used cigarettes if I wanted. After all, it was the least she could do for *me*. I lined the five different shaped cigarettes on the kitchen table and toyed with the tobacco leaves, which had fallen out. After staring at them for several minutes, I finally placed one between my lips and lit the crushed end. Lifting my coffee cup for a toast, I muttered, "Here's to another nail in my coffin." I inhaled the strong smoke. At first I coughed, but then I relaxed and felt only slightly dizzy. I exhaled my second cloud of smoke. It really tasted good. I'd forgotten how much I enjoyed it. After another drag, the tobacco reached the filter, and I stomped it out in the ashtray. Immediately, I picked up the next one in line and lit it.

After I finished all five cigarette stubs and three cups of coffee, I leaned back in my chair and tried to think what I was going to do next. I wasn't hungry; scratch off eating as one of my many events for the day. I could clean the house. No! What for? I could go for a drive. I looked out the window. David had my car—his was in the shop. I could take a walk. No. I did not feel like walking. I could call Lori. Yes! I could call Lori. Talk to her! Try to explain. Ask her for help.

I picked up the phone and dialed Elon's campus operator from memory. It rang a half dozen times before an unfamiliar voice answered.

"This is long distance calling for Lori Davis."

"What dorm is she in?"

"I'm not sure."

"Just a minute, please. I'll check the listing and connect you."

I felt the excitement build at the prospect of being able to talk with Lori again. Lori would listen. She would understand. I need you, Lori! I tried to remain calm. It would never do to have me fly into hysterics the moment she picked up the receiver. Relax! I had to relax.

Several minutes passed before I heard the unfamiliar voice speak again. "I'm sorry. Both of the lines on her hall are busy. Can I take a message?"

Tears stung at my eyes. I choked on the rising knot in my throat. The girl repeated herself several times. I finally managed an answer. "No . . . no message." I put the receiver in its cradle and leaned back in the chair. I bit my lip fighting back the tears. I wasn't going to cry. I would not allow myself that luxury.

I don't know how long I sat there before I heard keys jingling at the front door. When it opened, David and a burst of cold air came rushing into the house. I was still staring at the phone.

"Hi, Jennifer."

"Hello, David." I muttered still in my trance.

"What's for dinner?" he asked in a timid voice.

"Dinner?" I glanced at the clock over the refrigerator and noticed it was quarter past six. Where had the day gone? "I didn't know it was dinnertime."

"Would you like me to make something?" He was acting so pleasant— as if there had never been a last night. "I can whip up one of my fantastic sub sandwiches . . . you always liked them, Jennifer . . . remember?"

"Whatever you want. . . . " I took a deep breath and tried to take my eyes off the clock, but I just kept staring in that direction. "It doesn't matter. Whatever you want is fine with me."

David started working in the kitchen. I could hear the rattling of dishes, the opening of the refrigerator, the closing of cupboards and drawers. Watching the hands of the clock tick the minutes away, I was mesmerized by the magnifying sound each beat made. If I concentrated hard enough, I could make all the other noises disappear.

"Jennifer."

The spell was broken. I looked up. David was standing over me. He was holding a gigantic submarine sandwich. I automatically reached for it. "Thank you." I laid it on my lap, opened the contents, and nibbled at it.

"That was a hell of an election. Wasn't it?"

I didn't answer.

"The real laugh is on Massachusetts for being such fools to back McGovern."

I remained silent.

"Personally, I think Nixon's doing a damn decent job. He's been busting ass on foreign affairs, and it's starting to show. Who knows? According to Kissinger, he may get us out of this war before the end of the year."

I took another bite of my sandwich.

"That was a hell of a rainstorm we had this afternoon."

I chewed in silence. So! This was the way it was going to be. We were going to ignore what happened last night. All right. If that was the game plan, I guess I could go along with it. Ignorance is bliss. Who said that? Or was the adage, ignorance is no excuse?

"*The Godfather* is playing at Wisconsin Circle. I've heard Brando is sensational. Would you like to go see it tonight?"

I picked up my plate, rinsed it off in the sink, and walked out of the room. As I climbed the stairs, I could still hear his voice coming from the kitchen.

"You always complain that I never talk to you. Well, I am talking to you now . . . and you won't even listen."

3

Two weeks went by. I continued my routine of working at the dinner theater and keeping David's house. The only thing that changed in our schedules was that I had not returned to David's bed. I still remained locked in the guest room every night. David was always home when I was there. He always made small talk, but never mentioned the topic I was certain plagued his mind, even if he didn't speak of it. I didn't understand why, but I was not jealous. I harbored no resentment toward David or the woman he had taken to our bed. I had no anger, no hopes, and no dreams. I did not think about our future. Every day just slipped into the next. I smoked and drank the hours away.

One afternoon shortly before Christmas, the phone rang. I picked it up.

"Mrs. Henderson?"

I did not recognize the voice on the other end of the line. Who was Mrs. Henderson? Oh! I was Mrs. Henderson. I couldn't remember anyone calling me that before. "This is she." I responded mechanically.

"There's been an accident. Your husband is in the emergency room at Georgetown Hospital. Could you come right over?"

4

It was hours before they let me see David. I didn't know where the emotions came from— especially when I reflected upon our relationship—but I had a growing sense of panic at the idea of David dying. He couldn't die. Oh, God! Not David.

Finally, a police officer talked to me. He was a middle-aged man with a stoic expression on his face. "Mrs. Henderson, it was a hit and run. Your husband was in a crosswalk on M Street when it happened. We have no leads yet as to who was driving the car. There were no witnesses."

"How is he?"

"I don't know his condition, ma'am. But, rest assured, we'll continue to search for the responsible party."

"I don't give a shit who hit David! I just want to know if he's going to be all right." I lost control of my voice. Much to my surprise, I was screaming. I couldn't even remember the last time I'd raised my voice in anger. Emotions tore from my body—emotions I thought had been buried long ago. I covered my mouth trying to stifle the sudden outburst of abusive names and words. I was crying.

"Ms. Henderson." It was the nurse. Where did she come from? "Follow me, please."

I jerked at her shirtsleeve. "What is it? Is my husband all right?"

"You can see him now, Mrs. Henderson. The doctors are finished."

I walked down the corridor of stark white walls and glistening floors. I heard the nurse's shoes squeaking as she took each step. She stopped abruptly in front of a door, pointed, and directed me inside. The first thing I saw was the black-and-blue pulp that represented David's face. It was bloated with bruises and cuts. My God! I focused on all the wires and tubes that were connected to his body. I stared at him, unable to believe that what I saw was actually my husband. White sheets were blanketed over the parts of his body that were not covered with plaster of Paris. He looked pitiful.

"David." I ran to his bedside choking on his name.

"Mrs. Henderson."

I looked around the room. A gray-haired gentleman was standing in the corner. He was dressed in white. The only other color I saw was the dark blue portion of his tie, which stuck out from the top of his jacket. He had pens in his lapel pocket, two rings on his right hand, black horn-rimmed glasses, and a gentle smile on his face.

"I'm Dr. Klein. I was on duty when the ambulance brought your husband in."

"Is he going to be all right?"

"Your husband's a very lucky man. By all rights, he could have died before he ever got to the hospital, but I think with a little luck and good medicine, he'll get through this."

"What's the matter with him?"

"You want the good news first or the bad?"

"Don't joke around with me, doctor . . . "

"I'm not joking, Mrs. Henderson. I'm being perfectly serious." He continued, realizing that I was only acting out of stress. "The bad news is that both of his legs have been crushed in three places. One arm is broken, and he has multiple abrasions all over his body. He may never walk again." The doctor paused letting his message sink in. "The good news is that there is no internal damage, which is unbelievable under the circumstances, not even a broken rib . . . no internal bleeding and no spleen trouble. The arm will heal properly. The cuts and bruises will disappear in a few weeks. And maybe . . . I don't want to give you too much false hope . . . but *maybe*, his legs will heal with enough time and good physical therapy. With hard work and a lot of determination, he has a chance to walk again. You must work with me on this, Mrs. Henderson. Do you understand?"

"Yes." I nodded slowly. "Dr. Klein . . . may I stay with him?"

"Of course."

"How long will he be unconscious?"

"He's not unconscious. He's sleeping. When the drugs wear off a little, he'll wake up."

The doctor left the room. It was so quiet. I pulled the chair up beside David's bed. Resting my elbows on the mattress, I put my hands together and laid my head on top of the peak they made. I hadn't been to confession in years. I hadn't said grace or even so much as a Hail Mary. It had been nearly four years since I'd stepped foot in a church. I turned my back on the Catholic faith; I felt as if it abandoned me years before I stopped believing. I needed to believe now. I needed the strength that only faith could give. There had to be a God! Oh, please, God. Are you listening to me? I need your help. I have nowhere else to turn. I know I'm an unworthy follower. I know I don't deserve your blessings or your comfort. But please, please hear me. You've got to help David.

I began to pray and recite every scripture I could remember. I wished I had my rosary beads. I wanted to hold on to something—feel something concrete. God! God! Please help David. I beg you.

I felt warm fingers touching my hand. I raised my head. David's half-opened eyes were watching me. They were swollen and yellow around the lids. I could barely see the pupils because the puffy skin kept him from opening them completely. It pained me to see him look so helpless. His fingers slowly squeezed mine, as he attempted to show some sign of strength.

"Jen . . . "

"You're going to be all right, David. The doctors told me . . . everything is going to be fine."

He shook his head as he tried to speak. "Not . . . what I want . . . to talk . . . about."

"Don't talk, David. Rest. You need your rest."

He tried putting pressure on my hand again. I returned the warm feeling. Reaching over his confined body, I touched his lips and stroked the side of his face.

"Jennifer." He swallowed. "Forgive me." He made a grunting sound and attempted to form more words. "I don't know why I do those things. . . . I think I wanted you to catch me." He closed his eyes but then fought the sleep that was coming over him. Slowly, he blinked several times and moved his mouth without expressing any syllables. "I love you. . . . I know it doesn't seem like it, and I can't blame you if you don't believe me, but I do love you."

I gripped his hand as tightly as I could and held back the tears that were threatening to spill out. I didn't want him to see me cry. "Oh, David . . . "

"No . . . don't talk, Jennifer . . . let me." It was a physical effort for him to pronounce each word. Trying to moisten his lips, he ran his tongue over his parched mouth. The simple action seemed to pain him. "Don't leave me . . . please. Can we try again . . . can we start over?"

I laid my fingers on his free hand and squeezed it gently. "Yes, David . . . yes, we can."

13

Laura

IT WAS LESS THAN A MONTH UNTIL GRADUATION. LESS THAN FOUR WEEKS before I would hold a diploma in my hand. My one remaining dream was finally coming true; I soon would be a teacher.

Four years ago, I walked onto Elon's campus filled with aspirations for my future: hopes for Tommy and me, plans for a wedding, a career, and children. I thought everything would be so easy, so simple. My life was orderly and planned. What a fool I was—such a child with childish dreams! Four years! I had changed a lot in those four years. Surprisingly, I was even more lost and confused now than I was at eighteen. My heart ached with an empty feeling.

I missed Kurt. He was in Germany. Although I wrote him weekly, he replied only once. My brother was so bitter. The fact that the war ended in January didn't ameliorate his attitude at all. The draft was canceled, and the peace treaty was signed, which seemed to aggravate him even more. His words reeked of a hostile, negative perspective. "Why me?" He wrote in his one correspondence. Kurt didn't sound anything like the brother I knew.

I missed the warm, comfortable sanctuary I called home. I couldn't believe I was twenty-two years old, and I was homesick for my parents. I was certain if I could hide in those familiar protective walls nothing would change; therefore, nothing would hurt me again. Much to my surprise, I missed Tommy. He symbolized my lost innocence; a part of me wanted to crawl back into that safe cocoon he represented. Although I hated to admit it, I also missed those enchanting days I spent with Brad. I tried never to think of him. It hurt too much. Unfortunately, Brad still had the power to invade my thoughts from time to time; I had no control over the images. But mostly, I missed Jennifer. No one would ever be able to replace the friendship we had shared. The lack of it created a void in me that ached to be filled again.

At least, there was one silver lining in an otherwise dismal year: Jack Briskin. Jack and I met at the beginning of my senior year. Although we were not romantically involved, we made a pact to spend endless hours together. It was a platonic relationship that helped fill the vacuum in both of us. Jack was in love with Amy, his girl back home in Florida. He was totally committed to her. After graduation, they planned to get married. Because I dedicated most of my time to my student teaching position, and Jack remained forever faithful to Amy, neither of us had much of a social life. We were quite the odd couple.

Other than my student teaching class of fifth graders at Smith Elementary School and my relationship with Jack, there was only one highlight during my senior year. Last fall, the TKE fraternity nominated me to be their representative on the Homecoming Court. I was thrilled. The only drawback to the occasion was the fact that Brad Malone was my escort.

When Brad confronted me about the nomination, he exuded his usual confident manner. Smiling sarcastically, he said, "Well, Laura, I hear we are going to share the magic moment."

At first, I considered turning down their offer for fear I would not be able to handle being so close to Brad during the ceremony. I visualized verbally lashing out at him and making a complete fool of myself. I still hated him. Last fall, the scars hadn't even begun to heal from that awful trick he played on me the previous spring. Those caustic, unkind words still vibrated against my ears.

As I pondered my decision, Brad quietly grinned and tried to conceal his personal amusement. I wanted to scratch his eyes out and slap the smirk off his face; instead, I only commented, "Whose idea was this . . . for you to be my escort?" There were other people present. Because I felt uncomfortable under his scrutinizing stare, I focused all of my attention on keeping my voice as composed as possible.

"I can't imagine how it came about, Laura." He smiled mischievously as he traced a tender finger across my arm. "Of course, I must admit that I'm honored to have the privilege of your company." A playful chuckle emerged from his throat as he lifted his eyebrow and continued to speak. "But you certainly can't believe that I had anything to do with it."

I stepped back a safe distance, so he could no longer touch me. I still remembered his cocky demeanor and how I paused several seconds in order to catch my breath; the oxygen wasn't getting to my lungs, and my chest was heaving. "Just don't get the impression, Brad, that I'm enjoying this for one minute."

"You could always turn down the nomination, Laura."

I clenched my teeth. "You *are* taking pleasure in this! Aren't you?"

The right side of his lip curved upward in a lopsided grin, and his eyes twinkled merrily. "Yeah, I am." He radiated confidence.

"Damn you!" I whispered for his ears only. Moments later, I politely accepted the fraternity's proposal. Amidst the applause, I turned so I would not have to witness the victorious expression on Brad's face.

On the day of the ceremony, the stadium was packed. I strategically placed myself between two familiar faces and did not allow Brad the opportunity to sit next to me. I was not going to put up with his abusive comments or any part of his body touching mine.

It was an exciting game. Everyone cheered exuberantly as Joe West passed to Mike Lawton for two touchdowns in the second quarter; in addition, it appeared as if Lawton was on his way to breaking the school record for most yards rushing in a season. The team's combined efforts gave Elon a handsome lead before the gun went off announcing the end of the half.

As the ceremony began, Brad offered his arm and smiled proudly. I felt cold chills racing down my spine as we took the steps in unison across the field. Brad broke the silence between us. "You're looking exceptionally beautiful today, Laura."

"Thank you."

" . . . but I must admit, you look even better without your clothes on."

My entire face flushed as much from anger as embarrassment. I jerked my hand from around his arm. Brad threw his head back in laughter. I despised him! Every ounce of me wanted to blurt out my loathing; instead, I stifled my words thinking that anything I might say would only promote his amusement. Brad Malone would think it hysterically funny if I chose that particular moment to throw a punch in his direction. I had no intention of giving him any satisfaction.

We stood in silence as the intercom announced each girl and the group she represented. It felt like an army was performing somersaults in my stomach. Brad patted my hand lightly for encouragement. His trivial gesture seemed meaningless; I pulled away. It galled me that Brad was getting such an enormous amount of pleasure because I was trapped beside him.

"The Homecoming queen of 1972 is . . ." There was a hush in the audience. " . . . Miss Laura Davis representing TKE fraternity."

I heard the words, but they did not register in my mind. Loud clapping echoed throughout the stands. I was immobile—completely overwhelmed. I couldn't move. If it weren't for Brad, I may never have taken the initial step. There was a standing ovation in the bleachers. Everyone was cheering, whistling, and throwing confetti. Brad guided me forward. Someone handed me flowers—a dozen long-stemmed red roses. Last year's queen placed the crown on my head. My heart pounded so wildly, I barely noticed when Brad leaned over and kissed me gently on my cheek.

Flashbulbs went off in rapid succession. I was grateful for the support of Brad's arm.

"Congratulations, Laura." Brad whispered. "I don't know of another person who deserves it more than you." He said something else but the surrounding noise was so deafening I was not able to hear his words.

A few tears of joy emerged. A couple of them formed a trail down my cheek. Someone brushed them away. Was it Brad? I leaned against him, searching for support, and hoping my knees would not buckle under me. I could hear him chuckling as he squeezed my shoulder.

Together we walked off the field. I rejoined Jack and several other couples in the stands. Without a word, Brad disappeared.

Not once since the Homecoming ceremony did I speak to Brad. Not one single word. In the beginning of November, I heard that Brad broke his engagement to Cindy. It came as no surprise to the campus grapevine, but it was a total shock to me. I simply could not understand why Brad announced an engagement last spring only to cancel it several months later. Poor Cindy! She loved him so much. Her whole world was wrapped up in Brad. He was such a bastard! Cindy had not returned to Elon last fall, and Brad had obviously taken that opportunity to dump her in search of new meat, leaving Cindy in West Virginia to lick her wounds. Brad, on the other hand, seemed to glow in his newfound freedom. He dated all the freshman girls and ran through the list as if they were some kind of race he had to win. By the end of January, the gossip started to die down about his sexual antics. The rumor was, although he dated constantly, he never took the same girl out twice. He was described as considerate, polite, and even gentlemanly, but Brad Malone couldn't fool me. He was rotten to the core. No amount of positive hearsay could change my opinion of him. The only certainty I had regarding Brad Malone was that the woman who ended up with him deserved sympathy cards at her wedding instead of presents.

2

Every time I saw Jack Briskin, I was surprised that the two of us had ever formed a friendship. Physically, Jack was the exact opposite of most of the men I knew. He had shoulder length blond hair that was wonderfully thick and pleasant to touch. He wore beat up, faded, blue jeans, T-shirts with obnoxious sayings on them, and a string of beads around his neck. Jack was the only person I knew who had gone to Woodstock four years earlier. He said that the event changed his life. He dropped out of school for a year and drove across the country. During his academic hiatus, he saw the Grand Canyon, the Rocky Mountains, and the gigantic Oregon redwoods. He went to Mardi Gras, watched the sun rise at Cape Cod, and experienced white-water rafting in Utah before he returned to Elon.

Perhaps on a West Coast campus or on a large university up north, Jack would fit right in, but on a small-town, Southern, church-affiliated college campus like Elon he looked quite out of place. I never dwelled on Jack's physical appearance. I only saw what was inside of him. I liked his warm way of speaking, his genuine concern for mankind, his honesty, the gentle way he touched things, and his positive attitude about life. Jack was a lot like my brother—the brother I knew before the draft and before Jennifer married David Henderson.

Jack called after dinner. He asked if I wanted to see *The Poseidon Adventure*. I was finished with my lesson plan for the following day and thrilled to have a diversion from the mundane evening I had planned. Hurriedly, I changed and met him in the lobby.

"Mind if I smoke before we go to the movie?" Jack whispered as he opened the outside lobby door.

"No . . . go ahead." I didn't know why Jack asked. I wasn't even sure what he'd do if I said "no", but every time he wanted to light up a joint around me, he always asked for my permission.

Jack smoked a lot. At first, it frightened me. I'd never seen marijuana; I hadn't even smelled it. It was hard to believe that an entire generation was experimenting with grass, and I was oblivious to the drug. Was pot always around, or was it just now getting a strong foothold on our small campus? Times were changing. Instead of hiding the six-pack, the coeds were concealing their joints and claiming them to be a dynamite buzz with no morning hangover and easier to unload if the dorm mother went on the prowl.

My first experience with marijuana occurred last fall when Jack lit up a joint while we were parked in his little red Kadett. I leaned back in my seat as if it were a snake and said, "Don't you know that's illegal?"

Jack laughed. "Do you really think that stops anybody?" He struck a match. Before he lit the end, Jack glanced at me. Without a word, he blew out the flame. There must have been a look of total horror on my face because he put the joint in the glove compartment. "Hey, no sweat, Lori. I didn't know it would bother you so much. It's cool! I don't have to smoke. I can wait until I get back to my dorm."

Trying to conceal my embarrassment, I said, "It's okay. Really, Jack, I don't mind."

Taking me at my word, Jack retrieved the joint, lit it, and savored the moment as the smoke formed a cloud around him. I, on the other hand, sat in the passenger seat like a paranoid doe on the last day of hunting season. I looked around and waited for a cop to come along and catch us in the act. If I were naked and making love in the backseat, I wouldn't have felt more guilty or conspicuous than I did at that moment. Of course, in retrospect, my obsessive fear was ridiculous. After all, Jack was right; smoking pot was common practice.

Although Jack continued to smoke on nearly every occasion we were together, he never offered me another hit. Instead, he bought a bottle of Ripple or a couple Cokes for me.

Jack and I had thirty minutes to kill before *The Poseidon Adventure* started. He parked the car in a deserted area next to a cornfield and turned off the ignition. Without speaking, he shifted his pack of Salems and rotated the cigarettes until he found the one that was hidden in the back. He pulled the joint out of the pack and lit the end. I watched him as he inhaled. The bittersweet aroma burned the inside of my nose. Rolling down my window an inch or two, I let in fresh air. I sipped my Coke and continued to watch. Jack lay back against the headrest and closed his eyes.

"Can I have some?" Did I actually say that? I was just as surprised as Jack at my statement.

He turned slowly to face me. "What?"

"I guess my curiosity has finally gotten the best of me."

"You sure you want to do this?" Jack asked questioningly. His voice was pleasant.

"I want to try it." I paused. "For crying out loud, Jack. Everybody's doing it. Why can't I?"

He handed it to me. I held the joint between my fingers for a few seconds before lifting it to my lips. I gagged and coughed on the strong smoke. Choking, I struggled for air.

"Lori, breathe through your nose first, then inhale through your mouth. Hold the smoke in your lungs as long as you can . . . then let it out."

I followed his instruction and discovered that the urge to cough subsided. The smoke felt harsh on my throat, but it no longer caused involuntary gagging. I held my breath as long as I could before expelling it in one huge gush. Then I gasped for fresh oxygen. No reaction. I tried again. Then I tried a third time and a fourth. Nothing happened. I could barely breathe for all the excess smoke filling the inside of the car. I rolled the window down the remainder of the way; when that didn't help, I opened the door. A cool breeze splashed over my face. "I don't see what's so fantastic about this stuff," I mumbled.

Jack just chuckled as he rolled another joint, lit it, and handed it to me. "It takes longer the first time a person tries it. "

I continued the procedure, but still . . . nothing. I was just about to comment again on my lack of enthusiasm when out of the blue, my feet went numb. I looked down at them, kicked my shoes off, and watched my toes wiggle. Much to my amazement, I couldn't feel the movement. Seconds later, without any warning at all, my hands went numb. I pressed my thumb against my forefinger and felt nothing. As I forced my fingernails into my skin, I was certain I should be drawing blood, but I didn't feel any pain. The sensation started spreading. I opened my eyes wide and tried to focus on what was happening. I touched my cheeks with my hands. I neither felt the skin of my face nor the tips of my fingers. I looked over at Jack and saw that he was wearing a warm, friendly smile. I tried to smile back at him, but I wasn't sure if my lips were curved in the proper direction, so I used my fingers to force the corners of my mouth upward. Jack began to laugh. I laughed too. It seemed so silly, but I couldn't help roaring with amusement.

I moved languidly as I reached for Jack's hand. Everything was in slow motion. It seemed to take an eternity to touch fingers. I held his hand and smiled. I could actually feel his warm skin when I hadn't been able to feel my own. His hand was beautiful—warm and soft and beautiful. I clutched it.

This felt nothing like when I drank too much Ripple. Alcohol made me uncoordinated, sometimes sloppy, and often sleepy. I could feel each stage as I took each drink. Pot, on the other hand, just slowed everything down until it was almost at a dead stop without any warning at all. It was an odd sensation. One minute I was fine, normal. The next minute it was a totally different story. I had no control over the amount of uncontrol I felt.

"Just sit back and relax, Lori. Don't worry. Nothing's going to happen. It's clean stuff."

I didn't know what Jack meant by clean stuff; at the moment, I really didn't care. I took his advice, sat back, closed my eyes, and rested my body against the contour of the seat. It really was a unique feeling. The door of the car was still open. I felt a soft breeze surrounding me, enveloping me, loving me with tender caresses. I opened my eyes and concentrated on the beauty on the other side of the windshield. What a glorious night! "Look at those stars." I spoke more to myself than to Jack. "The first writer who ever said that stars were like diamonds must have been smoking pot when he put the words together. Twinkle, twinkle little star . . . like a diamond in the sky . . . how does that go? It doesn't matter. It's too beautiful for words . . . especially nursery rhymes."

"You really see things differently when you're stoned."

"Yeah . . . I understand. Everything is so . . . so pretty!"

Jack turned on the radio. I could hear every note. We weren't listening to Rock; the station was tuned to a symphony. I could hear violins, a trumpet, a flute; I even heard the faint tingle of bells. It sounded like stereo even though I knew that only one speaker worked in Jack's car. The music was every-where—loud and soft at the same time. Bass and treble magnified equally. I closed my eyes and relished the tones. All other images evaporated. I forgot Kurt . . . Jennifer . . . my family . . . Brad . . . the project I was working on for my fifth graders . . . the synopsis that was due in two days . . . tomorrow's lesson plan that wasn't quite finished yet. I heard and saw and felt nothing but the magnificent notes that encircled me. I even forgot where I was and whom I was with. I had no energy or desire to do anything, yet I felt won-derful . . . absolutely, positively, wonderful . . . freed.

"I think we missed the movie. Would you like to go to The Plus One for a beer instead."

Someone was talking. Who was that? "What?" I asked as I tried to get my bearings.

"I said . . . it's half past ten." He chuckled. "The movie's over. Would you like to go to Gibsonville and get a beer at The Plus One?"

"It can't be that late." I tried to sit up. "Where did the time go?"

"You've been in another world, Lori. How'd you like it?"

That was Jack's voice. I turned. Yes, it was Jack. He was smiling. He looked so nice . . . so nice . . . so very, very nice. Oh, Jack. I wish we weren't such good friends. I wish you'd put your arms around me and hold me, kiss me, love me. I'm so lonely. Where had that thought come from? A large knot began forming at the base of my throat. It felt as if gigantic tears were puff-ing out my eyelids. I was going to cry. Oh, God! I was going to cry. I hadn't cried in so long . . . such a long, long time.

My thoughts took verbal shape. "I don't want to go anywhere, Jack. I just want you to hold me. I feel so alone."

His warm arms wrapped tightly around me. I leaned my head upon his shoulder and forced the tears away. I would *not* cry. I would not allow myself to cry. Jack rocked me quietly. I could hear him humming softly against my ear. Tommy! No! That wasn't Tommy. Where was Tommy? My fault . . . it was entirely my fault. Poor Tom. If only I could have loved him. Rick! Rick was so good to me. Life could have been so easy. If only Rick could have kept me from discovering the truth. The truth? What truth? Jennifer! Why aren't you here? I need you. Kurt! Will it ever be the way it used to be? What's happened to you? You seem like another person. I miss you. Brad. No! Not Brad! Never Brad!

"Jack . . . love me." I encircled his neck with my arms and pulled his lips toward mine. "Make love to me . . . please. I need . . ." Before I could finish the sentence, I was crushed in his feverish embrace. Lips on fire, bodies pressed together, hands groping for a moment's pleasure. Suddenly, the bucket seats were put into a reclining position, giving us the required space. The tears dried in my eyes, and the knot in my throat disappeared. As the depressing wave vanished, I was overcome with passion.

Jack fumbled with the buttons on my blouse. He kissed my neck and used his free hand to massage the back of my head. Help me . . . help me! I began to jerk at the material and gave Jack the assistance he needed in order to disrobe me. We were both frantic. I pulled his shirt over his head and tossed it in the backseat. His skin felt wonderful against mine. I ran my fingers across the muscles of his back and pulled him closer to me. Without looking, I unbuckled his belt. As I struggled with the zipper on his pants, I felt the pressure of his body lift off me. I lay there panting . . . waiting for his next move . . . craving his touch.

"Lori." Jack's voice rang through the air as clear as the campus church bells in the distance: soft and sweet, yet firm and steady. "Not like this. We're friends . . . and I won't take advantage of you." He took a deep breath and stared directly into my eyes. "I'd be lying if I said that I didn't want you. You're so gorgeous—so incredibly sexy. I'd love to taste every ounce of you." He gently smoothed the hair away from my face. "Even though you drip with innocence, you are without a doubt the most alluring woman I've ever known. Don't test my control, Lori. Sit up . . . before I change my mind."

"I'm not a virgin." My God! Did I have no shame? "I know that everyone thinks I am. I hear what they say about me. Too innocent to know any better. All the girls think I'm weird—a castoff from a past generation. I don't want to be like that. I want to be like everybody else. I don't want to be different." The depression was washing over me again. Was it the marijuana taking me up and down like this? One minute I was flying high; the next, I was hitting rock bottom and crying. Why couldn't everything be beautiful and peaceful like it had been earlier in the evening? "Help me, Jack."

He held me tightly against his chest and whispered softly in my ear as he cradled me. "Lori . . ." He laughed quietly to himself as he continued to rock my body. "I should take you right here and now. Lord knows, I've thought about it enough." Quietly, he smirked. "Do you think it's easy being *just* friends with you?"

"Please, Jack . . . please."

"I'd make love to you in a heartbeat—without a second thought—if I didn't think it would hurt you in the end." He paused. "You forget—I love Amy. I'd be using you."

"I don't care. I don't care that you love Amy. I don't care about tomorrow." Huge tears spilled out onto my cheeks. "I'm so lonely, Jack." I moved my hand up his leg, curving inward and up his thigh.

"Stop it, Lori!" Jack imprisoned my hand with his and ceased my actions. "For Christ's sake! I'm only human. Don't push me too far!"

"Make love to me . . . I want you."

"It's not me you want, Lori."

"Yes it is . . . yes . . . it's you, Jack."

"No . . . you don't really want me."

"Hold me! Oh God, hold me." I buried my nose in his chest and gave in to the depressing sobs that were choking me. I could hear Jack speaking, but I didn't comprehend the words. What he said really didn't matter. The words weren't important. I just knew I felt better when his arms were wrapped around me.

An hour passed. Jack finally broke the silence, "Lori, I think I better take you back to campus. It's getting late."

"No . . . let's not move . . . let's stay right here forever."

"Can't do that, babe." He lifted me gently off his shoulder and eased me into my seat. "Gotta keep moving. We both have futures to think about . . . can't sit still and let time pass us by. In a couple months, I'll be in Florida—married to Amy and working for her father. And you'll be teaching a classroom full of kids and loving every minute of it. You'll probably have two or three guys knocking at your door—crazy about you—begging you to settle down, get married, have kids. Your biggest decision will be—which one? I don't know how someone like you could ever feel lonely. Sweet Jesus! Everyone likes you. I don't think I've ever heard one unkind thing about you . . . and that's next to a miracle on this small campus. You're so nice, Lori. Maybe you're too nice. I worry about you sometimes." Jack's voice trailed off into a soft whisper. He glanced out the window as he collected his thoughts. "It seems as if you don't really know what's happening. Everything smells like flowers to you, and they're all sweet and perfect." He returned his attention to me. "It's not like that out there in the real world. Life is not like that." Jack brushed a few strands of hair away from my face. "Try not to let it corrupt you, Lori. Someone like you could be swallowed up and spat out whole without even knowing what happened."

"What are you talking about, Jack? You're not making any sense at all."

He touched the side of my face with soft, tender fingers and then gently kissed my forehead. "I know you don't understand. That's what worries me." He turned and started the ignition. "You're so beautiful . . . so trusting . . . so damned idealistic. If I sat here all night and tried to explain it, you still wouldn't understand."

"What's wrong with being idealistic? You're idealistic."

"No, Lori." He laughed. "I'm not idealistic. I'm liberal. There's a difference." Jack paused as he shifted his car into drive. "It's a shame . . . a real shame . . . the rest of the world can't be like you. The world would be a terrific place if that were true."

3

May 20, 1973—Graduation Day! I sat with my classmates, listened to the speeches, and waited to receive my diploma. President Danieley, who would be retiring on June 20, was speaking. "What is past is only prologue . . ." I felt as if I were holding my breath in anticipation of the future as he continued, "greater days lie ahead. Let us go forward with an abiding faith in God that what we are doing is right and worthy of our best efforts."

Our special guest speaker was Captain Jeremiah Denton, the first POW to step off the plane last February and the father of the president of our Student Government Association. He was inspirational. As he spoke, I thought of all my yesterdays when I was living in this protective *womb* and working toward my future, while all those young men were fighting and struggling to stay alive one day at a time in Vietnam. The war was finally over. Our boys were home. Now we could think about our tomorrows . . . together. After more than a decade of war, we could finally embrace peace. We were the new generation, and together we could change the world . . . strive for a better life for everyone. We could make a difference!

My eyes wandered slightly to my left. I glanced at my classmates— those individuals with whom I had spent the last four years. Jack was up a few rows. His head was bowed as he concentrated on his own personal thoughts. I was going to miss him. Without Jack, I would never have gotten through my senior year. My eyes continued over the wave of caps and gowns. I saw guys I had dated, people I had studied with, sorority sisters. I glanced into the stands and focused on Rick Malone. He was holding Val's hand. In two years, it would be her turn to wear the cap and gown. They seemed wonderfully in love. I was happy for them. I looked across the aisle and slightly to my right. I saw Brad. When I realized he was watching me, I quickly looked away. Seconds later, my eyes were drawn to him again. He was still staring at me. As hard as I tried, I could not break away from the intangible contact our eyes made. There was an unreadable expression on his face. His eyes seemed to throw spears in my direction. I could almost feel the darts penetrate my skin. For a moment, I felt naked under his scrutinizing stare. I placed a hand on my chest and tried to cover myself, and then I realized that there was fabric at my fingertips. Nudity was in my imagination. I blushed. When he saw my reaction, he grinned slightly and nodded. Damn him! Determined not to glance in Brad's direction, I returned my attention to the podium. After today, I'd never have to see him again. Thank God!

4

A month after graduation, I moved into a one-bedroom apartment near Belle View Shopping Center, which was less than a mile south of Alexandria. The rent was $135 a month. I furnished it with crates for tables, bricks and boards for shelves, a couch I bought at a yard sale, and a brand-new bed I purchased on credit. My mother gave me a lot of hand-me-downs including plates, flatware, glasses, pots and pans, a few old curtains, some rather worn-out sheets, and a plastic ashtray in case a friend who smoked stopped by for a visit. But that was unlikely because I had no friends. No one ever came to visit.

I hung my posters—the same ones I had in my dorm at Elon—draped colorful cloths over the boxes, lined the shelves with books, and hung a few plants from the ceiling. My apartment was far from fancy, but it did feel like home. Despite its rather rustic decor, I loved it. Given time, I knew that I would replace the old stuff and buy new things along with a few extras. Perhaps after a couple of paychecks, I could buy the chair I saw at Sloan's and a reading lamp to put next to it, or maybe even a TV set or a stereo. I also bought—on borrowed money—an old beat-up '65 Ford Falcon. It was not much to look at, but it ran like a top, and I couldn't complain about that. I was out on my own and taking care of myself. I would soon be twenty-three years old. That sounded so ancient. And sadly, none of my dreams had come true.

For two months, I searched for a teaching job until I was completely positive there was none available. I laughed to myself as I remembered the counselor's words my freshman year: "Be a teacher, the country is in need of teachers." Counselors across America must have told everyone to pick that profession because whenever I knocked on a door, the first thing said was, "We have no available positions in the teaching field, but we can put you on a list." In the summer of 1973, rumor had it that in Fairfax County there was a list of over six hundred applicants searching for teaching positions: part time, half time, and full time. Unfortunately, the same rumor claimed that there were less than a few dozen spots to be filled. Even the private schools weren't hiring. I sent applications to different counties and other states, but heard no reply. I was beginning to realize that a good teaching credential wasn't going to guarantee me a job. I had thought it was going to be so easy.

Nearly all my money was gone. Even the nest egg I made working in the cafeteria at Harper Center had dwindled down to less than $200. I couldn't bring myself to ask a dime from my parents; they barely had enough to make ends meet. I needed a job to generate cash flow. I took a position as a cocktail waitress at Frank's Hideaway on Route One and promised myself that it was only temporary. In six months—maybe a year—things would be different, and schools would be hiring again.

I hated my new job. I couldn't stand wearing the uniform: a low-cut top and tight shorts. The white wet look boots I had to wear were not only sleazy, but they were uncomfortable too. The club catered to GIs from Fort Belvoir who were constantly pinching me and thinking I enjoyed it. I felt violated, but I couldn't do anything about it, because angry or harsh words meant a flat table—and that would defeat the purpose. So I smiled and pretended, playing along with their games, leaving plenty of leeway to avoid confrontations after closing hours. Every night when I returned to my apartment, I jumped into the shower and tried to wash away the snide comments, the "friendly" pinches, and the crude propositions. I hated the way men assumed that I was easy prey to their physical needs simply because I waited tables and delivered drinks; I hated the way they touched me as if I were part of the menu; but mostly, I hated the fact that I had a college degree, and I couldn't do a damn thing with it. It wasn't fair. I'd worked hard for my diploma, and now it all seemed worthless. What was I doing wrong? Nothing was working out the way I had planned and for the life of me, I couldn't understand why.

5

One day toward the end of August, I drove to my parents' house. Through most of the summer, I had dropped by unannounced several times a week in order to watch the Watergate hearings on their television. Nixon had really gotten himself into a mess this time. John Dean had spilled his guts in June and things weren't looking very good for the White House. The latest stink was over some tapes that the President refused to hand over to the Senate committee. No one seemed to know what was on the tapes, but everyone wanted to find out. The irony of it all was that Nixon had finally gained some popularity for his foreign policy, ending the war, and bringing our prisoners of war home. Now he was faced with this scandal.

People's attitudes reflected Nixon's actions. I heard, "Well, if the president can get away with bending the rules, why can't I?" The population felt betrayed, and everyone was angry. The press smelled blood. They were out for the kill.

It seemed as if the entire country was changing in front of my eyes. Strangers who had once appeared pleasant—greeting others with smiles, saying "please" and "thank you" when needed—were no longer behaving that way. They seemed aggravated while waiting in lines and often made negative remarks not worrying who might hear them. Manners and common courtesy were disintegrating. It appeared that everyone's priority was me, me, me! Respect for our country was at an all-time low, and few had anything positive to say for the future. It seemed as if a cancer was growing and decaying everything in its path. Had it always been like this? Or was this the beginning of a new era?

Washington is notoriously hot in August, but this particular day was unseasonably cool. As I drove into my parents' driveway, I noticed that their windows were open, which allowed a pleasant breeze to pass through the house. I loved this house. Whenever I felt sad, I knew I could come here and find a sanctuary filled with peace and harmony.

As I approached the door, I heard raised voices inside. I wondered who could possibly be talking in such a loud manner. Never in my life could I remember anger inside these walls: only patient, gentle tones. I took a few more paces and craned my neck.

"You can't do this, Joe." It was my mother's voice. I couldn't hear what my father was saying. His voice was much lower than Mom's. "Do you really think that you can walk out of here now that Lori and Kurt are grown?"

What the hell was going on? Why was my mother so upset?

"You leave the kids out of this!" My father's voice became audible. "I stuck around while they were young. We gave them a good place to grow up, but they're not here anymore, and I have a right to a life now. It's *my* turn!"

"You lousy son of a bitch! I put up with a lot of shit from you over the years, and I'm not going to let you walk out of here with everything going your way. Half of this is mine." Her boisterous voice bellowed through the yard. "You can take that sleazy whore of yours and get the hell out of here. But remember! If you walk out that door you won't take anything with you."

I clamped my hands over my ears but not before my father's voice pierced through the air one more time. "You listen to me, bitch! This is my house . . . my house! Do you hear me . . . mine! And I'm not going any fucking place. I've put every last dime I made into this house. Everything I own is here. Nobody is going to push me out of it."

What was happening? It seemed as if the cancer I noticed around me had festered and spread to my family. My God! My God! There was no safe place. No haven. There was nowhere to hide. I turned and raced back to my car. Several times, I stumbled over my feet. I dropped my purse and hurriedly bent over to pick it up. Everything fell out. In a panic, I shoved the contents back inside. I had to get away from here. My hand shook so badly; I could barely get the key in the ignition. I yanked the stick on the column and put the car in reverse. The world was filled with bitterness and hate. It was everywhere! Everywhere! I felt consumed by it.

Part II
The Changing Years

1

Brad

FOR THE FIRST TIME IN MY LIFE, I WAS DOING WHAT I WANTED TO DO. I moved out of my father's house after graduation, and I took everything that was mine with me. I never intended to return. I had my camera equipment, my clothes, a few pieces of beat-up furniture, and a cheap apartment in the Village. Not very much to call my own, but I was proud of it. I had my freedom, and I loved New York. For five months, I struggled, trying to get my foot in the door where my talent could be put to use, but I wasn't having any luck. I always knew it wouldn't be easy, but I had no idea that it was going to be this difficult. I was barely making ends meet. I worked as a dishwasher in a kitchen of a sleazy restaurant six nights a week; on Tuesday and Friday mornings, I knocked on doors, spoke with dozens of nameless secretaries, and tried to show my portfolio to their bosses—hoping for a break; on Tuesday afternoons and all day Monday and Wednesday, I moved around the city taking baby pictures in the subjects' homes; and on Thursday, I went back to those mothers whose babies I had photographed and tried to sell them the finished products. My dishwashing position paid minimum wage, pounding on doors paid zilch, and taking baby pictures was based strictly on commission. No one was interested in an up-and-coming professional photographer. But I wasn't going to give up that easily.

My professor at Elon gave me two names to look up when I arrived in New York. One listened to my speech, looked at my pictures, and even smiled pleasantly. After the interview, he simply muttered, "I'll give you a call if we need anyone." Needless to say, I hadn't heard a word from him. The second man referred me to the portrait service, which was connected with some kind of diaper business. They hired me.

The job was a referral of sorts. I was given a list every week of a dozen or more women with young children who used Day-by-Day Diaper Service. I called and asked each mother if she wanted her child's picture taken in her home. If the answer was "yes," I scheduled an appointment, lugged my equipment over to the address, and prayed the mother didn't stand me up, or the baby wasn't having a crying fit, or the kid didn't get sick all over me. It wasn't very glamorous, but at least I was taking pictures.

The problem with working for commission was that many times I shot a dozen or more jobs and barely broke even. I had a client who complained about every little thing. The mother demanded a Saturday appointment, which screwed up my only day off. She insisted on a certain time. When I arrived, the kid was sleeping. I had to wait over thirty minutes so she could get the kid ready, and then she constantly interfered with her child while I tried to pose him. And if that wasn't enough, the woman talked the entire time. I spent over an hour and a half—not including set up and travel time— taking the kid's pictures, and the damned mother bought the special of the week which was one stinking 5" x 7". It cost two dollars, and I made a frig- gin' thirty-five cents for my work. I was so pissed off, I couldn't see straight.

On another job, I photographed a pair of twins whose mother had hot pants. I couldn't believe it. The woman had five kids. Most of them cried in off-key tones while she propositioned me. At first, I thought she was kid- ding. But after the third time she rubbed her leg "accidentally" against mine, I got her message. Four times she repeated when her husband worked, when her little ones took their naps, and the hours the others were in school.

By the time I finished, I had her schedule memorized. I thought about taking her up on her offer, but decided against it. With my luck, she'd probably squeal, which would result in my termination. When I turned her down, she refused to buy anything, and I was stiffed again.

Most of the time, I made eight to ten bucks per family. Sometimes I made fifteen. And if I really hard sold an unsuspecting and proud new mother, I made twenty dollars. Once I hit the jackpot and sold over three hundred dollars worth of pictures to a single mom. My cut was seventy bucks. I felt rich.

My seventy-dollar commission came from the mother of one of the prettiest kids I'd ever photographed. She was about a year old, had curly, black ringlets all over her head, beautiful eyes, and a smile that could melt an iceberg. Her name was Ellie Woods. She was the perfect model. Most of the kids were nothing more than a royal pain in my ass, but this child was a pleasure to photograph. She actually flirted with me as I took her picture. There was something about her that looked vaguely familiar. I couldn't put my finger on it. Was it the smile or the eyes? Ellie's mother was nice too: pretty girl, about my age, with a soft-spoken voice, dark hair, and a pleasant personality. She was wealthy. I don't mean comfortably rich—I mean loaded.

As I entered her penthouse apartment, I wondered what her husband did for a living. When I inquired, she told me that she wasn't married. With that news, I proceeded with all my charms to get to know her. You couldn't blame a guy for trying; after all, she was even good looking. Unfortunately, Pam Woods wasn't interested in me, but she did purchase my most expensive package, which consisted of a plaque, an 8" x 10" of one pose, two 5" x 7"s of another, twelve wallets and an advanced order of Christmas cards with her daughter on the cover. It was a very lucrative day. The plaque alone sold for $220. It was more than a picture; it was a piece of furniture made of solid oak. The frame was freestanding, and it displayed a 16" x 20" picture of Ellie donned in a bright yellow dress with a matching ribbon in her hair. She was smiling and holding a tattered bear in her arms. I was very proud of that picture. It was one of the few times since I'd been taking pictures of children that I genuinely felt I captured my subject. I liked the photograph so much; in fact, I kept a small one for myself and put it in my collection of favorite shots.

The Woods commission was a nice bonus, but by no means did it solve my financial problems. I was flat broke 98 percent of the time. I ate tuna fish or peanut butter and jelly sandwiches and drank watered-down Kool Aid at almost every meal. On my "rich" days, I had a couple of eggs for breakfast or a cheap bottle of wine with dinner. Sometimes I splurged for a steak and starved the next few days in order to make up for it.

I couldn't afford to blow my money on luxuries. I had a landlady who didn't take "no" for an answer at the beginning of every month, creditors who were dying to repossess my new camera equipment if I failed to make a payment, and a father who was waiting for me to fall flat on my face. I wasn't going to give in—not now, not ever. My old man gave me a year to "find yourself," as he put it, and I was going to show the bastard that I could do it. More than anything in the world I wanted to open up *Time*, or *Vogue*, or *Newsweek*, or *National Geographic* and see my name at the bottom of a picture. "Photo by Bradley Malone." I'd show him; I'd show my old man that I could make it on my own.

Unfortunately, I hadn't had much of a social life since I'd left Elon. I was too busy, or too poor, or too disinterested. I wasn't sure which was the real truth—probably a combination of all three. But it didn't matter because I'd lost my fascination for women in general. They all seemed the same, and I couldn't be bothered with the trivial games that were played between the sexes. I'd heard it all, seen it all, and done it all. It just didn't seem worth the effort anymore. I'd had my fill. I was taking a vacation from all of them with the exception of Jill.

Jill and I had a unique relationship: one I enjoyed immensely. Fortunately, she made enough money to pay for a quick trip to New York once a week. I always looked forward to seeing her. Even though Jill never admitted it, I knew she was still in love with me. I also knew that she realized I wasn't in love with her. But it didn't seem to matter to either one of us. She seemed content with the arrangement, and so was I. I needed Jill's companionship. She needed to keep me around for reasons of her own. I didn't ask, and she didn't volunteer the information.

Jill and I were sleeping together again. It happened suddenly about three months ago while she was visiting me. We were sharing a couple of bottles of wine. Both of us were plastered. Before I knew what was happening, we were in each other's arms, our clothes peeled off. As always, sex with Jill was great. I had no complaint about our relationship in bed. The sexual part of our friendship was a physical outlet that both of us needed. For me, because I still needed sexual release and comforting arms. For Jill, because she felt that perhaps, eventually, I would have a change of heart. The relationship was two-fold: friendship and sexual. We enjoyed both.

I didn't want to hurt Jill like I'd hurt Cindy Wilder. It was nearly a year since I'd broken the engagement. My damned conscience was still gnawing at me. Cindy had loved me—really loved me, but she deserved better than I could offer. The duration of our relationship lasted much longer than I'd anticipated, but in the end I knew we were both better off this way. Neither one of us would ever be happy if we stayed together.

Since coming to New York, I'd received very little mail. In fact, other than Jill, Rick was the only person who wrote to me. My brother seemed genuinely happy with his life. His goals were so opposite my own. Working alongside my father and seeing Valerie a couple of times a month seemed to be the only important factors in his life. Even though I couldn't agree with his choice of occupations, I did have to admit that Rick found his perfect match with Valerie. I envied his happiness. The only thing that bothered me about Rick's letters was the countless times he hinted at my returning home. He never came directly out and said the words, but he was always writing that Dad asked about me, or Dad missed me, or Dad wondered what I thought about this idea or that concept. I ignored every word Rick wrote that was even remotely connected to our father. I knew it was all bullshit. My old man didn't want me home any more than I wanted to be there. And

I had no intention of disappointing either one of us.

In Rick's last letter, he mentioned that if I were interested, he would be more than willing to drive me to Elon for Homecoming Weekend; it was next week. At first, I snubbed the idea, thinking what a waste of time and precious money, but then I started pondering the trip. After all, it would be nice to see some old friends even if I wasn't the success I had bragged I would be. I hadn't left New York since May. I hadn't taken a day off from washing dishes since I started the job. And I hadn't seen Bill since graduation. I missed Bill. In fact, I missed all my fraternity brothers.

And then there was always Laura. More than likely, Laura would be at the festivities because she was last year's queen. Beautiful, lovely Laura! I tried never to think of her. The memories of her hostile expressions and trenchant words were far too painful. I knew now the hurt that was involved when a person's love was not returned. It had taken a long time to figure it out, but I finally realized that I loved Laura Davis. God help me, but I loved her more than I ever thought possible. I could kick myself in the ass for being such a fool, but I would have given anything to change those aloof, uncaring eyes of hers into passionate, ardent ones. But it was hopeless. Laura Davis hated me with as much fervor as I loved her, and there wasn't a damned thing I could do to change that fact.

I did everything I could think of to get over her. During my last year at Elon, I had dated dozens of girls, most of them freshmen, but I wasn't able to stop thinking about Laura, and a chain of new faces wasn't the cure. But finally I was getting over her. Hell! I could even go a full day—sometimes two—without thinking about her, and believe it or not, that was a small miracle.

Yes! I'd go with Rick to Elon. It might be fun.

2

The alumni came in hordes. Everywhere I looked, I saw old faces as well as new ones. Homecoming was the biggest campus weekend of the year. The students, as well as graduates, were celebrating it to the fullest. It was a gala starting off with a Stevie Wonder concert on Friday night, the football game on Saturday afternoon, and a special bonus outdoor concert with the Doobie Brothers on Sunday during the picnic. It was going to be quite an eventful weekend.

Rick made separate room reservations for both of us at the Holiday Inn. My brother insisted on loaning the money to me, because he simply could not let an entire weekend go by without privacy. I told him that I didn't want charity, and I had no idea when I'd be able to pay him back. Rick brushed my comment aside and said that it wasn't important. At first, I was a little pissed, but then I realized that Rick would be angry with me if I insisted on sleeping in the room he intended to share with Valerie. I grinned. My wholesome brother had changed. A few years ago, I never would have imagined that Rick would take a girl to a motel room.

After checking into the Holiday Inn, Rick dropped me off at the frat house, and then drove to Val's. Shortly after entering the fraternity house, I ran into Billy. We both grabbed each other by the shoulders as we each slapped the other on the back. He looked great. I remembered when Billy didn't have enough hair on his face to shave, and now he had a full beard and a thick mustache. Where had all the time gone? It seemed like yesterday that Billy and I played hooky from elementary school, rode our bikes to the river, and fished all afternoon. I couldn't remember when we weren't best friends. I didn't realize how much I missed him. We pulled a couple of beers out of the refrigerator, dropped a buck in the tin can on the counter, and sat down on two available chairs in the dining room.

As Billy and I talked about old times, I watched the people parading around us. The large room was packed with fraternity brothers, their dates, and several new pledges. The faces were beginning to change. There were a lot of new people. I recognized 70, maybe 75 percent of the guys. In a few years, if I came back to Elon, I probably wouldn't know anyone. It was sad. You went to a school for four years thinking it was your own private world, and when you graduated, the place was filled with new people, fresh ideas, and different pranks to pull. In a strange way, it made me feel lonely and out of place, as if I no longer belonged.

During the concert, I spotted Laura on the other side of the gymnasium. There were a couple thousand people jammed into a dimly lit room, and I still had the ability to pick her out of the crowd. She looked beautiful. I wanted to push my way down to her, but I knew that the attempt would only be met with a bittersweet exchange of meaningless words, and I would be left feeling even more depressed than if I didn't speak to her at all. Instead, I settled for watching her. I saw her lips move slowly as she spoke to the person next to her, and I watched as her smile captivated the ones around her. How many times over the last four years had I stood at a distance and watched Laura? Countless times. If there were a degree for staring, I would have earned it. The music stopped. After a five-minute standing ovation, Stevie Wonder came back onstage for an encore. The entire audience remained on their feet as he sang.

When the applause died down and people headed for the exits, I lost track of Laura. Everyone seemed to have a date with the exception of Billy and me. The two of us walked back to the TKE house and drank beer. We reminisced about our early years, roared at some of the antics we pulled, and wished we could be young again with no responsibilities, no bills, and no pressures. Our toughest problem back then was trying to figure out how we were going to pass our next spelling test. Finally, after consuming a six-pack, the frat house seemed oppressively overcrowded, so Billy drove me back to the Holiday Inn. I crashed on the bed and slept soundly during the remainder of the night.

The weather was absolutely perfect for an October afternoon: bright blue sky with huge, white, puffy clouds and just enough chill in the air to remind everyone that winter was approaching. It was real football weather. I had a full flask of Jim Beam in the pocket of my sports coat and was joining in with the rest of the half intoxicated, overly zealous young people bursting with the excitement of the day.

After Jacko White's marching band and feature twirler Mary Annie Harper performed the pregame show, everyone stood up for the kickoff. The game was under way. Joe West, the quarterback, was even better this year than last. He was fluid and precise—a treat to behold. If the season's winning streak continued, there was a rumor that Coach Red Wilson could take the Fighting Christians to the NAIA national playoffs. Needless to say, that goal inspired the crowd to cheer loudly for the team.

By halftime, I polished off four Cokes and half my bourbon. It was a good game. The crowd was exhilarated. I'd forgotten how much fun college ball was to watch. The fans were yelling and cheering as the team ran off to the locker room, and the halftime ceremonies began.

The Homecoming Court was presented. I vividly remembered a year ago when I stood next to Laura as the announcer spoke her name. Her hand trembled so much; I had a hard time holding on to it. She was completely floored by the fact that she was elected the queen, and I took great pleasure in wiping the shining tears from her cheeks. Laura didn't know it, but I paid off the guy who was supposed to be her escort. It cost me twenty-five bucks to trade places with him, but I couldn't pass up the chance to be near her.

I could still remember how angry Laura was when she discovered that I was to be her escort. She was more than upset; she was furious. There was actually a moment when I thought she might throw a jab in my direction. I was rather proud of the casual way I behaved. I certainly wasn't going to let her get the upper hand, and I definitely couldn't let her know how I felt; if I did, she'd only use it as a weapon against me. Instead, I was nonchalant and even made a few jokes.

As Laura walked onto the field, the announcer welcomed back last year's queen. The moment I saw her, I realized I could not leave North Carolina without at least attempting to speak with her. I swore I would never subject myself to her aloofness again, but the alcohol gave me the false courage I needed. The new queen was announced and crowned. I never heard the winner's name, because I was working my way past the crowded bleachers to the section of fence Laura had to cross in order to get back to her seat. Nervous as a schoolkid standing in front of an angry parent, I awaited Laura's return. Perspiration began to form on my upper lip. My left eye

Tesa Jones ❧ 325

twitched involuntarily. I put my hands in my pockets to conceal my shaking fingers. My toes were balled up inside my shoes; the pain it caused was a welcome diversion.

As she approached, I managed to speak. "Hi." I sounded more like an injured frog than a human.

"Hello, Brad." She had one hand on the railing, and her feet were on different steps.

Laura's lower lip seemed to be quivering, but I couldn't be sure. I did not know whether she was surprised, angry, or merely peeved at having to speak to me. "You're looking very well." I suddenly realized that I was holding my breath. I forced myself to breathe evenly.

"Thank you, Brad. You're looking rather fine yourself."

"Nice outfit . . . it looks pretty on you."

"Thanks." She was so stiff.

"Could I interest you in a drink and a little conversation . . . for old times' sake?"

"For old times' sake?" she muttered as she glanced over my shoulder. Her voice was very casual and soft. "I don't think so, Brad . . . but thanks for asking."

"Are you here with someone?"

"No."

I reached for her arm as she attempted to step past me, but all I managed to grab onto was the material of her sleeve. "Don't go, Laura." I watched her as she looked down at my hand. What was she thinking? "Please stay . . . just for a few minutes." I had never heard my voice sound so pleading, and I was embarrassed that I hadn't been able to conceal my emotions.

She returned her eyes to mine. Something changed in them. They were still crystal blue, still blank, and remote, but the callousness disappeared. I couldn't quite read the message that was held in them.

"All right," she nodded.

I steered her to an open section in the stands and mixed two light bourbon and Cokes. I cleared my throat before saying, "So, Laura, how's life been treating you since you left Elon?" I sounded too damned formal.

She looked down, masking her expression. After pausing a fraction of a second, she answered, "A lot differently than I expected."

"What grade are you teaching?"

"I'm not teaching. There weren't any positions available. I applied everywhere . . . private and public. I even sent applications as far away as Georgia, but I haven't heard a word. It's depressing."

"I know what you mean. I'm not having any luck either." I paused. "I'm in New York now. Believe it or not, I'm making a buck sixty an hour washing dishes. There's not a huge demand for rookie photographers."

"I always thought you had a lot of talent, Brad. I'm sure it will happen for you."

I grinned shyly. I was pleasantly surprised when I saw that she was returning my action. I loved Laura's smile. I watched her quietly for a moment before I continued, "Right now, I have this side job taking baby pictures for commission, but that's not really photography, and I certainly don't make very much money. If it weren't for my dishpan hands, I'd probably starve to death."

"I'm waiting tables." There was a wistful ring to the soft chuckle that emerged from her throat. She was pensive.

I desperately wanted to reach out and touch her. I wanted to see her smile again as she had done a moment ago.

"Nothing's like we thought it would be. Is it, Brad?" She glanced around at the activities surrounding us . . . the yelling, the cheers, the frivolous sheltered world we had left behind. "I'm just now realizing what it's really like out there . . . in the real world. It's so different. I must have been living in some kind of cocoon. I was so blind . . . and so stupid."

"I know what you mean." I touched the side of her face and lifted her chin as I silently ran my fingers over her smooth skin. With the exception of the slight quivering of her lower lip when I touched it with my index finger, Laura didn't move. Her eyes drooped shut and then flipped open again as she took a couple of steady, even breaths of fresh air. I continued tracing the line of her jaw. Even though hundreds of people surrounded us, I saw no one but Laura.

Slowly, she raised her hand, placed it firmly around mine, and lowered it back down onto her lap. I watched as her fingers drew patterns across my palm; she was lightly stroking each line. What was she thinking? Why was she touching me with so much tenderness?

Even though it had been a long time since Laura had shown any kind of physical affection toward me, I still remembered those magical moments we'd spent together: those countless hours I had rested my head in her lap, and she had stroked my hair as we shared our dreams, our struggles, our lives. I still remembered the way her lips tasted . . . the feel of her breast in my hand . . . how her body melded perfectly into mine when we danced . . . the way her eyelashes fluttered against my neck when I held her in my arms . . . the way my heart soared every time I saw her . . . how the very smell of her excited me. Every moment was still ardently clear. Not one memory had faded with time.

"Laura, let's get out of here . . . go some place where we can be alone. Come with me . . . please."

She never looked up from my hand; instead, she continued to trace my fingers with her own. Her voice was so soft. "All right," she whispered. Laura squeezed my hand, gently pulled it up to her lips, and pressed my fingers against her mouth. She closed her eyes and burned her lower lip into my thumb.

My God! Did she realize how much I wanted to wrap her in my arms—drink in her sweet scent? I didn't know why she was coming with me; I did not know where I was going to take her; I didn't even know the words I was going to say. I only knew that it was heaven to be so close to her again.

I borrowed Billy's car, and we drove to my motel room in silence. I did not ask her if she wanted to come, and she didn't comment when I pulled into the parking lot. Without saying a word, we got out of the car and walked slowly to the room that Rick had so graciously gotten for me. I closed the curtains and turned on the lamp. Loosening my tie, I pivoted to face Laura.

She looked fragile standing there in her light-blue wool suit. Her eyes focused on the floor, and her hair masked most of her expression. I took the steps between us and surrounded her with my arms. She, in turn, wrapped hers firmly around me. Holy Jesus! I must be dreaming. This couldn't be real! But it was. My body began to pulsate with anticipation and desire. I felt dizzy. It was intoxicating to be so close to her. I knew Laura could feel my erection penetrating through our clothes, but I didn't care. I pressed myself firmly against her hip and buried my mouth in her neck. Gathering her hair gently with both hands, I pulled it back behind her head, leaving her face free for my lips to taste.

My Laura! I was actually holding her in my arms, and for some unknown reason, she was responding. "Laura." I whispered her name. It was the first word spoken since we left the stadium.

"I can't fight you anymore, Brad." She muttered the syllables in a breathless, guttural manner.

I didn't know what she was talking about . . . and I didn't care. I only knew that she was undoing the buttons on my shirt. Her eyes captured mine as we slowly—methodically—removed each other's clothes. Although my breathing was erratic and my heart was pounding uncontrollably against the walls of my chest, I continued to move gingerly. I was savoring every moment. I couldn't believe it. This was really going to happen. I was finally going to make love to Laura. I'd waited more than four years!

The clothes lay in piles at our feet. Laura stood naked in front of me—displaying firm round breasts with taut nipples. I cupped them tenderly in my hands. They swelled at my touch. Laura took a shallow breath that stuck in her throat. For an instant, I saw panic in her expression. Seconds later, she flung her arms around me. As Laura kissed me, she cried out my name. I was overwhelmed by the passion—in her—in me. In one swift movement, I cradled her in my arms and carried her over to the bed. Gently, I placed her on the mattress. "I want you, Laura." My voice was husky and thick.

Her eyes had a misty film over the irises making them appear transparent. Her lips were slightly parted—inviting mine—and her arms were outstretched welcoming me to take her.

"Laura." I flung myself onto her. Before I knew what happened, I was entering her; I had only one split second to realize that there was no thin skin protecting her virginity. I brushed the thought aside. I couldn't think about that now. I could only think of Laura and possessing her. I heaved myself into her warmth two, maybe three, times before I could no longer control the sweeping desires that consumed me. Only moments after diving into her, I exploded from the tremendous excitement that had been building up inside me for years. I couldn't remember the last time I exhibited such a lack of self-control. I wanted it to be so different. I wanted to carry Laura over the brink with me. I wanted to share in the wild sensations it created—each of us stimulated and fulfilled.

I collapsed onto her chest completely exhausted and thoroughly satisfied. She clung to me, and I took satisfaction in the fact that at least she did not hate me anymore. I knew my sexual performance had been a physical disappointment, but next time . . . next time I'd pace myself.

Laura's nails traced circular patterns over my back. The soft, caressing movement sent shivers of delight throughout my body. She was humming quietly. It had a stimulating yet tranquilizing effect on me: a unique and exciting blend of sensations. I wrapped her in my arms and relished the moment.

It wasn't long before I felt aroused again. Being so near Laura was an aphrodisiac. Lightly, I brushed my lips across her neck. As I tenderly licked at the soft hairs of her skin, I was thrilled to feel her tremble beneath me. Little purring sounds emerged from deep within her throat. She pressed her body against mine, and I felt as if I might burst from the pleasure. This time, I was slow and deliberate in my actions as I searched each part of her body that I had dreamed of knowing. I teased her, toying with the areas that seemed to draw the most reward. Directly above her right nipple, there was a tiny pock mark. Fluttering my tongue around it caused her to whimper slightly. I buried my face between her breasts, and I was sure I'd gone to heaven. There had never been anything or anyone like Laura.

I continued moving down her body. She was sleek and firm. I wanted to memorize each inch, every detail, and frame it in my mind. Slowly, I ran my fingers over her legs, caressing them and nibbling at freckles I'd never seen before. The skin was soft and smooth as satin. On the inside of her right thigh, she had the most unusual birthmark. It was shaped like the profile of a cat with whiskers and a grin. I licked it twice before sucking it into my mouth, which created a tremor through Laura's entire body. I felt her pulse quicken and sensed the urgency in her movements. Her back arched invitingly, but I paced myself, knowing that she was not quite ready. Beads of sweat formed on her skin. I tasted the salty drops; as a result, her flesh swelled where my lips had been.

"Brad." She intertwined her fingers in my hair and forced me to look at her. She drew me so close to her that I could look deep into her eyes. "Kiss me." Laura forced our mouths together. Her pelvis arched to meet me. "Now, Brad . . . now." She muttered between the moments when are lips were apart.

"Laura . . . I've waited so long for this." As I pressed my mouth upon hers, I realized she had never tasted sweeter than at that moment. I entered her . . . this time slowly, rhythmically, blocking out everything but the very feel of her. She was hot. Burning. I continued pumping, concentrating on her pleasure, making sure that she was climbing the same mountain I was. Desperate sounds came from both of our throats as we matched each other's passion. When I reached the crest, I began to shudder. Oh, Jesus . . . sweet Jesus . . . Laura . . . I'm coming . . . I'm going to explode! I can't hold back any longer.

It seemed as if my head burst. The blackness surrounded me like it always did when I climaxed, but this time there was a peaceful feeling enveloping me that I'd never known before. It was magical, enlightening . . . . perhaps the most beautiful sensation I'd ever experienced.

In the aftermath, I felt as if I were glowing. It was wonderfully snug and warm in Laura's arms. Without either of us saying a word, I rested my head on her chest and listened to her heart beating. It was so comfortable being with Laura—quietly holding her—wishing that the moment would never end. I could not remember ever being so happy.

As time passed, I became curious about the fact that Laura was not a virgin, but I didn't broach the subject because I knew to do so might ruin the beauty of what just happened between us. But still, the thought gnawed at me. I began to feel jealous . . . even a little angry. The thought of Laura in another man's arms—Laura loving another man—it was pure torture. Who was it? Jack Briskin? Maybe. My God! Was it my brother? No! It couldn't have been. I'd have known if it were Rick. Wouldn't I? Perhaps it was someone else she'd dated at Elon. She knew lots of guys. Or maybe it was some asshole she met after graduation. If so, was she still involved with him?

Shit! Don't think about it! Push those negative thoughts away before I fucked up now—this minute—with Laura. What the hell difference did it make if she were a virgin? The important thing was that we were finally together.

"I can't believe you're really here." I almost choked on my words. "It was beautiful, Laura. You're beautiful." I kissed her cheek and looked into her smiling face. She was smiling. She was actually smiling. I had dreaded looking at the expression in her eyes, but I became completely ecstatic when I saw that there was only happiness reflected in them. I smothered her with warm, loving kisses and whispered endearments into her ears. Both of us were laughing, tickling, pinching each other, and kissing places on each other's body neither of us knew existed before today.

She nuzzled her nose into the side of my neck and whispered softly, "Hold me, Brad! Hold me. This isn't a dream, is it? If it is . . . don't ever wake me up." She was practically crying the words.

"Oh, Laura . . . you are mine." I kissed her passionately. "No one else can have you."

We made love a third time before I rolled off her body. Chuckling softly,

I said, "You are insatiable, my sweet Laura. I love it!" I kissed her playfully before adding, "I'm starving."

"If you think I'm going to let you go now . . . you're nuts." She jokingly pinned me down on the bed and straddled me.

I pretended to be too weak to move. "Food! I need food," I whispered as if I had no power to fight her. "A man needs his strength."

"Well, if you must," she responded teasingly as she leaped from the bed.

I was amazed at how uninhibited Laura was. I had always pictured her as shy and modest, but she paraded around, half dressed, singing merrily as she readied herself for our departure. It was a wonderful feeling to be in the same room with her. Cozy. Safe. Warm. I watched her as she brushed her hair and applied fresh blush on her cheeks. She didn't need to—her cheeks were already glowing. I hoped I was the cause of her radiant appearance. She looked exquisite and angelic simultaneously. I could not take my eyes off her.

While her back was to me, I strolled up behind her and encircled her tenderly in my arms. After kissing her neck, I whispered, "What do you say about returning Billy's car to the frat house? You pack your bags over at the dorm. I'll meet you. We can get some dinner at Harper Center. Then Rick can bring us back here." I ran my tongue enticingly over the edge of her ear. "I'm sure there are a few things we still haven't explored about each other. We can stay in bed for the rest of the weekend."

She twirled effortlessly in my arms and kissed me with a fervor I'd never known she possessed. If I weren't so hungry, I'd have picked her up and carried her back to the bed, disrobing her and making love to her for a fourth time today. But it could wait. We were finally together, and nothing was going to separate us again. "I do believe that I've opened Pandora's box," I said as I cupped her chin and playfully kissed her cheeks. Winking, I added, "Save some for later; we have plenty of time."

She laughed with me as we turned and walked out the door. During the ride back to campus, I had one hand on the steering wheel and the other securely on Laura's shoulder. Together, we sang along with the radio. Perfect songs were playing for the occasion. George Harrison's "Give Me Love", Roberta Flack's "Killing Me Softly", and my personal favorite, "You Are the Sunshine of My Life" by Stevie Wonder.

At a stoplight, Laura wedged herself between the steering wheel and me, pressed her body against mine, and kissed me in a provocative, alluring manner. I could feel her breasts swell as she breathed; it caused them to press suggestively against me. I wasn't sure if she was intentionally using her body in such a sensual manner or if she was merely being playful and oblivious to the effect it had on me. This was a side of Laura I had never seen before, and I loved it. The mixture of her innocence and her sexuality nearly took my breath away. While cupping her breast, I kissed her repeatedly and tasted the sweetness of her lips.

My God! She was real! I wanted to strip off her clothes. I couldn't get enough of her.

She giggled uncontrollably. "Brad . . . I think we're stopping traffic."

"Let 'em wait."

The horns blared behind us. It seemed we had caused quite a backup. There was a line of cars that wanted to get through the traffic light. Snickering, Laura sat up. I crossed the intersection and left the racket behind.

When we reached the outskirts of campus, Laura placed a chaste kiss on my cheek. "Brad, can you drop me off at Staley first? You can visit with your friends for a while . . . then come on over. I'll be packed and ready to go." She paused. "Rick doesn't need to take us back. I have my car in the lot."

"You're not going to disappear on me, are you?"

"Not a chance," Laura replied as she leaned over and instigated a sensuous kiss leaving us both craving more. "Come by and page me when you're ready. Don't be long, okay?"

I watched her jump out of the car. She was bouncing with energy and enthusiasm. Laura circled the front and came around to my side. Leaning her head in the window, she placed an enticing kiss on my lips. I gently trapped her neck with the back of my hand and paused several seconds before releasing her. She smiled, and then turned to go inside.

Laura took several steps. I called out to her. "Hey, Laura." She turned. I had so much I wanted to say—so many emotions I had yet to express. Instead of speaking, I just stared at her and framed her image in my mind. She looked exactly like the day I handed her wildflowers. I could still remember the way she looked at them: her face glowing, her eyes sparkling with excitement, and her hair blowing softly in the breeze. She was a combination of confidence and innocence. Her face shone with an inner beauty and strength I'd never seen in anyone. She intrigued me. When she smiled shyly at me that day, I had thought she looked like a ray of sunshine: warm and radiant. I still felt the same effects when I looked at her now.

"Yes, Brad?"

"Nothing . . . " I grinned. How could I possibly put it into words? "I'll tell you later. Okay, sunshine?"

"Okay." She smiled again before turning once more and taking the steps two at a time.

I watched until the door slammed behind her, and then I drove to the frat house. I wondered how Billy had gotten back to campus and hoped he'd hitched a ride with someone. With any luck, he wasn't too angry with me. I searched for him in each of the rooms and was disappointed; Billy was nowhere to be found. I wanted to talk to him. I wanted to tell someone what had happened. I wanted to shout it—ring bells, kick up my heels—and scream it to the skies; I wanted the whole world to know that Laura and I were finally together. She was mine!

I grabbed the ingredients for a sandwich out of the refrigerator. After making it, I plopped down on a chair in the living room and consumed it in several large bites. The place was packed with couples. People were everywhere—drinking, smoking, a few playing cards, several necking in the corners—a couple of brave souls were taking a hike up the stairs to the "den of iniquity." I sat there as patiently as possible and sipped on my Budweiser, ate potato chips, and tried to keep from pacing the floor. The guy next to me started talking, but I didn't hear a word he said. I was too excited to make small talk. Where was Billy? If I didn't talk to him soon, I was going to burst. I simply couldn't keep it in much longer.

"What?" I asked.

The guy had repeatedly said the same thing. "I said, 'it's nice to have open house on weekends.'"

"Yeah, I know . . . times sure change. When I first came to Elon, there was no such thing as open house or visitation. A person could get kicked out for being in the wrong place."

"They've changed the rules."

"Just my luck." I smirked remembering all the times I had used the great outdoors or the backseat of a car for my playground. "Of course, it really isn't that big of an improvement. Visitation is only on weekends . . . and only between the hours of noon and seven. You can still get your ass thrown out if you're caught at night."

We both laughed because each of us knew that visitation or not, girls and guys were still going to go where they weren't suppose to be. After all, rules were made to be broken. Right?

I finished my beer. As I walked toward the kitchen, Billy came into the house. "Hey, buddy . . . hold up."

"Well, Brad . . . how'd it go?"

I tossed him the keys. "Thanks for the use of the wheels."

"Don't mention it. What are friends for?"

"Hope I didn't put you out."

"Nah. Rick gave me a ride back."

We walked into the kitchen. Both of us selected a beer from one of the many coolers, popped the tops, and took a few long swallows. I was dying to talk, but I didn't know how to jump into the conversation.

"Brad, you look like the cat that ate the canary—grinning from ear to ear. What the hell happened after you so suddenly left the game? Find a new chick? Was she worth it?"

I sat down at the beat-up table that everyone used as a cutting board. It must have been around for three generations. As I leaned my elbow on the corner it rocked, and I had to grab my beer before it spilled onto the floor. A few guys paraded into the room, raided the refrigerator, and nodded in our direction. Trying to keep from blurting everything out in front of strangers, I waited until they left.

When Billy and I were finally alone again, I slammed my hand down on the table and let out a monstrous roar. "Billy . . . I did it . . . I finally did it, old buddy."

"Did what?"

"I got Laura into bed. I can't believe it, but I did. I got her . . . I really got her. And it was fantastic. No! It was better than fantastic."

"Where's the red sheet?"

"There isn't one."

"Are you kidding? I would have bet a fortune that Lori Davis still had it intact."

"Yeah. Me too."

"Disappointed?"

"Yeah . . . nah." I frowned slightly, trying to cover up the one disappointment of the day. "I wanted to be the first . . . but it's all right . . . I can handle it." I shrugged. "Do you believe it, Billy? Man, I can't. She actually came with me. Willingly! She was practically begging for it. It was incredible . . . like some kind of dream."

"I suppose you'll be wanting your ten bucks."

"What ten bucks?" I asked as I watched Billy grinning at me and holding back his own amusement.

"You know . . . the ten bucks you bet me when we were freshmen. You claimed that you could get into her pants; if I'm not mistaken, your exact words were 'Laura Davis is like putty in my hands.' Of course, it took longer than I thought, but you earned it." He reached into his pocket and withdrew his wallet.

About the time Billy pulled out two worn-out five dollar bills, there was a loud crashing from the hallway as if someone had slammed the door shut with so much force it had knocked down the curtain rod which hung over the window. Billy pushed the money toward me. "Jesus, they better cut that shit out. Someday, someone's going to break the glass. Hey, Brad, remember when Moose got drunk our senior year and put his head right through the door. Christ Almighty, I can't believe he didn't bleed to death. Thirty-seven stitches and he still hits that door like it is cardboard instead of glass and wood."

"Yeah, I remember." I pushed the bills back toward Billy. "I don't want your money. I'd forgotten all about that stupid bet. I made love to Laura because I'm crazy about her . . . not because I wanted ten lousy dollars." I stood up and started pacing the floor. "I love her, Billy. I'm wild about her."

"So, you finally figured it out. I was wondering how long it was going to take before you admitted it," Billy laughed.

It infuriated me that he was making light of something that I considered to be very serious. "Don't make fun of me, old buddy."

"Who's making fun? Not me, Brad. I think it's great! It's about time you opened your eyes. You were being such a damned fool when it came to that girl. Glad to see you wised up."

"I'm going to marry her. I'm going to marry her . . . now . . . tomorrow or the next day . . . but now."

"You're acting crazy, Brad. Don't freak out on me. Get serious!"

"I am serious! I've pissed away enough time. I want Laura, and I'm not going to take a chance of losing her again."

"You're nuts!" Bill's expression was one of total disbelief. "You can't even support yourself. How the hell do you suppose you'll take care of a wife too?"

"I've got it all figured out. I'll leave New York. I'll quit photography. Nobody wants me anyway. Hell! I'm probably not good enough to cut it. I'll go back to my dad's place and work for him. I can make good money there. Laura would love New Jersey. I just know she would."

"You can't do that, Brad. You hate working for your old man. You always have. And how the hell can you give up taking those pictures of yours? It's all you've ever wanted to do. You can't quit so easily."

"It doesn't matter. None of that matters, Billy! All I want is Laura. I swear to God, she's all I want. Ever since the first time I saw her . . . I can't explain it . . . I feel like she crept into my soul, and she has been tugging at my heart ever since." I took a deep breath and tried to sort my emotions. "I didn't want to fall in love with her. Hell! I didn't want to love anyone. I did not think it was possible." I stopped pacing and sat across the table from Billy. I continued to speak, but this time with a much calmer voice. "I don't feel like a whole person without Laura." I paused. "She's under my skin. When we're not together, I can't think straight! I feel like I'm missing something when I'm not with her. I can't explain it, Billy. I just know that I can't lose her again." After taking a deep breath, I continued, "I'm going to ask her to marry me . . . tonight. I know she'll say yes. I just know it. Damn it! She better say yes. I don't know what I'll do if she doesn't." We both laughed. I couldn't believe how nervous I was sitting there talking to Billy about it; I knew I'd be twice as apprehensive with Laura.

Of course, I wanted my pictures. I loved my cameras. I'd be a liar if I tried to deny it, but I wanted Laura too. I loved her. I'd loved her from the beginning, but I'd been too damn stubborn and stupid and afraid to admit it. It was all so clear now. I had made that snap decision to get engaged to Cindy my junior year because I was running away from my emotions. I was terrified of loving Laura and petrified of being vulnerable; therefore, I subconsciously—yet intentionally—sabotaged our relationship. But I knew in my gut I couldn't marry Cindy, and I could never marry Jill because they weren't the women I wanted. Laura was the only one! No other woman could replace her. I wasn't going to let her go, no matter what the cost.

"I'm happy for you, Brad. You and Lori belong together. Hell! Half the campus knew it. I've known it for years, but nobody could figure out how come the two of you didn't realize it."

"Will you stand up with me, Billy? Will you be my best man?"

"You bet; I'd be honored." He slapped me on the back. The two of us drank a toast to my future.

I felt as if I'd conquered the world.

After one additional beer, I jogged over to Staley dorm. On my way, I stopped by the Tiny Tote and bought a single red rose. I was overflowing with so much happiness that I actually felt as if my feet didn't touched the ground. I was in love. The words had a funny ring even to my own ears. Love! Imagine me, Brad Malone, in love. Love . . . I had sworn myself against the emotion. Love was for stupid fools who didn't know any better. I thought love was destructive, undependable, possessive, and for those who didn't have enough strength to stand on their own. Love wasn't like that at all. Loving Laura was the most beautiful thing that had ever happened to me. I was a fool to have wasted all those years fighting my emotions, but now I was going to glory in them for the rest of my life. I loved her! I loved her, and I didn't care who knew it. I stopped jogging and looked up toward the sky. "I love you, Laura Davis!" I screamed the words. After I said it, I felt better—not as tense and anxious. I walked the remainder of the way to Staley, my heart thumping in my chest. I opened the door and took the steps to the receptionist's desk.

"Will you please page Laura Davis for me?"

"Laura Davis . . . I don't think I know her. Wait a minute . . . didn't she graduate last year?"

"Yeah, but she's here for the weekend. It's Homecoming, you know."

"Let me see if she's on the list." The girl ran her finger down the names on the paper she was holding. "Here it is. She is in room 314 with Christie Hanlon. I'll ring the room for you."

Christie Hanlon? Name sounded familiar. She was one of Laura's sorority sisters. I thought she was a sophomore . . . no, a junior. I'd dated her last year—only went out with her once. She was a nice girl, fun date, but there just hadn't been any chemistry between us. Christ, there hadn't been any chemistry between me and another woman for a long time. Now I understood way.

"Laura Davis with you, Christie?" The receptionist's voice interrupted my thoughts. I couldn't hear the other end of the conversation. "Yeah . . .

okay. Lori Davis then. There's a guy down here asking for her." Silence. "All right, I'll tell him." She hung up the phone. "I'm sorry, I didn't catch your name."

"Brad . . . Brad Malone."

"Well, Brad, Christie said to wait right here. She'll be down in a minute."

"I don't want to talk to Christie. I want to see Laura." I was getting frustrated. This girl was dense. Well, it didn't matter. Christie would tell me where Laura was, and then I'd go get her. A moment later, I saw Christie coming toward me with a slip of paper in her hand. She smiled and waved. I returned the gesture.

"Hi, Brad. It's nice to see you again. How ya been?"

"Fine. How about yourself?"

"Doing pretty well. Enjoying the weekend?"

"Yeah, it's a lot of fun. Not to cut you short or anything, Christie, but do you know where Laura is?"

"She's not here."

"What?" Subconsciously, I gripped tighter on the stem of the rose I was carrying. One of the thorns drew blood. I did not feel the pain.

"She's gone."

"Oh. You mean she's somewhere else on campus?"

"No, I mean she's gone. She went home. We went to the football game together, but I couldn't find her when it was over. And when I got back a little while ago, she was in the room writing this note."

I felt a sinking sensation in the pit of my stomach. My knees became weak.

"I tried to convince her to stay for the Doobie Brothers' concert tomorrow, but she said she couldn't spend another minute on campus; she had to get home." Christie continued, "She said she had a previous engagement she couldn't miss."

"Was she upset?"

"No. She seemed fine."

Something was wrong! Something was very wrong! I watched silently as Christie placed the slip of paper in my hand. After unfolding it, I read the words.

> Decided to go home early. If anyone should ask, say
> that I had a change of plans.
>
> Zeta love, Lori

I smashed the paper into a wad and forced it into the smallest shape I could form. The left side of my face was twitching erratically. I was having difficulty breathing.

"Did you and Lori have a date, Brad?" Christie inquired.

"A date?" I took the balled-up piece of paper and straightened it out on the table. I pressed hard on the corners and smoothed out the wrinkles. "No, we didn't have a date." I ripped the paper over and over again until there was nothing left but tiny fragments. I started to put them in my pocket, but instead I tossed the paper and the rose in the wastebasket next to the desk.

Damn! Fool! I'd been a goddamned fool. I turned and walked out of the lobby. How could I have made such an idiot out of myself? I had actually thought that Laura cared about me. Loved me. Shit! The bitch didn't love me! She didn't give a damn about me! I reflected upon the day's events. I remembered how carefree, immodest, and seductive Laura had been. I remembered how surprised I was by her actions. She seemed experienced and beguiling when I had thought she would be more demure and timid. She knew what she was doing! She calculated her actions. She played me for a sucker. I was willing to bet that she laid with every prick from here to D.C., and like a total jerk I thought today was something special.

Obviously, I wasn't the first man to have her—that was for certain! More than likely, she had a string of affairs going—probably always had—and she didn't want to waste one precious weekend on me. In my mind's eye, I could see her roaring with laughter, loving how she humiliated me again! I played right into her hand—fell into her trap. I couldn't believe I had actually considered marrying her. She would have laughed in my face.

Love! I'd piss on the word. I was right all along. Love was for morons who were too blind to see. But my eyes were opened now. Never again! Never again!

2

Jennifer

It was David's voice on the other end of the phone. I was curious as to why he was calling me at work. He'd never done that before.

"No, Jennifer, instead of walking home, stay where you are. I'll come get you in the car."

"David! What's the matter?" He sounded anxious, which was very unlike my husband.

In the past year since David's near fatal accident, our relationship had slipped from bad to worse after only a few months of reconciliation. At first, while he was helpless in the hospital bed, both of us made a genuine effort to hold onto something, which actually never existed in the first place. After several months, I realized it was a lost cause. I tried to love David. He tried to remain faithful to me, but after his convalescence nothing seemed to work.

He spent a month in the hospital and two months on his back at home. Then, one day, against all odds, he stood up out of sheer determination and took a step. He still had a slight limp as a souvenir, but other than that, he appeared completely normal.

Three months later, I started seeing the signs of our failing marriage. I couldn't put all the blame on him. It was equally my fault. I was always too exhausted, and I never made a real stab at creating the type of atmosphere he wanted. David, on the other hand, was guilty of finding pleasure everywhere but at home.

The lack of money after the accident also created a burden. Insurance covered most of the bills, but we still had to lay out quite a few bucks to make up the difference. We always managed to pay the mortgage, but the utilities and credit cards were two and three months behind. I was furious when I discovered that David gambled away a lot of his paycheck. The worst part about it was that he never won. When he wasn't betting on horses, a ball game, or a rotten poker hand, David was drinking his pocket money or spending it on other women.

At first, I had turned a blind eye to his activities hoping that eventually he would voluntarily put a stop to it, but after a while even my silence did not suffice. There were no more women in my bed, but I knew David was unfaithful. That old cliché "lipstick on his collar" pertained to my husband. I knew his paramours weren't always the same girls, because the strands of hair I found on his clothes were not always the same color. Sometimes the hairs were short and brown; other times, they were long, curly, and red; once they were even kinky and black. David wasn't very good at hiding his affairs. When I did his laundry, I found matchbooks from local hotels in his pockets. I smelled perfume on his shirts. Once, there was even makeup on his underwear. Dozens of telltale signs condemned him of his ignominious acts.

David told me he loved me, but obviously he had a weird definition of love. My husband seemed to be pushing me, as if he wanted to find out what my breaking point was. But, as far as I was concerned, it didn't matter anymore. I didn't care. I stayed with David because I had nowhere else to go.

"David! Would you tell me what happened for Christ's sake? Don't keep me in suspense." I repeated myself as trepidation enveloped me.

"It's your parents, Jennifer."

"What? Are they all right?"

"I don't know any details, Jen. The hospital just called and told me they were in emergency. I'll be there in a minute, and we'll drive over."

I hung up the phone. Not again! It seemed as if every time I turned around someone was in the hospital. First me, two years ago, then David, last year, and now my parents. It was uncanny. I was beginning to believe that my family was single-handedly keeping the hospital in business.

I had not seen my mother or father in over a year and a half—not since I married David. Twice, I called my mother, but both times my father answered the phone. I hung up without saying a word. I made no other attempt to contact her. Why bother? My old man would beat my mother if he knew she spoke to me. As far as Dad was concerned, he no longer had a daughter. That was cool. I no longer considered him my father.

I informed my boss that I was leaving, put on my coat, and went out to the curb to wait for David. I was shaking as much from anxiety as from the cold November evening. I couldn't believe this was actually happening again. Life was so damned screwed up.

Within five minutes, David arrived. He pushed the passenger side door open, and I got in. We drove in silence to George Washington Hospital. Before parking, David let me out at the main door. I inquired at the desk. An elderly doctor came out to speak to me.

"Mrs. Henderson?"

"Yes. How are my parents?"

He took off his wire-rimmed glasses, folded them, and placed them in the pocket of his freshly starched white jacket. He looked despondent. "Let's sit down over here, Mrs. Henderson." He directed me to a hard wooden bench in the corridor. Simultaneously, we sat down. "I'm afraid I have some rather bad news." He paused. "Your father died about fifteen minutes ago. We did everything we could, but he was beyond help. Your mother is in critical condition. The officers who reported the accident said that it was a head-on collision on the Parkway. Your father was driving; he was crushed by the steering wheel. Your mother was thrown against the windshield. She wasn't wearing a safety belt. If she had been . . . well . . . it might have helped."

"Whose fault was it?" I could think of nothing else to say.

"According to the policeman, the driver of the other car was drunk. He lost control of his car near the Spout Run exit and broadsided your parents' car. It put them in a tailspin, forcing them off the road and into a tree. There's hardly a scratch on the other driver." The doctor shook his head and patted my hand tenderly as he muttered, "I don't understand how these things happen. It doesn't seem fair."

A combination of indescribable feelings raced through my mind: disbelief, sorrow, anger, remorse, guilt, and relief—such a variety of emotions. I couldn't seem to put any of them into perspective.

"Is my mother going to make it?"

"We don't know, Mrs. Henderson, but we are doing the best we can. She's been asking for you. She's very weak . . . lost a lot of blood. I'll give you a couple of minutes with her, but don't stay long."

My mother looked emaciated in the sterile, white bed. At first, I didn't think she was breathing, but then I noticed the slight rise and fall of her chest. I stood quietly beside her bed wondering whether or not I should speak.

"Is that you, child?" Her voice was barely audible.

"Yes, Momma."

She lifted her hand signaling me to take hold of it. Trying to give her my strength, I clung to her fingers. We were both trembling.

"I just want . . . "

I couldn't hear her very well so I leaned over and pressed my ear against her lips.

"I want to tell you . . . that I have always loved you, Jennifer."

"Yes, Momma."

"I tried to do my best."

"Don't talk, Momma. Please . . . just relax. It's going to be okay. We'll talk later, when you're feeling better."

"I know I made a mess of everything . . . "

"Shh."

"It's so hard . . . life is so hard."

"Yes, Momma." I couldn't think of any words to say. I wanted to tell her it was okay. I wanted to explain that I really understood. I wanted to tell her that I knew how difficult it was for her to leave my father, and that I understood why she stayed with him. Everything was suddenly crystal clear . . . it all made sense. I wanted her to know that I finally understood her. But none of the words came. I only held her fingers and used my other hand to wipe the hair from her eyes.

"I'm sorry, Jennifer."

"There's nothing to be sorry about, Momma."

"Yes, there is . . ." She swallowed. The effort looked painful. "I wish I could have been a better mother. You were such a sweet, little child. I would have given my soul for you, but I lost it somewhere along the way. I wish it could have been different." Tears welled up in her eyes. "I should have come to see you this year. You're married . . . and I never congratulated you. I should have given you my blessing. I should have . . . "

"Momma, don't talk. Save your strength."

"I want you to be happy, pumpkin." My mother hadn't called me that since I was five years old. It had a warm, pleasant sound to it. "That's all I've ever wanted."

"I know, Momma. I know."

"Don't cheat yourself out of a good life. Don't wait until you're old . . . too old . . . too set in your ways. Don't allow yourself to be in a position where you reflect back on your life only to wish you had done everything differently." She was struggling for breath. "Don't settle for less than your dreams. And Jennifer . . ." Her mouth stopped moving; her eyes remained opened, but her breathing ceased.

I instantly knew my mother was dead. I'd lost her before I'd ever had a chance to get to know her. I was angry and bitter—at my father because he had kept her from me—at my mother for putting up her own private barriers, and at myself for not having the courage to do anything about it. The real tragedy was that I would never get the chance to fix it. It was too late.

Slowly, I stood up. Without looking back, I left the room. David was coming toward me. Before he had the opportunity to speak, I passed him without even acknowledging his presence. I walked all the way home.

During the three days preceding the funerals, I spent the majority of my time sitting in my bathrobe on the big recliner in the living room. I didn't speak to David. I didn't eat. I rarely slept. I just stared blankly at the articles in the room and smoked cigarette after cigarette as I tried to decide what I was going to do with the rest of my life.

Masses of people showed up at Arlington Cemetery for my father's funeral. Men wearing military uniforms decorated with ribbons and stars, surrounded the grave. The Army, the Navy, the Air Force—they all were represented. There was even someone from the White House to pay respects. The twenty-one-gun salute, the horse-drawn carriage, the flag handed to me by the stoic soldier, the ceremony had all the window dressings. It was stately and magnificent, but all I really saw were false faces; they all wore false faces. They didn't know my father! If they had known him, they never would have given him respect or praise. They only saw the man my father wanted them to see. It was sick and perverted. I hated them for being so polite and sympathetic when I knew they didn't—couldn't—possibly comprehend or understand.

The following day, I stood at my mother's grave. Unlike my father's, there were very few people present to witness her burial. She never had many friends. A neighbor of hers came, one of her cousins from Annapolis, a few middle-aged women from the country club who actually had tears in their eyes, the owner of my mother's favorite boutique, and, of course, the priest. Each of them said how tragic it was. Each asked me if there was anything he or she could do for me. Each of them embraced me. None of them gave me any comfort.

I felt completely removed from the entire situation. It didn't seem real. My father received a glorious ceremony with a packed audience, while less than a dozen mourners—some of whom I'd never seen before—surrounded my mother. It didn't make any sense.

The following day, I met with Jonathan Lawrence, my father's lawyer, in his office on K Street in northwest Washington. What an experience! I sat quietly as he read the will. Lawrence was the executor. All expenses incurred for the funeral were to be paid from insurance policies; the house and other assets were to be liquidated and invested as the executor saw fit. A rather large donation was to be sent to West Point in my father's name, and my mother bequeathed an equal amount to three separate charities.

I heard David take a sharp breath when Mr. Lawrence mentioned my trust fund. All that money! When Lawrence was finished, he explained, "You do understand, Mrs. Henderson, that the money can't be touched until you are thirty years old?"

I only shrugged. "I don't care! It doesn't matter. To be perfectly honest, I'm shocked I'm even in the will." I spoke like a robot. "I thought he disowned me a while back."

"The will has not been rewritten in over fifteen years."

"No, of course not. Knowing my father, he didn't expect anything to happen to him. I imagine he thought he'd see one hundred."

"You can rest assured, Mrs. Henderson, that your money will be well invested. It's quite a tidy sum, which will grow handsomely. You can put your faith in us. We will look after you."

Defiantly, I stared directly at Lawrence. "I don't give a damn about that man's money."

"I realize you are under a great deal of stress." He paused for only a moment. "I know this is a difficult time. We will help you through it."

"Whatever you say."

"Jennifer, listen to the man. He's trying to help you." David spoke for the first time since we had taken our seats.

"You like this, don't you, David? This is what you've been hoping for . . . the money . . . this sham of a marriage has always been about the money! When you married me, you thought you'd roped the golden goose. But the laugh has been on you all along. He never acknowledged us. And now that he's dead, he still screws up your plan! You won't be able to touch that money for years. Poor David! You're going to have to live with me for seven more years in order to rake it in. Think it's worth it? Think you can stand me for that long?" I stood up, bent down next to the chair, and picked up my purse. "I don't know about you, David, but I have no intention of spending another day, much less years, with you." I nodded in the direction of the lawyer. "Good day, Mr. Lawrence."

"My deepest sympathies, Mrs. Henderson." John Lawrence reached across his desk, extending his hand.

"Save it for someone who cares." He looked shocked by my comment. Without waiting for David, I left the room.

"Jennifer, where are you going?" David followed. He caught up with me at the elevator.

"I'm going home." My voice was flat. "I'm going to pack, and then I'm leaving."

"You're leaving me?"

"How quick you are to figure that out."

"Jennifer . . . I love you."

"You have a rather strange way of showing it." I wasn't even looking at him as I spoke.

"I'll change. I promise."

"No, you won't, David. You'll never change. You've been like this since I met you. You used me. From the beginning, you got your kicks out of strutting around and telling people you'd reeled in the general's daughter. You thought that was some kind of ticket to class and money, didn't you?"

"Jennifer, it was more than that. You remember . . . we were good together."

"In whose memory?" I ran my eyes the full length of his body. As I spoke, my words were laced with resentment. "You took me for granted from the beginning. Every time you chipped away at our relationship with your incredible behavior, you always tried to make up for the damage by telling me you love me. You don't love me! You don't even know me. You never took the time to understand me or listen to me. You want a pet, not a wife. Someone you can play with at your convenience."

"You think it's easy living with you, Jennifer? Half the time you treat me like I am a piece of furniture."

"Give me a break! Now you expect me to feel sorry for you. I don't need to live like this anymore. My mother spent her entire adult life being someone else's doormat. She was too afraid to walk out. Well, I'm not going to waste my life like that."

"Where are you going? Where will you live? How will you take care of yourself?"

"I don't know. I really don't know. But all my life I let someone else make my decisions, write my rules, set my goals . . . whether I wanted them or not. I was always pushed into being someone that I wasn't and didn't want to be. I was never even allowed to have an opinion of my own. First, my father who was eternally disappointed that I wasn't the son he had hoped for; and then, there was my mother who went along with the charade because she was too weak to do anything about it. They told me how to dress, how to wear my hair, what to eat, who my friends should be, where to go to school, what courses to take. I had so few choices of my own." Pointing a finger at David's chest, I continued. "And you! You wanted me to be your toy! You never gave me credit for doing anything other than lying underneath you when you needed your horns clipped. It never occurred to you that I might have a mind—my own thoughts and opinions. You always laughed at me. I wasn't a person. I was some kind of decoration you liked to show off." Trying to gain my composure, I paused. When I spoke again, my voice was more controlled. "And then there was Kurt. Kurt wanted me to be a princess. At first, I enjoyed how he put me on a pedestal, but now I think that even he had it all screwed up. He wanted me to be perfect—some kind of angel that he could worship—but I'm not that either." I pounded at the elevator button, furious that the carriage still had not arrived. "Damn it! Why do people always want me to be who they want me to be? Why can't I be who I want to be?" I felt so tired. All I wanted to do was sleep—get away—lie down and sleep. "Don't you understand, David? I need to be me. I need to find out who I am. I couldn't be what my father wanted me to be. I can't be like my mother; I refuse to be like her. I'm not Kurt's dream; and I can't be what you want either. I'm none of those people. I'm almost twenty-three years old and damn it . . . I don't even know who Jennifer Carson is! I need my freedom! I need room to breathe!" The elevator finally arrived. The doors opened, and I stepped inside leaving David standing in the corridor.

"You can't do this. You can't just walk out on me."

"Oh, can't I?" The elevator started to close. "Watch me."

The double doors met in the middle. I was alone.

2

I wandered around aimlessly for two days without knowing what to do. Then I thought of Lori. I called her parents. Her father informed me that she lived in the Belle View Apartments on the outskirts of Alexandria. He gave me the address. Instead of calling her first and risking the chance that she might hang up on me, I drove over to see her. I couldn't believe I was actually standing outside Lori's apartment and waiting for her to answer my knock. Lori! Lori! Please don't let me down. I need you. I need you more now than I ever have in the past. The door opened slightly. Immediately, I saw the surprise register on her face. She didn't look angry, only pleased. The door swung completely open.

"Jennifer!" She spread her arms. I willingly fell into them. She was laughing and hugging me tightly. "Jennifer, it's so wonderful to see you.

Where have you been? My God! You look awful. Are you all right? Are you sick? What's the matter, Jennifer? Say something."

I couldn't speak. I was crying too hard to answer any of her questions. Between the sobs, I managed to say, "Can I come in?"

"Of course, you can." She guided me into the room. When I crossed the threshold, Lori noticed for the first time that my suitcases were perched on the stairs behind me. She didn't ask any questions; instead, she simply picked them up and carried them into the tiny foyer.

"Can I get you something to drink? You look hungry. Have you been eating? Would you like a sandwich?"

I finally got control of my sudden outburst. As I wiped the tears from my eyes, I nodded and muttered, "Yes, please . . . anything . . . I'm starved."

Lori hurriedly fixed a snack. I devoured the ham and cheese sandwich and drank three glasses of milk without saying a word. Lori! Good, patient, Lori! She sat there quietly while I ate. Leave it to Lori to give me the time I needed in order to pull myself together. I finished the last of my third glass of milk, dabbed my mouth with the napkin, and leaned back in my chair. I felt better—much, much better.

"Feel like talking now, Jennifer? Or would you rather just sack out on my couch? We can always talk another time."

"No. I want to talk. My only problem is, I don't know where to begin." I looked around her apartment and noticed that the L-shaped living room/dining room was lacking most of the tangible things a person normally saw in a home. There was a rather small couch that looked as if it had been in someone's family for generations, one lamp with a shade that didn't fit, crates for tables which had bright material covering them, and a beautiful arrangement of flowers sitting on top. Under the window was a makeshift combination of bricks and boards set up to form shelves with scores of paperback, as well as hard-backed, novels on them. I walked over to it and ran the tip of my fingers across the bindings. There were several mysteries, a few suspense thrillers, a couple of biographies, some historical romances, and at the end, standing on their own, were Lori's favorite novels—the books she read two and three times: *Gone With the Wind, Little Women, Wuthering Heights, The Flame and the Flower, Love Story.* Poor Lori . . . I wondered if she still believed there was truth in those books? Life was not like that. There was no Rhett Butler who waited years for his woman; rich men didn't fall in love with ladies from the poor side of town; Heathcliff and Catherine never met in heaven after they died. Fantasy! That was fantasy. Love didn't make the world go 'round, and there was no such thing as happily ever after. I tapped each book and made a steady rhythm as I hit them softly with my fingertips. Slowly, I turned around. The room was practically barren, but in a way it was filled with warmth. The plants, the flowers, the bright colors, the ruffled curtains, and the family pictures scattered about filled the room with Lori's personality. I felt welcomed and wanted. Although it was sparsely decorated, it was a beautiful room.

I walked over to the couch, sat down, and began to speak. "I left David." Lori made no comment. "My parents are dead. Both of them . . . last week . . . in a car accident."

"Oh, my God, Jennifer. I'm so sorry."

"So am I . . . but not for the right reasons." I saw the confusion on Lori's face, but she didn't interrupt me. "I'm sorry they're dead. I really am, but I didn't love them. Not the way I wanted to . . . not the way I should have. Isn't it awful? I feel so terrible. I wanted to love my parents. Or at least I wanted to love my mother. I stopped loving my father a long time ago. I wanted to feel their loss, but I don't . . . not really. I'm sorry they're dead—even my dad. I'm even sorry he's dead, but I don't miss them." I massaged my forehead with my fingers and pressed as hard as I could, trying to force away the headache that was threatening to strike. I rubbed my temples, closed my eyes, and dug my teeth into my lower lip. "I feel so old, Lori. I feel like I've lived a hundred years, and I didn't enjoy any of them."

Lori sipped her Pepsi. Silently watching me over the rim of her glass, she gave me the chance to speak my thoughts without interruption. Her company comforted me. I felt safe and protected. Those were feelings I had not experienced in so long I'd almost forgotten them. "I'm going to get a divorce. I never loved David, and he doesn't love me. It was wrong for us to get married." I thought of telling Lori of the day I'd overheard the conversation between Kurt and the dark-haired girl, but decided against it. I could have told Lori how lonely I had been at the time—how abandoned I felt—how much it hurt when she and I had drifted apart. I could have told Lori that I had run home to David only because I had been lost and confused. But that was ancient history. That was yesterday! I wanted to wipe the slate clean.

I talked for hours about David, his gambling, his women, his accident, our attempt at rebuilding the marriage, the fact that he had single-handedly forced himself to walk again, and finally, how I came to realize that I couldn't live with him any longer. Lori said little during my oration. I felt the painful emotion slowly draining out of me with each sentence I spoke. Lori was bringing me back to life. Quietly she sat with me as she helped restore my trust in her and in myself. I could feel her strength, and in doing so, I felt some of it within me. Finally, I sat back. I had said everything I could. No more words formed on my lips. I was exhausted—mentally, as well as physically, but I had not felt better in what seemed like an eternity. "Lori . . . I missed you so much. I was so afraid to come to you . . . so afraid that you'd never forgive me for what I'd done to you and your brother . . . for leaving without any explanation at all. I apologize for all those awful things I said in the past. I didn't mean them, really I didn't."

Lori surrounded me with her arms. She was smiling. "It's going to be all right, Jennifer. You should have known that I missed you too. Don't you realize you are the best friend I've ever had! I care so much about you. I worried about you. I missed you."

I clung to her as if she were giving me the courage to take each breath. Burying my head in her lap, I let Lori hold me. By easing the tension, she was erasing my pain.

After a few moments of silence I finally asked about Kurt. "How's your brother?"

"I suppose he's okay. He's in Germany. I don't hear very much from him."

Lori told me that Kurt seemed bitter and distant. She discussed a few of the details he had passed on about army life and German scenery. It didn't take long to conclude that Kurt was not married, and that Lori didn't seem to know anything about a dark-haired girl or a baby. I wondered if Lori realized that she was an aunt. I didn't think so. It felt awkward to keep this secret from her, but I vowed not to be the one to tell her. That was Kurt's business, not mine.

The subject changed again when I brought up my father's trust fund. "Do you believe it, Lori? All that money, and I can't touch it. I'm a pauper! I have two dollars in my purse and no job because I'm sure my boss fired me when I didn't show up as scheduled for an entire week. I have nothing, Lori, except what's in those bags and my car outside. Nothing else."

"It's okay, Jen. I'll take care of you until you can get another job. We'll work this out together."

"You know, at first I didn't want the money." I looked around Lori's simple apartment and thought of all the many things I could buy for her if I only had some extra cash. Some new furniture—or at least a chair—some rugs, a stereo, a decent light and most definitely, a television set. I couldn't believe she didn't have one. "If I had my old man's money we could set up in style. I could take care of you, instead of you taking care of me. We could have fancy stuff, maybe even take some trips together, and we would never have to worry about paying the rent or anything."

Very patiently, Lori commented. Her voice was soft and gentle. "We don't need that money. The two of us can do just fine. As soon as you're feeling up to it you can get a job, but you mustn't overwork yourself. You're not looking very well, Jennifer. It's been two years. I assumed you'd be fully recovered by now. You must not be taking very good care of yourself. You need the proper foods and a lot of rest. And for Pete's sake! You shouldn't be smoking. You know what the doctor said." She patted my hand and gave me an encouraging smile. "Don't worry about anything, Jennifer. The two of us are going to be just fine. You wait and see. In a couple of months, we'll both be back on our feet again—just like the good old days."

There was a strange, foreign quality in Lori's voice. For the first time, I noticed that Lori was looking unusually pale and drawn. Initially, I thought it was due to her concern for me, but then I realized that she included herself in her last statement. Lori had something troubling her on top of my problems. Something was wrong. There seemed to be pain etched in her eyes. I wondered what was going on in her life. She hadn't said a word about herself all night. Was she dating someone special? Was he causing her trouble? I didn't see any schoolbooks or papers lying around to give evidence of caring for pupils. Was she teaching? "Did you get a teaching job, Lori?"

"No, unfortunately, it's a little harder than I thought it was going to be." She responded as she brought out sheets and a blanket from the closet and started unfolding them on the couch.

"What are you doing?"

Lori paused as she straightened out the material on the sofa. Even though her face was cast downward, I still detected a forced grin on her lips. Her shoulders slumped in a way I'd never seen before, and her eyes were pensive.

"Let's hold that story for another night, okay, Jennifer? I think enough waters gone over the dam for one evening. Besides, you need your sleep . . . and so do I."

"What is it, Lori? I want to help. Hell! I'm always talking to you. Why don't you ever give me a chance to listen?"

"I will. We'll talk . . . I promise." As she crossed her arms over her chest, she placed her hands on her shoulders and cradled herself. "Not tonight though, Jen. I can't talk about it right now. Maybe tomorrow." She kissed me on the cheek as we embraced. "It's good to see you again, Jennifer. God knows I've missed you."

"I missed you too, Lori . . . more than I can ever say."

Tesa Jones ❀ 359

I slept around the clock. When I awoke, Lori was gone. There was a note on the refrigerator.

> Jennifer,
> I had to go to work. Be back around two. I bought some things at the store. Help yourself.
>
> > Lori

I wondered what Lori could possibly be doing that kept her out past midnight. The only conclusion I came up with was pushing drinks in a bar. Nothing else stayed open that late. I was upset at the idea that Lori was standing around a bunch of drunk and obnoxious men. Lori didn't know how to handle herself around guys like that. I was sure she hated it.

I scrambled a few eggs, fried some bacon, and toasted three pieces of bread. It tasted so good that I made a fresh batch when I had finished the first. It had been a long time since I'd enjoyed food. Instead of chewing and swallowing just for the nourishment, I kept each mouthful on my tongue and savored the taste. It was so good. I wanted a cup of coffee but noticed that there was none around. I looked in all the cabinets without success. Secretly, I wondered if Lori quit drinking coffee or if she had hidden the container to keep me from having any. It would be just like Lori to hide the things that she considered to be bad for me. I wanted a cigarette, too, but brushed the craving aside. Lori would be angry if I smoked. She'd been in the room when the doctor had warned me against the effects the nicotine had on my condition. No! I promised myself that I wouldn't smoke. I took those remaining cigarettes in my purse and flushed them down the toilet. At least now the temptation was gone. I smiled. It was wonderful to have someone around who genuinely cared about my health and me.

Actually, the specialists had been right. Those things—booze, tobacco, caffeine, pot—all those things that they had warned me about did have a negative effect on me. I really didn't feel well. In fact, there were days when I almost felt as badly as I did when I was recuperating in the hospital.

The door opened. I saw Lori enter the apartment dressed in clothes I'd never seen her wear before. She looked disgusting. Her black shorts were so tight when she bent over half her cheeks hung out the back. Her blouse was low and revealed more cleavage than it covered up, and her knee high boots were almost fluorescent. She had a lot of makeup on—more than I'd ever seen her wear. She didn't look at all like herself.

Without a word, Lori went directly to her room. A few moments later she reappeared, donned in a robe. Her face was freshly washed.

"Are you going to tell me what that was all about?" I said.

Lori took in a breath that flared her nostrils as color flushed over her cheeks. One eyebrow lifted. I could tell she was on the defensive. Whenever Lori felt guilty or angry, it always showed in the muscles around her eyes. They twitched involuntarily. She couldn't conceal her emotions. She could keep her eyes blank but she had no control over the area around them. Lori would never have made a good actress.

"It's my job, Jennifer. It's the only one I can get."

"What the hell do you do . . . strip or something?"

"It's not like I love what I'm doing. And . . . no . . . I don't strip for my paycheck, but I do feel like I'm naked."

"You're waiting tables in some dive, aren't you?"

"Well, don't look at me like I've committed a crime. You were doing it too, Jennifer." She was getting less guilty and more confrontational as her voice became raised.

"Yeah, I waited tables, but at least I was doing it in a nice respectable dinner theater. I wore a starched uniform that went below my knees."

"Are you going to get self-righteous on me? You're not my mother, damn it!"

I'd never seen Lori so upset. Was it only anger? Or was there something else causing this outburst?

"If I could have found a waitressing job where the dresses went below the knees, I would have taken it. I wanted to be a teacher. I looked every-where! I sent in applications to places I'd never even heard of before, but no one's hiring. I need money. I have bills to pay, expenses . . . I need to eat. Damn it! I had to get a job, so I took the only one that was available. Do you think I like men pinching my ass and asking me to go to bed with them when they don't even know my name? I think it reeks! I hate it."

"Lori . . . " I started softening. "I'll help pay the bills. I'll get a job. You can quit yours and get another one."

"No, I can't do that. I need the money more now than ever."

"I can support myself, Lori. You don't need to support me."

"It's not you, Jen. I need the money for me."

I watched Lori as she walked to the refrigerator and poured herself a Coke. When she finished, she leaned against the doorjamb between the kitchen and the living room. I could see tears welling in her eyes. When she spoke, her voice was low and shaky.

"You were right, Jennifer. You were right all along."

I had no idea what she was talking about. Right? Lori was always the one who was right. What could I possibly have been right about?

"You always told me . . ." Lori sniffed heavily at the moisture below her nose. "You always said that he was a bastard . . . but I didn't listen. Well, you were right! You were most definitely right. Brad Malone is a royal son of a bitch." Her words were spoken into the palms of her hands; each syllable was muffled.

What on earth was Lori talking about? What had Brad done now? What had happened in the year and a half since I last saw Lori? I thought Brad was married to Cindy Wilder. I figured Lori no longer had any con-nection with him. I was really getting confused; after all, Brad Malone did not even live in Virginia.

"I really screwed it up this time. Oh God, Jennifer! I've made such a mess out of my life." Lori was choking on her words. "He appeared out of nowhere. I didn't expect to see him. He took me by surprise. I lost control; I gave into him; I couldn't hold out any longer. He won. He finally beat me at his stupid, silly game. The worst part about it is, in spite of it all, I still love him. As much as I hate him, I'm still in love with him. God help me, I think I always will be."

Lori was in my arms and sobbing as she spoke each word. I held her as tightly as I could. It was my turn to comfort her, but I could find no sympathetic words to say about Brad Malone. Lori was intelligent. She had common sense—good judgment. How could she fall in love with a creep like Brad? I bit my lip, fighting back the urge to tell her "I told you so."

"All those times that I pretended Brad didn't exist and hoped that my feelings would die—all those years I built defensive walls in order to protect myself from him—and nothing I did mattered. He still won! I couldn't fight him anymore. I loved him too much, and he used my love to manipulate me . . . to crush me . . . and . . . I didn't have the strength to stop him."

"What did he do to you?"

"I was such a fool. You would have thought after all the times in the past, that I would have learned my lesson . . . but no! I wanted to believe him. I *wanted* to believe him so much. And for a few hours on a beautiful fall afternoon, I actually thought Brad Malone cared about me . . . loved me. I was so blind." She rubbed the sleeve of her robe across her nose. Tears were streaming down her face. "It was all a game. That's all I ever was to Brad. Just a game . . . a bet . . . a lousy ten-dollar bet. He destroyed me for ten damned dollars."

"What on earth are you talking about?"

"I heard him, Jennifer. I heard every word. Brad made love to me in order to get ten bucks from Billy. And the worst part about it is that the money didn't even matter to him. He just wanted to be victorious. Brad just wanted another piece of ass. Just like you always told me. You were right, Jennifer! You were right. I wish I had listened to you."

I handed her a tissue. Lori blew her nose several times and tried to steady her breathing. She sniveled as the heaving in her chest began to subside. I could see that her hands were shaking as she placed the tips of her fingers on her forehead and plastered them against her skin. It appeared as if Lori was trying to physically force Brad out of her head. I hated Brad Malone more now than ever. If he had been in the room at that moment, I would have run a knife through his heart.

Lori pointed her index finger at me, shook it several times, and then managed a pitiful smile. "At least I had one small victory of my own." A feeble laughing sound came from the base of her throat. "I wasn't a virgin. He expected a pure, unblemished woman—a cherry to pop, a red sheet he could display to his buddies—but I had a surprise of my own." She kept panting like she'd run a race and couldn't catch her breath. "He didn't win that victory."

"Lori, how do you know this? I knew Brad Malone was a first-class jerk, but did he actually come out and tell you this after he'd taken you to bed? I didn't think he was that low."

"No . . . No. He didn't tell me. I didn't wait around long enough for him to drop that particular bomb on me. I may be a fool, but I do have a little self-respect. No! There was no way I was going to stick around and let Brad laugh in my face. It would have killed me. I couldn't have taken it; instead, I packed my bags and got the hell out of there." She sat down on the couch and beat at the pillow; she hammered at it with both fists. Each time she connected a punch it seemed as if it were creating more hostility instead of easing it. "I went back to see Christie and to get my things, but she wasn't in the room."

Christie . . . Christie who? None of this made sense.

"I was so happy. I couldn't remember ever being that happy. I thought my whole world had finally come together. Everything was beautiful. Brad was beautiful. I felt beautiful. For one magnificent afternoon I was living in heaven. Not in my wildest dreams did I imagine that being with Brad could be so wonderful—so perfect. He was gentle and he was passionate at the same time. He touched me like I was very precious to him. He said things—wonderful things. I wanted to believe him. I thought he cared for me. And like a naive teenager, I started thinking of Brad and me and a future together." She paused. "I was supposed to wait for him, but I was so excited . . . I couldn't sit still . . . so I went to the TKE house."

Suddenly, I realized that Lori was talking about Elon. She must have gone back to campus for some reason, and Brad had been there at the same time. Why? When?

"The rules had changed. There was an open house so I walked right in thinking how nice it would be to surprise him." A fresh batch of tears sprang to Lori's eyes, overflowing and spilling out without her trying to stop them. She pointed aggressively to herself. "I was the one who was surprised! Me! Not him! I got the surprise shot with both barrels. Somebody told me he was in the kitchen. I couldn't believe it when I was standing there at the door listening to Brad boasting about his latest conquest. Me! I was his latest conquest. He didn't waste one precious minute. He raced back to Billy and told him all about it as if I were a movie he'd seen or a book he'd just finished reading. I wanted to kill him. I wanted to tear Brad apart, but instead all I did was turn around and walk out. I slammed the door behind me. I was so mad . . . so mad and hurt and humiliated." She got up and started pacing the floor again. "I hate him, Jennifer. I hate him! I hate him! I hate him! And, God help me, I love him too. From the first time I met him, he's jerked me around like some kind of yo-yo. He consumed my life. After everything . . . everything that he's done to me . . . I still love him." Lori was standing in the middle of the room, sobbing.

I embraced her trying to ease her pain. When her shoulders ceased the spasmodic jerks, I began to speak. "Well, at least now you know . . . and it's finally over." I tried to be as gentle as possible with my words.

"No! No, Jennifer, it's not. It's not over at all."

"The pain will go away. Someday this will only be a bad memory. I know you don't believe me now, but the pain will go away."

"Maybe . . ." Lori took a deep breath. "Maybe the pain will go away, but the baby won't. The baby won't just go away."

I was too stunned to speak. Lori was pregnant! And that son of a bitch was the father. Finally, I found words. "What are you going to do?"

"I don't know. I haven't thought about anything in over a month except Brad and this baby. I've always wanted children. When Tommy and I were dating, we talked about kids all the time. For as long as I can remember, I've wanted a family, a house full of children, four . . . maybe six . . . a bunch of them. I wanted to be a mother before I ever had any dreams of teaching." Lori cradled her stomach. "I love this baby."

"What about Brad?"

"What do you mean?" Lori replied.

"Will he take responsibility? Will he help you?"

"Are you kidding?" Lori smirked sadly. "I've run that conversation through my mind a thousand times." Her shoulders sagged. "If I told Brad, he wouldn't care. A baby . . . yeah, right! He's not interested in a life with me, and he certainly wouldn't want to be saddled with this child." Lori let out a pathetic, painful moan. "Oh sure, he might—if I were really lucky—he might offer to help by driving me to the doctor's for an abortion like he did with Cindy." Lori closed her eyes.

"So you have thought about an abortion."

"Oh, God! I don't think I can do that." There was panic in Lori's voice.

"How about adoption?" I inquired softy.

"I can't give it away, Jen. If I carried it for nine months, I know one thing for certain—I could not carry my baby to term and then give it away. I'd rather not have it at all."

"Then, you are considering an abortion."

"No, not really. I can't do that. Could you?"

"Yes, under the circumstances," I responded, trying not to push my opinion on her with too much force.

"But you're Catholic! It's against your religion."

"So are birth control pills, but I take them anyway. Besides I'm not a very good Catholic. I never have been. I think abortion is up to the woman. It's a personal choice. Nobody else should be involved, least of all not the government. Thank God they legalized it last January, so a woman can go to a hospital where it's safe, and there won't be any danger."

"I'm not for or against abortion, Jennifer. I never have been. When *Roe* vs. *Wade* was in the courts, I didn't wave a banner for either side. I've known quite a few girls who have gotten into trouble, and I never condemned or judged any of them. It was their decision—not mine! Some of the girls left school, some got married, and some had abortions. Those girls made their choices. But it's different this time. This time it's me! I don't know if I can ever forgive myself, no matter what I decide to do." Lori covered her face with her hands. "I can't believe this is happening."

"Don't think of it as a baby. Legally it's not—not until after the third month."

"What about morally, Jennifer? The hell with morality! What about what I think it is? I think it's a baby now."

I tried a different approach. "Do you really want Brad's baby? Do you want to be reminded of him every day?"

"It's my baby too!"

"Yes . . . yes, it is. But could you take care of it? I know you could love it, Lori. You have more than enough love, but could you feed it, clothe it, educate it, and keep a roof over its head? Hell, Lori! You can barely support yourself. How are you going to take on the added expense and responsibility of a baby? Where's the baby going to stay while you work? You want some stranger raising it? And how are you going to afford that? And how about the doctor's bills? Children are expensive, so is health insurance."

"I'll find a way. Whatever it takes . . . I'll find a way!"

"Lori! You are forgetting something very important." I paused to make sure I had Lori's full attention. "Society is never going to accept this child. According to the unwritten rules, babies have two parents . . . two *married* parents. Didn't you read *The Scarlet Letter* while you were in school? Every person in that town shunned Hester *and* her child. Is that what you want for your baby?"

"Hawthorne wrote that novel more than a hundred years ago, Jennifer, and it was about an era long before that. It doesn't have anything to do with *now*!"

"The hell it doesn't! Get real! Not that much has changed. Sure, you won't have to wear a big 'A' on your bodice like Hester, but you'll still be branded and so will the baby. Granted, a few things have changed with the passing of time. Women have the right to vote now." I laughed, but I knew it wasn't funny. "And women are leaving their homes and finding jobs in the business world, instead of being tied to the stove. Some of them are even doctors and lawyers. Hell! According to the liberated woman, she can bring home the bacon and fry it too! I guess that's some improvement." There was a sarcastic edge to my laughter. "And sure! Free love is spreading like wildfire. The hippies in their communes are reproducing like crazy, but they don't give a damn about fitting into society. And what's going to happen to their children when they decide to come back to reality and join the modern world?"

Suddenly, I realized that I didn't want Lori to have this baby. I didn't want her to have a constant reminder of Brad. It would only serve to hurt her even more. She had to get rid of it—either by adoption or abortion—because otherwise, she'd be attached to Brad for the rest of her life. She'd never be free of him. I had to find a way to convince her. "Some people think that the double standard is on the way out. They think that men and women can have the same rules in the bedroom; therefore, women can join this new sexual revolution—participate in free love without any ramifications. But the truth of the matter is, there is no equality in the bedroom—and there never will be—not when you're single." Memories of David flashed through my mind. "And not when you're married either! Men will never truly respect a woman who sleeps around. And any child born to that type of relationship will wear the brand and suffer the consequences. Is that what you want for your child, Lori?"

"When did you get so cynical, Jennifer?"

"I've always been cynical, Lori. You just never saw that trait in me. Don't mistake what I'm saying and think I'm some kind of puritan either. Hell! I've been around. You know that! But you haven't, Lori, and you are so naive!" Silence filled the room. "You have to think about yourself. Think about your future. If you have this baby, what kind of life will you have? Don't you want to get married someday and have that house full of kids you were talking about? You can have other babies, Lori." I looked at her expression and realized that the words I was speaking at the moment were not making any impact at all. It was the wrong strategy. I should have known that I couldn't use the selfish approach with Lori. She would never look at this problem from a selfish angle. I had to change my tactics. Lori couldn't have the baby. It would be a mistake! I had to make her see that. "I suppose you're thinking in the back of your mind that if you have this baby, someday Brad will find out about it and come back to you. Is that what you're hoping for? Do you really think that Brad Malone will take on the responsibility of a child he fathered in a moment of lust?" I paused to see if my words were making any impression on her. "You're right! What Brad did when Cindy was pregnant was appalling. He dragged her to some back alley to a butcher who wasn't even a doctor. Cindy's lucky she is alive. She couldn't go to a hospital. But, Lori, you can!" I raised my voice slightly. "Don't be a fool, Lori! Brad will never help you. I'd be willing to bet that he wouldn't even acknowledge it as his own."

Lori's eyes snapped open. The words I spoke burned their meaning in her expression. I could tell that I had struck her most vulnerable emotions. Poor, Lori! Now I knew more than ever that she couldn't have this baby. She would spend the rest of her life waiting for Brad Malone. I couldn't let her waste her future like that. I had to protect her from that fate.

Lori stood up and silently left the room. I could hear her rustling around as she paced the floor in her bedroom. I knew she was struggling within herself to find the decision that was right for her. I hoped my words were sufficient. I prayed she was listening.

Lori lived in such a rose-colored world. If she had this baby, I knew society would eat her alive. With all my heart, I knew that she couldn't have Brad's child. It would only be a cancer inside of her. I was not going to let this ruin Lori's life. I had to find a way to convince her, even if it meant brainwashing her every step of the way.

Ten days later, at breakfast, Lori broached the subject with only one sentence.

"I'm going to have an abortion." She spoke without looking up from her meal.

She didn't say anything else, and I didn't add to her comment. I was thankful that she didn't see the relief in my expression. I knew she was doing the right thing.

4

Three days passed. Lori and I pooled every dime we had for her operation, but it only totaled $50. Lori had $48, and I contributed $2. It wasn't enough. It wasn't even close. It might as well have been thousands because neither of us knew where we could possibly get more money. Lori told me that she thought of asking her parents, but she'd never lied to them in her life, and she couldn't start now. I thought about asking friends, but I realized I did not have any. There was no one to ask. Neither one of us had any credit references in order to take out a loan. We were in a real financial bind. I went to the only place I knew where I could get my hands on some quick cash.

I knocked on the door. David opened it.

His first reaction was a twisted, self-confident grin. "Didn't hold out for long, did you?"

"I'm not here to stay, David."

"Baby, you can't stay away from me. I know it, and you know it. It's as simple as that. We're good in bed, and that's what really counts."

"Shut up, David." I thought of the times before we'd been married when sex between us had been good. Then I thought of those pitiful half-minute quickies we'd had twice a week, and I became disgusted just looking at him. Sex! That was all he ever thought about. "I didn't come here to mince words with you, David. I want a divorce. I have grounds, and you know it. If you give me $250 right now, I promise I won't ask for another penny in settlement. You can have everything else. I won't fight for it if you just give me the cash I want today."

He looked at me suspiciously. "Whatcha up to, Jen?"

"I just need the money, David. Don't ask questions."

"Why $250? Why not $500 or $1,000?"

I didn't want him backing me into emotional corners. I made my voice strong and confident. "If I thought you had $1,000, David, I would have asked for it, but I'll be lucky if you have $250. I just need some quick cash. I need to get a place to live; I have to buy gasoline; and I have to eat. I lost my job. I need some money to tie me over until I get a new one."

"Why don't you come home, baby? I got a job for you right here." David put his hands on my face and made an attempt to kiss me. I jerked away from him. His touch repulsed me. "I don't want to be your whore, David. I'm not coming back."

"I tell you what. If you come upstairs with me . . . stay a while. Let's say an hour or so. Then if you still want the $250 and the divorce, you can have it."

I took two steps backward. I couldn't believe he was actually asking me to prostitute myself for the money. For Christ's sake! Legally it was my money too! I had every right to claim it. I could have slapped him; to be honest, I wanted to spit in his face. I should have walked away, but I didn't. I simply stood there wondering where else I'd be able to get that much money? Nowhere! If I wanted to help Lori, I had no choice.

David walked up the stairs. I followed. He chuckled all the way to his room, stripped off his clothes, and jumped into bed. When he patted the mattress next to him, I cringed. I couldn't believe this was happening. I sat beside him, closed my eyes, and gave in to his desires. I felt nothing. I knew he entered me; I even realized he was toying with my body, but I was too numb to feel his touch and too angry to give in to any physical sensations at all.

When it was over, I opened my eyes and received my only victory. He wanted me to fall victim to his powers. I hadn't, and he was angry. It was my turn to smile. "Can I have my money, please?"

"You think you've outfoxed me, don't you? You little slut."

"Just give me the money, David, or I'll sue you for much more." I watched as he walked over to his checkbook and started to write out the amount. "No checks, David. I'm not as dumb as you think I am. I know you don't have any money in the account. Do you really think I would have come here if I could have withdrawn it myself? My name is on that account too or have you forgotten that? Do you really think I'm that stupid? Cash, David! I want cash. And don't play anymore games with me."

"Okay." He opened the top drawer of his bureau and withdrew a leather-bound string bag, opened it, and dumped the contents out on the bed. Tens, twenties, a few fifties and a couple dozen ones floated down onto the mattress. It was David's gambling money. It looked as if his luck had finally changed. Or, maybe, he had just replenished his supply with money he should have been using to pay the bills. Either way, it didn't matter—just as long as I was the one who had it when I walked out the door. He counted it out and piled like bills on top of each other.

There was $443 plus a few pieces of change. David separated my cut and replaced the rest of it in his money pouch. I felt relieved when I was finally holding the cash in my hands.

"I'll file for divorce as soon as possible. I'll need money for that, too, so it'll take a while. I'll have my lawyer send you the papers." I stood up and dressed myself, grateful that the episode was over. I grabbed my coat and purse, wrapped a scarf around my head, and faced David for the last time. "Well, so long. Wish I could say it's been fun."

"You really mean it, don't you, Jennifer? You're not coming back?"

"No! I'm not. I was too weak to leave you before—too afraid. I didn't know where to go. I'm not frightened anymore. I don't need you. I'm not afraid to say it either. Good-bye, David." I left without giving him a chance to comment.

I raced home and showed Lori the money. She asked me where I'd gotten it. I told her that it had been in my savings account. She didn't pursue the subject. I hoped she'd be happy for my contribution, but instead she seemed aloof and somber. She went to her room, opened a book, and hid behind the pages for the rest of the evening. I didn't try to force her into a conversation. I figured it was better to leave her to her own private thoughts. Tomorrow she'd go to the clinic, and the problem would be solved; then she'd be the old Lori again. I got the pillow, sheets, and blanket from the closet and made up the couch. Hoping for a restful night's sleep, I crawled between the sheets, but it was hours before I dozed off.

The phone rang only once before I reached the receiver—still half asleep—and picked it up off the floor next to me. I glanced at my wristwatch. It was well past three o'clock in the morning. Who the hell was calling at this time of night?

"Hello," I muttered trying to shake the drowsiness.

"Who is this?" the male voice replied.

"Listen, buster. Do you know what time it is?" I tried to keep my voice down. I didn't want to disturb Lori. She was going to the doctor's in the morning, and if she laid awake in bed all night she might change her mind.

"Is that you, Laura?"

"No . . . it's Jennifer . . . Jennifer Carson." I had started using my maiden name again. I didn't want any leftovers from a bad memory.

"Oh, terrific! The last of the great white bitches." The masculine voice sounded agitated. There was a bit of a slur to the syllables as if he had been drinking. Who the hell was on the other end of this line?

"Don't you know it's the middle of the night, and some people like to get their sleep? Why don't you try calling in the morning at a decent hour."

"Wait! I want to talk to Laura. Put her on the phone."

"Listen, you jerk, I don't give a damn if you're Richard Nixon . . . you have no right to call anyone at this hour."

"I've had it up to my hair roots with you, Jennifer. Put Laura on the phone right now."

I knew that voice. There was no doubt in my mind. It had taken me a few moments but the identity of the stranger had finally come to me. "Who is this?" When I didn't get an answer, I continued. "Is that you, Brad?"

"What the hell difference does it make? Just put Laura on the phone."

"She isn't here." I lied. In no way was I going to let Brad Malone talk to

Lori tonight. He had done enough damage for a lifetime and tonight—of all nights—was definitely not a good time for him to make another attempt at causing Lori more pain.

"You bitch."

"You're drunk."

"I've been drinking. I'll admit that, but I'm not drunk." He was screaming. "I'm sick of playing games with you! Put Laura on this phone! I know she's there!"

"Get lost!"

"Jennifer! Don't hang up! Please, don't hang up on me. I've got to talk to her. I've got to tell her something."

"She's got company, Brad. She doesn't want to be disturbed."

There was silence on the other end of the line. I could hear his uneven breathing, but he did not speak. Seconds ticked by before I finally heard the phone go dead. He hung up. Good! The asshole deserved a slap in the face. I was glad that I could be the one to give it to him.

I nestled into the sheets. So I'd lied. I'd done worse things in my life. But at least I saved Lori any further abuse from that horrible man. I wondered what Brad Malone thought he could accomplish over the telephone. Perhaps he was in town and wanted a little free pussy. Well, he wasn't going to get it—not from Lori. If I had my way, he'd never hurt her again.

3

Laura

IT HAD BEEN NEARLY TWO MONTHS SINCE THE OPERATION. OPERATION! Whenever I spoke of it—which was not often and only with Jennifer after we'd both had a couple of shots of Southern Comfort—and whenever I thought of it—which was as little as possible because the pain plagued me— I used the word "operation" because I couldn't bring myself to call it by the real term. It was over! There was no more baby. It had been practically pain- less—except for the hurt that filled my soul. My poor child! Would God ever forgive me? Would I ever be able to forgive myself?

I knew in my mind that Jennifer was right. She was so pragmatic and analytical in her debates while, I was only thinking with my heart. I wanted to keep the baby. I thought I could raise it myself, but Jennifer made me see how foolhardy that would have been. A baby with no father! Society would never welcome the child. Jennifer was also right when she accused me of having a secret desire to have the baby in hopes that Brad would someday come back to me. And if he didn't—then the baby would be a part of Brad that even he could never steal from me. I could have loved the baby as I loved him. But that had been a foolish notion. Brad Malone would never care about a child born between us. I was no different from any of the others in the long line of women he used. After all, hadn't I sat in a car with Brad many summers ago when he had stated that *Cindy* was pregnant? He had admitted to being the one who had talked her into an abortion because he couldn't be bothered with a child. Why had I thought that my child would be any different? Brad Malone didn't care . . . not about Cindy, not about me, and not about either of our babies. It was obvious that the only person Brad Malone cared about was Brad Malone.

How in God's name had I ever fallen in love with him? I asked myself that question a thousand times.

In the beginning, he had seemed so honest and warm. I had been just naive enough to believe that his strategy and lies represented honesty and truth. I had been drawn to him from the first day. Even now, I could still remember how happy I had been just to be near him. It had been so easy to ignore others' warnings, because when I was with Brad, nothing else mattered. He had made me feel complete. In actuality, I had fallen in love with Brad Malone long before I'd realized what he really was like. The truth of the matter was, I loved the man Brad had pretended to be when he was with me. I knew that man only existed in my dreams. But that didn't help me love him any less. Now—without him—I felt as if something was missing in my life. I felt empty inside. What an ignorant fool I was.

2

It was a rude awakening when my parents announced that they were getting a divorce. I was shocked enough when I overheard their vicious quarrel last summer, but a divorce! I couldn't believe it. My mother and father seemed so happy while I was growing up. We were a family. What happened? How could I have been so blind?

Everything was falling apart. People were getting divorced as easily as they snapped their fingers. Just like that! They didn't want to be married, so they simply quit. What was it all about? Couples who were married for a few months or even decades were throwing in the towel, and many people weren't even getting married at all; instead, they preferred to live together without vows. It wasn't just my parents' marriage that bothered me. It was the lackadaisical manner in which everyone treated vows. The open marriage seemed to be popular. Husbands and wives were having affairs and bragging about it. People no longer felt it necessary to remove their wedding bands while they went on the prowl and looked for an evening's entertainment. Counting divorces seemed to be a joke. At work, I overheard conversations where people tried to outdo each other with the number of separations. The one who won was married and divorced three times during the course of two years. Why? It seemed as if fifty percent of everyone I met was either divorced or separated. They laughed about it. They thought it was funny. They seemed so callous. Were they? Or were they only pretending not to care? Where had I been all my life? I must have been walking around with my head in the clouds. I hadn't foreseen any of it. But this was reality. This was real life!

I made two promises to myself.

First, I was going to quit that filthy job. No more hustling drinks in a skintight outfit. No more jeering from men—married or single—who took for granted that I was an easy mark. No more fears of going home at night, because it was late and dark and I was alone. I needed a respectable job. I had postponed a desk job long enough thinking it would tie me down in case a teaching job became available, but not anymore. I was not going to wait any longer.

And second, I started taking birth control pills. I asked the doctor to prescribe them for me after the operation. He smiled at me knowingly. Needless to say, I was humiliated and embarrassed. But I swore to myself that I'd never again be caught in the situation from which I was now recovering. I'd take the Pill and be safe. Everybody was talking about sex. Free love had been around for almost a decade, but somehow I had escaped it. A person couldn't open a magazine without seeing the advertisements drip with sensuality. It was on the television and in the movies too. Whatever happened to chaste kisses and stroll, in the moonlight? I had been living in a time warp where the ideals of "Leave It to Beaver" and "Father Knows Best" were the ones I clung to, but those standards no longer existed.

Tesa Jones ✒ 377

Somehow I had totally missed the women's movement where they burned their bras and openly had affairs. I thought it was about equal pay for equal work and the fight to take women out of the kitchen and put them in the boardroom. But it was more than that. Women were demanding the right to have a sexual relationship without strings or guilt. Jennifer had told me that women would never be equal in the bedroom, but most of my female friends in college had emphatically told me for years that I was missing out on the sexual revolution. I didn't know who was right; I only knew that I was lonely—very lonely—and I didn't want to be lonely anymore. To date, I had only physically known—and cared about—two men. The first was Tommy; our inexperience and my guilt overshadowed any potential for pleasure. The second was Brad; he lifted me into another world where there was music, hot racing fluid, a floating sensation, and invisible waves that crashed against my ears. I had tasted the beauty of Brad, and now all I had left was a memory and an empty feeling inside of me created by his absence. I was trying desperately to tuck thoughts of Brad into the far recesses of my mind.

I decided what I really needed was a lover. Not someone to love, but someone to make love to me.

My first priority came a lot easier than anticipated. I quit my job at Frank's Hideaway, and after ten days of searching, I finally found a low-paying position as a receptionist at a law firm in D.C. I had no office experience and only rusty typing skills, so I was thrilled for the opportunity, and the benefits were good. I accepted the $6,000-a-year salary. Even though it was not much money, it was considerably more than minimum wage, which was what the other jobs offered. I was hoping, with time, that I'd acquire the knowledge I needed in order to advance in the corporation.

Robbins, MacMillan and Robbins had an entire floor of offices, some of which overlooked Farragut Square. There were dozens of secretaries and administrative help who buzzed around frantically all day working on their designated jobs. Needless to say, the clients of the firm suitably impressed me. They were major corporations from not only D.C., but New York, Los

Angeles, Chicago, Boston, Miami, even Paris and London. They consulted with political figures and celebrities from all over the country. It was a vibrant place with lots of action. Not only were the employees friendly, but also the decor was warm and welcoming, and the nine-to-five hours were perfect. I was hired to man the front desk, answer phones, address mail, sort envelopes, take messages, fix coffee, and handle light typing. Not a great deal of responsibility or challenge, but I was told that there was always room to move up if I dedicated myself properly. I'd never been afraid of hard work, and this was no exception. I plunged into my job. As the weeks passed, I decided that I liked my new career.

Shortly after I was hired, Jennifer found a job on Capitol Hill. Hers was a secretarial position that was a lot more glamorous and paid a great deal more money than mine. But then again, that was to be expected. After all, she had the skills. Those courses she took at Elon paid off. She typed well over seventy-five words a minute, and she'd learned shorthand. I was glad for Jennifer. She was proud of herself, and she had a right to be.

There was only one thing that bothered me. I was worried about her. She didn't seem well, and a full-time job wasn't going to give her the neces-sary time to relax and sleep all the hours her body required. I could tell just by looking at her that she had not recuperated from that illness which had laid her on her back for so many months.

Every night she dragged herself into our apartment and fell onto the couch in an exhausted slumber. She didn't even take the time to eat her din-ner or prepare for bed. She just crashed. I covered her with the blankets and wished I could get some food into her before she went to sleep. Despite my warnings, she still smoked well over a pack of cigarettes a day, drank cof-fee by the quart, and had cocktails. There were even a few occasions when I suspected she took pills to give her artificial energy. Jennifer was pushing herself too hard, and I was becoming increasingly concerned for her. Once I accused her of being self-destructive. Jennifer only laughed at me; she called me a worrywart and overprotective. Later, she was defensive and said harshly, "It's my life. I can live it the way I want." I backed off, confused and slightly hurt. Sometimes, I didn't understand Jennifer. On some occasions, I thought she wanted me to butt out of her life; while other times, I got the impression she longed for me to tell her what to do, as if she did not want to make her own decisions. The longer I knew Jennifer the more complex she became.

3

While winter raced by, and I was adjusting to my new job, I found that there was little time for a social life. Then one day, while I was waiting at the bus stop reading an article in the newspaper about the Patty Hearst kidnapping, I met Bob Johnson. I was so engrossed in the *Post* that I didn't notice when he nudged me. He tapped me several times before I looked in his direction. He asked me what I thought about the incident. As we waited for the bus, we began a conversation.

Bob Johnson appeared to be in his late twenties, amiable, and attractive. We continued talking for twenty minutes as traffic built up around us. It seemed that the bus was never going to come, so when Bob invited me for a drink at Trader Vic's, I responded with an unprecedented "yes," and we walked the distance to the restaurant. Even though I felt slightly awkward, I was enjoying myself. Bob was fascinating on any topic, even when he went on at length about his favorite team, the Miami Dolphins, and their victory at the Super Bowl last month. He discussed politics, movies, and sports. He told me a little bit about his college days when he played football and also his high school days when he'd played football, basketball, and baseball: a three-letter man. He bragged about a few legendary touchdowns he made, a basket in the last second of a game, and a home run that gave their team the division title. He told his tales in such a refreshing way that I could only be thoroughly entertained by them. It was a joy listening to him.

After watching him for several hours, I came to the conclusion that Bob Johnson had a lot of money. His clothes, his gold cigarette lighter, the medallion around his neck, his leather jacket, even his aftershave reeked of it. When I asked what he did for a living, he told me that his father had died and left him three car franchises—two Chevrolet and one Pontiac. He seemed quite proud of himself.

As time drifted by, I wondered why I had accepted his invitation. It was definitely out of character for me. After all, this was a whole new game to me, and I wasn't really sure I wanted to play.

Bob stopped in mid-sentence, leaned over the small table between us, and placed a finger gently under my chin. His voice was soft and purring. "You've never been—how shall I put this without sounding chauvinistic? You've never been 'picked up' before, have you, Miss Lori Davis?"

I lowered my eyes, embarrassed, wishing I could race from the table. I knew my cheeks were on fire with color, and I only hoped that the light was dim enough to conceal it. "Is it that obvious?" I wanted to appear sophisticated, but my voice sounded timid and meek.

"Yeah." He grinned. "I'm afraid so."

"Oh."

"Tell me, Lori. I'm really curious. Why did you come with me tonight?"

"I don't know."

He laughed. "Sounds like an honest answer to me." He called the waitress over and asked for the check before adding, "Can I give you a ride home?"

"A ride?" I questioned, slightly confused. "I thought you were waiting for the same bus I was."

He let out a loud chuckle. "No. I have my car. It's in a lot about two blocks away. I have a confession to make. When I saw you at the bus stop . . . I wanted to meet you."

"What would you have done if the bus had come?"

"That depends," he smiled.

"Depends on what?"

"If I thought that things were going well from the initial conversation and I wanted to get to know you better, when the bus arrived, I would have gotten on it and ridden with you."

"But your car is here."

"That's no problem. I would have gotten off after you, turned around, and taken another bus back. It would have been worth it."

I couldn't help but laugh. It was such a novel concept. "Do you do this often?"

"Actually, no. But you looked so pretty standing there, absorbed in the newspaper. I thought I'd give it a chance."

It was well past midnight when he drove me home and walked me to my apartment door. He kissed me innocently on the cheek and asked if he could call me. I said yes and gave him my number.

Two days later Bob telephoned and asked me to go dancing with him the following night. I accepted. We went to the Bayou. The evening was filled with easy conversation and pleasant jokes. I found myself beginning to relax around him.

Several days later, we went to see *The Exorcist*. I spent half the movie gripping Bob's arm. When that little girl's head turned totally around, I thought I was going to fly out of my seat. The movie shook me up so much that when Bob walked me home, I was constantly looking behind me and wondering if someone were following us. It gave me the creeps. That night I laid awake in bed for hours thinking about it and wishing Jennifer were home to keep me company.

On the third weekend after we'd met, Bob took me to the Rive Gauche in Georgetown. I'd never been any place so magnificent in my life. My menu didn't have any prices on it, and I was astounded when I discovered our bill was over $100. I couldn't believe anyone would actually spend that much money for a meal. Bob never batted an eyelash. He dropped money around as if it had no value.

I consumed a lot of wine with dinner. We finished two bottles, and I was definitely feeling the effects. But I was having such a wonderful time that the dizzy alcoholic feeling only served to heighten my mood. Bob told stories, and I giggled all the way back to my apartment.

When Bob walked me to the door, he politely asked if he could come in for a nightcap. I wasn't sleepy, and the night was still young, so I invited him in. Jennifer was out—probably on one of her overnight adventures. She had taken to hopping bars and finding her solace with strange men. I didn't understand her behavior. Not so long ago, Jennifer had preached to me that women would never gain respect from a man if they went looking for it in the bedroom. It was as if she had totally forgotten her own words. In a way, I felt a little sorry for her. Jennifer seemed more lost now than ever, and I did not understand why. It was almost as if she were trying to bury herself in the arms of men she didn't know or care about. When I tried to reach out to her, she invariably pulled back. I wondered what I'd done to upset her? Why was she clamming up on me? She never had before.

"Nice little place you have here," Bob said as he sat on the couch and watched me mix a couple of gin and tonics.

"Thank you. My roommate and I are trying to fix it up." I sat in the beanbag chair I'd purchased at a sale two weeks earlier.

"Don't sit all the way over there. Come sit down here next to me," Bob said as he patted the place next to him on the couch. "Where's your roommate?"

"She's out."

"That's nice." He edged over beside me and started rubbing the back of my neck and massaging my shoulders. "Lori."

"Yes." I didn't look at him. I was too nervous.

Slowly, he lowered me onto the couch. As Bob kissed me, he pressed his chest hard against mine. He'd never attempted to kiss me in that particular way before. I put my arms around him and tried to feel something. But no reaction came. Where were the skyrockets? Where was the music? He disrobed me between kisses: my scarf, my jacket, my shoes, and my blouse. I commanded my senses to react—to become involved. Wasn't this what I secretly wanted? Hadn't I taken the Pill purposely for a moment like this? Nothing was happening inside of me. No pulsating heat, no thrilling sensations rushing through my veins. Where were the crashing waves? The alcohol was making me extremely dizzy. I closed my eyes and tried to breathe evenly.

Bob stood up and started taking off his clothes. I kept my eyes tightly shut trying to envision something that would make the magic come. I crossed my arms over my chest and latched onto the straps of my slip. When I opened my eyes, Bob was standing over me; he was naked from the waist down. His shirttail covered most of his body. Slowly, he started shifting my skirt up to my hips, and I froze.

My God! He wasn't even going to bother to take all of our clothes off; in fact, he was still wearing his tie and his socks. I felt awful. My panty hose were pulled down to my knees and my skirt was up to my waist. We looked like something out of the funny papers. Only, I wasn't laughing! This was not right! Cold chills began to race through my body making me shiver all over. I curled my body into a ball and rolled onto my side.

"Come on, Lori! It's payoff time." He spoke softly but the meaning of his words was harsh and clear. Warm hands ran down my back as he chuckled to himself. "You want it—even if you don't know it. You've been begging for it. Your body's just aching for a cock, and I'm giving you mine."

I couldn't stand the words he was saying. How could someone who had appeared so pleasant, be so crude and vulgar? Did he actually think I owed him a reward for taking me to a couple of nice places? Was sex nothing more than payment in full for an evening's entertainment? Every place his hands touched, I began to feel filth. It wasn't just what he was doing; it was what he was saying.

I sprang off the couch and covered myself with the throw pillow that had been cast haphazardly onto the floor. "Get out! Get out of my home." My voice had a threatening quality to it, which was foreign to my ears.

"Damn it, Lori! I'm not leaving." He started walking toward me. He seemed massive—huge and overpowering in my small living room. "I've spent more money on you, woman, than the last five put together, and I want what's coming to me."

I started yelling at the top of my voice. "Get out! I'll call the police if you don't get out of here this instant." I was frightened. I was terrified. I knew I was equally to blame for what was happening—perhaps I had encouraged him. I hadn't meant to. And I certainly hadn't thought that he'd go from a chaste kiss to sex on a couch without even disrobing. I didn't want him to hurt me. When he took the steps toward me, I started to scream. My vocal cords were strained.

He stepped back, stunned by my reaction. I stopped yelling and stood in silence—gasping for air.

"You're nothing but a shitty prick teaser." He grabbed his pants and yanked them over his legs. "I shouldn't have wasted my time and money on you. Jesus Christ, what a poor investment you turned out to be." He picked up his coat and walked over to the door. "Do me a favor, bitch! If you ever see me coming, look the other way because I sure as hell don't want to waste any more time on you." He belted his buckle before adding, "I hope you like your beds cold—because you sure are." Bob slammed the door violently behind him.

I wasn't going to cry. That was a luxury I didn't deserve. Bob was right. They were filthy, unkind words he hurled at me; but he was right, and I was ashamed.

4

I put all thoughts of men from my mind for a while and concentrated solely on my job. I worked hard every day, and if there was any overtime available, I volunteered for it. I didn't want one single empty moment to think about my life. I worked, I ate, and I slept.

Washington is an exciting city. The hustle and bustle of the professional crowd was an atmosphere in which I could lose myself. Every morning at 7:20, Jennifer and I boarded the 11A bus outside our apartment building on Belle View Boulevard. She transferred at the Bureau of Printing and Engraving to go to the Hill, and I continued up Fourteenth Street, turned left on H Street, and got off at Farragut Square. I arrived at approximately 8:15, which gave me forty-five minutes to walk leisurely through the streets and peer in store windows. There was plenty of time left over to buy a cup of coffee from the vendor and organize my day once I got to my desk.

Periodically, Jennifer and I traveled across town and met for lunch. We longed for the day when the subway would be finished, but until then the mini-bus system worked well for us. The occasions usually coincided with payday when we felt rich and in the mood to splurge. We tried several restaurants, but our favorites were Harvey's and The Willard.

During working hours, I put every effort into the task at hand. If someone had an overflow, and I knew how to do the job, I asked for the responsibility. I wanted to broaden my horizons and learn as much as I could. During the times when the work slacked off, I read law books, reference material, and business vocabulary manuals. I practiced typing for speed, asked questions about the filing system, the office library, the VIP clients who needed kid-glove treatment, and toyed with the new computer. Robbins, MacMillan and Robbins was a company on the cutting edge of technology. Most of the partners' secretaries were extremely proud of their IBM Selectric typewriters, but a couple of the girls had computers. When I had a few extra moments, I offered to do work on those mysterious machines, just to get hands-on experience. I knew I was only a receptionist, but I wanted to be the best I could be, and I wanted to move up in the organization. Because I had become discouraged with the possibilities of ever getting a teaching position and I was determined to make the best of what I had, I even enrolled in a night course in order to learn shorthand.

One Wednesday night, I stayed well past five in order to finish some work for Larry Jenkins. He was a junior partner in the firm. He worked long hours, and he seemed to be pushing himself up the corporate ladder. Mr. Jenkins appeared courteous and professional, but in a way he seemed ruthless too. I didn't know him very well and hated to make judgments about people I barely knew, but Larry Jenkins seemed to be obsessed with impressing the firm and the partners.

Just about the time I finished my chores and was covering my typewriter for the night, Mr. Jenkins walked by my desk on his way out the door.

"Thank you for your help, Lori."

"You're welcome, Mr. Jenkins."

He put his hand on the doorknob, then turned, and approached my desk. "I suppose you've noticed that I demand excellence from the girls who work in my section?"

I didn't comment.

"I want you to know that you're doing a very good job at the front desk. You've proven to be a worthy and competent receptionist, but I think your talents are wasted out here."

"I like working for the company. I'm learning a lot. I know I didn't have much experience when I was hired, and I really appreciate the opportunity, Mr. Jenkins."

"Call me Larry." He leaned his hip on the side of my desk and started running his fingers over the top of it. Larry Jenkins was an attractive man in his mid-forties. He had brownish hair with just a touch of gray around the temples, sparkling green eyes, a slightly rounded face, a firm, confident jaw-line, and a wedding ring on his left hand. He stood almost six feet tall and walked as if he owned the world. "Would you like to join me for a drink?"

"Oh, thank you, but no. I can't. I promised my roommate I'd meet her at the Uptown. We're going to see *The Sting.*" I was glad that I hadn't needed to make up an excuse, because I didn't feel comfortable with his invitation.

"That's a fantastic movie. I saw it last month. Newman and Redford have done it again. They are a great duo. I enjoyed it very much. I'm sure you will too." Silently, he watched me for a moment before continuing, "You don't have to settle for sitting behind this desk, Ms. Davis. A girl with the right qualifications and attitude can find a lot more challenging work within the company. You seem to have drive. You're smart. You learn quick-ly, and you're pleasant on the eyes. There are quite a few positions here I think you might be interested in for the future." He gave me a long, appraising glance, during which time I felt a need to tug slightly at my hemline. He winked quickly before picking up his briefcase, turning, and walking out the door.

In the following weeks, I found myself working several extra hours at night for Larry Jenkins. The overtime was wonderful, but it was the learning experience that I found the most valuable. I started putting my newly acquired shorthand skills to use, plus I was constantly on the run doing errands for him. I even joined him in a couple of business meetings. I was not quite sure why I was there, but I did feel that it was adding to my book of knowledge.

The weeks kept flying by as Jennifer's and my lifestyles finally started taking hold. Together we saved almost $200. We sold my double bed and bought two single ones so that Jennifer would no longer have to sleep on the couch. Because we had successfully shared a room at Elon, we decided that we'd rather stay in a one-bedroom apartment for a while longer in order to save money.

On weekends, we usually drove around neighborhoods looking for yard sales and trying to find things we needed. Three Saturdays ago, I found a half-destroyed dining room table and three chairs for $20. I stripped off the paint, found natural oak underneath, and refinished them. They didn't look new, but they did look nice.

On another Saturday's outing, we purchased two lamps for less than $10 and an imitation Oriental rug for an incredibly low price. At another yard sale, we found a tattered chest of drawers. We instantly purchased it for Jennifer's use, and we tucked it neatly into the corner of the living room. We even managed to find a used television set. It was black and white and received only one channel. Thankfully, it was CBS so we got to see "M*A*S*H" and "Rhoda", which were our favorite shows. We were thrilled with all our new things, finding it so hard to believe that our treasures had been someone else's trash. Every new addition was special to both of us. We polished it, or cleaned it, or dusted it lovingly almost as if it had a soul. Our little apartment was beginning to be home for both of us.

5

When the oak trees started budding with a new year's growth, I met Stephen Shaw. He was unlike anyone I'd known before. Steve was of medium height and build; he had reddish-blond hair, a lazy drawl of an accent, and always had at least one day's growth on his face. He constantly punched me in a jovial way as if he didn't know his own strength, and his laughter practically rocked a room. He talked in a boisterous manner and used his hands when he spoke; his language was loaded with vulgar, distasteful words. After high school, Steve started working at the Hollin Hall Gulf Station on Fort Hunt Road; ten years later, he was still there—pumping gas. Steve had no drive, no motivation, and no desire to change anything in his life. He never tried to hide the fact that he would much rather play than work. Steve said countless times that working was strictly for a paycheck and playing was what life was really about. As far as he was concerned, every day was lived to its fullest; he didn't believe in making plans for the future.

Every week when I filled up my gas tank, Steve teased and cajoled me until I finally agreed to go out with him. He took me to the traveling carnival at Hybla Valley. It was fun. We rode on the Ferris wheel, went into the haunted house, ate cotton candy, and threw darts at balloons. Steve won a bright pink and green bear for me at one booth where he knocked down seven milk cans in a row. He offered to win more prizes for me, but I was content with one. It was an enjoyable evening, and when he invited me out a second time, I accepted.

Our second date was spent in front of his TV set drinking beer and watching Hank Aaron hit his 715th career home run, breaking Babe Ruth's long-standing record. Steve went nuts. His enthusiasm for baseball gave me goose bumps and flashbacks of another individual who loved the game. Push those memories away! Don't think of Brad!

On other occasions, Steve took me to the zoo, a drive-in movie on Route 1, and putt-putt golf. He had a wild, crazy zest for life. Sometimes, Steve let out a hoot without any warning; in fact, he often threw his head back in laughter at the slightest little joke. He was constantly hugging me as if I were a bear and picking me up off the ground. Occasionally, he even tossed me in the air and caught me again. Nothing ever seemed to bother him, yet nothing seemed of value to him either. He was different from the people I'd known in the past. He talked constantly, and he was filled with colorful stories, which I never knew whether to believe or not. Surprisingly, I enjoyed his carefree attitude.

As spring melted into summer, I realized that I had no strong feelings for Stephen Shaw, and I had the distinct impression that he really wasn't emotionally involved with me either, but we liked each other, and he took my mind off of being lonely. I was still religiously taking my birth control pills and was toying with the idea of consummating our relationship if he made any advance toward me. I figured that if I didn't love Stephen, then he couldn't hurt me, and that was the type of relationship I wanted right now.

One evening in late June, after dancing up a storm and drinking twice my normal capacity, I, willingly and without any hesitation, led Steve to my bed. He hurriedly undressed, and then helped me do the same. When I stood in front of him without one single piece of clothing to cover my body, I allowed him to carry me over to the mattress. Without a word, he lay down on top of me and proceeded to ease his own lust without the use of any foreplay to arouse my desires.

He was neither surprised nor disappointed when he discovered that I was not a virgin, but he was annoyed by the fact that I was not lubricated enough to ease the friction between our two organs. Without once kissing me, he jabbed and plunged himself into me until he finally got so aggravated by my dryness that he pulled himself out and got off the bed. "What the hell's the matter with you?" A frown covered his face and his tone accentuated his irritation. "You act like you want it. But shit! You have a box as dry as a desert."

I tried to hide my embarrassment. What was I doing wrong? I pulled the sheet up around my neck and looked away. I waited for Steve to say something else; but as the seconds ticked by in silence, I realized that I was alone. When I glanced back in the direction where he had been standing, I saw that the light was on in the other room. What he was doing rummaging around in the bathroom? I heard the door to the medicine cabinet open and close. Finally, the light was turned off, and I heard his footsteps coming toward me.

By the time he entered the room, my eyes had adjusted to the darkness. With the aid of the street lamp outside, I could see that Steve was holding a jar of petroleum jelly. He bent over my body, placed some between my legs, and forced the majority of it up inside of me. I was so shocked I didn't move. I gasped, trying to hide my embarrassment. No words were exchanged between us as he once again descended upon my body and entered me with a few strong thrusts. I bit down on my lower lip. He jerked spasmodically several times before shuddering and collapsing on top of me. Seconds later, I felt him shriveling inside me.

The moment he withdrew, Steve stood up and silently walked naked to the bathroom. A couple minutes later, he reappeared. He crawled into my single bed, circled me with his arms, and placed a rather chaste kiss on my forehead. "Not bad!" He rearranged his pillow and placed his head on it. "That was damn good, Lori. Damn good." He cuddled up to me and closed his eyes. A full minute had not passed before he was snoring and sound asleep.

So that was casual sex! Shit! I'd rather have an ice cream cone.

Something seemed very wrong. Why would girls boast and rave about this? Was there something the matter with me? Perhaps I had not done it right. Maybe next time, I'd ask questions and Steve could help me. I could not sleep. I wished Jennifer would come home. She'd be able to help me figure all this out. I lay quietly and watched my Baby Ben alarm clock make a full circle around its face, and still I was not drowsy. Steve's chest was rising and falling in the manner which indicated peaceful slumber. I resented his ability to fall into that state. I observed him for a while. It was so strange. I really didn't know Steve. Why had I chosen him? I wasn't in love with Steve. I wasn't even physically attracted to him. Why then? I stopped trying to psychoanalyze myself and stood up. After putting on my robe, I walked into the kitchen and looked in the refrigerator for something to eat.

I heard the key turning in the front door. Seconds later, I saw Jennifer standing in the foyer. I was surprised that she was home. My roommate's usual routine for Saturday night was to stay out until Sunday morning.

"You're up late." Jennifer stated as she saw me standing in the kitchen. "I didn't expect you home tonight." I poured us both a tall glass of milk and put a few oatmeal cookies on a plate. I bit into one. It tasted delicious.

"Well, there wasn't much going on tonight. The best-looking guys seemed to either have a date or just weren't interested. And I didn't want to waste my time on any losers." She ate three cookies in a row. She looked at me and suddenly noticed that I was extremely uncomfortable and squirming in my chair. She watched me for a few seconds, as if she were sizing up my reactions. She continued, "What's up, Lori?" Her voice was louder than usual.

"Shhh."

"Why do I have to be quiet? The neighbors are always playing their stereo at all hours, disturbing us. I'm certainly not going to whisper for their benefit." She drained her glass of milk, refilled it, and took a few more gulps before realizing that her high-pitched voice was only adding to my embarrassment. "What's going on, Lori? Is there a guy in the bedroom?" She stood up and began to pace the floor. She seemed more like a mother than a friend. "Did you sleep with someone? Who?" Jennifer demanded. "You have been, haven't you? I can see it on your face. Who is it?"

"Stephen Shaw."

"That creep! Jesus Christ, Lori. He's a total jerk."

"Shhh. He'll hear you."

"I don't give a damn. What the hell's gotten into you, Lori?"

"I can't explain it." I wanted to defend myself under Jennifer's cross-examination, but the words didn't come. I felt as if I'd committed a felony.

"He's a waste of time."

"You've got a lot of nerve, Jennifer. How can you stand there and pass judgment on me when you sleep with guys all the time? Occasionally, you don't even know their names. You don't see me accusing you of wasting your time, do you?"

"But Lori! Not you! You're not like that. I can't believe that you would sleep with someone you don't love." Her expression changed. It was as if she suddenly realized the impact of her own thoughts. "Do you love him, Lori? Are you in love with Stephen Shaw?"

I didn't want to admit that I'd actually slept with someone I had no real feelings for, so I simply smiled as warmly as I could and let Jennifer draw what conclusion she wanted. Silently, I finished the remainder of my drink and ate the last of the cookies on the plate.

"You are in love with him. You are such a fool, Lori. I can't believe that you . . . oh never mind." Jennifer looked furious. She continued to walk back and forth between the walls of the kitchen, clenching and unclenching her fists with each pace.

I was flustered and hurt. I wanted to ask so many questions and talk to Jennifer as a friend—part of me hoped she could unravel the confusion in my mind. But instead of giving me the support I longed for, Jennifer was looking at me as if I were a wicked woman.

"He's only going to hurt you, Lori. What do you want to mess around with guys like that for? He's trash! He's no better than Brad Malone—have you forgotten that little episode?"

I felt myself stiffen. "No! I haven't forgotten. I haven't forgotten one single moment." I got up, wiped the crumbs from my lips, and placed the dishes in the sink. "And you don't need to remind me either." I walked to the door. Before I left the kitchen, I mumbled, "Mind sleeping on the couch tonight?" Without waiting for a reply, I pivoted and left.

Silently, I crawled into the single bed next to Steve and left Jennifer's bed empty. He was still snoring—sleeping as if nothing could possibly go on in the world while his eyes were shut. He didn't move. I lay quietly, trying not to let his snoring bother me, but with each passing minute, it became more and more annoying. Damn! I poked him on the side and jabbed at him until he finally rolled over. The noise stopped. I nestled myself into the sheets and closed my eyes. Hours passed before I finally feel asleep.

The next morning, I was surprised when I rolled over and found someone beside me in my bed. At first, I didn't remember the events of the previous night. After blinking a few times, the memory came back to me. My stirring awakened Steve.

He turned to me saying in a husky voice, "Good morning, sunshine."

"Don't call me that." I immediately replied in a very unfriendly manner as flashbacks of Brad came to mind. Sunshine. I could hear his voice as clearly as if he were standing next to me. I could envision him tapping my nose with his finger and addressing me with that nickname. Sunshine. Go away! Go away, Brad! Leave me alone! I don't want to think about you anymore.

"A little grouchy this morning, huh?"

"I'm sorry. I didn't mean to snap at you. I guess I'm not in a very good mood."

"Let's see if I can fix that ill temper of yours." Steve laughed in a mocking way as he rolled me onto my back, mounted me, and got his own satisfaction one more time without pausing for so much as a good morning kiss. When Steve was finished, I took a shower and tried to wash off the invisible filth that was left on my body and in my mind. I scrubbed with hot water and plenty of soap, but the only thing I accomplished was to put a bright, healthy glow to my skin. After bathing and dressing, I made Steve an egg and bacon omelet. We ate in silence. It seemed that once we had lain together in a physical way, Steve no longer felt it necessary to make idle stabs at conversation. The funny, little stories he had told me in order to make me laugh were gone—of no further use—along with his charming mannerisms. When he was through with his meal, Steve kissed me on the cheek and said, "I'll call you soon." He left.

It didn't matter. It really didn't matter at all.

Sunday was spent with a tense silence between Jennifer and me. Out of the corner of her eye, she watched me as I buried my face in Michener's *Centennial*. I didn't speak to her and she, in turn, didn't try to make conversation with me. I missed our carefree, lazy Sunday talks. By early evening, I was willing to call a truce, but Jennifer was immersed in a magazine article and ignoring me. I figured perhaps it wasn't the proper moment.

The day passed without comment on the events of the previous night.

On Monday, while we commuted to work, Jennifer finally broke the silence. "Don't be mad at me, Lori. I can't stand it when you are angry with me." Jennifer was so pitiful when she got that sad look on her face. Her eyes pleaded for forgiveness.

I tried to stand firm. I wanted to make my point right at that moment. I wanted to tell her, 'I am a big girl now. I can live my own life and make my own mistakes!' but she looked so miserable. I smiled at her and smirked slightly. "I'm not mad, Jennifer. It wasn't really you I was mad at anyway. It was me. Besides I can't stay mad at you. You're the only friend I have." I laughed. I really did feel better now that we were speaking again. It seemed so juvenile to have wasted an entire day with the silent treatment.

"I'm really sorry, Lori. I didn't mean to hurt you."

"It's okay, Jen. Granted, perhaps you're not the most diplomatic person I know, but you do have a way of taking my head out of the clouds and bringing me down to earth." I placed my hand over hers and squeezed it slightly. "It'll be all right. I'm not mad at you anymore."

"Oh, thank God. I mean it, Lori . . . I really can't stand it when you are upset with me."

6

Weeks passed since Jennifer and I quarreled, and our relationship seemed back to normal again. I was glad the two of us were able to discuss some of my new frustrations. Jennifer enlightened me about a few of the mysteries surrounding sex. She told me that men are not really interested in giving women fulfillment; instead, they are simply content to reach their own satisfaction. So women, in turn, learn to climax during the man's short activities or else they must learn how to reach it by their own means. I commented that I didn't think that was very fair, and Jennifer replied, "More times than not, men don't know the meaning of fair."

Jennifer seemed bitter whenever I brought up the subject of sex, and when I inquired as to her attitude, she only shrugged saying, "David taught me a lot, and men in general reinforced it all." When I commented that it couldn't possibly be that bad, she referred to me as idealistic and naive. I was disappointed that Jennifer was unable to give me some kind of positive feedback; her answers only discouraged me all the more.

Steve and I shared a bed on a few occasions since our initial encounter. Each time it was relatively the same. We undressed and got into bed. He mounted me. A few seconds later, it was over. It seemed like such a waste of time. But I didn't want to give up too easily, so I tried to concentrate on the act—giving it my best shot. After all, there must be more to it than this!

Throughout the summer, I worked a lot of overtime for Larry Jenkins, but on August 8, I left as early as possible because I wanted to get home in order to hear Nixon's televised speech. Rumor had it that the president was going to resign in order to avoid impeachment. I didn't want to miss the historic moment.

Nixon had really painted himself into a corner. He'd lied so many times; I wondered if he even knew what the truth was anymore. It was sad too. Nixon had done a lot for our country. He'd ended the war as he had promised; he'd brought home our POWs; he'd opened the door to China and communications with them; and he and Brezhnev had signed the SALT Treaty, but I imagine as the years progressed, history would remember Nixon first for his scandal in Watergate. I never really liked the man, but I did feel sorry for him.

Hurriedly, I put the key in the door, twisted the knob, and went inside. The TV was not on yet. I figured Jennifer was taking a nap so I turned it on low and went into the kitchen to make myself a snack. As I opened the refrigerator, I detected a small laughing sound. Shaking my head, I passed it off as a noise from the next apartment. No, there it was again. I strained my ears and heard it a third time. It was Jennifer. What on earth was Jenny laughing to herself about? The sound was coming from our bedroom. I walked the length of the living room to the door and heard that chuckling sound again. Jennifer must be listening to the radio, and the announcer probably told an amusing joke. I turned the knob and walked in.

"Jennifer, what on earth is so funny? I could hear . . ." I stopped before I finished my sentence.

Jennifer was not alone.

Propped up in a sitting position, stark naked, was Jennifer. Sitting beside her in the same condition was Steve. They weren't even in Jennifer's bed; they were in mine! The shock nearly took my breath away as I stood there dumbfounded with my mouth gaping open. My mind functioned too slowly to speak. I couldn't believe that Steve had actually jumped into bed with my best friend. And Jennifer! What possessed her to be a party to this? The expressions on their faces could only be described as a combination of horror and confusion. No one spoke. We simply exchanged cold stares as each of us stayed motionless.

Seconds? Minutes? I had no concept of time. Finally I turned and walked from the room. As I slammed the door behind me, I overheard Steve speak. "I thought you said she wasn't coming home tonight."

What the hell did that mean? Slowly, I took the steps back into the kitchen. I was not going to be run out of my own apartment. I was definitely not leaving. I felt like a robot as I methodically poured a hefty portion of Jack Daniels into a glass. I added ice and water before downing it in one motion.

While sipping on my second drink, I stood at the window, pulled the curtain aside, and stared out into the distance. I could hear Nixon's voice coming from the television in the living room. I paid no attention to his words. I no longer cared what he had to say. I was too angry.

I heard soft footsteps in the next room, and then the front door opened and closed. Someone left. Steve? Jennifer? Both of them? The room held an oppressive silence. I felt as if I were being strangled by it.

A timid voice broke the stillness. "I only did it for you, Lori." Jennifer's voice cracked ever so slightly between words.

I refused to turn around and face her. Quietly, I filled the coffeepot with water and ignited the burner under it. After reaching for a cup, I inserted a tea bag and a teaspoon of sugar. With each action, I took special care not to show my anger by closing doors too loudly or banging utensils in a noisy fashion. Restraint! I was going to show restraint. I was not going to fill myself with liquor and start raging like a drunken fool. I took deliberate breaths in order to control my temper, but my pulse still seemed to be magnified as it pounded fiercely in my brain. I was afraid a vessel was going to pop from the pressure. I felt betrayed by the one person I was certain I could trust. Steve didn't matter; he wasn't the real issue here. At no point was Stephen Shaw of any importance to me. What really hurt was that Jennifer allowed herself to be party to it. Jennifer was my traitor—not Steve. Jennifer was my Judas. I felt as if she stuck a knife in my back but for the life of me, I couldn't understand why.

"Lori." Her voice sounded small and frightened. "I wasn't trying to hurt you. I only did it to prove what a bastard he is. I just had to show you that Steve isn't worthy of your love."

I could contain myself no longer. I turned to face her. My voice bellowed as each word blasted across the room. "I don't love him. I don't give a damn about Stephen Shaw." I banged the spoon I was holding. "Why the hell did you do it, Jennifer? Why? Do you have to sleep with every son of a bitch in pants? Aren't there enough men out there to satisfy you? God damn it! Why did you have to take mine?"

"You don't love him?" She looked more relieved than surprised. "You really don't love him?"

"Shit, Jennifer! You're missing the point."

"No." She shook her head and smiled weakly. "No, I'm not . . . that's exactly the point. All I wanted to do was prove what an asshole he is, and that he didn't deserve the love of a person like you. I didn't want you wasting your time on him. He wasn't good enough for you, Lori, and he didn't think a minute about you before falling into bed with me. Doesn't that prove what he's really like? I just wanted to show you that he wasn't worthy of your love."

"I told you, Jennifer. I don't love him. I never intended to love him." I was screaming. I could no longer conceal the volatile feelings inside me. "I

just wanted somebody to hold me! Hold me and pretend. Can't you understand that? For Christ's sake, why the hell did you ruin that for me? Damn
it, Jennifer. Why do you have to put a damper on everything I have ever
wanted?" I picked up the first object within my reach and slung it against
the wall. As it hit, the packets of tea bags scattered in every direction. I
watched them fall as the raging sensation inside me hit its peak. "You
planned this, didn't you, Jennifer? It was premeditated. You seduced Steve,
hoping I'd come in and see the two of you in bed. You wanted me to catch
you. Damn it, Jennifer! I thought you were my friend."

She took the steps between us—tears streaming down her face. She
reached for me, but I stepped aside. I didn't think I could bear her touch.

"Don't hate me, Lori. Please . . . please . . . please! Don't hate me. I only
did it for you. You've got to believe me."

I was too furious to care that Jennifer's face was distorted with anguish.
No amount of begging was going to ease my rage. I stepped aside as she
attempted to approach me a second time. Turning my back on her, I started
to leave the room. Before I managed to take three steps, Jennifer imprisoned
my ankles. I looked down only to discover that Jennifer had wrapped herself around my legs. I could not move. I tried to free myself, but the attempts
were futile.

Jennifer buried her head at my feet and began a fresh burst of pleas.
"Lori! Lori! Don't hate me. I'm begging you. I can't stand it when you're
angry with me. I'll do anything! Name it! Please . . . just don't leave me." She
was sobbing hysterically and repeating over and over again her last statements as she clung to my knees.

I could feel her tears streaming down my legs. The entire kitchen echoed
her sobs. I realized that my heart was beginning to soften. I could no longer
keep punishing her with my own private fury. I shouldn't forgive her. I really shouldn't, but in actuality she was right. Jennifer was always right. She
was only trying to protect me. I bent over and lifted Jennifer's trembling
body to her feet. "It's all right, Jen. It doesn't matter." I allowed her to fall
into my embrace as I tried to soothe her racking sobs. She clutched me as if

drawing strength from my arms. All of her weight seemed to be on me. I felt certain that if I stepped aside, Jennifer would surely collapse to the floor. "Jen." I spoke softly. "Stop crying now. It's okay. Come on, everything's all right. There's no need for tears."

Her body jerked with the force of her heaving cries. "You don't hate me? You forgive me? You really forgive me?"

I muttered quietly into her ear. "No, Jennifer. I don't hate you." I felt a part of my own tension ebbing. "Steve Shaw isn't worth destroying what the two of us have. A hundred men like him could never replace you, Jennifer. I'm angry, and I'm very hurt—I can't deny that—but if the two of us don't stick together, then neither one of us will have anything, will we?"

Jennifer wiped the base of her nose with the back of her wrist, and then used her palms to erase those tears that were still lying on her cheeks. "I'm sorry, Lori. I was only trying to help you." She flung her arms around my body as a fresh batch of tears formed in her eyes. "I need you so much. I would die if I lost you, Lori. You are the only person I care about in the whole world. I have no one but you. I can't lose you."

"Jen. Do me a favor."

"Yeah. Anything."

"Just let me make my own mistakes from now own. Okay? Don't try to fix everything for me." I held her for nearly an hour before she finally calmed down and ceased the spasmodic jerking of her body.

4

Kurt

THREE YEARS! IT HAD BEEN THREE LONG YEARS SINCE I WAS HOME. I spent two of those years in the 32nd Air Defense Command standing guard and pulling daily maintenance on Nike Hercules missiles in Hassloch, Germany. After a year of learning how to sleep standing up in the small guard tower, I was transferred to the mess hall and selected—lucky me—for the honor of what seemed at the time to be permanent KP duty. Actually, it was a rather cushy job as a cook making meals for the officers, and after a month or two, I decided that I liked it. Before my tour was up, I was promoted to E-4 and put in charge of meal preparation for the top brass. When the general wanted to entertain, I was the person who did the cooking. My lobster bisque and chicken Kiev were two of the most popular dishes with his wife, but the general raved even more about my baked Alaska. Their children were in the habit of stopping by on their way home from school to snack on my banana bread. I was told it was the best they'd ever eaten. My secret was the sour cream I added to the batter and the honey I poured over the top before baking it. Not only did I enjoy my new tasks, but I also discovered that I had a hidden talent for it.

Socially, Germany was a disappointment. I didn't have one single date until three months before my tour was up. Being celibate was the pits. The fact that I knew only a little German was definitely a handicap when it came to interacting with any of the native girls. It wasn't until Gretchen came into the local bar where my buddies and I were having a beer that I even had the chance to talk with a female. She was very proud of her broken English and loved the opportunity to try it out on me.

Our relationship developed quickly into one of a physical nature. I enjoyed losing myself in her plumb, ripe body. Gretchen was not beautiful. In fact, she was very plain. Although her hair was a lovely shade of spun gold and her eyes were a sparkling blue, her features were too sharp and angled to call her attractive. But she did have a gregarious nature, which helped pass the time and kept my mind off negative thoughts and home.

When my discharge came through, I elected to tour Europe instead of returning home to the United States. There was nothing and no one at home I wanted to see. Gretchen was thrilled with the idea of leaving family and responsibility behind, so she jumped at the opportunity to travel across the continent with me. We took odd jobs to pay our expenses. Together, we spent a year bumming around the countryside and seeing the sights. Often we slept under the stars and ate over a campfire. We got as far south as Rome before retracing our steps back up the "boot," turning west and heading through Switzerland into France, then south again to Spain. Italy was nice. I enjoyed the historical aspect, but Switzerland was more my style. We spent lazy days drifting in a rowboat and gazing at the Alps. I could not count the number of times we made love by the water's edge shielded only by darkness. While in Bern, we visited the zoo, which was perhaps Gretchen's favorite adventure. As a child, she had dreamed of going there, and the experience was even better than her dream. She was exhilarated as she interacted with the animals, made faces, and laughed uncontrollably. The fact that many of the animals were kept in natural-looking habitats rather than behind bars only enhanced her experience.

Paris was exciting, but expensive, so we didn't spend a lot of time there. Instead, we hitched a ride to Marseilles where we got jobs in a restaurant and worked for several months; subsequently, we blew all our money on the Riviera. When we were out of francs, we took another job in yet another restaurant until we had enough money to travel to Spain, where we ran with the bulls at Pamplona. That experience quickened my pulse and pumped my adrenaline.

It was in Spain that I started reading the news again. I paid little attention to international current events, and even less to what was happening in America. I didn't care about what was going on in the States anymore, and I wasn't sure if I ever wanted to go back again. While we were in Rome, I heard that Nixon resigned—thank God—and Gerald Ford was now president. Around Christmas, while we were in Marseilles, I heard that Nelson Rockefeller, Ford's choice for vice president, was sworn in to office. I found it amusing that this new administration was the first in U.S. history in which the people had not elected the president or the vice president. But I tucked the thought aside, because I really wasn't interested in what those Republicans were doing. I was enjoying my new life too much to care about the old one.

But now it was spring, and I was tired of Spain.

The chief chef in the restaurant where Gretchen and I were working was starting to be a real pain in the ass. One evening I got so angry with him that I threw a customer's dinner in his face, which, of course, resulted in the termination of my job. It was no great loss. I was ready to move on. We packed our bags and headed north again; a week later, we landed in Holland in time to see the tulips in full bloom. Gretchen and I got still another job in a restaurant, while we stayed in a small room about a block and a half away. I was getting restless and found myself glancing at headlines pertaining to the United States. I didn't actually pick up the papers, but I did hang around the newsstand and glance at a couple of articles. I read that Ford signed a tax cut bill of $22.8 billion in hopes that it would boost the U.S. into recovering from the recession. I also saw that the clemency program for draft evaders and military deserters had come to an end, which meant that over twenty-two thousand men would soon be going home. I could have been one of them. I was still bitter about what the draft had done to me.

Tesa Jones ❧ 403

I was in a foul mood more often than not, and Gretchen's warm body didn't seem to comfort me anymore. The harder she tried to please me, the more irritated I got. I found, instead of spending my money carelessly as I had done for nearly a year, that I was tucking it under the mattress and being more frugal.

On the weekend of July 4 1975, I watched Chris Evert and Arthur Ashe play incredible tennis matches on TV and win their respective Wimbledon singles titles. I wasn't sure if it was because I was spending another Fourth of July without fireworks or if it was because Evert and Ashe were Americans, but I suddenly felt nostalgic. I had an overwhelming desire to go home.

When I broke the news to Gretchen, she didn't seem upset at all. In fact, her first comment was that she, too, was homesick. That last night, we spent hours making love. It was the first time in several weeks that I enjoyed it. I realized, as did she, that although we would carry fond memories of each other, there would be no pain caused by our separation. What we had shared was good, but it was over.

2

On the flight home, I started pondering thoughts I had pushed aside for years. It would be nice to see Lori again. She wrote me quite often while I was in the army. I, of course, rarely returned her letters. During the year that I traveled, I sent her random postcards, but due to my drifting around, I had little news from her. I missed my parents, but I dreaded seeing them again. They were divorced. My mother was living in Delaware with her family, and my dad was in Alexandria somewhere between the Masonic temple and Landmark in a new home with another wife. Somehow, in spite of all the arguments I overheard as a kid, I never suspected another woman in my father's life. In the back of my mind, I always hoped that the two of them would work out their problems and keep our family together. No such luck. I suppose that was another dream that would never come true. I wondered how Lori was coping with the change.

Then, of course, there was Pamela. I fingered the letter and picture in my pocket that I'd carried around with me for three years. She'd written, as she had promised, a couple of months after the baby was born. It was a girl. Her name was Ellie. Pamela seemed thrilled to be a mother. I, in turn, was equally happy that I was let off the proverbial hook—no strings attached—safe at home plate. The last thing I wanted to be was a father.

And, finally, there was Jennifer. She and David Henderson were divorced. From what I heard, the marriage hadn't lasted very long. I had trusted Jennifer with my heart. No matter what her reasons might have been, I would never forgive her for betraying me. I had long since succeeded in wiping Jennifer from my mind; I had no intentions of replaying the past.

After arriving in New York, I discovered that I had a six-hour layover between flights. I pondered what to do with my time; in the end, I decided to hail a taxi. I read the return address from Pam's letter to the driver before he sped off in that direction. When I reached my destination, I stood silently by the elevator for several minutes before pressing the number of her floor. I was awed by the fact that she lived in the penthouse apartment in a gigantic building on Park Avenue. I'd completely forgotten about wealth in connection with Pam Woods. She never seemed rich to me. Her clothes did not look overly expensive; she rarely discussed money, and although she never seemed to be without cash, she certainly didn't flaunt it.

The elevator door opened. I stepped in and rode to the top. As I stood at the door, looking at the big brass knocker and the gigantic palm plants decorating the outside foyer, I realized that only a lot of money could buy this. I rapped heavily at the door and waited approximately a minute before it was slowly opened. A little dark-haired child peered out from behind it.

"Hi." She smiled. Ellie was absolutely adorable as she stood there in a spring green sun suit with a matching bow tied around her head. She resembled Pam, but she looked even more like Lori. She had curly black hair exactly the shade of Pamela's. The shape of the face was her mother's too. But the eyes, the nose, the smile—they were Lori's. There was no doubt about it: Ellie was my child. It was uncanny.

"Hello," I replied.

"I was hoping you were going to be my granddaddy," Ellie said, trying to hide her disappointment. "What's your name?" Her sweet voice asked. There was nothing timid about this child.

"Kurt Davis. I'm a friend of your mother's."

"What's that in your hand?"

I'd forgotten that I made purchases at Kennedy Airport. "Oh this?" I replied in a teasing manner as I knelt down to her level. "I figured that I couldn't possibly go visiting two such lovely ladies as yourself and your mother without bringing gifts." I handed her the doll I was holding.

"Oh, she is pretty."

Much to my surprise, Ellie threw her arms around my neck and squeezed me in gratitude. At first, I was slightly taken aback by her sudden movement but then I gave in to the fond embrace. She felt warm—so soft. And she smelled delightful. I buried my nose in the baby fresh texture of her hair and absorbed her fragrance. "I have a little something for your mother too. Is she home?"

Ellie's tiny head lifted off my chest. We pressed forehead to forehead as we exchanged smiles. "Mommy's in the kitchen."

I looked up after hearing footsteps and saw Pamela staring down at me with a surprised expression. I watched her as she dried her hands silently on a dish towel and then self-consciously raced her fingers lightly through her hair. She looked good. Although Pamela had never been as breathtakingly beautiful or possessed unique eye-catching features as Jennifer had, it was obvious that the last three years matured both Pamela's face and figure into a very attractive woman. The excess weight that I remembered was gone. Pamela had curves and angles to her now that gave her a sex appeal I never noticed before. The colorful backless sundress fit her nicely and flattered her summer tan. Her jet-black hair had grown quite long since I last saw her, and I liked the shag cut. The style made her appear more independent; in fact, it wiped out the childish first impression she used to give when I saw her walking toward me in Chapel Hill. Pamela still had those double layered, thick lashes circling the outside of her eyes, and she used only a touch of makeup to enhance them. As she smiled in my direction, I wondered if the slight coloring on her cheeks was from make-up or an involuntary blushing. Much to my surprise, she looked all grown up.

I stood up slowly and extended the box of candy I'd purchased for her. "Hello, Pamela. You're looking very well." We exchanged friendly smiles as she accepted my gift.

"Thank you." She blushed and averted her eyes so as not to look in my direction. "I didn't know you were coming. I didn't even know you were in the country." She seemed nervous. Unconsciously, she rubbed the tips of her fingers together. "It's good to see you, Kurt."

"Look, Mommy," Ellie pulled at the hemline of Pamela's dress. "Dollie! He gave me a doll."

Pamela looked first at the doll, then at her daughter. A pleasant smile spread over her lips. "Isn't that a pretty doll? Did you thank the nice gentleman for bringing it to you?" Pamela returned her eyes to mine and studied my every move.

Ellie threw her arms around my knees. "Thank you," she blurted before racing off into another room.

"That's very nice of you, Kurt. Ellie loves dolls, and there couldn't have been a more appropriate gift." She reached for my hand and guided me inside. As she closed the door behind me, she added, "I apologize for leaving you standing in the foyer, please come in. I hope you have enough time for a cup of coffee."

After leading me into the living room and offering me a chair, she disappeared with promises of a pot of fresh coffee and a tray of sweets. I looked around. The room was huge. I'd seen entire homes in Europe that were smaller than the room I was sitting in now. Surprisingly, even with all the crystal ashtrays and light fixtures, the silver tea sets and goblets, the brandy decanters and matching glasses, the paintings, the coordinating furniture in pale blues and contrasting darker colors, which probably cost more than most people made in a year, and the definite aura of affluence, I did not feel

oppressed by the wealth that surrounded me. It was impressive and magnificent, but it was far from overwhelming. I saw too much of Pamela's
warmth included in the decor to be intimidated by the room. I stood up from
my chair and took the paces to the window. The wool carpeting seemed to
spring with every step. I wondered how a cream colored pile was kept clean
when there was a three-year-old child around. The place was immaculate. I
parted the drapes and looked outside. My God! A person could see forever
from this vantage point! The smog was light, which was unusual for this
time of year. Visibility was exceptional; I could see for miles: hundreds of
buildings, thousands of cars. It was beautiful. Must be nice to be able to sit
on top of the world and watch it pass by without having to become involved
in the chaos below—a protective tower, a safe haven. Oh, to be out of harm's
way, tucked protectively in a nice comfortable world like this. Lucky, Pam!
No wonder she did not try to force me into any kind of commitment. She
didn't need me or anyone else for that matter. Shit! She had it all. There was
a slight sound behind me. Realizing I was no longer alone in the room, I
turned. Pamela stood at the door. She was holding a tray and watching me.
How long had she been standing there?

"Let me help you." I walked over to Pam and took the tray from her, then
set it on the marble table positioned in the center of the three matching couch-
es. I sat down and noticed that Pamela took a seat opposite me, reached for a
cup, filled it with hot, black coffee, and handed it to me. After doing so, she
filled a second cup, sat back in her seat, crossed her legs, and relaxed.

"I'm really glad to see you, Kurt. I think it's wonderful that you took the
time to stop by." She smiled warmly. There was a slight misting in her eyes
that was unreadable before she veiled them with her lids and concentrated
on sipping her coffee.

"What have you been doing, Pam?"

She chuckled. "I've taught myself how to cook. I take care of the apartment. I got rid of most of the servants a couple of years ago. A maid comes
in twice a week, but the rest are gone—the nanny too." She took another sip.
"And I'm trying to learn how to paint. I'm taking some courses, but I'm not

really very good. It's strictly amateur stuff, but it's fun. I read a lot in my spare time, but mostly I take care of Ellie. She keeps me pretty busy." She smiled proudly.

"I suppose a three year old is quite a handful."

"She is. She really is. But Ellie is such a good child. She's so happy all the time—so full of life. I love being with her; her happiness is contagious. Being a mother is a twenty-four-hour-a-day job—a lot of work, but I'm finding it very rewarding."

"Sounds like you're really enjoying it."

"Yes, I am."

"That's good! I'm glad for you, but don't you think you should do other things besides taking care of Ellie?"

"If you're trying to discreetly inquire as to whether I'm dating or not—or if I'm involved with anyone—I'm not." She glanced around the room refusing eye contact of any kind. Pam paused for a moment before continuing. "I don't have any desire to run in the social circle . . . especially not with men who think of me only as George Woods's daughter." She ran her fingers around the rim of her cup, crossed her legs at the knee, and bounced them irregularly as if she were nervous. "I have no real desire to date anyone; besides, Ellie takes up most of my time."

"That's not a very healthy attitude for someone your age, Pam. You can't channel your whole life in one direction. It's not fair to you. You're a very attractive woman." I saw her blush slightly at my words. "And you shouldn't trap yourself in this castle and pretend that the rest of the world doesn't exist."

"Don't!" she interrupted. She seemed to be holding herself in check. "Don't you come here to my home after three years and tell me how I should be running my life." Pamela sat her cup down on the table and clasped her hands together. Wringing her fingers silently, she continued, "Excuse me, I didn't mean to snap like that. I apologize. Why don't we change the subject? Tell me about yourself. Was the Army as bad as you thought it would be?"

"Yes . . . and no." I hadn't thought about the Army in almost a year. "I still get ticked off to think that they drafted me, interrupted my education, trained me to fight, and then sent me to some hole in the wall where I was little more than useless."

"Wasn't it better than being in Vietnam?"

"Yeah, I suppose," I replied. "Although there was a time during my training when I wanted to go. The sergeant really brainwashed everyone. I remember that I got a thrill out of the thought of killing. They pumped us up." I paused slightly as I remembered those old feelings. "And a part of me wanted to go over there for another reason. In analyzing it now, I think I might have had a death wish." I smirked slightly. "What a jerk I was; after all, there's more to life than just one woman." My voice dripped with sarcasm. "I suppose you don't know . . . Jennifer got married right before I was drafted. She didn't even have the decency to tell me."

"No! I didn't know." Pamela sat up in her seat almost as if she were straining to remain calm.

"It didn't last long. My sister told me she's divorced now. They're sharing an apartment."

"Oh." Pam's voice was soft. "I suppose you'll see her soon."

"I'd rather not, but I guess it can't be avoided."

After several moments of silence Pamela changed the subject. "So the Army wasn't that bad?"

"When I think about it now, Germany was okay. It was more boring than anything else. You know what really pisses me off? They took me out of college so that I could be a cook. Doesn't that beat all?"

"You could always go back to school."

"No! I don't think so." I contemplated my thoughts. "The desire's all gone."

"Mommy." Ellie came running into the room; her ringlets were bouncing on top of her head. "Cookie . . . I want a cookie."

"What do you say first, Ellie?" Her mother asked in a patient voice.

"Please," Ellie said, before reaching on the tray for the remaining treats. "Thank you."

"She really is adorable, Pamela." I grinned when I spoke the words.

"I think so, too, but I'm your everyday, average, prejudiced mother." That warm gentle smile that was so typical of Pamela's personality began to spread across her face again. She radiated love, and her face shone beautifully.

Ellie picked up the tray and offered it to me. "Cookie?"

"Thank you. I don't mind if I do," I responded as I selected the largest on the platter. "Mommy and I made them. Aren't they good?"

"Delicious," I said, before glancing at Pam. "You really have learned to fend for yourself. I'm sure that anyone who can make a cookie that tastes this good can do anything in the kitchen. You like to cook?"

"I enjoy it. Actually, I find it relaxing. I couldn't even boil an egg before Ellie was born, but I'm getting to be quite a gourmet now. Perhaps you'd like to stay for dinner."

"I can't. My plane will be leaving shortly."

Her disappointment was etched in her expression, but she quickly concealed it, and added, "If you're ever back in New York, please feel free to come by. I'll make dinner and show you how much I've learned. The invitation is open . . . anytime. And if you give me a little warning, I'll make you any dish you want."

I laughed. "Now there's an offer that's hard to turn down." I stood up, signaling my need to leave. She followed my lead and walked with me to the door.

"I want you to know, Kurt, that you're always welcome here."

"Bye, bye," Ellie waved as she came racing around the corner. She was cradling the doll I'd given her in one arm and waving her free hand. Before I knew what happened, she jumped into my arms. Closing my eyes to get full benefit from the tender embrace, I responded by wrapping my arms around her. It felt wonderful to hold her tiny frame against me. I rocked her back and forth several times before letting her go. "Now, Ellie. You take good care of that little doll because next time I'm here I want to see it, okay?"

"Okay."

"And you take real good care of your mommy, too, because she's my friend and I like her." I looked at Pamela. We exchanged warm smiles.

"Okay, Kurt." Ellie made an attempt at my name but butchered its one syllable. All three of us laughed.

"You take care of yourself, too, Kurt," Pamela stated as she touched me lightly on the cheek with her lips. "And don't be a stranger." After attempting a grin, she continued, "It really was a wonderful surprise to see you again."

I waved several times before the elevator came to take me down to the first floor. As I walked out into the late afternoon's activities, I thought that I hadn't felt this good in a long time.

3

I drove by the house where I had grown up only to see strangers there. Upon getting out of the car, I stood silently popping one old memory after another through my mind. I felt the oddest sensations as I watched three unfamiliar children playing in the front yard—a yard I had always considered my own. The place looked the same, yet everything was different. The building was still white, the shutters were still painted black, and the bushes still bordered the grounds. My old basketball hoop was still protruding from the oak tree where I'd missed more shots than made. The perennials were still adding color to the gardens and the massive clumps of impatiens were in full bloom—just as they were every year. The new occupants obviously took great pains to keep the yard pretty and neat as my parents had done.

But it wasn't home anymore—at least, not *my* home.

Yes! Everything did seem exactly the same; but in truth, it wasn't! Everything had changed! It was very different! It was as if I had stayed in the exact same place for three years, but the rest of the world kept on living and changing with each passing day.

I didn't fit in here anymore.

I had called my mother long distance from the airport, but I wasn't going to get the opportunity to see her until I purchased my own car. There was no way I could drive this rented one for such a long distance: no money for that expense! My father was on the other side of town living in a high-rise that wasn't even built three years ago. I wasn't sure I wanted to see him. Lori lived with Jennifer about two and a half miles away in their shared apartment. I was stalling, waiting to get the courage to face them both.

I glanced again at my once upon a time home, then turned, got back in the car, and drove off. Everything had changed. Three years had altered everything in the life I had left behind. A tiny fear nagged inside me as I wondered if there was a place anywhere in this world for Kurt Davis. I did not belong here. I didn't belong in Europe either—and I couldn't go back to North Carolina. What was I going to do now? I didn't have a place to live; I didn't have a job. I didn't even have a friend! Nothing was the same.

Without thinking where I was going, I drove north on Fort Hunt Road, turned right on Belle View Boulevard, and then left on Tenth Street. I pulled into the parking lot of the apartment where Lori lived. For well over an hour, I sat in my rented car. Finally, I got the courage to enter the building. I stood silently in front of her door. Minutes passed. Finally I tapped on the knocker. Maybe she wasn't home. Maybe I wouldn't have to see either Lori or Jennifer. I rapped on the door a second time.

The door opened. Before I could say a word, Lori squealed with delight and wrapped her arms around me. "Kurt, you're home! You're really home." She squeezed me several times and then picked me up an inch off the floor.

I was amazed at her strength and overjoyed by her reaction. Grateful for the warm reception, I returned her hug. "Lori, it's so good to see you."

"Let me look at you." She pulled herself away. "You look terrific, Kurt! You've let your hair grow back out. I like it. I can't believe it! My baby brother's all grown up." She kissed both of my cheeks and added, "I have missed you so much." She steered me into the living room. There were boxes, suitcases, and bags full of items scattered all over the floor. "Sorry about the mess. We're moving next week and getting a two-bedroom apartment." She glanced at me and waited to see if I were going to ask about

Jennifer. When I didn't, she changed the subject. "Can I get you something to drink?"

"Do you have a beer?"

"I certainly do. I bought it last week when I thought you were coming. Where have you been? I've been worried sick. Mom told me you were back and that she'd talked to you. I kept expecting you to show up. Daddy's called every day asking if I've seen you." She opened the refrigerator and pulled out a Budweiser. After using the bottle opener, she handed it to me.

"I've just been wandering around," I answered as I took a long swallow from the ice-cold brew.

Lori reached for a second beer, uncapped it, and took a drink. "Where have you been sleeping?"

"In the car."

"Why did you do that? You could have stayed here with me." Immediately after she'd said the words she knew the reason why I hadn't been by earlier. She covered up her embarrassment by adding, "If you did not want to stay here, you could have stayed with Daddy."

"I'm not too sure I want to crash there either, Lori. I don't think I'd fit in too well with our father's new bride." I couldn't keep the sarcasm out of my voice. Lori detected it instantly.

"I know what you mean," she answered as she flopped herself down on the couch and sipped her drink. It was odd watching my sister drink a beer. She looked different. It took me a moment to realize that it wasn't just a facial change. It was what she was wearing. Jeans. I'd never seen her wear jeans before. Her T-shirt was quite form fitting, even tight to some degree. In the past, Lori's attire was more on the demure side: loose-fitting outfits, coordinating colors, simple lines, pressed creases. She still had a fraction of wide-eyed innocence, but most of it was gone. I was certain during the last three years we had both done a lot of growing up.

"So . . . tell me, Lori. How do you like the new Mrs. Davis?" Even though I tried to sound nonchalant, my words came out laced with animosity.

"I don't know, Kurt. I want to like her—for Dad's sake." Lori paused. "She's nice, I guess."

"The divorce was a big enough surprise but, God, was I shocked when I found out that he remarried."

"I know. Me too." Lori pulled out a cigarette.

I was blown away when I saw her light it and exhale the smoke as if she had been doing it for years. Lori smoked cigarettes! Wow . . . that was a change I didn't expect!

She drew in on the filter several times in silence before adding to her comments. "Daddy invited me to Thanksgiving dinner last year. While I was there this strange woman came out of the kitchen." Lori puffed several times on her cigarette. "It was weird. Daddy was talking about politics . . . and then suddenly he introduced us. Can you imagine, Kurt? There I was— sitting on a chair that had been in our old home ever since I can remember— and Dad was saying, 'Lori, this is Judy.' He only paused a fraction of a second before he said, 'We were married yesterday. I know that the two of you are going to get along just fine.' I almost fell out of my seat. I was completely stunned. You won't believe this, Kurt, but I almost started laughing. I thought Dad was kidding. I really thought it was some kind of a joke. But when the new Mrs. Davis came right up to me and shook my hand without even a hint of humor, I stifled my surprise and tried to get to know her for Dad's sake." Lori leaned back in her seat and became lost in thought.

My poor sister. It must have been quite a jolt to her; it sure as hell was to me. How could my father have been so insensitive?

I gazed around the apartment looking for signs of Jennifer, but was relieved to see that she wasn't home. With a little luck, I wouldn't have to come face to face with her on my first visit with my sister. I needed a little time to prepare myself for that venture. "Well, you haven't told me," I said. "What's your opinion of our new stepmother?"

"I really don't know her that well. She's done her duty and had me over for Christmas and Easter dinner, and a couple of times this summer, but to be perfectly honest with you, Kurt, I'm not too sure I can be objective about this whole thing. She's nice enough, I suppose. She even appears to be in love with Dad, but it strikes a raw nerve as far as I'm concerned. I wonder if I'll ever be able to get used to it." A cloud of smoke encircled her head as she continued. She seemed to ponder each word before speaking. "Daddy looks happy; but then again, I thought he appeared happy all my life. I guess I'm not a very good judge of his inner emotions, am I? I think the thing that bothers me the most is that Judy—that's what I call her because I will never bring myself to refer to her as mother—well anyway, Judy doesn't seem to like to have me around. Maybe I'm being too sensitive; I don't know. But it's almost as if I'm in the way or something. Or maybe I make her as uncomfortable as she makes me."

"What about Dad?" I asked, wondering if he thought his children were just in the way now too.

"Daddy? He seems glad to see me when I come over. But it's all so different. I mean . . . well . . . it's like . . . I can't explain it. It's just not the same anymore. He seems so distant, and I feel out of place. Do you know, Kurt, there isn't even one picture of us in their home. Not one! It's really weird. It's as if she wiped out his past, and he let her do it."

"Poor Mom," I muttered, as I finished my beer and headed toward the kitchen. "Mind if I get another?"

"No, of course not. Help yourself," she said as she lit another cigarette. "You knew all along, didn't you, Kurt?"

I could hear Lori asking her question from the other room. I wasn't quite sure how to respond. Yes. I did know that our parents were not the happily married couple Lori imagined. But no! I had no idea there was another woman in the picture. Standing in the doorway, I leaned my shoulder against the frame, and watched her as she waited for my answer. I decided that it was a little too late to protect my sister. The damage was already done. "Yeah! I knew about Mom and Dad—at least part of it. You know, Lori, I really envied you for being so blind to it all. It must have made everything a lot easier for you as a kid. I wished I could have been that oblivious to their arguing. I wish I hadn't known."

Lori stared out the window for a while before she spoke. There was bitterness in her voice when she broke the silence. "Life's really a crock of shit . . . isn't it, Kurt?"

I couldn't believe optimistic, naive Lori actually made that statement. It was so out of character, but I refused to show my surprise."Yeah. It's the pits all right."

"We make a good pair—you and I," Lori muttered more to herself than to me. "A couple of life's dropouts—rejects from the Now generation. That's what we are. Misfits." She looked so sad. "We've come a long way, Kurt. Unfortunately, it seems as if it's all been backward. A step forward and two back. That's all I've ever done." Lori kept shaking her head in a pitifully depressing way.

I could tell by my sister's expression that even she was not the same person I knew before I left for Europe. Lori seemed more aware—cynical and uptight. She sounded like a hard-core realist instead of that naive creature with whom I shared adolescence. I always thought my sister would never be tarnished by a negative attitude, but I could tell by her expression that Lori was definitely not the innocent she was three years ago. She, too, had changed. I was about to comment on her negative statements when the apartment door opened, and Jennifer walked through the door.

The moment I saw her, my heart lurched. I thought all those old flames were extinguished, but it seemed that there were still a few left flickering inside of me. Jennifer looked beautiful, even more beautiful than my buried memories. Her hair was a little longer, and perhaps more blonde than I remembered. She was thinner and appeared slightly taller, but her eyes, her nose, the very shape of her face were all exactly the same.

"Hello, Kurt. Welcome back." Her initial comment seemed anything but welcoming. There were no readable signs in her expression. No sudden surprise in her eyes, no wide smiling grin—nothing.

"Hello, Jennifer." I watched her as she kicked off her shoes, walked into the kitchen, and returned with a glass of iced tea. She lit a cigarette. An oppressive silence filled the room.

"Can I get you another beer, Kurt?" Both Jennifer and I jumped—startled by the sound of Lori's voice. I had nearly forgotten that my sister was in the room.

"No, I think I'll be leaving shortly. Might as well go see our father and meet his bride." I had to escape. It was getting harder for me to breathe. Being in the same room with Jennifer was extremely oppressive. I stood up.

As my sister hugged me farewell, I glanced over her shoulder for one last glimpse of Jennifer. She was watching me. She looked as if she wanted to say something; in fact, her eyes seemed to be reaching out to me. Was it my imagination? Did she want me to make a move in her direction?

"It's nice to see you again, Kurt." Jennifer's voice was soft and sweet. "I hope you stop by often now that you're home."

She looked away before I could measure the expression on her face. I felt as if my heart were caught in the middle of my throat.

"Give me a call soon, little brother. And if you need anything—money, lodging, anything—just let me know." Lori kissed my cheek.

Before I could answer, I was standing in the hallway. I waved one more time. There was a plastic smile covering my face as I pretended to be calm and casual. The door closed, and I descended the stairs. Damn! Everything *had* changed! Everything except me! Everything except those old feelings I had for Jennifer! Obviously, it was going to take more than three years to banish them.

4

Lori was right about our new stepmother. She did seem to make our father happy. He did smile more and talk with less ice in his voice. He seemed more at ease. My sister was also correct about her impressions as to how our stepmother felt about us. Although I didn't feel that her reactions were intentional, the results were the same. I didn't feel welcome in my father's new home. I sat across from them on furniture I recognized from my youth. I felt self-conscious, distant, uncomfortable. As my father made polite stabs at conversation, I studied his new wife. Judy was an attractive woman in her mid-forties. She smiled a lot but the effort seemed obligatory. Judy Davis stood only a few inches shorter than my father, her black hair showed no traces of gray, her eyes were a very dark shade of green, and her cheekbones were set high on her face—so high, in fact, that they looked out of place. The new Mrs. Davis seemed like a nice enough woman, but I knew I would never really like her, because I would never give her more than half a chance. In all honesty, I wasn't being objective. I was just as guilty as Lori for jumping to conclusions before enough time had passed. My new stepmother must have sensed my feelings. Perhaps that was why she treated both Lori and me in an impassive manner. What the hell did she expect? Did she honestly think that I would welcome her with open arms into our family? Forget that shit! This was the woman who divided my family and destroyed my parents' lives. Granted my mom was far from an angel when it came to their marriage—perhaps she should shoulder some of the blame; after all, it takes two to make a marriage work, but damn it, somebody had to be at fault, and it was easier to blame Judy.

Judy Davis seemed to be able to read my mind. I watched as she frowned in my direction. I wondered what she was thinking. Our eyes met for the umpteenth time during the evening. Both our expressions were hostile. She made it quite plain that, if I couldn't act in a civil manner, I would no longer be a part of my father's life, and my expression clearly stated that I would barely tolerate her existence. There would definitely be no friendship between us.

"I'm glad you're home, son," my father stated again. He must have said that phrase at least a dozen times already tonight.

Everyone kept saying they were glad I was home. Why didn't I feel glad to be here?

Five minutes after I entered their new apartment, I knew I wouldn't find my roots with my father and his new wife. He might be glad I was home, but his interpretation of home was Virginia—not his honeymoon apartment. It was obvious to us all that I would not be staying here.

Before I had a chance to ask for a loan from the old man, he offered.

"Kurt, if you need any money to get settled, don't hesitate to ask. You know I don't have very much, but I'd be more than willing to give you a few extra bucks when I can."

"Thanks, Dad. I appreciate it. I might need some cash. I have a little left from my last job in Holland, but it's running out. I need to buy a car. I guess I'll need a month's advance on an apartment, and I'll have to stock some staples and necessities. Maybe tomorrow I can line myself up for an interview. If I get a job soon, I'll be all right."

"What kind of job are you looking for, Kurt?"

"Chef. The army didn't teach me a whole hell of a lot, but it seems, due to their effort, I'm a pretty good cook."

"There must be other jobs you can get—not that there's anything wrong with cooking but . . . "

"Sure, Dad . . . sure . . . I could dig ditches. Hell! Maybe I could sweep streets . . . or I could work construction. I understand the subway project pays well. I could put on a hard hat—go in the tunnels. Exactly what do you think I should do?"

"You could go back to school," Judy interjected politely with her first personal statement of the evening.

"Oh, sure!" I was being openly antagonistic. "Sure! Why not? How the hell am I supposed to do that?"

"Now that you're a veteran, the army will help pay for your education."

"Yeah, but what about the other bills? The army won't pay for those." I knew I was being stubborn. If I had really wanted to go back to school, I could have found a way, but at the moment, college was the last thing on my mind. I had a hell of a lot more things to worry about than finishing up an education that never should have been interrupted in the first place.

"You could take a few night courses at George Mason." My father was pushing. He wouldn't drop the subject.

"It would take me forever to get a law degree if I took one or two courses a semester," I mumbled as I continued sipping on my drink. Hopefully,

Judy and my father would change the topic before I lost my temper.

"It's a start, son. It might take a couple of extra years, but it would be worth it."

What the hell did he know? Cooks worked at night; they slept during the day. Hell! Who was I kidding? I'd probably have to take on two jobs just to be able to eat, and then there wouldn't be any time for classes or studying. Besides, I was no longer interested in being a lawyer. I'd lost sight of that goal a long time ago. College was for people who wanted to make something out of their lives. I no longer had that desire. I was a nobody who was going no place! What the hell did it matter anyway?

After a reasonable length of time, I excused myself, thanked both my father and his wife for dinner, and left. I felt only relief when I walked out the door. I knew one thing for sure—I wouldn't be coming back very often. I could barely stand the polite stifling aura between Judy and me. I didn't need that. They could both go to hell.

Thank God, my father gave me $100. I drove to a local bar and proceeded to drink $10 worth of booze. While I was there, I picked up an easy-looking chick who invited me to her place and nearly screwed my eyes out; consequently, I slept on a mattress instead of the backseat of my rented car.

5

By the time I helped Lori and Jennifer move into their new apartment, I already had a cooking job at a classy restaurant and secured a furnished efficiency of my own. The rent was $150 a month but I was certain I could afford it if I scheduled myself on duty six nights a week. I lucked out when the neighborhood bank loaned me $500 so I could buy a ragged old Buick. The car looked like hell but ran well enough to get around town. I had a place to live, a job, a little food on the table, and wheels. Life was far from rosy, but at least it was a start.

My sister and her roommate had a lot more things to move than I realized the first time I saw their place. It took the entire day for the three of us to carry everything they had from their Tenth Street apartment, down three flights of stairs, across the courtyard, down the street half a block, and back up three flights of stairs to their new two-bedroom apartment. Lori and I did most of the heavy transporting because we both noticed how tired Jennifer seemed. With Jennifer unpacking in the new place, Lori and I walked empty-handed back to the old apartment.

"Is Jennifer all right?" It was my first reference to my sister's roommate since the day began.

"She's still not much better than she was a few months after the pneumonia. I swear there's something wrong with her, Kurt, but she refuses to see a doctor, and she always tells me I'm acting like a mother hen."

"Well, Lori, we both knew when we met her that she didn't have much stamina. Maybe we're just expecting too much out of her. Jennifer was always short-winded even before her illness."

"I know, but I still worry about her all the same. It's not normal, and it drives me crazy when she pushes herself too hard."

"Has Jennifer said anything to you about me?"

At first, Lori tried to skirt the issue; in fact, she acted as if she didn't hear my question, but then she saw my expression and began to speak. "Not a word, Kurt. I could fib to you if you'd like, but the truth is that Jennifer has not mentioned a thing about how she feels. I was tempted to ask strictly for my own curiosity, but I haven't. I was surprised when she didn't even say anything that first day you came over. I thought she might bring it up then, but she didn't."

"What do you think?"

Lori shook her head as we mounted the stairs side by side. Pondering her next words, she crinkled her face slightly in a pensive frown. "I don't know, Kurt. Most of the time, I actually can tell what Jennifer is thinking even if she doesn't say a word. We've always been so attuned to each other. She knows me so well—better than anyone. And I know her equally well; but to be perfectly honest with you, there are times—and particularly in this case—that I haven't the vaguest idea what's going on inside her head."

We walked into the near-empty apartment and grabbed armloads of bags and suitcases. Most of the stuff had already been transported. A half dozen more trips and we'd be done. Before we left the apartment, Lori confronted me with a question. Even though her voice seemed timid, the words were spoken with frankness. "Are you still in love with her?"

I stopped in my tracks. At first, I was too shocked by her abrupt question to speak. I realized that I was silent because I didn't know the answer. Then suddenly, it became very clear. Once the first syllable was spoken, the words came pouring out. "I tried, Lori. I really tired to stop loving her. When Jennifer left me—I *hated* her, and I continued to hate her for three years. She betrayed me. I don't even know why. On my flight home, I was a hundred percent certain my head was screwed on straight where Jennifer was concerned; in fact, I didn't even harbor the hate anymore. But the moment I saw her, I realized that it isn't over—it never really was. God, it hurts!"

"Have you thought about telling her how you feel?"

"Hell, no! And don't you go yapping about it either, Lori! No, shit! Don't say one damn word to Jennifer about what I just said. I'll work this out myself."

"Okay . . . I promise."

Five long hours later, the move was completed. Dishes, pots, pans, and silverware were all stored away. Clothes were hung in their respective closets, and suitcases were unpacked. I used my inherent masculine abilities to screw in the holes for the curtain rods, hang pictures, and even put in a few molly bolts for hanging plants. I moved and shifted the heavier furniture until the girls were satisfied with the layout. It was an exhausting day, and Jennifer wasn't the only one showing signs of fatigue. Around ten o'clock, we all crashed in half reclining positions on the living room floor. It felt great just to be sitting still for a change.

The three of us shared a bottle of cheap wine; and then Lori stood up, brushed the back of her pants, and addressed both Jennifer and me. "I think I'll turn in now." She watched both of us quietly before placing a chaste kiss on my cheek. "Thanks a lot for your help, Kurt. We couldn't have done it without you."

"No sweat! What are brothers for?" My voice sounded a great deal more casual than my thoughts. Lori disappeared. I braved a glance in Jennifer's direction. She made no move. I wondered whether she wanted me to stay. I smiled—saying nothing—and waited for her to react. I didn't quite know what to expect. She returned my friendly grin, lifted her cup in a toasting fashion, and then took several long gulps. We made eye contact a few times, but before I could read her expression, one of us would look away. Finally, I broke the muted silence between us. "How do you like your job?" What a ridiculous question!

"Did Lori tell you I'm on Capitol Hill?"

I nodded.

"I work for Congressman Robinson."

"He's a Republican! Why do you want to work for him?"

"Doesn't really matter to me that he's a Republican. I like the job. It's fun. I can't believe it, but I'm actually good at what I'm doing. Thank God for those secretarial courses I took at Elon. If it hadn't been for them, I'd probably still be waiting tables. I never thought I'd be smart enough to get a job like this one."

"Quit knocking yourself, Jennifer."

"I'm not knocking myself. I'm being realistic. Things never came easily to me. I was never smart like you. All of that stuff was hard for me . . . and I didn't even enjoy most of it."

"You are too smart. You just never gave yourself any credit."

Jennifer became serious. Eyes cast downward, she traced the lip of her glass with her fingers. "You're the one who deserves a lot of the credit for getting me through the courses I took." It was Jennifer's first personal statement to me.

I was sitting on the floor several feet from her. I could feel the perspiration forming. It seemed as if I were choking on my thoughts and completely unable to respond to her statement.

"You and Lori," Jennifer continued, her face expressionless; her voice was unruffled and aloof. "The two of you are the only people who cared about me. Nobody else ever gave a damn." She laughed slightly as she lifted her paper cup. "You know, Kurt, I used to sit in front of the television and watch the news just so I would be able to talk intelligently to you. I even read the sports page so I'd know all the statistics about your favorite teams. I wanted you to be proud of me. I wanted you to think I was clever and witty and informed about the things that happened in the world." Jennifer paused. The expression in her eyes seemed defeated, lost. As she took another sip from her drink, she despondently added, "I actually believed that all those things were the answer. I really thought that if I knew dates, current events, public figures, foreign policy, all of the players on the Redskins' roster—if I knew all that stuff, then everything else would fall into place. Isn't that a crazy theory?"

I didn't know what the hell she was taking about. It all seemed like a riddle, but there were too many clues missing in order to get the solution. I was confused, desperate—I wanted to swing our discussion back to her and me. I didn't want to talk about world issues, football teams, or TV news. I wanted to talk about *us*. The wine warmed me—strengthened my resolve. It gave me a bit of courage to speak. "I don't understand, Jennifer . . ."

"Sometimes . . . " Jennifer interrupted my words; her voice sounded forlorn. ". . . neither do I."

I made another stab at courage. "Do you think . . . maybe on my next day off . . . would you like to go someplace? Anywhere. A movie or dinner. Whatever you'd like."

"Sure. Why not?" She smiled briefly, but her eyes didn't light up, and her face showed no sign of happiness.

I was too excited about our pending arrangement to ponder the reasons for her attitude. We had a start—a beginning. Everything was going to work out. After all, hadn't Jennifer stated in her own words that my sister and I were the only important people in her life? We were the only ones who cared. Didn't she just tell me that she, too, cared about me? I felt marvelous. I was determined not to lose Jennifer a second time.

Shortly after our conversation, I noticed Jennifer yawning and struggling to keep her eyes open. It had been a very long day. After telling Jennifer that I'd give her a call tomorrow, I excused myself and left. I was so happy—bursting with inner excitement. I simply had to talk with someone—anyone. At first, I couldn't think of a soul to call; but by the time I reached my apartment, a picture of Pamela formed in my mind. I'd call Pam. Even if it were nearly midnight I'd call her. Just to talk. Like the old days.

I dialed the area code and then the seven digits that I had written down on a slip of paper that was stashed in my wallet. She answered on the third ring.

"Hello."

"Hi, Pam." I immediately knew that she had been sleeping.

"Kurt? Is that you?" At the sound of my voice, Pam wiped the lethargy from her words. "How are you?"

"I'm fine."

"Is everything all right?"

"Yes," I paused a moment before laughing. "It's the silliest thing. I just had to talk to someone, Pam. I couldn't think of anyone but you. I don't really have any friends . . . you know what I mean?"

"I'm glad you called. Are you settled in yet? Did you get a job?"

I answered her questions. It felt so good to be talking with someone. I even started making jokes about my efficiency and the heap of junk I called my car. She laughed merrily at my words. Then I changed the subject. "How's Ellie?"

"She's fine. She learned a few new words since you were here. It seems like some kind of dam has been opened—all these new words are pouring out. She's always been very articulate, but I never realized how large her vocabulary is. It's just incredible how her mind works." Pam paused for a moment and when she continued her voice took on a more timid sound. "If you'd like, you could give me your new address, and I'd be glad to send you her recent photographs, and keep you up to date with her current antics."

"I'd like that, Pam." I gave her my current address and repeated again how much I liked hearing her voice. She seemed delighted, which only added to my own cheerful mood. We talked a few minutes longer about trivial events. "I better hang up now, Pam." I interrupted our airy conversation. "Long distance phone calls are not in my budget. Sorry I woke you up."

"Kurt, don't be sorry. You can call me anytime. I enjoyed hearing from you. And Kurt . . . I don't want to sound patronizing, and hope you don't take this the wrong way, but if you ever need anything—money, anything—you know, of course, that I have more than enough. I'd be glad to lend it to you or even give it to you. Please don't take offense by my offer. I mean it would be like from one friend to another."

"I'm not offended, Pam. It's okay. Who knows . . . maybe someday I'll take you up on it . . . but right now, I'm doing all right. It was great talking to you." I hung up the phone. It wasn't until the receiver was cradled that I realized I didn't even mention Jennifer during our conversation.

6

The following week I picked up Jennifer at her apartment and took her to The Crazyhorse in Georgetown. The place was packed as usual, but we still managed to get a table near the dance floor. Jennifer seemed distant. She only talked when I spoke to her, and she rarely smiled. We made polite conversation; we seemed more like coworkers than ex-lovers. I tried to draw her out, but she seemed to let the loud music and chaotic activity screen her from me.

I was annoyed by the fact that so many different men greeted her and stopped long enough at our table to exchange a few words. Whenever I asked who they were, Jennifer answered by saying "just a friend", which only aggravated me more. Where did Jennifer meet all of these men? Every individual who spoke to her increased in me a burning, jealous rage. I did not want to share Jennifer. I tried to suppress my resentment, and fortunately, my frustration was concealed.

We only danced three times the entire evening. Jennifer's endurance barely carried her through one song at a time. That, of course, made no difference to me. I didn't care what we did just as long as I had her full attention, but I wasn't getting that either. Her eyes wandered. Her thoughts seemed to skip from the subjects we discussed. Jennifer was somewhere else. As hard as I tried, I was not rewarded by a genuine smile on her face. I kept telling myself that it didn't matter as long as we were together.

It was well past one o'clock when I drove her home. Instead of walking her to the door, I stopped the engine and sat back in my seat. When I placed an arm gently around her, Jennifer neither cuddled against me nor pulled away. She sat there like a statue. I tilted her head toward mine and kissed her very tenderly on each cheek, then I covered her lips with my own. Initially, she showed no reaction; then slowly, I felt some response: warmth. Her lips were beginning to feel warm. I increased the pressure of my mouth upon hers. She did not push me away.

"Jennifer . . . " I traced her jaw with my lips. "Jennifer . . . I've waited so long . . . so long for this moment." I became more aggressive, as much to ignite her feelings as to satisfy mine. Trying to recapture the body I'd known so well, my hands started to explore. Jennifer seemed to be moving with me. I cupped a breast in my hand as I used the other one to cradle her neck. It felt so good to be touching her again. Nothing mattered. Nothing else mattered except holding Jennifer in my arms. I buried my nose in her fragrance. Every part of her had a scent I remembered and adored. Her hair was a combination of lemons and sea breeze; her skin smelled of springtime freshness, and her lips had the moistness of sweet morning dew, but the warmth seemed to be draining out of them. The more I kissed her the colder her mouth became. I closed my eyes and tried to take every part of her into my mind as I savored the moment and printed it into my memory. I struggled to coax sensations out of her, but I was not rewarded.

"Don't, Kurt."

At first, I wasn't sure she actually spoke the words; they seemed so distant. Jennifer's voice seemed detached from the wonderful smell and touch of her. I continued kissing her.

"Stop it, Kurt." She pushed me away and sat up straight on the other side of the car. "I really think I better go in now. It's been a long night, and I'm totally exhausted."

I smiled politely and tried not to show my irritation. I replied in a composed voice, "All right, Jennifer. I realize you've had a long day, but we'll go out again soon, okay?" I didn't want to plead with her, but I knew I would if it were necessary.

"Sure . . . we'll do it again real soon."

I relaxed. Everything was okay. She'd see me again. That was all that was important. I didn't want to force the issue. Give it time. All I needed was time to convince her that I truly still cared about her. Nothing to fear. I was sure that her aloofness was simply insecurity. I needed to show her that I really did love her, but I had to go slowly. Jennifer was acting like a frightened fawn, and I wasn't going to rush her into a relationship when she needed to build confidence in herself and in me. I must be patient. Patience was the key to our success.

Because Jennifer worked days and my job monopolized night hours, we could see each other only two days a week. My whole life seemed centered around sharing her company on those days. Every hour was spent looking forward to the moments I would be with her again. Weeks passed with the same pattern. I worked every night, called Jennifer as frequently as I could, slept most of the days away, and counted the minutes we were apart.

We saw *Jaws*, *The Great Waldo Pepper*, and *One Flew Over the Cuckoo's Nest*. We went to Wolf Trap to hear Olivia Newton-John. At Shady Grove, we saw The Supremes and The Temptations. At the Kennedy Theatre, we saw *Long Day's Journey into Night*. On the other evenings we spent together, we went to bars—sometimes to dance—but often just to listen to the music. It seemed that Jennifer always suggested places which were very crowded and often noisy; therefore, we didn't have much of a chance to be alone and talk. I tried to ignore what her reasons might be and focused mainly on the fact that at least we were together.

My biggest problem at the moment was that I was rapidly running out of money. I spent so much on Jenny that I didn't have enough to pay my bills. I went crazy in stores buying little gifts that caught my eye and picking up tiny things that were priced higher than I anticipated, but I couldn't resist them. I purchased a charm bracelet, a stuffed panda bear, and a porcelain figurine; in addition, I never went to see her without taking a handful of flowers. She rarely commented on anything I handed her, but I was certain that each present was bringing her closer to me. It was just that Jennifer was so introverted; if truth be told, she seemed even more withdrawn now than she did when we first met.

In September, when it was time to pay October's bills, I realized I did not have enough money to pay C&P Telephone much less the rent or the car payment. I was frantic to find a solution to my problem. After eliminating Lori, my father, and the banks as potential resources, I called Pamela. It wasn't as if she hadn't offered. She was the one who had suggested a loan if I ever needed one. I dialed her number and waited for the connection to go through.

"Hello."

"Pamela? It's Kurt."

"Hi, Kurt. Oh, by the way, Ellie loved the little musical doll you sent last month. That was really nice of you." She sounded cheerful. It was refreshing to hear a friendly voice. "She sleeps with it every night, and the tune it plays is delightful."

"How is she?"

Pamela told me of her daughter's latest feats. I listened trying to decide the most opportune moment to interject and ask for a loan. After Pam had spent several minutes accounting for Ellie's actions, she changed the subject on her own. "Is there anything I can do for you, Kurt?"

"Well, now that you mention it, Pam, I could use a little help. It's a bit more difficult down here than I imagined. The bills keep piling up, and the rent is due next week. I don't have enough cash to cover everything." I felt only slightly guilty about asking her for money. I repeatedly told myself that Pam Woods had more money than any fifty people put together.

Without even hesitating, Pamela asked, "How much do you need, Kurt?" Her voice was very trusting. There was no trace of contempt.

"I guess maybe . . . three hundred would cover it."

"I'll send you a check in the mail."

"I swear to you, Pamela, I'll pay every cent back by the end of the year. I promise. I wouldn't have asked if it weren't important."

"You don't need to apologize, Kurt."

Her voice was very comforting. I received my first twinge of conscience, but it only lasted a moment.

"And, Kurt, there's no need to pay me back in a hurry. In fact, consider it a gift. Really. I'm more than happy to help you out."

"Thank you, Pamela. You're a godsend. I really appreciate it."

"Anytime. All you need to do is call."

Feeling a mixture of relief and guilt, I hung up the phone. I was being a real cad, but I was too glad to be over the critical hump to dwell on the fact that I had purposely taken advantage of Pam.

When the check came the following day, it was made out in the amount of $400 instead of $300. I knew Pamela hadn't misunderstood my words. I was thrilled that she was so generous. I should have taken the extra $100 and paid off the loan on my car, but instead I bought Jennifer a gold chain necklace that had caught my eye in a jewelry store. It was beautiful. I knew Jennifer would love it.

With the rest of the extra $100, I decided to take Jenny to a quiet restaurant for dinner where we could talk without being interrupted. I wanted a place where she had to face me and express her feelings. I was flying high with the expectations of being able to spend a peaceful evening alone with her. It was all going to work out. Without telling Jennifer where I was taking her, I drove to a Japanese restaurant in Arlington. I had reservations for two in a secluded room. Everything was planned perfectly.

The waitress prepared our dinner right in front of us on a grill that also served as a table. When she was done, the waitress disappeared, which left the two of us completely alone. I was nervous and excited at the prospect of spending uninterrupted time with Jennifer. I planned to give her the necklace. It was wrapped in gold foil paper and topped with a matching bow. The timing had to be perfect; after all, timing was everything! I decided to declare myself after dinner. I wanted a commitment, and I was optimistic.

After eating our meal, we both leaned back on our cushions and sipped the remainder of the wine. Jennifer seemed relaxed and content. Even though we had not discussed anything serious, our conversation was steady. There were none of those silent spots that I dreaded.

The moment had arrived. I reached into my breast pocket for the tiny box. Without saying a word, I handed it to her. As usual, Jennifer made no comment when I presented her with the gift. She neither smiled nor spoke as she stripped the paper off, bundled it into a ball, and took off the lid. Jennifer picked up the chain. Silently, she ran the string of gold links around her fingers—draping it over and under each finger until the entire length was coiled around her hand. Instead of looking pleased, as I had expected, she appeared somber. I watched her as her eyes filled with tears.

"I can't accept this, Kurt."

"I want you to have it. I bought it for you."

"No . . . I can't take it."

"Please, Jennifer."

"It's too expensive. I simply can't allow you to spend that kind of money." Jennifer dropped it in the box and passed it over the table between us.

I wasn't going to take it back. Somehow, I knew that if I touched the gift she wanted to return, it would symbolize a backward motion in our relationship. I worked too hard getting us to this point. I didn't want to lose the little ground I had gained. "No, Jennifer. I won't take it back. It's yours. I want you to have it."

"Kurt . . ." She looked as if she were going to cry. "It isn't going to work."

I didn't want to hear what she was going to say. I wasn't going to allow her to speak. I interrupted. "I love you, Jennifer. I've always loved you." My voice sounded pathetic even to my own ears. "I'll do anything.

I know it'll take time. I'm willing to wait. Jennifer, please . . . just give us a little time."

Jennifer laughed in a forlorn way as she set the small box down in front of me. "Time! There's that damned word again. Time . . . the answer for everything . . . the cure-all. I'm sick to death of that word." She paused for a moment.

I was too stunned to speak. Jennifer glanced around our private room. She closed her eyes tightly as she bit down on her lips. I reached across the table to touch her; but when I laid my hand upon hers, she withdrew.

"Kurt, I'm afraid that time isn't going to be a healing factor here. No amount of time is going to help us." Her voice became more sympathetic as she stared directly into my eyes for the first time the entire evening. "I don't know how else to say it. Oh, Kurt . . . I know you don't want to hear this . . . but I simply don't love you."

"No! No! That's not true." I was suffocating. I felt as if I were pleading for my life. "You loved me once. I can make you love me again. Jennifer, you've got to let me. You've got to try." I reached for her hand again, but she pulled away. She looked rigid—hands clenched at her chest, mouth opened slightly—there was a misting over her eyes. "You're my whole life, Jennifer. I've lost everything else. There isn't anything in the world I want but you."

"Don't! Don't, Kurt." She held up a hand bringing my comments to a stop. "It's no use." She lowered the fingers she was using to silence me and clasped them with her other hand. She was trembling. "I wanted to love you. I really wanted to be in love with you, Kurt. An eternity ago, there was a chance for you and me, but I know now that it wasn't real . . . not even then. I tried to love you. I wanted to love you." She shook her head in pity. There were tears welling in her eyes.

Why was she pulling away from me? What could I say to convince her that she and I belonged together? "Jennifer . . . "

"It isn't going to work. I can't love you, Kurt. Can't you understand that? I don't want to hurt you anymore."

"I can't let you go, Jennifer. I can't lose you." I gripped her hand in mine making it impossible for her to stand up and leave.

As her eyes developed a cold rigidity, her voice became unemotional. "I shouldn't have led you on this way. It didn't take me long to realize that you still care for me, and I shouldn't have taken advantage of that. At first, I thought that we might get a second chance. I really hoped that it could be different. But I can't hold onto that anymore, Kurt, and neither can you. It's over, and you have to accept it." Her eyes softened slightly as she added her final words. "I wish I could spare you all this pain. I never meant to hurt you, but I can't go on lying to myself or to you. And I can't go on giving you false hope for a future that will never be." She stood up, pulled her hand from my grasp, and walked out of the room.

Before I was able to speak another word, Jennifer was gone. I looked down and saw the box she left behind. Cradling it in the palms of my hands, I added enough pressure to crush the cardboard into a ball. The necklace fell out. I picked up the chain and stared at it for a long time before breaking it into a dozen pieces and throwing them against the wall.

I drove home and drank myself into a stupor. My last thought before falling into bed was, I'll kill myself. I'll run a knife through my heart. I'll jump off a building. I'll buy a gun and blow my brains out. No! I couldn't do that. I didn't have the courage to die. Did I have the courage to live?

5

Brad

PHOTOGRAPHY HAD ALWAYS BEEN MY DREAM, BUT AFTER WHAT SEEMED like an endless chain of "don't call us, we'll call you," eating like a pauper, and living in a one-room flat furnished with only a bed, a chair, and table, I decided that I simply didn't have the necessary talent. I had to face the facts: taking pictures would always be nothing more than a hobby for me. I hated my father for being right. But what I hated even more than his accuracy was the fact that I knew I would eventually have to return to the family business. Where else could I go?

It was well over two years since graduation when I found myself knocking on my father's door, and asking for my old job back. Much to my surprise, he didn't rub it in. He didn't mention my failure or his opinion; instead, he welcomed me with a smile and open arms.

"The job's been waiting for your return," he said in an amiable manner.

I couldn't stand my father's confident attitude about my defeat when I had firmly told him for years that I would never work for him. Never! I hated him for acting as if he had known all along that I would eventually come home—practically on my knees—and yield to his will. I hated my father, but I hated myself even more. I was weak and lazy. I gave up on a lifetime dream. But I was tired of doing dishes, eating poorly, and scrimping for everything that I had once taken for granted. In the beginning, New York had been filled with excitement and hope. Unfortunately, now I saw those things that I had previously chosen to ignore: poverty and failure. I didn't want to become one of those people who spent decades searching for something they would never find. I copped out for easy living. I guess I wasn't the first person to do it; furthermore, I probably wouldn't be the last.

"The commercial arts' loss is my gain." My father smiled and wrapped an arm around my shoulder.

It made me sick——the way he was acting—so affable—almost nice!

In a way, if I was really honest with myself, I had to admit that it was good to be home. Not necessarily home with my father, but home: a decent roof over my head, three square meals, and the bar to look forward to every day. I couldn't believe I was admitting this—even to myself—but I missed the restaurant and especially the bar. I missed that sense of authority and that wonderfully rewarding feeling I had every night after a successful day's work; I missed the constant hectic activity and the feeling of self-importance. The truth of the matter was, part of me was glad to be back, even if it did mean giving in to my father and his wishes.

Another benefit of being back in New Jersey again was that it gave me the opportunity to see Jill more often. Her friendship and her bed were blessings. I still wasn't in love with Jill, but I did care about her, which was more than I could say about anyone else.

After living with my father in his house for a couple of weeks, I decided to move in with Jill. Thinking that it was probably the closest she would ever get to marriage, she was thrilled with the idea. We made terrific roommates. Jill was a marvelous cook, an average housekeeper, a good conversationalist, and dynamite in bed. I really couldn't ask for a better partner.

Leaving my father's home helped restore my self-esteem. I couldn't stand freeloading off of him. The fact that Rick was still home saving every penny before his marriage to Valerie in October didn't make it any easier for me to live under the same roof. I would turn twenty-five shortly before Christmas, and I certainly could take care of myself without any of my father's rules and regulations. Living with him was more than I could stand and moving in with Jill was the best decision I made since I'd graduated.

After a month with my father, I started rehashing those old theories I had contemplated when I was a freshman at Elon. I daydreamed about changing the banquet room into a dance floor. Discotheques were the latest craze in New York. Gloria Gaynor was nicknamed the "Queen of Disco," and she was hot! Music was shifting to a brand-new beat with a lot of drums and strong bass. The songs were double in length giving dancers ample time to feel the rhythm. I knew it wouldn't be long before the trend migrated to smaller cities and suburbia. I was certain that it was a money-making proposition, and I wanted to be a front-runner, not a follower, when the local population discovered it.

I laid out plans for a sound system, special lighting effects, and elaborate furnishings. I sketched a place for a new bar, the dance floor, the DJ's box, and seating for nearly two hundred people. I toyed with the layout and even went as far as pricing in round estimate figures for some of the more expensive things. When I discovered that the cost was well up into the tens of thousands, I stuffed my work into a drawer and abandoned the idea, thinking that my father would never buy it.

One night, while Dad and I were working the same shift and the restaurant was having a slow evening, I approached my father with a few of my thoughts. Much to my amazement, he was interested.

"So, Brad, you think if we knocked out that wall into the banquet room, close off that wall over there, and laid out a dance floor, we'd bring in a new type of crowd that would spend money on drinks instead of just food."

"Well . . . you know, Dad, you've always said the big money is in the booze, and there isn't as much profit in food." I could hardly contain my excitement. My father was actually talking to me as an equal, instead of a do nothing, no account, waste of a son.

He slapped me gently on the back. "I don't believe it, Brad. You actually *were* listening to me around the dinner table."

I started filling him in on my thoughts of converting to a discotheque. I told him about how a glimmering ball, twirling slowly as it hung from the ceiling, could reflect sparkling prisms over the entire room. I continued by describing an elaborate area where a DJ could spin his web, mixing music and personalities. Then I concluded with, "Well, right now, Dad, the music is basically black soul. The market hasn't been tapped yet, but I read in the paper that Hollywood is making this movie with John Travolta. The whole plot is centered on dancing. I know it's going to bust this concept wide open. If we hurry we can be the first place in town; therefore, we'd have a monopoly on it. We could make a fortune."

"It's a lot of money, Brad. We're doing very well the way it is now. Why do you want to shake things up?"

"That's what I thought you'd say," I shrugged, annoyed with myself for even broaching the subject with my father.

"You remind me of the way I was at your age. Your eyes even light up when you talk about it. Your mother always said that my eyes lit up like an electrical storm every time I got excited about a new idea. I was a little younger than you are now when I started putting this place together. I was so energized; I could barely contain myself. I was possessed by it until I finally convinced the banks that I was a good gamble." Lost in his own memories, my father looked around the room. He was smiling. "It's not much different than it was in the beginning." He paused. "Maybe it's time for a change." My father gave me a friendly hug. "I like your ideas, son. I think perhaps it's time I take a gamble on you. Get an architect in here. Call your friend, Bill. Doesn't he have his own construction company? Ask him for a bid. Compare it to a couple of others. Let's see if we can swing this brainstorm of yours."

I couldn't believe it. This could not be my father! This man was actually acting like a human being. And worse yet—I was even enjoying him. I waved to the bartender and signaled for a couple drinks. When they were delivered my father and I toasted the occasion.

"Brad, about your brother, Rick—he's good in this business. He works his heart out, and I appreciate it. I can see what an effort he is making, but he doesn't have your innate ability or your insight. None of it comes as naturally to him as it does to you. You're a lot like me, Brad. Even if you've never wanted to admit it—you are. And the business is in your blood." He patted me gently on the shoulder. "I'm glad you're back. While you and Rick were growing up, I always dreamed that someday we'd be here together." He paused. "Your mother says that you are a chip off the old block. I've never been sure whether or not she's complimenting either one of us."

I cringed slightly at the mention of my mother. I despised discussing her with him. It rubbed a raw nerve.

"Have you seen her?" he asked.

"Yeah. I had dinner with Mom last weekend."

"How is she?"

"She looks good," I replied, trying to think of a way to change the subject.

"Your mother's a mighty fine-looking woman. You know something, Brad, she's even prettier now than she was in high school. Caroline was in my English class; she could really light up a room—positively radiant, even as a teenager. I couldn't take my eyes off her."

"Let's cut the crap, Dad." I was livid that my father dared speak of my mother in such an intimate way. Without giving him a chance to add to his statements, I strolled off and left him standing by the bar.

That night, in spite of my irritation, I stayed up well past three o'clock arranging and rearranging the first plans I had drawn for the reconstruction. The next day I was off, and I took full use of it. First thing in the morning, I dropped by the job site where Bill was working and picked his brain for ideas and costs. He promised a rough bid by the end of the week. I could barely contain myself. I spent the entire day and every free hour during the following two weeks on my project. Then I presented it to my father.

He liked it.

As the autumn days slipped by, my father's favorite restaurant was closed for remodeling. I sold him my idea: lock, stock, and barrel. He agreed with all of it. I took pride in overseeing Bill's work. In less than six weeks, I knew we'd be in business again. I was praying that my judgments were good ones.

Because the restaurant was not in operation, the entire family was able to attend Rick and Valerie's wedding. Even Rosaline came from Pennsylvania with her husband. My little sister was all grown up and married. She had met Tony, her husband, during the first semester of her freshman year in college. Tony was a senior, majoring in English. Academics were never Rosaline's strong suit, so when Tony asked her to marry him, Rosaline dropped out of school. They were married the week after Tony's graduation. Needless to say, my mother was incensed, but there was no turning Rosaline around. When my sister made up her mind, she was steadfast and committed. She was also very happy.

It took Rick and Val a long time to finally set their wedding date, but when they did, Rick was nothing short of a basket case waiting for the event. The bride and groom were planning to live in New Jersey, but the ceremony was held in Winston-Salem, North Carolina, where Valerie's family lived. Rick was so excited at the prospect of sharing his life with Valerie.

I was truly happy for Rick and Rosaline. At least my siblings had found a niche in life that could give them contentment and joy. Even though I was somewhere in limbo and couldn't seem to locate what I really was looking for, I was pleased with their successes.

Rick and Valerie's wedding day was an exciting mixture of friends, food, music, and booze. Rick, Jill, and I started the day off with an all-you-can-eat champagne brunch. My problem with all you can eat places is that I hate to leave without getting full benefit from the cost. The ceremony was not until two o'clock, which gave us ample time to get our money's worth. It was just what Rick needed to calm his frazzled nerves.

When the time came to don our tuxedos, we hurried through the process and raced to the waiting room where we listened for the music that would summon us to the altar. I panicked for only one moment when I thought I'd forgotten the ring, but Rick reminded me that it was safely tucked inside my coat pocket. It seemed that, now, Rick was more relaxed than I was.

"You're as nervous as a cat in heat," Rick said with a charming grin covering his face.

"You sure are a cool one now, big brother! You were singing a different tune a little while ago," I joked as I poured the last of the black coffee from the thermos Jill had gotten for us. We both needed to sober up for the occasion.

"Why should I be nervous?" he replied in a more serious manner. "This is what I really want, Brad. I've waited a long time to marry Valerie, and now that it's finally here, I'm going to relax and enjoy it."

"You really love her?"

"I can't tell you how much, Brad. I can't explain it. It's as if I live and breathe for her. Valerie . . ." he paused for a moment and pondered on exactly the right words. "Valerie is everything. She's my whole world, and I'm the luckiest man alive." He slapped me twice gently on the face as he added, "Some day, baby brother, you'll understand what I'm saying. I know you probably think I'm nuts talking like this, but, trust me, someday you'll know. There's a woman out there who'll make living a whole new ball game for you. She'll open your eyes to things that you never saw before, and you'll wonder how you ever existed without her." Rick laughed confidently.

When had Rick gained such self-confidence? My brother had always seemed reserved and shy—even timid at times—but those traits seemed to have vanished, leaving him self-assured.

"I'm getting a little mushy here. I apologize, Brad. I guess I'm just so happy that I can't understand why every one in the world isn't riding on the same cloud I am."

"I'm happy for you, Rick. I really am." My statement was genuine. Over

Tesa Jones ❧ 441

the course of the last few years, our relationship—no, our friendship—had developed into a strong bond. I truly liked my brother. I found it hard to believe that there had actually been a day when the two of us barely spoke to one another. Times had changed. Perhaps we had both done a little growing up; as a result, we could appreciate being friends as well as siblings. It seemed as if the tables were turned on us. For so many years, I was the one who had what Rick considered confidence, self-esteem, and a knack for having a good time; but now my brother had all those things, and I was on the sidelines. I no longer felt so self-assured. I'd learned that life wasn't one big party, and I was having a hard time adjusting to that fact. Rick had something that I wasn't able to find; he had roots. He had substance to his life. Each day held meaning for him; whereas for me, with the exception of the restaurant, life still continued to be nothing more than a by-product with little challenge and less significance to it.

The bells started ringing in the chapel and musical notes from the organ began to filter back in our direction. We stood up. I reached my hand out to Rick. "Good luck."

"I don't need it, Brad. I have everything else on my side. Luck is no longer a factor." We exchanged grins. He really was happy. I opened the door. The two of us walked across the courtyard and entered the church where we took slow, tranquil steps up to the altar. The pews were packed with smiling faces. Everyone loves a wedding. I watched Rick as he waited to see his bride. He tried to appear composed, but he was unable to keep the exhilaration off of his face. He radiated vivacity. This was his moment as much as Val's, and he was just as eager as she.

As each of the bridesmaids measured her steps down the aisle, I glanced out into the congregation. I saw Valerie's mother muffing her sniffles. I saw my mother with soft tears in her eyes, biting her lower lip, and trying to control her fast approaching desire to cry. My father sat next to her in the family seat of honor. He reached for my mother's hand. She returned the gesture. I watched as they looked into each other's eyes with an expression I'd never seen before on either of their faces. He smiled. So did she. The tension between them seemed to vanish. Suddenly, they looked years younger. It was quite puzzling.

I glanced slightly to my right and saw countless, unfamiliar faces: a few smiling, several looking serene, some pensive. In the chain of nameless faces, my eyes became fixed on one person I recognized immediately. I froze; every ounce of me was immobile. I could feel my face growing white as each muscle in my body tensed. My heart began drumbeats so strong I was certain they were drowning out the wedding march.

Laura! Laura Davis was sitting in a pew alongside a string of unknown faces. As hard as I concentrated, I couldn't pull my eyes away. She was not looking at me. Instead, she was watching the procession of identically gowned ladies walking rhythmically down the aisle.

Laura looked beautiful. More than anything in the world, I wanted to reach out and touch her slightly flushed cheeks and brush a few strands of hair away from her face. I wanted to feel her skin with the tips of my fingers. I had almost forgotten the impact she had on me. Two years had dulled the pain. I thought I had long since banished her memories into the far recesses of my mind. She hadn't even invaded my dreams in the last several months. I had thought the victory won, but the moment I saw her, I realized that all my efforts to rid myself of her were futile. I loved her as much today as I had all the years before.

The entire congregation stood up as the bride entered. I never saw Valerie walking toward us, because I couldn't command my eyes to break away from Laura's petite form. Laura! She no longer looked like the innocent teenager she had been that first day I focused on her through my camera; instead, she'd grown into a beautiful woman. Her face had changed ever so slightly, giving it a mature and worldly look. I wasn't sure if it was makeup or the structure of her bones that gave me the impression, but her face no longer held that naive appearance I had always attributed to Laura. The natural girlish beauty was replaced with the glow of perfected features, which only served to enhance the delicate grace that surrounded her. Did everyone see Laura that way, or was I the only person who saw her as

Tesa Jones ❧ 443

some kind of untouchable, perfect goddess?

The guests seated themselves as Valerie joined hands with Rick. I ordered my body to turn slightly and participate in the activities around me. I would not allow myself to be caught up in thoughts of Laura and embarrass myself by staring at her when I was supposed to be listening attentively to the minister's words. Even though I acted as if I were involved in the sentences that were said, I actually didn't hear a syllable. My mind kept wandering into the past: a soft-spoken voice, shining blue eyes, a warm smile, arms clinging to me—returning a fevered embrace. I could feel her breast in my hand—swollen, taut nipple. I could smell her scent. I could taste her skin. Fragments of memories kept flashing uncontrollably in front of my eyes. Laura! Lips as sweet as honey, words that purred from her mouth, hands that touched with gentleness, laughter that sounded more like a melody than music itself, a face that radiated sunshine.

"The ring please."

"What?" I snapped back to reality as I fumbled for the gold trinket that I was holding for Rick. I almost dropped it before I managed to place it into my brother's hand.

He smiled at me and whispered in a jovial tone for my ears alone, "A fine best man you've turned out to be. Where has your mind gone, anyway?"

I sheepishly returned his grin. Concentrating solely on the activities at the altar, I controlled my thoughts long enough to get through the remainder of the vows. After the bride and groom exchanged a kiss, the minister announced, "I now present to you, Mr. and Mrs. Richard Malone Jr." The organ cued in on the exact moment. The wedding party began parading down the aisle. I paused only one moment as I saw Laura glancing at me for the first time. Nothing registered on her face. It was as if her expression were plastic: no recognition, no smile, no pleasant nod—nothing but a stone cold stare. I turned away and followed my brother and his new wife.

The hell with her!

The reception was a fun-filled dancing occasion where every guest delighted in fancy food and an open bar. Valerie's parents really knew how to throw a gala. The banquet hall was completely fringed with tables piled with food; there were gaps only where the gifts were placed, a band section, and a small stand where guests were supposed to sign their names. I did my job of mingling with people, introducing myself, and drawing out those guests who seemed introverted while we all waited for the receiving line to finish stopping up traffic.

I hadn't seen Laura since the ceremony, and with the aid of several bourbon and Cokes, I was beginning to feel relaxed again. It was a great party.

Rosaline and I enjoyed a few private moments during which time she let me in on her secret. My sister was pregnant. The baby was due in June. I was thrilled for her. Few people knew about her past—about her other baby; I was one of the few, and I would never tell. Rosaline loved Pennsylvania— she adored her husband and loved her new life. It seemed that time can heal old wounds.

As other guests joined us, we made polite conversation. I was having a grand time until I caught sight of Jennifer Carson. Jennifer Carson? What the hell was she doing here? Oh, shit! That's right! She was one of Val's sorority sisters. Damn it! One thing was for sure—if Jennifer Carson were in this room, then Laura would be somewhere close behind her. If I lived to be a hundred, I wouldn't care if I ever saw that Carson bitch again, and as for Laura . . . I certainly wasn't in the mood to be shrugged off as if I were a piece of lint. I wouldn't give either one of them the satisfaction.

The afternoon continued slipping away as I poured drink after drink down my throat, and danced with every woman within reach. My mother and I shared the first. Jill consented to dance two or three in a row, and then I lined up each of Valerie's bridesmaids twirling them around the floor. I was not going to allow myself one free moment to ponder the fact that Laura Davis was in the vicinity. I was in a terrific mood. She wasn't going to spoil it!

Not until I heard the band play the slow melody "If" by Bread, did I unconsciously scan the room for Laura. I caught sight of her halfway across the floor. She was standing perfectly still and staring at me. Her first impulse was to look away, but not before I saw the pink blush that covered her cheeks. Seconds later, she turned back around, and our eyes connected. She was my prisoner. Or was I hers? Neither one of us moved; finally, I started slowly toward her. I feared she would dart in another direction, but even when I reached her side, she made no attempt to flee. Without exchanging a word, I led her onto the dance floor and surrounded her with my arms. I couldn't believe that Laura was actually pressed against me. I could feel the palms of her hands resting on my back. It was almost as if her fingers were burning holes through my rented jacket. I closed my eyes and simply enjoyed the feel and smell of her. I laid my cheek upon her hair and savored the delicious aroma as my nose brushed lightly over the strands. Much to my amazement, despite the amount of bourbon I'd swallowed, my feet moved to the beat of the music, and Laura gracefully followed. It felt so good to hold her.

The music stopped. People were clearing the dance floor, but we continued to sway slowly to a melody no one else could hear. I didn't want to let her go. I didn't want to be forced into a conversation that would only break the spell; and mostly, I didn't want her to disappear into the crowd without ever once getting a chance to hear her voice. Without knowing how it happened, I was standing away from her, and Laura's face was tilted up toward mine. I wanted the music to resume, giving me an excuse to envelop her in my arms again, but when I turned to look, I noticed that the men in the band were taking a break. The entire dance floor was vacated. Laura and I stood alone. She was only inches from me. I couldn't find the words I wanted to say. I looked longingly into her eyes for some sign, but I was not rewarded.

"Can I get you a drink?" Was that really my voice?

"All right."

I gently placed my hand around her forearm and guided her over to the bar. We stood in silence as I waited to place our order. When it was my turn, I asked Laura what she would like, and she answered, "Gin and tonic, please . . . with a twist." I was surprised to hear even the most common of cocktails muttered on her lips. I'd always thought of Laura as drinking wine coolers.

When we had our drinks, I steered her toward a quiet corner and hoped that we could be alone for a few moments without interruption. "It's nice to see you again, Laura." There was so much I wanted to tell her, questions I had to ask, but none of the words formed.

"You're looking well, Brad." She seemed a bit on edge as she glanced everywhere but at me. Laura sipped at her cocktail and added, "What are you up to now? Still in New York?"

"Afraid not," I replied. At least our conversation had a topic. It was a foundation on which to build. I could stem off this subject once I felt more comfortable. "I gave it an All-American try, but I was spinning my wheels."

"You are good, Brad. Your pictures show a lot of talent."

"Yeah, I suppose I do have some talent, but do you know how many thousands of people out there have *some* talent."

"I'm sorry it didn't work out for you."

"If there's one thing I did learn in the years I was in New York, it's that my cameras can only be a hobby for me. I wanted to make a living out of it. It had always been a dream. It was a real blow to my ego when I discovered that I just plain wasn't good enough."

"I'm sorry."

"Yeah, so am I," I answered amiably as if it were no big deal.

After a pause that seemed infinite, Laura spoke again. "So what are you doing?" Her words were stiff and mechanical.

"I'm with my dad."

"You always said you'd never work for him."

"Well, sometimes you have to trade in your dreams and settle for an alternative." I was beginning to feel more comfortable with Laura. It had always been so easy to talk with her. I sipped at my drink before continuing, "I have this new idea for my dad's places." I told her about each aspect, and how excited I was. She seemed genuinely interested in what I was saying. "I couldn't believe my father actually took me seriously. He never listened to me when I was growing up. Now all of a sudden, he's following my lead.

It's hard to believe that he's the same man. He's changed so much."

"Maybe he hasn't changed. Maybe it's you who has changed, Brad."

"Oh, come on, Laura, give me a break. I told him how he could make more money, and I was convincing enough for him to trust me. Now we have a truce, but I'm not fool enough to think that anything's really changed between us."

"Do you honestly believe your father's that heartless?"

"You don't know him like I know him."

"Your father can't possibly be as bad as you think. When I met him, I thought he was very charming. He seemed considerate and kind. I rather liked him. And furthermore, he seemed a great deal more interested in you than you ever gave him credit for."

"Laura . . . " I was getting angry. Not only did she bring up an extremely sensitive subject, but she also interjected along with it a reminder of that weekend years ago when she came to visit my brother at our home. As if it were yesterday, I could see her standing in our family room with Rick's arm draped around her. She was smiling as if it were giving her some kind of personal satisfaction. "Damn!" There was a strained control in my voice. "Can we please change the subject?"

Laura stepped back a foot or two. She appeared stunned, as if I had slapped her. Her face flushed—eyes wide, almost glassy. She didn't speak. Laura started to walk away, but I gently reached for her arm and kept her from leaving.

"I'm sorry," I whispered. "I didn't mean to snap at you. You ought to know me well enough by now to realize that I'm not very polite when it comes to the subject of my old man. Let's talk about something else . . . anything . . . just not my father, okay?"

Her back was to me; I couldn't see her face. Softly, I ran my hand up and down her forearm. I wished there was no material between us. I wanted to touch her warm flesh. I took a small step behind her, bent down slightly, and breathed in her sweet scent. I nuzzled my nose in a few strands of her hair and savored the aroma. "You smell so good, Laura." My words were low, deep. They were barely audible. "Don't go." She turned around. As I leaned against the wall, I began to relax. Thank God, she wasn't going to leave. I cleared my throat and made an attempt at a new conversation. "So what have you been up to?"

"I work in Washington. It's a desk job for a law firm. They're pretty big. They have clients all over the country . . . a few on other continents." She veiled her eyes and lowered her voice. "I got a raise last week. Five hundred dollars."

"Congratulations . . . that's great!"

"Oh really? I don't know about that," Laura sounded depressed.

I wondered why an increase in salary created such an anxious expression on Laura's face. She was fidgeting with her fingernails and staring off in another direction as if I weren't even involved in the conversation. What was she thinking about? How could I reach her and keep her from drifting in and out of my life? "It sounds like an interesting job, but don't you miss teaching?" We were talking. At least *I* was talking, but we weren't saying the words I wanted to speak and hear.

"Yeah . . . yeah. It's interesting . . . and yes. I miss teaching."

"Have you thought about trying to get back into the field?"

"I just heard from a county in Georgia. They want to hire me."

"That's great, Laura. It's wonderful." Why didn't she look happy? Why did I feel like I was carrying on a discussion with a robot? She was barely responding to anything I had to say. She constantly left me dangling and uninformed.

"I turned it down."

"Why? It's what you've always wanted. I can still remember how excited you always got when you talked about kids and a classroom of your own."

"I didn't take it because . . . because Jennifer is afraid of moving."

"Jennifer? Jennifer Carson? What the hell difference would *she* make?" I tried very hard not to let the aggravation show in my voice, but Laura instantly noticed it. For a split second, I saw tiny bolts of angry lightning flash in her eyes, and then she pressed her lips together tightly and suppressed the sudden emotion. "If you really wanted to teach, Laura, then why let Jennifer Carson stop you?"

"Jennifer has this great job on the Hill. She's making buckets of money, and she loves it. I've never seen her so self-assured. She doesn't want to start over."

"So . . . why should that have anything to do with your choice?"

"It's hard to explain. Her parents are dead. She's divorced. She was dating my brother for a while after he came back from Germany, but that's over. I haven't a clue what happened between them. If I so much as broach the subject with Kurt, he bites my head off. And Jennifer isn't talking either." Laura sighed softly. "I think I'm her only friend. Jennifer has no one else."

"So? Does that mean you should change your life to accommodate her?"

"Jennifer is my friend, Brad. Friend! Do you know what that means? She needs me. I won't hurt her by deserting her now."

"I see she still has you riding a guilt trip."

"What's that supposed to mean?"

"For as long as I can remember, Jennifer Carson has led you around by the nose . . . and you've been too trusting to see it."

"Brad, please don't talk about Jennifer like that. Her friendship means everything to me. My life is so weird right now. I feel very disconnected from my family. My parents got a divorce. For God's sake, I never saw it coming. My mother doesn't even live in Virginia anymore. I never see her. We talk on the phone about once a month, but it's not the same. As for Dad, well, he's in another zone with his new wife. It is so bizarre to visit him. And Kurt, he's somewhere out in left field picking daisies. I don't know what's going on with him. I think he's doing drugs. I don't know how to reach him. We used to be so close and now he won't even talk to me." Even though Laura spoke the words in a regulated manner, there was a definite aura of despondency in her voice. "My sorority sisters are spread out all over the country. This is the first time I've seen some of them since graduation. We've had a great time today, but I know next week they will be back into their lives, and I will be involved in my own. It's sad how friendships seem to evaporate once you leave the college campus." Laura paused as she sipped casually on her drink. "I haven't made any friends at my office. It's almost like I don't fit in with their little cliques. Sometimes, I feel so lonely. My friendship with Jennifer is the only stable thing in my life right now. I need her! I need her as much as she needs me." Defiantly, Laura raised her eyes to meet mine. Her words turned caustic and combative as she continued, "But you wouldn't understand that, would you, Brad? You don't know anything about friendship or loyalty. You don't value other people . . . or their emotions. You don't even know what a real relationship is all about."

"That's not true!" My head was pounding. "And damn it, Laura, how can you be such a fool? Jennifer Carson is using you. She's always used you. She's a leach, and she's draining you of everything. Jesus Christ! Can't you live your own life? Can't you make a move without confiding in her and letting her make up your mind for you?" Laura made a motion to leave. I took hold of her arm and gripped it firmly with my hand. "For example, take this job in Georgia. Don't you realize it's a big break for you? You could get a couple of years experience and then transfer anywhere you want to go. With a little experience under your belt, you can go back to Virginia. Why are you letting Jennifer steal that from you?" Somewhere during my speech I started raising my voice; by the time I was through, I was practically yelling.

"Not another word . . . not one more word against her, Brad."

Laura was angry. So was I. This was all wrong. I had not intended to argue with her. The entire conversation had gotten out of hand. She was staring at me with volatile eyes. The muscle above her cheek was twitching involuntarily. Neither of us spoke for a moment as we tried to air our heated tempers. Damnation! There had never been a woman alive who could agitate me as Laura Davis did. I could be riding on clouds one moment, and flying into a fit of rage the next . . . and all without a second's warning. Shit! What did I ever do to deserve this kind of treatment?

"Hey, listen, Laura . . . I don't want to fight with you." I kept my voice calm. "Can we go someplace . . . away from all this chaos . . . someplace where we can talk?" I was sure that if only I could be alone with her . . . tell her how important she was to me . . . how much I loved her and wanted her to be a part of my life. If I bared my soul, maybe she would give me a chance. Perhaps I could convince her that my love was strong enough for both of us. In time, with a little luck, she might even learn to love me in return. I twisted a strand of her hair around my finger and smiled as pleasantly as I could. I used my other hand to trace the firm line of her jaw. "What do you say . . . let's split . . . go some place private."

"Don't you dare!" Laura spoke through clenched teeth. Her nostrils flared; the color of her eyes took on a deeper hue, and her voice sounded threatening and hostile. "Don't you dare pull that tactic! It worked once. I was just stupid enough to fall for it, but not again."

What the hell was she talking about? I watched her as she turned to walk away, then she pivoted and faced me again.

"You think you're so clever, don't you, Brad? Well, there are plenty of men here in this room who are far more interesting than you are. In fact, there are plenty of men *everywhere* who have more to offer than you do. I can think of at least a dozen . . . "

"I suppose you spread your legs for them too," I interrupted her. Why had I said that? All these feelings were boiling out of me, and I couldn't contain them. All I could see was Laura with another man . . . in another man's arms . . . making love to another man. Damn it! I was certain I'd go completely crazy if I couldn't block the images from my mind.

Laura faced me again. Her expression distorted her features. "Maybe I do . . . so what business is it of yours?"

She was rubbing it in! She was purposely baiting me, and it only served to increase my wrath. "You love it, don't you? I bet you dangle that body of yours in front of guys and hold them at bay until you're damned good and ready to ease your own cold cunt." What had possessed me to say those horrible things? I was so angry with her for teasing me with imaginary pictures of other men. I wanted to jerk her, shake her, and force her into caring about me! All I wanted was Laura's love; instead, she used my emotions to torture me. How could she be so cruel? I wanted to lash out at her. Hurt her. Make her suffer. "I always thought you were such an innocent, Laura . . . " My voice was low and deliberate. "But you're not! Are you? You're calculating and cold . . . You used that angelic face of yours to cover up the fact that you're nothing but a common slut." I saw her hand reaching out to strike me. Before it met its mark against the side of my face, I grabbed it and gripped her wrist so tightly I could actually see the pain registered on her expression. Our eyes darted spears back and forth, but neither of us looked away. "How many men did you sleep with before me, Laura? After all, you forget . . . I know for a fact that you were no virgin."

There was a spasmodic twitching around Laura's left eye. She took in a short, shallow breath and seemed to hold it for a long time before her lungs expelled the used oxygen. I could feel her body quaking with silent tremors as I held her wrists firmly and refused to let her go.

"No! I wasn't a virgin." Her speech was husky. "In fact, I wasn't a virgin the day you met me, but you waited over four years to find out." She spoke with a mordant tone. As a sneering smirk spread across her lips, she continued, "And you thought you were being so clever!" She jerked her wrist from my hold. Without saying so much as a good-bye, Laura spun around and walked away.

Before I could gain any kind of control over my fuming emotions, Jennifer materialized out of nowhere and confronted me. I stared at her and defied her to speak. The last person I wanted to see under the circumstances was Jennifer Carson.

"Hello, Brad," she said in a sarcastic manner. "I see you've been up to your usual charm, wit, and personality."

"Get lost!"

"Not a chance!" Jennifer spat out the words, as she stood in front of me; she did not give me the opportunity of a graceful exit. "So you think I'm a leach?" She chuckled more to herself than to me. "I'm the most important person in Lori's life right now. I stand by her when she needs me. I'm there when it counts. And you . . . " Jennifer jabbed me roughly with her finger. " . . .

with your Hollywood good looks and your macho attitude . . . you don't have a snowball's chance in hell with someone like Lori. She's too good for the likes of you." There was as much bitterness in Jennifer's words as there was contempt in her expression. "When are you going to realize that you're a zero in Lori's book? She isn't going to waste the time of day on you."

"Get fucked, Jennifer." I gritted my teeth. "You're nothing but a used-up tramp, and I don't need to listen to you about Laura."

"She doesn't need you, Brad. She doesn't even want you. It's probably hard for that overinflated ego of yours to believe that there is actually a woman in the world who doesn't give a damn about you, but it's true."

I started to make my way through the crowd. I had to patch things up between Laura and me. I had to apologize. I had to make her understand. Before I'd taken two steps, Jennifer yanked at the sleeve of my jacket and whirled me around to face her.

"You better start looking somewhere else for your one night stand, Brad, because Lori already has plans."

I freed myself from her hold and went in search for Laura. She had disappeared. I scanned the room three times before deciding that she'd left. I saw Jill sitting alone at a table. I walked over to her, flopped myself down on a chair next to her, and without a word, began draining the glass of champagne that was in front of me. Every nerve in my body was standing on edge. I blew it! Laura was in my arms, and I blew my chance.

"So . . . that's the mysterious Laura Davis." Jill's voice interrupted my thoughts. She sounded neither unkind nor avenging . . . just stating a fact. Her words started becoming a little more malicious as she continued. "You're still in love with her. Aren't you, Brad?" When she received no response, Jill continued, "You don't have to confirm it. I can tell by the way you held her while you were dancing, and I saw the way you looked at her."

I kept drinking from every half-empty glass on the table without caring what was in it. I'd had a lot to drink already: a lot of booze, a lot of champagne. And I was going to keep on drinking. I could hear Jill's voice. It sounded small and far away, but I could still hear her.

"You don't care about me, Brad. You never really cared about me. I've always been just some kind of replacement because you can't have what you really want. Brad . . . " She latched onto my hand. "Brad, listen to me. I love you . . . I love you more than she ever will. I'm the one who loves you . . . not her . . . I'd do anything for you. She's not worth it, Brad. She doesn't deserve you."

"Shut up, Jill. Just shut up!" I grabbed her roughly and started pushing her toward the door. By the time we reached the outside foyer, I was holding her hand and racing through the parking lot in the direction of my car. I didn't say a word as I practically threw her into the automobile. Barely allowing her enough time to get her legs in the car, I slammed the door. I got behind the wheel and drove as fast as I could back to our motel. Without speaking a word, I got out of the car. Jill followed. When we entered the room, I pulled her forcibly into my arms. Harshly, I kissed her as I fumbled with the belt of her dress. "I need you, Jill." As we struggled to disrobe, she sensed my urgency. We were ripping at each other's clothes, frantically removing them with little thought to the destructive sounds we were creating as the material tore and the buttons flew off. I bit at her neck and sucked in the smooth skin. She, in turn, copied my actions. Together we moved as one toward the bed. When our legs hit the frame, we fell uncontrollably onto the mattress. As if in a frenzy, we both licked and kissed those intimate, well-known areas on each other's bodies that created the most gratifying rewards. The moment before penetration, I made eye contact and spoke with a determined voice. "Don't leave me, Jill. Say you'll never leave me!"

Jill stared up at me with loving eyes. "Of course not."

I grabbed her tightly to reassure myself of her presence. "Swear it! Swear you'll never leave me." I was trembling.

"I love you, Brad. Don't you know that? I could never leave you."

I eased my grip. "I need you, Jill . . . I really need you." As I penetrated her haven, I kissed her again—this time with less force but the same amount of urgency. Mechanically, I made thrusting movements upon her body that began to veil my emotions. It felt good—wonderful. I wanted to bury myself in the utopia it created. Oh, thank you, Jill . . . thank you for being here . . . thank you for loving me.

As the movements became methodical and the rhythm began to mount, uncontrollable flashbacks started washing over me of times spent with Laura. It was always this way when I made love. It was always *her* face I saw . . . *her* body I touched, *her* lips I tasted . . . memories of *her* that invaded my mind. Oh God! When would it stop? When would I be free of her?

I tried to block the images and concentrate solely on Jill, but the pictures in my mind were too strong. I was holding Laura in my arms on the dance floor. We weren't saying angry words. Instead, we were holding each other with a gentle embrace. It wasn't Rick's wedding . . . it was mine. Mine and Laura's. She looked beautiful . . . smiling . . . loving me with her eyes. I pressed my face against her hair and pulled her closer. "Oh, Laura . . . you smell so sweet."

There was a sudden gasp that hung in the air. All action stopped. The fever-hot body that had been moving under me was now still. My mind blurred and then focused once again on the situation. Oh, my God! I had not only thought the words—I had said them! And it was not Laura I was holding; it was Jill.

I couldn't bear to look at Jill. I knew I'd hurt her, and I didn't want to see the pain. I felt, rather than saw, the tears streaming down her face. Gently, I cuddled her in my arms and held her as tightly as I could. "I'm sorry. I'm so sorry."

Jill pushed me away. Without a word, she rolled to her side—blocking me emotionally and physically from her sight.

3

Even though it had been two weeks since the wedding, Jill would not confront the incident. In spite of the fact that I was trying desperately to be tender, there was a strained silence between us. We still shared the same bed, and although our communication was at an all-time low, I did make a real effort to be gentle and tender, as I tried physically to apologize even if I couldn't verbally convince her. Unfortunately, she wasn't interested in my behavior or my sexual advances. Each night, without a word, she'd turn off the light and roll to her side of the bed. It was almost as if Jill wanted to sweep the memory under the rug.

The remodeling of the disco was coming along fine; in another week or two, we would be open for business. I was impressed with Bill's work. He suggested a few changes, which enhanced my original plans: a mirror here, an extra light there. It was all falling into place. I put my energies into one goal and refused to allow any other thoughts to invade my mind. I had a gut feeling that my project was going to work. It had to. I simply *had* to succeed at something.

Rick and Valerie were back from their honeymoon, and the new bridegroom was working standard hours again. It was nice to have my brother plugging along right beside me. I was thankful that he wasn't jealous of my ideas. Instead, Rick encouraged every new notion I discussed; nine times out of ten, he agreed with my plans. We made a good pair.

On Friday, after working well past midnight with Billy's overtime crew, I sipped some wine with Jill and read the evening paper. It had been a hell of a week with long hours and a lot of pressures as the last-minute details were finalized. It felt good to relax for a few minutes. I became absorbed in the sports page and only looked up from the print when Jill interrupted me by commenting on the events in her day. Periodically, she asked me a question, and I simply gave a yes or no response before delving back into the column. As I finished one article and started another, I noticed Jill perched quietly at my feet. Her fingers gently stroked the inside of my leg. She pulled the robe I had donned earlier to the side and began to lick seductively at the skin of my thigh. I felt myself growing hard with desire. I lowered the paper to watch her actions. Jill had a marvelous way of detouring me from my tasks at hand. I closed my eyes and let her work the magic she knew so well. When I couldn't stand her teasing lips any longer, I slipped to the floor and pulled her alongside of me. Her robe came off easily. I pressed myself against the full length of her nakedness. As I cupped her face in my hands,

I returned her kiss. Lifting her chin in order for her eyes to meet mine, I spoke. "I'm sorry, Jill. I am really sorry for what happened at the wedding. I can be such a jerk sometimes. I hope you can forgive me."

She was about to respond when the phone rang.

"Shit! Who the hell calls at this time of night?" I muttered as I regretfully stood up and answered the phone in the kitchen. "Yeah," I said as I grabbed the receiver from its cradle.

"Brad? This is Rick."

"Do you know what time it is? I thought honeymooners had special activities to do in the middle of the night." Rick didn't respond to my jovial comment, and I began to realize that my brother wouldn't be calling at this late hour if there weren't some kind of a problem. Something had happened to the restaurant. No! That wasn't it. He probably just had his first fight with his bride, and he needed a friend. Yeah, that was it. "Everything okay, Rick?"

He paused a long time before answering. "Brad . . . Mother died tonight."

"What?" It couldn't be true! There had to be a mistake.

"Mother had some kind of a stroke, or it could have been a heart attack. I don't know all the details yet. She died about an hour ago."

"How do you know, Rick?" I remained calm despite the inner turmoil racing through my body. This wasn't real! This was surely just a bad dream.

"John called. He asked me if I would tell you and Rosaline. He's calling Dad." Rick's words sounded choppy—almost apathetic—but I was certain he was acting out of shock.

"Are you sure, Rick? Are you sure Mother's really dead?"

"Why the hell would I call if I weren't sure?" It was the first time he raised his voice.

"Oh, my God! I can't believe it." The truth started sinking in. "Jesus Christ, Rick . . . she wasn't even fifty."

"I know. It doesn't seem fair . . . it just doesn't seem fair at all." His voice began to crack. "I got to go, Brad. I still have to call Rosaline." Neither of us said good-bye.

Before I returned the receiver to its resting place, I glanced around and saw Jill standing in the doorway. There was a concerned expression on her face. She tenderly encircled me with her body. I fell into her arms and took what comfort I could from her embrace.

4

The funeral was like a repetitive, stabbing pain. The church was crowded. My mother had a lot of friends. As I sat with my family in the front pew, I concentrated totally on the flower arrangement at the altar. I didn't focus on anything else. Unfortunately, the minister's words fell upon deaf ears. They gave me no solace. The organ played, but I didn't hear any of the notes. Afterward, I felt the handshakes and the sympathetic hugs. People spoke to me, but I took no comfort from their touch or their comments. I moved like a robot; in fact, I felt like a robot. Flashes of memories crossed my mind. I remembered the trip with Cindy to West Virginia all those years ago, and I finally understood her grief.

Oh, my God! I grabbed onto Jill's hand and squeezed it tightly. I was so afraid I was going to cry. To cause a distraction, I bit down as hard as I could on the inside of my cheek. I could taste blood. Surprisingly, the pain helped ebb the tears.

After the interment, I walked through the rooms of my father's house as if someone else were taking the steps. Every place I looked, I saw a memory, and I felt crushed. It had been years since my mother lived in this home—well over a decade since we were a family—but I could still see her around every corner. I pushed open the library door. Once I entered the room, I noticed that someone else already had the idea. It wasn't until after I closed the door behind me that I realized the other individual was my father. He was hunched in a chair—sobbing into his hands. Without warning, an odd sensation washed over me. I felt like a little boy: awkward, apprehensive, self-conscious. My stomach wrenched into a knot; my pulse raced; sweat began to form on my brow. At first, I didn't move, but then I turned slowly to exit the room.

Tesa Jones ❧ 459

My father heard my movements and lifted his head in time to call me back. "Brad," he muttered softly as he wiped his eyes and regained a close facsimile to his normal composure.

I froze. Realizing that he was the last person I wanted to see or talk with under the circumstances, anger and resentment became my dominant emotions. I arched an eyebrow and stubbornly remained silent.

"Please, son, sit down . . . share a brandy with me?"

I watched him pour the liquid into two snifters. He handed a crystal goblet to me and then proceeded to take a sip from his own. There were still remnants of tears in his eyes.

"What the hell are you so broken up about, Dad?" I was more than callous. I was vindictive and indignant and waiting for him to give me an excuse to lash out at him. I was absolutely certain that if my mother had been able to lead the life of leisure that my father had denied her, she would still be alive today. It was my father's fault! Now, I had someone to blame! Silently, I took a seat opposite him and leaned against the leather-backed chair. I watched him as he swirled the brandy around in his glass. As he contemplated his next statements, my father looked old—defeated.

"Why do you hate me so much, Brad?" He paused to take a deep breath. "If I'm guilty of anything in this world, I'm guilty of loving one son more than the rest of my children. I have loved you more than either Rick or Rosaline, and the only emotion you seem to be able to return is contempt for me."

"You destroyed my mother!" Oh, God! I said it. I actually said the words. I felt as if a gate were opened, and the words came pouring out. "You ruined her. You! You with your drive and thirst for money. You ruined her. My mother wouldn't be dead today if it weren't for you."

"What are you saying, Son? I loved your mother. I loved her more than anything in this world—even more than I love you. There could never be another woman for me. I did everything in my power to make her love me. I would have given every cent—every penny—I ever made if she would have just loved me in return."

"Stop it, Dad!" I stood up. I was screaming. "That's nothing but fucking bullshit. I know what you did to her! I know about illegitimate babies and shotgun weddings. I know how you forced her into bed and then demanded that she marry you when you discovered she was pregnant. You did it because her family had money, and you wanted it!" I pointed my finger at him and glared into his face. "She didn't want you. But you thought you could get a free ride if you married into her family. You destroyed my mother. You killed her!"

"I don't know how you found out about that . . . and it doesn't matter now." My father sounded calm, but his hands were shaking as he clasped the stem of his glass. "I have loved your mother since the first day I saw her. We were in the same English class in high school. I barely passed the course because I couldn't concentrate on anything but her. She was gorgeous." He seemed lost in thought. "She sat at the desk in front of me. Sometimes, she wore her hair in a ponytail. I wanted to undo the ribbon and let it all go free around her shoulders. But God! I wouldn't think to touch her. It was only a daydream—a fantasy." He made eye contact with me. "I admit that I did my share of running around when I was a kid. I always had a fling going with one girl or another, but all of them were meaningless. I never cared about any of them. But Caroline was different." He swallowed another sip of brandy. "She was so popular . . . so smart and beautiful. She was captain of the cheerleaders. Everybody adored her. Her family was wealthy. They lived on the hill—the one that overlooked the whole town. It was perched there like a castle." He paused to take another sip of brandy. "Her father owned the mill. He was an intimidating son of a bitch. My father worked for him. He was the janitor—when he was sober enough to show up for work. Hell! Everyone in the town worked for Caroline's father in one way or another." He stared directly at me. "Yeah! He was rich. But the money was never important to me. Even though my family could barely keep me in unpatched pants, I never wanted her money. I just wanted her. I followed her around like some poor, dumb turkey. I couldn't eat . . . I couldn't sleep. It made no difference that I already knew she was dating someone else—the quarterback of the football team; he was also captain of the baseball team. *His* father had a white-collar desk job working for Caroline's old man. That made him respectable . . . and acceptable! I, on the other hand, was from the other side of the tracks. Forbidden fruit! And, of course, let us not forget, she was going to college. She had already gotten her acceptance letter. Needless to say, I wasn't on that academic path. I didn't have the money or the grades." He glanced around the room in silence for several seconds. "But none of that mattered. I couldn't help myself. I was crazy about her. Unfortunately, she never even looked at me. Hell! I don't think she knew my name. Then one night, during a high school sock hop, she got angry with her boyfriend and left him standing on the dance floor. I saw her walk out the gymnasium door. I followed her and watched her for a while. I don't know how I got the courage, but I walked right up to her and started talking.

"She'd been drinking. I could smell it. It didn't take long to figure out that she was a little tipsy. Caroline kept leaning up against me, and I thought I was going to faint from the pleasure of her. We talked for fifteen minutes or so, and then she suggested that I take her for a ride. I couldn't believe it. It was like a dream come true." He smiled slightly before continuing, "I almost fell out of the car when she asked me to pull off the road and park a while. What a bumbling idiot I was! I stuttered; I stammered. I acted like such a loser. Hell! It wasn't like I hadn't been with girls before. I'd had my share and then some. I was probably the most sexually experienced guy in that entire school, but not that night. That night, I couldn't even string three words together that made sense. I was totally outclassed, and I knew it. " He closed his eyes. Silence filled the room. After taking several deep breaths, he continued, "But when Caroline kissed me, everything changed. The longer she kissed me, the more confident I became. It was like magic between us; there was this incredible chemistry. I was totally overcome by the way she opened her arms to me. She took her blouse off and encouraged me to touch her. Her beauty and her soft skin bewitched me. She was perfect."

It was almost as if my father didn't know there was anyone else in the room. He seemed so entranced by his memory that he didn't realize he was actually speaking his thoughts.

"Finally, I began to make advances toward her. She didn't stop me. She told me that she had been watching me for years. She actually said she had a crush on me. My head was swimming. Of course, now I realize it was the liquor that made her act that way." He paused to take a sip of his brandy. My father focused on me, suddenly remembering that I was in the room. Calmly, he proceeded, "We made love that night. I did not force her, as you seem to think, Brad. I never forced your mother—never." He stopped, stared directly into my eyes, and took several deep breaths before continuing. "Your mother had never made love to any other man before me . . . and I thought it was a sign. I was sure that she had to care for me or she would never have given up her virginity. I was in heaven." He set the glass down on the desktop. After putting his elbows on his knees, he laid his chin on his cupped hands and rubbed his thumb over his jawline. He closed his eyes. "I was devastated when I saw her talking with that other guy the next day. She totally ignored me. She treated me like I was a nuisance. God, it hurt." Gingerly, he stood up, drained his glass, reached for the decanter, and poured more into the goblet.

"When Caroline discovered she was pregnant, I immediately offered to marry her. I never even hesitated. I saw it as a message from God. Fate!" He swirled the brandy around in his goblet. "That creep she was dating didn't want anything to do with her. He ditched her even before she found out about the baby. He was such a jerk. And her father . . . what a jewel he turned out to be. Her dad disowned her. He didn't want a scandal. After all, he had his precious reputation at stake. He kicked her out—bag and baggage. She had nowhere to go.

"At first, she wanted nothing to do with me. But then when reality checked in, and she realized she had no one else . . . Caroline was more willing to listen to my plan." My father was quiet for nearly a minute before he continued, "She wanted to get rid of it. I'd worked since I was eleven, and I had the money in my savings account. I thought about giving it to her. But I couldn't. I knew if she got rid of the baby, I'd lose her, so I pleaded and begged until she finally gave in to me. She really had no other choice.

"Your mother and I left that one-horse town before Rick was born. We never looked back." He stared adamantly into my eyes. "While on the road, we stopped in Dover, Pennsylvania, and got married at a justice of the peace. Caroline didn't smile once during the ceremony. She looked like she was being tortured. I, on the other hand, was thrilled. I was positive I could make everything work out. We moved around to a couple of places before landing here. Both of us got jobs at this run-down take-out pizza joint. The owner was a nice guy, but he was a terrible businessman. He had no idea how to manage the place. A couple months after he hired us, he went bankrupt. Needless to say, Caroline and I lost our jobs. I had a pregnant wife who barely spoke to me, a one-room dump for a home, and no money coming in. I didn't think life could get any worse." My father glanced at me. A smile began to spread across his face, and his expression softened. His eyes actually sparkled. "That's when your mother showed me the shoebox she had hidden in the corner of our closest. It was filled with trinkets and cash. Some were gifts she had accumulated over the years. There was also a lot of jewelry, which had belonged to her mother before she died. And there were a few things she took from her father's house when she left. None of it was worth that much alone; but together, it was a pretty impressive stash. She offered to pawn it all. Her idea was to buy the pizza place. It was selling for a song. Much to my total surprise, we pulled it off. We worked side by side for the next several months. Caroline was amazing. Every idea she had worked like a charm. We were turning a profit within two months. There was a back room, which we converted into a bedroom. That saved a lot of money." He paused as he reflected upon his thoughts. "Those were trying, difficult times for us . . . lots of long hours . . . hard work . . . fear of failure. Most nights, after barely having spoken a personal word to each other throughout the entire day, we went to bed exhausted. But I was happy." My father took a long, laborious breath of air before continuing. "Unfortunately, I knew she wasn't. She detested being poor. She used to laugh at me because she always thought, along with her father, that I was only after the money. She called it irony—poetic justice. She said, more than once, that we deserved each other. Her contempt for me enhanced my drive. I *had* to succeed. I had something to prove . . . to her . . . to myself.

"When Rick was born, I was so proud. I thought if I worked hard enough . . . if I made enough money, Caroline would realize that I loved her . . . that I loved our family . . . that I never wanted her father's fortune. And maybe she would be able to love me. So, I did work hard. Miraculously, the pizza place thrived. We used it as collateral for the first restaurant and before I knew it, we had a flourishing business. Everything was running smoothly. Two years after you were born I sold the pizza place and bought this house. I hoped she would be proud of it . . . of me." He closed his eyes as he rubbed his fingertips against his forehead. "She hated it. I let her have all the money she wanted to decorate, but she didn't care. I bought her a car . . . she hated that too.

"A year later, I bought her a boat. That sailboat was the only thing I ever bought Caroline that she truly seemed to enjoy. She loved it. The best memories I have are on that boat. The Saturday afternoons we sailed on the river . . . sometimes alone . . . sometimes with you and Rick in the galley. It was so peaceful. During that period in our lives, there was a lot of laughter— for both of us. More times than not, Caroline had a smile on her face; she had a beautiful smile." My father became lost in thought. "If I could relive any time in my life, it would be those few years. I thought she was happy. I thought . . . maybe, maybe she had started loving me. When she got pregnant with Rosaline, she seemed thrilled. She actually glowed. We were a family . . . I thought the bad times were behind us.

"Then, a couple of years later, things went kind of rocky with the restaurants. I think, in retrospect, I tried to make the business too big, too rapidly. I had a lot of expenses. I had overextended myself, and there were so many bills—a lot of payments on luxuries I couldn't afford. As a result, I had to work twice as hard to make ends meet. I wasn't home much. She was running the house, taking care of the three of you, and I was struggling to keep the restaurants going. There didn't seem to be any time for us. I came home so late; often, she was already asleep. We developed a pattern of this kind of schedule. Weeks turned into months and months turned into years.

"Then, she started accusing me. She thought there was someone else. I swear to God, Brad, there was never anyone else. There could *never* be anyone else." He pressed his index fingers against his temples and massaged the side of his face for nearly a minute before continuing. "One day when I came home from work, I discovered that she'd taken all her things and moved into the spare bedroom. I didn't see it coming. I had been so happy with our lives that I never noticed her discontentment. I was frustrated and even angry. If it hadn't been for the fact that you and Rick were old enough to witness my rage, I would have broken the door down; instead, I let it slide and hoped it would pass with time," he sighed. "It didn't.

"When Caroline started having her affairs, I pretended I didn't notice. I looked the other way, and I didn't listen to the gossip; I never confronted her. I thought that if I ignored it, maybe it would stop. Can't you understand, Brad? Can't you understand one single word? I would have done anything to make her love me . . . anything! But Caroline never gave a damn about me. She didn't have any feelings for me except contempt." He started pacing the floor, staggering with every step. "And then when she wanted the divorce, I held the only trump card. She really loved the three of you. She wanted you with her. I was obstinate—totally unyielding. I felt that if I did not let her get custody of you, and if I didn't give her a penny to live on . . . then eventually, she'd come back to me. But she didn't! She never came back. She never gave me a chance. I would have given anything—anything for the opportunity to make her happy, but I couldn't even bribe her with the one thing in the world she truly loved: her children. It didn't take me long to realize that my money was no longer important to her. But I was so sure that she would come back for Rick, Rosaline, and you; unfortunately, she never did." He looked at me with a pleading expression on his face.

"When I finally admitted to myself that I lost her, I started lavishing all my love on you, Brad. You were the one person who reminded me of

Caroline. You actually look like her, and I started thinking that if I couldn't have my wife, I at least could have an imitation of her—but you didn't love me either. You hate me as much as Caroline ever did. I guess I pushed too hard. I've made such a hell of a mess out of my life."

"Caroline always accused me of spoiling you. She said that even though you look like her, you act like me. On more than one occasion she accused me of shaping you into an image of myself and in a way, you are, Brad." He paused. "For as long as I can remember, I gave you more time, more attention, more love than the other two children received. I tried to balance it out by giving Rick and Rosaline tangible possessions to make up for it, but I think they both have always known that I love you more, despite my attempts to be fair and equal." He stared directly at me. "I couldn't help myself, Brad. When I lost your mother, you became everything to me"

I did not respond. What could I say? An agonizing silence filled the room.

"Oh, God . . . " my father whispered. "I wish . . . I wish I had told her . . . just once. I wish I had told her that I loved her."

"You never told Mom that you loved her?" I couldn't believe it.

"Of course not. What would have been the point? I knew she didn't love me." His voice quivered. "Can't you understand, Brad? Isn't there any compassion in you? I would have given my soul for your mother's love . . . my life to spare hers. For so many years, I've held on to the hope that we might get back together—that eventually she'd love me . . . and now I have nothing." A tear formed in the corner of his eye. It glistened in the dim light. "Maybe, if I had told her . . . maybe if I had said the words . . . maybe then it wouldn't weigh so heavily on my chest."

A brief picture of Laura crossed my mind. Laura! I, too, would give anything for her returned affections. Anything! I knew what it was like to love so deeply, and for it to be futile. How ironic. I was more like my father than even he realized. I took a step toward him. I understood his anguish. I finally knew why he was such a driven man. I had compassion for the pain he was carrying inside of him. I laid a hand upon his shoulder and tried to console his grief. Before I knew what happened, my father was clinging to me, sobbing without speaking a word. I sheltered him with my arms, giving him what little comfort I could from my embrace. The library walls echoed our sorrowful moans as we began to draw strength from each other.

"I understand, Dad. I really do understand."

6

Laura

I WORKED FOR ROBBINS, MACMILLAN AND ROBBINS FOR NEARLY A year before I realized that the attention Larry Jenkins gave me was more than just that of an employer to an employee. At first, there were several implied comments, many suggestive, but seemingly accidental, brushes against my body, and numerous looks that gave me the impression he wanted more from me than my office skills. But I chose to ignore his subtle advances and concentrate on my job. As I acquired more and more responsibilities, I increased my duties to include dictation and typing skills. I even took a night course so I could operate the new office computer. Rumor had it that before long, these new bulky machines would make the IBM Selectric obsolete. This particular skill put me ahead of more than 90 percent of the other women in the clerical division of the office.

In spite of the fact that I was acquiring all of these new skills, I was disappointed I was still sitting at the front desk. I even asked several people, including Larry Jenkins, what the procedure was for advancement within the company. Their responses were always rather ambiguous.

It wasn't until an office party at the end of the summer of my second year that Larry Jenkins became more direct in his intentions toward me. On that particular occasion, he cornered me in a secluded office, trapped me against the wall with both arms, and forced me into kissing him. I was more than stunned by his actions; I was revolted. But my fears combated my good judgment; I simply stood there and waited for him to finish his physical advances.

When his mouth lifted off of mine, he said in a husky voice, "Given any thought to my ideas about how a girl can get promoted around here?" He smiled. "You do realize that there is more than one way to skin a cat."

I could still remember his smile. I wanted to slap the smirk from his face, but I simply stood motionless. The fact that he towered over me was intimidating. As I tried to think of something to say, I swallowed hard; in lieu of words, I used the back of my wrist to wipe his saliva from my lips in hopes he would realize my gesture was a sign of disgust. I didn't give him the satisfaction of answering his question; instead, I slipped out from under the barrier his arms created and left the room. Even now, I could still hear his sickening laughter vibrating inside my ears. I couldn't believe it. His wife was in the other room sipping cocktails with the wife of a senior partner as they discussed the colleges their children were attending. Did Larry Jenkins have no honor, no decency?

The following week I received an unexpected, $500-a-year increase in my salary. At first, I was delighted. I thought it was a reward for doing my job well. What a disillusioned fool I was! The next afternoon, I discovered that Larry Jenkins had instigated the financial increase. He passed my desk, grinning, "It was worth five hundred bucks." Instead of continuing on his way, he bent over and whispered, "There's a whole lot more where that came from, Lori. Keep it in mind." He winked. When he departed, I was left fuming in my own anger.

That was the beginning of a deluge of attention from Larry Jenkins. I thought about quitting. I even looked around for another job, but there did not seem to be anything available that wasn't a decrease in salary, so I decided that I could handle Mr. Jenkins. Everyone else in the firm seemed more than pleasant. All I had to do was stay out of Larry's way. Surely, if there were witnesses around, I had nothing to fear.

In the weeks that followed, I watched as a girl, with fewer skills than I had, replaced a secretary who had quit in order to have a family. Also in the same week, a girl from the typing pool moved to secretarial aid, and the girl didn't know the first thing about law much less shorthand or dictation. I would have liked a chance at either of those jobs. When I inquired, I was ignored. I kept trying to convince myself that there was a perfectly good reason why those girls were given the jobs instead of me, but I kept seeing how young and pretty they were, and how certain men seemed to be around their desks more often than not. Frequently, I also noticed that certain girls took an extra-long lunch hour when they went out with their bosses.

In the two years I'd been with the company, I studied the intricate jargon of the business, I was skilled on all the equipment, and I learned more by watching and listening than I was required to know. I was determined to be the best. I wanted a more challenging job, and I wanted to get it on my own merit. I was optimistic that eventually someone would notice I was overqualified for the menial job I was originally hired to do.

2

I awoke from a deep sleep. There was a muffled noise. Where was it coming from? I heard it again. Someone was crying. The sound was coming from Jennifer's room. After donning my robe, I knocked on her door. When I entered the room I saw her sitting in bed, cradling her pillow. It was damp from her tears. Her face was blotchy, and her eyes were red-rimmed and swollen from crying.

"Are you okay, Jen?" I asked.

She blew her nose several times and remained stubbornly silent.

I walked into the kitchen, grabbed a carton of milk, two glasses, and a bag of Oreo cookies; then I returned to her room. The two of us sat on her bed, drank all the milk, and ate every cookie before she broke the silence.

When Jennifer spoke, fresh tears streamed down her face. "Kurt's such a nice person. He was always so good to me. I don't know why he loves me. I don't deserve it." Jennifer stuttered and choked on each syllable. "I wanted to be in love with him. Lori, you must believe me. I don't understand anything anymore—nothing makes any sense."

Jennifer was an extremely private person when it came to her emotions. This was the first time she and I discussed her relationship with my brother—or any other man for that matter—since Kurt's return. I knew she was dating a lot of different guys. No—actually, dating wasn't an accurate description of the relationship she had with these guys. She met them in bars, often stayed out all night, but rarely invited any to our apartment. Even though she didn't talk about it, I knew she was sleeping with most of them.

Although I knew Jennifer hurt my brother, I gave her a lot of credit for not using Kurt in the way I was certain she was using all those other men. It was odd. Most of the stories I heard about casual sex always seemed as if the men used the women, but for some strange reason I thought it was reversed in Jennifer's case. It was almost as if she had no respect for the men she knew. She rarely talked about them; in fact, she didn't seem to be emotionally involved with any of them. There were even times when I doubted she knew their names. I worried about Jennifer. There seemed to be an emotional pain inside of her that kept growing like a tumor. I could see the hurt in her eyes, but she never talked about it; tonight was no exception. No matter how many times I coaxed her into divulging her feelings, she always replied, "It's not important." Once she even muttered, "Besides, I doubt you'd understand."

It hurt me that Jennifer felt she couldn't confide in me. She seemed to be pulling away. I didn't want to push, so I sat back and waited for the time when she'd be ready to talk.

I was very concerned for my roommate, but I was equally worried about Kurt. My brother was so messed up. There didn't seem to be any purpose in his life. He was strung out on more than just marijuana and booze. On several occasions, I found him flying off amphetamines or dragging from barbiturates. He didn't look like the same person I had known all my life. I had a feeling that it would be a long time before he would come to terms with himself and face the fact that he could have a perfectly good life without Jennifer. Kurt never came to visit me. The only times I saw him were when I made the attempt to seek him out at his job or in his apartment. He always pushed me away; often, he said he didn't need or want my consoling words or optimistic attitude. I persisted in visiting him. Unfortunately, neither my pep talks nor my hard-core, pragmatic speeches brought him down to earth. He kept using more and more of the drugs, which were only burying the problem instead of solving it.

I couldn't have been more concerned for my brother's mental health or for his life.

3

Jennifer and I had made a habit of unwinding several days a week in the bars on K Street. One Friday evening in late November, we went to a local pub for happy hour. The bars were basically all the same: smoked filled and so jammed with shoulder-to-shoulder activity a person could barely move. There were also loud voices, boisterous laughter, lively music, and secretly lonely individuals who were looking for a willing partner to share the evening.

Most days I enjoyed being involved in the activities and listening to the conversations, but tonight I was exhausted. It had been a long week, and I was perfectly content to sit alone on a barstool while Jennifer went off in a corner to seduce her next victim. I sipped my drink quietly as I pondered the idea of leaving early without Jennifer. I was sure she wouldn't mind. More times than not, she got a ride home instead of having to wait for the bus. I left a tip on the bar and turned to leave just as a man took two steps backward in order to let a waiter pass by; subsequently, he bumped into me. Immediately, he turned and apologized.

"Excuse me." As he turned around, his voice changed from simple politeness to curiosity. "Well . . . hello there." His eyes scanned my entire body.

There was once a time when I might have blushed under such a scrutinizing stare, but I had since become immune to the way a man's eyes stripped women. It was all part of the game.

"It could only be fate bumping into such a beautiful woman as you."

Lines. Guys were full of the same old bullshit. The words often changed, but the meaning was still the same. Men used compliments and soft-spoken words as if they were buying their next sweet treat. They thought women ate up their off-the-cuff comments and would fall obligingly into their beds. I smiled back into the stranger's face and played along with his game.

"Can I buy you a drink, miss . . ."

"Lori . . . Lori Davis."

"Lori . . . pretty name. It suits you. Do you know, Miss Davis, that you have the most beautiful eyes?"

Knowing full well that he had barely looked at my eyes, I brushed the comment aside. I started to turn away from him, but he began to speak again."The name's Gene Saunders." He extended his hand. I shook it politely. "It's a real pleasure to meet you."

In the dim light of the room, I could tell Gene Saunders was approximately forty. He was slightly gray at the temples. Only a few wrinkles—the kind that enhanced a man's good looks, but only served to hinder a woman's—surrounded his mouth and eyes. A tiny mole accented the crest of his cheekbone, and his pale green eyes twinkled when he smiled, which made him appear quite friendly. Gene Saunders was not handsome in the traditional sense of the word, but he was extremely sexy, and he radiated a type of virility that oozed of experience and pomposity. He wore an expensive three-piece gray suit that was tailored perfectly to fit his trim body. A pinstriped shirt and silk tie complemented his attire. I also noticed he was wearing cuff links. They were gold squares with a tiny star-shaped diamond in the center of each.

After my perusal, I returned a lukewarm smile and made another attempt to leave. I had decided I wasn't in the mood to fend off verbal or physical advances from Mr. Saunders or anyone else. Not tonight! Between an exhausting workload and Larry Jenkins's continuous propositions, it had been one hell of a day. "I was just leaving, Mr. Saunders."

"Don't go yet . . . you haven't even touched your drink. Besides, I want the opportunity to get to know you, and if you walk out that door, I may never see you again."

"I don't think that would be a grave loss to either one of us." I was being openly hostile and taking out my ill temper on a stranger.

"Come on, Lori. Stay." He stood in my way. "I promise to be on my best behavior. I really would like to get to know you. Come on, pretty lady . . . what do you say?"

I relaxed on my barstool knowing that he had won at least a few minutes of time. Hell! Why not? I didn't have anywhere else to go; if I left now, I would only spend a lonely evening in an empty apartment. That would serve to depress me even more. I decided to stay.

Gene and I discussed the two assassination attempts on President Ford last September; in addition, we talked about Sara Moore's and Lynette "Squeaky" Fromme's trial and impending sentencing. Gene hoped they both received life imprisonment. After that conversation, we switched to music. I brought up Bruce Springstein's *Born to Run* album; surprisingly, he admitted to having no knowledge of the new rock star. In fact, Gene confessed that he'd been too busy for Elvis in the fifties and too old for The Beatles in the sixties, but he was developing a love for rock 'n roll at this point in his life. After discussing The Rolling Stones for several minutes, the conversation melted into football. Gene said that although his favorite quarterback was Fran Tarkenton of the Vikings, he had already placed a bet that the Cowboys and the Steelers would be the teams to play in the upcoming 1976 Super Bowl in January. I commented that I only followed the Redskins. Gene replied that he had season tickets to RFK Stadium. He added, "I was a huge Sonny Jurgenson fan, but I'm not real impressed with Billy Kilmer as quarterback. He might be accurate, but in my opinion, his passes are a little too wobbly."

After forty-five minutes of polite conversation, Gene started interjecting comments on his own life story. I couldn't remember the number of men who had told me their personal history. Countless members of the opposite sex had packed my ears with anecdotes about wives who didn't care, success stories that never happened, projects they were working on, or the contract that didn't come through, previous sex lives, or the woman who got away. The faces changed, but they all sounded the same. Some were happier than others . . . some more prosperous than the next . . . others were pushing their way to the top . . . while some were just content with where they were. I always listened, but when the evening was over, the men had to settle for a pleasant good-bye or perhaps a simple kiss. Nothing more. I listened. I heard. I nodded. I even put in a comment now and then if the person asked for it. But I wasn't interested in sex of any kind as an extracurricular activity. There had been no more Steve Shaws in my life.

Gene Saunders told me about his ex-wife who had deserted him over fifteen years earlier to marry his best friend; consequently, Gene was left to raise their two children alone. He mentioned that his son and daughter were grown and only a few years younger than I was. "I don't even know why I married her in the first place. I suppose I must have loved her at the time, but I don't even remember anymore. When you're a kid, you really don't know the meaning of the word. We were married directly out of high school, had our first child a year later, and struggled just to make ends met. I got a degree in night school, which took eight years of hard work. While I was taking my classes, I was also working forty hours a week in order to put food on our table and keep a roof over our heads." He paused to order another drink. "I suppose it wasn't a very exciting life for her, but then again, it was no great shakes for me either. I was totally floored when I came home from work one day only to find a note pinned to the pillow; she'd left with Eric, my best friend. Some best friend he turned out to be. She also informed me that I could pick up the kids at the sitter. Her message was perfectly clear; she was never coming back. I haven't seen or heard from her in fifteen years . . . not even a Christmas card."

"That's awful. Do your children miss her?"

"The kids were devastated; after all, they were old enough to realize their mother had not just left me, she had deserted them too. Thankfully, I think even the kids have gotten over the pain now. Fifteen years can heal a lot of hurt."

"Do you have any idea where she is?"

"Not even the faintest notion. And I couldn't care less."

"What did you do when she left?" I found myself intrigued by his story. It was definitely more unique than the others I'd heard.

"I finished up the last of my classes, got my college diploma, and went into business for myself. I was a flop at thirty. Sometimes, I think I was more crushed by my own lack of success in that initial attempt at business than I was when my wife walked out on me. But I pulled myself together and got a good sales job at an office supplies store. Now, I'm the mid-Atlantic regional representative and living high on the hog. I make more money than any three young punks put together, and I've reverted back to adolescence. Since my kids are all grown up, I can finally take advantage of all the good times I missed when I should have been having fun instead of busting my ass to keep us all alive."

"That's so sad."

"I don't want your sympathy, young lady." He grinned as he took a sip of his drink without even once taking his eyes off me. "I'm very happy with my life right now. Most men my age are more financially strapped—like the position I was in when I was passing through my twenties—but that's all behind me. I'm the one having fun while they're all busting their fannies to keep their heads above water supporting teenagers and demanding wives. I never knew another woman before my ex-wife, and I didn't have the time for any sexual experiences when I was studying and working eighteen hours out of every day, but the last several years I've made up for it. And it's been heaven. I'm like a kid again. I can't get enough of women. I love them all. I take each one as a blessing in disguise." He gently ran two fingers over the side of my face. His words were tender as he traced the outline of my lip with his finger. "Every woman I meet is special; I treat a lady with the respect she deserves. I'm honest and direct. I don't believe in wasting time." He kept staring at me and even though I was becoming more nervous with each passing moment, I couldn't take my eyes from his. "I'm not going to lie to you, Lori Davis. I adore making love to beautiful women. I can't stand coyness or commitments of any kind. I don't like strings. I don't plan my tomorrows. I never intend to get married again or even fall in love with a woman; neither is a goal for the future. But I am terribly attracted to you. I won't lie about that." He stroked my cheek gently three times—each more softly than the last. "I want you, Lori."

The spell was broken. I immediately lowered my eyes as much for self-defense as from the tension that was mounting inside of me. "You're very blunt, aren't you, Mr. Saunders."

"Gene."

"Mr. Saunders."

"I told you, I don't like to waste time."

As I scanned the crowded room, I started to speak again. "I'm a wrong number as far as you're concerned, Mr. Saunders." I shifted slightly in my chair. "You're barking up the wrong tree. I'm not interested in any affairs, and if you don't want to waste your time, I suggest you find another girl." My head was lowered. "I'm no good at sex." Oh my God! What possessed me to say that? I stared only at the heels of my shoes as I tried to understand why I was confessing this to a stranger. "I've tried it before, and well, it's just not what it's cracked up to be as far as I'm concerned." I couldn't believe how candid I was on a subject that had always been taboo to me.

He tilted my chin up toward him. "Perhaps you've only known inexperienced little boys who don't know the art of pleasing a woman. What you need, Miss Lori Davis, is a man . . . not a kid who's still wet behind the ears. You have hidden treasures inside that gorgeous body of yours that even you don't know about; you only need the right key to unlock the doors."

I stood up. "I really think I ought to be going."

"No . . . not yet." He stuck his leg out in front of me to cut off my exit.

The room was packed. The roar of the music and voices was deafening; however, I felt completely alone with this stranger. I prayed that Jennifer would appear and help me escape. As I searched around the crowded room, she was nowhere in sight.

"I will see you again, Lori. We are going to cross paths . . . and I'm not letting you go until you give me your phone number. I want the right one. No made up numbers!" His words were hypnotic as each syllable rolled off his tongue in a gentle, provocative way.

He reached for a pen in his coat pocket and wrote down the digits on a paper napkin. Why was I giving this man access to my home? I'd never done that before. Dozens of men had asked for my phone number; it was a common practice every Friday night, but I had always brushed them aside with jokes or ambiguous responses. I had to face the fact that, like it or not, I was drawn to Gene Saunders. After I was finished, he removed his leg, and the exit was cleared for me to go. I picked up my purse and left without another word between us.

4

I was not surprised when Gene Saunders called me the following week and asked me to have dinner with him. I also was not surprised when I accepted. He took me out on three more occasions between Thanksgiving and Christmas before driving me back to his home and offering me a nightcap. I knew the moment he spoke the words that he was asking me to share more than just a relaxing, late-night drink in front of a fireplace. His motives were reflected in his eyes.

I did not turn him down.

Silently, he drove his car into the fir-lined driveway. Gene Saunders definitely lived well. Although the property was not large, his house was a huge two-story colonial with four big white pillars holding up the veranda. The subdivision was cluttered with gorgeous houses similar to Gene's. Even though they were all jammed together, I knew each had an expensive price tag, which labeled the owners as affluent.

As Gene built a fire in the fireplace, I roamed around his living room. Silently looking at the pictures on the wall, I tried to decide if I really should be here or not. Odd emotions kept doing flip-flops inside my mind. There was no doubt that Gene intended to have sex before the night was over. Did I want to share in that experience? Or did I want to go home? I had to admit—above everything else—I was intrigued. Quietly, I scanned the room. It was beautifully decorated. A built-in entertainment unit made of massive oak shelves took up one entire wall. In it was a television set, an eight-track tape deck, a turntable, dozens of albums, beautiful statues and figurines, and an assortment of the latest best-sellers. There was a couch with a matching love seat upholstered in a pattern of browns and beiges with a touch of harvest gold. The carpeting was the exact color of gold that was in the material of the furniture. The pile was so thick, I wanted to take my shoes off and run my toes through it. A gigantic spider plant hung from the ceiling in the corner. The coffee table and the end tables were chrome and glass. Everything was coordinated; even the ashtrays and table lighter were accent pieces.

I pulled out a cigarette and lit it as I watched Gene pour wine into crystal glasses.

"Did I tell you, Lori, you look very beautiful tonight?" He handed me a goblet and coaxed me into joining him by the fire. Gene placed an ashtray on the floor between us and lit a cigarette for himself. He was one of the few people I knew who actually looked sexy smoking on a filter. He inhaled, his cheeks sunk in slightly, eyebrow cocked, eyes stripping his subject, then he exhaled almost as if he had seduced the air that passed between his lips. "I want you, Lori . . . " He patted the rug between us and caressed it with his fingers as his voice purred each word. "I want you here . . . and tonight." He set both of our glasses down before drawing me into his arms and lowering me onto the carpet. "There will be no strings . . . no rules . . . no future and no past. There will only be a present for you and me." He cupped my cheek with his palm. "I am not going to fall in love with you. I don't want you to love me. You are free to do whatever you want when we are not together . . . and so am I. But when we are together, you will be the only woman on my mind, and I expect the same in return." The tone of his voice was mesmerizing and intoxicating. "I don't want you to misunderstand anything that I'm saying; I want honesty from the beginning."

He brushed his lips softly across my temples, my brow, and my lashes. I couldn't think. I only knew that I felt wonderful inside. Glorious. Hot! It had been an eternity since I had felt these sensations. My breathing quickened along with my heart rate. "Oh, yes."

"I will treat you well, Lori. We will make beautiful music together . . . I want you . . . I will make you feel like the lady you are. Beautiful . . . sensuous . . . " He licked with a feather-light touch at my ear.

I could no longer hear his words. I only saw him descending upon me. Closing my eyes, I waited for his next move. Instead of immediately stripping me of my clothing as I had expected, he simply started kissing me . . . everywhere. Gene lit fires inside of me that I had long since thought extinguished, and I melted toward his body. His hands touched me in more places than I imagined ten fingers could reach at the same time. Slowly and without any further conversation, he disrobed me as if it were an art instead of only a formality. I felt the material peeled from my body as hot flames rushed to my loins. When we both lay naked, I anticipated he'd mount me and release his own desire, but I was surprised once again when he spent wonderful, lengthy moments drawing out sensations from inside of me that made my mind climb intangible heights. I was going wild inside; pulsating, liquid fire was racing through every inch of me as I begged him to enter me and bring me to full awareness. He put me off even longer, as he teased me with his tongue and his touch. I was certain I would go completely mad from the exploding beauty that engulfed me until finally, I felt his hardness between my legs.

"Take me . . . take me. God, I can't stand it another moment." My voice was husky and filled with passion.

"Oh, yes you can, Lori . . . yes you can . . . I'm only beginning to unlock the treasures," he muttered as his organ teased the outside of my warm moist lips. Over and over again he touched the outskirts of my hidden secrets drawing back each time making me cry repeatedly to bury him inside of me. Finally, when I thought my sanity was about to take flight, he plunged into me as if he were filling up my entire abdomen. My hips arched to achieve full benefit from his thrusts. We moved as one . . . up . . . up . . . higher . . . higher . . . I could actually see the other side of the mountain. A vaguely familiar feeling washed over me. I had ridden this crest before . . . in another time . . . with another man. It had been a masterpiece of excitement. No! Push that thought away!

My hands, my body, and my limbs . . . everything exploded into a thousand little pieces and my mind went totally and blissfully blank. I felt his weight relax upon me as I circled him with my arms. I tried to block out all thought and concentrate only on the beauty of the moment, but reality started setting in. My first conscious thought was how thankful I was for the fact that I was still on the Pill. I smiled as I realized that consciously or unconsciously *this* was the reason I had renewed my prescription each month. The numbness in my legs receded as I began to gain feeling again, and my mind returned slowly to full awareness. The magic was over, but it was worth it . . . worth every ounce of anxiety and reluctance. I could not believe that I was capable of stepping over the peak and climaxing into oblivion as I had just done with Gene.

"Well, what do you think about sex now, my beautiful temptress?" Gene whispered softly, causing the hair on the back of my neck to stand up with renewed thrills. He rubbed my scalp with both hands massaging it gently. A deep chuckling came from his throat as he leaned over me and reached for our glasses.

I didn't want to open my eyes and ruin my mental picture with true realities. I wanted to hold onto its beauty forever, not letting any other factor corrupt or destroy what I had discovered.

"Open your eyes, Lori," Gene whispered as he kissed each lid softly with his lips. I knew the room was well lit not only by the fire but also by the lamp that remained on while we shared in each other's pleasures. When I remembered that I was lying completely naked on the living room floor, modesty began to envelop me. I wanted to cover myself. My bare back was to the pile when I finally unveiled my eyes. Keeping my vision on the ceiling, I grabbed for the seconds I needed to relax a bit in order to feel more comfortable with the situation.

"Look at me, Lori . . . don't be frightened. I will not hurt you. Wasn't I tender and gentle? I didn't hurt you in anyway, did I?" He spoke more as if he were answering his own questions instead of asking for a reply from me. "You should not be ashamed of your body . . . " He touched my shoulders, my breasts, my thighs and then made a small circular movement around my navel. "You should never hide yourself in darkness or behind blankets when you have sex. You should be proud of your beautiful body. Make love where there is light and you can get full benefit of every movement. Sex can be enjoyed at even greater heights if you are able to see what is actually going on." He traced my jaw with gentle touches of his fingers. "Look at me, Lori. Don't be ashamed. Don't pull away. I'm proud of my body just like you should be proud of yours."

Gene was sitting up as he helped me into the same position. He took my hand and tenderly folded my fingers around his organ. It seemed small and lifeless . . . not at all like the long, hard shaft that had been thrusting into me only a short time ago. His membrane was fleshy and soft with a combination of my own and his dampness surrounding it. I fondled it first with curiosity and then with loving fingers as I remembered the ecstasy it had created.

"My sweet, innocent, Lori . . . we have only just begun. I will teach you so much . . . wonderful things you never thought possible. Oh, Lori . . . you are going to love sex. You were born for it. Your body has been screaming for its release. I will teach you what it is like to wallow in its pleasures."

5

Gene was right. I really hadn't known even the beginnings of the art of sex— of movements, desires, stimulation, and satisfaction. Each time we saw each other, I learned something new and exciting. He was the teacher; I was the pupil. It was a revelation. I was with Gene at least twice a week, sometimes even more often, and the duration of each separation created a sexual tension within me that made it difficult to contain myself during the preliminary activities such as dinner, movie, or dancing. I wanted to make love all the time. I thought about it constantly. A new gate was opened up to me, and I craved sex, as most people needed food and drink.

Even though he told me to date whomever I wanted, I saw no one but Gene. He became part of my routine. I slept, I went to work, I waited for Gene to call. There was no room in my life for anything or anyone else.

Time slipped by. The Christmas season was a frenzy of activities. On New Year's Eve, as our country rang in its bicentennial year, we celebrated privately in his bedroom with a chilled bottle of champagne. In January, we traveled to New York for the weekend to see *A Chorus Line*. I was thrilled to have Gene to myself for two whole days. Also, during that month, we saw a ballet, went to a few movies, and out to dinner many times.

In February, we drove to Bryce Mountain where Gene attempted to teach me how to ski. We went to more restaurants and saw more movies, but my favorite dates were those we spent in bed as we watched Dorothy Hamill skate her heart out at Innsbruck, where she won an Olympic gold medal.

As spring flew by, I became engrossed in Gene's political views. He was behind a virtually unknown candidate from Georgia and swore that Jimmy Carter would be our next president. Gene felt that it didn't really matter who ran against the Republican ticket; Gene was certain that the Democrats would win, simply because America wasn't ready to forgive and forget the Republicans and Nixon's scandal. Carter's speeches seemed to win the hearts of many Americans as he promised never to lie, to reorganize our federal government, and to bring pride back to our country again. By the end of April, Carter had already come out on top in the Iowa, New Hampshire, Florida, Illinois, and North Carolina primaries. He dipped a bit in New York and Wisconsin, but then he took Pennsylvania. And on April 29 when Hubert Humphrey announced that he would not enter the race, Gene was positive that Carter would be the name on the Democrat ticket next November. Gene was so active in contributing to Carter's campaign that we went to quite a few dinners and parties in Carter's honor. It was fun, exciting, and definitely a new experience in my life. I loved being a part of it.

During the summer, we were extremely busy as Gene intermingled our social life with his political contributions. In addition to the Democrat functions, we went to Rehobeth Beach several times. He owned a house on West Street. Lying on the sand and listening to the ocean always made for a relaxing weekend. Also during the summer, I learned to water ski on the Potomac River behind Gene's nineteen-foot Mastercraft. Boating was a ball! In fact, the best boating adventure of the season was when we viewed, from the river, the impressive fireworks display at the Washington Monument on the Fourth of July. Ten days later we were absorbed in the Democratic National Convention as we watched Carter win the ticket. We finished off July with our eyes glued to the television set as we focused on Montreal and the summer Olympic Games where Romania's Nadia Comaneci acquired seven perfect ten scores in the gymnastics competition. I was so in awe of her that whenever she performed, Gene could not distract me with any of his usually successful moves.

Late August was oppressively hot; therefore, if we weren't out boating and baking in the sun, we were in air-conditioning working up our own sweat in his gigantic king-sized bed. It was wonderful. I learned how to excite him and tease his most sensitive areas making him moan and beg for release inside of me. In return, he gave me the same kind of fulfillment. I adored making love with Gene. There was so much chemistry between us. After all, when there was true emotion between two people, making love was a beautiful expression of that feeling. I was certain the depth of Gene's and my relationship was intensifying. I needed him. I wanted him. I even harbored the idea that I was in love with him. Gene Saunders was my reason for waking up in the morning, and I smiled all the time. He was so good to me. He made me feel beautiful. Intermingled in that splendor, I felt like a woman—a real woman—for the first time in my life.

In the beginning, I realized that Gene stated he would never love me— that I was not to destroy the beauty of our relationship by falling in love with him—but I was positive his attitude had changed. After all, Gene couldn't treat me with such warmth, such gentleness, so much compassion, if he did not care. Could he? No! Of course not! He was falling in love with me, too; of that I was certain. Oh, what a wonderful, wonderful feeling to be in love!

Unfortunately, Jennifer didn't like Gene Saunders. We had many arguments about him. She was certain that he was using me. How could Jennifer be so blind? Didn't she understand? Couldn't she see the love in our eyes? She even tried one time to persuade Gene into her bed, but only—as she said—out of a sense of duty and loyalty to me. When Gene told me about it, I was furious. I immediately confronted Jennifer and demanded an explanation.

"He doesn't care about you, Lori." Jennifer was screaming.

"He does! He *does* care about me. He couldn't treat me this way if he didn't have some feeling."

"You are confusing lust for love, Lori."

"Damn it." I was yelling, too, as I paced the floor trying to control my anger. I was too obstinate to see anything but the beauty in our relationship, and I wasn't going to let Jennifer ruin it. I kept remembering all the wonderful memories Gene and I were creating. Why couldn't Jennifer see it?

"You threw yourself at him, Jennifer. He told me about it. You literally threw yourself at Gene by taking your robe off in front of him while I was getting dressed for our date in the other room. How could you? You know how I feel about him."

"I was only trying to show you that he's just interested in anyone with a warm cunt."

"Stop it! Stop it! I won't listen to another word." I was so angry with Jennifer for trying to ruin one of the few happy times of my life. "Gene did not take you up on your offer, did he? Jen, can't you see that if he didn't care about me he would have slept with you—like Steve did. But he didn't. He didn't do it, and he even told me about your little ploy. That ought to prove how he feels."

"Obviously, Gene didn't tell you what he said to me after I slipped the robe off, did he? No, I'm sure he left that little part of the conversation out."

"I don't want to hear anymore, Jennifer."

"I've been right before, haven't I? I was right about Brad. I was right about Steve. I'm right this time too. Can't you see? For someone as intelligent as you are, Lori, you're pretty damn dumb. But if you won't take my word for it, let me tell you what happened between your true and faithful Gene Saunders and me." Her voice reeked of cynicism. "While you were in your room getting all dolled up for that creep, he was holding himself at bay in the living room with me by saying 'I'm sorry, Jennifer . . . not that you aren't a tempting morsel, but I never mess around with two women who are friends. It goes against the odds.' That's what your Mr. Wonderful said, Lori. He didn't say, 'I'm remaining loyal to Lori' and he didn't say, 'I'm not interested in anyone but Lori, and he most definitely didn't say, 'I'm in love with Lori.' Gene said, and I'll repeat myself so maybe some of it will sink in that thick skull of yours, 'I don't mess around with women who know each other.'"

"Shut up, Jennifer."

"Don't be such a fool, Lori! For Christ's sake . . . see it for what it's worth, but don't make something out of it that isn't there. The man's dating two other women that I know of and God knows how many more. He's sleeping all around town."

I blew my top at her last comment. Jennifer was lying. I knew it. She was only using that tactic because she thought I'd listen to her, but I won't.

"I don't want you to get hurt, Lori. Please, please . . . can't you understand that. I love you . . . I love and care about you. Please. I'm only trying to help. I can't stand to see you make a fool of yourself."

Jennifer and I had several arguments similar to that one, but most of the time my roommate stayed in the background. The two of us kept the peace by not dwelling on the subject. It caused an underlying tension in the air. Jennifer seemed too frightened of my wrath to make additional comments regarding Gene Saunders.

There were times when I was so angry with Jennifer I actually considered packing my bags and walking out without even leaving a note or an explanation. It galled me! It really galled me that Jennifer would be so overprotective. Didn't she realize that I was a full-grown woman? I didn't need someone hovering over my every move. I had a mind of my own. I could think and reason all by myself. I didn't need anyone to do it for me. Before I got one article of clothing packed, I remembered the good times we shared, and I put the suitcase away.

6

After Jimmy Carter was elected president, Gene and I started settling down a bit, and we spent more time at his house. One particular evening after spending over an hour wrestling around in bed and savoring each other's bodies, Gene and I lay back, lit up cigarettes, and sipped our drinks.

In the year we had dated, I had never mentioned to Gene the persistence of Larry Jenkins' advances. I feared that he would become so livid, he might demand that I quit my job. But finally, I broached the subject in hopes that Gene could give me some advice about how to handle Jenkins and keep the man away from me without losing my position.

"Gene, I have this little problem." I rested my head in the cubbyhole that his arm and chest made. "There's this guy at work who's been bothering me almost since I was hired."

"What do you mean?" Giving me his full attention, he lifted his head off the pillow and stared directly into my eyes.

"I don't know how to describe it, and I don't want to make you angry or anything, because with the exception of this one problem, I really like my job. I'm getting very good at it, and I hope I'll be promoted one of these days. I don't want to start over, Gene . . . so promise you won't get mad, okay?" I butted out my cigarette and immediately lit another one as I sat up Indian style on the bed and faced him. "This guy—he's one of the junior partners in the firm—and well, he keeps telling me that I can get promoted if I well, you know, if I accommodate him." I sipped on my drink and waited to see his reaction. When Gene didn't speak, I continued. "They keep promoting all these girls I know who aren't half as qualified as I am. Many of them haven't been there as long as I have; sometimes, they even put a brand-new girl in a position when I know for sure she's incapable of doing the job well. It's almost as if they are ignoring me."

"There's this job opening up. I'd be perfect for it, Gene. The girl's transferring out to the West Coast office. I just know that I'd be good in her place. Honest! I'm not being conceited or anything, but I've worked hard. I've learned a lot, and I simply can't believe that they're keeping me in that dinky receptionist job. This new job pays about $5,000 more a year, and even though the money would be nice, it really isn't that important. It's the job I want. It would be so much more challenging. I know I could handle the extra pressure and the longer hours. Those things don't bother me. I want those things. But when I mentioned that I'm interested in the job, I was referred to this guy who's giving me a hard time. It makes me feel as if I'm between a rock and a hard place." I lit another cigarette more from being nervous than from the actual desire for the nicotine. "And this partner . . . well, he made it perfectly clear the other day that the job could be mine . . . if I well, you know . . . if I slept with him."

"I don't see the problem," Gene stated as he drank the remaining liquid in his glass. "You want the job, right?"

I nodded, thinking Gene was going to give me a solution I had not yet contemplated.

"This guy says the job is yours . . . and all you have to do is lie on your back for five or ten minutes . . . and you get promoted. Doesn't sound like any problem to me."

"How can you say that, Gene?" I couldn't believe how casually Gene was speaking to me. "Doesn't it matter to you if I have to use sex to get a job that should rightfully be mine? It would be like prostitution—selling myself for a few extra dollars and more responsibilities."

"Lori, this is the big bad world you're dealing with—not some kind of fairy tale." He lit another cigarette. "You have to take what you want out of life. You're twenty-six years old. I'd think by now you would have learned that nothing comes easily and everything has a price. It seems to me that this partner fellow of yours has put a price tag on you, and you have to decide if the price tag on that job you want is worth the price that he wants in return. It's as simple as that. If you want the promotion . . . you pay the price . . . you get the job."

"I can't believe you're saying this, Gene. Doesn't it matter to you if I sleep with that bastard? I couldn't respect myself if I did something like that. How could I expect you to respect me?"

"My dear, adorable Lori . . . I have the highest regard for drive and motivation . . . and for success . . . no matter how it is achieved. This is a dog-eat-dog world, my fragile princess, and you have to learn to cut it any way you can. You roll with the punches, and you snap back out of it. Take the opportunity, Lori. You'd be dynamite in that position, and I'm sure you can keep going up if you want. Don't let a little barrier get in your way."

Tears burned my eyes. In order to force the emotional reaction away, I bit down on my lower lip. It would never do for Gene to see how badly he hurt me with his callous solution.

"As for respect, Lori, I have a great deal of admiration for you. You're beautiful, intelligent, witty, and talented . . . as much in bed as out there in the real world. I respect every inch of you—inside and out—but I respect people more when they take what they want and don't let golden opportunities slip by without grabbing at the brass ring." He lay back on the bed beside me and cradled my body in his arms as he drew patterns around my breast and made my nipples grow taut with involuntary desire. "The firm you work for is big . . . real big. I know some of the people there. You could go far with Robbins, MacMillan and Robbins, Lori. There's all kinds of room for expansion and growth with them. Secretaries and administrative aides are nothing. You can become a vital part of their firm, travel all over the country on business. You can become a right hand . . . and the benefits in that are infinite. You can sit in on conferences in cities you've only read about and have an expense account of your own. Their top girl makes forty-two grand a year and flies to more countries than you'll probably see in a lifetime. She works hard but she plays hard too . . . now that's the life. It could be yours. All you have to do is roll with a couple of punches."

I thought of Sally—the single woman who held the position Gene was talking about. She was an attractive, friendly, highly skilled woman in her mid-forties. I felt a stabbing pang of jealousy at the thought that Gene seemed to know Sally in more than just a business manner. How was he privy to her income? Had they dated? Were they lovers? "Do you know Sally?" I asked in a timid voice trying not to sound too demanding.

"Sure. Sally and I are friends from way back."

I tried to keep my voice calm. I looked away before speaking again. "Are you having an affair with her?"

He chuckled as he kissed my abdomen and traced his tongue across my navel. "You're sounding quite possessive tonight, Lori. Not a good sign." He smiled at me. "No, I'm not having an affair with Sally. That's been over for a couple of years, but we're still good friends. We have lunch together every once in a while and talk over old times." He fell back onto the pillow and chuckled some more to himself as he lifted the glass to his lips. "You are still so naive, my little lady. So fresh and young and naive. I bet you think Sally got her job by busting her fanny and just plain hard work." He flicked my nose with his fingers and continued, "You are just old-fashioned enough to believe that, aren't you, Lori?" He laughed again when he saw the realization of his words reflected in my expression.

I grew red from embarrassment and understanding. It didn't seem possible. Gene was telling me that Sally was a willing participant in the type of acts Larry Jenkins was offering me. Why did she do it? Sally was bright, intelligent, and hardworking. Why did she feel it necessary to sleep with someone in order to get her job? It didn't make any sense.

"Take the options you have, Lori. Get the job. Your mind is being wasted in the position you hold now. That guy's not asking much. Hell! You fuck with me and love it. He's only asking you to do something you'll enjoy. Be a sport . . . play along . . . it's only a game and you're the one who gets the real prize in the end." Gene finished speaking and started making love to me for the second time that night.

I closed my eyes and tried to find relief in the act we were sharing only to discover that the music was gone. For the first time since I'd lain with Gene in front of that roaring fireplace, I didn't reach climax. His fingers, his touch, his lips, and his arms . . . they no longer created that wonderful magic.

Instead of sleeping the rest of the night with Gene, as was my usual procedure, I insisted on going home. I drove back to my apartment, took a shower, and tried to wash the filth from my body. No matter how many times I scrubbed my skin with hot, soapy water, I didn't feel clean. The words kept echoing inside my head. "Take the job," "You're still naive," "Grab the brass ring," "not a fairy tale," "dog eat dog," "Don't let the golden opportunity slip by." My ears echoed the words and phrases over and over again until I was certain I'd scream.

By morning, after lying awake all night, I came to my decision. If Larry Jenkins wanted to sell a promotion for the price of my body . . . so be it. After all, what the hell difference did it make? I considered myself in love with Gene Saunders, and he didn't care; I discussed it with Jennifer, and she saw no real harm in acquiring a promotion in that way; Larry Jenkins was a married man, and he didn't even look at it as infidelity. Who the hell would give a damn if I lay with a man whom I didn't love and who wasn't in love with me? Gene certainly made it perfectly clear that he didn't give two cents about it. I believe it was his callousness toward the situation that hurt me the most. I was in love with Gene—head over heels crazy in love with him. And the worst part about it was, he didn't even return a crumb of affection. My decision came as much from a stabbing attack at Gene's uncaring attitude as it did from my own desire for the promotion.

I thought of leaving Gene—of terminating the relationship—but I knew I would never be strong enough to fulfill that goal. I was hooked, as much sexually as emotionally, and I couldn't let go. Jennifer was right! Jennifer was always right! But once again I hadn't listened. I hated Jennifer for being right, but I loved her for standing by me and helping me get through one more catastrophe in my life. Thank God, Jennifer was always there to help me pick up the pieces. Surprisingly—even though she had warned me repeatedly—Jennifer never said, "I told you so." She simply listened to my choking sobs, held me in her arms, and let me cry out the bulk of my tears. Jennifer was the only person I could truly count on—and once again—she didn't let me down.

The following day when I arrived at work, there was a note on my desk. It was from Larry Jenkins. The moment I entered his office, everything became crystal clear. He was wearing a victorious grin. It suddenly became obvious that Gene had clued in Larry on the discussion he and I had shared the night before. I stood dumbfounded, staring back into Larry Jenkins's snickering face. It had never dawned on me that Larry actually knew Gene. But why not? Of course, they knew each other. Hadn't Gene admitted to being acquainted with people in my office? I was shell-shocked as I realized that I was probably a topic of discussion between Gene and Larry while they had drinks during happy hour. More than likely, Gene even discussed our most intimate moments—times I considered sacred. My God! I felt sick to my stomach.

"Have you given any more thought to my offer, Miss Davis?" He was still smiling as he waited patiently for me to respond.

I stood quietly in front of him and stared out of the window behind his desk. It was a beautiful day outside. The sky was a rich blue. I couldn't see a cloud anywhere. The sun was so bright it made my eyes water, but I continued gazing out into the distance, hoping for an alternative.

I wanted to throw myself across the desk and rip Larry's eyes out for assuming that I'd answer affirmatively to his demands. Every ounce of me wanted to scream to anyone who would listen and talk about the predicament he was holding over me, but somehow, I instinctively knew that no one would even bat an eyelash. Obviously, I wasn't the first person to be propositioned in this way.

Larry Jenkins pushed a motel key over the top of his desk, leaned back in his chair, and smiled once again in a lazy manner. "The job will be yours tomorrow if you meet me in that room for lunch."

I stared down at the tiny brass key. The sun's rays caught it in exactly the right spot, reflecting beams of light into my eyes. The glittering prisms it created mesmerized me. I could hear the continuous squeaking of Larry's chair as he rocked slowly on its unoiled hinges. The noise was annoying; but in a strange way, it kept me calm as I stood completely still and contemplated my decision.

I had no idea how long I remained quiet before I finally reached down and scooped the key up in my hand. After glancing at it in my palm for only a fraction of a second, I returned my eyes to Larry's. I said nothing. What was there to say? I pivoted and left the room.

The job would be mine in the morning.

7

Jennifer

I FOUGHT THE FEELING FOR A LONG TIME, BUT FINALLY I CAME TO GRIPS with my emotions. It wasn't easy; in fact, discovering the truth caused me as much pain as fighting it had. I didn't quit school to escape facing Kurt or Lori; I didn't marry David out of revenge because Kurt had gotten a girl pregnant; my marriage didn't fail because of my husband's infidelities; I didn't go from bed to bed with strange men because I needed sexual gratification; lastly, I knew I could not return Kurt's love the second time around because I finally realized after all these years that I was not capable of loving Kurt—not even in the beginning.

The problem with psychoanalyzing oneself is—quite often—a person doesn't like what he or she finds. It would have been easier for me to keep on going through life with blind eyes, but I didn't. When I sorted out all my emotions—and all the pain—I finally realized that Kurt was only a male substitute replacing the love I felt for Lori. How ironic! Even though my father was dead, he still made a lasting impression on me. He always wanted a son—a boy to carry on the family name. He pushed me into masculine activities when everyone knew I was incapable of the physical strength necessary to excel. I wasn't able to play baseball. When he threw a ball at me, I always dropped it. I couldn't run. I couldn't do anything athletic. Hell! I wasn't even able to skip a rock across the water the way he showed me as a child. He was always disgusted with my lack of ability. And now—after all these years—I was actually more like the son my father desired than he would ever have wanted me to be. Physically, I was still inept, but emotionally . . .

I loved Lori the way a man loved a woman. I fought the suspicion for years, but it was always there, nagging at my subconscious thoughts.

At first, I believed that I really was in love with Kurt, and that he was my whole world, but I was wrong. Kurt Davis was nothing more than a masculine counterpart of the person I really loved. I tried to love Kurt. I even wanted to be in love with him, but the feeling just wasn't there. In fact, it probably never was. Lori picked up all the pieces of my chaotic life and made me whole—an independent person. Even in the beginning, it was Lori who shaped me, molded me, helped me, encouraged me, and created out of me an individual who never existed before our first meeting. It was Lori. It was always Lori. When I was sad, it was Lori who made me smile. When I cried, it was Lori who wiped away my tears. She made me laugh. She made me sing inside. She made me glad just to be alive. I loved her. Everything I did, I did for her. Every thought I had was centered on her. I was completely consumed by my love for her. Lori was my reason for living, and it pained me that I couldn't even tell her.

I hated it when men came into Lori's life. I was so jealous. I detested each one of them, especially those who were capable of possessing even the slightest piece of her heart or any portion of her mind. I hated Steve Shaw because he slept in her bed and experienced what I could never have. He made love to Lori, and that gnawed at my heart. I did not seduce Steve for my own sexual fulfillment; instead, it was out of a jealous rage. Steve didn't matter to me. If I had known that Lori wasn't in love with him, then perhaps I wouldn't have wedged myself into their relationship. Maybe then, I would have let her discover for herself what a bastard Steven Shaw really was.

I couldn't stand Gene Saunders! My loathing for him was not entirely because of the pain he caused Lori or the mental anguish he trapped her into, but because he was able to make her climb mountains I would never reach with her. Gene touched her in places I wasn't even allowed to see. He kissed her lips, cupped her breasts, and felt her warmth when I would never have the opportunity to know her intimately. And I hated the fact that he took advantage of the things that I would have treasured.

I detested Larry Jenkins. He hurt and humiliated Lori. He was scum! I was grateful that I'd never met the man because I knew that if we were ever in the same room, I would kill him for what he had done to her. I blamed myself for Lori's predicament because at first I had encouraged her to go ahead and screw Jenkins in order to get the job. I hadn't realized how much pain that choice created within Lori. Initially, I anticipated that he'd only be interested in a one-time affair; instead—months later—he was still involved with her.

I hated every man in Lori's life, but the one I despised the most was Brad Malone. I was more jealous of him than all the others put together because Brad had what none of the rest would ever claim. Brad had her heart. Lori was convinced she was in love with Gene Saunders, but I knew that wasn't true. Gene held only a poor imitation of her true emotions. I tried to explain to Lori the difference between sex and love—lust and commitment—but she was too old-fashioned and too down deep puritanical to separate the two. She wouldn't acknowledge the fact that one does not necessarily go hand in hand with the other.

Although she never admitted it, even to me, I knew that Lori's most private thoughts were still of Brad. The memories were so deep—so intense—I could still read them in her eyes. Lori didn't love Gene Saunders. No matter how many times she said it, I knew it wasn't true.

God, how I hated Brad Malone! He was such a bastard. It never ceased to amaze me how someone as good and kind and sweet as Lori could possibly get involved with such an asshole as Brad Malone. There wasn't a day that went by that I wasn't grateful he was yesterday's news. I could handle the Stephen Shaws and the Larry Jenkinses of Lori's life. I could even contend with the Gene Saunderses who might drift in and out as the years passed by, but I could never share Lori with Brad. I simply could not tolerate the way she looked at him with loving eyes, and he, in turn, abused that love.

Lori was so different now. All the warmth and joy seemed to vanish from her life, leaving her an empty shell. She acted more like a robot than a human. She rarely laughed anymore; sometimes days passed between her smiles. Her pain was my pain, and I hurt all the time. I wanted to hold her and force all the bad things away. Sadly, I knew I was not the answer; my confession could be of no comfort to her.

Even though I couldn't have Lori in the way I desired, I did cling to the fact that no one—not even her family—knew Lori as well as I did. She trusted no one, male or female, the way she trusted me. Not even Brad Malone could claim that part of her. Lori talked to me in a way that she never confided in anyone else. I latched on to that fact, knowing I could exist day to day for the rest of my life because I had Lori's confidence. After all, wasn't confidence and communication a part of love? Yes! There was a love between us, and in its own way . . . it was binding.

2

Even after five years of recuperation, I still felt run down and exhausted. Granted, I did abuse my body when the doctors repeatedly warned me against it, but booze, cigarettes, and men were the only outlets I had to make it through each day. I knew I was addicted to nicotine, but despite the large amounts of liquor and sex, I didn't consider myself an alcoholic or a whore. I wasn't the whore—the men were. Men were unpaid male prostitutes filling my need for sexual release. I didn't care about any of them. Strange men with no names—no pasts and no futures—were able to give me a few fleeting moments of normalcy. With each climax, I was granted a couple of seconds when Lori Davis did not torment and monopolize my thoughts.

Now that Lori spent most of her nonworking hours with either Gene Saunders or Larry Jenkins, I was left alone. I missed those lazy evenings and those wonderful Sundays we used to spend together. As a result of her busy schedule, I spent more and more time carousing in bars looking for a little action and hoping it would take the loneliness away. On this particular evening, I was too depressed to mix with the same old crowd, so I went home expecting the apartment to be dark and empty. When I opened the door, I was surprised to see Lori lying quietly on the couch. She was asleep. I was glad to see her. It had been such a long time since we had been in the apartment together. I crossed the room and turned off the television. The sudden change in noise created a stir from Lori. She sat up, rubbed her eyes, and smiled listlessly. She looked sad.

"Hi."

"Hi, Jennifer . . . have fun tonight?" she asked as she pulled herself into a sitting position and blinked her eyes several times.

"Nah. Nobody interesting was out tonight." I amazed myself when I was able to cover up my true feelings so well. "Want to have a beer with me?"

"Sure . . ." Lori paused. "Jennifer, it worries me that you go off with these men you don't even know. Doesn't it ever bother you?" She hesitated a moment before continuing, "I saw a movie last week with Gene. *Looking for Mr. Goodbar*. It scared the shit out of me. If you saw it . . . you'd be scared too."

Even though I was in the kitchen, pulling two Miller ponies out the refrigerator, I could still hear her voice. When I came back into the room, I answered her. "I don't worry about it, Lori. Whatever happens . . . happens. Who would care anyway?"

"I hate it when you talk like that. You know damn well that people care about you."

"Name someone!" I was in a depressed mood.

"Everyone on the Hill likes you."

"They don't like me. Hell, they don't even know me."

"Well, Jennifer, I care about you. I don't want anything to happen to you . . . and I wish you would be more careful about the men you run around with."

I was going to jump on her case about not running my life when I noticed for the first time that Lori had been crying. Her eyes were swollen and red. My temper ebbed as I spoke with soft words, "You okay?"

Lori reached across the coffee table and picked up her cigarettes. After taking a Virginia Slims out of the box, she lit it and inhaled in silence. "We've come a long way, baby." She twirled the package in her hand and repeated the slogan—more to herself than to me.

"Lori, what's the matter?" A lump started forming at the base of my throat. I couldn't bear to see Lori look so despondent. I tried to remain casual, as I suppressed my desire to run over to her and surround her with my arms. "What happened?"

"Nothing . . . everything." She exhaled the smoke in her lungs. "I was watching this old movie on TV. *The Sterile Cuckoo*. Have you ever seen it?" Lori did not wait for a response. "What a tearjerker. It's your typical boy meets girl . . . they fall in love . . . girl keeps loving boy even after the boy falls out of love with the girl . . . the girl suffers. First love is a beautiful hurt. Liza Minelli was sensational." Fresh tears sprang to her eyes.

I wondered who Lori was remembering.

"Jesus Christ!" Lori banged her fist against the cushion she'd been holding. "I don't know why I bother watching those stupid, mushy movies anyway. They don't do anything, but bring back old memories that are better left dead and buried." She touched her eyes with the tissue she was holding. "First love *is* beautiful . . . it is *so* beautiful . . . but God, how it hurts. It hurts so much you think you're going to die."

I wanted to shelter her from all the old pain, but I knew there was nothing I could do. Was she reminiscing about her past because she was trying to escape her present? Was she pondering on life with Gene? Was it the innocence she'd shared with Tommy? Or was it Brad and the pain he had caused her?

"Who are the tears for, Lori?"

"What the hell difference does it make?" She glanced quietly around the room before beginning to speak again. "I really know how to screw up my life, don't I, Jen? I thought the world was just jam-packed with wonderful things and beautiful people. Tommy was beautiful . . . Rick was beautiful . . . but I didn't see that. No! Not me! I couldn't settle for contentment and security. I had to go in search of vibrating, passionate love. I pushed Tommy's devotion aside. I practically walked over Rick. I was such a fool." She covered her face with both hands sobbing and choking on her words. "No, I didn't think I could be happy with them. No! Not me! I had to fall crazy in love with a creep like Brad Malone. I'm such a fool." She drained her beer before adding, "Do you know, Jennifer, how old I was before I figured out that people really don't give a shit about each other? Nobody cares . . . nobody gives a flying fig about anything just as long as they get what they want out of life." Lori was screaming hysterically. "It's all so damned ridiculous." She laughed in a sarcastic way. "I can't give up Gene. I'm hooked on him. He's like a drug to me. I don't know what I'd do if he stopped seeing me. He doesn't care about me—I know that—he probably never did. I wish I could tell him where to get off, but I can't. I need him. If two or three days go by and I haven't seen him, I start climbing the walls. He's an addiction. I have no pride left when it comes to Gene. I can't let him go. And then there's that bastard, Larry. God! I hate him. He won't leave me alone. He keeps pushing and pawing me until I don't think I can stand it another moment. I'm trapped. I'm trapped, and I don't know the way out."

I walked over to the couch and let Lori fall into my arms as I rocked her back and forth with steady even motions. I closed my eyes and savored the moment of just being able to hold her and feel her body pressed close to mine. It felt good to touch her even in this way. "You have me, Lori . . . you have me." She clung to me as I smoothed her hair and whispered inaudible words.

"What have I done to myself? Look at me, Jennifer! I'm a horrible excuse for a person. I don't know what to do or how to climb out of this hole. Help me, Jennifer. Help me."

"It's okay. It'll be okay," I repeated over and over again. We sat in the same position for well over an hour until Lori finally regained her composure. Lori needed me—that was the most important thing in the world as far as I was concerned. My Lori needed me, and I was here.

3

By the middle of August, I felt myself slipping in my job. I could no longer keep up with the strenuous, mental activity or the long hours. My nightlife was completely cut out because I didn't have the stamina to stay up even a few hours after I left the office at the end of each day. Lori was rarely home, so I spent most of my evening hours sleeping and trying to get enough rest to make it through the following day. I stopped drinking with the exception of a beer every now and then with Lori; I limited myself to a half pack of cigarettes a day and those were during working hours; and I hadn't slept with a man in three months. I was so tired all the time. My chest hurt. Sometimes, it was actually hard to breathe. No amount of rest helped. There were many days when I collapsed on the bed by half past six in the evening and slept for twelve hours, but I was just as exhausted the following day.

My boss was rapidly losing patience with my performance. He constantly had to return my work for corrections or revisions because of the errors I made, and more often than not, he needed to repeat himself because I'd forgotten his instructions. Twice last week, he even threatened to fire me if I didn't shape up and start producing accurate and timely work. He was right. Most of the things I did were sloppy or half finished. It was a struggle for me just to write a simple telephone message. When he dictated a letter, I was lucky if I got every fourth word, and when I made up the rest through connotation, he was so angry he literally wrote the letter himself. Typing was the most difficult. Every time I touched the keys, it felt as if the noise was vibrating inside my head. Several times when I felt the worst, I paid the girl down the hall a few bucks out of my own pocket to do my typing. And at lunch instead of eating, I looked for an empty office to curl up on the couch—instantly falling asleep for an hour.

Even though the subway had been open for over a year, I still elected to take the bus. During this particular evening, the 11A was so crowded by the time it reached the Bureau of Printing and Engraving, all the passengers were packed like sardines. The air was thick and oppressive which made it hard to breathe, and when I was capable of taking in oxygen, it smelled like hair spray, stale perfume, and body odor. I was gagging on the fumes. Usually, there was little conversation on the bus, but tonight people were buzzing about Elvis Presley. No one could believe that he was dead. His songs and movies were being remembered lovingly as strangers expressed their sorrow. I did not participate in the conversations because it was all I could do to keep from fainting.

Finally, the number of people on the bus began to thin out. I was able to sit down for a mile or two before reaching Belle View Boulevard. After I stepped out into the evening air, I began to feel a little better. Sweet Jesus! I didn't know I was claustrophobic. I stood there quietly for a few moments and got my bearings before walking home.

I climbed the stairs slowly. Stairs. I wasn't very fond of stairs. One flight was difficult enough; three were almost more than I could handle. By the time I reached the second-story platform, I could hear the phone ringing in our apartment. Hurrying up the last set of steps, I fumbled with my keys. I opened the door, unloaded my purse and keys on the couch, and picked up the receiver.

"Hello." I was out of breath.

"Hello, Lori?" It was a male voice.

"No . . . this is Jennifer." I didn't recognize the man on the other end of the wire.

"Is Lori there?"

"No . . . I don't think so. I just got home from work myself. I don't think she's arrived yet. Can I take a message?"

"Yeah. Tell her to call Larry at work . . . not at home . . . at work. Okay? Got that?"

I felt the hair on the back of my neck stand up when he mentioned his name. I'd never met Larry Jenkins. I'd never even spoken to him. I couldn't believe he was actually invading the privacy of Lori's home. The nerve of him! My heart was pounding. The tension began to boil. "Listen . . . you son of a bitch . . ." I knew I was probably going to get Lori into trouble talking like this to her boss, but I couldn't control my temper. "You may think you're God's gift to the ladies and have the right to bully Lori around in that high and mighty office of yours, but you have no right bothering her at home. Leave her alone, you bastard."

"Who the hell do you think you are? You can't talk to me that way."

"Leave her the hell alone!" I slammed down the receiver and sat on the couch as I strained to take in oxygen. I tried to relax and calm my erratically beating heart. I felt as if my chest was going to explode. My head was throbbing; I couldn't swallow. I tried again, but with no success. My fingers hurt. No . . . it was my arm. My entire arm hurt. There was a stabbing, painful sensation in my chest. I clutched at it trying to dull the overwhelming hurt centered in that one spot. I was sweating. No . . . I was cold. Oh, God . . . I hurt. I hurt so much. The room was whirling around me. I could not figure out whether I was standing or sitting. I opened my eyes as wide as I could and tried to get my bearings. What was happening to me? Everything was getting so fuzzy. I couldn't breathe. Help me! I can't breathe.

————

"Jennifer . . . Jennifer."

I kept hearing my name being said over and over again. Someone was slapping my face. I could not actually feel the hand hitting me, but I could hear the sound and my head moved slightly from the impact when the palm hit my jaw.

"Jennifer! Oh, my God! Jennifer!"

Who was that? I knew that voice. Slowly, I became aware of my surroundings. I could hear Lori. She was holding me, but she sounded so far away. She was crying. I could hear her crying. Why was she crying? Why did I feel so numb? Where the hell was I anyway?

"Jennifer . . . it's all right. I called an ambulance. It'll be here any minute. Just hold on. You're going to be all right."

I felt wet liquid between my legs. Oh, shit! I must have lost control of my bladder. Jesus! How humiliating. I tried to draw my legs together so Lori wouldn't be able to see what had happened. I was so wet. It was even damp around my knees. Shit!

"Lori . . . "

"Yes . . . I'm here . . . I'm here."

Why did she sound so concerned and worried? I tried to grip her arm, but nothing moved. I wasn't sure if my lips were even moving. I thought about the words I was thinking, but I wasn't sure if they were audible. I kept trying to speak. "Lori. Don't leave me! Don't let them take me away."

"It's okay, Jennifer . . . relax . . . just relax . . . don't let yourself get so worked up. I promise everything's going to be all right."

"Don't leave me, Lori."

"I won't leave."

She understood me. Oh, Mother of God. Thank you. Lori understood me. I tried to speak again. "Don't ever leave me. I couldn't stand it if you left me." Every word was an effort. "I love you, Lori. I love you."

"It's going to be okay, Jennifer. Everything's going to be all right."

She didn't understand. I concentrated as hard as I could on speaking the words again, but I couldn't even hear them in my own mind the second time. Strong arms picked me up. Higher, higher. I was being lifted . . . up . . . up . . . up. Who was that? Men . . . I heard men. There were male voices everywhere. I don't need you. I don't want any of you. Where was Lori?

8

Kurt

GOD! MY HEAD HURT; IN FACT, MY WHOLE BODY WAS IN PAIN. IT WAS agony just to lift my head off the pillow. My mouth tasted as if an entire army paraded through it in smelly, wet socks. I had a hangover. Not just an average, everyday, ordinary hangover, but one I was certain had the potential to kill. I drank more than two six-packs of beer last night, a few of which were boilermakers containing an ounce of bourbon dropped into the foamy brew. The only problem with alcohol was the disastrous way I always felt in the morning. Acid was rough on the body too; the trips were sensational, but the flashbacks were hell. Cocaine was nice for a treat, but I didn't want to make a habit out of it. It was too expensive. Pot was best. I never had a hangover from that blissful high. And if I sold a dozen ounces of it every couple weeks, my own personal stash was free. Couldn't beat that.

What I needed was a hot shower, about ten cups of coffee, and a couple of tokes off a jay. That would help make all the painful fuzziness go away. I struggled off the bed. I was still drunk. After staggering into the bathroom, I glanced at myself in the mirror and noticed several days' growth of beard on my face. I had shaved last night; I distinctly remembered doing it. Was it actually last night or was it a couple of days ago? Lately, all the nights and days ran into each other. I wondered what day it was.

I brushed my teeth three separate times, but was unable to get the foul taste out of my mouth. I ran my tongue over the inside of my cheeks and concentrated on keeping the bile down. Or maybe I'd feel better if I did throw up. I hung my head over the toilet purposely gagging as I tried to wretch the poison from my system. Nothing happened. Jesus! Just my luck! I wanted to puke my guts out and nothing happened. If I had decided against it, I probably would have involuntarily vomited all over myself. I turned the shower on full force with hot steamy liquid. Trying to clear my sinuses, I breathed in the warm mist. After stepping into the bathtub, I let the water splash over me as I leaned against the wall. It was helping . . . not a lot, but it was helping. Jesus! I sure tied one on last night, and today I was paying the full price in spades.

After standing in the shower for twenty minutes, I turned off the knobs and reached for the towel. Vigorously, I rubbed my scalp as I tried to massage blood back into my brain. I felt like shit!

It was moments like this when I begrudged my past. There was once a time when all the roads were open. I could have been a lawyer. Or I could have come back from North Carolina and worked for the government. There were a number of jobs available to those with a college degree. But all of that was gone now. Nobody wanted me. No one wanted to hire a burned out reject from the Vietnam era with only two years of college under his belt. It seemed as if everything that was once of value to me was gone. I lost all chances at succeeding at a profession other than flipping steaks. All my friends from Chapel Hill were developing careers; many were successful; some were even married; a couple of them had kids. Charlie, my old roommate, just finished taking the bar exam. They all seemed happy. Why was it so easy for them? Hell! I didn't even have my family anymore. I hadn't seen my mother in over a year. And my dad could drop dead as far as I was concerned. Oh, sure, Lori was still around, but sometimes her perky disposition made me nauseous. I was sick and tired of listening to her rattle on in her optimistic way. Most of the time when she called or tried to get in touch with me, I ignored her messages. I didn't care! I didn't need her! I didn't need anyone!

I made an attempt to shave, but only succeeded in nicking myself each time I ran the razor over my face. Shit! I couldn't do anything right. Staring into the mirror, I asked my reflection what the hell it was all about, but my image didn't answer me. I donned a robe and went to the corner of my apartment where there was a small stove. I turned it on as I filled the coffeepot with tap water and started fixing myself a cup of Maxwell House. I thought of making breakfast, but decided against it. Maybe—just maybe—with a little willpower I could starve myself to death. Nah! That wouldn't work.

Before the water started to boil, I picked up the phone and dialed the restaurant where I hoped I still had a job. The manager picked up his extension before the second ring.

"Jolly Ox, can I help you?"

"This is Kurt."

"You son of a bitch! Where have you been?"

"I wasn't on duty yesterday, sir. It was my day off."

"Listen, Davis, your day off was a week ago Thursday . . . not Friday, Saturday, Sunday, and Monday and the whole rest of the week. It was not your fucking vacation." He was royally pissed off.

I couldn't understand why he was yelling so much. It wasn't Tuesday; it was Friday! Or was it the following Friday? Had I actually lost ten days?

"You left us holding the bag, buster, and I was none too pleased about it. The restaurant was packed. We didn't even have a main chef to carry us through it. I had to cook! God damn it . . . all hell broke loose."

"I'll make it up to you, boss . . ." I was trying to joke about it and make light of the situation. "I'll work double shifts and make it all up to you."

"The hell you will, Davis! You're fired! You've been fired since the first night you didn't show up. I'm not putting up with any more of your crap. You've been nothing but a pain in my ass since I hired you. Don't bother showing up; you've been replaced."

"Listen . . . wait . . . listen, I can explain."

"Don't waste your breath! The decision has already been made." He hung up the phone before I could say another word.

I threw the receiver, the cord, and the base clear across the room along with everything else I could put my hands on. Shit! Now I didn't even have my fucking job. The rent was overdue; I owed my dealer twenty-five bucks; I didn't have a damned thing to eat in the refrigerator; my gas tank was on empty; worst of all, I didn't have two dimes to rub together. I thought about calling Pamela, but she'd already given me more money than I could ever repay in a lifetime of lousy cooking jobs. She'd loaned me at least five grand in the past two plus years, and never once did she ask when I was going to start returning it.

I could get into some heavy dealing, instead of the light stuff I was doing now. My supplier was constantly on me to branch out. Hell! If I played my cards right, I wouldn't have to go looking for another job. I could just sit back and let the other poor dumb bastards pay my rent and put money in my pocket. Yeah! It looked like that was my only solution at the moment.

I started cleaning up some of the mess. As I put the phone back into place, I wondered whether or not it was broken. Seconds later, it rang. I picked it up more to cease the loud tone than to find out who was on the other end. "Yeah," I muttered, furious that anyone would pry into my own private hell. Why didn't everyone just leave me alone?

"Where have you been, Kurt?"

It was my sister. Damn! I didn't want to talk to Lori. She'd left messages for me all over town, but today—like most days—I just wasn't in the mood for her prattle.

"I've been trying to reach you for weeks. You're never home, and you won't return my calls." She sounded extremely annoyed as she chastised me. "Where have you been?"

"What the hell is it, Lori?" My voice was agitated and loud. "I don't want any of your goddamned social visits . . . so just leave me alone."

"Kurt . . . stop talking . . . just stop talking for a minute and listen to me." Lori sounded upset. "Jennifer had a relapse. She was in the hospital for several weeks, but now they've sent her to a sanitarium in West Virginia to recuperate. She's still very sick."

I thought of Jennifer—my Jennifer—lying sick and in pain. God! I'd do anything to help her, but she didn't want me. She made that perfectly clear the last time we were together. "Well, what the hell do you want me to do about it?" I answered in a gruff voice as I tried to hide my own panic.

"My God! Kurt, she almost died! There were five days when the doctors didn't think she was going to pull through. You used to love Jennifer. Don't you have any compassion for her?"

Tears sprang to my eyes. Love her? God, yes! I still loved her. I would always love Jennifer. "What can I do, Lori?" My tone was a lot more sympathetic.

"Well, for starters, you could go see her."

"Does she want to see me?" I asked as I held my breath in anticipation of her answer. My sister hesitated for a few moments contemplating her reply. The urgency left her voice when she spoke again. "I don't know, Kurt. To be honest, Jennifer hasn't asked for you, but she needs all the friends she can get. She doesn't have anyone, except me, and she must be incredibly lonely in a strange place all by herself."

"What happened, Lori?"

"She had a heart attack. Do you believe it? A heart attack! Jennifer isn't even twenty-seven years old. The doctors think she had a mild stroke along with it. She's not paralyzed, but the doctors say she's very weak on her left side, and she's lost a portion of her sense of touch. They're hoping it will come back naturally on its own, given enough time. She can hear just fine, but she doesn't talk very well. I know she understands everything that's being said, but it takes her a long time to form words, and sometimes they are hard to understand." Lori paused. "My God, Kurt! She looks awful. I mean it. Jennifer looks absolutely dreadful. She wasn't following the doctor's instructions. She was drinking and smoking like there was no tomorrow. She was in this self-destructive mode. I noticed shortly before it happened that she didn't even have the energy to eat much less make it through a normal day. I should have seen the signs . . ." Lori paused again. "But I was so wrapped up in myself that I didn't pay any attention to Jennifer's problems. I feel so guilty. It's entirely my fault. I should have noticed all the danger signals. Kurt . . . she looks so helpless and pale. I've never felt so useless in my life. And those damn doctors keep telling me that they believe there has been too much damage to her heart. The odds are against her ever recuperating one hundred percent." Lori was crying. Her sniveling was distant, but audible. "I don't know what to do, Kurt . . . please come with me. You were so good for her the first time she was sick. Jennifer got better for you. Maybe this time it will happen again."

"But she hasn't asked for me."

"She didn't ask for you the first time either, but it worked, didn't it? You helped her get better."

"I don't know if I can do it, Lori. I don't know if I can go through that again."

"If you really love her, you'll stop thinking about yourself, and do what it takes to help her."

"Lori . . . I don't have enough money to drive around the block much less to take a trip to West Virginia."

"I'll take you. You can ride with me."

"Aren't you working?"

"I took the day off. Come with me! See Jennifer. God, she needs us, Kurt. Please come with me."

"Okay. Pick me up." I stared at the phone and wondered if my sister's idea was for the best. If Jennifer really wanted to see me, why didn't she call or try to contact me? She had to know that I was still in love with her. I made it perfectly clear two years ago that she was my whole life.

<hr>

Lori drove several miles in silence as I watched the scenery pass. We were on the Beltway near the Littler River Turnpike exit before she broke the silence. "I heard you lost your job."

"How'd you find out? I just heard about it this morning," I muttered as I watched cars zoom by in the left lane. I wished Lori would go faster. She always drove exactly the speed limit—not a mile above or a mile below. It was monotonous.

"I called the restaurant last week, and the manager informed me that he didn't want to ever set eyes on you again. He wasn't very polite about it either. What happened?"

"I don't know," I answered trying to figure it out for myself. "I must have been completely wasted or something because I sure didn't know it was Tuesday when I woke up this morning. I have a vague recollection of going to Good Guys. I can remember drinking a lot and talking to some girl at the table next to mine. She had red hair . . . no . . . no, it wasn't red. Hell, it doesn't matter. I think I got laid, but I can't really remember for sure. I don't know. It isn't important. I also remember playing cards. I had two full houses in a row. I made ninety bucks on those two hands, but I lost it all before the night was over."

"You mean to tell me, you spent ten days alternating between watching strippers and playing cards? And you don't remember what else?"

"Well, actually I do remember that I saw *Star Wars*. Jesus! What a show . . . especially when you're tripping. It seemed like all those space ships were coming off the screen and flying right at me. Now that I think about it . . . I watched it three times in a row. It was great."

"Kurt, I can't believe you're doing this to yourself."

"Damn it! I don't want a lecture. It's *my* fucking life."

"Kurt." My sister's voice was filled with concern. "You've got to snap out of this."

"None of your goddamned pep talks today, Lori!" I blurted out the words thinking if my sister was going to start lecturing me I'd surely throw myself out of the car door. Maybe that wasn't such a bad idea after all. In fact, if I leaned slightly on the door . . . and pulled the handle up . . . maybe I would fall out as we sped down the highway at fifty-five miles an hour. That might do it; with luck that would probably kill me. I rested my hand on the chrome handle. I fiddled with it. The metal felt cool against my palm as I caressed it and contemplated my act. Just one quick motion, and it would all be over. No more headaches, no more bills, no more pep talks, no more job hunting, and no more Jennifer haunting me.

I let go of the handle. I couldn't do it. Was it because I was a coward or did it have to do with the fact that I was beginning to gain hope at the thought of seeing Jennifer again?

Jennifer! Pretty flaxen-haired Jennifer—she had a sweet voice and sparkling eyes. No! That was the first Jennifer. The second Jennifer didn't have sparkling eyes. She didn't even have a purring voice. Where did my Jennifer go? The Jennifer who had clung to me as she whispered loving words while we shared exploding climaxes together. Where was the woman who threw herself into my arms each time we came together after a period of separation? Where was the Jennifer who smiled endlessly at me as I talked of silly little dreams and plans for the future. Where was she? Where was that Jennifer? She wasn't in the body of the second Jennifer. That Jennifer was aloof. There was no warmth in her eyes—no gentle loving words on her lips or tender arms to hold me. God! Give me back my Jennifer. I closed my eyes and let the time pass in silence.

The car stopped. I looked around. We had reached our destination. We were in a parking lot. There were three separate buildings forming a large horseshoe. The building in the center was three floors high; the side buildings were only two stories. All were freshly painted in white with kelly green shutters framing the windows. It looked very sanitary. The grounds were beautiful. Bushes outlined all the pathways, and huge redwood pots filled with annuals showing one last burst of summer's splendor sat on each side of every door. In the windows, there were fluffy white curtains drawn back with a sash. Gentle rolling mountains covered with trees all rich with autumn colors filled the background. Everything was neat and orderly. It didn't appear at all like I anticipated. It didn't look like a sanitarium; it looked like a resort.

"How's Jennifer paying for all this?"

"I worried about that too. She certainly doesn't have any money of her own, that's for sure. But when her lawyers found out, they informed the doctors about Jennifer's trust fund. What isn't covered by insurance will be paid by the executor when Jennifer reaches thirty."

"That's nearly three years from now."

"I know, but they are willing to wait as long as they get interest on their money."

"Yeah . . ." I said sarcastically. "I just bet they are. I'll also bet those good old doctors are all hovering over her just dying to puff up the total."

"Don't be so cynical, Kurt. You're beginning to sound just like Jennifer. That's exactly what she said when she found out."

"Why don't you grow up, Lori? You're so damned naive. I'm sure those doctors are foaming at the mouth and jotting down every dollar they can tag on to her chart knowing it'll all be paid in full without any problem. They'll drain her dry."

"At the moment, Kurt, I'm not nearly as concerned about her money as I am about her health. Come on, let's go."

My sister got out of the car, but I didn't move.

"Kurt . . . are you coming?" Lori opened the door on my side of the car and stood there waiting for me to join her. "Are you all right?"

"Yeah . . . yeah . . . I'm all right," I finally managed to answer. "I don't know if I can do this, Lori. I don't know if I can face Jennifer."

"Kurt . . . don't think of yourself . . . maybe that will help. Just think of Jennifer and how much she needs her friends right now."

Neither one of us spoke as we took the steps to the main building. I felt numb. We signed in at the desk. Lori asked the first available nurse where Jennifer Carson was.

"She's out on the terrace," the nurse answered in a pleasant but quiet voice. "We finally got her into a chair. She's getting some fresh air. By the way, Jennifer was asking about you, Miss Davis. She was hoping you'd be coming by today."

I opened the door for my sister. The two of us proceeded to cross the brick patio. There weren't many people around. An elderly-looking gentleman sat quietly in one corner; a pale middle-aged woman sipped on a cup and gazed out at the mountain view; and a group of people were gathered near the stairs. Other than that, Jennifer was alone. She sat in a wheelchair in a far corner, head leaning back, eyes closed, and hands crossed in her lap. My God! Lori was right. Jennifer looked awful. Her hair was much shorter. It looked as if it had been broken off at the shoulders instead of cut: straggling, unmanageable, and lifeless. She was so pale, chalky. There was no life to her expression. And she was very, very thin.

Jennifer didn't see me right away. She was so overcome by the fact that my sister was standing in front of her. I saw Jennifer's face light up as Lori bent down and placed a gentle kiss on her forehead. For one brief moment, I saw an old glimmer in Jennifer's eyes. She slowly reached for Lori's hand; the two of them exchanged a warm smile. It seemed as if every movement Jennifer made was an effort as she raised and lowered her hand to touch Lori's face. I wanted to knock my sister aside. I wanted it to be my face that Jennifer was touching so tenderly. I wanted to feel her soft fingers on my skin. I wanted to look in her eyes and see love.

"I've brought someone with me, Jennifer." My sister spoke. "Kurt's here."

My knees began to tremble. I was leery of her initial reaction. Slowly, Jennifer turned her head enabling our eyes to meet. I was not rewarded with the same joyous expression Jennifer had given Lori, but I didn't see anger or regret either. Instead of those reactions, I was confronted with apathetic eyes. My heart sank.

Soon after our initial greeting, Jennifer masked her reaction with an attempt at a welcoming smile. "Kurt . . . how nice to see you again." She spoke very slowly as if it were a strain to say the words.

We stood silently for several moments before Lori's voice broke the air. "I think I'll go inside for a minute."

"Don't go, Lori . . ." Jennifer pleaded as she reached for Lori's hand.

"I won't be long. I'll be right back, really. I want to talk to the doctor for a minute or two, and then I'll bring us back a tray filled with snacks, okay?"

My sister stood up and walked toward the patio doors.

With her eyes, Jennifer followed Lori's every step. I was alone with her. How many times had I prayed for an opportunity to be near her? How many little speeches did I rehearse? Unfortunately, all of those memorized words disappeared; I could not think of anything to say. I was left stumbling over my tongue and muttering half syllables under my breath.

"You look awful, Kurt." The words were choppy and strained.

"To be perfectly honest . . . I have felt better," I replied as I watched her for a sign—any sign—that would give me the strength to speak my thoughts and release my bottled emotions. "Things have been pretty bad."

"It's my fault, isn't it, Kurt?" There was an added sadness in her voice.

"It's nobody's fault, Jennifer." I ran the fingers of both hands through my hair as I stared at the mountain range in the distance. "You couldn't help it. I wanted something you simply couldn't give me. It's not your fault that I can't get back on my feet again."

"I am so sorry, Kurt. You'll never know how much I truly wanted to love you."

"For what it's worth, Jennifer . . . I'm still in love with you. I'll always be in love with you." I refused to look at her. I didn't want to see the expression on her face.

"You don't really love me, Kurt." Jennifer spoke softly, as she gazed into the distance focusing on some unknown object far away. "You don't even know me."

"But I do, Jennifer, I do know you. No one will ever know you and love you as much as I do. My God! You're my entire world."

"Kurt! Don't do this. Believe me! You really don't know me at all." She hesitated as much from pondering her thoughts as from the difficulty of speaking. "In fact, I don't even know myself. But . . . I'm learning. Each day I'm learning about me."

I knelt in front of her chair and gripped both her hands in mine. She tilted her head in my direction. We exchanged a moment of silence as the two of us searched each other's eyes. I rested my head tenderly in her lap while

Jennifer slowly stroked my hair in a friendly fashion. It felt so good to have her touching me. "Why did you leave me, Jennifer? Why did you go away and marry someone you didn't love?" I couldn't believe the floodgates to my thoughts had opened. All the questions were pouring out before I could form the sentences in my mind. "You couldn't have loved David. You just couldn't have. Why did you marry him?" I was begging for answers to unsolved mysteries. "I have a right to know."

"At first . . ." Jennifer started speaking as she smoothed the strands of my hair. " . . . I really thought I married David to lash out at you for . . . for fathering a child with someone else."

I was stunned. How did Jennifer know about Pamela and Ellie? No one knew about my Ellie . . . not even Lori. Had Pamela contacted Jennifer and told her the truth in order to punish me? Holy Jesus! It was too horrible an idea to contemplate.

"But then, Kurt . . . I realized . . . that your baby was not the reason. If I had really loved you . . . I would have fought for you . . . refused to let go; instead, I raced home and married David. It took me a long time to figure all of this out . . . and . . . it wasn't easy, Kurt. I realize that this is a cruel thing to say, but I don't think I loved you even in the beginning. I've finally realized that I used your infidelity as an excuse to terminate our relationship. If it hadn't been your baby, eventually . . . it would have been something else."

"I don't believe you. I can't believe that you never loved me, Jennifer. It isn't true! It just can't be true." Challenging her to take back her confession, I stared into Jennifer's eyes.

"It is true, Kurt. Believe me! It's true. I never really loved you . . . at least not in the way you wanted me to." She touched the side of my face with gentle hands and smiled weakly as she continued the uneven flow of her words. "I would give anything to fall in love with you. I tried. I really tried, but it just wasn't in the cards for us, Kurt. Unfortunately, the deck was stacked before it was ever dealt."

"Are you in love with David Henderson? Did you love your husband?"

"No . . . no, I didn't love David." She shrugged sadly. "I didn't even try to love David."

"Well, then damn it . . . who *do* you love?" I was agitated that she could be so callous.

Jennifer glanced away silently for a moment before returning her eyes to mine. They were unreadable. "No one. I don't love anyone. I don't even love myself."

"Jennifer . . . give me another chance. I can't live without you. I've tried. God, I've tried, but I'm screwing everything up. I'll settle for friendship. I'll settle for anything. Just let me love you. When you get better . . . when you get released from this place . . . I can take you home with me. I'll give you anything . . . *anything* . . . just give me a chance to make you happy. I need you in my life, Jennifer. I have love enough for the both of us. I want to marry you. I'd make you a good husband . . . just give me half a chance."

"Kurt! Don't! Don't do this. I've tried not to hurt you. I don't know how else to say it. No amount of love on your part can change me or alter the fact that I have nothing but friendly regard for you."

"But that can be enough to at least start building on, Jennifer. Give me a chance."

"Don't . . ." Tears sprang to her eyes. "Don't beg . . . I can't stand it. I never wanted this to happen. Please believe me . . . if I could change it, I would. I simply can't hurt you anymore by giving you false hope for something that will never happen." Jennifer cupped my chin between her thumb and fingers. Her touch was so light, I barely felt it. "Go back to the woman who has your child. She's the one who really needs you."

"Are you pushing me away because you think I owe Pamela? She does not need me. She has everything. She has her baby and her own life. She doesn't need me. Christ Almighty . . . she doesn't even want me. Jennifer . . . I won't lose you because you think I owe Pamela. I want you! Not her! I've never wanted her. I only made love to her because you left me. She just filled a void that you created when you left. She meant nothing to me! Nothing! You are the only person who has ever mattered."

"Oh, Kurt . . ." Jennifer seemed exasperated. "Don't mistake my words. I'm not playing the martyr." Her voice was weak, but clear. "I can't believe you are making me spell it out to you. I don't want to be cruel. Please, believe me. I can't let you waste your life waiting for something that will never happen. There will never be a future for you and me. You have to accept it."

"Would anybody like some tea?" Lori's voice interrupted our conversation. My sister was carrying a tray loaded with cups, a pot of steamy liquid, and sweet cakes.

I knew I would never be able to sit on that patio and make polite conversation with Jennifer after the words we'd just exchanged. "I'm going to take a walk, Lori. Stay as long as you like. I'll meet you at the car when you're ready to go back home." I turned, heading for the stairs. After taking three steps, I pivoted to face Jennifer. Not caring that Lori could hear every word, I said, "I love you, Jennifer. I have always loved you, and I will always love you . . . nothing you say can change that." Without glancing in Lori's direction, I turned again and descended the stairs.

2

I have no memory of how I came to be on the plane to New York. I did recall smoking a couple of joints in the backseat of Lori's car as I waited hours for our departure. And I did have a vague recollection of telephoning Pamela and begging her for support and/or money. I couldn't remember Pam's exact words, but I did recall her telling me to come to New York City and stay with her for as long as I needed. I was grateful to Pam for giving me a temporary sanctuary.

When I stepped off the plane, I saw Pamela and a child. Much to my amazement, it was Ellie. She looked so much older than I expected. I pictured her still a little toddler, but Ellie had outgrown all that baby fat stage. My daughter was five years old, and this was only the second time I'd seen her. Her long hair hung nearly to her waist. It was held back from her tiny, round face with miniature, plastic, pink clips that were in the shape of butterflies. The eyes were still the same color blue as I remembered; they looked remarkably like Lori's. The smile on Ellie's face was so magical. It temporarily made me forget my own personal heartache.

Ellie held the teddy bear I had given her for Christmas last year. She had it pressed firmly in one hand while her other hand loosely held on to her mother's. Pamela looked very pretty in her tailor-made suit of sky blue and yellow print. I stopped and watched them both for a moment wondering why I was here and how Pamela and Ellie could possibly help me out of my depression. Pamela Woods could offer me shelter, food, money, time . . . any of a number of physical needs, but she couldn't give me what I really wanted. Nothing she could do or say could bring Jennifer back to me. So . . . why did I come here?

Neither of them made an attempt to take the steps between us. They only smiled and waited patiently for me to cover the distance on my own. Slowly, one foot, then the next . . . I bridged the gap. She extended her hand. I took it firmly holding on to her fingers as if they could give me a reason to go on living. It didn't help. Even after touching her, I didn't feel any better. The pain didn't disappear; the depression didn't vanish. I guess I was hoping for a miracle.

"Hello, Kurt. I'm glad you decided to come."

Without exchanging a word with the dark-haired woman who paid my airfare, I knelt down and gently pinched the cheek of the little girl at her side. I smiled as I spoke to Ellie. "So, how do you like that little teddy bear?"

"I like it real good, sir. I sleep with it every night and take it everywhere with me. Mommy says you're the man who gave it to me."

I felt a pang. Ellie didn't remember me. "Yes, I'm the man. We met a couple of years ago. Do you remember?"

Ellie appeared puzzled for a moment then simply smiled shyly, "No, but Mommy shows me a picture of you everytime you send me a present. You're Kurt, because I remember you from the pictures."

I smiled at Pamela. She was watching the two of us exchange conversation. Pam looked like an angel staring down at me. The expression on her face was relaxed and gentle. I returned my attentions to Ellie and ruffled her hair with my hand. She really was an adorable child with a grin that could win anyone's heart. "So, you like all those presents?" I felt a little guilty knowing that each of them was purchased with money Pamela sent me instead of money I made on my own. "I enjoy buying you things, Ellie."

"Why?" her sweet voice asked.

"Well . . . because you are such an adorable kid, and I remember when I first met you. You were nuts about dolls and stuffed toys."

"My grandfather tells me I'm adorable too. He sends me toys from all over the world, from all the different countries he visits. But none of them are ever as nice as yours. I can't hug and play with his toys because they are always for show . . . like decorations. I have to put them on the shelf, and I only get to look at them. But I can hug your presents."

I had an overwhelming desire to hold her in my arms. Feel her tiny body pressed against me. "Would you be willing to give *me* a hug, Ellie?"

Before I finished my sentence she was cuddling herself in my arms. I didn't want to let her go. She was like medicine for my aching body and mind. I rocked her silently for a moment.

"Mommy says that maybe you'll come home and have dinner with us. Are you coming?"

"Would you like me to, Ellie?"

"Oh, yes, I want you to come to my house. Did you bring me a present this time?"

Ellie was searching my pockets. The curls in her hair were rubbing against my nose. She smelled wonderful. I had left in such a hurry, I did not think of buying anything for her. Ellie stuck her hand in my coat pocket and came out with a bag of peanuts the stewardess had given me on the plane. "Are these for me?" she asked joyfully as if she had found a fantastic treasure.

I returned her smile thinking how easily she was satisfied. "Of course, my little angel . . . you didn't think I came all the way up here empty-handed, did you?" I glanced at Pamela. She knew I was lying, but she seemed to approve.

"Thank you. I love peanuts."

"Kurt . . ." Pamela interrupted. "The limo is waiting. Let's get your bags."

"I don't have any baggage. This is it. What you see is all I brought with me."

"Then you won't be staying?" Pam looked disappointed.

"I have a few clothes in this bag here." I pointed to the bag next to me on the floor. "I was evicted." I paused, too embarrassed to admit my situation. "By the time I got back to my apartment, there was a lockbox on my door, and all my possessions were on the sidewalk. Actually, there wasn't much left after the neighborhood kids got done picking through it. What you see is everything I own." I hung my head. "I didn't have anywhere else to go, Pam."

"You're welcome to stay with us as long as you want, Kurt. All you need is just a little time to get back on your feet again." Her voice was calm; it had a soothing effect on me.

"After everything I've done to you . . . " I muttered trying to keep my words from falling onto Ellie's ears. "I can't believe you're actually willing to treat me with such kindness. I know I don't deserve it, but I really need a friend right now, Pamela." I avoided her eyes. I felt like a coward. "If I had not come here . . . I don't know what I would have done."

Pamela took my arm and guided me through the crowd. When we reached the car, the chauffeur held the door opened. I climbed into the backseat breathing deeply. I felt safe for the first time in years, and my mind was beginning to relax as if some of the strain was lifting.

3

Days passed. Each was filled with a new and different experience. I planned to stay only a night or two, but each day when I awoke, I pushed the thoughts of leaving away. I took Ellie to the zoo. Pamela packed us a picnic lunch. My daughter and I spent hours watching the monkeys, lions, bears, and birds. Much to my amazement, Ellie liked the bird section as much as any of the others. She loved to watch them fly around almost within reach.

It was especially nice because of the way the city set it up, allowing us to wander around among them. We thoroughly enjoyed every moment.

On another occasion, I took Ellie to see *Star Wars*. It was the fourth time for me, but the first for Ellie. Much to my surprise, I enjoyed the movie more watching it through a child's eyes and without the effect of drugs. The two of us ate popcorn and candy until we were sick. Pamela reprimanded me for allowing Ellie to eat so much junk food, but it was worth it. I loved every moment. Because Pamela trusted me with her daughter, I felt a renewed confidence.

There were times when the three of us went out together. One night we shared a pizza. Another time, we had triple-decker ice cream cones. Although neither Pam nor I could finish ours, we were both shocked when Ellie ate every bite of hers. Several times, the three of us took long walks in Central Park and shared peaceful afternoons. There was never a strain between Pamela and me. We were friends, and I was grateful for her friendship.

Three weeks passed before I finally decided that I had to start doing something with my life besides sponging off Pamela. I'd been sleeping in her guest room, eating her food, using her car and chauffeur, watching her television, and abusing her friendship. It was time I started living on my own. I needed a job, an apartment, and my own identity.

Ellie was tucked into bed while Pamela and I sipped on what was left of the bottle of wine we had been drinking during dinner. The two of us sat at the table. All the dishes were cleared, and the silverware was gone. There was soft, mellow music playing on the stereo in the living room. I felt comfortable. It was nice to pass the evening in such a tranquil way.

"About Jennifer . . ." I started to speak. Neither of us had even so much as spoken one word about Jennifer since I stepped off the plane.

"Kurt . . . you don't owe me any explanations. I don't know what happened, but . . . "

"I want to talk about it, Pam. I need to." I stared straight ahead without looking at her. There was no one I could confide in. Lori wouldn't understand. The relationship between my sister and me was too strained. I could never discuss Jennifer with her. My sister was too close to Jennifer . . . too involved . . . not objective. I needed a friend. "Jennifer doesn't love me, Pam . . . she said she never did." I hesitated. "God help me. I still love her. She was so sick; she still is. Like a fool, I thought she needed me. The first time Jennifer was ill, I went to her, and everything was all right. I thought it would be like that this time. But it wasn't. She made it perfectly clear that she doesn't love me; she doesn't need me. She said I wasn't important to her, and I never could be. What am I going to do with the rest of my life? I've loved her for so many years. It's almost as if my entire life began when I started loving her." I paused as I regrouped my thoughts. "Did you ever tell Jennifer about Ellie? She knows. And I wasn't the one who told her."

"My God, Kurt!" Pamela looked genuinely surprised. "I would never hurt you like that. I've always known how you felt about Jennifer . . . and I would never betray you. You have to believe me, Kurt. I never told anyone! No one knows."

"It doesn't matter how she found out. The fact of the matter is—Jennifer knows."

"I'm sorry. I know how you feel. It hurts. I wish there was something I could do to stop the pain."

"You don't know how I feel!" I was angry that Pam Woods was putting herself in my place by stating that she knew how I felt. "You have it all, Pam. You have money, prestige, this penthouse. You have a limousine and a driver to take you any place you want to go; that is, if you choose to leave this castle in the sky. You have more clothes in your walk-in closets than most women can wear in a lifetime. And I bet you don't even know how much this bottle of wine costs! You're trying so hard to be an ordinary person that you've become totally lost in your own private world. Nothing touches you up here. Hell! Everything is so easy for you. Oh sure . . . you cook when the spirit moves you; you clean part of the daily dust off the furniture; and you take care of your daughter. Big shit! You haven't a clue what living is all about. You don't know what's going on out there because you're up here in this pompous high-rise hiding from the rest of the world, so don't tell me you know how I feel!"

Pamela was too stunned to speak.

When I looked at her, I suddenly realized that I had hurt her with my harsh words. Pamela's eyes misted with tears that threatened to spill over. She stared quietly at her wineglass as she twirled it slowly between her fingertips. "I'm sorry, Pam. Christ! I didn't mean to be such an ass. You've been wonderful, and I really appreciate everything you've done for me. Please forgive me. I honestly didn't mean to say those awful things."

Her eyes did not meet my gaze. "Your apology is accepted."

"It's just that I haven't felt whole for such a long time. I don't know what I'm doing anymore. Not only am I lost, but I haven't the vaguest idea what I want to do, or who I want to be." I felt the bottled tears I had been holding back for so long begin to fill my eyes. I laid my head on the table and covered myself with my hands. The sobs came in torrents. My body wracked with each breath. It was not until I felt Pamela cradling me in her arms that I tried to control my own weeping. I was a man, not some babbling fool who had to release his frustration with tears. Where was my pride? I felt like such a child. I clung to Pam, letting out my pent-up pain—all the emotions screaming for escape. This was the second time I had collapsed in her arms and searched for comfort in her embrace.

Finally, I regained some semblance of control. I sat up in my chair. For several moments, Pamela remained kneeling on the floor next to me. Quietly, she watched me. I felt like such a fool. I was embarrassed. "I always seem to be at my worst around you, Pam. You're so easy to talk to, and I, unfortunately, seem to fall apart when I express things to you that I can't say to anyone else. Jesus! You must think I'm a sniveling idiot."

"I don't think any such thing, Kurt. You're a very strong and proud man." She reached over encircling my hand with hers and gently squeezed my fingers.

"I don't feel strong or proud right now. And I haven't for quite some time."

"Well, you are . . . even if you don't know it. You have so much to offer. Remember when we were in school, and you felt as if tomorrow always held something new and exciting? You were constantly striving to be the best you could be. You wouldn't settle for anything less. You were motivated and determined and wonderfully idealistic."

"That was a lifetime ago, Pam."

"So what if it was." Pam's voice was stern and strong. "Okay . . . you had a couple of bad breaks. I'll admit that. Are you going to wallow in it forever? Are you going to waste the rest of your life? I never thought of you as a quitter."

"You really know how to whip a guy when he's down, don't you?"

"Stop it! Stop feeling sorry for yourself. Remember the adage: Today's the first day of the rest of your life? Plant that thought in your mind. Forget about yesterday; think about today and tomorrow for a change. You can't live in your past; and you can't change it either. Spend some time thinking about your future."

"I don't know what I am qualified to do."

"That doesn't mean you shouldn't try."

"I suppose you're right."

"I tell you what, Kurt. There's a job opening up in my father's company."

"I don't want you lining up a job for me!" I was getting irritated with what seemed to be charity on Pam's part.

"I'm not going to get the job for you, Kurt. I know my father, and he won't listen to me when it comes to his business. What I can do is get you the interview. You will have to sell yourself to my father."

"Sounds fair enough."

Part III

The Awakening Years

1

Laura

GENE STRADDLED ME ON THE BED AND DROVE HIMSELF INTO ME WITH
steady continuous thrusts that made me climb up the mountain of pleasure.
I closed my eyes and concentrated all my efforts on reaching the peak as he
repeatedly pumped his organ into me. I prayed for the ultimate release. He
used his hands to prop himself up on my chest, which gave him the leverage he needed to work his magic, but he wasn't succeeding. Over and over
again, I arched my hips upward to join my body to his as I hoped to capi-
talize on the full effect of each movement. Unfortunately, when he reached
orgasm, I was not even close to feeling the beauty of grasping the summit.
Once again, I was disappointed and unfulfilled.

It wasn't the first time that our intimate act did not result in mutual fulfillment. In fact, I hadn't had an orgasm in three years . . . not since I slept
with Larry Jenkins. Each time Gene came near me, I begged him to make love
to me in hopes that he could take me over the edge of oblivion like he had
done so many times in the past, but every attempt was futile. I kept hanging
on to the fantasy that eventually the ecstasy would return. I knew I was com-
promising myself for a cheap thrill, but I couldn't let go. I wasn't able to leave
because I kept hoping and praying that next time I might find release again.

Gene collapsed onto my body and covered me with his weight and his sweat.

I closed my eyes blocking out the fact that I was here with him—sharing a bed with a man who didn't love me. Gene used me. I knew it . . . he knew it. Hell! Everybody knew it. No matter how hard I tried, I couldn't break away from Gene. It was as if I were addicted to him—like a junkie on heroin. I needed him. And I kept hoping that, given time, Gene would eventually develop deep feelings for me. But he had made up the rules from the beginning, and it was too late in the game to change them now.

Gene wasn't the only man to use me. Larry Jenkins used me too. Only with Larry, I felt even more ashamed. What Gene and I shared—what Larry and I shared—it was really both the same. Neither union could even remotely be described as making love. We didn't make love. We had what I was beginning to realize was raw sex. There was no love involved—just animalistic, mechanical lust.

"Oh, baby . . . " Gene interrupted my private thoughts. "I sure have taught you well. You are definitely the queen lay of my life."

He lifted his head off my body and kissed the side of my face. I tried to appear happy and pleased, but it was so difficult to return that reaction when I felt none of those emotions. I watched as Gene pulled out a joint from the chest next to his bed. He put it to his lips and lit the end. After taking several tokes, he handed it to me. I inhaled the smoke, leaving it in my lungs for several seconds. I hoped that the artificial high would replace the one I had unsuccessfully been searching for with Gene. I took another hit, sat back, closed my eyes, and waited for the numbing effects. I began to relax. That was better. Thank God for marijuana. Somehow the hits off the pot made it all fuzzy—not quite as humiliating or depressing—at least for a little while. Ever since Jennifer went to West Virginia, I'd been so lonely. Gene was hardly the suitable replacement for a friend like Jennifer. And Larry Jenkins didn't even deserve a mention in the same sentence as my old roommate.

Unfortunately, the marijuana wasn't helping. I still felt down. Where the hell was my high? I should have started feeling it by now, but I was only becoming more depressed.

"I mean it, babe, you are capable of fucking the eyeballs right out of my sockets. You're dynamite." When he received no response from me, he stood up and slapped me on the bottom before continuing. "Okay, sexy! Let's get that gorgeous ass of yours out of bed. I have dinner reservations for eight. It'll take us forty-five minutes to get there. Let's get a move on it."

I pulled the sheet over my body and glanced out the window. The sun hadn't even set yet. There had been a time when I would have been too embarrassed to sleep with a man in broad daylight and too shy to undress when I could be seen. Times had changed.

"I don't think I'll go tonight, Gene." As I gazed out the window, I wondered what possessed me to make that statement. "I'm not really in the mood. I wouldn't be very good company. I think I'll just drive home and spend a relaxing evening in front of the TV"

"Hey, doll, what's up? You know I like to take you places." He grinned in a teasing manner. "I don't want you to think I'm just after that fabulous body of yours. I like taking you out . . . showing you off."

I threw the covers aside and started picking up the clothes that had been haphazardly scattered around the room. "I'm not a whore, Gene. You don't have to spend money on me." I tried not to raise my voice so much as a notch from my normal manner of speaking. "I'm not some poor, stupid bitch who feels like you have to take me some place as payment for services rendered." I wasn't able to control my anger. The last few words were spoken in a hostile manner. I yanked my stockings up my legs. Then I shifted my body until the dress slipped over my head. I tied the sash of my new, rather expensive dress that I'd bought on my last trip to New York. It was an original; until recently, I'd never owned an original. Now my closet was jammed with brand-new clothes. Looking down at the hemline, I decided that I no longer liked the outfit; in fact, I suddenly discovered that I hated it. I fumbled through my purse and tossed things around as I tried to find my hairbrush.

"Damn!" Finally, I found it and ran it several times through my hair, before throwing it back into my purse again.

"Jesus! You sure have a hair out of place on your ass tonight." Gene started moving toward me, grinning and wiggling his hips as if he were trying to appear irresistible. "Come on, babe, we'll have fun. I'll take you out to dinner, maybe even a little dancing afterward. We haven't done that in months. What do you say? We'll paint the town . . . have a few laughs."

"I'm too tired . . . maybe some other time." It was a feeble excuse, but it was the only one I wanted to offer. Not caring what he thought about my statement, I turned to leave. "See ya later." I shut the door behind me.

I drove home in my car. It had become a habit to drive over to Gene's home—leave my car in his driveway, spend the night with him, and in the morning I had my own transportation to either get to work or return home without infringing on his schedule. I decided to use the George Washington Parkway along the Potomac River instead of driving through the subdivisions. Because of the damage Hurricane David had done earlier in the month, the Parkway was not as beautiful as usual for this time of year. Many trees were still down and branches cluttered the rolling grass and destroyed the flowerbeds. It was not quite time for the leaves to change color, but in a few weeks the road would be lined with yellows, oranges, and reds. By then, the damage would be cleared and forgotten, leaving a breathtaking sight. Ever since I could remember, The Parkway's beauty had a tranquilizing effect on me; unfortunately, tonight it wasn't any help at all. I felt strung out, beat, and on top of it all, I had a headache. I couldn't wait to get back to my apartment and take a few aspirin.

I pulled my car into the parking lot of my building and sat quietly for a moment as I let my body relax and my mind wander. I wished Jennifer were upstairs waiting for me. I missed her. It seemed so long since the two of us sat on that old tattered couch together. I missed the old days. Sometimes I wished I hadn't sold that broken-down couch; it was like selling memories. But I couldn't keep it. It didn't match all the new furniture I'd bought.

Jennifer wasn't getting much better. She had been in and out of that

West Virginia sanitarium for the last two years. It was great when she was home, but it never seemed to last for more than a month or two before the doctors sent her back. She was so weak. Dr. Lottman said that Jennifer's illness was more than a physical one. He said that she was extremely depressed, and the only time her spirits lifted was when I came for my weekly visits. The doctors were anxious about her disposition. They said that if Jennifer didn't get the right mental attitude, she might never be able to heal physically. I gave my old friend lecture after lecture saying that her doctors insisted she needed to help herself as much as she could before medicine or therapy could work. Jennifer only waved her hand at me and told me not to worry.

I was concerned for Jennifer. I worried about Kurt; his only contact with me was a Christmas card sent from New York City last year. And I was disillusioned about Gene, but the problem that really nagged at me was my dilemma with Larry Jenkins.

After the initial afternoon motel experience with Larry, which paid the price for my first promotion, Larry still pursued me with as much tenacity as before I agreed to sleep with him. I knew I prostituted my body for an increase in salary and a more challenging job, and I hated myself for it. In the last three years, I had received two promotions and four raises in salary. I made more money than I knew what to do with. In addition, several times a month, Larry left a hundred dollar bill by the bed in our motel room. I detested him for doing it. I felt as if his money was an added slap in the face, but after I rejected it several times, he started leaving it on my desk in the office; that humiliation was far worse than accepting it in the privacy of our room. I never spent Larry's money; instead, I put it in the bank and pretended I didn't know from where it came. I never looked at the bank statements, but I knew it had accumulated to quite a tidy sum.

The irony of it all was that I really liked my job. It was interesting, constructive, demanding, creative, and I was good at it. I enjoyed the PR work and the communications, but the most exciting aspect was the travel. In the last several years, I went to Chicago dozens of times for conferences; I flew to New York more times than I could count; I ate dinner in San Francisco; I went to Hollywood; I spent a few weekends in Boston; I flew on the Concord to London and Paris occasionally; and I spent many a cold winter's day on a sunny Miami beach. I met actors, politicians, and newspaper tycoons. It was never dull.

I even ran into Jack Briskin in Florida a year ago. Within a matter of hours, we started an affair. It lasted two and a half months as I traveled back and forth on business. For a brief moment, we reached into our pasts hoping to block out our present. At first, it was nice to be with an old college friend, but then the reality settled in. One day, after making love, it simply ended, as quickly as it started. I said that I felt sorry for him because he allowed himself to be drawn into the establishment. I accused him of ignoring all the dreams he had spoken so longingly about when we were at Elon. He had cut his hair, married his live-in girlfriend, purchased a coat and tie, labored at a nine-to-five job, and tossed away all those ideals he clung to as a student. When I finished with my critical oration, he calmly responded regarding his disappointment in me. He complained that I had allowed myself to be tarnished by the evils of the world that he had always hoped would never corrupt me. At the time, I laughed in his face and told him that I had never been happier in my life. But secretly, I wondered if there wasn't some truth to his words.

Shortly after the affair with Jack ended, I saw a potential pattern develop at work that frightened me. I traveled to New York several times during the spring to help Larry with a client who was backing a new Broadway play. On this particular occasion, Larry sent me on my own to deliver a contract. He asked me to stay overnight if necessary until all parties signed it. The principal client invited me to an opening. The problem arose following the cast party when the client brought me back to my hotel room and implied that I owed him something. I acted as naive as possible and politely ignored every advance he made. When I return to D.C., I confronted Larry, angrier than I'd ever been in my life. Finally, Larry confessed that he had given the client permission to sleep with me. I almost killed Larry that night. I threw a motel lamp at his skull and fortunately, or unfortunately, depending upon how a person looked at it, I missed him by only inches.

That night, I walked out on Larry Jenkins. He called me later in the evening to tell me that he promised never to put me in that position again. Larry jokingly said that he didn't think I would mind. I hung up the phone before he was able to speak again. He immediately dialed my number a second time. After a long conversation, Larry managed to smooth my ruffled feathers. I was thankful that the episode was not repeated. And, of course, there were two dozen red roses on my desk the following morning. No card. No explanation. But I knew who sent them. Immediately, I took the bouquet to the ladies room two floors below our office and dumped them in the trash. I would never accept roses from Larry Jenkins.

I wondered if Larry's wife was aware of the relationship between her husband and me. I wondered if she cared. In the beginning, I worried about the other employees in the office and their opinions of me; but I had long since put those fears to rest. I learned years ago that the office was loaded with "business mixed with pleasure" relationships. Many of the younger secretaries were locked into affairs. I felt compassion for those girls who truly believed they were in love. Sadly, they were in dead-end relationships, and they didn't realize it yet.

I never discussed my situation with any of the other girls. I realized they knew that I was sleeping with Larry, but I couldn't bring myself to talk about it. I never was the type of person to sit down and chat about the things going on in my mind . . . only with Jennifer. A few of the girls attempted to draw me into their conversations by admitting to their own affairs, but I still remained stubbornly silent. Several times, they invited me to lunch or to parties, but I always declined. Eventually, they stopped trying to be friendly. I was sure they all considered me to be a dreadful snob—and perhaps I was—but I could think of no other way to handle the situation. After a while, I no longer even cared. I didn't give a damn anymore. I had no friends; I didn't even have any acquaintances. I didn't encourage prospective male suitors; and I stopped going to the bars searching for someone I no longer believed existed. I became a solitary person. I did my job, earned my paycheck—which was double what most girls my age made—and I had my beautifully decorated apartment and gorgeous clothes. In addition, I had Gene and Larry who represented nothing but hopes and stabs at sexual fulfillment. I had my pot and my booze, which helped cover up all the unpleasantness that surrounded me, and I had my weekly visits with Jennifer. Hell! It wasn't so bad. All things considered . . . didn't I have more than most people? I laughed pathetically to myself and shrugged.

I grabbed my purse and overnight bag on the car seat next to me. After giving the door a good shove, it flew open. What I needed was a drink and a cigarette. I desperately wanted to get into my comfortable, terry cloth robe, turn on "Happy Days," smoke a joint, and relax. I wanted to make my mind go blank. I walked slowly toward the building. After all, what was the hurry?

As I entered the apartment, the phone began to ring. Dropping my bags, I picked up the receiver. "Hello."

"Lori? Is that you?"

"Yeah . . . who's this?"

"Tom . . . Tom Ladley."

"Tommy! Are you kidding? Really?" Never in my wildest imagination did I expect to hear his voice on the other end of the phone. "My God! It's been years."

"Nine . . . nine years to be exact. " He sounded distant for a moment and then masked it all by laughing softly. "I am in town for our tenth year high school reunion, but you weren't there."

"I didn't feel like going. Was it a good time?"

"Yeah! It was fun. Nice to see some familiar faces, but I really was hoping to see you."

"I got the invitation. Unfortunately, I had other plans," I lied. Actually, I didn't have any desire to go back to my high school years. Everything was so simple then, so easy. That was a lifetime ago.

"I'm only going to be in town for a few more days. Any chance we can get together . . . maybe for dinner or drinks?"

"Oh, Tommy, that would be great. I'd love it." The idea was uplifting. "How about tonight? Right now." I gave him directions to my apartment.

Tom Ladley! I hadn't thought about him in a long time. Tommy! Sweet, gentle Tommy. He was so warm and kind. It would be good to see him again even after so much water had gone under the bridge. I wondered if he'd changed and how he looked. We were just kids—kissing our teens good-bye—the last time I saw him.

I raced around the apartment and straightened up the clutter. I put ice in the bucket, fluffed up the couch pillows, and glanced in the mirror to see if I needed to redo my face. I touched my cheeks with blush and applied fresh lipstick before brushing my hair hurriedly. I was barely finished when there was a knock at the door. With more exuberance than I intended to express, I flung it open. Laughing joyfully, I threw myself in his arms and felt warmed by his gentle response. I kissed him on both cheeks and then placed a quick peck on his lips. Tommy looked fantastic. Perhaps a few extra pounds, a touch of premature gray, a mustache, which made him appear rather sagacious, but he was still the same Tommy I knew so well. We laughed in unison as I guided him into my apartment. I wasn't sure what to say and was grateful when he began the conversation.

"You look wonderful, Lori." He stepped back for a moment and appraised my full length in a very gentlemanly manner. "You really do look marvelous."

"Thank you, Tommy." I grinned a bit more confidently than I actually felt. "You look terrific too." I hugged him again before continuing. "Do you really want to go out? Why don't we just stay here?"

"Either way is fine . . . makes no difference." I steered him into the room and closed the door. "Let's stay here, then. I'll make you a cocktail. What would you like? I have scotch, bourbon, whiskey, gin, or vodka. Name your poison. I even have some pot in the other room if you're interested in a few hits."

"A beer's fine." He glanced over at my bar. The pleasant smile faded as a puzzled expression covered his face. "Looks like you really booze it up, Lori. When I knew you, you didn't drink at all."

"Well . . . shit. Times change, I guess." I laughed nervously as I handed him a beer and then proceeded to make a martini for myself. I felt a bit more uncomfortable than I had expected under his scrutinizing stare, so I downed my first drink and made myself a second. The vodka wasn't relaxing me so I rolled a joint, lit it, and offered a hit to Tommy. He declined. I became embarrassed by his constant appraisal of me as I puffed on the jay. Before I took a third hit, I put it out. Trying to be as nonchalant as possible, I waved the lingering smoke away.

"This is really a nice place you have here. You've decorated it beautifully." Tommy slowly walked around the room and touched different objects before returning to his seat and relaxing on the brand-new couch I had purchased from Sloan's. There was barely a piece of furniture left from my first apartment. I'd given it away or sold it. As my salary had increased, I'd bought wall-to-wall carpeting, contemporary matching furniture with straight lines, and a lot of chrome and glass. I'd even purchased custom-made curtains. I was surrounded by expensive, attractive possessions.

"I didn't know teachers made so much money," Tommy said hesitantly.

I cringed slightly. "I'm not teaching. There weren't any jobs available when I graduated so I took a position with a law firm in D.C. I've been promoted several times."

"Must be one hell of a good job." Again, there was that look of surprise on his face as his eyes wandered over the acquired luxuries. "Must pay well too." He kept staring at me.

"I manage."

"Why didn't you hold out for a teaching job? I know it was what you always wanted to do." He leaned back against the sofa as he began to relax.

"Well, Christ, Tommy," I answered as I pushed my hair back behind my shoulders and reached for a cigarette. "A girl's gotta eat you know. I waited around for as long as I could until I didn't have any money left, and then I settled for the best I could get."

"Yeah, I remember. In '73, it was hard finding a teaching job."

"Did you get one?" I asked.

"Yes. I went to Tennessee. It was a tough row to hoe, but I finally was hired by a small private school in Nashville. The salary was pitiful, but at least I was teaching. I'm in Bedford, Virginia, now teaching ninth grade history. The salary's still not that great, but I love it."

"That's fantastic, Tommy."

"I realize it was tough after we graduated, Lori, but it's not so bad out there now. There are jobs." He paused before sarcastically adding, "Or aren't you willing to take a cut in pay now that you have all these fine things surrounding you?"

"That's not fair! I work hard at my job. I've put a lot of energy and time into it, and I'm good at what I do." I was defending myself. Tommy kept looking at me as if he was waiting for me to continue pleading my case. I was on edge. I didn't want to talk about myself. I didn't even want to think about myself. I took a long drag off the cigarette and exhaled the smoke. Laughing nervously, I continued, "Let's not talk about me, Tommy. Tell me what you're doing."

He started to speak. I listened. He told me how he made his career move from Tennessee back to Virginia. I took in every word as if his sentences had a tranquilizing effect on me. His voice was soothing. If I didn't have to talk— if I only had to listen—then I was sure I could relax. I continued smoking cigarette after cigarette as he rattled on about the years between our last meeting. I watched him in silence and wondered why I felt so nervous around a person who, at one point in my life, was the only individual who gave me security? There was a pause in his conversation. Instead of speaking, I stood up and fixed myself a third drink. Finally, the martinis and the hits of pot began to calm my frazzled nerves.

"That sounds interesting. You've really come a long way, haven't you, Tom? I'm glad for you." I lit still another cigarette and noticed that he finished his bottle. "Can I get you another beer?"

"Please."

I walked to the refrigerator and back in silence. As I handed him the Budweiser, I waited a moment longer than necessary, hoping that he might encourage me to sit next to him. I didn't want to return to my original seat halfway across the room. Secretly, I wanted Tommy to pull me down next to him, hold me with warm arms, make love to me with tenderness, and speak ardent words that he had once said so sweetly all those years ago. I wanted to snuggle inside a cocoon with him and be protected. I wanted my old Tommy back—the one who surrounded me with a safe and secure feeling— the Tommy of my youth.

When he didn't encourage me, I turned around and stumbled slightly over my own feet before taking the necessary steps back to my original seat. I blinked my eyes several times. I felt a little dizzy. "I suppose you don't love me anymore." What possessed me to say that? I was embarrassingly blunt; in fact, I must have appeared pompous. I didn't mean to sound so arrogant, but the liquor and pot dulled my senses, and my words sounded cocky and conceited instead of a plea for comfort.

"No, Lori. Finally, I can honestly say that I don't love you anymore."

He watched me with a cold, apathetic gaze that made me immediately shiver. My lower lip began to twitch, and I bit down on it hoping Tommy wouldn't notice. Trying to hide my disappointment, I shrugged as if I didn't care about his response. "Damn! What a pity." Hoping to ease the tension, I laughed, but I stopped when I noticed Tommy was not amused.

"It took a long time for me to get over you, Lori. I thought I never would. I loved you more than anything in this world." He stated his words firmly, but without raising his voice. "Fortunately, I did get over you. I never would have believed it a few years ago, but I actually did stop loving you." He took a long pull off his beer, drained the bottle, and then placed it on the table. "I'm thinking about getting married. She's a nice girl . . . smart too. She told me she wouldn't give me an answer until I was sure I'd gotten rid of old ghosts. I came here tonight in order to be absolutely positive that you no longer haunt me."

"So, don't keep me in suspense. What's the verdict?" I felt my hands trembling so I gripped the arms of the chair. I didn't want to let Tommy see how disoriented I was.

He stared into my eyes for a long time. It seemed like an eternity before he answered the question. "There are no more ghosts. I'm positive."

"Well, shit!" I muttered as I extinguished another cigarette into an already overflowing ashtray. "It's no big deal. I was just curious. After all, a girl can ask, can't she?" Why was I acting so callous when I really wanted to be feminine and refined? I would have given anything if Tommy took the steps between us and held me in his arms, carried me off into the bedroom, and made love to me. I wanted to feel the security we had once shared. I stood up and walked toward him. I reeled slightly. I'd had too much to drink. Before I crossed the room, Tommy stood up and reached for his coat. I didn't want him to leave. I didn't want to be alone.

"Don't go, Tommy."

"It's time. I think we've said everything we can say to each other."

"Please . . . don't go." My head felt fuzzy, and my words were slurred. I tried to keep the conversation light by laughing; unfortunately, I could think of nothing witty to say. When I spoke again, there was a pleading quality to my voice. "You wouldn't consider making love to me, would you? I don't mean to be so forward, but I'd do anything to keep you here." To my horror, my voice quivered as I spoke. "I don't want to be alone." I diverted my eyes—too afraid that he'd see the burning tears welling up in them.

It felt like an eternity passed before Tommy spoke, "You're so different, Lori. You look basically the same—still beautiful, very beautiful—but you're so different. You're hard and callous. You smoke and drink. You use foul language that I never thought I'd hear from your lips. You get high off pot. You probably even sleep around. I think the thing that surprises me the most is your thirst for material possessions. You never cared about those things before. When I knew you, I bet your entire wardrobe didn't cost as much as the dress you have on now. And look at this place! It looks like a store showroom, and the ambience is just as cold and fake. You've turned into a real genuine sorority bitch, haven't you, Lori?" He sounded detached.

I couldn't bring my eyes to meet his gaze. I knew how he felt about cliques and elite organizations. I also knew that Tommy couldn't have said a more negative or demeaning statement. In his opinion, I could get no lower. I hung my head and stared at my thumb as it clipped repeatedly against the nail of my index finger.

"I barely recognize you, Lori. What happened to that pretty, little, innocent girl I loved so much? She certainly isn't in this room. God! I'm glad you can't hurt me anymore." He started buttoning his jacket. "By the way, thank you for your kind offer . . . " He paused, "but I'm not interested in sex with you—not anymore."

His caustic words were more painful than a slap in the face. I heard a pitiful choking sound coming from the base of my throat, and I struggled with my tears. Tommy stood at the door—hand on the knob—and stared at me for a long time before he began to speak again. "I don't know what's happened to you, Lori. And to be honest, I really don't care. But you better crawl out of the hole you're in before you get buried by it. Thanks for the beer . . . it's been a very enlightening evening."

The door closed quietly behind him. I sat down on the couch in a numb stupor for several minutes before the tears came. I let my head fall into the palms of my hands, and I cried. God! I cried! I wept for all the bastards I had known in my past: Bob Johnson, Steve Shaw, Brad Malone, Gene Saunders, Larry Jenkins. All the rotten men I allowed into my life. Trying to beat their images from my mind, I pounded my fists against my temples. They all looked alike. They were horrible and cruel. And I cried for myself—for what I had done to *me*, and for the foolish way I had gone about searching for something that didn't even exist. What had happened to me? How had I become the way I was today? How could I let all my integrity and principles fly out the window and destroy my self-esteem? Why did I attract men who were users and abusers? Why did I let all the gentle, kind men get away? Tommy had loved me. Rick had loved me too. Even Jack had cared about me in his own special way. They would have given me so much if I only had let them. But no! I had pushed them away in search of something else; ironically, I no longer knew what it was I had been looking for. A horrible image flashed in my mind. I saw myself twenty years from now. Beautiful wardrobe. Hot car.

Nicely furnished apartment. Expensive jewelry. Big savings account. But I was alone. I had no one in my life. I wept until I could cry no more. My body was completely drained of emotion.

I sat up straight trying to find myself again. Yes, I had changed, but it was not too late. I was only twenty-nine. It couldn't be too late! I dried the leftover tears from my eyes.

Some time during the night a part of the old Laura Davis returned. I felt a rebirth growing inside of me. I was not going to allow myself to drown in self-pity and neither was I going to let others' destructive attitudes take me down.

I didn't like myself anymore. That was my first goal! I wanted to like myself again—no matter what the cost. There would be no more Larry Jenkinses in my life. No more Genes who only teased me with false explosions that, when they occurred, only lasted for a fleeting moment. I would no longer degrade myself for a few seconds of hoped-for ecstasy. Jennifer was right. I didn't love Gene. I didn't even like him. In fact, the idea of being with him again made me sick inside. And as for Larry Jenkins . . . if I never saw him again, it would be too soon.

I vowed to start a new life.

2

The next morning—without any previous notice—I called the receptionist at the office and left a brief message: I quit. After I resigned, I walked into the kitchen and started the water boiling in order to make a cup of much-needed coffee. I saw a pack of cigarettes on the counter. Without thinking, I drew one of them out of its container and put it to my lips. Before I even struck the match, I crushed the tobacco in my hands and threw all the remaining sticks in the garbage disposal. I didn't need cigarettes. I didn't even like the taste. I only smoked because it made me feel less nervous among a crowd of people. No! That wasn't true. Cigarettes were just crutches: like booze and pot. I hid behind them. When I was unhappy, I drank; when I was nervous, I smoked; when I was disappointed, I got high; when I was tired, I drank; when I was bored, I smoked; when I was angry, I reached for a bottle; when

I was lonely, I lit up a joint. What had happened to me? I lived in a vicious circle of crutches. It seemed as if I couldn't get through an entire day without the use of one of them.

Carrying a plastic trash bag, I walked into the living room and placed each bottle of liquor—one by one—into it. Seventeen bottles of booze. Five different types! Fifteen different brands! Who in God's name needed seventeen bottles of alcohol? I drank too much. It seemed as if I drank all the time. When I wasn't working, sleeping, or screwing around with men I didn't care about, I was sipping on martinis, or gin and tonics, or scotch on the rocks, or bourbon and water. Tommy was right. I had changed. He didn't like the new me. He wasn't the only one. I didn't like the new me, either. However, I still had the power to change all that. I knew somewhere inside me, there was still the old Laura Davis struggling to get back out again. I was going to find her and bring her back to life.

All the bottles clanged and jingled as I lugged them down to the Dumpster outside the apartment building. The bag was too heavy to heave over the top; instead, I took each bottle—one at a time—and pitched it into the gigantic bin. I hummed quietly to myself as I listened to the bottles shatter on impact. I knew that my actions were strictly symbolic, but it actually felt as if each crashing of glass was easing a little more of the tension inside of me. When the last one was destroyed, I slapped my hands together and climbed back up the stairs to get a much-needed cup of coffee. I chuckled as I realized that I'd just thrown away well over $200 worth of near-empty, half-empty and completely full bottles of liquor. Five years ago, $200 would have seemed like a fortune. Now it didn't seem valuable at all—not because I had an overabundance of it—but because it was simply no longer important. For the last few years, it seemed that money had become an obsession with me. I worked for it. I pushed for it. I saved it. I lay on my back for it. I bought fancy things with it. And I even flaunted it. But now I knew that money wasn't what I wanted. Of course, I needed it. Everyone needed money. But I no longer had the insatiable craving to get more and more and more. I'd finally put money into perspective.

I sat down and relaxed with the morning paper scanning the classified ads. There was enough cash in my savings account to get through three or four months without any income. With a little luck, by that time, I'd have a new job and a new life. I circled the openings which required my qualifications. There were fifteen all together. That was a start. Typists, receptionists, secretaries, legal assistant—I could do any of those jobs.

I tossed the newspaper aside. That wasn't what I really wanted. That wasn't even what I was qualified to do. I was trained to be a teacher. It had been my dream, and there was no reason why I couldn't pursue that goal again. If there were no positions available, I would ask to be a substitute. Being a substitute didn't pay much; and it meant I wouldn't have a classroom of my own, but at least it was a foot in the door.

I thumbed through the telephone book and jotted down the number for the Fairfax County Public School System. After calling, I was informed that I could substitute throughout the county as soon as my paperwork was finished, and I could also apply for a permanent position. I set up a time for an interview. I put the receiver back into its cradle and smiled to myself. I was going to make my dream come true. I was no longer some little kid who was still wet behind the ears. I had learned how to fight in order to get what I wanted, and I wasn't going to give up as easily as I had the first time around. I planned to enroll in a couple of night classes to update my certification. The knowledge was all there; I just had to reclaim it and put it all to use.

I made an egg and cheese sandwich. As I put it to my lips to take the first bite, the phone rang interrupting my solitude.

"Hello."

"Lori? What the hell's gotten into you?" It was Gene's voice. He sounded perplexed and annoyed. "I just heard that you quit your job without giving notice. What are you . . . some kind of fool?"

"Yes. That's what I was, Gene . . . some kind of fool," I answered in a calm, steady tone. "But not anymore."

"Lori . . . for Christ's sake . . . that was a golden job you just kissed good-bye. I thought you liked the challenge and wanted the potential to get even higher in the firm."

"I thought I did too." I spoke with a new sense of awareness. It felt good to say the words instead of just think them as I had been doing since Tommy slammed the door on me the night before. "But I don't want that, Gene. I don't want any of it."

"Well, what the hell are you going to do, then . . . starve?" He was being sarcastic.

"I'm going to give teaching a second chance."

"Why do you want to be an old school marm? That would be a waste of your talents."

"Quite the contrary, Gene. It would be using my full potential. I don't intend to sell myself short any longer for something that isn't even what I want."

"How 'bout if I come over for lunch and try to talk some sense back into that crazy mixed-up head of yours." He was cajoling me by using a deep throaty voice to try and arouse what he considered to be a mutual attraction between us. "We can lounge around in bed for the rest of the afternoon and sort out whatever it is that seems to be bothering you. Did Larry push you too far? Is that the problem? Perhaps, he'll ease up a little bit if you stand your ground and demand only a periodic arrangement between the two of you. Jenkins is a reasonable man. He'll accept new terms. Lori, you don't seem to understand. You're an asset to him . . . and not just in bed. He needs you. You can't give up a job like that or the opportunities it can bring. I know sex was never as good with Larry as it is between us, but that shouldn't matter. I mean, Christ, Lori! You can't give up a goal just because there's a few obstacles in the way."

"Goal?" I muttered questioningly. "You don't understand . . . all my goals got confused. Somewhere in the last few years, I lost track of what my real goals are." I ignored the rest of Gene's conversation knowing that if I discussed it with him, I'd only become angry. Besides, I didn't owe Gene Saunders an explanation, and I didn't want to say things that would sound trashy and offensive. What would be the purpose? I had no desire to rehash my thoughts with him . . . I just wanted to forget all those awful things I did.

"I'll leave the office now. I'll be there in thirty minutes."

"I don't want you to come over, Gene."

"Well, then . . . how about tonight. I'll buy a couple of steaks and a bottle of wine. I'll make dinner for you. Afterward, we can play around a little bit. We can talk and put all this into prospective."

"No, Gene. I don't want you to come for lunch. I don't want you to come for dinner either. In fact, I don't want you to come at all. It's over. It's been over for a long time. In all honesty, it should have ended years ago when I could have kept a few fond memories. But I wasn't willing to let go. I kept trying to convince myself that you cared about me, and that there was more to our relationship than there actually was."

"Lori! What the hell are you talking about? We make beautiful music together. I'm good for you. You're good for me. We care about each other."

"We don't care about each other, Gene. There's never been any kind of emotional feeling between us. We had sex—and we had a few good times, but that was all." I pressed on with my little oration before I lost the courage to say the things that were foremost in my mind. "We played the game. We used *your* rules—no commitment, no strings, no love, no past, and no future. You called all the shots, Gene, and I followed. We played the game *your* way! But now the game is over."

"But Lori! I do care about you. I mean it wasn't just sex and good times. I thought we had a pretty good thing going for us. I can't believe you don't care about me. I mean . . . wasn't it good for you?"

"You don't care about me, Gene. Your pride's been hurt. That's all. But let's face it—you don't give a damn. I've known for years that I'm not the only woman in your life. You're out for a good time. And because of your past, I really can't blame you. But it's not what I want anymore. I want more than just a good time." I paused for a second or two in order to keep my voice steady. "There was a time, Gene, when I thought I'd fallen in love with you. I would have given anything for some kind of returned emotion, but it was never there. It hurt so much when I realized you didn't love me . . . but, thankfully, I don't care anymore. You used me . . . and in a way—if I'm really honest with myself—I suppose I used you too."

"Lori . . . let me come over right now. We'll talk . . . we'll straighten out this mess."

"No. Let it go, Gene. Let it go. It's over. There is no use trying to hold on to something that isn't worth a second thought."

"What the hell happened to make you change your mind?" He sounded surprised. "You changed overnight. I can't believe that you want to stop a beautiful thing like what we have shared."

"What we shared was not beautiful, Gene. It was convenient. And mostly, it was convenient for you. As for what happened . . . I finally realize what I have done to myself, and I don't need you dragging me down anymore."

"Wait a minute, Lori."

"Good-bye, Gene. There's nothing left to say." I hung up the phone.

The last remaining string holding me to the past I wanted to forget was finally broken. The job was gone; there would be no more Larry Jenkinses in my life; I dumped the booze, the pot, and the tobacco; and now even Gene was nothing more than a bad dream I could put out of my mind. I was free to start living again.

3

My interview went well. I was told that there was a chance that I might be able to fill a position in 1980 when the school year was halfway through. I held on to that hope and continued my routine of taking any substitute job offered within an hour's drive of my apartment. Five out of the next seven school days I spent substituting in various classrooms. One day, I did nothing but baby-sit a group of first graders; for three of the days, I felt in control of a classroom full of sixth graders; the fifth day, I instructed a gym full of boys in P.E. Each was a new experience in itself, but all were well worth the time and effort.

On the weekends, I spent at least one day visiting Jennifer in West

Virginia. I missed her so much. It seemed like an eternity since the last time she was home. She was always delighted to see me. The truth of the matter was—in spite of the long drive—I, too, enjoyed the few hours we shared. Jennifer was still the only person with whom I felt comfortable.

Saturday, I drove up earlier than usual in time to have lunch with Jennifer. We sat out on the patio and enjoyed the beautiful fall weather. There is nothing more splendid than watching the mountains change their complexion as each of the rolling hills was covered with patches of brilliant autumn colors. I loved the view.

"Despite the fact that I give all the nurses hell and I act like a bitch, I really am becoming rather fond of this place." Jennifer interrupted our silent thoughts as she sipped on her tea. "If you were here, Lori, it would be perfect . . . and I'd never want to leave."

"It certainly wouldn't be hard to lose myself in a wonderland like this," I answered as I, too, scanned the beauty around us. "When I close my eyes and listen, I can actually hear all the different animals, the leaves falling to the ground, and the wind whispering through the tree branches. It's almost as if there isn't a problem in the world. So tranquil . . . so relaxing." I must have sounded very plaintive because Jennifer immediately clued into my mood.

She reached for my hand, holding it for a moment before asking, "Is everything all right with you, Lori?"

"You'll be glad to know, Jennifer, that I told Gene to go fly a kite." A nervous laugh slipped from my lips.

"So you finally dumped good ol' Gene," Jennifer grinned in an amused manner. "That's the best news I've heard all year."

"Yeah." I smiled too. It felt good. "It was a lot easier than I thought. For the longest time, I didn't think I'd ever be able to let him go, but I just woke up one day and Gene didn't matter to me anymore. Just like that." I snapped my fingers. "I thought I was addicted to him, like a drug or something. He seemed like such a vital part of my life, but he wasn't. He wasn't important at all."

"Now all you have to do is give Larry Jenkins a good shove."

"I have some more news." I paused. "I quit my job."

"You're kidding." Jennifer seemed genuinely shocked.

"I called up the office . . . didn't even talk to Larry . . . I just told the first person who answered to give him the message."

"Lori, I know you don't want to hear this, but you should take him to court. What he did was wrong."

"Sure, Jennifer. Take a lawyer to court on formal charges! What kind of a chance do you think I'd have against a battery of lawyers who are protecting the firm's reputation?"

"You could try."

"No. I can't . . . I have to let go of it. As angry as I am . . . as much as I hate him . . . and hate what he did to me . . . I have to put it behind me." Tears welled up in my eyes. "I'm not a crusader, Jen. I can't change the way things are. Maybe someday a woman will come along and knock down a man like Larry Jenkins. And when that happens, everyone will see what's really going on in the business world. Maybe then, the workplace will be better for women. But I'm not that person. Right now, my priority is to save myself. I have to put this behind me, because I'm afraid if I don't . . . I'm going to drown in my guilt."

"I had no idea you were so miserable. Are you sure it wouldn't be more therapeutic to stick it to Larry Jenkins?"

"It wouldn't work, Jen. I accepted his offer. I knew what I was getting into and not only did I go along with it the first time, but I continued for years."

"You still have a case."

"Probably . . . but what about the money I took? And I don't mean the salary raises . . . I deserved those." I stared at Jennifer letting her absorb the full meaning of my words. "Larry gave me several thousand dollars while we were together. I thought in the beginning that it was his way of alleviating his own guilt, but now I realize that it was part of the trap. Do you honestly think that I wouldn't be eaten alive in a courtroom if that little tidbit of news ever got out?"

"I can't believe you're going to let him get away with this."

"I knew what I was doing, Jennifer. I hated it . . . but I knew what I was doing. And if I'm perfectly honest with myself . . . I was just as guilty as he was. He used me, Jennifer . . . but I used him too. I couldn't take Larry to court without dragging myself down with him. No! I want to forget about it . . . put it behind me." I threw my hands up into the air. "Can we change the subject? I don't want to talk about it anymore." A small smile spread across my face. "I want to think about tomorrow . . . and next week . . . next year . . . my future. I'm going to teach, Jen. I have a substituting job, which helps pay some of the bills, and there's a chance that this coming January I'll get my own classroom—full time. The hell with the money, Jen. I'm going to do what I want to do for a change, and if it means dwindling down my savings account . . . I don't care. This feels right; this feels good!"

Jennifer smiled and patted the top of my hand gently. "I'm glad you're not seeing either one of those bastards anymore."

"Once again, you were right. Gene Saunders was exactly what you said he was. Thanks for not rubbing my nose in my mistakes." I paused as I filled my cup with more of the steamy brew and sipped twice before recapping the events of Tom Ladley's visit. I told Jennifer about how wonderful he looked and about what he was doing with his life. I also mentioned that I drank more than I should have and that I made a fool of myself before he walked out on me without so much as a kind word. "When he left, Jennifer, I finally realized that Tom was right on the mark. I had changed. I deserved all those nasty words he said to me. It was a hell of a way to wake up to my own destruction, but I'm thankful to him for helping me finally see the light."

"I suppose you quit smoking, too, or are you just not going to let me sneak anymore cigarettes just because those silly doctors tell me it's not good for my condition." She put an innocent yet sheepish expression on her face as she alternated between glancing at me and at my purse on the table between us.

"Sorry! There are no cigarettes in my purse. I quit. So . . . " I smiled in her direction. "You're out of luck, pal. I can't help you out this time. I'm glad, too, because it always made me feel guilty when I let you have drags off mine." We both laughed.

Jennifer and I sat quietly for a few minutes as we watched other patients and listened to the wonderful sounds that penetrated the air: crickets, birds, rustling leaves, and an occasional footstep or two. "Have you heard from your brother?" Jennifer's question came as such a surprise; she hadn't mentioned Kurt in years.

"No, not in a long time. I got a Christmas card last year. He told me he was taking some night courses, and he was finishing up his degree. He said he was working for Woods Enterprises in their New York branch. But that's all he wrote . . . just the basics . . . nothing personal. I wish he wrote more often. When we were kids, Kurt and I used to talk and laugh and do things together all the time. We were close. But then after the Army . . . well, I suppose he got tired of me calling all the time, checking up on him, acting like a mother hen. He said I was smothering him, and he resented it. I can't blame him." I signed softly to myself. "I miss Kurt. We were more than just brother and sister. What we had was special."

"Don't worry about Kurt. He'll be all right. I'm sure he's just trying to find himself in New York. Things will all work out for the best in the long run."

"Do you want him to come back? I know he would if you just gave him the word." I spoke carefully, knowing that Jennifer was extremely peculiar on the subject of my brother.

"No," she muttered. "No, I didn't mean to give the wrong impression. There could never be anything between Kurt and me. It's just that I know how much you care about him." Jennifer's mind seemed to wander for a moment. She circled the rim of her cup with her index finger. Her brow crinkled into a frown. "Someday . . . someday Kurt will be happy. At least, I hope he will. All I know is that he could never be happy with me."

"Are you sure, Jennifer? I know how much he loves you. When you get better . . . when you get out of this place for good, I'm certain Kurt would still want you back."

"Yes, Lori . . . I'm sure. What I'm not sure of is whether or not I'll ever get out of here. It's been four months since the last time they let me go home. I want to try again. I want to be with you. I get so lonely here."

"We have to trust the doctors, Jennifer. So far, they seem to know what they're doing."

During the afternoon, we played a few hands of gin rummy. I drank coffee, and Jennifer sipped on a concoction that the doctors prescribed for her. We strolled through the gardens. Actually, I did all the walking while Jennifer sat in her wheelchair. We paused long enough in a few areas to pick some of the last remaining button mums. Most of them had been killed by the early frost, but the few that survived made a pretty bouquet. It was a lazy, relaxing afternoon.

Before leaving, I took the opportunity to speak with one of Jennifer's doctors. Dr. Lottman seemed optimistic. Jennifer was improving. She had regained most of her muscle control. Her speech was completely recovered. She could even walk a few steps without help. Jennifer had come a long way. I was grateful that all the signs were pointing in a positive direction. Money was no longer an obstacle. Jennifer's lawyers had gone to court, making her trust fund available to pay the bills. She even had enough left over to start again.

4

Sunday, I went to the public tennis courts to hit a few balls against the backboard and practice my serve. It had been a long time since I'd stepped foot onto a court. I was surprised at the number of people who were already there. Tennis had become very popular. Years ago, when I played regularly, few individuals seemed interested in participating, but now it seemed as if every other person I met owned the latest graphite tennis racket and had at least a half dozen stylish outfits. I felt a little out of place wearing my cutoffs and T-shirt, but I ignored the others and started to practice my forehand on the massive pieces of plywood that were fastened securely against the fence. I repeatedly hit the tennis ball for about fifteen minutes before I noticed that

I had an audience. At first, I only smiled and continued doing my exercises; but after a short time, I became nervous under his scrutinizing stare. As far as I could tell out of the corner of my eye, he appeared to be around my age, dark hair, lean build, and still tanned from the summer months.

I lost my concentration, and much to my embarrassment, my racket completely missed the ball as it leapt by me and traveled several yards away. Before I had a chance to retrieve it, my male spectator picked it up and walked in my direction.

"Hi . . . been watching you." He had a pleasant voice and a warm smile.

"I noticed." I smiled back trying to act friendly even though I didn't particularly want any company at the present time.

"There's a court available. Would you like to play a couple of sets?"

"I'm kind of rusty. I haven't played in years. I won't be able to give you much of a workout," I answered, delighted at the idea of having someone to hit with, but reluctant to accept the offer of a stranger. If there was one thing I'd learned in the last few years it was that most of the time men expected a whole lot more than just friendly conversation. I wasn't ready to become involved with anyone even if it were just on the tennis court.

"You look like you know what you're doing against the backboard. Come on, give me a chance. I can use any kind of workout you can give me."

"All right, I'll give it a try," I grinned, as I noticed for the first time that he was a rather pleasant-looking person. I studied him while he walked to the opposite side of the court. His gregarious smile and warm eyes were very charming. He carried himself with confident strides, and his shoulders were held in a way that made him appear larger than his average height.

We played two sets. I lost both, which was no big surprise. Even though I hadn't been on a court in several seasons, I was pleased that my natural ability was holding strong. I couldn't break his serve, but I managed to hold mine a couple times. I knew that he was going easy on me. It was obvious that if he wanted to, the score would be 6-0 and 6-0. I laughed after the end of the match as I made him admit that he was a lot better than he was displaying.

He chuckled, "I didn't want to be rough on you. After all, you said it was your first time out in a while. Besides," he added, "if I whipped you too badly, you might not want to play with me again." He bent over and picked up his bag, placed the balls in the can, and put his towel into the side pocket. "Would you consider playing with me tomorrow after work? I get home about five thirty. There's still an hour or so of ample light."

I had not intended to give the gentleman the opportunity to form any kind of relationship. But what harm could a little tennis do? One thing was for sure: I could use the exercise, and I definitely was in dire need of the practice. "Okay, I'll meet you here tomorrow at five thirty."

"Sounds good to me." We both walked off the court in silence. He closed the gate behind us. I started heading in the direction of my building, and he went the opposite way. "So long, see you tomorrow."

I took several steps before he called out to me. "Hey, stop . . . wait a minute." I turned around and saw that he was waving me down. "I didn't catch your name."

"Lori . . . Lori Davis."

"I'm Bruce Dailey," he yelled back and waved a second time. "It's nice to meet you, Lori. See you tomorrow."

We played every evening for two weeks, except Wednesday, when it rained. Each time, the two of us met on the court. When the sets were finished, I walked back to my apartment alone. There was not even the slightest suggestion on his part encouraging anymore between us. At first, I was relieved that he didn't expect anything but a friendly game, but as each day passed, I became more interested and curious about him as a person instead of just an opponent.

Bruce didn't have a wedding ring on his finger, but I'd learned from past experience that the absence or presence of a gold band was not necessarily a sign of a single man or a married one. My curiosity was starting to get the best of me, but I didn't even hint at any details about his life . . . neither did he. We simply hit the ball in silence and rescheduled another time to play when the match was over.

There was one thing, however, that I did know about Bruce Dailey. He lived either in my apartment complex or somewhere close by because he never drove up to the court or left in a car. When it rained on Wednesday, neither one of us had the other's telephone number so we couldn't make arrangements to play on another day. When Thursday evening came, instead of staying home, I took the chance that Bruce would be at the court without previously setting up a time. As I approached the gates, I saw him sitting patiently on a bench. Without exchanging a word, we started to play.

The following week, we did the same thing. Each night at five thirty I met him at the gate, and the two of us exchanged volleys. I even took a set off him for the first time. After that, I noticed he no longer patronized me. Bruce was impressed that I could return his most difficult topspinning serve, even if I had to use a flat forehand to get it over the net. Of course, he most definitely wasn't pushing himself to his limit, but there were several points and even a few games that I won all on my own.

When the sun nestled below the tree line, and it became too difficult to see the little yellow ball, Bruce and I quit playing. Instead of our usual quiet and rather formal good-bye, he started a conversation.

"You're pretty good, Lori . . . I mean . . . for a girl."

I laughed. "That sounds like a chauvinistic statement if I ever heard one," I joked trying to keep the conversation light.

"I didn't mean it like that. I mean you're really good." He stuttered slightly as if he were a bit nervous. Perhaps Bruce Dailey was more bashful than his initial impression. "Did you ever play on a team or anything, Lori?" He leaned back on the bench.

"Oh, goodness no. I just play tennis for fun. Besides, there were no tennis teams for girls in my high school or college."

"I really have enjoyed playing with you, Lori. It's been fun." He fumbled with his bag and shifted back and forth on his feet as if he wasn't comfortable talking with me. Bruce said something, but the words were not clear.

"Excuse me? I didn't hear you."

"You wouldn't be interested in having a drink with me sometime, would you?" he repeated in a little louder voice.

It wasn't until he actually said the words that I realized how much I wanted to hear them. "Yes, I'd like that," I answered even before I had the chance to think about it.

Bruce seemed even more apprehensive than a few moments earlier. His eyes wandered off into another direction as he muttered, "You're not married or anything, are you?"

"Heavens no! I thought you were married." I laughed as it finally dawned on me why he was being so standoffish.

"You have a boyfriend?" There was confidence in his voice again. I shook my head and he smiled. "I just thought all this time that you were married or living with someone. I mean, it's hard to believe that a pretty girl like you could possibly be unattached."

"No. There isn't anyone in my life right now," I confessed as I stuck my racket under my arm and leaned against the bench.

"That's good. So, you'll have a drink with me, huh? Maybe Friday night or would Saturday be better?"

"Friday's best for me," I answered, as I remembered that oftentimes I didn't return from my visit with Jennifer until late on Saturday evenings. Bruce jotted down my phone number and asked where I lived. I gave him my address.

"We're practically neighbors. I live on Wakefield, take a right and down three buildings." We both laughed simultaneously. He offered to walk me back to my garden apartment two and a half blocks in the opposite direction. "It's too dark for a girl to be strolling around without a friend. I'll walk with you. That way, I'll know where to pick you up Friday night."

He left me at the door without even asking if he could come inside.

Several weeks went by as Bruce and I spent many evenings playing tennis under lighted courts because daylight savings time was over. We also went out to dinner on two occasions. We saw *Kramer vs. Kramer* and *10*. On one occasion, we even went dancing. I was teaching at least three days out of the week and had enrolled in a night class that wouldn't start until after the Christmas vacation. I was beginning to feel safe and relaxed in Bruce's company. I even allowed myself the luxury of feeling happy.

Over the Thanksgiving holidays, I took Bruce to meet Jennifer. It was a lazy Indian summer Saturday afternoon. The weather was wonderful, and the ride was enjoyable. The only thing that put a damper on the day was—much to my amazement—Jennifer didn't seem to like Bruce, which took me totally by surprise. I figured that Bruce Dailey would be exactly the type of person everyone liked . . . even Jennifer. I couldn't understand why she was so reserved; in fact, twice during the day she was actually obnoxious. I was having a hard time imagining what Jennifer could possibly find at fault with Bruce. He was not only a perfect gentleman, but personable and intelligent as well. On top of that positive combination, he was also good looking, and owned his own business.

I could tell that even though Bruce made an attempt to like Jennifer, he didn't really warm up to her any more than she cared about him. They were merely polite to one another as they smiled and nodded at all the proper times, and even shook hands while exchanging a brief cheek-to-cheek kiss. There was definitely friction in the air between them.

It wasn't until Jennifer and I were alone that she broached the subject with an acerbic tone. "Don't you go getting yourself hurt again, Lori."

Immediately, I felt defensive. "Bruce isn't like those other guys. He's very nice."

"There's no such thing as a nice guy, Lori . . . or haven't you figured that out yet?"

"My God, Jennifer, you could at least try to like him." I refused to listen to any more of her undermining comments about Bruce, and after a few more minutes of visiting alone with Jennifer I suggested that Bruce and I leave. It was a lot earlier than my normal departure time.

Jennifer clung to me when I bent down to kiss her cheek. "You'll come back, won't you? Please, Lori," she whispered in my ear not allowing Bruce to hear her words. "I'll be good. I promise, I won't say another word against him. Just promise you'll come back."

"Of course I will, Jennifer. You know how important you are to me." She smiled and released my arm from her firm grasp.

Bruce and I drove back to D.C. without commenting on Jennifer Carson. At first, I hoped that they could be friends, or at least friendly, but I instinctively knew that they would never be able to form any kind of relationship. Thankfully, Bruce had the good sense not to make negative comments about my closest friend. I appreciated his tactfulness.

Between Christmas and New Year's, Bruce took me to meet his parents. I was relieved when they welcomed me warmly. I felt comfortable in their home and enjoyed the dinner we shared. Bruce's father was retired from the family hardware store, which was now operated by his only son. They talked business, and I enjoyed listening to the male conversation as we passed mashed potatoes, candied yams, roast duck, and gravy.

Occasionally, Bruce's mother interrupted them by asking me a personal question. "Bruce tells me that you're a teacher. Where did you go to school?"

"I attended a small school in North Carolina. Elon College."

"Did you enjoy it?"

"Oh, yes. It's a very nice place. I think I was the type of person who needed a small southern school. I probably would have drowned at one of those big northern universities."

"My son went to the University of Maryland."

"Yes, I know." I felt a little self-conscious, but I knew that Mrs. Dailey didn't intend to make me to feel that way.

"I guess he also told you that he played football for two years."

"Mom!" Bruce interjected. "Lori doesn't need to hear about my benchwarming days. I'm sure you can find something else to talk about."

"You played," she added in defense of her son.

"Not enough for it to be significant."

"All right . . . ," Mrs. Dailey smiled as she continued to make friendly conversation. "I hear that you play tennis, too, Lori. My son was on the high school team years ago. He was very good, but now he only does it for recreation. I understand that you met on the courts."

We spoke of a few of Bruce's high school tennis matches, Bjorn Borg and Martina Navratilova's successes at Wimbledon the previous summer, and two relatively new stars, Tracy Austin and John McEnroe, before the conversation changed to politics.

"I've been a Republican most of my life," Mr. Dailey stated. "But in '76, I voted for Carter. I can't believe what a mistake that was. In retrospect, Ford would probably have been better, but hindsight is always easier than predicting the future. I guarantee, in November, I won't be voting for Carter a second time."

"Dad, I don't think you're being very fair to the man," Bruce interrupted. "Granted, I thought he was too idealistic to be president, but I think his biggest mistake has been that he didn't surround himself with strong, experienced people in his administration."

"He hasn't done a damn thing about the energy fix we're in. Inflation is worse than it's ever been. And last month when Iran's crazy ayatollah seized the American embassy in Teheran and took all those hostages, Carter should have done something."

"Yeah, I agree with you there. Khomeini is bad news." Bruce sipped on his coffee. "I think he believed that because we had once been allies that Iran could extradite the shah while he was in New York for medical help. But you can't give in to terrorism. If you do, there will be no end to it. Well, I doubt Iran and the United States will be on friendly terms again for quite a while."

"And if that's not bad enough . . . the Russians just marched into Afghanistan, and Carter's not doing a damn thing about that either! Where's it going to stop?"

I remained quiet. I didn't want to admit that I had helped on Carter's campaign. Silently, I grinned to myself as I thought of Gene and how hard he had worked for the man. I was certain that he, too, was disillusioned with Jimmy Carter. Where once Gene had viewed Jimmy Carter as a white knight filled with hope for a fresh start in rebuilding American pride, I was sure that now Gene criticized Carter for being weak. There was no doubt in my mind that Gene had eaten a great deal of crow in the last three years.

"I'm bringing in dessert now." Mrs. Dailey interjected. "And I want all this serious talk to stop. Haven't you two learned yet that you can't solve the world's problems over dinner?" She spoke lovingly to both of the men at the table. "Let's change the subject and give poor Mr. Carter a break." She turned to me. "Lori, would you like a piece of pie?"

"Yes, thank you. It looks delicious."

The evening continued with less serious conversation as we discussed the Redskins, the course I was going to take in January, and the Winter Olympics to be held in Lake Placid in February. After dessert and several cups of coffee, both of Bruce's parents hugged me affectionately and asked me to return soon. It was a very pleasant evening.

The weeks blended together. By a stroke of luck, I was given a position at Waynewood Elementary School, which was less than five miles from my apartment. The previous teacher was taking maternity leave. Hopefully, I would be able to stay at Waynewood for the remainder of the school year. It was a wonderful class of third graders who seemed excited about learning. Needless to say, I was thrilled.

Two nights a week, I took classes at George Mason University to brush up on my skills, and the rest of the time I spent with Bruce. We were developing a solid relationship. He came over almost every evening. Sometimes I cooked for him, and other times he showed off his talents by cooking for me. We went to movies. We listened to music. Several times—when the snow provided us with a winter wonderland—we went sledding on the steep hill by the Parkway.

In February, we watched Eric Heiden win an unprecedented five gold medals in speed skating. And if that wasn't enough to raise goose bumps on our flesh, we also sat on the edge of our seats as the U.S. hockey team shocked the world by beating Finland four to two and winning the gold medal.

I could not help but compare my life now with the one I had been living four years ago when I had been watching the last Winter Games. Life with Bruce was so much better than it had been with Gene. I felt as if I were reborn, and I credited that feeling to Bruce. He never pressured me either emotionally or physically, which gave me a secure feeling. For the first time in a very long time, I felt in control over what was happening to me. I no longer had the sensation that I was riding at breakneck speed on a roller coaster destined for doom. It was nice to be safe and warm in Bruce's arms.

In March, after a wonderful evening of listening to Kenny Rogers albums and sipping wine, I encouraged Bruce into my bed. We became lovers. Life was finally coming together for me. I was very happy.

5

In June, I went to West Virginia.

"Hello, Jennifer," I spoke in a cheerful voice.

She immediately smiled, her face covered with a radiant expression. I was afraid—after staying away for three weeks in a row—she'd be angry with me for neglecting her.

"Lori, I've missed you. You haven't even called or written. You're not angry at me, are you?"

"Of course not. I've just been very busy . . . but now that school's out, I'll have a little more free time."

"I'm so glad you're here. I have some terrific news."

"So do I," I chimed in directly after she had spoken.

"You do? What is it?"

"No, Jennifer, you first."

"I couldn't wait to tell you. Yesterday, the doctor said I could go home next week. Isn't that terrific? It'll be just the way it used to be. You and me. It's been so long. I feel so good. I can even walk again. Not very far, mind you, but I'm building up. Maybe someday, I'll even be able to jog with you." She laughed knowing full well that she had never—nor would she ever—have the desire to jog. "Isn't it marvelous?"

"Oh, Jennifer. I'm so happy for you. This is terrific news." I hugged her tightly. She no longer looked fragile and pale. It had been a long time since I'd seen Jennifer appear so healthy. Her hair had grown out again. It was thick and shiny like it had been while we were in college. Her eyes danced merrily, and her cheeks were splashed with a natural shade of pink.

"So, tell me. What's your news?" Jennifer said excitedly as she held my hand.

"You were wrong, Jen."

"Wrong about what?"

"Wrong about Bruce. You know I'm not one to say I told you so, but this time I'm going to." I clasped my hands together and let out a hoot of a laugh. "He loves me. He really loves me." I was trembling from sheer joy. "We're going to get married in August."

Jennifer's reaction wasn't at all what I anticipated. Instead of being overjoyed for me, she looked dismal and dejected. The color I had seen on her cheeks only moments ago vanished. She was as pale as the day I discovered her unconscious on the living room floor.

"Jennifer, are you all right?"

"Yes . . . yes," she muttered quietly. "I'm just surprised."

"I want you to be happy for me." I reached for her hands and cupped them in mine. "I feel wonderful about this. Bruce is giving me back something I thought was lost forever. Please don't look so horrified." I spoke gently knowing that I made the mistake of jumping into the conversation instead of easing our way into it. "Be happy for me, Jen."

Jennifer regained her composure. I realized that she was probably just a little bit envious that I was going to share my life with a wonderful man. Perhaps a part of her also thought that I might desert her, and maybe there was even a fraction of her that remembered her own marriage to David.

She stared straight at me. "I'm happy for you, Lori. Really I am. Bruce Dailey seems like a fine person. I wish you the best."

"You're acting like we'll never see each other again."

"We probably won't."

"Don't be such a silly goose. We'll see each other all the time. It's not like I'm going into a convent. I'm only getting married. Bruce isn't going to hold me prisoner." I laughed, trying to make light of her uneasiness. "And, Jennifer, will you be my maid of honor? If you take good care of yourself, you'll be well in August and you can stand up with me. Please . . . will you? Say yes."

"Of course." Jennifer still hadn't regained her coloring. "Do you love him, Lori?"

"Yes," I answered. "I do, Jennifer. I do love him. It's not quite the same as bells ringing or heartbeats skipping or music everywhere. But I do love him. Bruce makes me feel good. He makes me feel wanted and safe. I need that, Jennifer. I've been so lost . . . so lonely. He gives me companionship, loyalty. He's so devoted. I'm going to make him a good wife. I've finally realized that I don't have to have a whirlwind love or a passion that is electrifying. Those are not the important things. I feel secure with Bruce. Be happy for me, Jennifer. I've finally found someone who can make me smile again."

"I'm very glad for you, Lori. Really I am."

2

Brad

FINALLY, LIFE WAS BEGINNING TO TAKE A POSITIVE SHAPE FOR ME. IT WAS nearly five years since my mother's death. I thought of that moment as a turning point in my life. It took a long time to get over the shock of losing her, but as the weeks and months drifted by after the funeral, I began to put her life, my father's life, and my own life into perspective. I was guilty of placing my mother on a pedestal without ever giving my father the chance to be anything but a selfish, possessive man. I discovered that my mother wasn't the goddess I made her out to be, and my father was not the horrible, vindictive creature I imagined for most of my life. I was so wrong. They were simply two human beings. Both with faults and virtues. Why did it take me so long to see that?

The transition was not an easy one for me. I didn't discover my love or my respect for my father overnight. At first, I felt only pity for him, but as the resentment began to dissipate, I started feeling a growing admiration for the man who had sired me. Eventually, as the months passed, and we worked side by side for countless hours, the two of us became close with a mutual respect for one another's business intelligence, personal thoughts, and creative ideas. We worked well together, rarely even arguing. I gave in to his opinion on several occasions, but he, also, gave in to mine.

After the first restaurant was turned into a disco, I spent a shaky couple of years waiting for it to take hold in the community. It was not the instant success I had hoped it would be. It seemed that suburbia wasn't ready to behave as the big cities did, and we rarely filled fifty percent of our seats. It was hard to look my father in the eye. He never begrudged me my ideas. In fact, he often lovingly joked about the disco by calling it Brad's folly.

Toward the end of 1977, I was just about to admit defeat when a miracle happened. *Saturday Night Fever* hit the big screen, and overnight the disco had lines of people out the door waiting to dance to tunes by The Bee Gees. I was amazed at the effect one silly movie had on my confidence. All of a sudden, I was a genius!

Shortly after the phenomenon, my dad presented me with my birthday gift. He was excited and laughing as he blindfolded me, drove me to the club, stood me across the street, and took the blindfold off. There it was in bright lights, arced over the club: Brad's Follies. I was in awe.

"Happy birthday, son." My dad shook my hand. "I thought it was the perfect name. Besides I was getting kind of used to calling it that."

"Thank you, Dad." I was stuttering from surprise. "Not just for changing the name and putting up the sign. Thanks for believing in me."

"I've always believed in you, Brad." He hugged me with strength and warmth. "Now . . . what do you say we start spreading this around like you originally wanted. With a little luck, by spring we could have two more."

For the better part of the next three years, we did little else but rake in the money. Then another movie hit the box office, and I had a fresh idea. It seemed as if John Travolta was once again a major factor in my life. He played the lead in *Urban Cowboy*. After I saw the movie with Jill, I knew that everything was about to change, and I wanted to be sure that we were the front-runners.

"Dad, you have to trust me on this," I said over the phone. I didn't even wait for our regular weekly meeting. I was too excited. "People are getting tired of the disco sound. Granted, it was great, but it was short-lived. Times are changing . . . and fast! We have to get a new sound in the club. A little country flavor maybe. And tomorrow I'm going to see where I can dig up a few mechanical bulls. There wasn't a man in that audience tonight who did not get off looking at Debra Winger doing her thing on that riding machine. Dad, I'm not kidding. This is it!"

I loved it when new ideas took shape in my mind. Sometimes, it was even better than sex. Actually, it enhanced sex. After the discussion with my father, I drove straight home. I had one thing on my mind when I scooped Jill in my arms and carried her to bed; my cravings needed immediate attention.

I didn't sleep the whole night. Instead, I sat at my desk, writing and rewriting new layouts for the club. The prism ball that hung from the ceiling had to go. It had more than paid for itself, but it was obsolete now. With a little imagination, the renovations could be done quickly and effortlessly without digging too deeply into our pockets. Hot damn! I was on a roll!

2

Rick and Valerie were starting a family. My brother was strutting around like a proud father in spite of the fact that Valerie was barely showing her condition. I envied Rick his happiness and wished that a little of it would rub off on me. He and Valerie seemed to have the ideal life. Secretly, I wished I could love Jill in the way Rick cared for Val.

Jill and I had been living together over five years, and although we had a solid relationship, I was not able to return those emotions I knew she craved from me. Every once in a while I considered finding release in another woman's arms, but I never did. There was a time when I would have run rampant over Jill's heart without giving much thought to her pain, but after I learned firsthand how much it hurt, I stopped inflicting Jill with that torture. I had Laura Davis to thank for that lesson. It was Laura who taught me how to love; consequently, it was Laura who changed that beautiful emotion into a painful one. She had given me something magical and then snatched it away. I often wished I had never discovered my true feelings for Laura

Davis. There were days when she still wedged herself into my mind. I found that it was *those* days that I had to dedicate myself the most to my work.

Rick and Val weren't the only happy couple in my life. Bill had gotten married the previous March. We saw each other often, including our weekly Wednesday night poker parties. We were both pleased that Jean, his new wife, didn't restrict him from his afternoon beers, which we shared, or his one night out with the boys.

Everyone's life was falling into place. Even my father was starting to date. He wasn't serious about anyone, but at least he was getting out and enjoying himself. I was glad to see that he was breaking out of his shell.

Sometimes, I felt as if I were the only person not delighted with life. Of course, I had the clubs. They were a challenging aphrodisiac, and I had Jill who was a wonderful companion, but I still felt empty inside most of the time.

3

Every Tuesday and Thursday, I visited the club Rick managed on the outskirts of Newark. We went over paperwork, discussed the weekly business, tallied up the profits and expenses, and often there was enough time afterward to share a late lunch and light conversation. We sat at our table in the corner where no customers or employees infringed on our few moments of privacy. Our conversation was filled with new ideas for the clubs, the fact that the U. S. wasn't participating in the Summer Olympics in Moscow, and Val's pregnancy. I thoroughly enjoyed Rick's company.

"So, tell me. How's the little pregnant momma coming along?" I asked as I sat back in the booth and sipped on my soda.

"Val's doing fantastic. Even though she's gaining a little weight here and there, I don't think I've ever seen her look better. This baby is just what we both have always wanted. I can't tell you how happy I am. I'm scared to death and thrilled at the same time. I'm going to be a dad!" He was grinning and blushing as much from his statements as from the joy that was bursting inside of him. "I bet you think I'm nuts."

"I don't think you're nuts," I answered as I let his happiness rub off on my mood. I liked being around Rick. He had a positive effect on me. "I mean . . . you have to remember that you're not the only one who has a reason to wave banners. You're going to be a father, but I'm going to be an uncle."

"Have you ever thought about being a father?"

"Yeah." I remembered Cindy's baby. I let out a long, pensive sigh. Then I had flashbacks of Laura, and how for one brief moment in time I wanted nothing but Laura Davis and a family. "I've thought about it."

"So you want kids?" Rick seemed delighted with this revelation.

"I suppose so . . . someday. I haven't given much thought to it recently."

"It'll come. One day you and Jill will decide to start a family. You'll get married, and it'll happen for you." Rick took a bite out of his triple-decker sandwich before continuing. "Speaking of new families . . . did you get a wedding invitation?"

"Wedding invitation . . . who's getting married?" Rick had shifted the topic of conversation so quickly I had only a mild interest in his question.

"I guess you didn't get one. But then again—all things considered—I suppose you wouldn't be invited to the wedding. You remember Lori Davis?"

Instantly, my attention returned. Laura! Laura was getting married? It wasn't possible. Laura couldn't be getting married! Even though it had been years since I'd seen her, I couldn't imagine her married to anyone. I had wanted her to marry me—not someone else! Jesus Christ! I couldn't stand knowing that someone else was going to spend a lifetime with Laura—not my Laura. I knew it was absurd, but I had subconsciously always dreamed that one day she would simply appear out of nowhere and come running into my arms as if she had always loved me.

"What?" I replied realizing that Rick had asked me a specific question.

"Jeez, Brad! You're in another world. You haven't heard a word I've said. Well, anyway, Valerie called Lori and explained that we wouldn't be able to attend the wedding, but we sent our regards, a gift, and wished her the best. Val said that Lori sounded wonderful. She seemed to be genuinely happy. She has a teaching job in a public school. Valerie asked about her fiancé and from what I hear he must be a pretty solid type of guy. But that doesn't surprise me any."

"Yeah . . ." I muttered as I drained my glass. "Yeah . . . knowing Laura . . . he's probably a real nice guy." I felt sarcastic, but I was surprised that my words actually sounded nonchalant. I couldn't believe I appeared so apathetic about a subject that was tearing my guts out. My God! Laura! Laura couldn't get married. She must love him. Good Lord! That was a thought which was pure torture in itself. Laura loved a man enough to marry him!

"You know something, Brad. It's kind of funny in a way. There was a time when I thought I loved Lori. But I didn't really. I just wanted her because I thought . . . I thought you were in love with her . . . and I wanted to take her away from you." Rick sat back in his seat waiting for a reaction from me. When there wasn't one, he continued, "I was really jealous of you back when we were kids. Everything was so easy for you. I thought if I could win one victory over you, then I'd feel better about myself. Of course, at the time I wasn't quite this objective and analytical about it all. I really didn't understand what was going on in my mind. I really believed at the time that I loved Lori. When I found out that she didn't care about me, I thought my life was going to go all to hell, but then I found Val. That's when I discovered that I never really loved Lori. She only symbolized some kind of contest for me . . . and the prize was beating you. This sounds awful, doesn't it? I can't believe I'm confessing it to you. I hope you realize that was all in the past. Those are old wounds! I've gotten beyond them. I don't feel like that anymore. You and I . . . I don't know how to say it. I love you, Brad . . . not just as a brother . . . but as a friend."

"I know, Rick. You weren't exactly my favorite person either when we were kids." I grinned sheepishly. "I'm glad that's all in the past."

"And as for Val—there isn't another woman in the world—including Lori Davis, who could possibly make me happier. Life has a lot of little quirks, but if it hadn't been for Lori's honesty, I might never have met Valerie. It's strange the way things work out." He smiled. "I could have sworn when we were at Elon that you and Lori had something going. There seemed to be such a magnetic attraction between you. You wouldn't believe how jealous I was."

I clenched my teeth silently. When would Rick get off this subject? The last thing I wanted to hear was anything on the topic of Laura Davis.

"Just out of curiosity, Brad—did you love her?"

"What?" I almost choked on the word.

"I just wondered. You seemed happier when you were around her. Your entire personality changed when the two of you were dating." He sipped at his drink. "Then when you weren't together, you were so angry. No one could mention her name in your presence, yet you were protective of her too. And sometimes, when I watched you look at her, there was an expression on your face—I don't know how to say it—you looked different when you looked at her." He paused several seconds. "Were you in love with her?"

"Hell, no!" I couldn't talk about it. I felt like I was smothering. It was difficult to breathe. I found it hard to believe that even after all these years those old emotions still weighed too heavy for words. "Laura Davis wasn't anything special. Besides that's ancient history." I choked on the sentences.

Rick watched me silently for a while as he finished the remainder of his lunch. He smiled politely as he dabbed his lips with the napkin. Pushing the table slightly to the right Rick stood up. "Well, Brad . . . I better get back to work. Looks like the happy hour crowd is starting early today."

"Sure . . . sure. Go ahead."

"Brad . . ." He paused slightly as he placed his hands on the edge of the table and lowered his voice. "All that hostility and anger I had for you when we were younger . . . it's gone. I mean it, Brad. I haven't felt like that in years. We're friends, you and I . . . good friends, and if you ever need someone to talk to . . . I'm more than willing to listen."

"Yeah . . . sure." I quickly shook Rick's hand before he went about his duties. I was glad he left. I focused on the paperwork in front of me. I was not going to let his news affect me. I was over Laura. I had finally started to live without her, and I wasn't going to let her memories destroy the life I had created for myself. Damn it! Damn it! Damn it! Shit! It was her life! She could do whatever the hell she wanted with it. Why did I care anyway? I stood up and left the restaurant without even signaling a good-bye to my brother.

Slowly, I walked in a daze. Passing a couple of stores along the way, I looked pensively into all the windows and tried to avoid thinking. It was not until I saw a beautiful gold-trimmed 8" x 10" picture frame perched in the showcase of a gift shop that I stopped in my tracks and stared at it. It was magnificent with its tiny little floral decorations on the outside rim. I just kept looking at it and thinking how much like Laura it was: dainty and pretty. I wanted to touch it—run my fingers over it—thinking perhaps by doing so I could feel her warm skin. As if in a trance, I walked into the shop and purchased the frame without even so much as asking the price. I used their phone to call Valerie and get Laura's address off the invitation. I jotted it down on a scrap of paper and then handed it to the salesclerk. Before I could change my mind, I instructed the woman to ship the package along with a short note.

> Laura,
> I heard about your wonderful news and wish you
> a lifetime full of joy and happiness.
>
> > > Brad

The moment I left the store, I had the urge to return and demand the package. Before I gave in to my thoughts, I picked up my pace until I was jogging down the street back to my car. The hell with it! It was done and so be it!

I drove around for hours before finally returning to Jill's and my apartment. It was late when I opened the door and saw Jill sitting on the sofa with a concerned look on her face as if she was worried—and perhaps fearful—of where I had been. Jill knew better than to inquire, and I appreciated her silence. I walked into the kitchen. There was a plate in the refrigerator that contained my dinner. I took off the plastic wrap and popped it in the microwave; then I sat down to eat. Jill quietly came into the kitchen, poured herself a glass of juice, and pulled out the wrought-iron chair opposite me.

After taking several bites in silence, I put down my fork and stared directly into her eyes. "How would you like to get married, Jill?" My voice was flat and had no vibrancy to it, but I immediately saw that the quality in which my question was asked had no ill effect on Jill's expression.

"Are you kidding? Yes! When? Where? You know I'll marry you anytime, and anyplace. I've always loved you, Brad."

"How 'bout Friday? That will give us the time to get a marriage license and blood tests. We can do it at the county courthouse and then go away someplace for the weekend." I proceeded to finish my meal.

"I kind of always wanted a pretty church wedding, Brad." She hesitated as she watched me continue to put one fork full of peas into my mouth after another. There was a long, heavy silence in the air. "But that doesn't matter. Nothing matters except that we'll be married, right?" She tried to make her voice sound cheerful. "I don't need all that fancy stuff. I just want you."

Her words sounded small and distant to my ears. She kept chatting away. I pretended to listen: nodding occasionally, smiling, answering with a "yes" or a "no." Jill was finally getting what she wanted. Me! Well, she could have me. It was certainly obvious that no one else wanted Brad Malone.

3

We said our vows in a small chapel surrounded by a dozen of our closest friends and family. I felt numb. Each word I spoke sounded as if it were coming from the mouth of someone else. Jill was radiant and ecstatic with the ceremony. She was clutching a nosegay of flowers I bought for her. The small bouquet was the least I could do since the atmosphere was definitely far from romantic. The lack of music, gowns, crowded pews, and all the elements of a traditional wedding didn't seem to bother Jill. She was happy and completely oblivious to the fact that I stood next to her like a statue: cold and resigned.

A couple of minutes, a few words spoken and suddenly, I was a married man. Jill was my wife. I kissed her and smiled letting my bride take as much beauty as she could from the moment. She was bubbling with enthusiasm and joy.

I took Jill to New York for the weekend. We had dinner at the hotel and went to see the Broadway hit, *Children of a Lesser God.* Phyllis Frelich and John Rubinstein were incredible, and for a couple of hours, I lost myself in their love story. When the play was over, Jill and I went outside to hail a cab. As we stood there in the crowd with the humid air surrounding us, I felt a nudge on my shoulder. Turning around, I faced a rather tall, attractive, dark-haired woman. She looked no older than me. Her clothes were chic. I recognized her, but I couldn't place the face, and I certainly couldn't remember the name.

"I don't mean to be rude . . ." Her voice was very pleasant. "But I think I know you."

I returned her pleasant smile as I studied both the woman speaking and the man standing next to her. For the life of me, I couldn't figure out who she was. Even her escort looked familiar. Who was he? He seemed to recognize me too, but he couldn't remember my name any more than I could remember his.

"Didn't you take baby pictures?" The dark-haired girl spoke again.

"Yes! Yes, I did, but that was years ago." I looked at her a second time and instantly I remembered. I still couldn't recall her name, but I did remember her baby girl. "You have a daughter. She was about a year old when I took her picture. Her name was . . . let me see if I can remember . . . Ellie . . . . that was it. Ellie. She was the prettiest little baby I've ever seen. Gorgeous eyes. Cute little smile. I even saved one of her proofs. Usually, I pitch them or give them back to the company, but I kept one of Ellie. She made quite an impact on me. The perfect model." We all laughed. After the sound echoed away, the air became awkward once again as we realized we still could not remember each other's names. "So, how is your daughter?" I questioned politely. I could almost see those little girl's eyes. It was just about as clear as if I had seen them only a moment ago.

"Oh, she's fine, but she's not little anymore. She's eight and will be going into third grade this fall."

"You're kidding! It's been that long?"

"Kids grow up so fast. It's almost like you turn around once or twice and they aren't kids anymore." There was silence again. Suddenly, the dark-haired girl extended her hand and smiled shyly. "I really must apologize, but I don't remember your name. I'm Pamela Woods."

"Brad Malone." I shook her hand firmly. This is my wife, Jill." The women nodded at each other.

"This is Kurt . . . Kurt Davis," Pamela Woods said as she pointed to her escort.

My stomach twisted into a knot. Sweet Jesus! No wonder I recognized him! He was Laura's brother. I'd seen him dozens of times. He dated Jennifer Carson. My God! Of all the luck! Running into him—of all people—and tonight of all nights! I stared silently at Kurt Davis for several moments. It suddenly dawned on me why I was so taken with Ellie Woods. Everything came into focus—crystal clear! I recalled the child's smiling eyes. No wonder I was drawn to her! Kurt Davis was her father, which made Laura her aunt. The resemblance was uncanny. After recalling the introduction and realizing that the couple in front of me did not claim the same last name, I thought better not the mention my discovery. I wondered if Laura knew about her niece. Interesting question. As I tried to quiet my nerves, I swallowed several times. "So . . ." I shifted from one foot to the other. "How's your sister?" It was a polite question . . . one that would be expected of two acquaintances after so many years had passed.

"I haven't seen her in a long time," he replied casually. "She's getting married later this summer. I suppose I'll be going home for the wedding."

"Please give her my regards," I replied.

"I will," Kurt responded. He seemed as stiff as I was.

"Are you still in photography?" Pam asked.

"No. I gave that up years ago," I answered. "It's just a hobby now."

"What a shame. You showed a lot of talent."

"Brad owns clubs," Jill interjected. "He has a chain of them in New Jersey. Brad's Follies. Have you ever heard of it? They are fantastic."

I jabbed Jill in the side trying to quiet her. I'd been to Pam Woods' home. One thing I knew for sure, women like her didn't hang out in clubs like mine.

"Would you care to join us for a late supper or a drink?" Pamela Woods asked.

"No," I muttered.

"Yes that would be very . . ." Jill replied.

Both of us simultaneously responded to the dark-haired woman's kind offer. Jill immediately cut off the remainder of her response. She looked up at me, eyes searching, questioning my attitude.

"I appreciate your invitation, but you see . . ." I gave Jill a firm squeeze. "My wife and I . . . we were just married today. I'm sure you can understand why we would rather pass up your offer." The last thing I wanted to do was spend an evening with Laura Davis's brother. Aside from my own feelings, I knew that my brand-new bride would not be able to contain herself from asking questions. She obviously had made the connection between Kurt and Laura, and her curiosity would definitely spoil the evening.

"Oh, so you're newlyweds," Pamela Woods smiled. "How romantic. Congratulations."

"Thank you," Jill nodded.

"Yes, thank you," I responded.

"And you picked New York for a honeymoon. Great city."

"Yes, it is." About the time I finished my comment a large, black limousine pulled up to the curb.

Kurt Davis opened the door and Pamela made a move toward it. "Are you sure we can't change your minds about coming with us?" she inquired again, but this time there was a teasing quality to her voice.

"No, we'll pass. But thank you."

"It was nice talking with you," she said before shutting the door.

Jill and I waved as the car pulled out into the street. I took a deep breath and let it all out. Thank God they were gone. "Let's go get a drink some-place."

"Let's go back to the hotel," Jill's voice purred suggestively

The next morning over room service, Jill started the first serious con-versation of our married life. Both of us were still dressed in our robes. My head was buried in a newspaper. I sipped on my second cup of coffee when her words broke the silence. "I know why you married me, Brad," she said quietly as she used her fork to toy with the remaining food on her plate. "That guy last night . . . he was Laura's brother, wasn't he?" When I didn't respond, Jill continued. "You already knew Laura was getting married, did-n't you?"

I felt every muscle in my body tense at the thought of discussing Laura with anyone . . . much less Jill. I did not want to be reminded of Laura. I did not want to talk about her. I didn't even want to think about her. Laura Davis was part of the past, and I wanted to leave it behind me. But how could I for-get Laura if my wife was going to insist on rehashing the memory?

Jill pressed the issue without altering her calm voice. "I know you still love her, Brad. And I'm not a fool. I realize that you only married me on a whim to try and get even because of what she did to you. But I'll make you a good wife. You won't be sorry you married me. I promise. You must know—I'll do anything to make you happy."

"Jill . . ." I spoke my first words of the morning. I was trying to get a grip on my rising irritation so I paused long enough to consider my next words. "If you really want to make me happy you will never, never say her name again." I placed my cup down in the saucer in front of me. I kept my voice firm and my expression blank. "Laura Davis is dead. The subject of her will not be spoken between us any more. Is that perfectly clear?" I reached for Jill's hand, gently squeezing it. "Let's start off fresh—just you and me—all of our yesterdays are over. We just have tomorrows. I don't want to look back. I just want to look forward."

Jill nodded. We continued to eat our meal in silence.

3

Kurt

THREE YEARS IN NEW YORK DID WONDERS FOR ME. WITH PAMELA'S help, I succeeded in finding a job with her father's company. Although I truly felt comfortable in the position for the present, I knew it was not what I wanted to do with the rest of my life. As for the other aspects of my life, I still drank occasionally. Who didn't? But I was off the drugs and rarely smoked pot. I had enrolled in night classes, and earned my degree in business administration a couple of years before. I was continuing my education. With a little luck I'd be a qualified CPA by the end of the following year, which would enhance my job opportunities.

When I started with Wood's Enterprise, I was a gofer in his New York office, but over the years I worked my way up. Now I was more of a troubleshooter and a right arm for his personal as well as business dealings in the New York area. Although George Woods rarely made an appearance in New York, scarcely a day went by that I didn't have to perform a crucial task for him.

I was grateful that my boss didn't know of my relationship to his granddaughter or my friendship with Pam. Despite the fact that he was rarely in town to give his time and affection to Ellie, I discovered that she was crazy about him. George Woods was generous, loving, and attentive during the few occasions a year they had the opportunity to see each other. When they were together, they shared wonderful experiences, which Ellie described to me at length.

Last August, I went to my sister's wedding. It was a pleasant affair. Bruce Dailey seemed like a nice guy, and I was happy for Lori. Even though it was good to see her again, I was not ready to rekindle our sibling bond. Lori reminded me of youth, college days, and Jennifer; they were things and people I was trying to put behind me. I didn't need Lori's sunny disposition as a constant reminder of what might have been. As for Jennifer, she had yet another relapse shortly before the wedding and was unable to attend. That was fine by me. My parents were at the wedding too. Although I visited my mother on occasion, I seldom saw my father. I still felt ambivalent toward him. I had no desire to renew any kind of relationship, and I remained stubborn, holding fast to my original opinion that he and his wife could drop dead as far as I was concerned.

After the weekend's festivities, I returned to New York. Between my job, my visits with Pam and her daughter, and my studies, I found little room for anything else. Then, in November, shortly before the 1980 presidential election, I met a girl in one of my night classes. Her name was Helen. We discovered during a short conversation that we were of the same opinion about Jimmy Carter and Ronald Reagan. Over wine and steaks one evening, we held our own debate. Although we both planned to vote for Carter a second time around, we each knew in our hearts that he didn't stand a chance at reelection. It wasn't just the double-digit inflation, the recession levels of unemployment, or the interest rates that plagued him; it was the unfavorable decision he made to boycott the Summer Olympics in Moscow and the fact that he still was not able to get the hostages out of Iran that angered the population the most.

"If he can get those fifty-two Americans out of there before Election Day," Helen commented between sips of wine, "then I honestly feel he has a chance."

"It'll never happen!" I stated. "That asshole ayatollah is super pissed off at Carter for freezing all those billions of dollars in Iranian assets that they have here in America. There is no way he'd give Carter an inch. I think the ayatollah is taking great pleasure in watching the Carter administration fall. I wouldn't be surprised if Khomeini didn't wait until Reagan is inaugurated, then make a deal with him to let the hostages go."

"You're probably right. I wish Americans would make up their minds," Helen declared. "They all called the President a wimp because he never took a stand on anything. Well, he did in this case and look what it got him. Carter wouldn't give in to terrorism and hand over the shah in exchange for the Americans. And furthermore, even though I don't agree with the fact that Carter made our athletes boycott the Olympics because the Soviets moved troops into Afghanistan, at least he stood his ground."

"Now, Helen, Carter was wrong about that! The Olympics should never be part of the political arena. It's the mistake that will ruin his political career."

"You're right! You'll get no argument from me. I'm just saying that he finally had the guts to take a stand, and he's being crucified for it." She refilled her wineglass. "Let's talk about something else."

During the months between Ronald Reagan's landslide victory and his inauguration in January 1981, Helen and I spent endless hours together. Most of them were filled with conversation, but other times we listened to jazz on her stereo or watched television. It was only natural that our relationship bloomed into a physical one. I knew we were not in love with each other, but we did like being together, and for me, that was good therapy. Winter passed by quickly, and so did spring. In May, Helen told me that she had tickets to see *The Little Foxes* on Broadway with Elizabeth Taylor's debut on stage. She said it was a celebration and invited me to join her. It wasn't until after the performance that she announced what we were celebrating. Helen received a promotion and was being transferred to Los Angeles. For a brief moment, I wondered what she might say if I asked her to stay, but I could already see the answer in her eyes. What Helen and I shared was good

while it lasted, but it was time for her to move on. This was a career opportunity she wasn't going to compromise. We spent the following two weeks
basking in each other bodies, but when I drove her to the airport I did not
feel even the slightest tug at my heart. We promised to write, and perhaps
we had honest intentions to do so, but I knew by Christmas we'd be lucky if
we exchanged cards.

Another chapter in my life was over.

2

"Hi, Ellie. Is your mother home?" I hugged her in my arms and carried her
into the living room. I breathed deeply of her scent. Children always smelled
so good—clean and fresh. I adored nestling my nose in her hair and drinking in the delightful fragrance of youth and innocence.

"Mommy's making dinner for us. She told me that you were coming
over. I've been excited all day," her little voice answered with a happy
squeal. "Is that a present for me?" She pointed to the package I cradled
under my arm.

"So, you think this is for you, Ellie?" I teased as I made her wait to open
it. "What makes you think that I'd bring you a present?"

"Because it's my birthday. I'm nine," she answered, as I saw the pouting
lines start forming around her mouth at the possibility that I might have forgotten the day.

"Is it really your birthday?" I continued to tease her, but she already
guessed at the game I was playing.

"You remembered, Uncle Kurt! I know you remembered. You're just
teasing me," she said as she grabbed gently at the wrapped box I was holding in my hand. "What's inside?"

"I don't know. Why don't you look and see?" I coaxed, as I finally consented to give it to her. I watched as she ripped off the paper. Obviously
thrilled with delight, Ellie pulled from the box a soft, furry, stuffed bear with
a bright red bow around its neck.

"Oh, Uncle Kurt, it's beautiful. Thank you so much." She lovingly hugged her new treasure, embraced me several times, and then disappeared into the kitchen to inform her mother that I had arrived. I poured a drink from the crystal decanter that was sitting on the table in the corner. Shortly after I took my first sip, Pamela appeared dressed in a stylish outfit with an apron around her waist. It never ceased to amaze me that Pam chose to do daily tasks herself when she could have numerous servants catering to her needs.

"Good evening, Kurt. I'm so glad you could come. Ellie already had a small birthday party this afternoon with some of her friends from school, but what she was really looking forward to is your visit. She asked me weeks ago to invite you to dinner. I'm sorry I put it off until the last minute, but I thought you might want to make other plans."

"Don't be silly! I wouldn't miss Ellie's birthday for anything. You ought to know that by now." I became more pensive as I continued, "I'm crazy about that little girl of yours."

"She's pretty wild about you, too, Kurt."

The three of us ate a leisurely meal centering the conversation on Ellie. I found it heartwarming and amusing to watch her chattering away about the events of the last week. She pleaded with me to take her to the zoo again; it didn't take a second's time for me to give my consent. We set a date to see the monkeys and lions on Saturday afternoon. I invited Pamela to go along with us, but she said she already had plans.

When dinner was finished, Pam excused herself leaving Ellie and me alone at the table. I watched her as she spoke. It was hard to believe that Ellie was nine years old. She was so precocious. Ellie looked a lot like Pamela. She had her mother's dark hair. It was thick, yet fine. She had the same skin tone, the same nose, the same shape of face. Ellie was even going to get her mother's above-average height. But she looked like me too. It was becoming more and more obvious—even to a stranger—that she had some of my features. She had the Davis eyes, perhaps slightly more like Lori's than my own, but nonetheless they were definitely the Davis eyes: the color, the shape, the size, even the way they crinkled when she smiled.

"Uncle Kurt," Ellie interrupted my thoughts. "I wish you were my daddy."

My entire body reacted. Every nerve tightened expressing the tension that her sweet, innocent words created inside me. I felt a thin layer of perspiration forming over my lip. I knew that one side of my face was twitching involuntarily from a nervous spasm. Pamela entered the room in the middle of Ellie's statement; I glanced in her direction. I saw a strained look on her face as her eyes filled with a combination of shock and embarrassment. Without giving me the opportunity to read her expression any further, Pam pivoted and left the room.

I *was* Ellie's father. It was odd. I felt so much pride in knowing that there was someone who carried my blood. Years ago, when I heard the news of Pam's pregnancy, I never would have guessed I could be affected this way. I smiled. It was both strange and pleasant. A part of me wanted to inform her of that fact. But then my pragmatic nature took over, and I backed down. My daughter was old enough and intelligent enough to realize that I had deserted both of them. I took the paces between us and gathered her into my arms. As I held her tiny frame, I spoke, "I love you, Ellie. You're my little princess." I cleared my throat so she wouldn't become aware of the knot that was growing inside of it. As I smiled into her face, I gently kissed both cheeks. "I think of you as my own special little girl . . . isn't that enough?"

Ellie returned my smile with one of her own. "I guess so, Uncle Kurt. It's just that I don't like the guy that Mommy's been going out with. He's not like you. He's not nice, and he doesn't take me to fun places. And if Mommy marries him, he'll be my daddy, and I don't want him to be my father. I'd rather have you, Uncle Kurt."

"I didn't know your mother was seeing anyone special. What's his name?"

"Ned somebody . . . I don't remember. He's real creepy, and he always brings Mommy flowers and junk. He gives me stuff, too, but I don't like them as much as your presents."

"Does your mother like him?" I felt as if I were interrogating Ellie, but the words she was saying came as such a shock to me. I couldn't resist asking questions. Much to my surprise, I was experiencing a twinge of jealousy.

"I don't really know how Mommy feels, but I do know that Ned is always coming around here. I could have invited him to my birthday party tonight, but I wanted it to be just you and Mommy. I don't think you'd like him, Uncle Kurt. He talks real loud, and he never lets me say anything. And Mommy always has to ask him if I can come along, instead of him asking me if I want to go. Most of the time he doesn't want me to come, but when I do, he just pretends I'm not there. Uncle Kurt, will you talk to Mommy and ask her not to marry Ned? I don't want him for my daddy."

I grinned at her candid approach and brushed the hair away from her face. "Okay, princess, I'll talk to your mother, but I can't make any promises."

Her smile radiated delight. She looked like a miniature angel. I wanted to hold her and protect her from all the evils of the world. Ellie was so trusting and loving, so gentle and kind. She was a model child. Pamela had done wonders rearing her all alone. Ellie never talked back, never threw tantrums, never pushed or shoved like most kids her age. She was always well behaved, but not stifled or stiff. She was far more intelligent than the norm. And she had a wonderful sense of humor. Pamela was definitely a good mother.

"I just called the chauffeur. How would you two like to go out for ice cream?" Pam said as she entered the room.

"Oh, could we, Mommy?" Ellie's joy was apparent in her voice.

"Do you have any plans, Kurt? Would you like to join us?"

"It would be my pleasure." I winked at Ellie.

We piled into the limousine and drove several blocks to Ellie's favorite ice cream parlor. Mr. Bryant, the chauffeur, dropped us off, and Ellie raced in to get us a booth. She patted the seat next to her and asked me to join her. Pam sat on the opposite side. After ordering, Ellie whispered in my ear, "Uncle Kurt, I'm going to excuse myself and go to the ladies room. I think now is the perfect time for you to talk to Mommy about those things I was telling you earlier."

I chuckled to myself. "You do, do you?"

"Yes," she replied. "There's no time like the present."

I couldn't help but laugh warmly at Ellie's comment. She was utterly delightful. "I'll see what I can do."

Ellie politely excused herself. Pam watched me in silence for several moments before she spoke. "I'm sorry, Kurt, about Ellie's comment earlier this evening. Children are so honest about their emotions. She's very attached to you."

"There's no need for an apology," I spoke gently. "I don't feel threatened by the fact that Ellie wishes I were her father. She is so sweet. Perhaps, subconsciously, I have wanted to hear her say that for a long time." I waited for a response, but Pamela didn't look up from the napkin she was shredding. "Would you please stop that? It's terribly frustrating to carry on a conversation with you when you won't even look at me."

Slowly, she pushed the pieces of paper aside. After resting her hands in her lap she faced me. "I'm sorry, Kurt. I didn't mean to be rude."

"Who's this Ned guy Ellie's been telling me about?" My voice was steady yet I had a hard time controlling the tiny bit of irritation that was developing in it.

Pamela looked as if she were on trial and guilty as sin. She stammered on her words and paused frequently as she informed me of the nature of their relationship. "Ned is just a fellow I've been seeing. He has a good, steady job. Ned's a nice person, and he seems to like me. I suppose he talks too much, and he's probably only interested in me for my money, but I enjoy his company—and surprisingly enough—I feel comfortable around him."

"Are you sleeping with him?"

"I don't think that's any of your business." For the first time Pam directed her eyes at me. There was a hint of rebellion in them. "You have no right to dictate my life."

"I didn't mean to sound that way, Pam." Trying to get a grip on my rising emotions, I reminded myself that the purpose of this inquisition was to aid Ellie in her quest, but an unexpected thought was forming in the back of my mind; much to my surprise, I was actually jealous. "Now it's my turn to apologize, Pam. You're right. It isn't any of my business. It's just that Ellie told me she didn't like this guy, and she's afraid you might go and get yourself married to him leaving her with a father she doesn't want."

"Oh . . . " Pam looked disappointed. "So, that is what this conversation is all about." She hesitated before continuing. "I can't spend the rest of my life alone, Kurt. Ellie gives me so much happiness and joy, but you have no idea how lonely I get. Especially at night . . . I think the nights are the worst. Ellie goes to sleep, and the apartment is so quiet. I go to bed with the television or a book. Either way it's unbearably lonely." She paused to clear her throat. "I'm grateful to Ned. He's good company."

"Do you love him?" I had no right to ask the question, but I couldn't resist.

Before Pamela could answer, our waitress brought our order. She placed it in front of us and then disappeared. It seemed to give Pamela the time she needed in order to form her words. "Maybe not in the way you consider a person should love another person, Kurt. But I love him in a different way. He fills a void."

"You can have anybody, Pamela. You're intelligent, pretty, nice. Why are you settling for something less than you deserve?"

Pamela took several sips from her soda. "Not anybody I want, Kurt. Sometimes a person has to settle for second best in life; if not, he or she is stuck with nothing at all."

I was about to respond to her comment when there was a loud crashing noise that came from the back of the room. It was followed by a muffled scream. All heads turned in that direction. "Did you hear that?" I strained to see what was going on. "Was that Ellie?" The hairs on the back of my neck stood up as an odd tingling sensation ran down my spine. Without waiting for a reply, I leaped from my seat and raced to the back of the room in search of Ellie. After locating the ladies room, I flung the door open without bothering to knock. "Ellie . . . Ellie. Are you in here?" It was empty. A sick sensation was developing in the pit of my stomach. I searched the room rapidly with my eyes and detected her tiny purse on the floor. "Oh, shit!" I reached down to pick it up. When I left the room, gripping the purse in my hand, I turned right looking for a rear exit. I found it, and the door was ajar. As I glanced outside, I saw a dark sedan speeding away.

"Did you find her, Kurt?" Pam said as she reached my side.

"No, she's not here." I turned my attention to the purse in my hand.

Pam followed my eyes. After taking it from my grasp, Pam turned it over several times in her own hands before speaking in a choked voice. "This is Ellie's. Where did you find it? Where is my little girl? My God, Kurt! What's happened?"

4

We spent hours in the ice cream parlor. During the commotion, someone called the police, and they began their investigation, but nothing was resolved. Pamela was frantic; so was I. Together we paced the floor as the officer questioned us repeatedly.

Finally, he dismissed us, telling Pam that the best thing for her to do now was to return to the apartment and wait, hoping for a ransom demand. There was unspoken fear in both our minds: What if Ellie was not abducted for a monetary purpose? If that were the case, would we ever be contacted? I was afraid the bastards might harm her before we even had the chance to bargain for her life.

The chauffeur materialized at her side the moment Pamela called for him. "Bryant, could you please take us home now?" Her voice sounded so defeated.

"Yes, ma'am," he tipped his hat. "The car's right outside."

We drove to the penthouse in silence. An officer accompanied us to Pamela's apartment. It wasn't until we went inside that we realized he intended to stay with us. The policeman explained that he and his partner were assigned to tap the phone and wait for the call. Without speaking, Pamela nodded, pointed in the direction of the living room, and then headed toward the kitchen. I followed. When we were alone, she leaned against the counter and buried her face in her hands. Her shoulders jerked from silent tears.

I took the paces between us, then wrapped her in my arms. She spun her body to face me and gave way to her sobs. I tried to comfort her, hoping by doing so it would also comfort me, but I felt no solace. Before I knew what was happening, I, too, was crying pitifully. We clung to each other desperately, trying to gain strength.

We remained in that position for quite some time before Pamela finally spoke. "This is a nightmare. Who would do this?"

Just as Pamela spoke, an officer walked into the kitchen. "I'm afraid, Ms. Woods, that people with your kind of money are always targets."

"I'll give them anything they want . . . anything . . . just make sure I get my baby back." She began to rock in my arms. "Oh, God, Kurt! I can't stand it! What if they hurt my little girl? What if something happens to her? She must be so afraid." Pamela was getting hysterical.

"I took the liberty of calling a doctor," the policeman said. "You should probably have a sedative."

"No! No! Absolutely not! I can't go to sleep. No doctors . . . no sedative. Kurt! You can't let them." Pamela was losing control.

"It's okay, Pam. Calm down. You've got to calm down." I squared off a look at the officer. "I'll handle this; just give me some breathing space." I guided Pam from the room and headed toward the bedroom.

"Hey, Davis," the officer called behind me. "When you've got a minute, I want a few words with you."

"Okay." I led Pam down the hall as if she were blind. She seemed incapable of standing on her own. After lowering her onto the bed, I took off her shoes and gently moved her into a comfortable position.

"Don't leave me."

"I won't," I replied, as I slid next to her and cradled her with my warmth. She began to weep quietly again, so I stroked her hair and whispered words of encouragement. Hours passed before I heard Pam's steady breathing indicating that she'd fallen asleep. Quietly, I removed myself from her firm grip and slid off the bed. As I watched her lying on the mattress, I raked my fingers through my hair. I envied her slumber. I left the room in search of a glass of bourbon. When I entered the living room, I was met with a chaotic scene of several police officers and their equipment. The noise was deafening. I couldn't imagine why I hadn't noticed it from the bedroom. Ignoring the commotion, I made myself at home at the bar.

"Davis," the detective in charge called to me. "Come over here."

"Yeah. What do you want?"

"I'm Detective Shipman." He extended his hand. "How's Ms. Woods?"

"Not too well . . . but at least she's asleep for a little while."

"The doorman found this lying on the floor by the main entrance." He handed me an envelope with magazine letters spelling Pam's name pasted on it. "It's been dusted for prints, but it was clean. What do you make of it?"

I opened it and read the contents aloud. "Will contact you. Get rid of police."

I glanced at Shipman. "Looks like it's straight out of a low-budget movie to me."

"Yeah . . . " he paused. "I don't think the people we're dealing with are professionals. In fact, I'd venture to guess they've never done this before and don't really know what they are doing."

"Sounds feasible to me."

"How well do you know Ms. Woods?" Shipman asked.

"Pretty well . . . very well. Why?"

"I'm asking the questions here, Davis." He jotted something down in his notebook. "How often do you see her?"

"Weekly. Sometimes more, sometimes less."

"What do you do?"

"I work for Pam's father"

"How much do you make in a year?"

"My salary is none of your damn business!"

"Don't give me a hard time, Davis." He wrote something down on the paper. "Had any financial problems recently?"

"Just what the hell are you getting at?" My nerves were frazzled, and I didn't like the direction this conversation was going.

"The way I see it," Shipman stared directly at me. "We're dealing with amateurs here. And there's no way they could have done it without having someone on the inside. Someone who could tip off the kidnappers about where and when to snatch Ellie. It wasn't like she was taken from a scheduled event in her routine. It had to be someone who knew where you were going tonight, and from what I gather you were the only guest at the party."

"You think I had something to do with this?" I pointed at him fiercely. "You son of a bitch! I didn't have anything to do with this." I wanted to deck the guy with a right cross. I was totally out of control. "She's my daughter! She's my blood! Do you think I'd hurt her?" I was screaming. "I love her. I would never hurt her."

"Kurt." Pamela was standing in the doorway. Her face was ashen. She wore an expression of sheer horror.

"My God! Pamela, you don't think I had anything to do with this . . . do you?"

Tears glistened in her eyes. Slowly, she shook her head. "Do you know, Kurt . . . that's the first time you've ever called her that."

"Called her what?"

"Your daughter." A small smile spread across Pam's face. "No, Detective Shipman, Kurt didn't have anything to do with this. I'm sure of it." Pam walked toward me. "You do love her, don't you, Kurt?"

"Of course, I do. Was there ever any doubt?"

"Yes . . . in the beginning," she paused. "It was years before you gave her an ounce of attention. I thought she was a burden to you."

I hung my head as the guilt washed over me. Yes. I'd spent the first several years of Ellie's life ignoring her existence and hoping she'd disappear, alleviating me of my responsibility. But she hadn't. Somehow, over the years, the most overwhelming attachment developed between us. She was the only good thing in my life. I couldn't lose her. "Ellie's no burden. I love her. You have to believe me. "

Pamela enveloped me with her arms. "I believe you."

For the first time since this ordeal started, I felt as if Pam was giving me her strength instead of me giving her mine. I closed my eyes for a moment, relishing it. When I opened them again, I focused on the box on the couch and the crushed wrapping paper next to it. "Where's the bear?"

"What bear?"

"The bear! The one I gave Ellie for her birthday." I walked over to the couch and looked inside the box. It was empty. I pulled the cushions aside. No bear! "Did any of you see a stuffed bear around here? Pamela, do you know where it is?"

"I don't know, Kurt. Who cares?" Pam seemed agitated.

I raced to Ellie's room and rummaged through it, throwing the contents in all directions. When I returned to the living room, I was distraught. "Listen to me. I've looked everywhere! It's not in her room. It's not in the box, and she didn't take it with her when we went to get ice cream. Think about it! It couldn't have just disappeared."

"You on to something, Davis?" Shipman interjected.

"Don't you get it? The bear was here when we left, but it's gone now. Someone had to come into the apartment and take it. Someone Ellie knows. Someone *you* know, Pam . . . someone with a key."

All eyes turned to Pam. "Not very many people have a key to this place. My father, of course, but he's in Japan. He doesn't even know what's happened yet. I should send him a telegram. And there's Francis—the maid. She comes a couple of times a week. But she's been with me for years. I can't believe she'd have anything to do with this."

"Anyone else?" the officer asked.

"I can't think of anyone," Pam replied.

"How about the chauffeur?" I inquired.

"Mr. Bryant? Yes, I think he does have a key."

"How long has he been working for you?" Shipman stepped into the conversation.

"Five or six months. But there have never been any problems."

"Do you know where he lives?"

"Yes, it's in my address book, but I'm certain he would never hurt Ellie. He's always been so good to her."

"Smith. Cronin." Shipman pointed to his men. "Go check it out." Policemen began moving in every direction.

I led Pamela away from the activity. The quiet of the kitchen seemed a million miles away from the frenzy in the living room. The two of us sat at the table. Often, as I firmly held her hand in silence, our eyes met. I saw such anguish on her face. I wished only that I could erase her expression and replace it with her usual cheerful countenance.

It could have been minutes—or perhaps hours—we spent sitting in that position. Eventually, the phone interrupted the silence. Detective Shipman raced into the room and yanked Pam away from the phone before she could answer it.

"I want you to take the call in the living room where all the equipment is," he spoke in a harried fashion.

By the fourth ring Pam was picking up the receiver simultaneously with the detective. "Hello." Her hand was shaking so badly she had to cup it between her shoulder and her cheek. Tears filled her eyes in anticipation. I couldn't hear the other end of the conversation, which only added to my trepidation. Time seemed to stand still as I watched the look on Pam's face change from fear to delight. Tears mixed with perspiration streamed down her cheeks. She dropped the phone and ran to me.

"Ellie's okay . . . she's coming home."

5

Several weeks had gone by since the horrible incident on Ellie's birthday. Two of the culprits had been apprehended and the third, the chauffeur, had been killed on the night Ellie was rescued. Apparently, Mr. Bryant had gotten into debt by playing the numbers, then to make matters worse, he had borrowed from loan sharks to cover himself. When payment came due, he found himself in a mess he couldn't get out of. It seemed that he then became mixed up with the two other men. They had planned the kidnapping, hoping each would get a sizable cut. Fortunately for Ellie, Bryant had a conscience the other two had not counted on. It was true that the chauffer had informed them from the car telephone where to find Ellie, but when he had seen how frightened she was, Bryant had returned to the penthouse and gathered a few of her belongings hoping it would console her. My birthday bear had been one of those articles. That was not the only mistake Bryant made. The fools had worn stocking masks, but they had used the chauffeur's apartment to conceal her, and Ellie had recognized photos on the wall, which meant that she would be able to identify her captors when released. Just as the police were arriving, one of the kidnappers was about to drag Ellie out with plans to dispose of her. Bryant's loyalty had won in the end. He protected Ellie; subsequently, he took the bullet that had been intended for her. The police, of course, were instantly on the scene and miraculously able to save Ellie from further harm.

My heart beat so wildly when Ellie ran into the apartment that night, I was sure I'd crumple from an attack. I'd never had such an adrenaline rush in my life. She raced to Pam's arms, crying for me to join them. Together we shed an enormous amount of tears.

The week following the incident had been chaotic, but life was beginning to return to normal. Instead of my weekly visits, I found myself dropping by Pam and Ellie's daily: after work, on my lunch break, after my class, as often as I could. If Pam was busy, I spent time with Ellie. If Ellie was occupied, I talked with Pam. As always, I received tremendous pleasure in their company.

One particular evening, after I took Ellie to see *Raiders of the Lost Ark*, I found myself resting lazily beside her in bed reading from a junior version of *The Wizard of Oz*. Ellie adored stories whether they were made up, on the screen, or in books. We were just getting to the part where Dorothy met the scarecrow when Ellie blurted out, "Uncle Kurt, remember that night those bad men took me."

"Yes. I remember it very well."

"Do you also remember that you promised me you would talk to Mommy about something for me. Do you remember?"

"Yes, I remember."

"Well, did you?"

"Yes, I did. But if you'll recall a lot happened that night, and we never were able to finish our conversation."

"Well, obviously, Uncle Kurt, Mommy wasn't listening to you."

"Oh, she wasn't, huh?"

"No, and now you have to talk to her again before she marries Ned. She told me today that he asked her, and she said yes. You gotta stop her, Uncle Kurt."

"I don't know if I can, Ellie. Your mom's a big girl. She has a right to make her own decisions."

"Can you try?" Ellie pleaded.

"We'll see." I kissed her on the forehead and tucked her blankets around her neck. "Goodnight, sweetheart. You sleep tight now."

"I love you, Uncle Kurt."

My heart swelled with joy. I ran my fingers gently over the smooth skin of her cheek. "I love you too." I whispered the words for fear that I might choke on them as they erupted from my throat. The moment I spoke them I felt freed. I repeated myself. "I do love you, Ellie."

"I know."

What was a revelation to me was more than obvious to Ellie. Children are so much brighter than adults give them credit for being.

I slowly left the room in search of Pam. I discovered her in the kitchen finishing the dinner dishes. I appraised the situation, trying to find the proper statement to begin my conversation. "Pam, got a minute?"

"Sure. What can I do for you?" She placed another plate in the dishwasher.

"First of all, you can turn around so I can see your face." I waited. "Ellie just told me about your plans."

"I was afraid she might do that. I wanted to tell you myself."

"You can't marry him," I spoke with a monotone voice.

"I can, and I will." She turned her attention back to the sink as she continued rinsing dishes. "You can't stop me, Kurt." There was a stubborn determination in her tone.

"Yes, I can!" My statement hung in the air for several seconds.

With a jutting chin and a demeanor of tenacity, Pam faced me again. Neither of us spoke. Her eyes flashed defiantly as she challenged me to question her resolve. Time seemed to stand still. As if by instinct, I took the paces to the counter and placed both hands on her shoulders. I had no idea what my intentions were. Before I could rationalize my behavior, I covered her mouth with my own. I was losing myself in the flavor of her lips. I could not remember them tasting so sweet all those years ago when we were both young and innocent. It seemed different. Her mouth was warm and yielding. She was clinging to me with a greater fever than the one that was erupting inside of me. Without taking my mouth from hers, I picked her up in my arms and carried her the length of the hallway to her bedroom. No words were spoken as I slowly disrobed her and then myself. There was no doubt in my mind. I wanted Pamela. I craved her like I'd never desired her in the past. Our first intimate acts were performed out of mutual loneliness, comfort, and friendship. At that point in time, Pamela had been my savior in an hour of need. But what I felt at this moment had nothing to do with salvation. I wanted Pamela as a woman. She was sexy, provocative, beautiful, with passionate arms and fiery lips. I explored her body with a completely different insight than the first time we became physically acquainted. She was no longer the inexperienced virgin, and even though I was relatively certain she hadn't known many men, if any, since our union, she was by no means shy or reserved about her actions. She greeted me with warmth and ardent caresses. We made explosive love to each other, and I found the experience to be passionately fulfilling.

After our desires were quenched, I lay beside her and drew her into my arms. I felt a tear drop onto my chest; I knew Pamela was crying. Was it from joy or regret? I snuggled closer to her, tightening my hold on her body and feeling protective of her. I wanted to speak, but I didn't know what to say. Was she happy or sad? I only knew that I was completely satisfied. I hadn't felt this good in a long time—years.

As the minutes ticked by, I became increasingly apprehensive about her feelings. I decided to make light of the moment and perhaps with a joking attitude we could clear the air. I smiled and laughed heartily as I broke the silence. "I suppose I could marry you and make an honest woman out of you." Had I really said that? Sweet Jesus! Where had the idea come from? I had meant to say a little joke, not suggest matrimony. Why couldn't I have simply said "did you hear the one about the . . . " Why the hell did I spoil it by saying something stupid like that? Marriage? Pamela! It was ludicrous. An eternity passed in silence.

"No, Kurt." She wasn't looking at me, but I felt a tension in her body that matched my own.

For one brief second, disappointment washed over me, but then I felt only relief. I didn't want to get married. It was the passion of the moment that drove me to say such a crazy thing.

"I can't marry you, Kurt." She paused as she cleared her throat and pondered her thoughts. "Marrying you now would be the same as marrying Ned, except on opposite ends of the pole. If I marry Ned, I will be settling for a relationship where the man loves me, but I don't return the affection. If I marry you, it will mean . . . " she stopped. After taking several deep breaths Pamela continued to speak. "I won't cheat myself. I can't do that. At least I know you were right about one thing, Kurt. I can't marry Ned. You've opened my eyes to that fact. Ellie was right to confide in you and use you as her comrade in her attempts to dissuade me. No one else but you could have shown me what a mistake it would be to marry a man I don't love."

I stroked her head and enjoyed the pleasant silence that had fallen between us. "The man who finally ends up with you, Pamela, is going to be a very lucky fellow. You are terrific."

Pam curled up in my arm, nestling against me. "Do you remember a song called 'Angel in the Morning'? It was really popular in the late sixties?"

"Yeah, sure . . . pretty tune."

"That night . . . that first night we made love . . . it was playing on the radio," she paused. "I've always thought of it as "our" song. There were many times I cried when I heard it, especially while I was pregnant with Ellie." She stroked the hair on my chest. "Juice Newton has a remake of that old song. Her version is popular now," she paused several additional seconds. "I find that rather ironic . . . especially after what just happened."

"I've hurt you," I sighed quietly. "I'm so sorry, Pam. I don't know what came over me. I just sort of went crazy when Ellie told me you were going to marry that jerk. You have a right to be happy. I just don't think he's what you need."

"You must realize, Kurt, that you're the only man I really want. Not just because you're Ellie's father—although I'm sure that might be part of it—but because I've been . . . I've been in love with you since long before Ellie was conceived. I know you could never care for me the way that you love Jennifer Carson . . . and I understand . . . really I do. That's why I've always been able to settle for friendship. I'd rather have that than nothing at all." She blushed slightly as she continued. "I hope what just happened won't jeopardize our relationship. I won't force myself on you. I don't really know what happened tonight. I guess you just caught me at a weak moment. I never expected this—I swear I didn't! It's not necessary for us to be lovers. I'd understand if you aren't interested in that kind of relationship with me—but please, let's stay friends." Her words had a pleading quality that seemed foreign to her voice.

"You're very important to me, Pamela." I wiped away the few tears I saw traveling down the side of her face. "Unfortunately, you're right. I do still love Jennifer. I probably always will. I don't know what it is about her that makes me want to go back in time—relive memories, start over—but I do. It's almost as if she symbolizes my youth—a time when I was idealistic. Sometimes, I think that if I had her, I'd never grow old. Does that make any sense? No, of course not! It doesn't make any sense to me either." Without realizing it, I started a steady rhythm of strokes up and down Pamela's arm. In a way, it had a calming effect on me. "It's strange. As much as I love

Jennifer . . . you've given me more comfort than she ever did. You and I are closer in so many different ways than Jennifer and I ever were. You've always stood by me when no one else gave a damn, and you never asked anything in return." I kissed her softly on the mouth tasting the beauty of her lips. "I respect you, Pamela, more than anyone else in this world. You are the most gentle, honest, decent person I know."

"I love you so much, Kurt." She threw her arms around me and buried her face in my chest. I cradled her body against me and rocked her quietly as her muffled words were spoken into my shoulder. "I'm not as honest as you think, Kurt. Most of the things I did were done for selfish reasons. I listened to you talk about Jennifer because it kept you coming back to me. I sent you money because I wanted you to need me, even if it were only financially. I got you the job with my father to keep you in New York. And I begged my dad to keep you out of the draft."

"What?" I couldn't believe her last statement.

"When I found out your lottery number was so low, I asked my father to use his influence to keep you from being drafted."

"Well, it didn't work. I was still drafted."

"I know. My father told me that General Carson was using his pull to have you sent to Vietnam even though the troops were coming home."

"Are you kidding?" I sat up, shocked by the news. "I didn't even know that Jennifer's father knew I existed."

"Apparently, he did," she replied.

"Jesus! He must have really hated me. Or maybe he just couldn't stand to see his daughter happy. I can't believe he did that."

"It seems that my dad and General Carson were playing their own private tug of war with your life. But it ended in a stalemate. General Carson got you drafted, but my father, thank God, kept you out of combat."

"I always wondered why I was sent to Fort Polk for combat training, but I never got orders for 'Nam." I glared at Pam for the first time during our conversation. "Did you tell your old man that I was Ellie's father? Has he known all this time?"

"I never told him, Kurt. I swear. I think he guessed because I was so adamant about the whole thing, but I never told him. I was just so worried about you. I was sure I'd never see you again. I figured that you'd eventually marry Jennifer, but I didn't care. I just couldn't let you get killed in that stupid war."

"I guess you didn't know that Jennifer was already married when I was drafted." I leaned back on the headboard.

"No. I didn't. I had no idea. I wasn't concerned about her. I was only concerned for you. Please don't hate me, Kurt. I couldn't stand that."

"I don't hate you, Pamela," I paused trying to take in all the new facts that I was learning. "In all honesty, I probably would have despised you at the time. After I finished my training, I remember that I actually wanted to fight. I think for a while, I had a death wish . . . and the easiest way to fulfill it was to get myself killed honorably in a battle. When I was sent to Germany instead, I was so damned mad. I do believe I would have wrung your pretty, little neck if I had found out then." I pulled her up beside me and encircled her with my arms. "A lot's happened since those days." After placing a kiss on her forehead I continued, "It appears that I owe you a great deal more than I thought I did. It seems as if—aside from everything else you've done for me—you have also saved my life. Literally, as well as figuratively."

"I love you, Kurt. I would have done anything for you."

"So, your dad knows about me?" I frowned. "He must think I'm the scum of the earth."

"I don't think Daddy remembers, Kurt." Some of the tension seemed to ease from her body. "When I asked him to find a position in his company for you, he didn't even bat an eyelash. I really don't think he connected the name. After all, it had been years, and my father's a very busy man. He doesn't have the time to recall the name of every person—even me—that he does a favor for. He certainly has never approached me about the subject."

Pamela looked very enticing sitting on the bed with half of one breast peeking out from behind the sheet she had wrapped around her. Her jet-black hair was flowing loosely over her shoulders, and I suddenly had an overwhelming urge to stroke her. As I reached for Pam, she willingly fell into my arms. It felt good to hold her. I didn't love Pamela Woods, but I did care for her. I liked everything about her; perhaps that would be enough, at least for the present. I could worry about the future tomorrow.

4

Jennifer

SOMETIMES IT FELT LIKE I SPENT MORE OF MY LIFE IN THIS GODFORSAKEN sanitarium than out of it. And even on those rare occasions when I was able to leave West Virginia, I was still, more often than not, a prisoner in my wheelchair. I was tired of feeling this way: sick, weak, depressed. And I was so damned lonely. The doctors were always fluctuating with their opinions on my health. They think I'm getting better; they think I'm getting worse; they think I'm stabilizing; they see signs of improvement; they're disappointed with my progress. Hell! I wished they'd make up their minds.

Since my initial admittance, I had been released seven times in order to attempt living on my own. All of them were before Lori's wedding in the summer of 1980, and none of them lasted for more than three months. Before Lori met Bruce, I worked hard to get well so that I could go back to living with her, but since I no longer had anywhere to go, I didn't care if I ever got out of West Virginia. Lori pleaded with me prior to her wedding to be strong enough to participate in it, but I feigned difficulties and didn't attend. I couldn't bear to see her taking the vows. Lori was two years into her marriage; and just as I had anticipated, her visits dwindled down to once a month. It wasn't fair. All I ever wanted in the whole world was Lori. She meant everything to me—everything—but I couldn't have her. I missed her so much.

I turned thirty over a year ago, and on that day my trust fund became available to me. It was quite ironic. During the course of one afternoon, I was penniless, wealthy, and then middle class with nothing but a stroke of the pen from my lawyers. Through the duration of my illness, I didn't have a single dime to my name. Insurance covered the majority of the doctors' bills, but the cost of the sanitarium was another story. When I first arrived, the facility was priced at $20,000 a year. It was now $35,000. At those rates, it would take less than a decade for me to be a pauper again.

The doctors encouraged me to walk. They were so sure that if I just tried, I'd be able to. What the hell for? I was too depressed to care if I ever took another step again. They kept insisting that if I wouldn't exercise my body, my heart was never going to be strong enough to functional normally. Two years ago, I improved enough to take numerous steps. There were even days when I could walk the entire patio, but I had a relapse. Now it was a struggle just to get in and out of the wheelchair. I was ill-tempered, frustrated, and angry, which agitated all the people around me. My refusal to work with the nurses only served to weaken an already ill-functioning, crucial organ of my body. They threatened me with death on several occasions; but I didn't care, I always turned away and muttered statements they'd heard a thousand times before. I was antagonistic. But what the hell! Nobody really gave a damn about me. So why should I even try?

The doctors told me that if I didn't show signs of improvement within the next year, they would have to put me on a list for a heart transplant because the heart I had couldn't take the pressure of another stroke or attack. I laughed in their faces. A heart transplant! That would be the day! I'd rather die than let anyone treat me like a guinea pig. There was no way I'd ever give consent to that operation. The doctors could talk until they were blue in the face, and I still wouldn't sign any form allowing them to experiment on my body with that relatively new procedure.

I knew Dr. Lottman was right about one thing. I was in bad shape—very bad shape. He blamed my condition on the fact that I refused to cooperate, but I realized that wasn't the entire truth. I was sick . . . really sick. He kept asking me to help myself. What a jerk he was! Lottman was always pretending to be my friend. And I knew damn well he didn't want anything but money from me. He didn't care about me; he didn't care about anyone! All he wanted was his precious paycheck. I fought him tooth and nail on everything. I resented his patronizing attitude and his plastic smiles. I used up a lot of my energy screaming at him, but he was so damned patient it was unnerving. Some days when Dr. Lottman came in to talk to me I wouldn't say anything at all. I was completely silent and stared holes through him. He would sit there quietly, sipping on his coffee, waiting for me to respond. Often an entire hour passed without one single word exchanged between us. He silently watched me over the rim of his mug. At the end of these sessions, he always said, "When you want to talk, Jennifer . . . I'll be here to listen. I want to be your friend." Typically, I laughed in a sarcastic manner. It was an absurd idea—Lottman and me—friends? Impossible!

Once I even came on to him while he was giving me my biweekly physical. I was lying on the table, wearing my white dressing gown with nothing underneath, and he was standing next to me. He took my pulse, my blood pressure, and the usual blood sample. After eyeing him for quite a while I sat up and let the gown slip suggestively off my shoulder. Lottman was standing right beside me. I moved over a little bit allowing my breast to rub against his arm. When he looked up from my chart, I smiled. He gave no reaction. He didn't even have the damned decency to blush. I was so pissed off. I thought that if I could seduce him, I could prove what a lousy doctor he was and that he was using his patients for sexual activities, but he didn't fall for my ruse. Three times I tried to steer him into sex. Three damn times! And the third time I was downright blatant about my moves. We were alone in his office. Dr. Lottman was inquiring about my marriage to David, and I was being my usual silent self. He came around his desk and leaned against the side of it—watching me, studying me, staring at me. I couldn't stand his cold, professional manner. He was like a rock, and I wanted to chip his façade a little bit. I crooked my fingers as if I wanted him to bend down so I could whisper something in his ear. When he was at my level and only inches away from me, I encircled him with my arms and planted a firm, sensual kiss directly on his lips. He didn't jerk away. He didn't even act shocked. When I was finished, he simply stood up, walked around his desk, and sat down in his chair. The only sound in the room was the drumbeat tapping of his fingers on the desk.

He took a deep breath before he finally spoke. "I imagine you don't think I'm clever enough to figure out exactly what's going on inside your head. I'm not as dumb as you seem to think I am. Listen here, young lady, I've about had it with you. You're rude, insensitive, selfish, and downright bitchy. But I'm not going to give up. You don't seem to realize that I'm a very tenacious man. You can fight me all you want. You can push me away; you can remain silent; you can use your filthy language; you can even dangle sex in front of me. In fact, you can fight me all the way to your grave, if that's what you really want. It's up to you, Jennifer. But remember one thing: I'm not a quitter—and I'm not giving up." His words were a combination of firm and tender. He spoke softly but each syllable was clear and distinct. He leaned across the desk and pointed a finger in my direction. "I want to make one point perfectly clear. I do not want to be your lover. I want all this crap to stop. In all honesty, Jennifer, if I thought that sex was the way to reach you, then perhaps I would have taken you up on your offer; however, I know you better than you think. I want to be your doctor, Jennifer. I want to help you."

"Oh, come on, Doc! Don't give me that crap."

"You shut up just one minute and listen to me. I'm sick and tired of you sitting silently in that chair and wasting my valuable time. I have something to say, and I'm not going to let you interrupt me just because you feel like talking for a change. Now . . . this is the way it's going to be from here on out. You are going to come to my office three times a week. You are going to sit in that chair and talk. I don't give a damn what you talk about. You can spout off about Brezhnev's death, or the new Vietnam memorial that was dedicated last week in Washington, a movie you saw on television or punk rock music. I don't give a damn what you talk about! But you are going to talk! No more silent treatments. And we're going to continue physical therapy. I will no longer accept your excuses. There isn't going to be any more of this rubbing up against me crap, either. That's all going to stop! I want to help you, Jennifer. I demand your respect. And damn it, if it's the last thing I do, I'm going to get it."

"Dr. Lottman . . . "

"You're dismissed, Jennifer! I'll see you on Wednesday." His words were terse and final.

I was fuming. How dare he talk to me that way! I pushed the buttons on my wheelchair, spun it around, and left the room. I was so angry, I didn't talk to anyone for two days.

2

On New Year's Day 1983, there was a skeleton crew on duty. I was feeling particularly depressed. Lori had been to visit me only twice in December, and Dr. Lottman had been on vacation the last couple of weeks, which meant I didn't even have him to aggravate. Actually, I'd grown quite attached to the antagonistic relationship we shared. Even though I pretended to detest our conversations, I did look forward to the sessions. Now, without them, the days melted together in a monotonous string of lonely, boring hours.

"Aren't you Jennifer Carson?" A voice interrupted my thoughts.

It was far too cold to be outside, so I was gazing at the snow-covered mountains from the main lobby window. I turned to see who was speaking to me. "Yes, I'm Jennifer."

"I'm Cindy Sherwood."

"Sorry. The name doesn't ring a bell."

"My maiden name was Wilder."

"Yes. I remember you. Cindy Wilder. You went to Elon."

"That's right."

"Do you work here?" I asked.

"I'm a nurse. I used to work in Wheeling, but my husband was transferred here for temporary work a month ago, so I applied for a part-time position. I got lucky. They hired me last week. I'll be staying until spring. I'm surprised I didn't run into you earlier."

"I don't get out of my room very often, especially when the patio's not accessible."

"We're just going to have to get you up and around more often."

I stared her down. "The doctors didn't send you over here to give me a lecture, did they? I'll tune you out if you start. I don't need any rookie with a sunny smile and positive vibes."

"First of all, I'm not a rookie. I've been a nurse for six years." Her voice remained very professional. "And secondly . . . no one sent me to you. I haven't even seen your chart."

I appraised the situation. "Okay, I believe you." I relaxed. Although I hated nurses and their constant busywork, it was nice to see a familiar face. "So, you're married. Any kids?"

"Yes. We have one. Jim—my husband—he wants a huge family. Personally, I'll settle for two, maybe three."

"Is it a boy or a girl?"

"A girl. She'll be two next month." Cindy continued her friendly chatter by telling me in great detail how she and her husband met, courted, and married. She described his mother, father, and brothers. Then, she went into an elaborate description of her home.

I was enjoying every word Cindy spoke. It was a refreshing change from my everyday humdrum existence. I was taking great pleasure in Cindy's warmth. It was odd. When I was at Elon, I never would have been caught dead in Cindy's room passing the time with friendly conversation. We had nothing in common. In fact, the only feeling I ever had for Cindy was pity because of her unfortunate situation with Brad Malone. Before I realized what I was saying, words, slipped out, "So what ever happened to Brad?"

Cindy's face made a complete transformation from a pleasant smiling expression to one of despondent contemplation. "I think he's still in New Jersey. Apparently, he's part owner in a few nightclubs. I heard he married some girl he'd been living with for years. That's all I know."

"I'm sorry. I didn't mean to be so blunt."

"No problem. Forget about it." Cindy waved her hand nonchalantly. "It's no big deal. To be honest, I haven't thought about him in years. You just took me by surprise, bringing him up out of the blue like that."

"I'm glad you didn't end up with him. He was real bad news."

"It took a long time." Cindy paused. "But I finally figured out that a relationship with Brad was a no-win situation for me."

"You're a bright girl. I knew you'd eventually come to that conclusion." I was a bit more sarcastic than I had intended to be. I smiled sheepishly and apologized.

"I loved him. God, how I loved him." Cindy lowered her head and hesitated for several seconds before her soft voice began to speak again. "Brad could have loved me. I'm sure that he really was capable of loving me if it hadn't been for that awful Lori Davis. How I hated her! She was so beautiful, so confident . . . so chic even with her plain clothes and old-fashioned deportment. Brad loved her—not me. He was so crazy about Lori. He was so wild in love with her that I never even had a chance to make him feel that way about me. And Lori Davis didn't even care. She didn't want him. Haughty little bitch! But I wanted him. A lot of good that did me. How I remember the torture Brad put me through! It used to hurt so badly every time I saw him watching Lori. He didn't know I noticed, but I did. He never stared at me that way. Some nights when I snuck up into his dorm room and spent the night with him he called out her name in his sleep. I would lie there quietly and listen to him repeat it over and over again. Once I even tried to kiss her name off his lips but instead, he made love to me as if I were Lori. He was passionate yet savage . . . almost violent. He was rough and gentle at the same time. It was as if he were in another dimension. Then, when he woke up, he didn't even remember." Cindy smiled in a forlorn manner. "Oh, he remembered making love, but he didn't remember that he called out her name . . . or at least he didn't admit it. He worshipped her . . . and I hated her for that." Suddenly, Cindy's eyes snapped open as the recollection of an old memory began to replace the sad expression she had been wearing. She put her fingers to her lips and closed her eyes firmly. "I'm sorry, Jennifer. I just remembered that Lori Davis was a good friend of yours. I didn't mean to get so carried away. Truly, I didn't. In fact, that's all behind me now. I'm really very happy. I haven't thought about Brad in years. You have to believe me. I don't love him anymore. I know that sounds ridiculous especially after the way I was just carrying on, but I really don't. I guess I just kind of got melancholy when you mentioned his name. You might find this hard to believe, but I really am very happy with my life the way it is. I wouldn't want to change it one little bit."

"Oh, I believe you, Cindy. Your husband sounds a hell of a lot better than Brad Malone; you're lucky to be rid of him. You might have loved Brad, but he would never have made you happy." I paused and smiled as I added in a joking tone. "I suppose I hated Brad Malone about as much as you despised Lori. He was such a bastard, and you seemed so nice. I never could figure out how the two of you got together in the first place. He didn't deserve anyone like you."

"Is that a compliment?"

"Yeah, I guess it is." I laughed again. I couldn't remember the last time I laughed twice in a row. It would be nice to have a friend in this lonely place.

"In all honesty, Jennifer, Brad wasn't that bad. I can be objective now that it's all over and tucked neatly away in my past. Brad was really not a bad person at all. He could be very sweet and gentle sometimes. And believe it or not, he was very sensitive. Of course, he probably wouldn't agree with me—he pretended to be such a hard-ass; but it's true. Toward the end—I didn't see it at the time, but I can understand it all now—but toward the end of our relationship, Brad sacrificed a lot of time to help me over some hurdles. It was a rough point in my life. He didn't desert me when I needed him the most. He could have; he even wanted to—I can see that now—but, thankfully, he didn't. He stuck it out. If it hadn't been for Brad, I probably would have cracked up."

"I still think he's a bastard."

"Well, that's okay . . . " Cindy laughed. "I still think Lori Davis is a bitch."

"Well, I guess you can say we are both a little prejudiced." We laughed simultaneously.

Cindy and I continued talking, but the topic of discussion changed. I began to open up to her. I told her how long I'd been stuck in this place. I explained to her about how my heart kept weakening, and how the doctors were hinting at the possibility of a transplant at some point in the future if my condition didn't correct itself. And I admitted for the first time—to someone other than Lori—that I was lonely. I also told Cindy that I would kick her on her butt if she ever told anyone else what I had just confessed. She laughed. I did too. It had a wonderful sound to it. Before Cindy left to continue her rounds, she gave me a gentle hug. "Happy New Year, Jennifer. Perhaps 1983 will be a better year for you."

3

"You have a visitor, Miss Carson," the nurse said cheerfully. My spirits were immediately lifted at the thought of seeing Lori again. It was late April and the last time I'd seen her was during Super Bowl XVII when she and Bruce came to watch the Redskins beat the Dolphins 27 to 17 on the big screen television in the main lobby. I still didn't care much for football, but I had been delighted with Lori's company.

It seemed as if I spent every day waiting for Lori to come. Since Cindy Wilder had taken a permanent position at a nearby hospital, the only highlights of my life were the hours I spent with Lori. I moved my head slowly to the side so I could watch her approach, but it wasn't Lori walking toward me.

"Hello, Jennifer," Kurt said as he stood in front of me. He looked good—much better than the last time he stood on the patio and faced my frank, honest statements. He was taller than I remembered, and much more masculine, as if he had filled out with the passing of years. That young, adolescent mien had vanished from his appearance. His hair was styled and cut much shorter. He had a thick, brown mustache that made him appear quite sophisticated. And his blue eyes—once faded and dull—were sparkling again as they had when we were young.

Lori had written that Kurt was semi-living with the woman I knew to be the mother of his child. Perhaps that was the reason for his confident strides and healthy appearance. I was glad for him. Lori, of course, to the best of my knowledge, still did not know about the fact that she had been an aunt for over a decade. I imagined that was the way Kurt wanted it. It was one of the few secrets I kept from Lori, and the only one that I felt she had a right to know. But I wouldn't hurt Kurt by telling his sister. When he was ready, he would tell Lori.

"Hello, Kurt. You're looking well." I watched him as he sat down in a hardback chair in front of me. It was difficult to recall that there was once a time when I basked in his gentle warmth. My God! It seemed like an eternity ago when we had quenched our desires in his cozy single bed in Chapel Hill. I strained my mind to remember what he looked like without his clothes, but I wasn't able to form the memory. A gentle breeze blew a few strands of his hair, and for a fraction of a moment, I saw the young man he was when we first met. For a brief segment in time, Kurt and I were happy. Perhaps it was an artificial happiness, but both of us were happy. What a shame it was not possible to go back in our past and freeze ourselves in the moments of time when we were filled with innocence—when we smiled the most, when we laughed a lot, when problems seemed small or even nonexistent, when days were filled with music, laughter, and warmth—and when the word loneliness had no meaning.

I was another person then. I couldn't remember that Jennifer Carson. What ever happened to her? In retrospect, I honestly believe she never really existed. That Jennifer Carson was a figment of Kurt's imagination. She was *his* dream . . . a dream that never had a chance to come true. For a couple of short years, someone else lived inside my body, motivated my actions—instigated my thoughts. It was someone else who struggled for a foothold on my life. That Jennifer Carson died. I tried! I really wanted to be that Jennifer Carson. Oh well, it didn't matter anymore. It was all too late now. There were no real choices for me. I couldn't fight the way I felt. I couldn't fight who I was.

Kurt stood silently staring at me. What was he thinking? Was he wondering what happened to his pretty little angel with the long flaxen hair? Was he gathering up memories that were better left unspoken and buried inside both our minds? Or was he simply taking pity on a poor, worn-out woman who looked far older than her years?

"How are you, Jen?" He looked pensive as he spoke.

"Oh, just peachy," I smiled sarcastically. "I feel grand. And don't bother telling me that I don't look the part. That's the nurse's job."

"You sound very bitter, Jennifer."

"Bitter? Me?" I thought of how fate put me in this wheelchair. I recalled the times I was released from this barless prison only to reenter it after a few short weeks of freedom. I wondered what would happen if I ever did get well: Where would I live, and what would I do? I thought of my father: Why was I chosen to be the "lucky duck" to be his daughter? I thought about my health: Why was I given a heart that wasn't worth a shit? Then there was always David: Why did I self-destruct with him and waste those precious months—time I had taken for granted? And finally, I thought of all the years I spent loving Lori: Why?

"Give me one good reason why I shouldn't be bitter?" I said caustically.

"You're alive."

"Oh, Christ! Did your sister send you here to pump me up with optimism?"

"I haven't seen Lori." He paused. "What do the doctors have to say?"

"Screw the doctors, Kurt. I don't want to talk about me. I don't even want to think about me." I paused and tried to smile apologetically. "Let's talk about you. You look marvelous! What are you doing now? Still living in New York? Are you seeing . . . what was that girl's name?"

"Yes, I'm still in New York. In June, it'll be official. I'll be a CPA. I put some feelers out, because I think I'll leave Woods Enterprises and work for a private firm. There will be more money in it for me. Besides, I don't think under the circumstances, I should stay with Woods." Kurt seemed stilted. He stopped long enough to pour himself a cup of coffee before adding, "The girl's name is Pamela."

"Pamela, huh? Pretty name. She still in love with you?" I was being awfully blunt. I smiled inwardly as I realized that I was beginning to sound like Doctor Lottman. It was just the type of frankness he would use.

"You know Pamela?"

"No. We never met, but I saw her once . . . in Chapel Hill . . . under a tree . . . a lifetime ago."

"Oh . . . " He paused. "How could you have known that she loved me? I didn't even realize it myself until a couple of years ago."

"I saw the way she looked at you, Kurt. It was written all over her face. I didn't understand at the time—and I was far too hurt to be objective about the whole affair—but I have had a lot of time to think about my life—and your life—and a lot of other people's lives. I know what I saw in your Pamela's eyes. She loved you. Does she still?"

"Yes, I suppose she does. She's wonderful. Her love's very important to me. I feel needed with her. I respect and admire her more than anyone in the world."

"But . . . "

"But . . . what?" Kurt inquired as he stared through me.

"But you don't love her. Is that what you're trying to say?"

He glanced out at the rolling hills in the distance and scanned the line of trees on the horizon. There was a long moment of silence before he answered. "I want to love her, but it seems that I can't quite let go of what you and I shared. I still have these overwhelming feelings for you, Jennifer. There are days when I think I love you as much now as I did then."

"I don't think it's me you're in love with, Kurt." I spoke slowly. "I think you're in love with the memories." I paused to let my message sink in.

"Somehow over the course of time those memories developed into a fantasy. You loved the person you wanted me to be."

"Maybe." He responded quietly.

"I also think that perhaps you are clinging to the way *you* were then. It's hard growing up—letting go of youth—knowing that it will never return. And along with maturing, you lose those idealistic values you treasured so much." I chuckled. "I bet you aren't even liberal anymore. In fact, I'll wager that you're beginning to think Ronald Reagan isn't such a bad president after all."

"Why do you say that?"

"The signs are obvious! You resemble a classic conservative. Look at the way you're dressed. Silk tie. Gorgeous suit. Nice fabric! Bet it cost you a pretty penny too. Do you know that until today, I've never seen you in a suit? The only thing lacking is a pair of designer sunglasses resting on the bridge of your nose. And your hair . . . you used to be able to put it in a ponytail. My guess is that you don't go to a barbershop. I bet you go to a stylist. Am I right?"

"Yeah." Kurt lowered his head.

"Look at those wing tips. Whatever happened to the tennis shoes with holes in them? I'll make another bet. I'll bet you own several pairs of Reeboks, you jog, and you work out at a private club."

"Guilty of all of the above."

"That's what's bothering you! Isn't it, Kurt? You feel guilty because you've changed. You're afraid to become what you always despised when you were young. You hated the establishment! You hated big business! You wanted to be a lawyer, so you could defend the poor and needy. Now you're a CPA with nice clothes and a comfortable life. And what's more—you like it! Poor Kurt, don't take it to heart! It was fashionable to be liberal in the sixties. In fact, I heard a few doctors talking the other day. One of them said that if you were not liberal in the sixties you had no heart; and if you were still liberal in the eighties you had no brain. I think by the end of the decade that's probably going to be very true for the majority of people. So, you see, being liberal is no longer the "in" thing to be—conservative is the way the pendulum is swinging. It's OK, Kurt! The whole country's doing it. You're not alone. You don't have to feel guilty."

"When did you become so analytical?"

"If you had someone tapping on your brain for nearly six years, you'd be able to analyze people too." I smirked. "Don't hang on to yesterday, Kurt. Look at yourself! You aren't the same anymore! And guess what? That's okay! You wouldn't be happy going back to being that person. Those days are over! Live for now; live for tomorrow; don't live for yesterday."

A half smile formed over his lips. "You're quite astute, Jennifer." He leaned toward me, cupped my face in his hands and gently stroked my cheeks with his thumbs. "I'm glad I came to see you."

I closed my eyes as he placed a chaste kiss on my cheek.

"Good-bye, Jennifer," he said as he smiled warmly. "Thanks for putting everything into perspective for me."

"Take care of yourself."

"If you ever need me, I'll come. All you have to do is call." Without another word, he pivoted, and walked away. Kurt Davis was gone.

I bit my lower lip in order to keep the stinging sensation from burning my eyes. Chills ran down my spine. I felt more alone at that moment than any other time in my life. Jesus Christ! There was no one . . . no one in the world for me.

4

Two weeks later Lori came to visit me without her husband. I was delighted to see her. In spite of the fact that she'd put on a couple of pounds, Lori looked wonderful; actually, the increased weight seemed to enhance her beauty. Her eyes were shining, and there were splashes of natural color on her cheeks.

We spent hours talking in the gardens before Lori started lecturing me about my health and the fact that I wasn't contributing to my own improvement. I felt like a naughty child, and Lori was my parent instead of my friend. At first, I was angry. I didn't want to listen to her. Then, I realized that she was only trying to help. She cared.

"Jennifer, I had a long talk with Dr. Lottman before I came out to the patio. He tells me that you are fighting him tooth and nail on everything. What the hell's gotten into you? You want to die or something?" There was not a trace of joking in her voice when she made her statement. Every line in her face was etched with concern, and there were big tears welling up in the corners of her eyes. She seemed genuinely upset.

"What do you care? You probably couldn't give a shit if I died or not." I laughed slightly as my words were spoken. They dripped with cynicism.

"Damn you, Jennifer! How can you say such a vile thing. You know that's not true."

"You've been married how long? Almost three years. I bet I can count on my fingers the number of times you've been to see me since the wedding."

"You're exaggerating, Jennifer. Granted, I don't get to come as often as I want, but I've been here more than that."

"You don't care about me! You don't care what happens to me!" There was an intentional whine in my voice. I knew I was fishing for compliments. There was no doubt that I was behaving childishly; I only hoped that Lori couldn't see through me.

"Jennifer Carson! You can't possibly believe one word of that." She bent down on her knees in front of my chair and cupped both of my hands in hers. "How can you assume that I don't care what happens to you? You are the best and dearest friend I have ever had. The only real friend in my entire life. I've told you that so many times it ought to be engraved in your brain by now. I love you as much, if not more, than anyone I've ever known."

"Including your husband?" I asked making her measure and pinpoint her devotion.

Lori glanced away and then gave a feeble smile as she returned her eyes to mine. "I'm very happy with Bruce. Our relationship gives me contentment and security—aspects in my life I never thought I'd have. Perhaps, I don't love him as much as I should, but I do love him. Bruce gives me a reason to wake up each morning, which is something I had lost a few years ago." She hesitated slightly as she squeezed my fingers and smiled mischievously into my eyes. "I suppose, Jennifer, that in a way, I probably do love you more than Bruce. You understand me. You've helped me over more hurdles than most people see in a lifetime, and you've always stood by me, despite everything. I don't think Bruce could have done that for me. And if the tables were turned—truth be told—I doubt I could have done it for him. But, thank God, you were always there."

"How about Brad Malone?" I asked after several moments of silence. I held her eyes waiting to see the reaction his name would have on her expression. "Do you love me more than him?" The ultimate question was hanging in the air.

Her features transformed from a warm, amusing glow to that of pondering memories. Her eyes actually changed color slightly from a crystal blue to a darker shade as they became misted with a haze of glittering moisture. The line of her jaw tightened as a muscle flexed against her cheek. She used her tongue to dampen her lower lip. "You know, Jennifer, I thought for a while that I was truly over Brad. I really did. Sometimes months went by when I wouldn't even recall a single memory: good or bad. But, recently, I realized that Brad's still there—somewhere in the recesses of my mind. It seems that no amount of effort on my part can banish him from my thoughts. My God . . ." She let out an enormous amount of air from her lungs. As she heaved the breath, she glanced upward to the sky. "He still invades my dreams. He has a way of creeping into my daily life without my having any control over it. For instance, I was washing dishes the other night—up to my elbows in suds—and I heard him laugh. There wasn't anyone home. The house was completely silent, but I could actually hear his laugh. And sometimes, when I close my eyes, I can see him smiling. How I remember that smile. There were times when I loved it, and there were other times when I hated him for it." She stopped a moment, smiling to herself. "The other day I was walking through Springfield Mall. I thought I saw Brad ahead of me. I went weak; every part of me felt like Jell-O. I raced after the man and practically tackled him from behind. I was so embarrassed. The guy turned around. He was a perfect stranger."

"Do you know he's married?" I asked.

"Yes. Kurt told me he saw Brad in New York—on his honeymoon. I never thought of Brad as the type of person to love anyone enough to get married. His wife must be a remarkable woman. I hope he's happy." Lori shook her head sadly as she unconsciously twisted her wedding band. "Did you know that Brad sent me a wedding gift? Can you believe the audacity of the man? I got a wedding gift from him while he was on his honeymoon! I thought about sending it back to him—unopened; instead, I stuffed it in a drawer. I'll never use it."

"What was it?" I inquired.

"A picture frame. It's actually quite beautiful." Lori became quiet—lost in memories.

I considered telling Lori about the conversation that I had with Cindy Wilder, but decided against it. Brad Malone had sucked enough of Lori's time and attention. I wasn't going to give her any more food for thought.

"It's all so silly." Grinning sheepishly, Lori broke the silence. "I know what the problem is, Jennifer. I'm getting old. I mean, I don't think thirty-two is ancient; but let's face it, I'm not a kid either. My twenties are behind me, and my life is about to change drastically. I need to let go of the past." Her face lit up with enthusiasm. "I'm going to have a baby, Jen." She giggled happily. "I'm so happy about this. I've never wanted anything more in my life. I love it." She cupped her abdomen. "I can't wait until I can actually hold it in my arms."

Lori was pregnant! The shock was staggering. I sat back in my chair and simply stared at her, completely dumbfounded by her news. I felt as if someone had ripped out my heart. A baby! A baby was living proof that

Lori had found joy and contentment in her life. She would no longer have any need for me. Lori always wanted children. She wanted Brad Malone's child. I was positive, in the back of her mind, even though Lori hadn't mentioned it, she was contemplating their child that might have been. That was probably one of the reasons for her reflecting so much on Brad and their past together.

But now Lori would have a legitimate child. There was nothing I could do to prevent it.

"Don't look so unhappy, Jennifer. Ignore all that other stuff I was saying before. I was just rambling. I don't know what got into me. All expectant mothers get emotional and think weird thoughts. They have no control over it. I must admit that I do get a little apprehensive about all the responsibilities of raising a child, but the joys are far more rewarding." She smiled as she smoothed the material over her belly. "This baby is a whole new beginning for me. An entire new world. It's a time where I can let the past die, and the future will have a chance at a real start. Can you understand what I'm trying to say, Jennifer?"

"Yes . . . yes, I understand," I answered even though inside I was screaming. No! No . . . I don't understand. Can't we go back to the way it was when we lived together—sharing our lives, before I got sick, before Bruce, before a baby could tear you away from me forever? Brad's child was the biggest threat, but now Bruce was giving Lori what I would never be able to give her. They were going to have a family. A child would make it binding. There would be no room for me in Lori's life.

I mustn't be so selfish. God! Forgive me, Lori! Lori, please forgive me. What had happened to me? How had I become so corrupted by my love to deny Lori the one dream that would make her happy? She always longed for a baby. She loved children. I had to put a stop to my vindictive and selfish thoughts.

"I am happy for you, Lori. Really I am. I guess I'm just a little surprised." I managed a smile and immediately was rewarded by her firm embrace.

"I love you, Jennifer. I really do love you. In fact, I consider you to be more my family than my family actually is. I haven't told anyone about the baby yet. I haven't told my parents or Bruce's family. To be perfectly honest, Bruce doesn't even know he's going to be a father yet. I just had to come here first and share it with you."

"When is the baby due?" I tried to act interested.

"Sometime around Christmas."

"Do you think Bruce will be excited?" I kept trying to think of pertinent questions that would show enthusiasm.

"I'm sure he'll be ecstatic. He's wanted a baby from the beginning. Bruce loves kids. He'll be thirty-five next month, and he thought all along that we should start our family right away. He doesn't want me to work after the baby's born. I can understand that even though I'll miss teaching and the classroom, but he's right. If we couldn't afford the luxury of me staying home, maybe I'd disagree with him, but he makes plenty of money. We're lucky."

"You're going to be a terrific mother, Lori." I paused. "I really am happy for you."

Later, after Lori had left, I pondered my own problems. Everything had changed. For so many years, I lived off of Lori's life, taking what morsels I could get from her. But it was all going to be different now. The baby would alter everything. Lori had her own future. And now even her present was on steady ground. I was going to have to learn to live without her . . . make a life of my own. It didn't seem fair. It didn't seem fair at all. I hurt inside. I didn't know what to do. But I did know that I wanted a chance. I wanted a real honest to God chance at life. Maybe the nurses and doctors were right. Perhaps I could recover if I just made the attempt. Help myself, as they always said to me. Maybe if I could get better I could get out of here and start over. There must be some place out there for me. There must be a Jennifer Carson somewhere inside of me that could fit into the outside world. I felt like talking. I mean *really* talking. I had so many thoughts inside of me that were screaming to get out. There must be someone besides

Lori I could confide in. The feelings were overflowing inside of me. I wanted to talk. I needed someone. Where could I go?

I pushed the buttons on my wheelchair and headed in the direction of Dr. Martin Lottman's office. He always told me he wanted to listen. Now was the time to prove it.

5

Brad

As I entered the room, I read the banner hanging on the wall. "Welcome to the 10th reunion of the Class of 1973." It was hard to believe that a decade had passed since graduating from Elon. It was great to be back. Homecoming Weekend. Football. Fraternity brothers. The smell of fall in the air. It was amazing how quickly I could chop off ten years of my life and revert back to the memories of being a student. Everywhere I looked, I felt a flashback wash over me.

A few moments earlier, Jill and I went through the Alamance Building where, as a freshman, I had taken that mandatory religion course and slept through more classes than I attended. I also showed Jill the Long Student Union. We ordered a Coke, sat in the booth, and watched all the activities around us. In addition, we strolled around the main campus holding hands, as I pointed to this spot or that place and recalled one anecdote after another. Jill laughed at my stories. In the morning, we visited the frat house. It looked exactly the same, with the exception of the fact that the second step on the front porch was in need of repair and a new paint job wouldn't hurt its facade. Excitedly, I dragged Jill through each room, reminiscing the entire time. During the social for the current and alumni fraternity brothers,

I quietly snuck out the side door, leaving Jill in the company of several wives. I suddenly felt a need to be alone. I walked to Harper Center. On my way there, I discovered that a new dorm had been built—Story Center. It stood directly in the path that led from main campus—the same path Laura had walked when I used to watch her from my dorm window. To my amazement, I was actually disturbed by the addition. It was odd; I wanted everything to be *exactly* the same as I remembered it, and the change bothered me.

After circling the lake, I sat under the old oak tree at the edge of the water. Colorful leaves were scattered around me. I leaned against the trunk as I raked my fingers through the grass. Plucking dozens of blades, I made a pile, concentrating my efforts on the task. I felt as if I'd been transported in a time machine, and at any moment, Laura would come racing out of Staley Dorm, smiling, her hair springing softly off her shoulders, arms outstretched, ready to throw herself into my embrace.

I shook my head. I couldn't believe how real the image was in my mind. I scanned the entire area unconsciously hoping that Laura really would appear, but all I saw were students absorbed in their own lives. They looked so *young!*

I remained by the lake for almost an hour, not quite sure what I was waiting for, but not willing to leave either. Melancholy emotions encompassed me. Finally, I stood up, brushed the grass from my pants, and returned to the frat house. Jill didn't even notice my absence.

I read the sign again, this time out loud. "Welcome to the 10th reunion of the Class of 1973." Scanning the room, I saw a number of familiar faces. It was nice of the college to provide a pregame brunch to gather everyone together. In the crowd, there were dozens of girls I had dated, most of whose names I could not recall. I spied three guys from my hall. I hoped the weekend didn't pass without a chance to speak with each of them. Over by the buffet table, I saw Janie Council. Tugging slightly at Jill's arm, I coaxed her in that direction. "There's someone I want you to meet." When I introduced them, I told Jill that Ms. Council was—without a doubt—my favorite professor at Elon. I found that as the conversation continued and the room filled with still more alumni, I became distracted; my eyes roamed from one side of the room to the other in search of one particular face.

I didn't see her.

As the function was winding down, I came to the conclusion that Laura did not make the trip back for Homecoming. A quiet depression fell over me as I realized how much I was looking forward to seeing her again. After finishing a conversation with the roommate I had in Moffit during my sophomore year, I suggested to Jill that it was time to head for the stadium. We slowly made our way through the thinning crowd. Before I reached the door, I noticed Jack Briskin in our path. Jack Briskin. What a creep! It was no great loss if I spent the entire weekend without speaking to him. I began guiding Jill more to my left in order to avoid contact with him. When I ventured another look in his direction, I strained to focus on the individual who was lost in conversation with Jack. I could only see the back of her head. I shifted direction again and headed toward them. My hands were clammy; my heart raced; I swallowed three separate times because my throat was so dry. The closer I got, the more certain I became. I meandered around groups of people, dragging Jill behind me. The hair was the same color. The height was right. As I got closer, I heard the laugh. That wonderful sound. Yes! It was Laura. I didn't need to see her face. I could tell by the warm chuckling that drifted through the air. I stopped short, watching her as she spoke with Jack and two strangers. After taking several long breaths to steady my nerves, I took the remaining steps between us and stood directly behind her. She couldn't see me. I leaned over to whisper in her ear. "Bet you can't guess who this is?" Even though I finished speaking, I didn't pull away. She smelled so good. I couldn't see her expression, but I sensed her stiffen. The conversation died. There was only silence.

Finally, she spoke. "Yes . . . I know who it is." She paused. "Hello, Brad."

"Hi, Laura . . . let me get a good look at you." She spun around slowly.

My God! She was gorgeous—even more beautiful than any of my memories. Her irises were every bit as blue as the sky outside. Her warm smile created tiny crinkles at the corners of her eyes, which only seemed to enhance the sparkle in them. I loved the way she was wearing her hair—shoulder length, full, and brushed away from her face. "You look wonderful, Laura," I said. It wasn't until I reached for her hands that I gazed downward. Spellbound, I stood stock-still. "You're pregnant!" I nearly choked on my words.

"I am?" she chuckled. "I thought I swallowed a giant watermelon." Everyone laughed.

"I . . . I . . . I didn't know." I couldn't believe I was stuttering so badly.

"I want you to met my husband, Bruce . . . Bruce Dailey . . . this is Brad Malone." She paused. "And you know Jack Briskin . . . this is his wife, Amy." She pointed to the woman standing next to her.

"It seems that Brad has lost his manners and isn't going to introduce me. I suppose I'll have to do it myself. I'm Jill Malone . . . Brad's wife." Jill shook hands with everyone. "Brad, darling, are you all right?"

"Yes . . . I'm fine," I replied to Jill before turning my attention back to Laura. "I'm just surprised. I don't think I have ever thought of you as pregnant. It becomes you."

"Thank you." She lowered her gaze as a soft blush spread over her face.

"You must be due shortly."

"Six more weeks," she responded.

"I bet you're excited," Jill interjected.

"We are," Laura answered as she automatically latched on to her husband's arm. "Bruce and I are very excited about this little critter."

"Not to interrupt you all," Jack spoke for the first time. "If we want to get to the game before kickoff, we should leave now. Laura, would you and Bruce like to ride with us? We have a van."

"Sure," Bruce responded.

"Can we have a lift too?" I inquired ignoring the tug on my arm from Jill. "My car is clear across campus." Jack didn't seem pleased by my question, but to avoid being rude he included us. I wanted to sit with Laura in the car, but Bruce took his rightful place next to her. At the game, I tried to get close to Laura again, but Jill positioned herself between us making verbal or physical contact of any kind impossible during the entire time. I turned my attention to the plays on the field, but discovered that as hard as I tried, my eyes continued to wander in Laura's direction. It seemed as if she were purposely refusing to look my way no matter how much I willed her to do so.

After the game, the six of us made plans to eat dinner at a new steak restaurant in Burlington called The Cutting Board. I arrived at the table before Jill or Bruce and grabbed the seat next to Laura. All of us made small talk as we waited for the food to arrive. Jack discussed his business at length. His wife described her assistant managerial position with the Hilton in their hometown. Bruce told everyone about his hardware store before Jill finally started talking.

"I'm so proud of Brad. His father had three quaint, little restaurants before Brad got involved in the business. He changed them into gold mines. Brad completely renovated the original three, converting them into clubs. Now there are six of them. Brad's Follies. That's the name . . . isn't it cute? Three in New Jersey, one in Delaware, one in Pennsylvania, and he just opened the latest one in New York City."

"Brad, that's fantastic." Laura seemed genuinely impressed. "You really have a gift."

"Remember when I couldn't stand the thought of working for my father?"

She laughed softly. "I certainly do. You cringed at the idea. What happened?"

"I don't know exactly. I think I grew up. My father and I are a lot alike. Perhaps when I was a kid I fought those very aspects of his personality that I so much admire now. I love him very much. I bet you never thought you'd hear me say that." There were six people at the table, but I saw no one except Laura. We continued talking—our heads together—so engrossed in our conversation that we barely touched the food in front of us. I told her about how we almost lost our shirts when I renovated the first club into a disco. "My timing was off by a year, and we couldn't fill the club at first. Do you know that my father never said a word? He gambled on me . . . I took his entire life's work and almost dumped it down the toilet, and he never said a negative word. He stood by me. Then, of course, it skyrocketed at the end of '77, and we converted the other two. The clubs were packed the majority of the time with standing room only." I paused long enough to take a sip of my drink. "But disco didn't last long; so a few years later, I changed the concept again to a country sound that quite often crossed over the line into pop. It was a good thing I saw it coming or we probably would have gone bust. We were in the middle of dealings for a building in Delaware and construction from scratch on the club in Pennsylvania." I took a bite of my steak, but I didn't even taste it. I was too excited. "Now, I think it's time for another change. I've thought about converting the sound system to compact disc. It's state of the art. The acoustics are tremendous, but there isn't that much available right now on CD, which means we'd be limited to the songs we can play. And I don't think it's wise to switch over yet. So I put that idea on the back burner for now."

"What do you think about the music these days?"

"Today's sound is saturated with heavy metal and new wave. We tried catering to that age group last summer, but it didn't work. That style of music has no lasting substance to it. I doubt if, in another year or so, it will even be around."

"Have you thought about focusing on our age group instead of trying to appeal to this new generation?" Laura asked, completely immersed in our conversation. "Everyone who was born in the post-World War II era—what's that nickname we've acquired—The Baby Boomers—we're all whizzing through our thirties. Perhaps you should tap that market, instead of punk rock."

"Yeah . . . I see what you mean. A lot of oldies. Maybe even specialize on certain nights." I could feel the adrenaline rush through me. I loved it when new ideas took shape.

Laura placed a warm hand on mine. She seemed comfortable with our conversation. "Maybe one night a week," she spoke excitedly, "there could be nothing but Beatles' tunes. I know for a fact that my brother would go absolutely bananas over a place that had all Beatles' music. There must be millions of fans like him."

"That's a great idea." I gripped her hand, bringing it to my lips and kissing the palm. "You're a genius." I laughed. "And, on top of that, I could get a couple of large screens, strategically located, and play their old movies. *Hard Day's Night* one week . . . the next, *Help!* or *Yellow Submarine*. And I could make the dance floor smaller. It doesn't need to be so big anymore now that disco died. A smaller dance floor means more seating . . . which of course, means more booze sold and more money . . . more profit."

"But Brad, you can't play Beatles every night. Can you?"

"No . . . but that's the beauty of it. Each night will be different. Music videos seem to be popular right now . . . perhaps a night with them bouncing off the walls is an idea. Saturday night would be great for that! But Friday would be a perfect night for Beatles . . . draw the working people. TGIF happy hour. The college kids don't leave campus as much on Friday night as they do on Saturday. Three of our six clubs are close to universities. So Saturday could be geared to the younger set. *Flashdance* was a huge success this year. The sound track off that movie is sensational. And have you heard Michael Jackson's LP, *Thriller*? It sold twenty million copies. On Saturday, we could concentrate on what's hot at the moment." My body was trembling with excitement. "And Sunday we could have a jazz brunch. Maybe live music in the New York club . . . I know that would be a hit. And it would draw still another clientele."

"How about the rest of the week?" Laura was caught in the same fever I was. "You could have a ladies' night. Women's drinks half price . . . that draws in the singles. And all the music can be hits from female vocalists."

"The men might not like that . . . "

"So what!" she laughed. "They're only coming to hit on the women . . . not to hear the music."

"You're right," I said as I continued to stroke her fingers. Her skin felt so warm. "And another night could be strictly Motown."

"Wouldn't it be terrific to hear nothing but the Supremes, the Temps, The Four Tops, Stevie Wonder . . . I could go on forever."

"*I Heard It Through The Grapevine, Tears of a Clown, Sitting on the Dock of the Bay.*"

She joined in, "And how about . . . *I Second that Emotion, Ain't Too Proud to Beg.*"

"*Standing in the Shadows of Love.*"

"Don't forget, *My Guy* and *My Girl*. They are great tunes." She was laughing. It had such a pleasant ring to it.

"*Just My Imagination.*"

"*I Wish It Would Rain.*"

"*You Are the Sunshine of My Life.*" The moment I spoke the words, I saw the effect they had on Laura. She froze. So did I. I instantly flashed back to a time we sang that song together during a car ride long ago.

She jerked her hand away as if I had stung her. She looked in the other direction, not allowing me the benefit of seeing her expression. I was just about to reach for her when the waitress came to our table.

"Could I interest anyone in dessert?"

"No, thank you . . . but I'll have a cup of coffee please." Jill was the first to speak.

The others chimed in with the same order. I asked for another bourbon and Coke. No matter how many times I tried to pull Laura back into a conversation, she refused to give me her full attention. Deciding that I wasn't going to make a fool out of myself, I finally stopped trying. I sat quietly as I sipped my drink and watched the others.

When the check arrived, we paid the bill. Jack's wife suggested we go straight to the dance, but Laura feigned exhaustion saying that what she really needed was a good night's sleep. I tried to catch her eye, but was unsuccessful. It seemed that she was no longer interested in my company.

We went our separate ways.

After freshening up in our room, Jill and I walked over to the Ramada's ballroom where the alumni dance was being held. I spent hours listening to music, dancing with numerous women, and wishing Laura was with us. Finally the smoke, the noise, and the crowd began to annoy me. While Jill was doing the bump on the dance floor with a fraternity buddy, I excused myself and went outside. I walked around the courtyard, eyeing the moon, and enjoying the fresh, crisp air. It was a gorgeous evening. I reached the pool area. Although the water was partially drained, the lounge chairs were still circling the pool, and it looked quite inviting. I was just about to take a seat when I glanced to my right and noticed a shadow by the fence.

It was Laura.

"Hi." I approached her. "Thought you were tired."

"I was. I am. It's hard to sleep these days. It's a little uncomfortable being this huge."

"Where's Bruce?"

"He's in the room . . . asleep . . . has been for hours."

"Can I join you?"

"Of course."

I pulled up a chair next to hers. There was a crescent moon, which did not lend to a great deal of light; as a result, it was difficult to see her face. I had so much I wanted to say—years of bottled thoughts and dreams I hoped to discuss, memories I wanted desperately to relive—some I wished I could alter, making her part of my life instead of only a reflection in my mind. "I really enjoyed our conversation tonight." I waited for her to reply. When she didn't respond, I continued. "It's so easy to talk to you, Laura. Just like the old days." I paused again. "Remember all those hours we used to lounge around the lake outside the dorm?"

"Yes . . . I remember."

"I was there today. I half expected you to be there too. I was disappointed when you weren't." I sipped on the drink I brought with me. Her silence was stifling. I changed the subject. "How do you like being pregnant?"

"It's okay. In fact, most of the time I feel great . . . it's just lately I've had trouble sleeping." She seemed more comfortable on this topic. "I've waited a long time to have a baby."

"You're going to be a terrific mother, Laura," I said. "You're so patient and kind. That's one lucky kid." I paused. "Jill's had two miscarriages in the last couple of years. She wants a baby so badly. The doctors say there's not much hope. Apparently, her cervix isn't strong enough."

"I'm sorry." Laura squirmed in her chair. "Have you considered adoption?"

"No," I replied. "Jill wants *our* baby."

"And you . . . what do you want?" She seemed reserved as she asked her question.

Before I had a chance to answer, she jerked in her seat. "Oh!" She clutched her belly.

"Are you all right?" I was alarmed.

"Yes. I'm fine." She grinned. "The baby just jabbed me. I think it would rather run races than stay cooped up inside of me."

"It's moving?"

"Quite a bit. I do believe it has its days and nights confused. That's why I don't get a lot of sleep."

"Could I . . . could I feel it?" I sat on the edge of my seat. For some reason, I had an overwhelming urge to experience what Laura was telling me about.

"Okay," she replied shyly. "Come here."

I knelt beside her and allowed Laura to take my hand. She placed it over the smooth roundness of her stomach. "It's so hard. I had no idea it would feel quite like this." She continued moving my fingers gently in a rotating fashion. Nothing happened. I was about to ask why I couldn't feel anything when a solid push knocked against my palm. "Oh, my God!" I jerked away. "Did you feel that? I felt that!" I looked up into her face. She was smiling. I could even see a twinkle reflecting in her eyes. "Can I feel it again?"

"Sure."

I used both hands, moving them strategically around her stomach hoping for an instant replay. I was rewarded within moments by several jarring hits to my left hand. Instead of pulling away this time, I remained still, feeling the full effect of the move. "God! That's beautiful." Without asking consent, I leaned forward and placed my ear where my hand had just been. The noises were fascinating. My lobe took a direct hit before I pulled away. I was so mesmerized by the experience that I was speechless. Silently, I stared at Laura, wishing with all my heart that the baby she was carrying were mine. I stroked the material of her dress. She, in turn, began to run her fingers gently through my hair. A tingling sensation ran down my spine. I lay my head in what space there was left on her lap, hoping that this moment would last forever. I missed her so much.

"Brad?"

I wasn't sure I'd heard the voice until it rang through the night air a second time.

"Brad . . . is that you?" It was Jill.

I sat up at the same moment that Laura pulled away from me.

"I've been looking everywhere for you." She walked over to me. "Oh, Laura . . . I didn't see you." She was taken by surprise and her voice became guarded. "Is everything all right?"

"I better go." Laura stood up.

"No . . . wait, Laura. Don't go." I moved toward her, but she was too quick. Laura was already out of my reach.

She turned, her expression wary. "I can't stay. Bruce is waiting for me." She nodded at Jill. "Good night. It was good seeing you again, Brad. Nice to meet you, Jill." She turned, walked away, leaving Jill and me in silence.

2

"Get off my back, Jill."

It seemed as if every time I came home from work my wife was nagging at me about something. In the last year, things had gone from bad to worse around our apartment. I resented her constant bickering and suggestive innuendoes about what I did with my free time. I wasn't really what anyone could call a faithful, true blue husband, but it wasn't all my fault. We'd been married over four years, but during the last year, our marriage slid down hill like an avalanche.

I shouldn't have married Jill. It was unfair to her, and it was definitely wrong for me. I actually thought in the beginning that there might be a chance for the two of us, but I was wrong. Every little argument we had, Jill invariably threw Laura's name in my face. God, to be free of Jill's constant cornering me with that painful memory.

After we came back from Elon last fall, my wife was frantic about having a baby. I feared that her desire to conceive stemmed more from a need to create a bond between us than because she actually wanted to have a baby. But I went along. Thanksgiving and Christmas went smoothly. Shortly after the new year, Jill announced she was pregnant. Needless to say, she was ecstatic. Her exuberance was contagious. I was happy too.

But then last March, Jill miscarried for the third time. The doctors informed us that there was little hope she would ever carry a baby full term. In fact, they suggested that we stop trying. Jill was depressed, bitter, and antagonistic. Numerous times, she accused me of being grateful that she could not have children. She shrieked constantly. I felt like our home was a battle zone. I tried to be sympathetic and understanding, but it was futile.

In the middle of May, we had an explosive argument. While Jill was cleaning out my closest, she discovered a large box of my old mementos. She rifled through it and found an English paper I'd written in high school and a couple others from my college days, a few letters from my dad, several first edition stamps, some torn movie tickets, about a dozen old coins, a pamphlet on the Jefferson Memorial, a used pass to Mt. Vernon, and a lot of pictures: some proofs, some snapshots. Among them was a photograph of Laura. I'd forgotten all about it; in fact, I thought I'd destroyed all of the pictures I'd taken of Laura years ago. I recognized the photo immediately. It was taken at Elon. Laura was posed in front of the lake. Her hair was long, straight, and parted down the middle. She sat

Indian style, with her elbows on her knees. Her warm smile made her eyes dance. It was a fantastic picture.

My wife was furious when she found the photograph. She waved it at me, screaming and cussing. "It's not bad enough that you literally foamed all over the woman at your homecoming. Not only was she married, but pregnant as well. But that didn't stop you! Now I discover that you even keep a picture of her. What do you do? Sneak it into the bathroom and jack off while you look at it, wishing you were with her instead of me?"

I tried to convince Jill that I had forgotten about the picture long ago, but she wouldn't believe me. She was making life miserable for both of us. It wasn't just the photograph of Laura either. Anything and everything that even remotely resembled Laura Davis was thrown in my face. If Jill and I walked down the street and there was a girl who had features like Laura, my wife watched for my reaction and then picked a fight; if there was a love song on the radio, or a sentimental movie, or romantic television show, Jill somehow converted it into an argument, baiting me constantly until I fought back. It drove me crazy.

During the summer, I got into the habit of leaving the house whenever she started one of her screaming tirades. I found refuge in the movie theaters. I saw *Star Trek III: The Search for Spock*, *Ghostbusters*, *Gremlins*, *The Karate Kid* and *Footloose* over the course of a five-week period. Then I noticed that I was not the only single, unattached person in the theater. There were single, lonely women there too. It wasn't until late August when I saw *Tightrope* that I picked up my first extramarital affair. There were two more faceless women in September. And then I stopped going to the movies. The fleeting, peaceful haven those women gave me could not balance the guilt I felt. I stopped going to the matinees; instead, I spent countless hours at my clubs. I became a workaholic. What free time I did have I spent with Rick or Billy. We shot pool or played cards; sometimes we talked, but I never divulged my private thoughts. They were too personal to share.

On Election Day 1984, Jill planned a victory party for her Reagan political friends. They had a lot to celebrate. It was a slaughter. A record number of electoral votes defeated Mondale. In fact, Reagan's opponent only took his home state of Minnesota and the District of Columbia. Reagan's reelection was a landslide. Within seconds after the polls closed, he was declared the victor. Jill's party was a huge success, except for one thing. I wasn't there.

It wasn't that I didn't support Reagan; because I did—100 percent. He was my man all the way. It was just that I had no interest in celebrating with Jill's friends in such a boisterous manner; instead, I chose to play cards with Billy and Rick.

Jill met me at the door when she heard my key turning in the lock. All her company was gone. "Where have you been this time, Brad, out with some slut? Or did you have to pay for it?"

She looked awful: hair disheveled, no makeup, a robe that I'd seen her wearing on every occasion that I'd been home for the last ten days, a glass of liquor in one hand and a cigarette in other. She reeked of booze and smoke.

"Still pining over your lost love? Are you still trying to find her in every whore in town? Do you think, Brad, that if you close your eyes you can pretend that the woman you're screwing is your precious Laura?"

"Jill! Not tonight. For Christ's sake. Give it a rest. I was a playing cards with Bill, Rick, and a couple of the fellows from the club. If you want to call them . . . go ahead." I was telling the truth.

"I will. I'll do just that." Jill waltzed over to the phone and banged on the numbers to my brother's home.

"Jill! Are you crazy?" I slammed down the receiver. "What the hell's gotten into you? It's two o'clock in the morning. If you call Rick now, you'll wake up Valerie and the kids."

"So you are lying. You weren't with them tonight! Where were you?" She started throwing things around. The apartment was a disaster. She had not cleaned up a thing after her party. Jill was only adding to the mess that was already surrounding her.

"Jill . . ." Trying to get her to listen to reason, I lowered my voice. "I was with my brother. I swear. You can call him tomorrow morning, but for Pete's sake, don't wake up an entire household because you don't believe me."

She became silent for the first time since I entered the room. Jill was standing in a pile of two-day-old newspapers, dirty dishes, and beer bottles that were left on the floor. There was black makeup smeared under her eyes, and her hair didn't look as if it had been brushed in weeks. She appeared to be in her forties instead of only thirty-four.

My God! I'd done that to Jill. I was the culprit. Jill was slowly chipping away at her self-esteem, and it was my fault. The truth of the matter was . . . I wasn't really in a whole lot better shape than my wife. I didn't look quite as unkempt as she appeared, but my guts were just as torn apart as hers; and I was equally confused and bitter about our relationship.

"I'm going to bed, Jill. Are you coming?"

"Shit no!"

"Come on . . . it's late."

"Do you actually think I'm going to sleep next to a man who dreams about another woman?" She threw something at my head. I ducked. It crashed inches from my temple and shattered into tiny pieces.

"We've been over this a million times. All this crap is in your imagination. Why don't you just let it die?"

"My imagination, huh? I suppose all those sluts are in my imagination too?"

"Jill, please," I begged.

"So, then, you admit it."

"Damn it, Jill. I don't care about anyone else."

"You son of a bitch."

"Can't you stop screaming all the time, and then maybe the two of us could call a truce."

"So you could go on living in the past?"

"Oh, come off it, Jill. I think you're being melodramatic about all this. I am not living in the past! I've been trying to make a future—for us—but, damn it, you won't let me." I turned to go in the direction of our room, undoing the buttons of my shirt as I took the steps.

"Where the hell are you going?"

Tesa Jones ❧ 639

"To bed. I'm exhausted. Why don't you come with me, and we can talk about this in the morning after we've both simmered down a little?"

"Don't you dare walk out on me, Brad! You stay here and fight."

"There isn't anything left to fight about, Jill. We've said it all. Can't you just drop it for one lousy night? Come on; come to bed."

"What's the matter? Are you horny or something? You can't find it outside so you decided to come home and get it from your wife."

I turned to face her. "You haven't slept in our bed in six months! I certainly am not expecting tonight to be any different." I was livid. In order to calm down a little bit, I took several deep breaths. I watched Jill silently for several moments realizing for the first time that the only emotion I felt for my wife was pity. No love, no admiration, not even any respect. I'd lost all those old feelings I used to have for her; they had died. Now all I felt was pity. Softly, I spoke again. "Jill, take a long look in the mirror. I've been doing just that lately. I don't like what I see. I don't think you will either. We're tearing each other apart. I can't live like this much longer, Jill. We've got to find some mutual ground where we can start over again. Can't you see that we're drifting further and further apart? We're destroying everything that was ever good between us . . . and we're destroying each other right along with it. We've got to do something, Jill. We certainly can't go on like this." I pivoted and left the room. I entered the bedroom. Our bedroom. Only I knew that I would be sleeping alone. As was the norm of late, Jill slept on the couch with her blanket and pillow. It was her way of rebelling. I knew that Jill wanted me to take all the steps in her direction. She didn't want to compromise; she didn't want to meet me halfway. She wanted me to love her more than I was capable of feeling. But I couldn't do that. A person can't make love happen. There was often no rhyme or reason for the emotion. I couldn't help it if I didn't love Jill with the fiery passion she desired. I may not have cared for Jill in that special way she craved, but I'd always liked her. I enjoyed her company, respected her, and desired her physically. For years, we had a strong, stable relationship between us. If only she could be that person again, we could have a successful marriage. If only Jill weren't so insecure. If she could just revert back to that wonderful carefree individual she had once been. I was certain Jill and I could find contentment with each other. And wasn't that enough?

I woke up the next morning well past my usual hour. When I went out to make myself breakfast and coffee, I discovered that the entire apartment—with the exception of the bedroom—was cleaned up. The place looked good. Not immaculate, but at least it was neat and tidy. Maybe something I'd said the night before had actually clicked inside Jill; perhaps there was still a chance for the two of us after all. I hoped so; I really hoped so. I didn't want to quit.

When I reached for the handle on the refrigerator, I noticed a note on the door. It was in Jill's handwriting.

Brad,
I'm going away for a little while. I need
some time to sort things out. Will be in touch.
                    Jill

3

Several weeks went by without a word from my wife. I worried about her. I pondered our past, and I tried to sort out things in my mind. What a mess it had become! There had to be a way to fix it. If only we could talk logically, I was certain we could work it out.

It wasn't until I came home from work early on Thursday night that I discovered my wife sitting on the couch waiting for me. She looked a lot better than she had in over a year. Jill was wearing a stylish outfit of beiges and browns that accented her honey-brown hair color. Her features were highlighted with just a touch of makeup enhancing her natural beauty. I'd forgotten what an attractive woman she was. After I closed the door, I noticed the suitcases lined up in the small foyer between our living room and the kitchen. I glanced at Jill a second time. I didn't know what to say.

"Hello, Brad."

"Hi." I wanted to say so much more, but none of the words came out. I simply stood there watching my wife; she, in turn, stared back at me. I felt as if we were in limbo.

"I'm leaving, Brad." Jill's words finally broke through the air. Her voice was calm. "I'd stay and ask you to leave, but I know for a fact that I can't afford the rent on this place with the salary I make."

I took several steps toward her. I didn't want to have this conversation. There had to be a way to repair the havoc that had come into our lives. I tried to speak.

"Don't say anything, please. I've been doing a lot of thinking since I went away, and I've come to the conclusion that you and I were never meant to be. I would have given anything to make it work, Brad . . . anything. But last year when I saw you with Laura . . . holding her. The aura that surrounded you was far more intimate that any moment we have ever shared before or during our marriage." She paused. "I thought if we had a baby . . . maybe it would change things. Maybe you'd love me more if I were the mother of your child. After the first two miscarriages I still believed in us. But I'm sure now . . . even if I hadn't lost that third baby . . . there was never any hope for you and me." She shifted in her seat. "Years ago, when you talked about your photographs, you said that a picture wasn't any good if it didn't speak to you. When I walked in on you and Laura at Elon it was like looking at one of your pictures. I didn't need any words. Watching you said it all." A single tear streamed silently down her cheek. "I'm not a total innocent here. I'm just as much to blame for this mess. I realize that I've been guilty of pushing you. I couldn't stand competing with memories, and my insecurities created such a wedge between us that I was a pretty hard person to live with, much less love."

I walked toward her. Jill stood up, once again keeping me from commenting by gently placing her fingers on my lips to hush me. I felt like an outsider witnessing the scene instead of one of the two members involved in it.

"You can't help how you feel, Brad. And I can't change the way I am. I really thought that I would be able to live with the fact that you were not in love with me. I was even naive enough to imagine that I could make you love me, but that didn't work either." Jill touched the side of my face and smiled. There was warmth in her expression—a warmth that hadn't been there since before we were married. "Basically, Brad, we are both good people. Of course, we have our weaker points; I guess everyone does. But, on the whole, we are two decent individuals. Unfortunately, I've finally learned that those are not the elements to make a marriage work. We don't have the potential to live a happy life together." She took a deep breath. "It's not your fault; it's not mine. It's just the way it is."

"But, Jill . . . " I was stuttering. "I need you."

"I know that, Brad. I really do know that, but somehow it just isn't enough to be *needed* anymore. I want to be *loved*." A sad smile spread over Jill's face. "I have to find someone in this world who can love me and want me for who I am. I don't want to settle for being second prize. Because that's what I've always been to you, Brad. Second prize. I've always known. I would have been a fool not to see it. But I don't resent it anymore. I'm not even sure that after all these years that I'm as crazy in love with you as I used to be. You can only love someone so much . . ." Jill stood up tall. Her eyes glassed over with a fresh batch of tears. She smiled bravely and continued to speak. "I'm going to make it, Brad. I'm going to get through this, and I'm going to come out of it just fine." She hesitated only a second before kissing me on the cheek. "I wish the same for you."

My wife started walking toward the door with a suitcase in each hand.

"Jill, wait. You can't just quit like this. You can't just throw away all the good years."

"We did have some good years, didn't we?"

"Yes . . . yes we did. And you can't just throw those away."

"Brad, I know you don't really give a damn if I walk out that door or not, but I appreciate your attempts at trying to keep me here. It helps my ego a little bit."

"How can you say that? I don't . . . I don't want you to leave."

"Let's not be foolish. Let's not hang on to something that should have been allowed to die a long time ago. It took me an eternity to face the facts, but I've finally learned that I can't live this way. I still love you, Brad. I'm not going to lie about that. I do still love you, but I'm not going to allow my love to destroy me—or you either, for that matter—not anymore." She stood in the doorway for several seconds as if she were framing my image in her mind. Then, she left.

6

Laura

JENNIFER LOOKED SO PALE. TUBES UP HER NOSE. MONITORS EVERYWHERE.

I'd been sitting by her hospital bed for an hour holding her hand while she slept. Of all the relapses she'd had since that first attack, this was definitely the worst. Jennifer had been in intensive care for nine days, and things weren't improving as the doctors anticipated. It seemed that each attack stressed her heart to the max, depleting whatever reserve energy she had.

Everything had been going so well for Jennifer before this happened. For nearly a year, she had been living with Bruce and me in our spare bedroom. Over the course of that time, she had developed a little more stamina, and her health seemed to be improving. In fact, Jennifer seemed so well that she had actually worked during the holiday season at a boutique in Beacon Hill Mall. After the Christmas rush was over, Jennifer had continued working two four-hour days a week. It gave her a sense of independence. Unfortunately, she was not strong enough for the task. It was during her part time job that she had her latest attack, which sent her by ambulance to the George Washington Hospital.

As I sat by Jennifer's bed holding her hand, I thought of how wonderful it had been to have my old roommate living with me during the past year. Jennifer was great with Joey. I never thought of Jennifer as enjoying children, but when I watched the two of them together it was magical. Last month, on Joey's first birthday, Jennifer dressed up like a clown and strutted around the living room; consequently, Joey nearly burst from peals of laughter. And on Christmas, it was Jennifer—not Bruce—who donned the Santa outfit. I took the cutest picture of the two of them. Of course, I made a copy for Jennifer. Twice when I entered her room without knocking, I discovered her lying across the bed, smiling as she looked at it.

Because Jennifer and Joey got along so famously, I never hesitated to leave Joey with her when I needed to go to the store or to run a few errands. My dear friend was not only good company for me, she was also a terrific buddy for my son. The only person who didn't seem thrilled with our living arrangements was Bruce. My husband didn't like Jennifer; in fact, he didn't like her from the first time they met. Unfortunately, nearly five years later, their relationship had not improved.

"Lori." Her voice broke through the stillness.

"I'm here, Jennifer." I stroked her hand.

"Am I still at G.W. Hospital or did they move me to West Virginia again?"

"No, Jen . . . you're still at the hospital."

"Good. I hate that place . . . it's so lonely." She struggled to speak. "How long have I been asleep?"

"Almost an hour."

"Have you been here the whole time?"

"Yes . . . rest, Jen. You need your rest."

"Will you stay?"

"I can't. The nurses won't let me." I paused. "Besides, I have to pick up Joey at Bruce's parents' house by six."

"How is Joey?"

"He's fine, but he misses you."

"Give him a big hug for me, and a kiss too." She made the attempt to swallow several times. She seemed to be in pain. "Is it still snowing?"

"Yeah . . . it's coming down pretty hard."

"Is it sticking?"

"Not too badly yet, but the weatherman's calling for a foot by morning."

"You know that little pan sled I gave Joey for Christmas?"

"Of course I do," I replied.

"That little, bumpy hill in your backyard is going to be perfect for him; he can ride that pan sled. I wish I could see him in his tiny snowsuit. Please take pictures, Lori. Promise me you will take lots of pictures." She whimpered slightly from the pain before she attempted to speak again. "Maybe next year I'll be able to help him build a snowman. You tell him Auntie Jenny is going to help him next year . . . okay, Lori?"

"Yes, I will." Her eyes fluttered as her head rolled slowly to the side.

"Jennifer!" I spoke in a panic.

"Yes, Lori," she whispered.

I relaxed slightly. Her movements had frightened me.

"I'm so tired, Lori."

I gently smoothed her hair away from her face. "Close your eyes. Sleep. I'll come see you tomorrow. Same time . . . okay?"

"I'll be here," she chuckled with a weak smile. "Any chance you could sneak Joey in to see me?"

"I don't think so, Jen. I tried it Saturday, and they cut me off before I even got the question out." Before I finished my statement, I noticed that Jennifer was already asleep. I waited several additional minutes before leaving.

There was an accident on Memorial Bridge, which created such a backup that it took me an hour and a half to go two miles. By the time I crossed into Virginia, there was at least five inches of snow on the grass and a heavy layer on the street as well. Even with my snow tires, I was having difficulty keeping the car steady.

It was 8:30 before I reached the Dailey's. Joey had already eaten his dinner and changed into his pajamas. Granddaddy was reading him a bedtime story. He was dozing; it didn't look as if Joey would be awake much longer.

"I really wish you'd stay the night, Lori," June Dailey said with a wary tone. "The roads must be awful by now."

"I'd consider it, but the phones are out. If I don't get home soon, Bruce will be worried sick about us." I zipped Joey into his snowsuit. Making sure his ears were covered, I tied the hat. "We'll be fine, Mom. It's less than five miles home from here, and most of the cars are off the roads."

"You be careful."

"Thanks for watching Joey." I started the car, put it in reverse, and pulled out into the street. Visibility was terrible. I couldn't see more than thirty feet in front of me. Thankfully, as I noticed earlier, there were few vehicles left on the road, which made driving much easier than it could have been. I glanced in Joey's direction. My son was fast asleep. He looked adorable. In the last thirteen and a half months, I had yet to tire of watching my precious child.

The night Joey was born, I was so elated from the experience that sleep eluded me. After lying in my bed until 3:00 in the morning, I finally got up, wandered down the hall until I discovered the nursery, then ventured inside. The nurse was a warm, friendly individual who welcomed me enthusiastically. After pulling up a chair, I sat next to my newborn son and observed him until the morning shift arrived and shooed me back to bed. Even now, all these months later, I still adored walking into his room at night, standing over his crib, and watching him dream his little boy dreams. His tiny lips moved, forming a grin, making me wonder what his thoughts were. When I was pregnant with Joey, I knew that I would be completely devoted to him, but I had not anticipated the force that would be behind the emotions I felt for my son. It was overwhelming and all consuming. He was the joy of my life.

The snow was building up on the windshield, making it difficult for the wipers to complete a full cycle. Only a small area was wiped clean with each movement. Visibility was diminishing. Straining, I kept my attention on the lane ahead of me. I was thankful that the light on Richmond Highway was green because I noted that the icy patch before the intersection made it difficult to stop.

"Oh, my God!" There was no time for me to step on the brakes—no time to swerve—no time to react at all when I suddenly saw the truck coming at me from my right. It hit me square in the passenger side and spun me around as if I were in a teacup carnival ride. After what seemed like an eternity, I slammed into a telephone pole.

Then everything stopped.

I laid my head on the steering wheel, motionless. I swallowed. After breathing deeply, I realized that my chest hurt. I opened my eyes. At first, I couldn't see. Upon touching my forehead, I felt moisture and realized that I was bleeding so badly that it was impairing my vision. I wiped my lids and focused. My left wrist was broken. I could see the bone protruding through the skin, but I couldn't feel any pain.

Joey! Oh, shit! There were red stains all over his snowsuit. The window beside him was shattered; dozens of pieces of glass were sprinkled all over his small frame. I could see a steady stream of blood oozing from his head. He wasn't moving! He wasn't even crying!

"Joey! Joey! My God, Joey . . . " I unlatched my safety belt and moved toward him. The sudden motion created a torturous pain in my rib cage, which knocked the breath out of me. Before I could reach my baby, I blacked out.

2

I could hear voices. Lots of them. They were low and mumbled. I seemed to be swirling in a thick, heavy mist and couldn't get my bearings. It was such an effort to open my eyes. I took a breath of air. Ouch! There was a sharp pain in my side. My head hurt too. I moaned slightly.

"Lori."

My lips were dry and cracked. The task of opening my eyes seemed immense, but I kept trying. Finally, I succeeded. I was in bed. Bruce was next to me. Dark circles surrounded his eyes. He looked exhausted. His father was behind him, so was my father and Judy. I opened my mouth, but no words came out.

"Hi, honey!" Bruce spoke. "You're going to be okay. You're pretty banged up, so you'll be sore for a while, and you have a few broken ribs. Your arm's a real mess, but they set it in emergency and put it in a cast."

"Joey?" I whispered the word. I didn't like the concerned expression on Bruce's face. Everyone in the room wore a matching demeanor. I dreaded what my husband was going to say. "Is he OK?"

"It was a bad accident, Lori. That truck had no business going so fast under those conditions."

"It wasn't my fault." I choked on the words.

"Settle down, Lori. No one's blaming you."

"Oh, God . . . Joey's dead." I was already crying.

"No! No, he's not. He's in surgery. The doctors said he's lost a lot of blood. Things don't look too good. He's been up there for hours, and we haven't heard a word for a long time. But he is alive."

"We're all praying, honey." My father's words were soothing. "I know he'll pull through. He's a tough little guy." Dad latched on to Judy's arm as if it gave him strength. His skin appeared gray, which aged him far more than his years.

"Daddy!" Gigantic tears formed in my eyes. "Don't let them take my little boy away. Daddy, please . . . please don't let them." Jerking spasms racked my body. I tried to control them, but I couldn't. "I have to see my baby." Using all my strength, I tried to get up. "Honey," Bruce patiently spoke. "You can't get up. And even if you could, they wouldn't let you see Joey. Not until the surgery's over."

"I've got to see my baby! Get me out of here! I've got to see my baby!" As I frantically thrashed around in my bed, I ripped out the IV.

"Nurse! Nurse!" Bruce screamed. "Nurse!"

An elderly woman raced into the room.

"Do something! Hurry before she hurts herself."

"I'll give her a sedative. That will calm her down."

"No!" I cried. "No sedative! No drugs! I want to see my baby."

Three people held me down as the nurse injected the needle.

3

Three months later, as I cut the last of the daffodils from my garden, no one could have guessed that Joey and I had been in such a terrible traffic accident. Both of us recovered completely from our wounds.

Unfortunately, Jennifer was not as lucky. She was out of G.W. Hospital, but she was back in West Virginia recuperating at the sanitarium. It seemed as if she was on a vicious treadmill. When she got better, she came home, only to have yet another attack sending her to the intensive care unit at the hospital where they treated her as best as they could until she was well enough to go to the sanitarium, where they patched her up so she could come home again—until the next attack. How many times could Jennifer's body be put through such trauma?

I wrapped the flowers in a damp cloth, placed them on the seat of the car, and headed for a visit to see Jennifer. Upon my arrival, I cornered the doctor and demanded that he be frank with me. I was shocked by his comments. Dr. Lottman said that Jennifer's only chance at a productive, normal life was a heart transplant.

"Isn't that a drastic measure?" I responded.

"Yes, but under the circumstances I don't think Jennifer has any other options. She's practically an invalid now, and she will never recover without the surgery."

"You don't give her much of a choice." I was frustrated and annoyed that there was nothing I could do to help. "She lives as an invalid or she dies from the transplant."

"Do you actually think, Lori, that Jennifer's body can stand much more of this? It will be a miracle if she lives two more years under these conditions. Every time she becomes ill, whether it's an attack or even just a simple virus, she becomes weaker and weaker. Eventually, everything will stop." He paused in order for me to digest what he said. "Jennifer had a heart murmur from birth; that's in her records. It's also a fact that she had pneumonia while she was in college."

"Yes. That's true. She almost died."

"Along with the pneumonia, she also had a virus that attacked her cardiovascular system and destroyed the majority of the muscle tissue surrounding her heart. That virus went undetected for so long that it weakened her heart even more, which makes her prone to the attacks. Jennifer's heart is swollen much larger than it should be. And the tissue is deteriorating. We've tried every medication; we've used different diets, combining vitamins and rest. We've used physical therapy and every new technique we have, but nothing has helped. It's getting worse. It's possible that she won't live to have the operation."

"What?" I felt weak from shock. "The last time I saw Jennifer she looked much better."

"Actually, she looks pretty well right now, but it's purely cosmetic. Surface, not internal. I think the reason she seems better is that she isn't fighting her therapy anymore like she used to for so many years. She actually wants to get better. In fact, the nurses no longer call her the terror of the ward." He chuckled. "She had quite a reputation for many years because she fought us tooth and nail the entire time she was here." The doctor removed his glasses and placed them in his jacket pocket. "I think that's changed now. I truly believe that Jennifer wants to recover. She has hope. And hope is a powerful medicine."

"This can't be real! A heart transplant!" I shifted to my right leg taking the pressure off my hip. Sometimes it ached from the bashing I took last winter during the accident. "Does Jennifer agree to this? Does she understand?"

"I've talked at great length with Jennifer. She knows exactly what's going on. She knows the percentages and her chances. She's agreed to give me full reign on her future. I've put her name on a waiting list at the Medical College of Virginia. When the time comes, the doctors are going to perform the surgery."

"What are her chances?"

"Not that great, but a hell of a lot better than if she doesn't have the operation. If . . . and I said *if* we can find a suitable donor before Jennifer dies, she has about a 50-50 chance of pulling out of it." He steered me over to the edge of the hall out of the way of traffic. "In the United States, the first transplant occurred in 1967; the patient died. The next year four out of fifty-four heart transplant patients lived. The following few years the specialists performed fewer transplants, but the success ratio was better. Unfortunately, it still was less than 25 percent. In the last several years, about half of the patients who underwent the surgery lived. They predict that in the years to come, the percentage of survival will increase. In fact, so far this year, the charts already show that the success ratio is over two to one."

"You sound so cold, so unfeeling, as if Jennifer is nothing more than a statistic. I can't stand here and talk about her as a number on a chart. She's my friend! A human being! She deserves more than an insensitive listing of figures and odds."

"I didn't mean to give that impression, Lori. I most definitely do not consider Jennifer Carson a statistic. I have been working with her for almost seven years . . . most of them have been uphill struggles just to get her to communicate with me. In the beginning, I was convinced that she didn't want to get well . . . that she was just wasting away the rest of her life sitting in a wheelchair and waiting to die, but I think I've finally gotten through to her. She trusts me. God knows, it took years to develop that kind of relationship with her, but finally I can honestly say that Jennifer trusts me, not only as her doctor, but as her friend."

"I understand what you're saying, Dr. Lottman. Jennifer is not an easy person to get to know. She fights strong relationships, and she doesn't bend as most people do. Life has not been easy for her. She doesn't want anyone around her who isn't willing to give her 100 percent. She's had too many lukewarm relationships in her life—her parents, for instance, and her ex-husband. She won't settle for false affections from anyone—including you. Jennifer has a way of forcing those she needs and cares about the most into proving their devotion. In a way, it's extremely selfish of her, but you have to understand Jennifer to realize why she does it. I hope you can reach her, doctor, because she needs someone like you. I don't think Jennifer has ever had any friends except my brother and me. Mark my words, Dr. Lottman, don't cross her. I can guarantee you won't get a second chance."

"I think she trusts me; in fact, I know she does. We talk. I can tell she's hiding things, keeping thoughts to herself, holding back a little bit, but a couple of years ago she started opening up to me. Over time, she let me see more and more of what makes her tick. That's a mountain I thought I would never climb. Jennifer is working with us now. She's trying to get better. I'm sure you must realize that's the first step to getting her healthy again."

"Can you fill me in on this operation? I don't mean the odds and the percentages but the facts. What's going to happen?"

"Like I already told you, Jennifer's name is on a waiting list in Richmond. The Medical College of Virginia, which is affiliated with VCU— Virginia Commonwealth University—is where the operation will take place. They are specially equipped, and the surgeons have experience in the field. It's one of the few places in the country that performs this type of surgery. Jennifer will have to wait her turn and then wait even longer until they can locate a suitable donor. Unfortunately, it will probably take quite a while because the donor must be between the ages of fifteen and thirty-five. He or she can't have died from any heart malfunctioning; in fact, an ideal condition would be for the donor to die of some kind of brain failure. Only one out of every one hundred people dies that way. The person donating the heart cannot have any blood pressure problems or any other kind of malfunctioning of the heart. Not to mention the fact that both Jennifer's and the donor's blood type must match. On top of all that, the donor must live within a few hundred mile radius of Richmond."

"Why?"

"The heart can't be kept pumping outside the human body for more than four hours, which means only four hours in order to take the heart out of the donor, transport it, and put it into Jennifer. Meanwhile, Jennifer also has to be moved to Richmond, prepped, and ready in the same amount of time." He paused. "Unless the donor can be kept alive by machines . . . then we have a little more time to play with."

"And you've explained all this to Jen?"

"Yes. She understands. I haven't colored it to give her any false sense of security. That's why I'm telling you all this now, so you'll know exactly what she knows and there will be no confusion. But please, Lori, for Jennifer's sake, don't try to talk her out of the operation. It's her only chance."

"All right, doctor. I promise I'll back you up. Thank you for being honest and straightforward with me. I know that you're not legally bound to confide in me at all about Jennifer's condition. I really appreciate your honesty."

"You're right. I don't have to discuss this matter with you, but I feel, as I'm sure Jennifer feels, that you *are* her family."

"Thank you again, Doctor." I extended my hand, and we exchanged a firm shake. I noticed that he managed a pleasant smile, but I could tell that he manufactured it only for my benefit. It seemed as if Jennifer had become a personal challenge to Dr. Lottman. He must have worked very hard to win her over. I wondered if perhaps there weren't a little something more to his story than met the eye.

I turned and went in search of Jennifer. She wasn't in her room; I headed for the patio. It was a gorgeous day. When I opened the double doors, I saw her sitting in her wheelchair at the edge of the patio. She was staring out into the distance unaware of my presence. What was she thinking about? The doctor? Her illness? The odds? Her future? Dr. Lottman was right. Jennifer did look physically better. Her skin was still fleshy—almost hanging on her face. There were premature lines surrounding her eyes and mouth. Her hair still lacked life, and her body weighed pounds less than it should, but there was a color to her cheeks—a blush I hadn't seen in years—and her shoulders didn't sag.

"Hi, Jen."

She started smiling even before she looked in my direction. Her lips curled upward in a grin, and I could actually see that there were tiny flecks glittering in the corner of her eyes.

"Hello, Lori." Jennifer looked happier than I'd seen her in a long time.

"You're looking pretty well. How are you feeling?"

"Didn't the doctor tell you? I'm in training for the Boston Marathon?"

"No! I think I must have missed that part of the conversation." We both chuckled.

"I've missed you, Jennifer."

"I've missed you too. How's Joey?"

"Pretty well. It's amazing how children bounce back. You can hardly see the scars. The doctors say that even those will disappear with time."

"Where is he?"

"I would have brought him but he has this terrible cough he can't seem to shake; I didn't want to expose you."

"You mean you didn't bring him?" Jennifer looked genuinely upset. "I was really looking forward to seeing the little tike."

"Maybe next time." I became more serious. "But, under the circumstances, Jennifer, after what Dr. Lottman just told me, I don't think it's wise to expose you to anything that might be viral right now."

"So the good doctor filled you in on the scoop." Jennifer adjusted her chair in order to face me directly. "Good. I'm glad. I didn't want to be the one to tell you."

"Seems as if Dr. Lottman has taken quite an interest in you."

"Yeah. He has. At first, I thought he was a royal pain in the ass. He rubbed me the wrong way. But after a while, I guess I just kind of got used to having him around. When he told me about his wife and how she died of a heart disease similar to mine, I noticed that he sort of took me under his wing. Sometimes, I think he's making a personal crusade out of my case. I guess I can't blame him. When his wife died, there were no options."

"Sounds like he's been telling you a lot about himself."

"Yeah. I think he figured it was a good technique to reach me. I have to admit that it worked. In the beginning, he did all the talking, and I ignored the hell out of him. He got so pissed off. Oh, he tried to cover it up and be cool about it, but I could tell. I used to get the biggest kick out of seeing him get infuriated as I sat with him through entire sessions and never said a word. I think I did that for a couple years before he started using his own personal problems to draw me out. Sometimes, I wonder whether or not he made it up. It would have been a good trick, but I think he's telling the truth. If not, he should have been an actor instead of a doctor. I trust him, Lori, and you know me well enough to realize that's quite an accomplishment in itself."

"So you're going to have the operation?"

"What choice do I have?" She smiled as if we were discussing trivial matters. "Did I tell you, Lori, that David came by to see me? All these years and he drops by completely unannounced. Can you believe it?"

"What did he want?"

"I'm not sure." She paused. "He claimed that he wanted to see how I was doing. He's been married and divorced again since the last time I saw him. David told me that he'd been thinking about me and wondering how come we'd trashed our lives so much. We had a long talk. I told him about the operation. He said he wants to be involved as much as possible and for me to keep in touch. David said he didn't want to push me, but he'd like to try our hand at friendship. I couldn't believe my ears when he actually said that. If I could have walked, I would have left him sitting there, but I was stuck. I told him that my trust fund was damn near dry and if it was money he wanted he'd have to go somewhere else. He answered that he hadn't even thought of the money; he just wanted to see me." Jennifer chuckled in a wistful manner. "Can you just imagine? All those damned years and he picks now to show up and act friendly! I listened to him as he tried to explain why he acted the way he did while we were married. David said he knew about Kurt. David told me that he was crazy jealous about it. And listen to this! He said that my father had shown up on his doorstep while I was at Elon. Apparently, my dad told David about Kurt and me. In fact, David said my dad rubbed his face in the news, taking great pleasure in watching him squirm. Jesus Christ! I knew my old man was a son of a bitch, but I never realized he was that bad. Can you believe it, Lori? I had no idea." After taking a deep breath, she continued, "Surprisingly, I enjoyed talking to David. It was weird. The entire time I knew him—before and during our marriage—he never gave me credit for having more than a pea for a brain, but when he came to visit me, he actually asked me about my opinion on things. I was shocked. I asked him why he never bothered to carry on a decent conversation with me before, and he said that he did not know I wanted to talk. Do you believe that? Hell, it's not important what David and I discussed; the only thing that is important is that the two of us actually cleared the air between us. I can't say we love each other, but I like him a hell of a lot more than I ever did in the past. Who knows! Perhaps we can be friends. After all, bigger miracles have happened, right?"

It was a wonderful visit. I felt optimistic when I left.

4

As the summer progressed, Joey's cough developed into a chesty congestion and a low-grade fever. He was on several antibiotics, but nothing seemed to help. His condition was compounded by one ear infection after another, which only made matters worse. The pediatrician recommended a specialist for ear tubes, but suggested a few in-office tests first. Bruce and I both agreed to whatever procedure she recommended.

In mid August, the results of Joey's tests were in. Bruce and I were sitting in the lounge waiting for our turn to see Joey's doctor. Our son was curled in my lap; his normal vivacious demeanor was far more subdued than his usual comportment. The constant fever caused lethargy. Bruce accompanied us because he was as concerned as I was. Hopefully, the doctor ascertained the problem; and it would only be a matter of time before we could tackle it.

"Mr. and Mrs. Dailey." The receptionist was a cute girl in her early twenties.

"Yes."

"Could you follow me, please?" She smiled warmly as she guided us down the corridor to the pediatrician's office.

After entering, we took seats across from her desk.

"Linda," Dr. Thompson spoke to her aid. "Could you take Joey into the play room for a few minutes while I confer with his parents?"

"Of course," she responded in a friendly manner. "Joey, will you come with me? I have some terrific toys I'm sure you'll love."

Joey slowly crawled off my lap and willingly went with the girl. Suddenly aware of her concerned expression, I turned my attention to Dr. Thompson. Consternation enveloped me. My fingers started to shake.

"I'm afraid I have some bad news," Dr. Thompson said. "I don't know of an easy way to say this. We ran over a dozen tests on Joey. Only one came up positive."

"What is it?" Bruce asked.

"HIV. It's a virus."

"Isn't that another word for that disease . . . what is it? AIDS?" Bruce sat up straight in his seat, instantly alert.

"Yes," the doctor replied.

"I heard on the television last week that Rock Hudson has it. He looks awful." Bruce snapped. "My son can't have that! It's a homosexual's disease! Joey's just a baby." Bruce seemed to be losing control.

"I'd like to test you and your wife." The doctor's voice remained calm.

"You think we have it?" Bruce was near hysterics.

"No. Actually, I think the results will be negative. I just want to be sure."

"Well, then, explain to me how the hell my boy can have this godforsaken disease!"

"Unfortunately, I think Joey was given contaminated blood while he was in surgery last January after the car accident."

"Oh, my God!" It was the first time I spoke. I put my hand over my mouth. I was going to be sick. I could feel the bile rising from my stomach.

Without saying another word, I leaped out of my chair, ran from the room, and raced down the hall to the private bathroom. I stood over the toilet and vomited everything I'd eaten for lunch.

"Oh my God! Not Joey! Not my baby!"

5

For five months I watched as my child became more and more listless, and increasingly thinner. He was so frail; it was hard to believe that he was the same energetic child he was before the accident. I held him constantly. For hours at a time, I rocked him in the chair and sang his favorite tunes—stubbornly ignoring his wheezing cough.

On Joey's second birthday, we had a small family party, but Joey felt so sick that he wasn't even able to blow out the two candles, and he went to bed directly after the cake was cut. I left the Daileys, my father, and Judy in the living room in search of privacy. I couldn't stop crying. It was very difficult to keep my eyes dry around Joey, but I always managed. When he was sleeping, I no longer tried to stifle my tears. I sobbed uncontrollably.

We spent Christmas in the emergency room because Joey's condition became so poor that he needed an oxygen tent to breathe. I brought his presents, in case he expressed a desire to open them, but he only had the strength to unwrap one. Bruce and I did the rest as he watched. We flooded him with toys. Trucks, cars, balls, coloring books, and a Fisher-Price cassette recorder, which was the one thing he asked Santa to bring him. He continuously played a *Sesame Street* tape; Joey loved Bert and Ernie.

Under circumstances like these, many couples find strength in each other. Husbands lean on wives. Wives find support from their husbands. It was not the case for Bruce and me. Instead of drawing together, we unconsciously built a wall; each day it became thicker and sturdier. I discovered no comfort in Bruce's company. And he found no solace from me. He never said it, but I knew he blamed me for what happened. He wasn't the only one; I, too, blamed myself. If I had not been out that night—driving in a blizzard—I wouldn't have had the accident, and Joey wouldn't have gone to the hospital; therefore, he wouldn't have needed a blood transfusion, and he wouldn't be sick today.

The guilt ate at my soul.

Joey was in and out of the hospital constantly until finally on January 28, 1986, two and a half hours after the space shuttle *Challenger* exploded over Cape Canaveral, he died. It was one year and one week after the accident.

The entire hospital was in mourning over the tragic disaster in the sky. The sorrow blanketed every room, which only enhanced the anguish that filled my heart. Staff, visitors, and patients alike roamed the halls in stunned silence. Joey was a well-liked patient, and nurses cried openly as much for my son as for Christa McAuliffe and the crew of the *Challenger*.

I did not shed a tear.

Joey was in so much pain; I was actually relieved that his suffering was over—thankful he could finally rest in peace. He was so brave even in the end, trying desperately to smile when everyone knew even that small action was sapping his strength. I held his tiny hand, pressed the fingers to my lips, and prayed to a God I feared no longer existed.

Now I'd lost two babies!

Bruce and I drove home from the hospital in silence. We buried our son three days later, still in silence. I cried no tears at the funeral. Two days after the ceremony, Bruce began his attacks. Callously, he lashed out at me with words, stating what I already knew was true. It was my fault . . . *all* my fault!

As the months slipped by—winter melted into spring and spring into summer—I rarely left the house. I sat in the nursery rocking chair wearing the same blue jeans and T-shirt every day. It was my uniform. I stared out the window doing little other than watching the seasons change. I realized how destructive I was being, both to Bruce and to myself, but I didn't care. Bruce no longer represented my savior. Where he had once been a white knight rescuing me from loneliness, giving me contentment and security, he was now at the center of my empty life representing nothing more than a shadow of what could have been.

For a while, Bruce continued his barrage of malicious words, yelling at me whenever he was home. As the months slipped by, he became more restrained. The two of us settled into the pattern of living in the same house without any communication. Frequently, I smelled liquor on his breath and perfume on his clothes. Many nights, he didn't come home at all. I knew what he was doing, but I didn't care.

Finally, five months after burying Joey, I woke up and donned proper street clothes. I brushed my hair and put on makeup. It was June. I was thirty-five years old. And I knew that I could no longer hide behind walls and pretend that the real world didn't exist outside my door. I grabbed my purse and my keys.

Much to my surprise, my old car still started. The battery actually had enough juice to turn over the engine even though two seasons had passed since the last time it was driven. I got behind the wheel and began my journey. At first, I didn't know where I was going, or what I was going to do, but as miles flew past me, I realized that I was—consciously or unconsciously—headed in the direction of West Virginia and Jennifer.

Dr. Lottman had called me earlier in the week, stating that Jennifer was dangerously close to returning to the hospital. She was extremely weak, and there was still no donor in sight. I knew two things: Jennifer needed me, and I needed her. In every crisis in my life, it was Jennifer who pulled me through. She was always there for me. I felt so guilty, because I had not been there for her—especially these last few months. I had deserted her for so long, leaving her alone and waiting for her fate. As I traveled the distance between us, I hoped that she could forgive me for my absence and prayed that somehow she would help me overcome my pain. Maybe together we could each be healed.

When I reached the sanitarium, I went in search of Jennifer. She was not in her usual spot on the patio, so I flagged down the first available staff member who told me that Jennifer was in her room. Upon entering it, I found her wheelchair empty. Jennifer was in bed sleeping, or so I thought until she moved slightly and opened her eyes.

"Lori . . . am I dreaming?"

"No. It's me. I'm here." I pulled up a chair and sat next to the bed.

"I'm so sorry about Joey." Tears sprang to her eyes. "He was such a special little boy." She reached for my hand and cupped it with her own, giving me reassurance. "I wish I could have been there for you."

"I know you loved him too, Jennifer."

"Yes, I did. When he was born, I thought I might be a little jealous of him. But you were wonderful, Lori." Jennifer managed a smile. "You shared him with me. You made me feel like I was part of his life too." A single tear rolled down Jennifer's cheek. "I didn't know I could love a child so much. Joey was the baby I knew I would never have. I miss him." Jennifer squeezed my hand. "I'm sorry, Lori. Here I am going on and on about me when you must be devastated. How are you holding up?"

"Not very well, I'm afraid. I've been feeling sorry for myself and wallowing in my own self-pity." Before continuing, I took several deep breaths. "I locked myself in the house; I didn't leave at all. I refused to talk to anyone . . . see anyone. I wanted to die."

"Don't say that, Lori." Jennifer tightened the grip on my hand.

"It was my fault, Jennifer. I knew the weather reports, but I went out anyway. If it weren't for the accident, Joey wouldn't be dead. God is punishing me."

"Don't be an ass." It was difficult for Jennifer to speak, but she was able to make it sound firm. "You can't really think Joey died because of you. If you truly believe that, then you have to transfer the blame to me. After all, it was me you came to see in the hospital. If I hadn't been in the hospital . . . you wouldn't have been out that night. Can't you see how ridiculous it sounds? It wasn't your fault! It wasn't my fault! It was an accident."

"I knew I'd be punished eventually. I knew what I did was wrong. Now God took my little boy away."

"Stop it! I know what you're thinking! You're thinking about Brad's baby . . . about the abortion."

"I killed one of my babies, and God killed the other."

"I'm not going to listen to this horseshit anymore." Jennifer struggled to sit up. She wedged the extra pillow behind her back so she could get more comfortable. "That's the most asinine thing I've ever heard. God isn't punishing you, Lori. Even though I let go of my Catholic upbringing, and I don't believe in the church anymore, I do still believe in God. In spite of everything that's happened to you and me, I know that God would never take vengeance against anyone as good and kind as you, Lori. You didn't lose your son because of your past mistakes, and you must never think like that again." She cradled my hands. "Promise me you will put that horrible thought away. It isn't true! I know it!"

"Oh, Jennifer, I really wish I could believe you." I lowered my forehead onto her hands and sat quietly for a moment. I closed my eyes and relaxed as I felt Jennifer's free hand stroking the back of my head in silence. Feeling as if Jennifer were my confessor, I began to speak again. Opening up the floodgates, I poured out the poison and finally the tears came. "I'm not a good person, Jennifer. I've been awful and selfish. Somewhere along the line, I lost all my values—my principles. I've done things that I'm ashamed of, and I've hurt people who didn't deserve my abuse. There was that terrible chapter in my life when I allowed money and greed to consume me. I was so caught up in Gene's world that I couldn't see the good, intangible things I left behind. Then, I married Bruce for all the wrong reasons; I know that now. I didn't really love him. I married him out of fear and loneliness. In the beginning, he gave me security and contentment like I used to feel with Tommy. I honestly believed that it would be enough to build a marriage. I wanted to make Bruce happy, and I really tried. But when I was pregnant with Joey, and we went down to Elon for our tenth reunion, I saw Brad. Instantly, I knew I was lying to myself." I sighed softly, as I allowed all the old memories to flood through my mind. "Brad always had a way of popping into my life and turning it into total chaos."

"What happened at Elon? You've never mentioned this before."

"Nothing really. Six of us had dinner, we talked, we laughed . . . for a while it even felt as if we were young again. I got caught up in the moment." I paused, reflecting on hidden memories I had not allowed myself to dwell upon for many years. "I met his wife. She's lovely. She seems to adore him. They're trying to have a family . . . perhaps, by now, they do." Tears threatened to spill out. "I can't talk about this, Jennifer."

"But you're going to . . . it's the only way you'll feel better." She smiled warmly before continuing. "So after that weekend at Elon . . . your life with Bruce changed?"

"Yes. Not at first . . . it was gradual. Joey was born. Without realizing it, I focused all my time, all my love, all my energy, on the baby. Bruce became just someone who lived in the house. Perhaps if Joey had lived, Bruce and I could have found a common ground on which to rebuild. But now so much has happened. I think he's having an affair with the store's bookkeeper. I should be outraged, but I don't feel anything at all."

"Are you sure?"

"Yeah, pretty sure. He doesn't come home for days. And there are phone calls at night. Plus, do you remember all those things you used to tell me about David?" I didn't wait for a reply. "All that evidence is piling up against Bruce. We haven't discussed it, but I know it's true."

"Maybe you could have another baby."

"No." I sat in silence for a long time. My head still in Jennifer's hand. "No, that would be like grabbing at straws in the wind." I looked up. "There isn't anything left to recapture. Bringing a baby into that type of situation would do nothing but cause all three of us pain."

"Are you going to get a divorce?" Jennifer's voice showed no sign of emotion. The only implication of any inner stress was the sound her teeth made as she ground them together; other than that, she remained silent.

Divorce! I was sure the idea was already in the recesses of my mind, but I hadn't allowed it into any of my conscious thoughts. "I hate divorce, Jennifer. I've always thought it was such a cop-out. All my life, I felt as if wedding vows were forever, and there were no exceptions to the rule. But my parents didn't follow that path, neither did you, Jen. I was so idealistic as a kid. I always believed that when two people got married, they naturally lived happily ever after. I never took into consideration that people change—a wedding band doesn't assure the couple that life is going to be all rosy and beautiful. It isn't. Life isn't like that at all, and neither is marriage. I don't know how I could have been so foolish as to think that marrying Bruce would solve all my problems. I imagine that marriage between two people who love each other is difficult and hard work even when it's at its best, but a marriage when there is not even love and friendship to fall back on is next to impossible." I twisted my wedding band as I spoke. "Neither Bruce nor I have broached the subject." I stood up and walked to the window, looking but not seeing what was outside. "I don't know, Jennifer. I just don't know. I haven't really thought far enough into my future to decide about a divorce or not." I returned to my chair.

"You know something, Jennifer . . . I feel better. Just talking to you makes it so much easier. I feel as if bricks have been taken off my shoulders. Thank you, my friend . . . thank you so much for being here." I chuckled genuinely for the first time in months. "What would I ever do without you? You've always said that I was the strong one. You're wrong! You've always given me my strength. You and I are so different—how did we ever become friends?" I laughed again, but I noticed that Jennifer wasn't joining in my amusement. "You've always been able to keep my feet planted firmly on the ground. You make me see things realistically when my head's in the clouds. You're so much more spontaneous and exciting than I ever was. And even when I've been angry with you, I've been able to draw strength from that emotion. You make me laugh when I'm depressed, and you lift my spirits when I think no one can possibly help me. You're the best friend anyone could ever have. You were a terrific roommate. You're a great confidant, a good guidance counselor. Hell, you were even a good set of parents wrapped in one when my mom and dad split up. If it weren't for you, I would have fallen apart. You are so wonderful, Jennifer. Do you have any idea how much I need you? I'm sure I don't say it enough, but I hope you know how much I love you."

A strange expression passed over Jennifer's face. I could never remember seeing her look quite so taken aback by a statement of mine. It was almost as if I'd slapped her instead of spoken of my devotion. Her reaction aroused my curiosity, but I refrained from speaking.

"I love you too, Lori." Her voice was melancholy.

"I know you do, Jennifer. I know you do."

She shook her head and pressed both her lips inside her mouth as her teeth bit down on them. After pausing in silence for several seconds, she finally replied. "No, you don't, Lori . . . you don't know at all." She folded her hands and laid her chin on top of the pyramid they formed. "I love you . . . I mean I really love you." Her eyes locked on to mine.

I was speechless as I listened to the deep throaty noises of Jennifer's voice.

"I love you the way you have always loved Brad Malone," Jennifer paused, took in oxygen without even wavering her eyes once from my gaze. "I despised him simply because you were in love with him. I was so jealous of that love. I hated Brad even more for taking advantage of a love that I wanted for myself. You can't imagine what it's like, Lori. All these years . . . It took me a long time to figure it out. I tried to replace you with men. I even used your brother. In the beginning, I actually believed that I loved Kurt, but then I realized—when he came back from Europe—that he was nothing but your male counterpart. He represented the normal way of life, and as hard as I tried to fit into that mold . . . it didn't work. I used other men—strings and strings of other men—but it didn't help. All the faceless men . . . They weren't you, and no amount of trying could make me fall in love with any of them. I hated hurting Kurt. I saw what I did to him, and I hated myself for being party to his pain, but I had no other choice."

I was having a difficult time grasping the meaning of Jennifer's words. Love? Was she confusing friendship with physical passion? Was she asking for some kind of a response from me? Why was she confessing to this emotion when she must realize that I didn't mean for her to misinterpret my use of the word? Oddly, I was not repulsed by her confession. In a unique way, I drew comfort from the knowledge that there was someone . . . someone in the world who truly loved me for who I was. When did all this happen? Was it something Jennifer discovered while she was in West Virginia or was it in her thoughts long before she arrived? I couldn't speak. I only listened to her calm, steady voice as she spoke, and her warm, glistening eyes shone with each word.

"I don't expect anything from you, Lori, and I've always known that there could never be anything between us but friendship and the devotion that goes along with it. I did not intend to ever tell you about how I feel. I didn't want to burden you. I didn't want to repel you or upset you, either. I guess you kind of caught me off guard today." She paused to catch her breath. "I've loved you for so long, Lori. For so many years, all the words lay dormant, but I can't hide them any longer. I realize that I'm putting our relationship in jeopardy by confessing what is probably a very repugnant topic for you to discuss, but I feel as if I will explode if I don't talk about it." She ran her fingers through the back of her hair and let out a long exasperated breath of air. Her head hung down hiding her expression.

Minutes passed as I watched Jennifer. She scanned the walls. I noticed that a tension ebbed from her body, and the drawn expression vanished from her face. I wanted to speak; I wanted to say something—anything—but words didn't form on my lips.

"I find it hard to believe that you never guessed my emotions. All these years, Lori . . . didn't you notice? I've done everything any jealous lover would do except scream my emotions at you. And, in spite of it all, you're still the unblemished, old-fashioned princess. So much has happened to you, and even though you are not quite as naive and innocent as you were that first day I walked in on you at Elon—sitting cross-legged on the bed looking like a babe in the woods—you are still the same beautiful, virtuous individual, living behind an unrealistic veil in a world that I don't think exists for anyone else but you. If I hadn't told you, you never would have guessed, would you, Lori? No! You wouldn't. I'm a mutation! A freak! But you have never seen that, have you? You see my devotion and love as friendship. You only see the good in people. Because that's the type of person you are. Unless someone points out the bad, you only see the beauty.

"You may disagree with me at the present, Lori, but you have not been corrupted by all the tragedy and depravity you've experienced . . . and I doubt you ever will be. Granted, you had a rough time of it when you discovered life was not the bowl of cherries you thought it was, but I honestly believe that it didn't destroy you or warp your perspective on life as you think. You are not hardened. I'm certain that there will be a time when you will see beauty in everything again. It's just the way you are, Lori. You can't help it . . . just like I can't help the way I am.

"Life's been unkind to both of us . . . perhaps it's been in different ways, but it's still been a tough road for you and me. The wonderful thing about it, Lori, is that eventually I know you will snap out of it and return to that optimistic, loving, warm person you always were before the scars scratched your heart. The genuinely good people like you can't be held down for long." Jennifer tapped her fingers together and clicked her tongue several times before continuing. "Unfortunately, I doubt that I'll be going that route. I never saw life the way you did . . . and I'm not capable of doing it now or even in the future. But I am going to do the best I can with the opportunities that come my way. I intend to live, and Martin Lottman has convinced me that I can do just that if I put myself in his hands. I'm going to have the transplant, and when it's over, I'm going to start living again. David says he wants to be my friend—I'll give that a shot too. I've been extremely rough on people. I've expected too much out of relationships. I wanted all take and little give. I've been wrong. Perhaps I had my reasons, but I've been wrong all the same. When I finally get out of here, I'm going to try to start over and not make the same mistakes. I've done a lot of thinking while I've been here. God knows, thinking is just about all I can do . . . and now, I know what I've done wrong. I'm not going to waste my life making the same errors over and over again." She paused. "I need to find another purpose in life besides loving you, Lori. I know there's an answer out there. All I have to do is find it."

"Oh, Jennifer." I finally found my voice, but I wasn't sure what I wanted to say. "I didn't know . . . I really didn't understand. I wish . . ." I didn't know what I wished. Did I wish that I could return her love? How simple life could be if I loved Jennifer in the way she loved me. The two of us could probably be happier together than any of the men I've known in my life. Tommy and Bruce weren't capable of giving me the inner peace I craved. Rick Malone was a wonderful friend, but that was all he was. Gene Saunders, Stephen Shaw, and Larry Jenkins certainly weren't able to give me any kind of mental fulfillment. Jack Briskin was not the answer. And even Brad—whom I still loved with all of my heart—was not capable of returning the kind of love I wanted in my life. "I wish . . . I really wish there was something I could do to make the pain go away, Jennifer, because I know how much it hurts to love someone and never get that love returned. I'm sorry, Jen." It sounded like such a weak response. I felt terrible that I wasn't able to communicate in a better way than those pathetic few words.

"Don't hate me, Lori, please. Whatever you feel about what I've said . . . please just don't hate me." A thick mist covered Jennifer's eyes as her body became rigid with a new type of tension. She watched and waited for a response.

"I don't hate you. I don't even hate the words you've just said. I only wish that I could take the pain away. I don't know how this freak of nature happened, and I suppose it doesn't really matter now. But it won't change how I feel about you. I love you. In a way, I wish I could love you in the manner you want. But my love is not the type of love you're looking for, and I can't change that. But I certainly don't hate you. How could I? You are the dearest and best friend I've ever had. I love you in the way that I always have . . . nothing will change that." I stopped and watched her reaction. Jennifer didn't move. She sat completely still staring into my eyes searching for some kind of solution. Unfortunately, I didn't know any of the answers.

"You do still love me? You really do? I mean, you care about me as a person? I'm not asking you to love me in the way I love you, but it would kill me to lose the friendship we have always shared. I couldn't bare that loss, Lori."

"Yes, I love you, Jennifer. Most people live their entire lives without truly loving anyone. I mean really and completely loving anyone including themselves, but I've loved two people aside from Joey: you . . . and Brad." I closed my eyes for a moment, lost in private thoughts. "In retrospect, I realize that loving Brad was a mistake." Tears burned my eyes. "But for one little moment in time, I was so happy. When we were together I felt like a whole person. It was like fitting in the last two puzzle pieces to finish the picture. Complete! I was euphoric when I was with him. I wouldn't trade that blissful feeling for anything in the world . . . even to free myself from the pain that losing him caused. And loving you, Jennifer . . ." I paused reaching once again for her hands as I searched for exactly the right words. "You are worth all the other people I've known put together. You are so valuable to me. I don't know how else to say it. You are always there for me . . . always! Of course, we've had our arguments and our uphill struggles from time to time, but you and I invariably pull through it together. I don't know what I would have done if you hadn't been there." I saw the tears swell in Jennifer's eyes, then spill out and roll down her cheeks. She was silent. I leaned over and tenderly slid my fingers across her face erasing the drops before they had the chance to complete the path down her jaw. We smiled at each other knowing that the moment was a special one exchanged only between two people who truly care for one another. I wanted so much to reach out to Jennifer . . . give her some kind of comfort in exchange for all the occasions she helped me, but there were no more words to express the thoughts in my mind.

How ironic life was. If it weren't so sad, it might actually be amusing. Kurt, my poor, lost brother, spent years loving Jennifer. And she, by some fluke, chose to fall in love with me when my heart belonged to a man who didn't know how to love anyone but himself. It seemed that the fantasies we created over time crumbled along with the memories we held bottled in our minds. All our dreams and hopes died leaving us little to hold on to for the future. It would take time for each of us to put the past behind us and allow cobwebs to weave around our memories.

7

Kurt

"I WANT TO MARRY YOU."

"What?"

"I want to marry you, Pamela." It was not my intention to blurt it out so comically, but I was feeling quite jovial after watching Paul Hogan's antics in *Crocodile Dundee*. When the actor walked on top of all those people's shoulders in the New York subway in order to declare his love to his leading lady, I was inspired. "I am a sucker for a happy ending."

In actuality, marriage was a subject I had been pondering for quite some time. Ellie was a high school freshman. I couldn't believe it. It didn't seem possible. Where had the time gone? My daughter wasn't the only reason for my proposal. Initially, I wanted to love Pam solely because she was the mother of my child, but as the years passed I discovered that I truly held deep affections for her. Perhaps it was a different kind of love than the emotion I once shared with Jennifer, but it was still love all the same.

Pamela! Faithful, wonderful, warm, gentle Pamela. She always stood by me. Not once in our five-year affair did Pamela put any kind of pressure on me. We were a good match.

"Well, damn it," I said playfully. "Answer me . . . don't leave me in suspense." I laughed as she stared at me with her mouth hanging opened in total amazement.

Pamela was completely flabbergasted. "Don't joke with me, Kurt, not about this. You must know how much I've wanted to hear you ask me all these years. I couldn't stand it if you made a joke out of it."

"I'm not joking, Pam. I realize that I wasn't very romantic about my proposal, but I mean every word." I left her standing alone in order to run to the corner where a vendor was parked. He was selling flowers by the bunch. I bought an armload before returning to Pam. Kneeling at her feet, I took one flower out at a time; I laid them in a circle around her. "Marry me."

"Kurt, everyone's looking at us."

I continued surrounding her with the red roses, "I don't care. In fact, I want the world to know that I love you." I turned to a couple on my right who had stopped to witness my actions. "I love this woman!" I said to them. "I want her to marry me." They nodded approvingly and smiled.

"Kurt!" Pamela was giggling.

"Darling, can't you see that I'm on bended knee? I'm pleading my case. My heart will surely break if you will not grant me the answer I want to hear." I plucked the petals off several of the roses and tossed them in the air like confetti. "I will shower you with love." I was chuckling. "Say you will marry me, or I will stand here and create a scene."

"You already *are* creating a scene." Pam was openly laughing.

I turned to my audience. "Don't you think this lovely lady should marry me?" The crowd applauded, cheering their enthusiasm. I handed Pam the remainder of her flowers before scooping her into my arms. As I paraded down the sidewalk carrying her, I asked, "You are going to marry me, aren't you?"

"Of course, I am. Oh, Kurt, I love you."

I smothered her mouth with my lips. This was sheer joy.

2

Pam and I were sleeping, nestled in each other's arms. Until the light flicked on invading our dreams, I was completely unaware that another person entered the room. Immediately, I sat up, caught between the dimension of heavy slumber and complete awareness. It was not until I heard the thunderous voice storming through the silence that I shook sleep from my mind. I became guarded.

"You!" The male voice boomed. "You son of a bitch. I take you in . . . give you a job . . . treat you with respect. And like some kind of conniving bastard you jump into bed with my daughter. I'll kill you." George Woods came flying across the mattress; rage masked his face.

I cringed at the sight of him coming toward me, but I couldn't speak or even move in my own defense. His clenched fist smashed against my jaw. God, it hurt! Instinctively, I warded off the second blow with my right hand. I heard screaming in the distance, but I couldn't make out the words. I was just about to slug him with my own fists when all the commotion stopped. My hand froze for a second in midair before I dropped it to my side. Shifting my jaw back and forth, I discovered that nothing was broken, and all my teeth were still intact. I blinked several times and shook my head to get my bearings.

"Honestly, Daddy, you're acting like a teenager. For goodness sake! Get a hold of yourself." Pam seemed calm despite the hectic activity around us. "I'm a grown woman. I don't need protection. Besides, Kurt and I aren't doing anything wrong. It's perfectly normal for a husband and wife to sleep together."

My brand new father-in-law stared silently, first at his daughter and then at me. There was nothing I dreaded more than this moment. I waited for his reaction. At first, he was angry. Then, a pleasant smile spread across his face. "It's about time you got around to marrying my little girl. You sure wasted enough years getting her to the altar." He sat on the edge of the bed and slapped me fondly on the back. "I thought you'd never come to your senses, boy."

He knew! Pamela's father knew all along. I actually blushed like a kid when I realized George Woods held that piece of knowledge inside his head for all this time without ever once saying a word.

"I love your daughter."

"Any fool can see that, Kurt. I've known how you felt about Pamela since the first time I saw the two of you together, but I didn't say anything. I figured my daughter knew what she was doing by letting you come to your own conclusion in your own time." He tapped my jaw. "Did I hurt you?"

"Nah . . . I'll be all right."

"I'm sorry."

"It's okay . . . I think I probably had it coming."

"So . . . tell me. When did the two of you tie the knot?"

"You must have missed our telegram, Daddy. We wanted you to be here, but I imagine you and the message must have crossed paths. We were married yesterday, right here in the apartment. There were only a few guests. Kurt's sister and her husband were here. Kurt's mother came too. I wish you could have met them. I hope you're not disappointed, Daddy. We tried to reach you."

"I'm certainly not disappointed that you're married, but I do wish I could have given away the bride." He kissed his daughter's face. "I know it's late or perhaps I should say it's very early in the morning, but do you think you could humor your old man and get up, fix us some coffee, and tell me all about it?"

"I love you, Daddy." Pamela smiled as she circled her father with her arms.

"I love you too, sweetheart."

"I know . . . I know." Tears misted over Pamela's eyes.

My wife and I donned robes before we joined her father in the kitchen for danish and coffee. It was nearly dawn. The three of us sat around the circular table and discussed the past and the future. We told Pam's father about Ellie's parentage. He admitted to having knowledge of it from the beginning, keeping quiet only for his daughter's benefit.

After my confession, Woods spoke. "Does Ellie know?"

"Last Tuesday I took Ellie out to dinner. I informed her that her mother and I were getting married and then struggled with the words to tell her that

I was her biological father." I grinned as I recalled the incident. "Her response was amazing. Ellie told me, 'When I was very little, I used to cry at night because I didn't have a father like all the other kids in kindergarten. When you came to New York to live, I was instantly infatuated with you. You'd take me to the zoo, movies, fun places. Remember? You not only became my friend, but you were my hero as well. Every night, before I fell asleep, I prayed that you'd be my daddy.' It was at that moment," I told Pam and George, "Ellie became pensive. Then she said, 'For the longest time, I was very angry at God for not listening to my prayers.' Then, Ellie smiled. 'I guess, Uncle Kurt,' she said, 'God really did hear me after all.' At that moment, Ellie threw her arms around me and laughed uncontrollably. 'I have always, for as long as I can remember, thought of you as my father. Now it will not only be legal but true as well.' I couldn't believe that Ellie was not judgmental or angry. She was so elated by my news." I smiled at my father-in-law. "Ellie and I are going to be okay. It seems as if she is a lot more forgiving and understanding than I would be. I'm a very lucky man." I reached across the table and squeezed Pam's hand.

Before anyone had the opportunity to add to the conversation, the phone rang. Pam answered it. I checked the time on the wall clock over the door. It was shortly before seven.

"Hello." Pam spoke into the receiver, then paused. "Lori . . . I hope you and Bruce made it home all right?" Still another pause. "Yes, he's right here . . . I'll put him on." She handed me the receiver.

"I'm sorry to bother you, Kurt."

"It's no bother. Is everything all right?" I replied.

"You told me that you wanted to know if and when Jennifer was going to have her operation." There was a moment of silence. "The doctors found a suitable donor last night. If everything goes as planned, the transplant is scheduled for ten this morning."

"So soon? I mean just like that?"

"It really isn't soon, Kurt. I mean, Jennifer's known for a long time, but she was just waiting for the opportunity. The doctor had to find a match.

Tesa Jones ❧ 677

They're keeping the donor alive on a respirator, and they are transporting Jennifer by helicopter even as we speak."

"She could die?"

"Yes, she could."

"I don't understand why the doctors are doing this. I mean . . . at least she's alive now, but if . . . "

"Kurt," my sister's voice was stern as she jumped back into the conversation. "You haven't seen Jennifer in several years. Granted she's alive, but just barely. She wants a chance to live a normal, healthy life. The odds aren't the best, but if she doesn't take them, Jennifer won't live out the year."

"I didn't know that . . . "

"I know. I never told you. I'm sorry to be laying it all on you now, but I figured you had a right."

"I understand. I didn't realize how serious her condition was." I glanced over at Pamela, who had a concerned expression on her face. I wanted to smooth away the lines on her forehead. I wanted to reach out and touch her skin, feel its warmth, but Pam was too far away. Instead, I extended my hand, and she touched it with her fingers. I squeezed her tenderly in return. I admired my wife so much. Pamela could have shown anger or jealousy or disappointment at the fact that I was discussing the one woman who—for more than fifteen years—had been a silent wedge between us; instead, Pam looked saddened at the aspect of another individual's personal struggle.

"What do you want me to do, Lori?"

"You don't have to do anything, Kurt. I wouldn't even have called if you hadn't specifically asked me to notify you when the operation was going to take place."

"Thanks, I appreciate it," I answered, still unsure of my own emotions on the subject. "What hospital? The one you told me about in Richmond?"

"Yes, they've already taken her. Jennifer will probably be there within the hour. I'm driving down as soon as I hang up. I want to be with her."

I said good-bye, and the phone went dead. As I placed the receiver in the cradle, I glanced first at my father-in-law and then at my wife. I got the distinct impression when I looked at George Woods that he knew a great deal more about the situation than what he had just overheard. Had Pamela told him? No! I was certain that Pam never said a word. Ostensibly, her father knew everything I did since the moment Pam begged him to keep me out of the draft. My guess was that he knew me better than I knew myself. In fact, George Woods probably had a file on me thick enough to fill a cabinet. For a moment, I was angry that he infiltrated my life, but in an odd way, I respected his silence, and I appreciated the fact that he was not watching me with a condemning, disapproving expression. Woods was a better man than I had given him credit for being. For years, I thought he was the rich bastard with a heart of steel. I was wrong. I studied my father-in-law. For the first time, I could see his emotion written in his eyes. George Woods loved his family; he just had a different way of showing it.

"Daddy." Pamela spoke first. She placed a gentle kiss on her father's forehead before adding, "I think Kurt and I need to be alone for a few minutes. Would you mind?"

Both of us watched him leave quietly without even exchanging a glance. Finally, when we were alone Pamela walked up to me and reached for my hands. Her gesture had a calming effect on me.

She smiled peacefully before speaking. "Kurt, I think you ought to go to Richmond."

"How can you say that, Pamela? This is the first day of our honeymoon. We're supposed to leave for Hawaii this afternoon."

"It's not an issue of whether or not we go to Hawaii today. We can do that another time. Tomorrow . . . next week . . . next year. But today, Kurt, you must go to Richmond . . . for your sister, who—I'm sure—needs you very much right now . . . for Jennifer, because she has no family of her own . . . but mostly for you and me, Kurt. You have to go down there for yourself and for our future. I do not want a black cloud hanging over our marriage before it even has a chance to get off to a good start. If you don't go, it will always be there between us. I realize that at the moment you don't think it's important. You've told me that you've put Jennifer and those memories behind you. But it *is* important, Kurt. I know you love me. I'm not afraid to let you go. I know you'll come back."

"I can't believe you're saying this, Pam. You actually want me to go. Why?" I was confused. Jennifer and I made our break a long time ago. I had come to terms with my feelings. Why was my wife pushing me in Jennifer's direction again?

"I love you, Kurt. I love you more than anyone . . . except maybe our daughter. I also understand you. Trust me on this, Kurt."

"All right," I muttered as I circled her with my arms.

"Take the jet; it will be quicker. I'm sure Father won't mind."

3

"Hi, Jennifer." The drugs were already taking effect. She was extremely drowsy. Luckily, I was in time to have the opportunity to speak to her before the orderlies wheeled her into the operating room. She looked so pale. Her eyelids opened and closed several times.

At first, Jennifer didn't recognize me; finally, she managed a faint smile. "Well, hi there, stranger. Long time, no see." She faded for a moment and then continued. "What are you doing here? Huh? I thought you just got married."

"I did."

"So why are you here?"

"I heard you needed a friend."

"Lori's here . . . somewhere," she mumbled.

"Well, then . . . if you don't need my support," I tried to make my voice sound light and joking. "I'll give it to my sister."

"Thank you . . . I mean . . . thank you for being here. I'm grateful." She closed her eyes as if the drug finally took full effect, but then opened them again as she spoke. "I'm happy for you, Kurt . . . I really am. You've come a long way. We both have. I . . . I am . . . I was never the right person for you. You know that now . . . don't you?"

"Yes, I know." I gripped her fingers. Strangely enough, I did. I really did know exactly what Jennifer meant. It was just my own obstinacy that kept me in that emotional vacuum for so long. But now I was finally free. Jennifer was only a sick friend who needed comfort. She no longer represented anything else to me. Touching her hand didn't give me any symbolic feeling. Being so close to her did not create any turmoil in my body or my mind. And hearing the truth didn't hurt at all.

"I'm . . . I can't seem . . . to stay awake . . . any longer. I'm glad you're here, Kurt."

I started to walk away in search of my sister, but Jennifer wouldn't let go of my hand. As I tried to pry her fingers away, she surprised me by speaking when I thought she was asleep.

"I don't want to die." Her words got caught in her throat. "Lori! Stay with me, Lori." Jennifer's lips barely moved, but the syllables were definitely audible. It was obvious that she was no longer aware of her surroundings. "Please God . . . I don't want to die."

I knew that Jennifer was no longer aware of my presence, but I was certain that she could draw strength from my hands. I clung to her fingers hoping she could feel my warmth. "You're not going to die, Jennifer. Everything's going to be fine. You wait and see. Everything is going to be just fine." Before they wheeled her gurney away, I kissed her softly on the cheek.

I paced the floor for several minutes before Lori came racing to my side. She buried her face in my shoulder. Together we walked to the assigned waiting room and sat down in silence. An hour ticked by; neither of us spoke. I simply held her hand and gave it a firm squeeze every now and then to remind her that I was still here.

There was only one other person in the room besides Lori and me. He appeared to be around our age. I felt sympathy for him because the expression on his face was one of great concern. Obviously, he, too, was waiting for the results of a patient. I thought of making an attempt at conversation with him, but decided against it.

"I was surprised to see you, Kurt. I never expected you to show up." Lori moved and spoke like a robot.

"I didn't think I'd be here, either," I answered in a numb stupor. "It was Pamela's idea. I didn't understand her logic at the time, but now I do. When I stood over Jennifer . . . I realized that Pamela was right. It was important that I come. It seems as if my wife knows me very well . . . very well indeed."

"Do you still love Jennifer?"

"No. No, I don't . . . I really don't." Words came out of my mouth. I was astonished at my candor. "When I was young, I honestly believed I loved her, and maybe I did in the very beginning. But I think all those years ago, Jennifer became someone I invented in my mind. I created her because I wanted to love her. She was some kind of a dream . . . an illusion . . . and then, I allowed the memories to magnify into something that never truly existed. The strange thing about a lost love is that a person always forgets the painful, bad memories and only clings to the beautiful ones. If I rationalize everything, I realize that Jennifer's and my relationship was never the blissful union I remember. There were many rocky roads between us—a lot of fighting about things that I didn't understand." I rubbed my temples quietly for a full minute before continuing.

"For a long time, I believed Pamela was only a replacement for what I really wanted. There was a tiny thought in the back of my mind taunting me, nagging at me, telling me that Pamela was a substitute because I couldn't have what I really wanted. I was always pushing the idea away, pretending it didn't exist. But I know now that it isn't true. Pamela's not a substitute. She's never been a substitute!" I ran my fingers slowly through my hair. "It's funny . . . the heart really does heal." Pausing, I took several deep breaths. "I love Pam . . . all the way to my soul, I love her." A small chuckle emerged from the base of my throat. I smiled warmly. "My wife is an amazing woman. What's been a mystery to me has always been very clear to her. She just waited until I pulled myself together and finally discovered what she must have known all along—I was really in love with her and have been for years. She is my life."

Lori reached for my hand and squeezed it tenderly. She smiled, but her eyes did not light up in the way that I remembered as a child.

"How are you holding up?" I changed the subject.

"I'm fine," Lori responded, but it was obvious she was lying.

"Jennifer's going to be all right."

"God, I hope so, Kurt. I don't think I can stand it if anything happens to her. I need her so much. I suppose in a lot of ways, I've been a burden to Jennifer, but she was always there for me. Always! I never really learned how to handle a crisis on my own. My whole world has fallen apart. I can't take it if I lose Jennifer too."

"Joey's death was such a tragedy."

"It's been almost a year, and the pain hasn't gotten any better. I miss him so much." Tears welled up in Lori's eyes. She swallowed several times before continuing. "Sometimes I think that my sweet baby is still alive, and all I have to do is go in his room and touch him. I actually take the paces and stand by the crib. And for an instant . . . I have hope. But he's not there." She paused. "I touch his blankets, turn on his music box, read his books." Lori's voice quivered. "I cling to the memory of his laughter. Sometimes, I'm afraid I will forget what he looked like . . . his smile . . . his tiny, little hands . . . those beautiful, enchanting eyes." Lori dabbed her nose with a tissue. "There are even times when all the memories get fuzzy, almost as if he was never part of my life at all. There are actually moments when I can't conjure up his face in my mind . . . it's so frightening. I run to the photo album and stare at the pictures because I can't bear for his image to fade." Although her voice seemed relatively strong, the tears traveled in a steady stream down her face. "There were so many experiences I wanted to share with him. So many things I never got to say. I wanted to give him the world, but I wasn't even capable of giving him tomorrow." Lori was silent for a long time. "It seems like I always lose the people I love the most."

"Come on, Lori . . . don't dwell on it . . . it's too painful."

"But, it's true. With the exception of Jennifer, everyone I've loved is no longer a part of my life. Even you, Kurt." She grinned sadly. "You and I used to be so close. When we were kids, I truly believed that I could read your thoughts. Sometimes I knew what you were thinking before you said anything. Most brothers and sisters fight like cats and dogs, but not us. You were my best friend. If I had a nickel for every game we played, every story we told each other before bedtime, and every secret we shared, I'd be a rich woman. I so treasured the companionship we had. But somewhere down the road it all fizzled. We changed. You and I no longer needed each other. We drifted apart."

"Yeah . . . I know what you mean . . . I miss those days." I was pensive as a flood of long-forgotten childhood memories swept over me. "Maybe we could change things . . . bring back that old relationship . . . or better yet . . . start over . . . build a new one."

"We could try." She didn't look up. Instead, she continued to stare at her hands.

"How's Bruce? You talk as if he's not a part of your life."

"That's because he's not. Granted, we still live in the same house. We're even civil to each other. But we don't have a marriage. We don't even have a friendship. Bruce and I tried to start over. A few months ago, we talked it out, and we really made an effort to rebuild our lives together. But it's not working. I can't see any alternative but divorce. We certainly can't go on living this way. Neither one of us is happy. Bruce was having an affair shortly after Joey's death. It stopped for a while. I thought it was over, but it isn't." Lori looked at me. "I don't want to give you the wrong impression, Kurt. Bruce tried; I have to give him credit for that much. I tried too. But there was just nothing left." She opened her purse, pulled out a fresh tissue, and wiped her eyes. "Life's really a bitch, isn't it?"

The tone in my sister's voice and the expression on her face took me by surprise. I looked over at her questioningly and saw deep creases around her eyes and on her forehead. Before I had the chance to speak, she continued. "Everything's gone wrong. When we were kids, teachers, our parents, the minister at our church—everyone told us how beautiful life was going to be. They told us about growing up—about falling in love, getting married, having children, liking our jobs. They taught us history, the degrees of a right angle, how to dissect a frog, how to balance a checkbook. They taught us the Ten Commandments and the Golden Rule. They told us to have ethics and values, honor and integrity . . . everything else would fall into place. I was just naive enough to believe them. But they didn't tell us about the pain. They never warned us that there are people out there who make up their own rules—people who don't care who gets hurt or who gets pushed aside. They didn't teach us how not to trust everyone."

"You sound bitter, Lori."

"Well, I guess I am. I don't know. Things never really work out the way we plan. Do they? Somehow . . . it's like . . . we're dealt cards from a marked deck. I sound full of self-pity, don't I? Like I'm trying to place the blame on anyone but myself. I don't mean to. It's no one else's fault but my own, and I know it. All the decisions were mine . . . all the choices . . . mine. I could have done it differently, but I didn't. They were my mistakes . . . not Mom and Dad's . . . not some elementary school teacher's or our pastor's . . . or Jennifer's . . . or Bruce's. They were my decisions, my choices, my mistakes, my fault." She took a deep breath as she rubbed her temples with her index fingers. "All I ever wanted were the simple things: love, friendship, happiness."

"What? No power or fame or money?" I responded in an almost joking tone.

"No, just the simple things."

"Ah, the intangibles."

"Yes, I suppose you could look at it that way." Lori paused for a moment contemplating her thoughts. "I guess I got sidetracked somewhere along the way. Money seemed important for a time; so did the things it could buy. My goals and principles got all screwed up, and I didn't even know who I was anymore. I had no integrity! I had no pride! It was awful." Lori took a deep breath. "Then like a miracle, Bruce and Joey came into my life. I thought— maybe—maybe I was going to get a chance at happiness. But they're gone now. Everything's gone now . . . everything except Jennifer. If I lose her, there'll be nothing left." Silent tears rolled down her cheeks. Lori didn't push them away. "Jennifer always said that I was the strong one . . . I was the one she turned to . . . I was the one who could handle anything. She was wrong, Kurt. She is the strong one. I need her! God, I need her so much."

"She's going to be okay, Lori. I just know it. Jennifer is going to pull through this."

She leaned over silently and rested her head on my shoulder. "Thanks, Kurt."

"For what?"

"For being here." She continued laying her head on my arm. "It's been a long time since the two of us talked . . . I mean really talked."

"Too long."

"I know you're not going to like what I'm about to say, but hear me out, okay?" Lori waited until I gave her a positive nod. "This problem between Bruce and me . . . it's not like Mom and Dad's problems, but it helped me to understand why they chose to go their separate ways. I know it's been hard for you to forgive them or to understand why they got a divorce, but maybe my life can shed some light on their situation. Maybe they were wrong to stay together all those years, but they stuck it out for you and me. They wanted us to grow up in a healthy, normal family unit. They thought they were doing what was best. They loved us enough to push their problems and their desires aside. If the tables were turned and I was in Mom or Dad's shoes, I don't think I could have been as unselfish as they were. I know you've patched things up with Mom, but you ought to know that Dad loves you too."

"I don't know, Lori. I'm not sure I can be as objective as you are."

"Dad misses you so much. If you could see his eyes when he talks about you. It's really heartbreaking, Kurt."

"I miss him too." I couldn't believe I actually said it aloud. I was thinking about Dad a great deal lately; in fact, I even considered inviting him to the wedding, but decided against it because so many years had passed without a word between us. I didn't know whether I wanted to make a fresh wound out of an old scar or not.

"I'm sure he'd love a visit if you felt like dropping by on your way back to New York."

"I'll think about it." I looked at my sister, holding her attention with my eyes. "Thanks, Lori." I was leaning over and giving her a warm squeeze when a doctor donned in all white entered the room. Lori's face froze, and for one moment, I thought her heart stopped beating. She was going to faint. I let her lean on me. She took in several deep breaths. Slowly, she regained her composure.

"Doctor Lottman." Lori spoke first. "Is it over?"

"Yes," he responded. "I just left the observation booth. They're wheeling her out now. She'll be in recovery for quite some time. I think a celebration is in order. The operation was a success. All her vital signs are good. Jennifer has made it this far, and she's holding her own."

"That's wonderful! Oh, that's awesome news!" Lori grabbed my shoulders and both of us were grinning.

I noticed that the stranger, who was sitting quietly in the corner of the waiting room, stood up and joined our little group. I was curious about his identity.

"Doctor?"

The doctor turned in his direction. The two men shook hands. Obviously, Dr. Lottman knew who the stranger was.

"Mr. Henderson, nice to see you again."

"I was wondering if I could see Jennifer . . . when she regains consciousness, of course."

"I'm sure you can. That would be good. She'll be in intensive care for quite a while. The visiting time will be limited, but Jennifer's going to need a lot of support, so feel free to come as often as you can. Remember to keep the visits short." Dr. Lottman turned to us and spoke again. "Lori, Kurt . . . have you met David Henderson?" As I extended my hand for a friendly shake, I watched the man silently. So that was David Henderson—Jennifer's ex-husband. There was once a time when I would have considered killing him, but now all I felt was compassion. He was obviously very distressed. It was odd. The missing pieces of the puzzle seemed to be falling into place. Apparently, Jennifer was in love with her husband. Strange! Why had I never figured that out? She loved him—not me. And now they seemed to be together again. Funny how things worked out.

"Nice to meet you, Kurt," David said. He had a gentle voice, but his eyes seemed to be piercing holes through me. "Lori. Nice to meet you too."

After the formalities of the introductions, Dr. Lottman began to speak again. "I've already told you that Jennifer is doing well at the moment. The transplant was a success. But whenever a foreign substance is placed inside a body everything inside that body fights to expel it. Jennifer's white blood count will magnify in order to combat the new heart. It usually takes about three months for a body to adjust. If Jennifer can make it through that period of time, she'll more than likely live for many more years."

"What do you think, doctor?"

"So far, the odds look good."

I felt wonderful. Lori was crying with relief. David Henderson was smiling, and there were tears staining his cheeks. Optimism filled the room. Jennifer was going to pull through this. She was going to be just fine.

4

Pamela and I had been married for five weeks; many of those days we'd spent basking in the sunshine on the beaches of Maui. Each day had been as blissful as the day before, but it was good to be home again. I sat in my recliner with one ear on the NBC Nightly News, while the other enjoyed the family sounds of Pam humming in the kitchen and Ellie's stereo blasting to the latest Whitney Houston album. On the television, Tom Brokaw was commenting about an American C-123K cargo plane, which was shot down over Nicaragua. Apparently, three crewmembers were killed and one American, Eugene Hasenfus, was captured. There were weapons on board, which were bound for the contras. According to the news, there was a hint of CIA involvement, but the Reagan administration denied knowledge of the affair.

I whistled to myself. "Pam . . . Pamela . . . come out here. You've got to see this. Sounds like one huge can of worms has just been opened."

"Yes, honey." Pam was wiping her hands on a dishtowel.

"Check this out." I pointed to the television. "Looks like someone's been caught with his pants down. "We both turned our attention to Tom Brokaw.

Moments later the phone rang. Pam picked it up. "It's for you, Kurt."

I spoke into the mouthpiece. "This is Kurt."

"Kurt . . . Lori."

I had not spoken to my sister since the day we returned from our honeymoon over two weeks ago. Our last conversation consisted of Jennifer's improvement and the optimism the doctors conveyed regarding her recovery. I was grateful to Lori for her weekly updates. Pamela and I had sent flowers to Jennifer every Friday since the operation. A nurse had taken dictation from Jennifer returning a thank you note each time. A couple of the letters had sounded quite chipper.

But this time, my sister's voice didn't sound as perky as usual. Normally, she asked how the "happy honeymooners" were doing, but there was no mention of Pamela or Ellie or me—not a word about the weather or Bruce or herself. There was a long heavy silence before I heard Lori speak again.

"She's dead, Kurt! She died an hour ago." My sister's voice cracked slightly. Lori cleared her throat and swallowed several times before trying to speak again. "Jennifer's dead. The doctors did everything they could, but the procedure just didn't take. She kept getting weaker and weaker until finally everything stopped. I can't believe it, Kurt. It's like a nightmare . . . only I can't wake up. I just can't believe she's gone."

8

Laura

EVEN THOUGH SPRING WAS MY FAVORITE SEASON OF THE YEAR, I WAS having difficulty enjoying the gentle breezes and the warm sunshine. I found it therapeutic to dig in the earth, weeding out last year's remnants and planting the coming summer's annuals. It was the only form of relaxation I had to pacify the depression that was inside of me. Joey's death had ripped out a chunk of my heart, leaving a void that would never be filled. I instinctively knew that time would not heal me; I would go to my grave with the pain.

And I missed Jennifer too. Exactly seven months had passed since her death. It was so hard to believe she was actually gone. Jennifer was the only person in my entire life with whom I had ever truly found friendship. I needed her. Even though she'd said countless times that I was her strength; the fact of the matter was, she'd been mine. Her confession about loving me had not changed any of that. Strangely enough, Jennifer's words had in no way jeopardized our relationship.

It didn't seem fair. Jennifer had always been handed the short end of the stick. And then when she'd finally been given the hope for a second chance, some quirk of fate had once again put her on the receiving end of another raw deal. Lady Luck had never been on Jennifer's side.

God, I missed her. I missed her so much.

Two weeks after the funeral, I had taken my stand with Bruce and told him that there was no future for us. Initially, I was surprised when he had not fought the idea of divorce, because a part of me had thought that he would refuse. Bruce was the type of person who didn't want a failed marriage on his record. But finally he had agreed with me. We both knew we had made a mistake. I'd married Bruce because I'd felt the need for security, and he had married me because he wanted a wife—any wife. The separation papers had been filed several months ago. It was only a matter of time before I would become Ms. Laura Davis again.

Both Bruce and I were civil about the whole process. My husband got to keep his business intact, the bulk of our savings, and his classic '62 convertible T-bird. In spite of the fact that I could have sued him for divorce on the grounds of adultery, I hadn't. I asked for no alimony either. My part of the settlement consisted of the '87 LeBaron along with its two and a half years of payments, $4000 in government savings bonds, the house in Stratford Landing, which had very little equity, and most of its furnishings. The house was all I really wanted. I had no desire to make Bruce's life miserable by demanding that he divide the business equally. Most of what we had was his to start with anyway. And it didn't seem fair to make him pay a higher price when we both wanted the divorce.

Times change; people change; sometimes neither change. I finally figured out that I was the exception to the rule. I was not able to change along with the rest of my generation. I lived in fantasies and dreams. How naive I had been! How naive I was even now! In the fall, I would turn thirty-seven. Thirty-seven years old! I'd seen a lot; I'd done a lot too. But, in actuality, I'd only gone full circle. No. That wasn't really true. I'd gone beyond full circle. Full circle was when I'd married Bruce. Now, after all that had happened, I was a great deal more aware and not nearly as idealistic. I missed my old philosophies. Perhaps, they were naive, but they were easier to live with than the bitter, lost feelings I had now.

I wasn't going to compromise anymore. I had my teaching job at Fort

Hunt Elementary, the house, and my brother in New York. Perhaps, given enough time and a little bit of luck, one day in the future there would be room for something or someone else. Until then, I would have to be content with what I had.

I got on my hands and knees. Being careful not to damage the growth of this year's bulbs, I picked through the debris that winter had left in my garden. The daffodils were nearly finished, and the tulips were magnificent. The buds on the forget-me-nots were about to pop, spilling touches of blue all through the yard. They were my favorite. As I plucked a Grecian wild-flower to examine its petals, a shadow crossed over my own. I froze.

"Hello, Laura."

I didn't look up. I was too afraid. I was certain that the voice I heard was only a figment of my imagination. There wasn't anyone standing behind me. That voice was only a recurring dream . . . a fantasy . . . a long-awaited wish. I watched the dark image cast by the person behind me. It moved slightly to my right. I felt numb, yet my skin tingled with a prickling sensation. Even after so many years, I still knew to whom that voice belonged. No one spoke my name the way he did. Never before him and never again would my name roll off another individual's tongue and have the ability to send charges of electricity throughout my body.

It was Brad.

"Don't you have anything to say to an old friend?" His voice had a charming, yet joking, quality to it.

I kept staring at the flower I was about to pluck before his words invad-ed my thoughts. My back was still toward him. What was he doing here? Why had he come into my life again with no warning at all? It wasn't fair. I was in enough turmoil; I didn't need him creating more.

"I've been watching you." He paused. His shadow shifted back and forth as if he were changing from one foot to another. Brad spoke so soft-ly that his voice seemed to blend in with the chirping of the birds and the rustling of the branches. "I saw you from the driveway. I stood there for a long time wondering what you were thinking . . . whether or not I should step closer and speak to you. You look beautiful, Laura." His voice cracked.

I found it hard to believe that I could possibly look anything close to his description. I was wearing filthy jeans and a worn-out Zeta T-shirt; my hair was tied haphazardly into a ponytail, and my hands were covered with dirt. My vanity began to overpower my confidence; as a result, I became even more insecure. I couldn't face Brad. More than likely he was in town on business and just decided to drop by to see an old college friend. I knew I was not up to making polite conversation with the only man I'd ever loved, just to have him disappear again after sharing a cup of coffee or a bit of lunch. I couldn't stand being teased that way.

"Laura . . . please . . . please look at me."

All over my body tiny goose bumps formed. I shivered with the hot and cold sensation they created through my nervous system. Slowly, I rose to my feet and turned to face him. I'd forgotten how tall he was—how tan and beautiful his skin appeared—how wonderfully brown his eyes shone. But, mostly, I'd forgotten the effect his warm, confident smile had on me. Brad was even more handsome than the pictures in my memory. I swallowed, praying that my voice would not betray the emotions that were swirling around inside of me.

"Hello, Brad." Miraculously, I even managed to smile. "It's nice to see you again. Are you in town on business?"

"Business?" He shook his head without taking his eyes off mine. "No . . . not business."

Brad appeared slightly nervous. Why was he on edge? *I* was the one who was being put in an awkward situation . . . not him! I was the one who was finding it difficult to breathe because he was standing so close to me. I was the one who had the shaky knees and the quaking voice . . . not him!

I finally remembered my manners. "May I offer you some coffee, a Coke . . . ?" I felt so uncomfortable. I didn't know what to say. The only thing I did know was that I loved him. I couldn't bear to be so close to him again. It was so incredibly painful that I wanted to flee from his quiet appraisal of me. Without realizing why I said it, words came flooding out. "What are you doing here, Brad? Why did you . . . " I sounded impatient.

Before my sentence was completed he was already answering it. "Jennifer called me."

I knew that was a lie! Why was he lying? Jennifer didn't call Brad. She couldn't have. Jennifer had been dead for seven months. And aside from that, Jennifer despised Brad more than anyone in the world. She would never have telephoned him. Never!

"That's impossible, Brad. Jennifer's dead." My words sounded so cold. Immediately, I saw confusion register on Brad's face. Or was it despondency? I wanted him to leave—go away before I lost control of my fettered emotions. I didn't want any more of his lies and tricks. I couldn't bear to hear him say words that had the potential to weasel their way back into my life. I did not want a brief moment of his time only to have him turn around and leave me barren and miserable again.

"I'm sorry about Jennifer. I didn't know. You two were always such close friends. I'm sure it was very hard on you. Was it sudden? " He sounded truly sympathetic.

I kept telling myself not to fall for his ploy. Don't let him maneuver me. And definitely, above everything else, I couldn't let him see how much he was affecting me. "No." I slapped my hands together ridding them of the dirt particles that were clinging to my fingers. "No . . . it wasn't sudden . . . it was long and painful." I glanced away from him hoping he didn't see the tears burning my eyes. "There was an operation that could have saved her, but it didn't work." I licked my lips and stopped speaking long enough to gather the courage I needed to speak again. "I don't know what you're doing here, Brad . . . and to be honest, I don't care. I just wish you'd leave. Please . . . just go away." I started walking toward my house, praying that I'd get into the sanctuary of its walls before I broke down.

"Jennifer told me about our baby."

His words echoed in my ears—over and over again—vibrating with the meaning of every syllable. Jennifer was the only person, aside from me who knew about Brad's child. I stopped dead in my tracks. If Brad knew about the baby, he could have found out about it only from Jennifer. She *must* have called him. When? Why?

"You should have told me, Laura. My God! I had a right to know!" He sounded angry.

I couldn't see the expression on his face because he was behind me. Why was Brad doing this to me? Why was he bringing up the past and opening all my old wounds? Why? Why didn't he just leave me alone and let me live in peace?

9

Brad

LAURA SPUN AROUND. I SWORE I COULD SEE SPARKS FLYING FROM HER eyes. She was angry, but even with her distorted features, she was still the most beautiful woman I had ever known.

"And why the hell, Brad, should I have told you?"

I saw the tears spring to her eyes. I wanted desperately to take the paces between us and hold her in my arms. My Laura! I couldn't stand to see her look so resentful and forlorn.

"If I had told you about our baby . . . what would you have done?" She did not wait for my answer. "You would have forced me into the decision that I made on my own. You wouldn't have wanted my baby any more than you wanted Cindy's. You would have told me to get an abortion just the way you insisted she have one." Laura continued but this time her voice dripped with sarcasm. "Oh, granted . . . perhaps you would have been will-ing to split the bill, but I didn't need that from you. I never wanted any of your damned money. I never wanted anything from you but . . . " She stopped.

What was Laura about to say? I wanted her to finish the sentence. Was she about to speak the word "love?" Could it be true that Laura wanted love from me as Jennifer implied when she made that surprise phone call so many months go?

I was so shocked when I answered the phone last fall only to discover that Jennifer Carson was on the other end of the line. It was quite a puzzling moment when Jennifer addressed me with a voice that was barely audible. Even today—after all the months that had passed—I could still remember her statements.

"Don't talk . . . just listen." Those were Jennifer's first words to me after announcing her name. "I realize you and I have never seen eye to eye about any goddamned thing in this world, Brad, but we both love and care for the same person. I don't want Lori to suffer any longer."

Even after all the years, the sound of Laura's name still caused passion to race through my body. Was Jennifer going to tell me that Laura was ill . . . hurt . . . dying? What was the reason for her call? Those initial questions flashed rapidly through my mind. I didn't speak as Jennifer demanded with her first statement; instead, I listened with consternation flooding over me.

"I think I've misjudged you, Brad." I could still remember how feeble Jennifer's voice sounded. "I don't like you very much and God knows, I never will; however, I do feel that you deserve some benefit of the doubt."

"Jennifer! Is Laura all right?" There was a sinking sensation in the pit of my stomach. I was anxious for Jennifer to get to the point.

"Please, Brad . . . listen to me. I love Lori more than anyone will ever know. And I want to see her happy. For some unknown reason, I think you're the key to her happiness. I don't know why the hell she fell in love with you, and I guess that's not important now. The point is that Lori loved you. She still does. Personally, I don't think you deserve her, but Lori does not seem to be able to make a life for herself without you." It was at that moment that Jennifer coughed continuously for over a minute. When she spoke again, she seemed weaker. "When you got her pregnant, Brad . . . I wanted to kill you."

"Pregnant?" I could still remember my confusion. "What the hell are you talking about?"

"Yes! Damn you! You got Lori pregnant."

"Are you sure it was my child?" I didn't mean for my words to sound caustic. My hostile, questioning attitude surfaced when I reflected upon Laura's nonvirginal state the day we made love. And to add to that memory, I could still recall the way she flaunted images of other men in front of me, pushing me close to the brink of insanity on more than one occasion.

"You son of a bitch!" Jennifer answered. "Yes, I'm sure. Lori was never the type of girl to go screwing around with just anyone . . . especially back then. It was your kid, Brad. I'll guarantee it. Besides, why the hell would I want to lie about something like that?"

Laura? Laura was pregnant with my child? Why didn't she tell me? Didn't she realize how much I loved her, how very much I would have loved any child born between us? "Laura and I have a child?" I could feel my heart swelling with a tremendous sense of elation. It was an overwhelming emotion. "Is it a boy or a girl? A boy, I bet. Is he a nice kid? Smart? Does he like sports? I bet he plays baseball. Or . . . wait . . . maybe a girl? Pretty like Laura . . . sweet and gentle. Oh, God, Jennifer! Why didn't Laura tell me?"

"No! You don't have a kid, Brad. Lori wanted your baby." Jennifer sounded very sad while she spoke the words. Was it grief in her tone? Anger or anguish? "Lori really wanted to keep the baby."

"She gave it up for adoption?" Imaginary pictures of my child flashed through my mind. How old would it be? Around thirteen . . . a teenager! A smile formed on my lips.

"No! She didn't give it up for adoption." Jennifer paused for what seemed like an eternity. "I talked her into an abortion."

"What?" I found it difficult to breathe. It felt as if an intangible vice gripped my chest.

"Why didn't Laura call me?" My immediate reaction was anger; mixed with my rage was a feeling of betrayal. I could understand Jennifer's reactions. But Laura? Did she hate me so much that the idea of bearing my child was inconceivable to her? "You mean to tell me that

Laura was pregnant with my child, and she didn't give me the chance to help decide its future? Shit!"

"Lori didn't think you'd care. In all honesty, neither did I. But I think now . . . after all these years . . . perhaps I've been wrong about you, Brad." Jennifer hesitated as she gathered her strength to speak again. "I'm certain that she still loves you. And I want more than anything in this world for her to be happy. Don't misunderstand me, Brad. I don't give a shit about you. I never have, and I never will . . . but perhaps, now, I understand you better. Lori needs you. She needs you now more than ever, but if you don't love her in the way I believe you do, then for Christ's sake, don't go to her. Don't hurt her any more than you already have."

I could not recall the rest of the conversation—it had something to do with Cindy Wilder—but I was too wrapped up in her first statements to concentrate on the remainder.

For seven months, I battled the thoughts of seeing Laura again. Did she really love me as Jennifer professed or was this some kind of sick joke? The question of whether I still loved Laura never entered my mind. Of course, I still loved her! I would always love Laura. The real question was whether to believe Jennifer's words and risk the pain of seeing Laura again, only to be pushed away one more time.

There was definitely some truth to Jennifer's words. Of that, I was now certain. Laura had been pregnant with my child. Jennifer had not lied about it. I could see the truth in the pained look in Laura's eyes and the antagonistic way in which she had blurted out her words. There had been a baby. *My* baby! *Our* baby!

"You really should have told me, Laura." I spoke firmly. She didn't respond. She didn't move. "That was *our* child!"

Laura visibly jerked. It was almost as if I had slapped her with my words. Tears burned her eyes. A single drop rolled down her cheek. Even though her expression did not change, and she remained silent, I instinctively knew what Laura was thinking. I could see her pain. I could feel it in my heart. It tore through me like a thunderbolt. In spite of my frustration and anger, compassion emerged. I wanted to comfort her. I took a step toward her.

"Please," Laura whispered with a quaking voice. "Please leave. I'm hanging on by a thread, and I can't do this."

"Laura! We have to talk."

"I have a life of my own now, Brad." Laura's voice was suddenly strong. She jutted her chin upward, and her eyes shone defiantly. "I don't need you."

Her words were like tiny knives stabbing at my heart. I wanted to turn and walk away before she could see the visual effect that her statements were having on me. I pivoted, took three steps, and then faced Laura again. No! I could not leave now. If I did, Laura would haunt me for the rest of my life. "I'm not leaving, Laura. Not until we talk." I took two steps toward her and noticed that she immediately stepped backward as if my touch repelled her. "You're going to listen to me, Laura. You're going to listen to everything I have to say and then—if you want me to go—I will. But not until I've said my piece." I stepped away from her allowing her the room she seemed to need. I watched her and saw the tension start to ease from her expression. She seemed slightly more relaxed when I was not within reach. What was I going to say? How could I express my thoughts and make her understand that she was more important to me than everything else in my life?

"I love you, Laura." My voice was throaty and deep with both physical and emotional passion.

"Don't!" The word sounded like the cry of a wounded animal. Her eyes glazed with fresh tears. "Don't toy with my feelings, Brad. I won't let you hurt me again. I'm immune to the pain you have caused me. I won't let you lie and trick and cheat your way back into my life—not again. I don't know what you're doing here . . . and I don't care . . . just go away."

"Damn it, woman! Would you listen to me! I'm not lying. I love you. I've always loved you. You were a fool if you didn't know it." I was finding it difficult to control the frustration that was welling up inside me. I reached for her again. She, in turn, stepped back. "Don't fight it, Laura."

"You don't love me! You don't love anyone! You don't even know how to love. Love is nothing more than a game you play. That's all it ever was." Laura spat out each word as if it were venom. She seemed to draw satisfaction from the speech she made.

"Where the hell did that come from?" I was baffled by her bitterness. "Loving you has never been a game to me. It has been beautiful and all consuming . . . and more times than not, it's been painful, but it's never . . . never been a game." I was having trouble putting a leash on my rising anger. Laura was infuriating me with her lack of understanding.

"Why didn't you tell me you loved me before? Why have you waited all these years?"

"Me!" I let out a sarcastic laugh. "Damn it, Laura! I wasn't going to say it. All those years at Elon and afterward . . . you were nothing but aloof toward me. Even when we were together, you always held me an arm's length away. You kept such a tight reign on your emotions. I never knew what you were feeling; I only knew that I wanted to be with you. I said everything I could think of to let you know how I felt. Hell! I thought you always knew I loved you, but you just didn't give a damn. You were the ice princess—up in that royal castle of yours—cold and condescending and distant. I wanted to crush you more times than I care to remember. No way! No, Laura. I would never have given you the satisfaction of saying it . . . not back then. But now . . . now, I simply can't stay prisoner to the words any longer."

"Stop it! Stop playing with me, Brad Malone. I will not stand for it! From the moment I met you, you had the power to turn my life upside down . . . and you did it too . . . several times. And I kept making the same mistake over and over again. You toyed with my heart until you came out the victor. You won! You always won! As hard as I tried, you still succeeded in taking my heart and my body. You raped my mind until I couldn't think of anything but you, and I will not tolerate you back in my life again. I fought you with everything I had, but you still beat me. You tore down my defenses and got what you wanted. And then you couldn't wait to go running back to your best friend to brag about the victory and get the ten lousy dollars you bet Billy for screwing me. Sex! Sex is all you ever wanted. Another bitch in bed. I was nothing more to you than a conquest. I hated what you did to me. And . . . I hated you!"

"What are you talking about, Laura?" Nothing made any sense. What ten-dollar bet? What victory? Laura was the one who always turned out the victor. She was the one to play me for the fool, lulling me into a false sense of security, then departing without a word—leaving me with an empty heart and bruised pride.

"You know damn well what I'm talking about, Brad. You bet Billy—probably the first year we were at Elon—that you'd succeed in getting into my pants. Isn't that how you guys say it? What a disgusting term. Well, you won. At Homecoming, I heard you talking to Billy about it, so don't you dare stand here and deny one word. I heard every damn thing you said. Stop this charade! Don't lie to me anymore." She bit into her lower lip. A tiny drop of blood trickled out. "I can't believe . . . even after all these years . . . that it still hurts as if it happened yesterday."

Ten dollars? Billy? Homecoming weekend? Virginity. Red sheets. Yes, I did remember that conversation, but I didn't take the money! The bet was made out of vengeance years before I slept with Laura . . . long before I realized I was in love with her. I had lashed out at Laura for leaving me, for turning her back on me and staying with that high school boyfriend of hers. My God! I made that bet seventeen years ago. What did it have to do with the day we made love? It certainly was the furthest thing on my mind at the time.

"If you heard all that crap about $10, and you're so damn good at eaves-dropping, Laura, then you must have also heard that I told Billy how much I loved you, and that I intended to ask you to marry me. Or didn't you bother to stick around long enough to give me the benefit of the doubt?"

Something changed in her expression. Was it surprise? Reluctance? Curiosity? What was she thinking? Why didn't she say something? She had to believe me! "Laura . . . we've wasted too many years. We've crossed paths so many times. Give us one last chance to build upon what's inside our hearts. I know you loved me once; Jennifer told me, and I believe her. I have to believe her! I need you, Laura. Most of my life, I've run away from loving people . . . especially you. But not anymore! I'm not leaving until we've discussed this all the way through." I stopped to collect my thoughts, trying not to raise my voice. "I've turned my back on you in the past, but as far as being a fugitive from the emotion—you're just as guilty as I am. You never stood up to me. You never confessed your feelings! You never even gave me a clue! You always ran like hell . . . scared to death I'd hurt you. Both of us were fools not to see what was so obvious to everyone but us. Rick knew how I felt! Christ, my own brother's known all along. He probably knew before I did. Cindy knew—I tried to deny it—but she knew. And Jill knew from the beginning how I felt about you. She tried so hard to compensate . . . and for a while, I tried too, but I couldn't make my marriage work because I was so obviously in love with you. My best friend knew too. Bill used to make nonchalant cracks at my protective walls. He used to goad me unmercifully. Shit! Even Jennifer knew. What I can't figure out is why she never told you how I felt or why she finally was compelled to call me after all these years. For Christ's sake, Laura. Everyone knew I loved you. Why the hell didn't you know it?" I was exhausted from our one-sided conversation. I felt as if I were pleading my case to a jury and all twelve of the members were wearing condemning, negative expressions.

"If you loved me like Jennifer said, then you must still have some feeling left. Laura, there must be something we can build upon. I need you so much. I can't imagine spending the rest of my life without you."

"I don't know when Jennifer called you, Brad, but I do know it was at least seven months ago. Why did you wait so long if I was so important to you?" She was still being defensive.

"I did call. Last fall. Your husband answered the phone. I hung up." I paused, reflecting upon the past. "A few months later, I was working with my dad. It was late. We were sharing a couple of beers . . . talking . . . about nothing in particular . . . just talking. Then, out of nowhere, I started telling him about you. I'd never told my dad about you before—not one word." I chuckled slightly under my breath. "He remembered you. He remembered that weekend you came home with Rick. His memory was incredibly accurate." I shifted my weight from one foot to another. "I must have talked to my dad for hours that night. I let out a flood of emotions. He didn't interrupt me . . . not once. I just kept talking on and on. When I was finished, he finally spoke. My father looked me right in the eye and said, 'Brad, don't make the same mistake I made.' Then he told me something I will never forget. He told me that since my mom's death he had been doing a lot of thinking about and analyzing his life. And in retrospect, he finally figured out that his wife—my mother—had loved him too . . . from the beginning and even after their divorce. Only they were both so stubborn . . . so terrified and insecure about their relationship that they built barriers to hide behind, and they never said the words. My father never told my mom that he loved her—not even once—and she never said the words to him either. And now, for them, it's too late." I swallowed several times. There was a knot in my throat making it difficult to speak.

"I spent the next couple of months, Laura, wondering if it was worth the risk to confront you again. I heard you were separated. I tried to get more involved with my work, but each day that passed I became more and more obsessed with seeing you. I couldn't stay away any longer. I had to find out. For God's sake! Don't just stand there. Say something! I'm baring my soul, and you're just looking at me as if I'm some kind of fool."

"I want to believe you, Brad. More than anything in this world . . . I want to believe you."

"Believe it!" I demanded with more force than I intended to display. "Believe me, it's all true. I've never loved anyone the way I love you. I remember the day I heard that you were getting married. I was so bitter. I wanted to ring your neck! I was angry enough and jealous enough to tear you apart; but instead, I immediately married Jill, thinking that at least I could get some kind of satisfaction by marrying before you did. But I did more damage to Jill and to myself than anyone else. I messed up my life by compounding one mistake with another because I simply wasn't able to block you out of my mind. My marriage never had a chance. Jennifer told me that yours wasn't any good either. Don't you see? Isn't it plain enough for you? We are the right two people for each other. We always have been; we always will be. There was never a right time for us before, but now we have that chance. We really have one more chance. I want that opportunity! I want a life with you, Laura. Not one night . . . not just a week or a month . . . but a lifetime."

"We're not the same people we were, Brad. We were just kids then. Things aren't as simple as they used to be. It's been a long time. Perhaps we've built too much on memory. I've changed. A lot's happened to me. Perhaps you won't like the Laura I am now. Maybe you're still in love with an innocent, naive teenager. I've done a lot of things that I'm not very proud of—some of which helped me to grow and understand, and others that were nothing but wild, painful stabs into the dark—learning experiences I wish I'd never had. I don't know whether the Laura you claim to love is still here. I'm afraid she might have died when I grew up. I liked the old me much better than the one I am now. I haven't really liked myself for quite some time. I often wonder what happened to that sweet, pathetically blind little girl I once was, but she's gone. I guess I outgrew her. Or maybe she outgrew me. Either way, I'm definitely no longer innocent, and I certainly don't look at life through rose-colored glasses anymore." Laura's shoulders slouched. She released a long, low sigh. She seemed defeated. "It's so sad; it's all so very sad."

"Laura, we've both changed. Perhaps, when we first met, I wasn't mature enough to handle a lasting relationship with you. I'll admit that. Perhaps I was afraid of a commitment of any kind. And maybe I just plain wasn't ready for any type of love. I had a lot of growing up to do . . . more than most people. I was stubborn, egotistical, and downright selfish, but I've learned a lot since we first met. I have realized that I'm just one person in a world of many. The earth doesn't revolve around me. It was a rude awakening, but I adjusted. For years, I hid behind my arrogance hoping that I wouldn't get hurt, thinking that if I hurt other people then I would never be inflicted with pain. I was wrong, Laura! Seems as if I've been wrong all my life. But I'm not wrong about one thing. I love you. I always have. If I analyze it, I have to admit that I fell in love with you at the beginning of our freshman year at Elon, but I was so damn stupid that I didn't see it. I've loved you for so long that I can't remember what it was like *not* to be in love with you. You've become my life. Almost everything I've done since we met was centered around you—sometimes because of my love and often because I thought I hated you—but nevertheless, I did them because of you. I can't go on like this any longer, Laura. I've fought my feelings for you until I thought I'd choke on them, but not anymore."

As I reached Laura's hand, I saw her cringe and step backward a foot or two. I was exasperated by her apparent fear of me. Did she think I was going to hurt her? My God! I'd never hurt her! Never. What would it take to convince her?

"When we were both kids, Laura, maybe we didn't have the right ingredients to mold and shape our love into a lifetime contract. Maybe we weren't mature enough to handle it, but I think that's all changed now. I think we're old enough and wise enough to face reality. I loved you then, Laura. Perhaps it was a young, selfish type of love that wouldn't have lasted at the time. I was selfish; I've admitted that. Back then, I did take everything for granted. And you're probably right about the fact that I didn't know how to handle love or responsibility. I wasn't ready for the impact you'd have on my life." I smiled, shyly, hoping she would return a similar reaction. She did not.

"Our relationship started out as nothing more than a new experience, but then it grew into a strong love that even after all these years has not gone away." I hesitated. During my silence, I tucked my hands in my pockets for a lack of any other gesture. "Yes! I had a lot of growing up to do. But damn it, Laura . . . so did you! You expected a man to be perfect . . . flawless. There isn't anybody like that, Laura. Those are dreams and fantasies. I never could have fit into that mold you made for me. You wanted a knight in shining armor . . . someone to carry you into the sunset. You were so unrealistic. All

those years ago, you never would have been able to accept me for who I really am."

"I suppose you're right about that, Brad. I did expect too much from the
people I cared about . . . maybe I still do. Maybe I'll never be able to cope
with anything less than my dreams. I don't know. I just don't know."

Laura bent her head. I could no longer see her face. I waited for her to
continue, but she remained silent. Minutes passed. When I couldn't stand
the silence any longer, I began to speak again in a hushed, soft-spoken
manner.

"I tried everything I could think of to rid myself of your memory, but
Laura, I can't stop loving you. I'm not going to give up without a fight. Not
this time! I'm not a kid anymore, Laura. I know what I want. I want you! I
intend to court you, follow you, chase after you, beg you if I have to—whatever it takes—because I'm convinced that we belong together. And I believe
. . . in my heart . . . you know it too."

I pulled a small package from my pocket. I fluffed up the yellow bow
and handed it to Laura. "I know it's not your birthday, but I took a gamble
and bought this hoping that . . . " I stuttered not knowing the appropriate
words to say. "Go ahead . . . open it."

Laura unwrapped the box. Slowly, she took off the top. Inside was a delicate gold chain. There was an oblong charm connecting the links. Laura
mouthed the engraved words. *I love you.* She flipped it over to the reverse
side where she found additional engraving, *Yesterday, Today and Always.*

"It's beautiful, Brad." She seemed to choke on the syllables.

"Remember when we were freshmen? I gave you a similar one."

"Yes, I remember." She seemed lost in thought. "After you took it back,
you gave it to some dizzy blonde within the week."

"I was pretty angry with you. I'm surprised I didn't flush it down the
toilet." I chuckled nervously, waiting for some kind of similar reaction from
her. "I only wish I'd had the courage to say how I felt when we were kids;
then maybe it wouldn't have taken us so long to climb this hurdle."

I saw Laura's eyes mist with fresh tears. I took the steps between us.

This time she didn't pull away. Gently, I kissed her cheek as I slid my arms around her small frame. Laura quietly rested her head upon my chest. She was trembling. Her body felt good in my arms. I could actually feel her heart pounding against mine. How many times had I dreamed of this moment? Dozens . . . hundreds . . . thousands!

"I love you, Brad." Her words were like a melody. "I've always loved you." Laura paused for a moment. "But I'll be honest. I'm not as optimistic as you are. I don't know whether or not we can have a successful relationship. I am not sure our love can outweigh the other elements involved. But you're right. We at least have to give it a chance. I do love you, Brad. We have to try."

I knew I had been reborn. Her words were drawing out all the tension that the years had created. With my fingers, I traced the line of Laura's jaw and lifted her chin so our eyes could be connected. I could sense Laura's pessimism, but I wasn't worried. There was no doubt in my mind that Laura and I belonged together. And now—finally—we were going to get the opportunity to prove it. I was certain there was nothing that could come between us but a lifetime of love and happiness. Enveloping her in my arms, I savored the joy of holding Laura again.

Epilogue

"HI, LAURA. I THOUGHT I MIGHT FIND YOU HERE," BRAD SPOKE SOFTLY AS IF HE didn't want to disturb the aura surrounding him. He leaned against the massive trunk of the old oak tree. From behind his back, he produced a long-stemmed red rose and handed it to Laura.

"Oh, Brad, it's beautiful. Thank you."

"I never look at a rose without thinking of you." His smile brightened his expression. Brad sat down beside her and softly kissed her cheek. "Penny for your thoughts."

"A lot of memories . . . everywhere I look . . . I see you . . . I see me. We were so young . . . innocent . . . full of dreams."

"I know what you mean. There is nothing like a twenty-fifth reunion to bring on a nostalgic mood."

"So, how was the golf tournament?"

"Putts were good; drives stunk up the course," Brad chuckled. "I saw a lot of old buddies. I was hooked up with Bob Palmer, Barry Baker, and Terry Harker. A few of your Zeta sisters were there: Chris Maley, Carol Leone, and Rexanne Bishop. They can't wait to see you tonight at the reception."

"You're kidding! I didn't know they were coming," Laura responded enthusiastically. "That's great."

"I also saw Jane Kiger and Carolyn DeLuca. They'll be at the football game tomorrow. I think Nick Angelone will be there too. They all look great—older maybe—but good."

"I suppose we do look older. This aging business is a bit depressing."

"You haven't aged, Laura. You don't look a day older." Gently, he touched her face before continuing, "Not you! You look exactly like you did the first time I saw you. As the saying goes, you take my breath away . . . then and now . . . every time I look at you." Brad paused to smile. "Your hair's shorter. And you have a line or two around your eyes when you smile . . . and maybe, if I'm honest, I might be able to find a gray hair if I look hard enough, but other than that, to me, you haven't changed a bit."

"Oh, my sweet husband . . . married over a decade and you still know exactly the right words to say." Laura kissed him with tenderness, parting her lips slightly. "Thank you."

"Don't you realize, Laura, even after all of these years, I'm still totally enchanted by you."

"Now, Brad, you're being silly."

"Are you kidding! There has never been and there never will be anything silly about the feelings I have for you." He wrapped his arm protectively around her shoulders and pulled her close. "You are the one true magic in my life. And I will never take you or our love for granted."

Laura nestled her head on his chest. Listening to his heartbeat, she closed her eyes and enjoyed the steady flow of his words. "Can you believe how gorgeous Elon is now? When we went here, it was a quaint campus; but now I guess majestic is a better description. Mosley Center is incredible. It's gigantic! There was nothing like it in the 70s. Certainly, Long Student Union didn't hold a candle to this new center." Brad paused as he scanned the area.

"Did you get a chance to go into Koury Center? On my way here, I walked through the building. I stood in the small rotunda at the front entrance. It's quite regal and maybe a little overwhelming. Gigantic pictures of Mike Lawton, Tommy Cole, Joe West, and Richard McGeorge fill the room—a hallowed hall. They were our heroes! It's a wonderful tribute to the stars of years past." As Brad spoke, he rhythmically stroked the line of Laura's jaw, as if he didn't even realize he was doing it.

"I heard now that Elon is in Division I, they're going to build a new stadium, probably in the year 2000. This one will be on campus . . . no more games at Walter Williams High School in Burlington. That will be another change separating our memories from the present campus." Again, he paused. "At least the lake is still here." He scanned the area with his eyes. Most of the autumn leaves were resting on the ground in circled rings around each tree.

"Did you know that the lake has a name?" Laura whispered.

"Really? I don't remember it having a name in the past."

"Yes, it does. I walked all the way around it . . . like I used to do when I needed to clear my mind. And there, over by the street, there is a sign. It's called the Mary Nell Lake. I wonder who Mary Nell is?"

"Probably someone who loves this place as much as we do."

"Brad, the forest is gone. Our place, where we used to picnic in the woods, it's gone. When I saw the change, it tugged a little bit at my heart. They built a soccer field, a baseball diamond, and an entire street of sorority and fraternity houses. There's even a Zeta house." Laura's voice was somber. "It's beautiful, but it made me a little sad. It's as if the places that hold our memories have been wiped clean." She glanced to her left.

"And, have you seen Harper Center? Wow! What a difference. Remember when we used to sit in the lobby and talk for hours, remember that couch in the corner? Oh, the number of hours we spent nestled there. And the TV room . . . it's gone. And the receptionist's desk where you called for me . . . it's gone too. They don't need a receptionist anymore. The kids—boys and girls—walk freely in all the dorms. There are no concrete rules like we had . . . no need for visitation hours. The lobby, the TV room, the receptionist's desk . . . they're all gone. That whole area is a food court now. It's nice, but it is very different."

"Reunions can be bittersweet. Don't be sad, honey. They can change Elon all they want. It won't change us—or our memories."

Again, Brad stroked Laura's cheek in a calming fashion as he spoke. It was a gesture of comfort that had endured for nearly three decades. Both seemed to find solace in the contact.

"At least our tree is still standing." Brad patted the trunk and smiled. "This spot sure brings back memories. We spent a lot of time here . . . some good . . . some not worth remembering. One thing I could always count on in the past: I could find you here. For as long as I can remember, I've thought of it as our tree. They can do what they want to the rest of the campus—as long as they don't cut down this oak. It will always be a part of us, and we will always be a part of it."

He paused and watched the ducks swim quietly across the water. A gentle breeze rustled the leaves. When the sun slipped behind a cloud, it caused a slight drop in temperature. "You're right though, Laura. Elon has changed. It's another generation's campus now. There is a whole new set of rules . . . an entire new list of dreams . . . their dreams . . . their goals. We're just part of its history." He gave Laura a gentle squeeze while letting out a long, slow sigh.

"Are you sorry, Brad, that you put your cameras away? You always dreamed of taking that special picture. You know the one . . . the picture that everyone would remember . . . the one that would be in *Newsweek,* or *Vogue,* or *National Geographic.* Do you ever wish you had stayed in photography?"

"No. In fact, I haven't thought about professional photography in years. I like what I do. I love our clubs. And although it sounds silly saying it here . . . on this spot where I proclaimed so defiantly years ago that I would never work for my father . . . turns out I love it, and I love him."

"So, you're not sorry?"

"No, not a bit. Besides, I didn't put my camera away, and I *have* taken that special picture. In fact, I've taken dozens of them—you and the twins at the zoo, on the river, at the picnic table in our backyard. My favorite picture is the one I took of you and the kids in the rocking chair the week after they were born. It captures every dream I ever had." Brad gently nestled his nose into Laura's hair, breathing in her scent. "How about your dreams?"

"I'm living my dreams, Brad. Surely you know that by now." The two of them sat quietly for several moments as the nostalgic memories washed over them.

Finally, Laura spoke again, "It's kind of nice that Ellie graduated from here. Kurt and Pam have said over and over again that Ellie loved Elon. I'm not surprised. It is a little far away from New York, but Elon was the perfect college for her. It gave her a great foundation in business. She sure is a confident, determined, young lady. From what I hear, she will be ready to take over Woods Enterprises from her grandfather before too much longer."

"Hey, according to Kurt, she's more than capable, but George Woods isn't ready to retire just yet." Laura grinned as she looked into her husband's eyes. "Wouldn't it be wonderful if the twins decided to go to Elon too?"

"Now, Laura, don't rush it. Let's not push them. They're only in the third grade."

"You're right. But if I close my eyes and use a little imagination, I can actually see Jennifer and Richard walking across main campus."

"They are cute little rascals, aren't they?" Brad brushed his lips across Laura's forehead. "Have I thanked you lately for bringing such joy into my life? You and the kids . . . you are my life. When I was young I never, not even in my wildest dreams, thought I could ever be this happy." Brad pressed his lips against Laura's cheek. He whispered softly, "Thank you for making all my dreams come true."

"Sometimes," Laura paused. "I think about what-ifs. What if I had gone to James Madison or East Carolina? What if I hadn't gone to Elon? We never would have met."

"Now look who's being silly? Of course, we would have met! It did not matter what college we went to, Laura. It didn't matter what jobs we took . . . where we lived . . . or what roads we drove on . . . none of that mattered. Don't you realize that eventually—one way or another—we were destined to be together? If we hadn't met at Elon, it would have been somewhere else. I know that with all of my heart. You and I belong together—always have, always will. There was no luck involved. No choices or highways that needed to be traveled. It was our destiny . . . you and me."

"You're right, Brad. It took us long enough to figure it out, but I know with all of my heart, that we were meant to spend our lives together." She took hold of his hand, raised it to her lips, and gently kissed each finger. "While you were playing golf, I was running through all of our memories here on this campus. And do you know what? I think I knew the first moment I saw you." Laura grinned. "I didn't understand it at the time, and God knows I would have been terrified had I figured it out right away, but subconsciously . . . I knew in that first instant. There would never be anyone else for me but you. Although it was terrifying and overwhelming, it was also intoxicating and totally euphoric."

The breeze blew a few strands of Brad's hair out of place. Laura gently stroked his brow, running her fingers slowly across his face. "I remember the first time you kissed me. I was totally beguiled. I have loved you ever since." She traced his lips with her fingers. Their eyes locked in an intangible embrace. "Thank you, Brad, for making my dreams come true."